ANNE TYLER

A NEW COLLECTION

ANNE TYLER

A NEW COLLECTION

THREE COMPLETE NOVELS

THE ACCIDENTAL TOURIST

BREATHING LESSONS

SEARCHING FOR CALEB

WINGS BOOKS

NEW YORK • AVENEL, NEW JERSEY

This 1994 edition is published by Wings Books, distributed by Random House Value Publishing, Inc., 40 Engelhard Avenue, Avenel, New Jersey 07001, by arrangement with Alfred A. Knopf, Inc.

Printed and bound in the United States of America

Library of Congress Cataloging-in-Publication Data
Tyler, Anne.
    Anne Tyler : a new collection.
      p.   cm.
    Contents: The accidental tourist — Breathing lessons — Searching for Caleb.
    ISBN 0-517-06459-6
    I. Title.
PS3570.Y45A6   1991
813'.54—dc20
                                                 91-16589
                                                      CIP

10 9 8 7

CONTENTS

THE
ACCIDENTAL
TOURIST

1

They were supposed to stay at the beach a week, but neither of them had the heart for it and they decided to come back early. Macon drove. Sarah sat next to him, leaning her head against the side window. Chips of cloudy sky showed through her tangled brown curls.

Macon wore a formal summer suit, his traveling suit—much more logical for traveling than jeans, he always said. Jeans had those stiff, hard seams and those rivets. Sarah wore a strapless terry beach dress. They might have been returning from two entirely different trips. Sarah had a tan but Macon didn't. He was a tall, pale, gray-eyed man, with straight fair hair cut close to his head, and his skin was that thin kind that easily burns. He'd kept away from the sun during the middle part of every day.

Just past the start of the divided highway, the sky grew almost black and several enormous drops spattered the windshield. Sarah sat up straight. "Let's hope it doesn't rain," she said.

"I don't mind a little rain," Macon said.

Sarah sat back again, but she kept her eyes on the road.

It was a Thursday morning. There wasn't much traffic. They passed a pickup truck, then a van all covered with stickers from a hundred scenic attractions. The drops on the windshield grew closer together. Macon switched his wipers on. Tick-*swoosh*, they went—a lulling sound; and there was a gentle patter on the roof. Every now and then a gust of wind blew up. Rain flattened the long, pale grass at the sides of the road. It slanted across the boat lots, lumberyards, and discount furniture outlets, which already had a darkened look as if here it might have been raining for some time.

"Can you see all right?" Sarah asked.

"Of course," Macon said. "This is nothing."

They arrived behind a trailer truck whose rear wheels sent out arcs of spray. Macon swung to the left and passed. There was a moment of watery blindness till the truck had dropped behind. Sarah gripped the dashboard with one hand.

"I don't know how you can see to drive," she said.

"Maybe you should put on your glasses."

"Putting on my glasses would help you to see?"

"Not me; you," Macon said. "You're focused on the windshield instead of the road."

Sarah continued to grip the dashboard. She had a broad, smooth face that gave an impression of calm, but if you looked closely you'd notice the tension at the corners of her eyes.

The car drew in around them like a room. Their breaths fogged the windows. Earlier the air conditioner had been running and now some artificial chill remained, quickly turning dank, carrying with it the smell of mildew. They shot through an underpass. The rain stopped completely for one blank, startling second. Sarah gave a little gasp of relief, but even before it was uttered, the hammering on the roof resumed. She turned and gazed back longingly at the underpass. Macon sped ahead, with his hands relaxed on the wheel.

"Did you notice that boy with the motorcycle?" Sarah asked. She had to raise her voice; a steady, insistent roaring sound engulfed them.

"What boy?"

"He was parked beneath the underpass."

"It's crazy to ride a motorcycle on a day like today," Macon said. "Crazy to ride one any day. You're so exposed to the elements."

"We could do that," Sarah said. "Stop and wait it out."

"Sarah, if I felt we were in the slightest danger I'd have pulled over long ago."

"Well, I don't know that you would have," Sarah said.

They passed a field where the rain seemed to fall in sheets, layers and layers of rain beating down the cornstalks, flooding the rutted soil. Great lashings of water flung themselves at the windshield. Macon switched his wiper blades to high.

"I don't know that you really care that much," Sarah said. "Do you."

Macon said, "Care?"

"I said to you the other day, I said, 'Macon, now that Ethan's dead I sometimes wonder if there's any point to life.' Do you remember what you answered?"

"Well, not offhand," Macon said.

"You said, 'Honey, to tell the truth, it never seemed to me there was all that much point to begin with.' Those were your exact words."

"Um . . ."

"And you don't even know what was wrong with that."

"No, I guess I don't," Macon said.

He passed a line of cars that had parked at the side of the road, their windows opaque, their gleaming surfaces bouncing back the rain in shallow explosions. One car was slightly tipped, as if about to fall into the muddy torrent that churned and raced in the gully. Macon kept a steady speed.

"You're not a comfort, Macon," Sarah said.

"Honey, I'm trying to be."

"You just go on your same old way like before. Your little routines and rituals, depressing habits, day after day. No comfort at all."

"Shouldn't I need comfort too?" Macon asked. "You're not the only one, Sarah. I don't know why you feel it's your loss alone."

"Well, I just do, sometimes," Sarah said.

They were quiet a moment. A wide lake, it seemed, in the center of the highway crashed against the underside of the car and slammed it to the right. Macon pumped his brakes and drove on.

"This rain, for instance," Sarah said. "You know it makes me nervous. What harm would it do to wait it out? You'd be showing some concern. You'd be telling me we're in this together."

Macon peered through the windshield, which was streaming so that it seemed marbled. He said, "I've got a system, Sarah. You know I drive according to a system."

"You and your systems!"

"Also," he said, "if you don't see any point to life, I can't figure why a rainstorm would make you nervous."

Sarah slumped in her seat.

"Will you look at that!" he said. "A mobile home's washed clear across that trailer park."

"Macon, I want a divorce," Sarah told him.

Macon braked and glanced over at her. "What?" he said. The car swerved. He had to face forward again. "What did I say?" he asked. "What did it mean?"

"I just can't live with you anymore," Sarah said.

Macon went on watching the road, but his nose seemed sharper and whiter, as if the skin of his face had been pulled tight. He cleared his throat. He said, "Honey. Listen. It's been a hard year. We've had a hard time. People who lose a child often feel this way; everybody says so; everybody says it's a terrible strain on a marriage—"

"I'd like to find a place of my own as soon as we get back," Sarah told him.

"Place of your own," Macon echoed, but he spoke so softly, and the rain beat so loudly on the roof, it looked as if he were only moving his lips. "Well," he said. "All right. If that's what you really want."

"You can keep the house," Sarah said. "You never did like moving."

For some reason, it was this that made her finally break down. She turned away sharply. Macon switched his right blinker on. He pulled into a Texaco station, parked beneath the overhang, and cut off the engine. Then he started rubbing his knees with his palms. Sarah huddled in her corner. The only sound was the drumming of rain on the overhang far above them.

2

After his wife left him, Macon had thought the house would seem larger. Instead, he felt more crowded. The windows shrank. The ceilings lowered. There was something insistent about the furniture, as if it were pressing in on him.

Of course Sarah's personal belongings were gone, the little things like clothes and jewelry. But it emerged that some of the big things were more personal than he'd imagined. There was the drop-leaf desk in the living room, its pigeonholes stuffed with her clutter of torn envelopes and unanswered letters. There was the radio in the kitchen, set to play 98 Rock. (She liked to keep in touch with her students, she used to say in the old days, as she hummed and jittered her way around the breakfast table.) There was the chaise out back where she had sunbathed, planted in the only spot that got any sun at all. He looked at the flowered cushions and marveled at how an empty space could be so full of a person—her faint scent of coconut oil that always made him wish for a piña colada; her wide, gleaming face inscrutable behind dark glasses; her compact body in the skirted swimsuit she had tearfully insisted on buying after her fortieth birthday. Threads of her exuberant hair showed up at the bottom of the sink. Her shelf in the medicine cabinet, stripped, was splashed with drops of liquid rouge in a particular plummy shade that brought her instantly to Macon's mind.

He had always disapproved of her messiness but now those spills seemed touching, like colorful toys left on the floor after a child has gone to bed.

The house itself was medium-sized, unexceptional to look at, standing on a street of such houses in an older part of Baltimore. Heavy oak trees hung over it, shading it from the hot summer sun but also blocking breezes. The rooms inside were square and dim. All that remained in Sarah's closet was a brown silk sash hanging on a hook; in her bureau drawers, lint balls and empty perfume bottles. Their son's old room was neatly made up, as sleek as a room in a Holiday Inn. Some places, the walls gave off a kind of echo. Still, Macon noticed he had a tendency to hold his arms close to his body, to walk past furniture sideways, as if he imagined the house could barely accommodate him. He felt too tall. His long, clumsy feet seemed unusually distant. He ducked his head in doorways.

Now was his chance to reorganize, he told himself. He was struck by an incongruous little jolt of interest. The fact was that running a house required some sort of system, and Sarah had never understood that. She was the sort of woman who stored her flatware intermingled. She thought nothing of running a dishwasher with only a handful of forks stacked inside. Macon found that distressing. He was opposed to dishwashers in general; he believed they wasted energy. Energy saving was a hobby of his, you might say.

He started keeping the kitchen sink filled at all times, adding some chlorine bleach for disinfectant. As he finished using each dish, he dropped it in. On alternate days he pulled the plug and sprayed everything with very hot water. Then he stacked the rinsed dishes in the empty dishwasher—which had become, under his new system, a gigantic storage area.

When he hunkered over the sink to let the spray attachment run, he often had the feeling that Sarah was watching. He sensed that if he slid his eyes just slightly to the left, he would find her with her arms folded across her chest, her head tipped and her full, curved lips meditatively pursed. At first glance she was simply studying his procedure; at second glance (he knew) she was laughing at him. There was a secret little gleam in her eyes that he was all too familiar with. "I see," she would say, nodding at some lengthy explanation of his; then he'd look up and catch the gleam and the telltale tuck at one corner of her mouth.

In this vision of her—if you could call it a vision, considering that he never did glance over at her—she was wearing a bright blue dress from the early days of their marriage. He had no idea when she had given that dress up, but certainly it was years and years ago. He almost felt that Sarah was a ghost—that she was dead. In a way (he thought, turning off the faucet), she *was* dead, that young, vivid Sarah from their first enthusiastic apartment on Cold Spring Lane. When he tried to recall those days, any image of Sarah was altered by the fact that she had left him. When he pictured their introduction—back when they were barely out of childhood—it seemed nothing more than the beginning of their parting. When she had looked up at him that first night and rattled the ice cubes in her paper cup, they were already moving toward their last edgy, miserable year together, toward those months when anything either of them said was wrong, toward that sense of narrowly missed connections. They were like people who run to meet, holding out their arms, but their aim is wrong; they pass each other and keep running. It had all amounted to nothing, in the end. He gazed down at the sink, and the warmth from the dishes drifted gently up into his face.

Well, you have to carry on. You have to carry on. He decided to switch his shower from morning to night. This showed adaptability, he felt—some freshness of spirit. While he showered he let the water collect in the tub, and he stalked around in noisy circles, sloshing the day's dirty clothes underfoot. Later he wrung out the clothes and hung them on hangers to dry. Then he dressed in tomorrow's underwear so he wouldn't have to launder any pajamas. In fact, his only real laundry was a load of towels and sheets once a week—just two towels, but quite a lot of sheets. This was because he had developed a system that enabled him to sleep in clean sheets every night without the trouble of bed changing. He'd been proposing the system to Sarah for years, but she was so set in her ways. What he did was strip the mattress of all linens, replacing them with a giant sort of envelope made from one of the seven sheets he had folded and stitched together on the sewing machine. He thought of this invention as a Macon Leary Body Bag. A body bag required no tucking in, was unmussable, easily changeable, and the perfect weight for summer nights. In winter he would have to devise something warmer, but he couldn't think of winter yet. He was barely making it from one day to the next as it was.

At moments—while he was skidding on the mangled clothes in the bathtub or struggling into his body bag on the naked, rust-stained mattress—he realized that he might be carrying things too far. He couldn't explain why, either. He'd always had a fondness for method, but not what you would call a mania. Thinking then of Sarah's lack of method, he wondered if that had got out of hand now too. Maybe all these years, they'd been keeping each other on a reasonable track. Separated, demagnetized somehow, they wandered wildly off course. He pictured Sarah's new apartment, which he had never seen, as chaotic to the point of madness, with sneakers in the oven and the sofa heaped with china. The mere thought of it upset him. He looked gratefully at his own surroundings.

Most of his work was done at home; otherwise he might not have cared so about the mechanics of the household. He had a little study in the spare room off the kitchen. Seated in a stenographer's chair, tapping away at a typewriter that had served him through four years of college, he wrote a series of guidebooks for people forced to travel on business. Ridiculous, when you thought about it: Macon hated travel. He careened through foreign territories on a desperate kind of blitz— squinching his eyes shut and holding his breath and hanging on for dear life, he sometimes imagined—and then settled back home with a sigh of relief to produce his chunky, passport-sized paperbacks. *Accidental Tourist in France. Accidental Tourist in Germany. In Belgium.* No author's name, just a logo: a winged armchair on the cover.

He covered only the cities in these guides, for people taking business trips flew into cities and out again and didn't see the countryside at all. They didn't see the cities, for that matter. Their concern was how to pretend they had never left home. What hotels in Madrid boasted king-sized Beauty-rest mattresses? What restaurants in Tokyo offered Sweet'n'-Low? Did Amsterdam have a McDonald's? Did Mexico City have a Taco Bell? Did any place in Rome serve Chef Boyardee ravioli? Other travelers hoped to discover distinctive local wines; Macon's readers searched for pasteurized and homogenized milk.

As much as he hated the travel, he loved the writing—the virtuous delights of organizing a disorganized country, stripping away the inessential and the second-rate, classifying all that remained in neat, terse paragraphs. He cribbed from other guidebooks, seizing small kernels of value and discarding the rest. He spent pleasurable hours dithering over questions of punctuation. Righteously, mercilessly, he weeded out the passive voice. The effort of typing made the corners of his mouth turn down, so that no one could have guessed how much he was enjoying himself. *I am happy to say*, he pecked out, but his face remained glum and intense. *I am happy to say that it's possible now to buy Kentucky Fried Chicken in Stockholm. Pita bread, too*, he added as an afterthought. He wasn't sure how it had happened, but lately pita had grown to seem as American as hot dogs.

"Of course you're managing," his sister told him over the phone. "Did I say you weren't? But at least you could have let us know. Three weeks, it's been! Sarah's been gone three weeks and I only hear about it today. And by chance, at that. If I hadn't asked to speak to her, would you ever have told us she'd left you?"

"She didn't *leave* me," Macon said. "I mean it's not the way you make it sound. We discussed it like adults and decided to separate, that's all. The last thing I need is my family gathered around me saying, 'Oh, poor Macon, how could Sarah do this to you—' "

"Why would I say that?" Rose asked. "Everybody knows the Leary men are difficult to live with."

"Oh," Macon said.

"Where is she?"

"She's got a place downtown," he said. "And look," he added, "you don't have to bend over backwards, either, and go asking her to dinner or something. She does have a family of her own. You're supposed to take my side in this."

"I thought you didn't want us to take sides."

"No, no, I don't. I mean you shouldn't take *her* side, is what I'm trying to say."

"When Charles's wife got her divorce," Rose said, "we went on having her to dinner every Christmas, just like always. Remember?"

"I remember," Macon said wearily. Charles was their oldest brother.

"I suppose she'd still be coming, if she hadn't got remarried to someone so far away."

"What? If her husband had been a Baltimore man you'd have gone on inviting them both?"

"She and Porter's wife and Sarah used to sit around the kitchen— this was before Porter's wife got *her* divorce—and they'd go on and on about the Leary men. Oh, it was the Leary men this, the Leary men that: how they always had to have everything just so, always so well thought out beforehand, always clamping down on the world as if they really thought they could keep it in line. The Leary men! I can hear them still. I had to laugh: One Thanksgiving Porter and June were getting ready to leave, back when their children were small, and June was heading toward the door with the baby in her arms and Danny hanging onto her coat and this load of toys and supplies when Porter called out, 'Halt!' and started reading from one of those cash-register tapes that he always writes his lists on: *blanket, bottles, diaper bag, formula out of the fridge* . . . June just looked over at the other two and rolled her eyes."

"Well, it wasn't such a bad idea," Macon said, "when you consider June."

"No, and you notice it was alphabetical, too," Rose said. "I do think alphabetizing helps to sort things out a little."

Rose had a kitchen that was so completely alphabetized, you'd find the allspice next to the ant poison. She was a fine one to talk about the Leary men.

"At any rate," she said. "Has Sarah been in touch since she left?"

"She's come by once or twice. Once, actually," Macon said. "For things she needed."

"What kind of things?"

"Well, a double boiler. Things like that."

"It's an excuse, then," Rose said promptly. "She could get a double boiler at any dime store."

"She said she liked ours."

"She was checking to see how you're doing. She still cares. Did you talk at all?"

"No," Macon said, "I just handed her the double boiler. Also that gadget that unscrews bottle tops."

"Oh, Macon. You might have asked her in."

"I was scared she'd say no," he said.

There was a silence. "Well. Anyhow," Rose said finally.

"But I'm getting along!"

"Yes, of course you are," she told him.

Then she said she had something in the oven and hung up.

Macon went over to his study window. It was a hot day in early July, the sky so blue it made his eyes ache. He rested his forehead against the glass and stared out at the yard, keeping his hands stuffed deep in the rear pockets of his khakis. Up in one of the oak trees, a bird sang what sounded like the first three notes of "My Little Gypsy Sweetheart." "Slum . . . ber . . . on . . ." it sang. Macon wondered if even this moment would become, one day, something he looked back upon wistfully. He couldn't imagine it; he couldn't think of any period bleaker than this in all his life, but he'd noticed how time had a way of coloring things. That bird, for instance, had such a pure, sweet, piercing voice.

He turned away from the window, covered his typewriter, and left the room.

He didn't eat real meals anymore. When he was hungry he drank a glass of milk, or he spooned a bit of ice cream directly from the carton. After the smallest snack he felt overfed and heavy, but he noticed when he dressed in the mornings that he seemed to be losing weight. His shirt collar stood out around his neck. The vertical groove between his nose and mouth had deepened so that he had trouble shaving it. His hair, which Sarah used to cut for him, jutted over his forehead like a shelf. And something had caused his lower lids to droop. He used to have narrow gray slits of eyes; now they were wide and startled. Could this be a sign of malnutrition?

Breakfast: Breakfast was your most important meal. He hooked up the percolator and the electric skillet to the clock radio on his bedroom windowsill. Of course he was asking for food poisoning, letting two raw eggs wait all night at room temperature, but once he'd changed menus there was no problem. You had to be flexible about these matters. He was awakened now by the smell of fresh coffee and hot buttered popcorn, and he could partake of both without getting out of bed. Oh, he was managing fine, just fine. All things considered.

But his nights were terrible.

It wasn't that he had trouble getting to sleep in the first place. That was easy. He'd watch TV till his eyes burned; then he'd climb the stairs. He would start the shower running and spread his clothes in the tub. At times he thought of skipping this part, except there was such a danger in falling behind with your system. So he carried out each step: hanging the laundry, setting up the breakfast things, flossing his teeth. He couldn't go to bed without flossing his teeth. For some reason, Sarah had found this irritating. If Macon were condemned to death, she'd said once, and they told him he'd be executed by firing squad at dawn, he would no doubt still insist on flossing the night before. Macon, after thinking it over, had agreed. Yes, of course he would. Hadn't he flossed while in the depths of pneumonia? In the hospital with gallstones? In a motel the night his son was killed? He checked his teeth in the mirror. They were never entirely white, in spite of all his care. And now it seemed his skin was taking on a yellowish cast as well.

He turned off the lights, moved the cat over, helped the dog up onto the bed. The dog was a Welsh corgi, very short-legged, but he did love to sleep in a bed, and so every night he stood erect and propped his elbows on the mattress and gazed at Macon expectantly till Macon gave him a boost. Then they'd all three settle themselves. Macon slipped into his envelope, the cat fitted her shape to the warm spot under his arm, and the dog plopped down near his feet. Then Macon closed his eyes and drifted off.

But eventually he found himself conscious of his dreams—not borne along by them but tediously constructing them, quibbling over details. When it dawned on him that he was awake, he would open his eyes and squint at the clock radio. But it was only one a.m. At the latest, two. There were all those hours still to be survived.

His brain buzzed with little worries. Had he left the back door unlocked? Forgotten to put the milk away? Made out a check for his bank balance instead of his gas bill? He remembered all in a rush that he'd opened a can of V-8 juice and then put the can in the icebox. Oxidation of the metal seams! Resulting in lead poisoning!

The worries changed, grew deeper. He wondered what had gone wrong with his marriage. Sarah had been his first and only girlfriend; now he thought he should have practiced on someone else beforehand. During the twenty years of their marriage there'd been moments—there'd been months—when he didn't feel they had really formed a unit the way couples were supposed to. No, they'd stayed two distinct people, and not always even friends. Sometimes they'd seemed more like rivals, elbowing each other, competing over who was the better style of person. Was it Sarah, haphazard, mercurial? Was it Macon, methodical and steady?

When Ethan was born, he only brought out more of their differences. Things they had learned to ignore in each other resurfaced. Sarah never got their son on any kind of schedule at all, was lax and unconcerned.

And Macon (oh, he knew it, he admitted it) had been so intent on preparing him for every eventuality that he hadn't had time to enjoy him. Ethan at two, at four floated up into his vision as clearly as a color film projected upon the bedroom ceiling. A chortling, sunny little boy, he'd been, with Macon a stooped shape above him wringing his hands. Macon had been fierce in teaching him, at age six, how to swing a bat; it would have wrenched his soul to have Ethan chosen last for any team. "Why?" Sarah had asked. "If he's chosen last, he's chosen last. Let it be, why don't you." Let it be! Life was so full of things you couldn't do anything about; you had to avert what you could. She laughed when Macon spent one fall collecting Wacky Packs, which had these jokey stickers inside that Ethan liked to plaster his bedroom door with. He'd have more than anyone in the whole third grade, Macon vowed. Long after Ethan had lost interest, Macon was still doggedly bringing them home. He knew it was absurd, but still, there was this one last sticker they had not yet managed to get hold of . . .

Ethan went away to camp when he was twelve—a year ago, almost exactly. Most boys started earlier, but Macon had kept delaying it. Why have a child at all, he asked Sarah, if you were only going to ship him off to some godforsaken spot in Virginia? By the time he finally gave in, Ethan was in the top age group—a tall blond sprout of a boy with an open, friendly face and an endearing habit of bouncing on the balls of his feet when he was nervous.

Don't think about it.

He was murdered in a Burger Bonanza his second night at camp. It was one of those deaths that make no sense—the kind where the holdup man has collected his money and is free to go but decides, instead, first to shoot each and every person through the back of the skull.

Ethan wasn't even supposed to be there. He had snuck away from camp with a cabinmate, who waited outside as a lookout.

Blame the camp for not supervising. Blame Burger Bonanza for poor security. Blame the cabinmate for not going in too and altering, perhaps, what took place. (Lookout for what, for God's sake?) Blame Sarah for allowing Ethan to leave home; blame Macon for agreeing; blame even (hell, yes) Ethan. Blame Ethan for wanting to attend that camp and for sneaking off from it, and for entering Burger Bonanza like some headstrong fool while a holdup was in progress. Blame him for so meekly moving to the kitchen with the others, for placing his hands flat against the wall as he was ordered and no doubt bouncing slightly on the balls of his feet . . .

Don't think about it.

The director of the camp, not wanting to break the news on the phone, had driven to Baltimore to tell them in person. Then he'd driven them back to Virginia. Macon often recalled that director. Jim, his name

was, Jim Robinson or maybe Robertson—a burly, white-whiskered man
with a crew cut, wearing a suit coat, as if in respect, over a Redskins
T-shirt. He'd seemed uncomfortable with silence and did his best to
fill it with abrupt little fragments of chitchat. Macon hadn't listened,
or he'd thought he hadn't; but now all the fragments came back to
him. How Jim's mother had been a Baltimorean herself, born the year
Babe Ruth was playing for the Orioles. How Jim's tomato plants had
been acting queerly, producing only tiny green marbles that fell off the
vines before they ripened. How Jim's wife was terrified of driving in
reverse and avoided any situation that required it. Macon gave a lot
of thought to that now, lying in his bed at night. Could you really
drive a car without reversing? What about at intersections, where a bus
driver pokes his head out his window and asks you to roll on back a
few yards so he can turn? Would she refuse? Macon imagined her,
staunch and defiant, glaring straight in front of her and pretending not
to notice. The driver escalating into curses, horns blowing, other drivers
shouting, "Aw, lady!" It made a nice picture. He kept it firmly in mind.

Finally he would sit up and wriggle out of his sheet. The dog,
sighing, roused himself and dropped off the bed to pad downstairs
behind him. The floorboards were cool underfoot, the kitchen linoleum
cooler still; there was a glow from the refrigerator as Macon poured
himself a glass of milk. He went to the living room and turned on the
TV. Generally some black-and-white movie was running—men in suits
and felt hats, women with padded shoulders. He didn't try to follow
the plot. He took small, steady sips of milk, feeling the calcium traveling
to his bones. Hadn't he read that calcium cures insomnia? He absently
stroked the cat, who had somehow crept into his lap. It was much too
hot to have a cat in his lap, especially this one—a loose-strung, gray
tweed female who seemed made of some unusually dense substance.
And the dog, most often, would be lying on top of his feet. "It's just
you and me, old buddies," Macon would tell them. The cat made a
comma of sweat across his bare thighs.

At last he would slip out from under the animals and turn off the
TV. He would put his glass in the chlorine solution in the kitchen sink.
He would climb the stairs. He'd stand at the bedroom window looking
over the neighborhood—black branches scrawled on a purple night sky,
a glimmer of white clapboard here and there, occasionally a light.
Macon always took comfort if he found a light. Someone else had
trouble sleeping too, he assumed. He didn't like to consider any other
possibility—a party, for instance, or a heart-to-heart talk with old friends.
He preferred to believe that someone else was on his own, sitting up
wide awake fending off his thoughts. That made him feel much better.
He returned to his bed. He lay down. He closed his eyes and without
even trying, he dropped off the edge into sleep.

Sarah telephoned Macon and asked if she could come get the navy blue rug from the dining room.

"Navy blue rug," Macon repeated. (He was stalling for time.)

"I wouldn't mention it except you never liked it," Sarah told him. "You said it was a mistake to have a rug where people were eating."

Yes, he had said that. A crumb catcher, he'd said. Unsanitary. Then why did he feel this sudden, wrenching need to keep the rug for himself?

"Macon, are you there?"

"Yes, I'm here."

"So would you mind if I came and got it?"

"No, I guess not."

"Oh, good. My apartment has these bare floors and you've no idea how—"

She would stop by for the rug and he'd invite her in. He'd offer her a glass of sherry. They would sit on the couch with their sherry and he would say, "Sarah, have you missed me?" Or no, he'd say, "I've missed you, Sarah."

She would say . . .

She said, "I thought I'd drop over Saturday morning, if that's convenient."

But people don't drink sherry in the morning.

And besides: He wouldn't even be here then. "I leave for England tomorrow afternoon," he said.

"Oh, is it time for England again?"

"Maybe you could come this evening."

"No, my car's in the shop."

"Your car? What's wrong with it?"

"Well, I was driving along and . . . you know that little red light on the lefthand side of the dash?"

"What, the oil pressure light?"

"Yes, and so I thought, 'Well, I'll be late for the dentist if I stop and see to it now and anyway, the car does seem to be running all right, so—'"

"Wait. Are you saying the light lit up? And then you went on driving?"

"Well, nothing sounded any different and nothing *acted* any different, so I figured—"

"Jesus, Sarah."

"What's so terrible about that?"

"You've probably ruined the engine."

"No, I did not ruin the engine, for your information. I just need this single, simple repair job but unfortunately it's going to take a few days to do it. Well, never mind. I've got a house key; I'll just let myself in on Saturday."

"Maybe I could bring the rug over."

"I'll wait till Saturday."

"That way I could see your apartment," Macon said. "I've never been inside, you know."

"No, it's not fixed up yet."

"I don't care if it's fixed up."

"It's a disaster. Nothing's been done."

"How could nothing be done? You've been living there over a month."

"Well, I'm not so wonderfully perfectly efficient as you are, Macon."

"You wouldn't have to be efficient to—"

"Some days," Sarah said, "I can't even make it out of my bathrobe." Macon was silent.

"I should have agreed to teach summer school," Sarah said. "Something to give some shape to things. I open my eyes in the morning and think, 'Why bother getting up?' "

"Me too," Macon said.

"Why bother eating? Why bother breathing?"

"Me too, sweetheart."

"Macon, do you suppose that person has any idea? I want to go see him in prison, Macon. I want to sit on the other side of the grid or the screen or whatever they have and I'll say, 'Look at me. Look. Look at what you did. You didn't just kill the people you shot; you killed other people besides. What you did goes on and on forever. You didn't just kill my son; you killed me; you killed my husband. I mean I can't even manage to put up my curtains; do you understand what you did?' Then when I'm sure that he does understand, that he really does realize, that he feels just terrible, I'm going to open my purse and pull out a gun and shoot him between the eyes."

"Oh, well, sweetheart—"

"You think I'm just raving, don't you. But Macon, I swear, I can feel that little kick against my palm when I fire the gun. I've never fired a gun in my life—Lord, I don't think I've ever *seen* a gun. Isn't it odd? Ethan's seen one; Ethan's had an experience you and I have no notion of. But sometimes I hold my hand out with the thumb cocked like when kids play cowboy, and I fold my trigger finger and feel what a satisfaction it would be."

"Sarah, it's bad for you to talk like this."

"Oh? How am I supposed to talk?"

"I mean if you let yourself get angry you'll be . . . consumed. You'll burn up. It's not productive."

"Oh, productive! Well, goodness, no, let's not waste our time on anything unproductive."

Macon massaged his forehead. He said, "Sarah, I just feel we can't afford to have these thoughts."

"Easy for you to say."

"No, it is not easy for me to say, dammit—"

"Just shut the door, Macon. Just walk away. Just pretend it never happened. Go rearrange your tools, why don't you; line up your wrenches from biggest to smallest instead of from smallest to biggest; that's always fun."

"Goddammit, Sarah—"

"Don't you curse at me, Macon Leary!"

They paused.

Macon said, "Well."

Sarah said, "Well, anyhow."

"So I guess you'll come by while I'm gone," he said.

"If that's all right."

"Yes, certainly," he said.

Although he felt a curious uneasiness when he hung up, as if he were letting a stranger come. As if she might walk off with more than just the dining room rug.

For his trip to England, he dressed in his most comfortable suit. *One suit is plenty,* he counseled in his guidebooks, *if you take along some travel-size packets of spot remover.* (Macon knew every item that came in travel-size packets, from deordorant to shoe polish.) *The suit should be a medium gray. Gray not only hides the dirt; it's handy for sudden funerals and other formal events. At the same time, it isn't too somber for everyday.*

He packed a minimum of clothes and a shaving kit. A copy of his most recent guide to England. A novel to read on the plane.

Bring only what fits in a carry-on bag. Checking your luggage is asking for trouble. Add several travel-size packets of detergent so you won't fall into the hands of foreign laundries.

When he'd finished packing, he sat on the couch to rest. Or not to rest, exactly, but to collect himself—like a man taking several deep breaths before diving into a river.

The furniture was all straight lines and soothing curves. Dust motes hung in a slant of sunlight. What a peaceful life he led here! If this were any other day he'd be making some instant coffee. He would drop the spoon in the sink and stand sipping from his mug while the cat wove between his feet. Then maybe he'd open the mail. Those acts seemed dear and gentle now. How could he have complained of boredom? At home he had everything set up around him so he hardly needed to think. On trips, even the smallest task required effort and decisions.

When it was two hours till takeoff, he stood up. The airport was a thirty-minute drive at the most, but he hated feeling rushed. He made a final tour of the house, stopping off at the downstairs bathroom— the last *real* bathroom (was how he thought of it) that he'd see for the next week. He whistled for the dog. He picked up his bag and stepped out the front door. The heat slammed into him like something solid.

The dog was going with him only as far as the vet's. If he'd known that, he never would have jumped into the car. He sat next to Macon, panting enthusiastically, his keg-shaped body alert with expectation. Macon talked to him in what he hoped was an unalarming tone. "Hot, isn't it, Edward. You want the air conditioner on?" He adjusted the controls. "There now. Feeling better?" He heard something unctuous in his voice. Maybe Edward did, too, for he stopped panting and gave Macon a sudden suspicious look. Macon decided to say no more.

They rolled through the neighborhood, down streets roofed over with trees. They turned into a sunnier section full of stores and service stations. As they neared Murray Avenue, Edward started whimpering. In the parking lot of the Murray Avenue Veterinary Hospital, he somehow became a much smaller animal.

Macon got out of the car and walked around to open the door. When he took hold of Edward's collar, Edward dug his toenails into the upholstery. He had to be dragged all the way to the building, scritching across the hot concrete.

The waiting room was empty. A goldfish tank bubbled in one corner, with a full-color poster above it illustrating the life cycle of the heartworm. There was a girl on a stool behind the counter, a waifish little person in a halter top.

"I've brought my dog for boarding," Macon said. He had to raise his voice to be heard above Edward's moans.

Chewing her gum steadily, the girl handed him a printed form and a pencil. "Ever been here before?" she asked.

"Yes, often."

"What's the last name?"

"Leary."

"Leary. Leary," she said, riffling through a box of index cards. Macon started filling out the form. Edward was standing upright now and clinging to Macon's knees, like a toddler scared of nursery school.

"Whoa," the girl said.

She frowned at the card she'd pulled.

"Edward?" she said. "On Rayford Road?"

"That's right."

"We can't accept him."

"What?"

"Says here he bit an attendant. Says, 'Bit Barry in the ankle, do not readmit.' "

"Nobody told me that."

"Well, they should have."

"Nobody said a word! I left him in June when we went to the beach; I came back and they handed him over."

The girl blinked at him, expressionless.

"Look," Macon said. "I'm on my way to the airport, right this minute. I've got a plane to catch."

"I'm only following orders," the girl said.

"And what set him off, anyhow?" Macon asked. "Did anyone think to wonder? Maybe Edward had good reason!"

The girl blinked again. Edward had dropped to all fours by now and was gazing upward with interest, as if following the conversation.

"Ah, the hell with it," Macon said. "Come on, Edward."

He didn't have to take hold of Edward's collar when they left. Edward galloped ahead of him all the way across the parking lot.

In that short time, the car had turned into an oven. Macon opened his window and sat there with the motor idling. What now? He considered going to his sister's, but she probably wouldn't want Edward either. To tell the truth, this wasn't the first time there had been complaints. Last week, for instance, Macon's brother Charles had stopped by to borrow a router, and Edward had darted in a complete circle around his feet, taking furious little nibbles of his trouser cuffs. Charles was so astonished that he just turned his head slowly, gaping down. "What's got into him?" he asked. "He never *used* to do this." Then when Macon grabbed his collar, Edward had snarled. He'd curled his upper lip and snarled. Could a dog have a nervous breakdown?

Macon wasn't very familiar with dogs. He preferred cats. He liked the way cats kept their own counsel. It was only lately that he'd given Edward any thought at all. Now that he was alone so much he had taken to talking out loud to him, or sometimes he just sat studying him. He admired Edward's intelligent brown eyes and his foxy little face. He appreciated the honey-colored whorls that radiated so symmetrically from the bridge of his nose. And his walk! Ethan used to say that Edward walked as if he had sand in his bathing suit. His rear end waddled busily; his stubby legs seemed hinged by some more primitive mechanism than the legs of taller dogs.

Macon was driving toward home now, for lack of any better idea. He wondered what would happen if he left Edward in the house the way he left the cat, with plenty of food and water. No. Or could Sarah come see to him, two or three times a day? He recoiled from that; it meant asking her. It meant dialing that number he'd never used and asking her for a favor.

MEOW-BOW ANIMAL HOSPITAL, a sign across the street read. Macon braked and Edward lurched forward. "Sorry," Macon told him. He made a left turn into the parking lot.

The waiting room at the Meow-Bow smelled strongly of disinfectant. Behind the counter stood a thin young woman in a ruffled peasant blouse. She had aggressively frizzy black hair that burgeoned to her shoulders like an Arab headdress. "Hi, there," she said to Macon.

Macon said, "Do you board dogs?"

"Sure."

"I'd like to board Edward, here."

She leaned over the counter to look at Edward. Edward panted up at her cheerfully. It was clear he hadn't yet realized what kind of place this was.

"You have a reservation?" the woman asked Macon.

"Reservation! No."

"Most people reserve."

"Well, I didn't know that."

"Especially in the summer."

"Couldn't you make an exception?"

She thought it over, frowning down at Edward. Her eyes were very small, like caraway seeds, and her face was sharp and colorless.

"Please," Macon said. "I'm about to catch a plane. I'm leaving for a week, and I don't have a soul to look after him. I'm desperate, I tell you."

From the glance she shot at him, he sensed he had surprised her in some way. "Can't you leave him home with your wife?" she asked.

He wondered how on earth her mind worked.

"If I could do that," he said, "why would I be standing here?"

"Oh," she said. "You're not married?"

"Well, I am, but she's . . . living elsewhere. They don't allow pets."

"Oh."

She came out from behind the counter. She was wearing very short red shorts; her legs were like sticks. "I'm a divorsy myself," she said. "I know what you're going through."

"And see," Macon said, "there's this place I usually board him but they suddenly claim he bites. Claim he bit an attendant and they can't admit him anymore."

"Edward? Do you bite?" the woman said.

Macon realized he should not have mentioned that, but she seemed to take it in stride. "How could you do such a thing?" she asked Edward. Edward grinned up at her and folded his ears back, inviting a pat. She bent and stroked his head.

"So will you keep him?" Macon said.

"Oh, I guess," she said, straightening. "If you're desperate." She stressed the word—fixing Macon with those small brown eyes—as if giving it more weight than he had intended. "Fill this out," she told him, and she handed him a form from a stack on the counter. "Your name and address and when you'll be back. Don't forget to put when you'll be back."

Macon nodded, uncapping his fountain pen.

"I'll most likely see you again when you come to pick him up," she said. "I mean if you put the time of day to expect you. My name's Muriel."

"Is this place open evenings?" Macon asked.

"Every evening but Sundays. Till eight."

"Oh, good."

"Muriel Pritchett," she said.

Macon filled out the form while the woman knelt to unbuckle Edward's collar. Edward licked her cheekbone; he must have thought she was just being friendly. So when Macon had finished, he didn't say good-bye. He left the form on the counter and walked out very quickly, keeping a hand in his pocket to silence his keys.

On the flight to New York, he sat next to a foreign-looking man with a mustache. Clamped to the man's ears was a headset for one of those miniature tape recorders. Perfect: no danger of conversation. Macon leaned back in his seat contentedly.

He approved of planes. When the weather was calm, you couldn't even tell you were moving. You could pretend you were sitting safe at home. The view from the window was always the same—air and more air—and the interior of one plane was practically interchangeable with the interior of any other.

He accepted nothing from the beverage cart, but the man beside him took off his headset to order a Bloody Mary. A tinny, intricate, Middle Eastern melody came whispering out of the pink sponge earplugs. Macon stared down at the little machine and wondered if he should buy one. Not for the music, heaven knows—there was far too much noise in the world already—but for insulation. He could plug himself into it and no one would disturb him. He could play a blank tape: thirty full minutes of silence. Turn the tape over and play thirty minutes more.

They landed at Kennedy and he took a shuttle bus to his connecting flight, which wasn't due to leave till evening. Once settled in the terminal, he began filling out a crossword puzzle that he'd saved for this occasion from last Sunday's *New York Times*. He sat inside a kind of barricade—his bag on one chair, his suit coat on another. People milled around him but he kept his eyes on the page, progressing smoothly to the acrostic as soon as he'd finished the crossword. By the time he'd solved both puzzles, they were beginning to board the plane.

His seatmate was a gray-haired woman with glasses. She had brought her own knitted afghan. This was not a good sign, Macon felt, but he could handle it. First he bustled about, loosening his tie and taking off his shoes and removing a book from his bag. Then he opened the book and ostentatiously started reading.

The name of his book was *Miss MacIntosh, My Darling,* and it was 1,198 pages long. *(Always bring a book, as protection against strangers. Magazines don't last. Newspapers from home will make you homesick, and newspapers from elsewhere will remind you you don't belong. You know how alien another paper's typeface seems.)* He'd been lugging around *Miss MacIntosh* for years. It had the advantage of being plotless, as far as he could tell, but invariably interesting, so he could dip into it at random. Any time he raised his eyes, he was careful to mark a paragraph with his finger and to keep a bemused expression on his face.

There was the usual mellifluous murmur from the loudspeaker about seatbelts, emergency exits, oxygen masks. He wondered why stewardesses accented such unlikely words. *"On* our flight this evening we *will* be offering . . ."* The woman next to him asked if he wanted a Lifesaver. "No, thank you," Macon said, and he went on with his book. She rustled some little bit of paper, and shortly afterward the smell of spearmint drifted over to him.

He refused a cocktail and he refused a supper tray, although he did accept the milk that was offered with it. He ate an apple and a little box of raisins from his bag, drank the milk, and went off to the lavatory to floss and brush his teeth. When he returned the plane was darker, dotted here and there with reading lamps. Some of the passengers were already asleep. His seatmate had rolled her hair into little O's and X-ed them over with bobby pins. Macon found it amazing that people could be so unself-conscious on airplanes. He'd seen men in whole suits of pajamas; he'd seen women slathered in face cream. You would think they felt no need to be on guard.

He angled his book beneath a slender shaft of light and turned a page. The engines had a weary, dogged sound. It was the period he thought of as the long haul—the gulf between supper and breakfast when they were suspended over the ocean, waiting for that lightening of the sky that was supposed to be morning although, of course, it was nowhere near morning back home. In Macon's opinion, morning in other time zones was like something staged—a curtain painted with a rising sun, superimposed upon the real dark.

He let his head tip back against the seat and closed his eyes. A stewardess's voice, somewhere near the front of the plane, threaded in and out of the droning of the engines. "We just sat and sat and there wasn't a thing to do and all we had was the Wednesday paper and you know how news just never seems to happen on a Wednesday . . ."

Macon heard a man speaking levelly in his ear. "Macon." But he didn't even turn his head. By now he knew these tricks of sound on planes at night. He saw behind his eyelids the soap dish on the kitchen sink at home—another trick, this concreteness of vision. It was an oval china soap dish painted with yellow roses, containing a worn-down sliver of soap and Sarah's rings, her engagement ring and her wedding band, just as she had left them when she walked out.

"I got the tickets," he heard Ethan say. "And they're opening the doors in five minutes."

"All right," Macon told him, "let's plan our strategy."

"Strategy?"

"Where we're going to sit."

"Why would we need strategy for that?"

"It's you who asked to see this movie, Ethan. I would think you'd take an interest in where you're sitting. Now, here's my plan. You go around to that line on the left. Count the little kids. I'll count the line on the right."

"Aw, Dad—"

"Do you want to sit next to some noisy little kid?"

"Well, no."

"And which do you prefer: an aisle seat?"

"I don't care."

"Aisle, Ethan? Or middle of the row? You must have some opinion."

"Not really."

"Middle of the row?"

"It doesn't make any difference."

"Ethan. It makes a great deal of difference. Aisle, you can get out quicker. So if you plan to buy a snack or go to the restroom, you'll want to sit on the aisle. On the other hand, everyone'll be squeezing past you there. So if you don't think you'll be leaving your seat, then I suggest—"

"Aw, Dad, for Christ's sake!" Ethan said.

"Well," Macon said. "If that's the tone you're going to take, we'll just sit any damn place we happen to end up."

"Fine," Ethan said.

"Fine," Macon said.

Now he did turn his head; he rocked it from side to side. But he kept his eyes tightly closed, and in time the voices stopped, and he found himself in that edgy twilight that passes for sleep when you're traveling.

At dawn he accepted a cup of coffee, and he swallowed a vitamin pill from his bag. The other passengers looked frowsy and pale. His seatmate dragged an entire small suitcase off to the lavatory and returned all combed, but her face was puffy. Macon believed that travel causes retention of fluids. When he put his shoes on, they felt too tight, and when he went to shave he found unfamiliar pillows of flesh beneath his eyes. He was better off than most people, though, because he hadn't touched salted food or drunk any alcohol. Alcohol was definitely retained. Drink alcohol on a plane and you'd feel befuddled for days, Macon believed.

The stewardess announced what time it was in London, and there was a stir as people reset their watches. Macon adjusted the digital alarm clock in his shaving kit. The watch on his wrist—which was not digital but real time, circular—he left as it was.

They landed abruptly. It was like being recalled to the hard facts— all that friction suddenly, the gritty runway, the roaring and braking. The loudspeaker came on, purring courteous reminders. The woman next to Macon folded her afghan. "I'm so excited," she said. "I'm going to see my grandchild for the very first time." Macon smiled and told her he hoped it went well. Now that he didn't have to fear being trapped, he found her quite pleasant. Besides, she was so American-looking.

At Heathrow, there was the usual sense of some recent disaster. People rushed about distractedly, other people stood like refugees surrounded by trunks and parcels, and uniformed authorities were trying to deal with a clamor of questions. Since he didn't have to wait for his luggage, Macon sailed through the red tape far ahead of the others. Then he exchanged his currency and boarded the Underground. *I recommend the Underground for everyone except those afraid of heights, and even for them if they will avoid the following stations, which have exceptionally steep escalators . . .*

While the train racketed along, he sorted his currency into envelopes that he'd brought from home—each envelope clearly marked with a different denomination. *(No fumbling with unfamiliar coins, no peering at misleading imprints, if you separate and classify foreign money ahead of time.)* Across from him a row of faces watched. People looked different here, although he couldn't say just how. He thought they were both finer and unhealthier. A woman with a fretful baby kept saying, "Hush now, love. Hush now, love," in that clear, floating, effortless English voice. It was hot, and her forehead had a pallid shine. So did Macon's, no doubt. He slid the envelopes into his breast pocket. The train stopped and more people got on. They stood above him, clinging not to straps but to bulbs attached to flexible sticks, which Macon on his first visit had taken for some kind of microphone.

He was based in London, as usual. From there he would make brief forays into other cities, never listing more than a handful of hotels, a handful of restaurants within a tiny, easily accessible radius in each place; for his guidebooks were anything but all-inclusive. ("Plenty of other books say how to see as much of a city as possible," his boss had told him. "You should say how to see as little.") The name of Macon's hotel was the Jones Terrace. He would have preferred one of the American chain hotels, but those cost too much. The Jones Terrace was all right, though—small and well kept. He swung into action at once to make his room his own, stripping off the ugly bedspread and stuffing it into a closet, unpacking his belongings and hiding his bag. He changed clothes, rinsed the ones he'd worn and hung them in the shower stall. Then, after a wistful glance at the bed, he went out for breakfast. It was nowhere near morning back home, but breakfast was the meal that businessmen most often had to manage for themselves. He made a point of researching it thoroughly wherever he went.

He walked to the Yankee Delight, where he ordered scrambled eggs and coffee. The service here was excellent. Coffee came at once, and his cup was kept constantly filled. The eggs didn't taste like eggs at home, but then, they never did. What was it about restaurant eggs? They had no character, no backbone. Still, he opened his guidebook and put a checkmark next to the Yankee Delight. By the end of the week, these pages would be barely legible. He'd have scratched out some names, inserted others, and scrawled notes across the margins. He always revisited past entries—every hotel and restaurant. It was tedious but his boss insisted. "Just think how it would look," Julian said, "if a reader walked into some café you'd recommended and found it taken over by vegetarians."

When he'd paid his bill, he went down the street to the New America, where he ordered more eggs and more coffee. "Decaffeinated," he added. (He was a jangle of nerves by now.) The waiter said they didn't have decaffeinated. "Oh, you don't," Macon said. After the waiter had left, Macon made a note in his guidebook.

His third stop was a restaurant called the U.S. Open, where the sausages were so dry that they might have been baked on a rooftop. It figured: The U.S. Open had been recommended by a reader. Oh, the places that readers wrote in to suggest! Macon had once (before he'd grown wiser) reserved a motel room purely on the strength of such a suggestion—somewhere in Detroit or was it Pittsburgh, some city or other, for *Accidental Tourist in America*. He had checked out again at first sight of the linens and fled across the street to a Hilton, where the doorman had rushed to meet him and seized his bag with a cry of pity as if Macon had just staggered in from the desert. Never again, Macon had vowed. He left the sausages on his plate and called for his bill.

In the afternoon (so to speak), he visited hotels. He spoke with various managers and inspected sample rooms where he tested the beds, flushed the toilets, squinted at the showerheads. Most were maintaining their standards, more or less, but something had happened to the Royal Prince. The fact was that it seemed . . . well, foreign.

Dark, handsome men in slim silk suits murmured in the lobby while little brown children chased each other around the spittoons. Macon had the feeling he'd got even more hopelessly lost than usual and ended up in Cairo. Cone-shaped ladies in long black veils packed the revolving doors, spinning in from the street with shopping bags full of . . . what? He tried to imagine their purchasing stone-washed denim shorts and thigh-high boots of pink mesh—the merchandise he'd seen in most shop windows. "Er . . ." he said to the manager. How to put this? He hated to sound narrow-minded, but his readers did avoid the exotic. "Has the hotel, ah, changed ownership?" he asked. The manager seemed unusually sensitive. He drew himself up and said the Royal Prince was owned by a corporation, always had been and always would be, always the same corporation. "I see," Macon said. He left feeling dislocated.

At suppertime, he should have tried someplace formal. He had to list at least one formal restaurant in every city for entertaining clients. But tonight he wasn't up to it. Instead, he went to a café he liked called My American Cousin. The diners there had American accents, and so did some of the staff, and the hostess handed out tickets at the door with numbers on them. If your number was called on the loud-speaker you could win a free TV, or at least a framed color print of the restaurant.

Macon ordered a comforting supper of plain boiled vegetables and two lamb chops in white paper bobby socks, along with a glass of milk. The man at the next table was also on his own. He was eating a nice pork pie, and when the waitress offered him dessert he said, "Oh, now, let me see, maybe I will try some at that," in the slow, pleased, coax-me drawl of someone whose womenfolks have all his life encouraged him to put a little meat on his bones. Macon himself had the gingerbread. It came with cream, just the way it used to at his grandmother's house.

By eight o'clock, according to his wristwatch, he was in bed. It was much too early, of course, but he could stretch the day only so far; the English thought it was midnight. Tomorrow he would start his whirlwind dashes through other cities. He'd pick out a few token hotels, sample a few token breakfasts. Coffee with caffeine and coffee without caffeine. Bacon underdone and overdone. Orange juice fresh and canned and frozen. More showerheads, more mattresses. Hairdryers supplied on request? 110-volt switches for electric shavers? When he fell asleep, he thought anonymous rooms were revolving past on a merry-go-round. He thought webbed canvas suitcase stands, ceiling sprinklers, and laminated lists of fire regulations approached and slid away and approached again, over and over all the rest of his days. He thought Ethan was riding a plaster camel and calling, "Catch me!" and falling, but Macon couldn't get there in time and when he reached his arms out, Ethan was gone.

It was one of Macon's bad habits to start itching to go home too early. No matter how short a stay he'd planned, partway through he would decide that he ought to leave, that he'd allowed himself far too much time, that everything truly necessary had already been accomplished—or almost everything, almost accomplished. Then the rest of his visit was spent in phone calls to travel agents and fruitless trips to airline offices and standby waits that came to nothing, so that he was forced to return to the hotel he'd just checked out of. He always promised himself this wouldn't happen again, but somehow it always did. In England, it happened on his fourth afternoon. What more was there to do? he started wondering. Hadn't he got the gist of the place?

Well, be honest: It was Saturday. He chanced to notice, entering the date in his expense book, that at home it was Saturday morning. Sarah would be stopping by the house for the rug.

She would open the front door and smell home. She would pass through the rooms where she'd been so happy all these years. (Hadn't she been happy?) She would find the cat stretched out on the couch, long and lazy and languid, and she'd settle on the cushion next to her and think, *How could I have left?*

Unfortunately, it was summer, and the airlines were overbooked. He spent two days tracking down faint possibilities that evaporated the instant he drew close. "Anything! Get me anything! I don't have to go to New York; I'll go to Dulles. I'll go to Montreal! Chicago! Shoot, I'll go to Paris or Berlin and see if they have flights. Are there ships? How long do ships take, nowadays? What if this were an emergency? I mean my mother on her deathbed or something? Are you saying there's just no way out of this place?"

The people he dealt with were unfailingly courteous and full of chirpy good humor—really, if not for the strain of travel he believed he might actually have liked the English—but they couldn't solve his problem. In the end he had to stay on. He spent the rest of the week huddled in his room watching TV, chewing a knuckle, subsisting on nonperishable groceries and lukewarm soft drinks because he couldn't face another restaurant.

So he was first in line, naturally, at the check-in counter on the day of his departure. He had his pick of seats: window, nonsmoking. Next to him was a very young couple completely absorbed in each other, so he didn't need *Miss MacIntosh* but sat staring out at the clouds all the long, dull afternoon.

Afternoon was never his favorite time; that was the worst of these homeward flights. It was afternoon for hours and hours, through drinks and lunch and drinks again—all of which he waved away. It was afternoon when they showed the movie; the passengers had to pull their shades down. An orange light filled the plane, burdensome and thick.

Once when he'd been away on an unusually difficult trip—to Japan, where you couldn't even memorize the signs in order to find your way back to a place—Sarah had met his plane in New York. It was their fifteenth anniversary and she had wanted to surprise him. She called Becky at the travel agency to ask his flight number and then she left Ethan with her mother and flew to Kennedy, bringing with her a picnic hamper of wine and cheeses which they shared in the terminal while waiting for their plane home. Every detail of that meal remained in Macon's memory: the cheeses set out on a marble slab, the wine in stemmed crystal glasses that had somehow survived the trip. He could still taste the satiny Brie. He could still see Sarah's small, shapely hand resolutely slicing the bread.

But she didn't meet him in New York today.

She didn't even meet him in Baltimore.

He collected his car from the lot and drove into the city through a glowering twilight that seemed to promise something—a thunderstorm or heat lightning, something dramatic. Could she be waiting at home? In her striped caftan that he was so fond of? With a cool summer supper laid out on the patio table?

Careful not to take anything for granted, he stopped at a Seven-Eleven for milk. He drove to the vet's to pick up Edward. He arrived at the Meow-Bow minutes before closing time; somehow, he'd managed to lose his way. There was no one at the counter. He had to ring the service bell. A girl with a ponytail poked her head through a door, letting in a jumble of animal sounds that rose at all different pitches like an orchestra tuning up. "Yes?" she said.

"I'm here for my dog."

She came forward to open a folder that lay on the counter. "Your last name?"

"Leary."

"Oh," she said. "Just a minute."

Macon wondered what Edward had done wrong this time.

The girl disappeared, and a moment later the other one came out, the frizzy one. This evening she wore a V-necked black dress splashed with big pink flowers, its shoulders padded and its skirt too skimpy; and preposterously high-heeled sandals. "Well, hi there!" she said brightly. "How was your trip?"

"Oh, it was . . . where's Edward? Isn't he all right?"

"Sure, he's all right. He was so good and sweet and friendly!"

"Well, fine," Macon said.

"We just got on like a house afire. Seems he took a shine to me, I couldn't say why."

"Wonderful," Macon said. He cleared his throat. "So could I have him back, please?"

"Caroline will bring him."

"Ah."

There was a silence. The woman waited, facing him and wearing a perky smile, with her fingers laced together on the counter. She had painted her nails dark red, Macon saw, and put on a blackish lipstick that showed her mouth to be an unusually complicated shape—angular, like certain kinds of apples.

"Um," Macon said finally. "Maybe I could pay."

"Oh, yes."

She stopped smiling and peered down at the open folder. "That'll be forty-two dollars," she said.

Macon gave her a credit card. She had trouble working the embossing machine; everything had to be done with the flats of her hands, to spare her nails. She filled in the blanks in a jerky scrawl and then turned the bill in his direction. "Signature and phone," she said. She leaned over the counter to watch what he wrote. "Is that your home phone, or your business?"

"It's both. Why? What difference does it make?" he asked.

"I was just wondering," she told him. She tore off his copy, in that splay-fingered style of hers, and put the rest of the bill in a drawer. "I don't know if I mentioned before that it so happens I train dogs."

"Is that right," Macon said.

He looked toward the door where the first girl had disappeared. It always made him nervous when they took too long bringing Edward. What were they doing back there—getting rid of some evidence?

"My speciality is dogs that bite," the woman said.

"Specialty."

"Pardon?"

"Webster prefers 'specialty.' "

She gave him a blank look.

"That must be a dangerous job," Macon said politely.

"Oh, not for me! I'm not scared of a thing in this world."

There was a scuffling sound at the door behind her. Edward burst through, followed by the girl with the ponytail. Edward was giving sharp yelps and flinging himself about so joyfully that when Macon bent to pat him, he couldn't really connect.

"Now, stop that," the girl told Edward. She was trying to buckle his collar. Meanwhile, the woman behind the counter was saying, "Biters, barkers, deaf dogs, timid dogs, dogs that haven't been treated right, dogs that have learned bad habits, dogs that grew up in pet shops and don't trust human beings . . . I can handle all of those."

"Well, good," Macon said.

"Not that he would bite me, of course," the woman said. "He just fell in love with me, like I think I was telling you."

"I'm glad to hear it," Macon said.

"But I could train him in no time not to bite other people. You think it over and call me. Muriel, remember? Muriel Pritchett. Let me give you my card."

She handed him a salmon-pink business card that she seemed to have pulled out of nowhere. He had to fight his way around Edward to accept it. "I studied with a man who used to train attack dogs," she said. "This is not some amateur you're looking at."

"Well, I'll bear that in mind," Macon said. "Thank you very much."

"Or just call for no reason! Call and talk."

"Talk?"

"Sure! Talk about Edward, his problems, talk about . . . anything! Pick up the phone and just talk. Don't you ever get the urge to do that?"

"Not really," Macon said.

Then Edward gave a particularly piercing yelp, and the two of them rushed home.

Well, of course she wasn't there. He knew it the instant he stepped inside the house, when he smelled that stale hot air and heard the muffled denseness of a place with every window shut. Really he'd known it all along. He'd been fooling himself. He'd been making up fairy tales.

The cat streaked past him and escaped out the door, yowling accusingly. The dog hurtled into the dining room to roll about on the rug and get rid of the scent of the kennel. But there was no rug—only bare, linty floor, and Edward stopped short, looking foolish. Macon knew just how he felt.

He put away the milk and went upstairs to unpack. He took a shower, treading the day's dirty clothes underfoot, and prepared for bed. When he turned off the light in the bathroom, the sight of his laundry dripping over the tub reminded him of travel. Where was the real difference? *Accidental Tourist at Home*, he thought, and he slid wearily into his body bag.

4
=

When the phone rang, Macon dreamed it was Ethan. He dreamed Ethan was calling from camp, wondering why they'd never come to get him. "But we thought you were dead," Macon said, and Ethan said—in that clear voice of his that cracked on the high notes—"Why would you think *that*?" The phone rang again and Macon woke up. There was a thud of disappointment somewhere inside his rib cage. He understood why people said hearts "sank."

In slow motion, he reached for the receiver. "Yes," he said.

"Macon! Welcome back!"

It was Julian Edge, Macon's boss, his usual loud and sprightly self even this early in the morning. "Oh," Macon said.

"How was the trip?"

"It was okay."

"You just get in last night?"

"Yes."

"Find any super new places?"

"Well, 'super' would be putting it a bit strongly."

"So now I guess you start writing it up."

Macon said nothing.

"Just when do you figure to bring me a manuscript?" Julian asked.

"I don't know," Macon said.

"Soon, do you figure?"

"I don't know."

There was a pause.

"I guess I woke you," Julian said.

"Yes."

"Macon Leary in bed," Julian said. He made it sound like the title of something. Julian was younger than Macon and brasher, breezier, not a serious man. He seemed to enjoy pretending that Macon was some kind of character. "So anyway, can I expect it by the end of the month?"

"No," Macon said.

"Why not?"

"I'm not organized."

"Not organized! What's to organize? All you have to do is retype your old one, basically."

"There's a lot more to it than that," Macon said.

"Look. Fellow. Here it is—" Julian's voice grew fainter. He'd be drawing back to frown at his flashy gold calendar watch with the

31

perforated leather racing band. "Here it is the third of August. I want this thing on the stands by October. That means I'd need your manuscript by August thirty-first."

"I can't do it," Macon said.

In fact, it amazed him he'd found the strength to carry on this conversation.

"August thirty-first, Macon. That's four full weeks away."

"It's not enough," Macon said.

"Not enough," Julian said. "Well. All right, then: mid-September. It's going to knock a good many things out of whack, but I'll give you till mid-September. How's that?"

"I don't know," Macon said.

The dullness of his voice interested him. He felt strangely distant from himself. Julian might have sensed this, for after another pause he said, "Hey. Pal. Are you okay?"

"I'm fine," Macon told him.

"I know you've been through a lot, pal—"

"I'm fine! Just fine! What could be wrong? All I need is time to get organized. I'll have the manuscript in by September fifteenth. Possibly earlier. Yes, very possibly earlier. Maybe the end of August. All right?"

Then he hung up.

But his study was so dim and close, and it gave off the salty, inky smell of mental fidgeting. He walked in and felt overwhelmed by his task, as if finally chaos had triumphed. He turned around and walked out again.

Maybe he couldn't get his guidebook organized, but organizing the household was another matter entirely. There was something fulfilling about that, something consoling—or more than consoling; it gave him the sense of warding off a danger. Over the next week or so, he traveled through the rooms setting up new systems. He radically rearranged all the kitchen cupboards, tossing out the little bits of things in sticky, dusty bottles that Sarah hadn't opened in years. He plugged the vacuum cleaner into a hundred-foot extension cord originally meant for lawn mowers. He went out to the yard and weeded, trimmed, pruned, clipped—stripping down, he pictured it. Up till now Sarah had done the gardening, and certain features of it came as a surprise to him. One variety of weed shot off seeds explosively the instant he touched it, a magnificent last-ditch stand, while others gave way so easily—too easily, breaking at the topmost joint so their roots remained in the ground. Such tenacity! Such genius for survival! Why couldn't human beings do as well?

He stretched a clothesline across the basement so he wouldn't have to use the dryer. Dryers were a terrible waste of energy. Then he disconnected the dryer's wide, flexible exhaust tube, and he taught the cat to go in and out through the empty windowpane where the tube had exited. This meant no more litterbox. Several times a day the cat leapt soundlessly to the laundry sink, stood up long and sinewy on her hind legs, and sprang through the window.

It was a pity Edward couldn't do the same. Macon hated walking him; Edward had never been trained to heel and kept winding his leash around Macon's legs. Oh, dogs were so much trouble. Dogs ate mammoth amounts of food, too; Edward's kibble had to be lugged home from the supermarket, dragged out of the car trunk and up the steep front steps and through the house to the pantry. But for that, at least, Macon finally thought of a solution. At the foot of the old coal chute in the basement he set a plastic trash can, with a square cut out of the bottom. Then he poured the remainder of a sack of kibble into the trash can, which magically became a continuous feeder like the cat's. Next time he bought dog food, he could just drive around to the side of the house and send it rattling down the coal chute.

The only hitch was, Edward turned out to be scared of the basement. Every morning he went to the pantry where his breakfast used to be served, and he sat on his fat little haunches and whimpered. Macon had to carry him bodily down the basement stairs, staggering slightly while Edward scrabbled in his arms. Since the whole idea had been to spare Macon's trick back, he felt he'd defeated his purpose. Still, he kept trying.

Also with his back in mind, he tied the clothes basket to Ethan's old skateboard and he dropped a drawstring bag down the laundry chute at the end of a rope. This meant he never had to carry the laundry either up or down the stairs, or even across the basement. Sometimes, though—laboriously scooting the wheeled basket from the clothesline to the laundry chute, stuffing clean sheets into the bag, running upstairs to haul them in by the long stiff rope—Macon felt a twinge of embarrassment. Was it possible that this might be sort of silly?

Well, everything was silly, when you got right down to it.

The neighborhood must have learned by now that Sarah had left him. People started telephoning on ordinary weeknights and inviting him to take "potluck" with them. Macon thought at first they meant one of those arrangements where everybody brings a different pot of something and if you're lucky you end up with a balanced meal. He arrived at Bob and Sue Carney's with a bowl of macaroni and cheese. Since Sue was serving spaghetti, he didn't feel he'd been all that lucky. She set his macaroni at one end of the table and no one ate it but Delilah, the three-year-old. She had several helpings, though.

Macon hadn't expected to find the children at the table. He saw he was somebody different now, some kind of bachelor uncle who was assumed to need a glimpse of family life from time to time. But the fact was, he had never much liked other people's children. And gatherings of any sort depressed him. Physical contact with people not related to him—an arm around his shoulder, a hand on his sleeve—made him draw inward like a snail. "You know, Macon," Sue Carney said, leaning across the table to pat his wrist, "whenever you get the urge, you're welcome to drop in on us. Don't wait for an invitation."

"That's nice of you, Sue," he said. He wondered why it was that outsiders' skin felt so unreal—almost waxy, as if there were an invisible extra layer between him and them. As soon as possible, he moved his wrist.

"If you could live any way you wanted," Sarah had once told him, "I suppose you'd end up on a desert island with no other human beings."

"Why! That's not true at all," he'd said. "I'd have you, and Ethan, and my sister and brothers . . ."

"But no people. I mean, people there just by chance, people you didn't know."

"Well, no, I guess not," he'd said. "Would you?"

But of course she would—back then. Back before Ethan died. She'd always been a social person. When there was nothing else to do she'd stroll happily through a shopping mall—Macon's notion of hell, with all those strangers' shoulders brushing his. Sarah thought crowds were exciting. She liked to meet new people. She was fond of parties, even cocktail parties. You'd have to be crazy to like cocktail parties, Macon thought—those scenes of confusion she used to drag him to, where he was made to feel guilty if he managed by some fluke to get involved in a conversation of any depth. "Circulate. Circulate," Sarah would hiss, passing behind him with her drink.

That had changed during this past year. Sarah didn't like crowds anymore. She never went near a mall, hadn't made him go to any parties. They attended only quiet little dinners and she herself had not given a dinner since Ethan died. He'd asked her once, "Shouldn't we have the Smiths and Millards over? They've had us so often."

Sarah said, "Yes. You're right. Pretty soon." And then did nothing about it.

He and she had met at a party. They'd been seventeen years old. It was one of those mixer things, combining their two schools. Even at that age Macon had disliked parties, but he was secretly longing to fall in love and so he had braved this mixer but then stood off in a corner looking unconcerned, he hoped, and sipping his ginger ale. It was 1958. The rest of the world was in button-down shirts, but Macon wore a black turtleneck sweater, black slacks, and sandals. (He was passing through his poet stage.) And Sarah, a bubbly girl with a tumble of copper-brown curls and a round face, large blue eyes, a plump lower lip—she wore something pink, he remembered, that made her skin look radiant. She was ringed by admiring boys. She was short and tidily made, and there was something plucky about the way her little tan calves were so firmly braced, as if she were determined that this looming flock of basketball stars and football stars would not bowl her over. Macon gave up on her at once. No, not even that—he didn't even consider her, not for a single second, but gazed beyond her to other, more attainable girls. So it had to be Sarah who made the first move. She came over to him and asked what he was acting so stuck-up about. "Stuck-up!" he said. "I'm not stuck-up."

"You sure do look it."

"No, I'm just . . . bored," he told her.

"Well, so do you want to dance, or not?"

They danced. He was so unprepared that it passed in a blur. He enjoyed it only later, back home, where he could think it over in a calmer state of mind. And thinking it over, he saw that if he hadn't looked stuck-up she never would have noticed him. He was the only boy who had not openly pursued her. He would be wise not to pursue her in the future; not to seem too eager, not to show his feelings. With Sarah you had to keep your dignity, he sensed.

Lord knows, though, keeping his dignity wasn't easy. Macon lived with his grandparents, and they believed that no one under eighteen ought to have a driver's license. (Never mind if the state of Maryland felt otherwise.) So Grandfather Leary drove Macon and Sarah on their dates. His car was a long black Buick with a velvety gray backseat on which Macon sat all by himself, for his grandfather considered it unseemly for the two of them to sit there together. "I am not your hired chauffeur," he said, "and besides, the backseat has connotations." (Much of Macon's youth was ruled by connotations.) So Macon sat alone in back and Sarah sat up front with Grandfather Leary. Her cloud of hair, seen against the glare of oncoming headlights, reminded Macon of a burning bush. He would lean forward, clear his throat, and ask, "Um, did you finish your term paper?"

Sarah would say, "Pardon?"

"Term paper," Grandfather Leary would tell her. "Boy wants to know if you finished it."

"Oh. Yes, I finished it."

"She finished it," Grandfather Leary relayed to Macon.

"I do have ears, Grandfather."

"You want to get out and walk? Because I don't have to stand for any mouthing off. I could be home with my loved ones, not motoring around in the dark."

"Sorry, Grandfather."

Macon's only hope was silence. He sat back, still and aloof, knowing that when Sarah looked she'd see nothing but a gleam of blond hair and a blank face—the rest darkness, his black turtleneck blending into the shadows. It worked. "What do you *think* about all the time?" she asked in his ear as they two-stepped around her school gym. He only quirked a corner of his mouth, as if amused, and didn't answer.

Things weren't much different when he got his license. Things weren't much different when he went away to college, though he did give up his black turtlenecks and turn into a Princeton man, crisply, casually attired in white shirts and khakis. Separated from Sarah, he felt a constant hollowness, but in his letters he talked only about his studies. Sarah, home at Goucher, wrote back, *Don't you miss me a little? I can't go anywhere we've been for fear I'll see you looking so mysterious across the room.* She signed her letters *I love you* and he signed his *Fondly.* At night he dreamed she lay next to him, her curls making a whispery sound against his pillow, although all they'd done in real life was a lengthy amount of kissing. He wasn't sure, to tell the truth, that he could manage much more without . . . how did they put it in those days? Losing his cool. Sometimes, he was almost angry with Sarah. He felt he'd been backed into a false position. He was forced to present this impassive front if he wanted her to love him. Oh, so much was expected of men!

She wrote she wasn't dating other people. Neither was Macon, but of course he didn't say so. He came home in the summer and worked at his grandfather's factory; Sarah worked on a tan at the neighborhood pool. Halfway through that summer, she said she wondered why he'd never asked to sleep with her. Macon thought about that and then said, levelly, that in fact he'd like to ask her now. They went to her parents' house; her parents were vacationing in Rehoboth. They climbed the stairs to her little bedroom, all white ruffles and hot sunlight baking the smell of fresh paint. "Did you bring a whatchamacallit?" Sarah asked, and Macon, unwilling to admit that he hardly knew what one looked like, barked, "*No,* I didn't bring a whatchamacallit, who do you think I am?"—a senseless question, if you stopped to examine it, but Sarah took it to mean that he was shocked by her, that he thought her too forward, and she said, "Well, excuse me for living!" and ran down the stairs and out of the house. It took him half an hour to find her, and longer than that to make her stop crying. Really, he said, he'd only been thinking of her welfare: In his experience, whatchamacallits weren't all that safe. He tried to sound knowledgeable and immune to passions of the moment. He suggested she visit a doctor he knew—it happened to be the doctor who treated his grandmother's Female Complaint. Sarah dried her tears and borrowed Macon's pen to write the doctor's name on the back of a chewing gum wrapper. But wouldn't the doctor refuse her? she asked. Wouldn't he say she ought to be at least engaged? Well, all right, Macon said, they would get engaged. Sarah said that would be lovely.

Their engagement lasted three years, all through college. Grandfather Leary felt the wedding should be delayed even further, till Macon was firmly settled in his place of employment; but since his place of employment would be Leary Metals, which manufactured cork-lined caps for soft drink bottles, Macon couldn't see himself concentrating on that even briefly. Besides, the rush to and from Sarah's bedroom on her mother's Red Cross days had begun to tell on them both.

So they married the spring they graduated from college, and Macon went to work at the factory while Sarah taught English at a private school. It was seven years before Ethan was born. By that time, Sarah was no longer calling Macon "mysterious." When he was quiet now it seemed to annoy her. Macon sensed this, but there was nothing he could do about it. In some odd way, he was locked inside the standoffish self he'd assumed when he and she first met. He was frozen there. It was like that old warning of his grandmother's: Don't cross your eyes, they might get stuck that way. No matter how he tried to change his manner, Sarah continued to deal with him as if he were someone unnaturally cool-headed, someone more even in temperament than she but perhaps not quite as feeling.

He had once come upon a questionnaire that she'd filled out in a ladies' magazine—one of those "How Happy Is Your Marriage?" things—and where it said, *I believe I love my spouse more than he/she loves me,* Sarah had checked *True.* The unsettling part was that after Macon gave his automatic little snort of denial, he had wondered if it might be true after all. Somehow, his role had sunk all the way through to the heart. Even internally, by now, he was a fairly chilly man, and if you didn't count his son (who was easy, *easy;* a child is no test at all), there was not one person in his life whom he really agonized over.

When he thought about this now, it was a relief to remind himself that he did miss Sarah, after all. But then his relief seemed unfeeling too, and he groaned and shook his head and tugged his hair in great handfuls.

Some woman phoned and said, "Macon?" He could tell at once it wasn't Sarah. Sarah's voice was light and breathy; this one was rough, tough, wiry. "It's Muriel," she said.

"Muriel," he said.

"Muriel Pritchett."

"Ah, yes," he said, but he still had no clue who she was.

"From the vet's?" she asked. "Who got on so good with your dog?"

"Oh, the vet's!"

He saw her, if dimly. He saw her saying her own name, the long *u* sound and the *p* drawing up her dark red mouth.

"I was just wondering how Edward was."

Macon glanced over at Edward. The two of them were in the study, where Macon had managed to type half a page. Edward lay flat on his stomach with his legs straight out behind him—short, pudgy legs like the drumsticks of a dressed Long Island duckling. "He looks all right to me," Macon said.

"I mean, is he biting?"

"Well, not lately, but he's developed this new symptom. He gets angry if I leave the house. He starts barking and showing his teeth."

"I still think he ought to be trained."

"Oh, you know, he's four and a half and I suppose—"

"That's not too old! I could do it in no time. Tell you what, maybe I could just come around and discuss it. You and me could have a drink or something and talk about what his problems are."

"Well, I really don't think—"

"Or you could come to *my* place. I'd fix you supper."

Macon wondered how it would help Edward to be dragged to supper at some stranger's house.

"Macon? What do you say?" she asked.

"Oh, why, um . . . I think for now I'll just try to manage on my own."

"Well, I can understand that," she said. "Believe me. I've been through that stage. So what I'll do is, I'll wait for you to get in touch. You do still have my card, don't you?"

Macon said he did, although he had no idea where it had got to.

"I don't want to be pushy!" she said.

"No, well . . ." Macon said. Then he hung up and went back to his guidebook.

He was still on the introduction, and it was already the end of August. How would he meet his deadline? The back of the desk chair hit his spine in just the wrong place. The *s* key kept sticking. The typewriter tapped out audible words. "Inimitable," it said. His typing sounded just like Sarah saying "inimitable." "You in your inimitable way . . ." she told him. He gave a quick shake of his head. *Generally food in England is not as jarring as in other foreign countries. Nice cooked vegetables, things in white sauce, pudding for dessert . . . I don't know why some travelers complain about English food.*

In September, he decided to alter his system of dressing. If he wore sweat suits at home—the zipper-free kind, nothing to scratch or bind him—he could go from one shower to the next without changing clothes. The sweat suit would serve as both pajamas and day wear.

He bought a couple of them, medium gray. The first night he wore one to bed he enjoyed the feel of it, and he liked not having to dress the next morning. In fact, it occurred to him that he might as well wear the same outfit two days in a row; skip his shower on alternate evenings. Talk about saving energy! In the morning all he had to do was shave. He wondered if he ought to grow a beard.

Around noon of the second day, though, he started feeling a little low. He was sitting at his typewriter and something made him notice his posture—stooped and sloppy. He blamed the sweat suit. He rose and went to the full-length mirror in the hall. His reflection reminded him of a patient in a mental hospital. Part of the trouble, perhaps, was his shoes—regular black tie shoes intended for dressier clothes. Should he buy sneakers? But he would hate to be mistaken for a jogger. He noticed that without a belt around his waist, he tended to let his stomach stick out. He stood up straighter. That evening when it was time to wash the first sweat suit, he used extra-hot water to shrink out some of the bagginess.

He felt much worse in the morning. It had been a warm night and he woke up sticky and cross. He couldn't face the thought of popcorn for breakfast. He laundered a load of sheets and then, in the midst of hanging them, found himself standing motionless with his head bowed, both wrists dangling over the clothesline as if he himself had been pinned there. "Buck up," he said aloud. His voice sounded creaky, out of practice.

This was his day for grocery shopping—Tuesday, when the supermarket was least crowded with other human beings. But somehow, he couldn't bring himself to get going. He dreaded all that business with the address books, the three tabbed books he shopped with. (One held data from *Consumer Reports*—the top-rated brand of bread, for instance, listed under B. In another he noted prices, and in the third he filed his coupons.) He kept having to stop and riffle through them, muttering prices under his breath, comparing house brands to cents-off name brands. Oh, everything seemed so complicated. Why bother? Why eat at all, in fact?

On the other hand, he needed milk. And Edward was low on dog food, and Helen was completely out of cat food.

He did something he'd never done before. He telephoned The Market Basket, a small, expensive grocery that delivered. And he didn't order just emergency rations. No, he called in the whole week's list. "Shall we bring this to the front or the back?" the clerk asked in her tinselly voice.

"The back," Macon said. "No, wait. Bring the perishables to the back, but put the dog food next to the coal chute."

"Coal chute," the clerk repeated, apparently writing it down.

"The coal chute at the side of the house. But not the cat food; that goes in back with the perishables."

"Well, wait now—"

"And the upstairs items at the front of the house."

"What upstairs items?"

"Toothpaste, Ivory soap, dog biscuits . . ."

"I thought you said the dog biscuits went to the coal chute."

"Not the dog biscuits, the dog *food!* It's the food that goes to the coal chute, dammit."

"Now, look here," the clerk said. "There's no call to be rude."

"Well, I'm sorry," Macon told her, "but I just want the simplest thing, it seems to me: one puny box of Milkbone biscuits up beside my bed. If I give Edward my buttered popcorn it upsets his stomach. Otherwise I wouldn't mind; it's not as if I'm hoarding it all for myself or something, but he has this sensitivity to fats and I'm the only one in the house, it's me who has to clean up if he gets sick. I'm the only one to do it; I'm all alone; it's just me; it seems everybody's just . . . fled from me, I don't know, I've lost them, I'm left standing here saying, 'Where'd they go? Where is everybody? Oh, God, what did I do that was so bad?' "

His voice was not behaving right and he hung up. He stood over the telephone rubbing his forehead. Had he given her his name? Or not. He couldn't remember. Please, please, let him not have given her his name.

He was falling apart; that much was obvious. He would have to get a grip on himself. First thing: out of this sweat suit. It was some kind of jinx. He clapped his hands together briskly, and then he climbed the stairs. In the bathroom, he yanked off the sweat suit and dropped it into the tub. Yesterday's hung from the shower curtain rod, still damp. There wasn't a chance it would dry by tonight. What a mistake! He felt like a fool. He'd come within an inch, within a hairsbreadth of turning into one of those pathetic creatures you see on the loose from time to time—unwashed, unshaven, shapeless, talking to themselves, padding along in their institutional garb.

Neatly dressed now in a white shirt and khakis, he gathered the damp sweat suit and carried it down to the basement. It would make good winter pajamas, at least. He put it in the dryer, wedged the exhaust tube in the window again, and set the dials. Better to consume a little energy than to fall into despair over a soggy sweat suit.

At the top of the basement stairs, Edward was complaining. He was hungry, but not brave enough to descend the stairs on his own. When he caught sight of Macon he lay flat, with his nose poking over the topmost step, and put on a hopeful expression. "Coward," Macon told him. He scooped Edward up in both arms and turned to lumber back down. Edward's teeth started chattering—a tickety-tick like rice in a cup. It occurred to Macon that Edward might know something he didn't. Was the basement haunted, or what? It had been weeks now, and Edward was still so frightened that sometimes, set in front of his food, he just stood there dismally and made a puddle without bothering to lift his leg. "You're being very silly, Edward," Macon told him.

Just then, an eerie howl rose from . . . where? From the basement's very air, it seemed. It continued steadily; it grew. Edward, who must have been expecting this all along, kicked off instantly with his sturdy, clawed hind legs against Macon's diaphragm. Macon felt the wind knocked out of him. Edward whomped into the wall of damp body bags on the clothesline, rebounded, and landed in the center of Macon's stomach. Macon set one foot blindly in the wheeled basket and his legs went out from under him. He stepped down hard into empty space.

He was lying on his back, on the clammy cement floor, with his left leg doubled beneath him. The sound that had set all this in motion paused for one split second and then resumed. It was clear now that it came from the dryer's exhaust tube. "Shoot," Macon said to Edward, who lay panting on top of him. "Wouldn't you think that idiot cat would know the dryer was running?"

He could see how it must have happened. Attempting to enter from outside, she'd been met by a whistling wind, but she had stubbornly continued into the tube. He pictured her eyes pressed into slits, her ears flattened back by a lint-filled gale. Wailing and protesting, she had nonetheless clung to her course. What persistence!

Macon shook Edward off and rolled over on his stomach. Even so small a movement caused him agony. He felt a lump of nausea beginning in his throat, but he rolled once more, dragging his leg behind him. With his teeth set, he reached for the door of the dryer and pulled it open. The sweat suit slowly stopped revolving. The cat stopped howling. Macon watched her bumbling, knobby shape inching backward through the tube. Just as she reached her exit, the entire tube fell out of the window and into the laundry sink, but Helen didn't fall with it. He hoped she was all right. He watched until she scurried past the other window, looking just slightly rumpled. Then he drew a breath and began the long, hard trip up the stairs for help.

5
=

Oh, I've erred and I have stumbled," Macon's sister sang in the kitchen, "I've been sinful and unwise . . ."

She had a tremulous soprano that sounded like an old lady's, although she was younger than Macon. You could imagine such a voice in church, some country kind of church where the women still wore flat straw hats.

> I'm just a lucky pilgrim
> On the road to Paradise.

Macon was lying on the daybed in his grandparents' sun porch. His left leg, encased in plaster from mid-thigh to instep, was not painful so much as absent. There was a constant dull, cottony numbness that made him want to pinch his own shin. Not that he could, of course. He was sealed away from himself. The hardest blow felt like a knock on the wall from a neighboring room.

Still, he felt a kind of contentment. He lay listening to his sister fix breakfast, idly scratching the cat who had made herself a nest in the blankets. "I've had trials, I've had sorrows," Rose trilled merrily, "I've had grief and sacrifice . . ." Once she got the coffee started, she would come help him across the living room to the downstairs bathroom. He still found it difficult to navigate, especially on polished floors. Nowadays he marveled at all those people on crutches whom he used to take for granted. He saw them as a flock of stalky wading birds, dazzlingly competent with their sprightly hops and debonaire pivots. How did they do it?

His own crutches, so new their rubber tips were not yet scuffed, leaned against the wall. His bathrobe hung over a chair. Beneath the window was a folding card table with a wood-grained cardboard top and rickety legs. His grandparents had been dead for years, but the table remained set up as if for one of their eternal bridge games. Macon knew that on its underside was a yellowed label reading ATLAS MFG. CO., with a steel engraving of six plump, humorless men in high-collared suits standing upon a board laid across the very same table. FURNISHINGS OF DECEPTIVE DELICACY, the caption said. Macon associated the phrase with his grandmother: deceptive delicacy. Lying on the sun porch floor as a boy, he had studied her fragile legs, from which her anklebones jutted out like doorknobs. Her solid, black, chunky-heeled shoes were planted squarely a foot apart, never tapping or fidgeting.

He heard his brother Porter upstairs, whistling along with Rose's song. He knew it was Porter because Charles never whistled. There was the sound of a shower running. His sister looked through the sun porch door, with Edward peering around her and panting at Macon as if he were laughing.

"Macon? Are you awake?" Rose asked.

"I've *been* awake for hours," he told her, for there was something vague about her that caused her brothers to act put-upon and needy whenever she chanced to focus on them. She was pretty in a sober, prim way, with beige hair folded unobtrusively at the back of her neck where it wouldn't be a bother. Her figure was a very young girl's, but her clothes were spinsterly and concealing.

She wrapped him in his bathrobe and helped him stand up. Now his leg actively hurt. It seemed the pain was a matter of gravity. A throbbing ache sank slowly down the length of the bone. With Rose supporting him on one side and a crutch on the other, he hobbled out of the sun porch, through the living room with its shabby, curlicued furniture. The dog kept getting underfoot. "Maybe I could stop and rest a moment," Macon said when they passed the couch.

"It's only a little farther."

They entered the pantry. Rose opened the bathroom door and helped him inside. "Call me when you're ready," she said, closing the door after him. Macon sagged against the sink.

At breakfast, Porter was cheerily talkative while the others ate in silence. Porter was the best-looking of all the Learys—more tightly knit than Macon, his hair a brighter shade of blond. He gave an impression of vitality and direction that his brothers lacked. "Got a lot to do today," he said between mouthfuls. "That meeting with Herrin, interviews for Dave's old job, Cates flying in from Atlanta . . ."

Charles just sipped his coffee. While Porter was already dressed, Charles still wore his pajamas. He was a soft, sweet-faced man who never seemed to move; any time you looked at him he'd be watching you with his sorrowful eyes that slanted downward at the outer corners.

Rose brought the coffeepot from the stove. "Last night, Edward woke me twice asking to go out," she said. "Do you think he has some sort of kidney problem?"

"It's the adjustment," Macon said. "Adjustment to change. I wonder how he knows not to wake *me*."

Porter said, "Maybe we could rig up some sort of system. One of those little round pet doors or something."

"Edward's kind of portly for a pet door," Macon said.

"Besides," Rose said, "the yard's not fenced. We can't let him out on his own if he's not fenced in."

"A litterbox, then," Porter suggested.

"Litterbox! For a dog?"

"Why not? If it were big enough."

Macon said, "Use a bathtub. The one in the basement. No one goes there anymore."

"But who would clean it?"

"Ah."

They all looked down at Edward, who was lying at Rose's feet. He rolled his eyes at them.

"How come you have him, anyway?" Porter asked Macon.

"He was Ethan's."

"Oh. I see," Porter said. He gave a little cough. "Animals!" he said brightly. "Ever considered what they must think of us? I mean, here we come back from the grocery store with the most amazing haul—chicken, pork, half a cow. We leave at nine and we're back at ten, evidently having caught an entire herd of beasts. They must think we're the greatest hunters on earth!"

Macon leaned back in his chair with his coffee mug cupped in both hands. The sun was warming the breakfast table, and the kitchen smelled of toast. He almost wondered whether, by some devious, subconscious means, he had engineered this injury—every elaborate step leading up to it—just so he could settle down safe among the people he'd started out with.

Charles and Porter left for the factory, and Rose went upstairs and ran the vacuum cleaner. Macon, who was supposed to be typing his guide-book, struggled back to the sun porch and collapsed. Since he'd come home he'd been sleeping too much. The urge to sleep was like a great black cannonball rolling around inside his skull, making his head heavy and droopy.

On the wall at the end of the room hung a portrait of the four Leary children: Charles, Porter, Macon, and Rose, clustered in an armchair. Their grandfather had commissioned that portrait several years before they came to live with him. They were still in California with their mother—a giddy young war widow. From time to time she sent snapshots, but Grandfather Leary found those inadequate. By their very nature, he told her in his letters, photos lied. They showed what a person looked like over a fraction of a second—not over long, slow minutes, which was what you'd take to study someone in real life. In that case, said Alicia, didn't paintings lie also? They showed hours instead of minutes. It wasn't Grandfather Leary she said this to, but the artist, an elderly Californian whose name Grandfather Leary had somehow got hold of. If the artist had had a reply, Macon couldn't remember what it was.

He could remember sitting for the portrait, though, and now when he looked at it he had a very clear picture of his mother standing just outside the gilded frame in a pink kimono, watching the painting take shape while she toweled her hair dry. She had fluffy, short, brittle hair whose color she "helped along," as she put it. Her face was a type no longer seen—it wasn't just unfashionable, it had vanished altogether. How did women mold their basic forms to suit the times? Were there no more of those round chins, round foreheads, and bruised, baroque little mouths so popular in the forties?

The artist, it was obvious, found her very attractive. He kept pausing in his work to say he wished she were the subject. Alicia gave a breathless laugh and shooed away his words with one hand. Probably later she had gone out with him a few times. She was always taking up with new men, and they were always the most exciting men in the world, to hear her tell it. If they were artists, why, she had to give a party and get all her friends to buy their paintings. If they flew small planes on weekends, she had to start pilot's lessons. If they were political, there she was on street corners thrusting petitions on passersby. Her children were too young to worry about the men themselves, if there was any reason to worry. No, it was her enthusiasm that disturbed them. Her enthusiasm came in spurts, a violent zigzag of hobbies, friends, boyfriends, causes. She always seemed about to fall over the brink of something. She was always going too far. Her voice had an edge to it, as if at any moment it might break. The faster she talked and the brighter her eyes grew, the more fixedly her children stared at her, as if willing her to follow their example of steadiness and dependability. "Oh, what is it with you?" she would ask them. "Why are you such sticks?" And she would give up on them and flounce off to meet her crowd. Rose, the baby, used to wait for her return in the hall, sucking her thumb and stroking an old fur stole that Alicia never wore anymore.

Sometimes Alicia's enthusiasm turned to her children—an unsettling experience. She took them all to the circus and bought them cotton candy that none of them enjoyed. (They liked to keep themselves tidy.) She yanked them out of school and enrolled them briefly in an experimental learning community where no one wore clothes. The four of them, chilled and miserable, sat hunched in a row in the common room with their hands pressed flat between their bare knees. She dressed as a witch and went trick-or-treating with them, the most mortifying Halloween of their lives, for she got carried away as usual and cackled, croaked, scuttled up to strangers and shook her ragged broom in their faces. She started making mother-daughter outfits for herself and Rose, in strawberry pink with puffed sleeves, but stopped when the sewing machine pierced her finger and made her cry. (She was always getting hurt. It may have been because she rushed so.) Then she turned to something else, and something else, and something else. She believed in change as if it were a religion. Feeling sad? Find a new man! Creditors after you, rent due, children running fevers? Move to a new apartment! During one year, they moved so often that every day after school, Macon had to stand deliberating a while before setting out for home.

In 1950, she decided to marry an engineer who traveled around the world building bridges. "Portugal. Panama. Brazil," she told the children. "We'll finally get to see our planet." They gazed at her stonily. If they had met this man before, they had no recollection of it. Alicia said, "Aren't you excited?" Later—it may have been after he took them all out to dinner—she said she was sending them to live with their grandparents instead. "Baltimore's more suitable for children, really," she said. Did they protest? Macon couldn't remember. He recalled his childhood as a glassed-in place with grown-ups rushing past, talking at him, making changes, while he himself stayed mute. At any rate, one hot night in June Alicia put them on a plane to Baltimore. They were met by their grandparents, two thin, severe, distinguished people in dark clothes. The children approved of them at once.

After that, they saw Alicia only rarely. She would come breezing into town with an armload of flimsy gifts from tropical countries. Her print dresses struck the children as flashy; her makeup was too vivid, like a foreigner's. She seemed to find her children comical—their navy-and-white school uniforms, their perfect posture. "My God! How stodgy you've grown!" she would cry, evidently forgetting she'd thought them stodgy all along. She said they took after their father. They sensed this wasn't meant as a compliment. (When they asked what their father had been like, she looked down at her own chin and said, "Oh, Alicia, grow up.") Later, when her sons married, she seemed to see even more resemblance, for at one time or another she'd apologized to all three daughters-in-law for what they must have to put up with. Like some naughty, gleeful fairy, Macon imagined, she darted in and out of their lives leaving a trail of irresponsible remarks, apparently never considering they might be passed on. "I don't see how you stay married to the man," she'd said to Sarah. She herself was now on her fourth husband, a rock-garden architect with a white goatee.

It was true the children in the portrait seemed unrelated to her. They lacked her blue-and-gold coloring; their hair had an ashy cast and their eyes were a steely gray. They all had that distinct center groove from nose to upper lip. And never in a million years would Alicia have worn an expression so guarded and suspicious.

Uncomfortably arranged-looking, they gazed out at the viewer. The two older boys, plump Charles and trim Porter, perched on either arm of the chair in white shirts with wide, flat, open collars. Rose and Macon sat on the seat in matching playsuits. Rose appeared to be in Macon's lap, although actually she'd been settled between his knees, and Macon had the indrawn tenseness of someone placed in a physically close situation he wasn't accustomed to. His hair, like the others', slanted silkily across his forehead. His mouth was thin, almost colorless, and firmed a bit, as if he'd decided to take a stand on something. The set of that mouth echoed now in Macon's mind. He glanced at it, glanced away, glanced back. It was Ethan's mouth. Macon had spent twelve years imagining Ethan as a sort of exchange student, a visitor from the outside world, and here it turned out he'd been a Leary all along. What a peculiar thing to recognize at this late date.

He sat up sharply and reached for his trousers, which Rose had cut short across the left thigh and hemmed with tiny, even stitches.

No one else in the world had the slightest idea where he was. Not Julian, not Sarah, not anyone. Macon liked knowing that. He said as much to Rose. "It's nice to be so unconnected," he told her. "I wish things could stay that way a while."

"Why can't they?"

"Oh, well, you know, someone will call here, Sarah or some-one—"

"Maybe we could just not answer the phone."

"What, let it go on ringing?"

"Why not?"

"Not answer it *any* time?"

"Most who call me are neighbors," Rose said. "They'll pop over in person if they don't get an answer. And you know the boys: Neither one of them likes dealing with telephones."

"That's true," Macon said.

Julian would come knocking on his door, planning to harangue him for letting his deadline slip past. He'd have to give up. Then Sarah would come for a soup ladle or something, and when he didn't answer she would ask the neighbors and they'd say he hadn't shown his face in some time. She would try to get in touch with his family and the telephone would ring and ring, and then she would start to worry. *What's happened?* she would wonder. *How could I have left him on his own?*

Lately, Macon had noticed he'd begun to view Sarah as a form of enemy. He'd stopped missing her and started plotting her remorsefulness. It surprised him to see how quickly he'd made the transition. Was this what two decades of marriage amounted to? He liked to imagine her self-reproaches. He composed and recomposed her apologies. He hadn't had such thoughts since he was a child, dreaming of how his mother would weep at his funeral.

In the daytime, working at the dining room table, he would hear the telephone and he'd pause, fingers at rest on the typewriter keys. One ring, two rings. Three rings. Rose would walk in with a jar of silver polish. She didn't even seem to hear. "What if that's some kind of emergency?" he would ask. Rose would say, "Hmm? Who would call *us* for an emergency?" and then she would take the silver from the buffet and spread it at the other end of the table.

There had always been some family member requiring Rose's care. Their grandmother had been bedridden for years before she died, and then their grandfather got so senile, and first Charles and later Porter had failed in their marriages and come back home. So she had enough right here to fill her time. Or she made it enough; for surely it couldn't be necessary to polish every piece of silver every week. Shut in the house with her all day, Macon noticed how painstakingly she planned the menus; how often she reorganized the utensil drawer; how she ironed even her brothers' socks, first separating them from the clever plastic grips she used to keep them mated in the washing machine. For Macon's lunch, she cooked a real meal and served it on regular place mats. She set out cut-glass dishes of pickles and olives that had to be returned to their bottles later on. She dolloped homemade mayonnaise into a tiny bowl.

Macon wondered if it ever occurred to her that she lived an odd sort of life—unemployed, unmarried, supported by her brothers. But what job would she be suited for? he asked himself. Although he could picture her, come to think of it, as the mainstay of some musty, antique law firm or accounting firm. Nominally a secretary, she would actually run the whole business, arranging everything just so on her employer's desk every morning and allowing no one below her or above her to overlook a single detail. Macon could use a secretary like that. Recalling the gum-chewing redhead in Julian's disastrous office, he sighed and wished the world had more Roses.

He zipped a page from his typewriter and set it face down on a stack of others. He had finished with his introduction—general instructions like *A subway is not an underground train* and *Don't say restroom, say toilet*—and he'd finished the chapter called "Trying to Eat in England." Rose had mailed those off for him yesterday. That was his new stratagem: sending his book piece by piece from this undisclosed location. "There's no return address on this," Rose told him. "There's not meant to be," Macon said. Rose had nodded solemnly. She was the only one in the family who viewed his guidebooks as real writing. She kept a row of them in her bedroom bookcase, alphabetized by country.

In midafternoon, Rose stopped work to watch her favorite soap opera. This was something Macon didn't understand. How could she waste her time on such trash? She said it was because there was a wonderfully evil woman in it. "There are enough evil people in real life," Macon told her.

"Yes, but not wonderfully evil."

"Well, that's for sure."

"This one, you see, is so obvious. You know exactly whom to mistrust."

While she watched, she talked aloud to the characters. Macon could hear her in the dining room. "It isn't *you* he's after, sweetie," she said, and "Just you wait. Ha!"—not at all her usual style of speech. A commercial broke in, but Rose stayed transfixed where she was. Macon, meanwhile, worked on "Trying to Sleep in England," typing away in a dogged, uninspired rhythm.

When the doorbell rang, Rose didn't respond. Edward went mad, barking and scratching at the door and running back to Macon and racing again to the door. "Rose?" Macon called. She said nothing. Finally he stood up, assembled himself on his crutches, and went as quietly as possible to the hall.

Well, it wasn't Sarah. A glance through the lace curtain told him that much. He opened the door and peered out. "Yes?" he said.

It was Garner Bolt, a neighbor from home—a scrawny little gray man who had made his fortune in cleaning supplies. When he saw Macon, every line in his pert, pointed face turned upward. "There you are!" he said. It was hard to hear him over Edward, who went on barking frantically.

"Why, Garner," Macon said.

"We worried you had died."

"You did?"

Macon grabbed at Edward's collar, but missed.

"Saw the papers piling up on your lawn, mail inside your screen door, didn't know what to think."

"Well, I meant to send my sister for those," Macon said. "I broke my leg, you see."

"Now, how did you do that?"

"It's a long story."

He gave up blocking the door. "Come on in," he told Garner.

Garner took off his cap, which had a Sherwin-Williams Paint sign across the front. His jacket was part of some long-ago suit, a worn shiny brown, and his overalls were faded to white at the knees. He stepped inside, skirting the dog, and shut the door behind him. Edward's barks turned to whimpers. "My car is full of your mail," Garner said. "Brenda said I ought to bring it to your sister and ask if she knew of your whereabouts. Also I promised your friend."

"What friend?"

"Lady in pedal pushers."

"I don't know any lady in pedal pushers," Macon said. He hadn't realized pedal pushers still existed, even.

"Saw her standing on your porch, rattling your doorknob. Calling out, 'Macon? You in there?' Skinny little lady with hair. Looked to be in her twenties or so."

"Well, I can't imagine who it was."

"Squinching in and shading her eyes."

"Who could it be?"

"Tripping down the porch steps in her great tall pointy high heels."

"The dog lady," Macon said. "Jesus."

"Kind of young, ain't she?"

"I don't even know her!"

"Going round the back of the house to call out, 'Macon? Macon?'"

"I barely met her!"

"It was her that told me about the windle."

"Windle?"

"Windle to the basement, all broke out. Fall sets in and it'll turn your furnace on. Waste all kinds of energy."

"Oh. Well. Yes, I suppose it would," Macon said.

"We thought you might've been burglarized or something."

Macon led the way to the dining room. "See, what happened," he said, "I broke my leg and I came to live at my family's till I could manage for myself again."

"We didn't see no ambulance though or nothing."

"Well, I called my sister."

"Sister's a doctor?"

"Just to come and take me to the emergency room."

"When Brenda broke her hip on the missing step," Garner said, "she called the ambulance."

"Well, I called my sister."

"Brenda called the ambulance."

They seemed to be stuck.

"I guess I ought to notify the post office about my mail," Macon said finally. He lowered himself into his chair.

Garner pulled out another chair and sat down with his cap in his hands. He said, "I could just keep on bringing it."

"No, I'll have Rose notify them. Lord, all these bills must be coming due and so forth—"

"I could bring it just as easy."

"Thanks anyway."

"Why don't I bring it."

"To tell the truth," Macon said, "I'm not so sure I'll be going back there."

This hadn't occurred to him before. He placed his crutches together delicately, like a pair of chopsticks, and laid them on the floor beside his chair. "I might stay on here with my family," he said.

"And give up that fine little house?"

"It's kind of big for just one person."

Garner frowned down at his cap. He put it on his head, changed his mind, and took it off again. "Look," he said. "Back when me and Brenda were newlyweds we were awful together. Just awful. Couldn't neither one of us stand the other, I'll never know how we lasted."

"We aren't newlyweds, though," Macon said. "We've been married twenty years."

"Brenda and me did not speak to each other for very nearly every bit of nineteen and thirty-five," Garner said. "January to August, nineteen and thirty-five. New Year's Day till my summer vacation. Not a single blessed word."

Macon's attention was caught. "What," he said, "not even 'Pass the salt'? 'Open the window'?"

"Not even that."

"Well, how did you manage your daily life?"

"Mostly, she stayed over to her sister's."

"Oh, then."

"The morning my vacation began, I felt so miserable I like to died. Thought to myself, 'What am I doing, anyhow?' Called long distance to Ocean City and booked a room for two. In those days long distance was some big deal, let me tell you. Took all these operators and so forth and it cost a mint. Then I packed some clothes for me and some clothes for Brenda and went on over to her sister's house. Her sister says, 'What do *you* want?' She was the type that likes to see dissension. I walk right past her. Find Brenda in the living room, mending hose. Open my suitcase: 'Look at here. Your sun dress for dining in a seafood restaurant,' I tell her. 'Two pairs of shorts. Two blouses. Your swimsuit.' She don't even look at me. 'Your bathrobe,' I say. 'Your nightgown you wore on our honeymoon.' Acts like I'm not even there. 'Brenda,' I tell her. I say. 'Brenda, I am nineteen years old and I'll never be nineteen again. I'll never be *alive* again. I mean this is the only life I get to go through, Brenda, so far as I know, and I've spent this great large chunk of it sitting alone in an empty apartment too proud to make up, too scared you'd say no, but even if you did say no it can't be worse than what I got now. I'm the loneliest man in the world, Brenda, so please come to Ocean City with me.' And Brenda, she lays down her mending and says, 'Well, since you ask, but it looks to me like you forgot my bathing cap.' And off we went."

He sat back triumphantly in his chair. "So," he said.

"So," Macon said.

"So you get my point."

"What point?"

"You have to let her know you need her."

"See, Garner, I think we've gone beyond little things like letting her know I—"

"Don't take this personally, Macon, but I got to level with you: There's times when you've been sort of frustrating. I'm not talking about myself, mind; *I* understand. It's just some of the others in the neighborhood, they've been put off a little. Take during your tragedy. I mean people like to offer help at occasions like that—send flowers and visit at the viewing hour and bring casseroles for after the service. Only you didn't even have a service. Held a cremation, Lord God, somewheres off in Virginia without a word to anyone and come home directly. Peg Everett tells you she's put you in her prayers and Sarah says, 'Oh, bless you, Peg,' but what do *you* say? You ask Peg if her son might care to take Ethan's bike off your hands."

Macon groaned. "Yes," he said, "I never know how to behave at these times."

"Then you mow your lawn like nothing has happened."

"The grass did keep on growing, Garner."

"We was all dying to do it for you."

"Well, thanks," Macon said, "but I enjoyed the work."

"See what I mean?"

Macon said, "Now, wait. Just to insert some logic into this discussion—"

"That's *exactly* what I mean!"

"You started out talking about Sarah. You've switched to how I disappoint the neighbors."

"What's the difference? You might not know this, Macon, but you come across as a person that charges ahead on your own somewhat. Just look at the way you walk! The way you, like, *lunge*, lope on down the street with your head running clear in front of your body. If a fellow wants to stop you and, I don't know, offer his condolences, he'd be liable to get plowed down. Now, I know you care, and you know you care, but how does it look to the others? I ask you! No wonder she up and left."

"Garner, I appreciate your thoughts on this," Macon said, "but Sarah's fully aware that I care. I'm not as tongue-tied as you like to make out. And this isn't one of those open-shut, can-this-marriage-be-saved deals, either. I mean, you're just plain goddamned *wrong*, Garner."

"Well," Garner said. He looked down at his cap, and after a moment he jammed it abruptly on his head. "I guess I'll fetch your mail in, then," he said.

"Right. Thanks."

Garner rose to his feet and shuffled out. His leaving alerted Edward, who started barking all over again. There was an empty spell during which Macon looked down at his cast and listened to the soap opera from the living room. Meanwhile Edward whined at the door and paced back and forth, clicking his toenails. Then Garner returned. "Mostly catalogs," he said, flinging his load on the table. He brought with him the smell of fresh air and dry leaves. "Brenda said we might as well not bother with the newspapers; just throw them out."

"Oh, yes, of course," Macon said.

He stood up and they shook hands. Garner's fingers were crisp and intricately shaped, like crumpled paper. "Thanks for stopping by," Macon told him.

"Any time," Garner said, looking elsewhere.

Macon said, "I didn't mean, you know—I hope I didn't sound short-tempered."

"Naw," Garner said. He lifted an arm and let it drop. "Shoot. Don't think a thing about it." Then he turned to leave.

As soon as he did, Macon thought of a flood of other things he should have mentioned. It wasn't all his fault, he wanted to say. Sarah had a little to do with it too. What Sarah needed was a rock, he wanted to say; someone who wouldn't crumble. Otherwise, why had she picked him to marry? But he held his peace and watched Garner walk out. There was something pitiable about the two sharp cords that ran down the back of Garner's neck, cupping a little ditch of mapped brown skin between them.

When his brothers came home from work, the house took on a relaxed, relieved atmosphere. Rose drew the living room curtains and lit a few soft lamps. Charles and Porter changed into sweaters. Macon started mixing his special salad dressing. He believed that if you pulverized the spices first with a marble mortar and pestle, it made all the difference. The others agreed that no one else's dressing tasted as good as Macon's. "Since you've been gone," Charles told him, "we've had to buy that bottled stuff from the grocery store." He made it sound as if Macon had been gone a few weeks or so—as if his entire marriage had been just a brief trip elsewhere.

For supper they had Rose's pot roast, a salad with Macon's dressing, and baked potatoes. Baked potatoes had always been their favorite food. They had learned to fix them as children, and even after they were big enough to cook a balanced meal they used to exist solely on baked potatoes whenever Alicia left them to their own devices. There was something about the smell of a roasting Idaho that was so cozy, and also, well, *conservative*, was the way Macon put it to himself. He thought back on years and years of winter evenings: the kitchen windows black outside, the corners furry with gathering darkness, the four of them seated at the chipped enamel table meticulously filling scooped-out potato skins with butter. You let the butter melt in the skins while you mashed and seasoned the floury insides; the skins were saved till last. It was almost a ritual. He recalled that once, during one of their mother's longer absences, her friend Eliza had served them what she called potato boats—restuffed, not a bit like the genuine article. The children, with pinched, fastidious expressions, had emptied the stuffing and proceeded as usual with the skins, pretending to overlook her mistake. The skins should be crisp. They should not be salted. The pepper should be freshly ground. Paprika was acceptable, but only if it was American. Hungarian paprika had too distinctive a taste. Personally, Macon could do without paprika altogether.

While they ate, Porter discussed what to do with his children. Tomorrow was his weekly visitation night, when he would drive over to Washington, where his children lived with their mother. "The thing of it is," he said, "eating out in restaurants is so artificial. It doesn't seem like real food. And anyway, they all three have different tastes. They always argue over where to go. Someone's on a diet, someone's turned vegetarian, someone can't stand food that crunches. And I end up shouting, 'Oh, for God's sake, we're going to Such-and-Such and that's that!' So we go and everybody sulks throughout the meal."

"Maybe you should just not visit," Charles said reasonably. (He had never had children of his own.)

"Well, of course I want to visit, Charles. I just wish we had some different program. You know what would be ideal? If we could all do something with tools together. I mean like the old days before the divorce, when Danny helped me drain the hot water heater or Susan sat on a board I was sawing. If I could just drop by their house, say, and June and her husband could go to a movie or something, then the kids and I would clean the gutters, weatherstrip the windows, wrap the hot water pipes . . . Well, that husband of hers is no use at all, you can bet he lets his hot water pipes sit around naked. I'd bring my own tools, even. We'd have a fine time! Susan could fix us cocoa. Then at the end of the evening I'd pack up my tools and off I'd go, leaving the house in perfect repair. Why, June ought to jump at the chance."

"Then why not suggest it," Macon said.

"Nah. She'd never go for it. She's so impractical. I said to her last week, I said, 'You know that front porch step is loose? Springing up from its nails every time you walk on it wrong.' She said, 'Oh, Lord, yes, it's *been* that way,' as if Providence had decreed it. As if nothing could be done about it. They've got leaves in the gutter from way last winter but leaves are natural, after all; why go against nature. She's so impractical."

Porter himself was the most practical man Macon had ever known. He was the only Leary who understood money. His talent with money was what kept the family firm solvent—if just barely. It wasn't a very wealthy business. Grandfather Leary had founded it in the early part of the century as a tinware factory, and turned to bottle caps in 1915. The Bottle Cap King, he called himself, and was called in his obituary, but in fact most bottle caps were manufactured by Crown Cork and always had been; Grandfather Leary ran a distant second or third. His only son, the Bottle Cap Prince, had barely assumed his place in the firm before quitting to volunteer for World War II—a far more damaging enthusiasm, it turned out, than any of Alicia's. After he was killed the business limped along, never quite succeeding and never quite failing, till Porter bounced in straight from college and took over the money end. Money to Porter was something almost chemical—a volatile substance that reacted in various interesting ways when combined with other substances. He wasn't what you'd call mercenary; he didn't want the money for its own sake but for its intriguing possibilities, and in fact when his wife divorced him he handed over most of his property without a word of complaint.

It was Porter who ran the company, pumping in money and ideas. Charles, more mechanical, dealt with the production end. Macon had done a little of everything when he worked there, and had wasted away with boredom doing it, for there wasn't really enough to keep a third man busy. It was only for symmetry's sake that Porter kept urging him to return. "Tell you what, Macon," he said now, "why not hitch a ride down with us tomorrow and look over your old stomping ground?"

"No, thanks," Macon told him.

"Plenty of room for your crutches in back."

"Maybe some other time."

They followed Rose around while she washed the dishes. She didn't like them to help because she had her own method, she said. She moved soundlessly through the old-fashioned kitchen, replacing dishes in the high wooden cabinets. Charles took the dog out; Macon couldn't manage his crutches in the spongy backyard. And Porter pulled the kitchen shades, meanwhile lecturing Rose on how the white surfaces reflected the warmth back into the room now that the nights were cooler. Rose said, "Yes, Porter, I know all that," and lifted the salad bowl to the light and examined it a moment before she put it away.

They watched the news, dutifully, and then they went out to the sun porch and sat at their grandparents' card table. They played something called Vaccination—a card game they'd invented as children, which had grown so convoluted over the years that no one else had the patience to learn it. In fact, more than one outsider had accused them of altering the rules to suit the circumstances. "Now, just a minute," Sarah had said, back when she'd still had hopes of figuring it out. "I thought you said aces were high."

"They are."

"So that means—"

"But not when they're drawn from the deck."

"Aha! Then why was the one that Rose drew counted high?"

"Well, she did draw it after a deuce, Sarah."

"Aces drawn after a deuce are high?"

"No, aces drawn after a number that's been drawn two times in a row just before that."

Sarah had folded her fan of cards and laid them face down—the last of the wives to give up.

Macon was in quarantine and had to donate all his cards to Rose. Rose moved her chair over next to his and played off his points while he sat back, scratching the cat behind her ears. Opposite him, in the tiny dark windowpanes, he saw their reflections—hollow-eyed and severely cheekboned, more interesting versions of themselves.

The telephone in the living room gave a nipped squeak and then a full ring. Nobody seemed to notice. Rose laid a king on Porter's queen and Porter said, "Stinker." The telephone rang again and then again. In the middle of the fourth ring, it fell silent. "Hypodermic," Rose told Porter, and she topped the king with an ace.

"You're a real stinker, Rose."

In the portrait on the end wall, the Leary children gazed out with their veiled eyes. It occurred to Macon that they were sitting in much the same positions here this evening: Charles and Porter on either side of him, Rose perched in the foreground. Was there any real change? He felt a jolt of something very close to panic. Here he still was! The same as ever! *What have I gone and done?* he wondered, and he swallowed thickly and looked at his own empty hands.

H elp! Help! Call off your dog!"

Macon stopped typing and lifted his head. The voice came from somewhere out front, rising above a string of sharp, excited yelps. But Edward was taking a walk with Porter. This must be some other dog.

"Call him off, dammit!"

Macon rose, propping himself on his crutches, and made his way to the window. Sure enough, it was Edward. He seemed to have treed somebody in the giant magnolia to the right of the walk. He was barking so hard that he kept popping off the ground perfectly level, all four feet at once, like one of those pull toys that bounce straight up in the air when you squeeze a rubber bulb.

"Edward! Stop that!" Macon shouted.

Edward didn't stop. He might not even have heard. Macon stubbed out to the hall, opened the front door, and said, "Come here this instant!"

Edward barely skipped a beat.

It was a Saturday morning in early October, pale gray and cool. Macon felt the coolness creeping up his cut-off pants leg as he crossed the porch. When he dropped one crutch and took hold of the iron railing to descend the steps, he found the metal beaded with moisture.

He hopped over to the magnolia, leaned down precariously, and grabbed the leash that Edward was trailing. Without much effort, he reeled it in; Edward was already losing interest. Macon peered into the inky depths of the magnolia. "Who *is* that?" he asked.

"This is your employer, Macon."

"Julian?"

Julian lowered himself from one of the magnolia's weak, sprawling branches. He had a line of dirt across the front of his slacks. His white-blond hair, usually so neat it made him look like a shirt ad, stuck out at several angles. "Macon," he said, "I really hate a man with an obnoxious dog. I don't hate just the dog, I hate the man who owns him."

"Well, I'm sorry about this. I thought he was off on a walk."

"You send him on walks by himself?"

"No, no . . ."

"A dog who takes solitary strolls," Julian said. "Only Macon Leary would have one." He brushed off the sleeves of his suede blazer. Then he said, "What happened to your leg?"

"I broke it."

56

"Well, I see that, but how?"

"It's kind of hard to explain," Macon told him.

They started toward the house, with Edward trotting docilely alongside. Julian supported Macon as they climbed the steps. He was an athletic-looking man with a casual, sauntering style—a boater. You could tell he was a boater by his nose, which was raw across the tip even this late in the year. No one so startlingly blond, so vividly flushed in the face, should expose himself to sunburn, Macon always told him. But that was Julian for you: reckless. A dashing sailor, a speedy driver, a frequenter of singles bars, he was the kind of man who would make a purchase without consulting *Consumer Reports*. He never seemed to have a moment's self-doubt and was proceeding into the house now as jauntily as if he'd been invited, first retrieving Macon's other crutch and then holding the door open and waving him ahead.

"How'd you find me, anyway?" Macon asked.

"Why, are you in hiding?"

"No, of course not."

Julian surveyed the entrance hall, which all at once struck Macon as slightly dowdy. The satin lampshade on the table had dozens of long vertical rents; it seemed to be rotting off its frame.

"Your neighbor told me where you were," Julian said finally.

"Oh. Garner."

"I stopped by your house when I couldn't reach you by phone. Do you know how late you're running with this guidebook?"

"Well, you can see I've had an accident," Macon said.

"Everybody's held up, waiting for the manuscript. I keep telling them I expect it momentarily, but—"

"Any moment," Macon said.

"Huh?"

"You expect it any moment."

"Yes, and all I've seen so far is two chapters mailed in with no explanation."

Julian led the way to the living room as he spoke. He selected the most comfortable chair and sat down. "Where's Sarah?" he asked.

"Who?"

"Your wife, Macon."

"Oh. Um, she and I are . . ."

Macon should have practiced saying it out loud. The word "separated" was too bald; it was something that happened to other people. He crossed to the couch and made a great business of settling himself and arranging his crutches at his side. Then he said, "She's got this apartment downtown."

"You've *split*?"

Macon nodded.

"Jesus."

Edward nosed Macon's palm bossily, demanding a pat. Macon was grateful to have something to do.

"Well, Jesus, Macon, what went wrong?" Julian asked.

"Nothing!" Macon told him. His voice was a little too loud. He lowered it. "I mean, that's not something I can answer," he said.

"Oh. Excuse me."

"No, I mean . . . there *is* no answer. It turns out these things can happen for no particular reason."

"Well, you've been under a strain, you two," Julian said. "Shoot, with what happened and all . . . She'll be back, once she's gotten over it. Or not gotten *over* it of course but, you know . . ."

"Maybe so," Macon said. He felt embarrassed for Julian, who kept jiggling one Docksider. He said, "What did you think of those first two chapters?"

Julian opened his mouth to answer, but he was interrupted by the dog. Edward had flown to the hall and was barking furiously. There was a clang that Macon recognized as the sound of the front door swinging open and hitting the radiator. "Hush, now," he heard Rose tell Edward. She crossed the hall and looked into the living room.

Julian got to his feet. Macon said, "Julian Edge, this is my sister Rose. And this," he said as Charles arrived behind her, "is my brother Charles."

Neither Rose nor Charles could shake hands; they were carrying the groceries. They stood in the center of the room, hugging brown paper bags, while Julian went into what Macon thought of as his Macon Leary act. "Macon Leary with a sister! And a brother, too. Who'd have guessed it? That Macon Leary had a family just never entered my mind, somehow."

Rose gave him a polite, puzzled smile. She wasn't looking her best. She wore a long black coat that drew all the color from her face. And Charles, rumpled and out of breath, was having trouble with one of his bags. He kept trying to get a better grip on it. "Here, let me help you," Julian said. He took the bag and then peered into it. Macon was afraid he'd go off on some tangent about Macon Leary's groceries, but he didn't. He told Rose, "Yes, I do see a family resemblance."

"You're Macon's publisher," Rose said. "I remember from the address label."

"Address label?"

"I'm the one who mailed you Macon's chapters."

"Oh, yes."

"I'm supposed to send you some more, but first I have to buy nine-by-twelve envelopes. All we've got left is ten-by-thirteen. It's terrible when things don't fit precisely. They get all out of alignment."

"Ah," Julian said. He looked at her for a moment.

Macon said, "We wouldn't want to keep you, Rose."

"Oh! No," she said. She smiled at Julian, hoisted her groceries higher, and left the room. Charles retrieved his bag from Julian and slogged after her.

"The Macon Leary Nine-by-Twelve Envelope Crisis," Julian said, sitting back down.

Macon said, "Oh, Julian, drop it."

"Sorry," Julian said, sounding surprised.

There was a pause. Then Julian said, "Really I had no idea, Macon. I mean, if you'd let me know what was going on in your life . . ."

He was jiggling a Docksider again. He always seemed uneasy when he couldn't do his Macon Leary act. After Ethan died he'd avoided Macon for weeks; he'd sent a tree-sized bouquet to the house but never again mentioned Ethan's name.

"Look," he said now. "If you want another, I don't know, another month—"

Macon said, "Oh, nonsense, what's a missing wife or two, right? Ha, ha! Here, let me get what I've typed and you can check it."

"Well, if you say so," Julian said.

"After this there's only the conclusion," Macon said. He was calling over his shoulder as he made his way to the dining room, where his latest chapter lay stacked on the buffet. "The conclusion's nothing, a cinch. I'll crib from the old one, mostly."

He returned with the manuscript and handed it to Julian. Then he sat on the couch again, and Julian started reading. Meanwhile, Macon heard Porter come in the back way, where he was greeted by explosive barks from Edward. "Monster," Porter said. "Do you know how long I've been looking for you?" The phone rang over and over, unanswered. Julian looked at Macon and raised his eyebrows but made no comment.

Macon and Julian had met some dozen years ago, when Macon was still at the bottle-cap factory. He'd been casting about for other occupations at the time. He'd begun to believe he might like to work on a newspaper. But he'd had no training, not a single journalism course. So he started the only way he could think of: He contributed a free-lance article to a neighborhood weekly. His subject was a crafts fair over in Washington. *Getting there is difficult,* he wrote, *because the freeway is so blank you start feeling all lost and sad. And once you've arrived, it's worse. The streets are not like ours and don't even run at right angles.* He went on to evaluate some food he'd sampled at an outdoor booth, but found it contained a spice he wasn't used to, *something sort of cold and yellow I would almost describe as foreign,* and settled instead for a hot dog from a vendor across the street who wasn't even part of the fair. *The hot dog I can recommend,* he wrote, *though it made me a little regretful because Sarah, my wife, uses the same kind of chili sauce and I thought of home the minute I smelled it.* He also recommended the patchwork quilts, one of which had a starburst pattern like the quilt in his grandmother's room. He suggested that his readers leave the fair no later than three thirty, *since you'll be driving into Baltimore right past Lexington Market and will want to pick up your crabs before it closes.*

His article was published beneath a headline reading CRAFTS FAIR DELIGHTS, INSTRUCTS. There was a subhead under that. *Or,* it read, *I Feel So Break-Up, I Want to Go Home.* Until he saw the subhead, Macon hadn't realized what tone he'd given his piece. Then he felt silly.

But Julian Edge thought it was perfect. Julian phoned him. "You the fellow who wrote that hot dog thing in the *Watchbird?*"

"Well, yes."

"Ha!"

"Well, I don't see what's so funny," Macon said stiffly.

"Who said it was funny? It's perfect. I've got a proposition for you."

They met at the Old Bay Restaurant, where Macon's grandparents used to take the four children on their birthdays. "I can personally guarantee the crab soup," Macon said. "They haven't done a thing to it since I was nine." Julian said, "Ha!" again and rocked back in his chair. He was wearing a polo shirt and white duck trousers, and his nose was a bright shade of pink. It was summer, or maybe spring. At any rate, his boat was in the water.

"Now, here's my plan," he said over the soup. "I own this little company called the Businessman's Press. Well, little: I say little. Actually we sell coast to coast. Nothing fancy, but useful, you know? Appointment pads, expense account booklets, compound interest charts, currency conversion wheels . . . And now I want to put out a guidebook for commercial travelers. Just the U.S., to begin with; maybe other countries later. We'd call it something catchy, I don't know: *Reluctant Tourist* . . . And you're the fellow to write it."

"Me?"

"I knew the minute I read your hot dog piece."

"But I hate to travel."

"I kind of guessed that," Julian said. "So do businessmen. I mean, these folks are not running around the country for the hell of it, Macon. They'd rather be home in their living rooms. So you'll be helping them pretend that's where they are."

Then he pulled a square of paper from his breast pocket and said, "What do you think?"

It was a steel engraving of an overstuffed chair. Attached to the chair's back were giant, feathered wings such as you would see on seraphim in antique Bibles. Macon blinked.

"Your logo," Julian explained. "Get it?"

"Um . . ."

"While armchair travelers dream of going places," Julian said, "traveling armchairs dream of staying put. I thought we'd use this on the cover."

"Ah!" Macon said brightly. Then he said, "But would I actually have to travel myself?"

"Well, yes."

"Oh."

"But just briefly. I'm not looking for anything encyclopedic, I'm looking for the opposite of encyclopedic. And think of the pay."

"It pays?"

"It pays a bundle."

Well, not a bundle, exactly. Still, it did make a comfortable living. It sold briskly at airport newsstands, train stations, and office supply shops. His guide to France did even better. That was part of a major promotion by an international car-rental agency—slipcased with *The Businessman's Foreign Phrase Book*, which gave the German, French, and Spanish for "We anticipate an upswing in cross-border funds." Macon, of course, was not the author of the phrase book. His only foreign language was Latin.

Now Julian restacked the pages he'd been reading. "Fine," he said. "I think we can send this through as is. What's left of the conclusion?"

"Not much."

"After this I want to start on the U.S. again."

"So soon?"

"It's been three years, Macon."

"Well, but . . ." Macon said. He gestured toward his leg. "You can see I'd have trouble traveling."

"When does your cast come off?"

"Not till the first of November at the earliest."

"So? A few weeks!"

"But it really seems to me I just did the U.S.," Macon said. A kind of fatigue fell over him. These endlessly recurring trips, Boston and Atlanta and Chicago . . . He let his head drop back on the couch.

Julian said, "Things are changing every minute, Macon. Change! It's what keeps us in the black. How far do you think we'd get selling out-of-date guidebooks?"

Macon thought of the crumbling old *Tips for the Continent* in his grandfather's library. Travelers were advised to invert a wineglass on their hotel beds, testing the sheets for damp. Ladies should seal the corks of their perfume bottles with melted candlewax before packing. Something about that book implied that tourists were all in it together, equally anxious and defenseless. Macon might almost have enjoyed a trip in those days.

Julian was preparing to go now. He stood up, and with some difficulty Macon did too. Then Edward, getting wind of a leavetaking, rushed into the living room and started barking. "Sorry!" Macon shouted above the racket. "Edward, stop it! I figure that's his sheep-herding instinct," he explained to Julian. "He hates to see anyone straying from the flock."

They moved toward the front hall, wading through a blur of dancing, yelping dog. When they reached the door, Edward blocked it. Luckily, he was still trailing his leash, so Macon gave one crutch to Julian and bent to grasp it. The instant Edward felt the tug, he turned and snarled at Macon. "Whoa!" Julian said, for Edward when he snarled was truly ugly. His fangs seemed to lengthen. He snapped at his leash with an audible click. Then he snapped at Macon's hand. Macon felt Edward's hot breath and the oddly intimate dampness of his teeth. His hand was not so much bitten as struck—slammed into with a jolt such as you'd get from an electric fence. He stepped back and dropped the leash. His other crutch clattered to the floor. The front hall seemed to be full of crutches; there was some splintery, spiky feeling to the air.

"Whoa, there!" Julian said. He spoke into a sudden silence. The dog sat back now, panting and shamefaced. "Macon? Did he get you?" Julian asked.

Macon looked down at his hand. There were four red puncture marks in the fleshy part—two in front, two in back—but no blood at all and very little pain. "I'm all right," he said.

Julian gave him his crutches, keeping one eye on Edward. "I wouldn't have a dog like that," he said. "I'd shoot him."

"He was just trying to protect me," Macon said.

"I'd call the S.P.C.A."

"Why don't you go now, Julian, while he's calm."

"Or the what's-it, dogcatcher. Tell them you want him done away with."

"Just *go*, Julian."

Julian said, "Well, fine." He opened the door and slid through it sideways, glancing back at Edward. "That is not a well dog," he said before he vanished.

Macon hobbled to the rear of the house and Edward followed, snuffling a bit and staying close to the ground. In the kitchen, Rose stood on a stepstool in front of a towering glass-fronted cupboard, accepting the groceries that Charles and Porter handed up to her. "Now I need the *n*'s, anything starting with *n*," she was saying.

"How about these noodles?" Porter asked. "*N* for noodles? *P* for pasta?"

"*E* for elbow macaroni. You might have passed those up earlier, Porter."

"Rose?" Macon said. "It seems Edward's given me a little sort of nip."

She turned, and Charles and Porter stopped work to examine the hand he held out. It was hurting him by now—a deep, stinging pain.

"Oh, Macon!" Rose cried. She came down off the stepstool. "How did it happen?"

"It was an accident, that's all. But I think I need an antiseptic."

"You need a tetanus shot, too," Charles told him.

"You need to get rid of that dog," Porter said.

They looked at Edward. He grinned up at them nervously.

"He didn't mean any harm," Macon said.

"Takes off your hand at the elbow and he means no harm? You should get rid of him, I tell you."

"See, I can't," Macon said.

"Why not?"

"Well, see . . ."

They waited.

"You know I don't mind the cat," Rose said. "But Edward is so disruptive, Macon. Every day he gets more and more out of control."

"Maybe you could give him to someone who wants a guard dog," Charles said.

"A service station," Rose suggested. She took a roll of gauze from a drawer.

"Oh, never," Macon said. He sat where she pointed, in a chair at the kitchen table. He propped his crutches in the corner. "Edward alone in some Exxon? He'd be wretched."

Rose swabbed Mercurochrome on his hand. It looked bruised; each puncture mark was puffing and turning blue.

"He's used to sleeping with me," Macon told her. "He's never been alone in his life."

Besides, Edward wasn't a bad dog at heart—only a little unruly. He was sympathetic and he cared about Macon and plodded after him wherever he went. There was a furrowed W on his forehead that gave him a look of concern. His large, pointed, velvety ears seemed more expressive than other dogs' ears; when he was happy they stuck straight out at either side of his head like airplane wings. His smell was unexpectedly pleasant—the sweetish smell a favorite sweater takes on when it's been folded away in a drawer unwashed.

And he'd been Ethan's.

Once upon a time Ethan had brushed him, bathed him, wrestled on the floor with him; and when Edward stopped to paw at one ear Ethan would ask, with the soberest courtesy, "Oh, may I scratch that for you?" The two of them watched daily at the window for the afternoon paper, and the instant it arrived Ethan sent Edward bounding out to fetch it—hind legs meeting front legs, heels kicking up joyfully. Edward would pause after he got the paper in his mouth and look around him, as if hoping to be noticed, and then he'd swagger back all bustling and self-important and pause again at the front hall mirror to admire the figure he cut. "Conceited," Ethan would say fondly.

Ethan picked up a tennis ball to throw and Edward grew so excited that he wagged his whole hind end. Ethan took Edward outside with a soccer ball and when Edward got carried away—tearing about and shouldering the ball into a hedge and growling ferociously—Ethan's laugh rang out so high and clear, such a buoyant sound floating through the air on a summer evening.

"I just can't," Macon said.

There was a silence.

Rose wrapped gauze around his hand, so gently he hardly felt it. She tucked the end under and reached for a roll of adhesive tape. Then she said, "Maybe we could send him to obedience school."

"Obedience school is for minor things—walking to heel and things," Porter told her. "What we have here is major."

"It is not!" Macon said. "It's really nothing at all. Why, the woman at the Meow-Bow got on wonderfully with him."

"Meow-Bow?"

"Where I boarded him when I went to England. She was just crazy about him. She wanted me to let her train him."

"So call her, why don't you."

"Maybe I will," Macon said.

He wouldn't, of course. The woman had struck him as bizarre. But there was no sense going into that now.

On Sunday morning Edward tore the screen door, trying to get at an elderly neighbor who'd stopped by to borrow a wrench. On Sunday afternoon he sprang at Porter to keep him from leaving on an errand. Porter had to creep out the rear when Edward wasn't watching. "This is undignified," Porter told Macon. "When are you going to call the Kit-Kat or whatever it is?"

Macon explained that on Sundays the Meow-Bow would surely be closed.

Monday morning, when Edward went for a walk with Rose, he lunged at a passing jogger and yanked Rose off her feet. She came home with a scraped knee. She said, "Have you called the Meow-Bow yet?"

"Not quite," Macon said.

"Macon," Rose said. Her voice was very quiet. "Tell me something."

"What's that, Rose?"

"Can you explain why you're letting things go on this way?"

No, he couldn't, and that was the truth. It was getting so he was baffling even to himself. He felt infuriated by Edward's misdeeds, but somehow he viewed them as visitations of fate. There was nothing he could do about them. When Edward approached him later with a mangled belt of Porter's trailing from his mouth, all Macon said was, "Oh, Edward . . ."

He was sitting on the couch at the time, having been snagged by an especially outrageous moment in Rose's soap opera. Rose looked over at him. Her expression was odd. It wasn't disapproving; it was more like . . . He cast about for the word. Resigned. That was it. She looked at him the way she would look at, say, some hopeless wreck of a man wandering drugged on a downtown street. After all, she seemed to be thinking, there was probably not much that you could do for such a person.

"Meow-Bow Animal Hospital."

"Is, ah, Muriel there, please?"

"Hold on a minute."

He waited, braced against a cabinet. (He was using the pantry telephone.) He heard two women discussing Fluffball Cohen's rabies shot. Then Muriel picked up the receiver. "Hello?"

"Yes, this is Macon Leary. I don't know if you remember me or—"

"Oh, Macon! Hi there! How's Edward doing?"

"Well, he's getting worse."

She tsk-tsked.

"He's been attacking right and left. Snarling, biting, chewing things—"

"Did your neighbor tell you I came looking for you?"

"What? Yes, he did."

"I was right on your street, running an errand. I make a little extra money running errands. George, it's called. Don't you think that's cute?"

"Excuse me?"

"George. It's the name of my company. I stuck a flyer under your door. *Let George do it,* it says, and then it lists all the prices: meeting planes, chauffeuring, courier service, shopping . . . Gift shopping's most expensive because for that I have to use my own taste. Didn't you get my flyer? I really stopped by just to visit, though. But your neighbor said you hadn't been around."

"No, I broke my leg," Macon said.

"Oh, that's too bad."

"And I couldn't manage alone of course, so—"

"You should have called George."

"George who?"

"George my company! The one I was just telling you about."

"Oh, yes."

"Then you wouldn't have had to leave that nice house. I liked your house. Is that where you lived when you were married, too?"

"Well, yes."

"I'm surprised she agreed to give it up."

"The point is," Macon said, "I'm really at the end of my rope with Edward here, and I was wondering if you might be able to help me."

"Sure I can help!"

"Oh, that's wonderful," Macon said.

"I can do anything," Muriel told him. "Search and alert, search and rescue, bombs, narcotics—"

"Narcotics?"

"Guard training, attack training, poison-proofing, kennelosis—"

"Wait, I don't even know what some of those things are," Macon said.

"I can even teach split personality."

"What's split personality?"

"Where your dog is, like, nice to you but kills all others."

"You know, I think I may be over my head here," Macon said.

"No, no! Don't say that!"

"But this is just the simplest problem. His only fault is, he wants to protect me."

"You can take protection too far," Muriel told him.

Macon tried a little joke. " 'It's a jungle out there,' he's saying. That's what he's trying to say. 'I know better than you do, Macon.' "

"Oh?" Muriel said. "You let him call you by your first name?"

"Well—"

"He needs to learn respect," she said. "Five or six times a week I'll come out, for however long it takes. I'll start with the basics; you always do that: sitting, heeling . . . My charge is five dollars a lesson. You're getting a bargain. Most I charge ten."

Macon tightened his hold on the receiver. "Then why not ten for me?" he asked.

"Oh, no! You're a friend."

He felt confused. He gave her his address and arranged a time with the nagging sense that something was slipping out of his control. "But look," he said, "about the fee, now—"

"See you tomorrow!" she said. She hung up.

At supper that night when he told the others, he thought they did a kind of double take. Porter said, "You actually called?" Macon said, "Yes, why not?"—acting very offhand—and so the others took their cue and dropped the subject at once.

7

When I was a little girl," Muriel said, "I didn't like dogs at all or any other kinds of animals either. I thought they could read my mind. My folks gave me a puppy for my birthday and he would, like, cock his head, you know how they do? Cock his head and fix me with these bright round eyes and I said, 'Ooh! Get him away from me! You know I can't stand to be stared at.' "

She had a voice that wandered too far in all directions. It screeched upward; then it dropped to a raspy growl. "They had to take him back. Had to give him to a neighbor boy and buy me a whole different present, a beauty-parlor permanent which is what I'd set my heart on all along."

She and Macon were standing in the entrance hall. She still had her coat on—a bulky-shouldered, three-quarter length, nubby black affair of a type last seen in the 1940s. Edward sat in front of her as he'd been ordered. He had met her at the door with his usual display, leaping and snarling, but she'd more or less walked right through him and pointed at his rump and told him to sit. He'd gaped at her. She had reached over and poked his rear end down with a long, sharp index finger.

"Now you kind of cluck your tongue," she'd told Macon, demonstrating. "They get to know a cluck means praise. And when I hold my hand out—see? That means he has to stay."

Edward stayed, but a yelp erupted from him every few seconds, reminding Macon of the periodic bloops from a percolator. Muriel hadn't seemed to hear. She'd started discussing her lesson plan and then for no apparent reason had veered to her autobiography. But shouldn't Edward be allowed to get up now? How long did she expect him to sit there?

"I guess you're wondering why I'd want a permanent when this hair of mine is so frizzy," she said. "Old mop! But I'll be honest, this is not natural. My natural hair is real straight and lanky. Times I've just despaired of it. It was blond when I was a baby, can you believe that? Blond as a fairy-tale princess. People told my mother I'd look like Shirley Temple if she would just curl my hair, and so she did, she rolled my hair on orange juice tins. I had blue eyes, too, and they stayed that way for a long long time, a whole lot longer than most babies' do. People thought I'd look that way forever and they talked about me going into the movies. Seriously! My mother arranged for tap-dance school when I wasn't much more than a toddler. No one ever dreamed my hair would turn on me."

Edward moaned. Muriel looked past Macon, into the glass of a picture that hung behind him. She cupped a hand beneath the ends of her hair, as if testing its weight. "Think what it must feel like," she said, "waking up one morning and finding you've gone dark. It near about killed my mother, I can tell you. Ordinary dull old Muriel, muddy brown eyes and hair as black as dirt."

Macon sensed he was supposed to offer some argument, but he was too anxious about Edward. "Oh, well . . ." he said. Then he said, "Shouldn't we be letting him up now?"

"Up? Oh, the dog. In a minute," she said. "So anyway. The reason it's so frizzy is, I got this thing called a body perm. You ever heard of those? They're supposed to just add body, but something went wrong. You think *this* is bad! If I was to take a brush to it, my hair would spring straight out from my head. I mean absolutely straight out. Kind of like a fright wig, isn't that what you call it? So I can't even brush it. I get up in the morning and there I am, ready to go. Lord, I hate to think of the tangles."

"Maybe you could just comb it," Macon suggested.

"Hard to drag a comb *through* it. All the little teeth would break off."

"Maybe one of those thick-toothed combs that black people use."

"I know what you mean but I'd feel silly buying one."

"What for?" Macon asked. "They're just hanging there in super-markets. It wouldn't have to be a big deal. Buy milk and bread or something and an Afro comb, no one will even think twice."

"Well, I suppose you're right," she said, but now that she'd got him involved it seemed she'd lost interest in the problem herself. She snapped her fingers over Edward's head. "Okay!" she said. Edward jumped up, barking. "That was very good," she told him.

In fact, it was so good that Macon felt a little cross. Things couldn't be that easy, he wanted to say. Edward had improved too quickly, the way a toothache will improve the moment you step into a dentist's waiting room.

Muriel slipped her purse off her shoulder and set it on the hall table. Out came a long blue leash attached to a choke chain. "He's supposed to wear this all the time," she said. "Every minute till he's trained. That way you can yank him back whenever he does something wrong. The leash is six dollars even, and the chain is two ninety-five. With tax it comes to, let's see, nine forty. You can pay me at the end of the lesson."

She slipped the choke chain over Edward's head. Then she paused to examine a fingernail. "If I break another nail I'm going to scream," she said. She took a step back and pointed to Edward's rump. After a brief hesitation, he sat. Seated, he looked noble, Macon thought—chesty and solemn, nothing like his usual self. But when Muriel snapped her fingers, he jumped up as unruly as ever.

"Now you try," Muriel told Macon.

Macon accepted the leash and pointed to Edward's rump. Edward stood fast. Macon frowned and pointed more sternly. He felt foolish. Edward knew, if this woman didn't, how little authority Macon had.

"Poke him down," Muriel said.

This was going to be awkward. He propped a crutch against the radiator and bent stiffly to jab Edward with one finger. Edward sat. Macon clucked. Then he straightened and backed away, holding out his palm, but instead of staying, Edward rose and followed him. Muriel hissed between her teeth. Edward shrank down again. "He doesn't take you seriously," Muriel said.

"Well, I know that," Macon snapped.

His broken leg was starting to ache.

"In fact I didn't have so much as a kitten the whole entire time I was growing up," Muriel said. Was she just going to leave Edward sitting there? "Then a couple of years ago I saw this ad in the paper, *Make extra money in your off hours. Work as little or as much as you like.* Place was a dog-training firm that went around to people's houses. Doggie, Do, it was called. Don't you just hate that name? Reminds me of dog-do. But anyhow, I answered the ad. 'To be honest I don't like animals,' I said, but Mr. Quarles, the owner, he told me that was just as well. He told me it was people who got all mushy about them that had the most trouble."

"Well, that makes sense," Macon said, glancing at Edward. He had heard that dogs developed backaches if they were made to sit too long.

"I was just about his best pupil, it turns out. Seems I had a way with animals. So then I got a job at the Meow-Bow. Before that I worked at the Rapid-Eze Copy Center and believe me, I was looking for a change. Who's the lady?"

"Lady?"

"The lady I just saw walking through the dining room."

"That's Rose."

"Is she your ex-wife? Or what."

"She's my sister."

"Oh, your sister!"

"This house belongs to her," Macon said.

"I don't live with anybody either," Muriel told him.

Macon blinked. Hadn't he just said he lived with his sister?

"Sometimes late at night when I get desperate for someone to talk to I call the time signal," Muriel said. " 'At the tone the time will be eleven . . . forty-eight. And fifty seconds.' " Her voice took on a fruity fullness. " 'At the tone the time will be eleven . . . forty-nine. Exactly.' You can release him now."

"Pardon?"

"Release your dog."

Macon snapped his fingers and Edward jumped up, yapping.

"How about you?" Muriel asked. "What do you do for a living?"

Macon said, "I write tour guides."

"Tour guides! Lucky."

"What's lucky about it?"

"Why, you must get to travel all kinds of places!"

"Oh, well, travel," Macon said.

"I'd love to travel."

"It's just red tape, mostly," Macon said.

"I've never even been on an airplane, you realize that?"

"It's red tape in motion. Ticket lines, customs lines . . . Should Edward be barking that way?"

Muriel gave Edward a slit-eyed look and he quieted.

"If I could go anywhere I'd go to Paris," she said.

"Paris is terrible. Everybody's impolite."

"I'd walk along the Seine, like they say in the song. 'You will find your love in Paris,' " she sang scratchily, " 'if you walk along the—' I just think it sounds so romantic."

"Well, it's not," Macon said.

"I bet you don't know where to look, is all. Take me with you next time! I could show you the good parts."

Macon cleared his throat. "Actually, I have a very limited expense account," he told her. "I never even took my wife, or, um, my . . . wife."

"I was only teasing," she told him.

"Oh."

"You think I meant it?"

"Oh, no."

She grew suddenly brisk. "That will be fourteen forty, including the leash and the choke chain." Then while Macon was fumbling through his wallet she said, "You have to practice what he's learned, and no one else can practice for you. I'll come back tomorrow for the second lesson. Will eight in the morning be too early? I've got to be at the Meow-Bow at nine."

"Eight will be fine," Macon told her. He counted out fourteen dollars and all the change he had loose in his pocket—thirty-six cents.

"You can pay me the other four cents tomorrow," she said.

Then she made Edward sit and she handed the leash to Macon. "Release him when I'm gone," she said.

Macon held out his palm and stared hard into Edward's eyes, begging him to stay. Edward stayed, but he moaned when he saw

Muriel leave. When Macon snapped his fingers, Edward jumped up and attacked the front door.

All that afternoon and evening, Macon and Edward practiced. Edward learned to plop his rump down at the slightest motion of a finger. He stayed there, complaining and rolling his eyes, while Macon clucked approvingly. By suppertime, a cluck was part of the family language. Charles clucked over Rose's pork chops. Porter clucked when Macon dealt him a good hand of cards.

"Imagine a flamenco dancer with galloping consumption," Rose told Charles and Porter. "That's Edward's trainer. She talks nonstop, I don't know when she comes up for air. When she talked about her lesson plan she kept saying 'simplistic' for 'simple.' "

"I thought you were going to stay out of sight," Macon told Rose.

"Well? Did you ever see me?"

"Muriel did."

"I guess so! The way she was always peering around your back and snooping."

There were constant slamming sounds from the living room, because Edward's new leash kept catching on the rocking chair and dragging it behind him. During the course of the evening he chewed a pencil to splinters, stole a pork-chop bone from the garbage bin, and threw up on the sun porch rug; but now that he could sit on command, everyone felt more hopeful.

"When I was in high school I made nothing but A's," Muriel said. "You're surprised at that, aren't you. You think I'm kind of like, not an intellect. I know what you're thinking! You're surprised."

"No, I'm not," Macon said, although he was, actually.

"I made A's because I caught on to the trick," Muriel told him. "You think it's not a trick? There's a trick to everything; that's how you get through life."

They were in front of the house—both of them in raincoats, for it was a damp, drippy morning. Muriel wore truncated black suede boots with witchy toes and needle heels. Her legs rose out of them like toothpicks. The leash trailed from her fingers. Supposedly, she was teaching Edward to walk right. Instead she went on talking about her school days.

"Some of my teachers told me I should go to college," she said. "This one in particular, well she wasn't a teacher but a librarian, I worked in the library for her, shelving books and things; she said, 'Muriel, why don't you go on to Towson State?' But I don't know . . . and now I tell my sister, 'You be thinking of college, hear? Don't drop out like I dropped out.' I've got this little sister? Claire? *Her* hair never turned. She's blond as an angel. Here's what's funny, though: she couldn't care less. Braids her hair back any old how to keep it out of her eyes. Wears raggy jeans and forgets to shave her legs. Doesn't it always work that way? My folks believe she's wonderful. She's the good one and I'm the bad one. It's not her fault, though; I don't blame Claire. People just get fixed in these certain frames of other people's opinions, don't you find that's true? Claire was always Mary in the Nativity Scene at Christmas. Boys in her grade school were always proposing, but there I was in high school and no one proposed to *me*, I can tell you. Aren't high school boys just so frustrating? I mean they'd invite me out and all, like to drive-in movies and things, and they'd act so tense and secret, sneaking one arm around my shoulder inch by inch like they thought I wouldn't notice and then dropping a hand down, you know how they do, lower and lower while all the time staring straight ahead at the movie like it was the most fascinating spectacle they'd ever seen in their lives. You just had to feel sorry for them. But then Monday morning there they were like nothing had taken place, real boisterous and horsing around with their friends and nudging each other when I walked past but not so much as saying hello to me. You think that didn't hurt my feelings? Not one boy in all that time treated me like a steady girlfriend. They'd ask me out on Saturday night and expect me to be so nice to them, but you think they ever ate lunch with me next Monday in the school cafeteria, or walked me from class to class?"

She glanced down at Edward. Abruptly, she slapped her hip; her black vinyl raincoat made a buckling sound. "That's the 'heel' command," she told Macon. She started walking. Edward followed uncertainly. Macon stayed behind. It had been hard enough getting down the front porch steps.

"He's supposed to match his pace to anything," she called back. "Slow, fast, anything I do." She speeded up. When Edward crossed in front of her, she walked right into him. When he dawdled, she yanked his leash. She tip-tapped briskly eastward, her coat a stiff, swaying triangle beneath the smaller triangle of her hair blowing back. Macon waited, ankle-deep in wet leaves.

On the return trip, Edward kept close to Muriel's left side. "I think he's got the hang of it," she called. She arrived in front of Macon and offered him the leash. "Now you."

He attempted to slap his hip—which was difficult, on crutches. Then he set off. He was agonizingly slow and Edward kept pulling ahead. "Yank that leash!" Muriel said, clicking along behind. "He knows what he's supposed to do. Contrary thing."

Edward fell into step, finally, although he gazed off in a bored, lofty way. "Don't forget to cluck," Muriel said. "Every little minute, you have to praise him." Her heels made a scraping sound behind them. "Once I worked with this dog that had never in her life been housebroken. Two years old and not one bit housebroken and the owners were losing their minds. First I can't figure it out; then it comes to me. That dog thought she wasn't supposed to piddle *any*place, not indoors or outdoors, either one. See, no one had ever praised her when she did it right. Did you ever hear of such a thing? I had to catch her peeing outdoors which wasn't easy, believe me, because she was all the time ashamed and trying to hide it, and then I praised her to bits and after a while she caught on."

They reached the corner. "Now, when you stop, he has to sit," she said.

"But how will I practice?" Macon asked.

"What do you mean?"

"I'm on these crutches."

"So? It's good exercise for your leg," she said. She didn't ask how the leg had been broken. Come to think of it, there was something impervious about her, in spite of all her interest in his private life. She said, "Practice lots, ten minutes a session."

"Ten minutes!"

"Now let's start back."

She led the way, her angular, sashaying walk broken by the jolt of her sharp heels. Macon and Edward followed. When they reached the house, she asked what time it was. "Eight fifty," Macon said severely. He mistrusted women who wore no watches.

"I have to get going. That will be five dollars, please, and the four cents you owe me from yesterday."

He gave her the money and she stuffed it in her raincoat pocket. "Next time, I'll stay longer and talk," she said. "That's a promise." She trilled her fingers at him, and then she clicked off toward a car that was parked down the street—an aged, gray, boatlike sedan polished to a high shine. When she slid in and slammed the door behind her, there was a sound like falling beer cans. The engine twanged and rattled before it took hold. Macon shook his head, and he and Edward returned to the house.

Between Wednesday and Thursday, Macon spent what seemed a lifetime struggling up and down Dempsey Road beside Edward. His armpits developed a permanent ache. There was a vertical seam of pain in his thigh. This made no sense; it should have been in the shin. He wondered if something had gone wrong—if the break had been set improperly, for instance, so that some unusual strain was being placed upon the thighbone. Maybe he'd have to go back to the hospital and get his leg rebroken, probably under general anesthesia with all its horrifying complications; and then he'd spend months in traction and perhaps walk the rest of his life with a limp. He imagined himself tilting across intersections with a grotesque, lopsided gait. Sarah, driving past, would screech to a halt. "Macon?" She would roll down her window. "Macon, what *happened?*"

He would raise one arm and let it flop and totter away from her. Or tell her, "I'm surprised you care enough to inquire."

No, just totter away.

Most likely these little spells of self-pity (an emotion he despised ordinarily) were caused by sheer physical exhaustion. How had he got himself into this? Slapping his haunch was the first problem; then summoning his balance to jerk the leash when Edward fell out of step, and staying constantly alert for any squirrel or pedestrian. "Sss!" he kept saying, and "Cluck-cluck!" and "Sss!" again. He supposed passersby must think he was crazy. Edward loped beside him, occasionally yawning, looking everywhere for bikers. Bikers were his special delight. Whenever he saw one, the hair between his shoulders stood on end and he lunged forward. Macon felt like a man on a tightrope that was suddenly set swinging.

At this uneven, lurching pace, he saw much more than he would have otherwise. He had a lengthy view of every bush and desiccated flower bed. He memorized eruptions in the sidewalk that might trip him. It was an old people's street, and not in the best of repair. The neighbors spent their days telephoning back and forth amongst themselves, checking to see that no one had suffered a stroke alone on the stairs or a heart attack in the bathroom, a broken hip, blocked windpipe, dizzy spell over the stove with every burner alight. Some would set out for a walk and find themselves hours later in the middle of the street, wondering where they'd been headed. Some would start fixing a bite to eat at noon, a soft-boiled egg or a cup of tea, and by sundown would still be puttering in their kitchen, fumbling for the salt and forgetting how the toaster worked. Macon knew all this through his sister, who was called upon by neighbors in distress. "Rose, dear! Rose, dear!" they would quaver, and they'd stumble into her yard waving an overdue bill, an alarming letter, a bottle of pills with a childproof top.

In the evening, taking Edward for his last walk, Macon glanced in windows and saw people slumped in flowered armchairs, lit blue and shivery by their TV sets. The Orioles were winning the second game of the World Series, but these people seemed to be staring at their own thoughts instead. Macon imagined they were somehow dragging him down, causing him to walk heavily, to slouch, to grow short of breath. Even the dog seemed plodding and discouraged.

And when he returned to the house, the others were suffering one of their fits of indecisiveness. Was it better to lower the thermostat at night, or not? Wouldn't the furnace have to work harder if it were lowered? Hadn't Porter read that someplace? They debated back and forth, settling it and then beginning again. Why! Macon thought. They were not so very different from their neighbors. They were growing old themselves. He'd been putting in his own two bits (by all means, lower the thermostat), but now his voice trailed off, and he said no more.

That night, he dreamed he was parked near Lake Roland in his grandfather's '57 Buick. He was sitting in the dark and some girl was sitting next to him. He didn't know her, but the bitter smell of her perfume seemed familiar, and the rustle of her skirt when she moved closer. He turned and looked at her. It was Muriel. He drew a breath to ask what she was doing here, but she put a finger to his lips and stopped him. She moved closer still. She took his keys from him and set them on the dashboard. Gazing steadily into his face, she unbuckled his belt and slipped a cool, knowing hand down inside his trousers.

He woke astonished and embarrassed, and sat bolt upright in his bed.

"Everybody always asks me, 'What is *your* dog like?' " Muriel said. " 'I bet he's a model of good behavior,' they tell me. But you want to hear something funny? I don't own a dog. In fact, the one time I had one around, he ran off. That was Norman's dog, Spook. My ex-husband's. First night we were married, Spook ran off to Norman's mom's. I think he hated me."

"Oh, surely not," Macon said.

"He hated me. I could tell."

They were outdoors again, preparing to put Edward through his paces. By now, Macon had adjusted to the rhythm of these lessons. He waited, gripping Edward's leash. Muriel said, "It was just like one of those Walt Disney movies. You know: where the dog walks all the way to the Yukon or something. Except Spook only walked to Timonium. Me and Norman had him downtown in our apartment, and Spook took off and traveled the whole however many miles it was back to Norman's mom's house in Timonium. His mom calls up: 'When did you drop Spook off?' 'What're you talking about?' Norman asks her."

She changed her voice to match each character. Macon heard the thin whine of Norman's mother, the stammering boyishness of Norman himself. He remembered last night's dream and felt embarrassed all over again. He looked at her directly, hoping for flaws, and found them in abundance—a long, narrow nose, and sallow skin, and two freckled knobs of collarbone that promised an unluxurious body.

"Seems his mom woke up in the morning," she was saying, "and there was Spook, sitting on the doorstep. But that was the first we realized he was missing. Norman goes, 'I don't know what got into him. He never ran off before.' And gives me this doubtful kind of look. I could tell he wondered if it might be my fault. Maybe he thought it was an omen or something. We were awful young to get married. I can see that now. I was seventeen. He was eighteen—an only child. His mother's pet. Widowed mother. He had this fresh pink face like a girl's and the shortest hair of any boy in my school and he buttoned his shirt collars all the way to the neck. Moved in from Parkville the end of junior year. Caught sight of me in my strapless sun dress and goggled at me all through every class; other boys teased him but he didn't pay any mind. He was just so . . . innocent, you know? He made me feel like I had powers. There he was following me around the halls with his arms full of books and I'd say, 'Norman? You want to eat lunch with me?' and he'd blush and say, 'Oh, why, uh, you serious?' He didn't even know how to drive, but I told him if he got his license I'd go out with him. 'We could ride to someplace quiet and talk and be alone,' I'd say, 'you know what I mean?' Oh, I was bad. I don't know what was wrong with me, back then. He got his license in no time flat and came for me in his mother's Chevy, which incidentally she happened to have purchased from my father, who was a salesman for Ruggles Chevrolet. We found that out at the wedding. Got married the fall of senior year, he was just dying to marry me so what could I say? and at the wedding my daddy goes to Norman's mom, 'Why, I believe I sold you a car not long ago,' but she was too busy crying to take much notice. That woman carried on like marriage was a fate worse than death. Then when Spook runs off to her house she tells us, 'I suppose I'd best keep him, it's clear as day he don't like it there with you-all.' With *me*, is what she meant. She held it against me I took her son away. She claimed I ruined his chances; she wanted him to get his diploma. But I never kept him from getting his diploma. He was the one who said he might as well drop out; said why bother staying in school when he could make a fine living on floors."

"On what?" Macon asked.

"Floors. Sanding floors. His uncle was Pritchett Refinishing. Norman went into the business as soon as we got married and his mom was always talking about the waste. She said he could have been an accountant or something, but I don't know who she thought she was kidding. He never mentioned accounting to *me*."

She pulled a dog hair off her coat sleeve, examined it, and flicked it away. "So let's see him," she said.

"Pardon?"

"Let's see him heel."

Macon slapped his hip and started off, with Edward lagging just a bit behind. When Macon stopped, Edward stopped too and sat down. Macon was pleasantly surprised, but Muriel said, "He's not sitting."

"What? What do you call it, then?"

"He's keeping his rear end about two inches off the ground. Trying to see what he can get away with."

"Oh, Edward," Macon said sadly.

He pivoted and returned. "Well, you'll have to work on that," Muriel said. "But meantime, we'll go on to the downstay. Let's try it in the house."

Macon worried they'd meet up with Rose, but she was nowhere to be seen. The front hall smelled of radiator dust. The clock in the living room was striking the half hour.

"This is where we start on Edward's real problem," Muriel said. "Getting him to lie down and stay, so he won't all the time be jumping at the door."

She showed him the command: two taps of the foot. Her boot made a crisp sound. When Edward didn't respond, she bent and pulled his forepaws out from under him. Then she let him up and went through it again, several times over. Edward made no progress. When she tapped her foot, he panted and looked elsewhere. "Stubborn," Muriel told him. "You're just as stubborn as they come." She said to Macon, "A lot of dogs will act like this. They hate to lie down; I don't know why. Now you."

Macon tapped his foot. Edward seemed fascinated by something off to his left.

"Grab his paws," Muriel said.

"On crutches?"

"Sure."

Macon sighed and propped his crutches in the corner. He lowered himself to the floor with his cast in front of him, took Edward's paws and forced him down. Edward rumbled threateningly, but in the end he submitted. To get up again, Macon had to hold onto the lamp table. "This is really very difficult," he said, but Muriel said, "Listen, I've taught a man with no legs at all."

"You have?" Macon said. He pictured a legless man dragging along the sidewalk with some vicious breed of dog, Muriel standing by unconcerned and checking her manicure. "I don't suppose *you* ever broke a leg," he accused her. "Getting around is harder than it looks."

"I broke an arm once," Muriel said.

"An arm is no comparison."

"I did it training dogs, in fact. Got knocked off a porch by a Doberman pinscher."

"A Doberman!"

"Came to to find him standing over me, showing all his teeth. Well, I thought of what they said at Doggie, Do: Only one of you can be boss. So I tell him, 'Absolutely not.' Those were the first words that came to me—what my mother used to say when she wasn't going to let me get away with something. 'Absolutely not,' I tell him, and my right arm is broken so I hold out my left, hold out my palm and stare into his eyes—they can't stand for you to meet their eyes—and get to my feet real slow. And durned if that dog doesn't settle right back on his haunches."

"Good Lord," Macon said.

"I've had a cocker spaniel fly directly at my throat. Meanest thing you ever saw. Had a German shepherd take my ankle in his teeth. Then he let it go."

She lifted a foot and rotated it. Her ankle was about the thickness of a pencil.

"Have you ever met with a failure?" Macon asked her. "Some dog you just gave up on?"

"Not a one," she said. "And Edward's not about to be the first."

But Edward seemed to think otherwise. Muriel worked with him another half hour, and although he would stay once he was down, he flatly refused to lie down on his own. Each time, he had to be forced. "Never mind," Muriel said. "This is the way most of them do. I bet tomorrow he'll be just as stubborn, so I'm going to skip a day. You keep practicing, and I'll be back this same time Saturday."

Then she told Edward to stay, and she accepted her money and slipped out the door. Observing Edward's erect, resisting posture, Macon felt discouraged. Why hire a trainer at all, if she left him to do the training? "Oh, I don't know, I don't know," he said. Edward gave a sigh and walked off, although he hadn't been released.

All that afternoon and evening, Edward refused to lie down. Macon wheedled, threatened, cajoled; Edward muttered ominously and stood firm. Rose and the boys edged around the two of them, politely averting their eyes as if they'd stumbled on some private quarrel.

Then the next morning, Edward charged the mailman. Macon managed to grab the leash, but it raised some doubts in his mind. What did all this sitting and heeling have to do with Edward's real problem? "I should just ship you off to the pound," he told Edward. He tapped his foot twice. Edward did not lie down.

In the afternoon, Macon called the Meow-Bow. "May I speak to Muriel, please?" he asked. He couldn't think of her last name.

"Muriel's not working today," a girl told him.

"Oh, I see."

"Her little boy is sick."

He hadn't known she had a little boy. He felt some inner click of adjustment; she was a slightly different person from the one he'd imagined. "Well," he said, "this is Macon Leary. I guess I'll talk to her tomorrow."

"Oh, Mr. Leary. You want to call her at home?"

"No, that's all right."

"I can give you her number if you want to call her at home."

"I'll just talk to her tomorrow. Thank you."

Rose had an errand downtown, so she agreed to drop him off at the Businessman's Press. He wanted to deliver the rest of his guidebook. Stretched across the backseat with his crutches, he gazed at the passing scenery: antique office buildings, tasteful restaurants, health food stores and florists' shops, all peculiarly hard-edged and vivid in the light of a brilliant October afternoon. Rose perched behind the wheel and drove at a steady, slow pace that was almost hypnotic. She wore a little round basin-shaped hat with ribbons down the back. It made her look prim and Sunday schoolish.

One of the qualities that all four Leary children shared was a total inability to find their way around. It was a kind of dyslexia, Macon believed—a geographic dyslexia. None of them ever stepped outside without obsessively noting all available landmarks, clinging to a fixed and desperate mental map of the neighborhood. Back home, Macon had kept a stack of index cards giving detailed directions to the houses of his friends—even friends he'd known for decades. And it used to be that whenever Ethan met a new boy, Macon's first anxious question was, "Where exactly does he live, do you know?" Ethan had had a tendency to form inconvenient alliances. He couldn't just hang out with the boy next door; oh, no, it had to be someone who lived way beyond the Beltway. What did Ethan care? *He* had no trouble navigating. This was because he'd lived all his life in one house, was Macon's theory; while a person who'd been moved around a great deal never acquired a fixed point of reference but wandered forever in a fog—adrift upon the planet, helpless, praying that just by luck he might stumble across his destination.

At any rate, Rose and Macon got lost. Rose knew where she wanted to go—a shop that sold a special furniture oil—and Macon had visited Julian's office a hundred times; but even so, they drove in circles till Macon noticed a familiar steeple. "Stop! Turn left," he said. Rose pulled up where he directed. Macon struggled out. "Will you be all right?" he asked Rose. "Do you think you can find your way back to pick me up?"

"I hope so."

"Look for the steeple, remember."

She nodded and drove away.

Macon swung up three granite steps to the brick mansion that housed the Businessman's Press. The door was made of polished, golden wood. The floor inside was tiled with tiny black and white hexagons, just uneven enough to give purchase to Macon's crutches.

This wasn't an ordinary office. The secretary typed in a back room while Julian, who couldn't stand being alone, sat out front. He was talking on a red telephone, lounging behind a desk that was laden with a clutter of advertisements, pamphlets, unpaid bills, unanswered letters, empty Chinese carryout cartons, and Perrier bottles. The walls were covered with sailing charts. The bookshelves held few books but a great many antique brass mariners' instruments that probably didn't even work anymore. Anybody with eyes could see that Julian's heart was not in the Businessman's Press but out on the Chesapeake Bay someplace. This was to Macon's advantage, he figured. Surely no one else would have continued backing his series, with its staggering expenses and its constant need for updating.

"Rita's bringing croissants," Julian said into the phone. "Joe is making his quiche." Then he caught sight of Macon. "Macon!" he said. "Stefanie, I'll get back to you." He hung up. "How's the leg? Here, have a seat."

He dumped a stack of yachting magazines off a chair. Macon sat down and handed over his folder. "Here's the rest of the material on England," he said.

"Well, finally!"

"This edition as I see it is going to run about ten or twelve pages longer than the last one," Macon said. "It's adding the business *women* that does it—listing which hotels offer elevator escorts, which ones serve drinks in the lobbies . . . I think I ought to be paid more."

"I'll talk it over with Marvin," Julian said, flipping through the manuscript.

Macon sighed. Julian spent money like water but Marvin was more cautious.

"So now you're on the U.S. again," Julian said.

"Well, if you say so."

"I hope it's not going to take you long."

"I can only go so fast," Macon said. "The U.S. has more cities."

"Yes, I realize that. In fact I might print this edition in sections: northeast, mid-Atlantic, and so forth; I don't know . . ." But then he changed the subject. (He had a rather skittery mind.) "Did I tell you my new idea? Doctor friend of mine is looking into it: *Accidental Tourist in Poor Health.* A list of American-trained doctors and dentists in every foreign capital, plus maybe some suggestions for basic medical supplies: aspirin, Merck Manual—"

"Oh, not a Merck Manual away from home!" Macon said. "Every hangnail could be cancer, when you're reading a Merck Manual."

"Well, I'll make a note of that," Julian said (without so much as lifting a pencil). "Aren't you going to ask me to autograph your cast? It's so white."

"I like it white," Macon said. "I polish it with shoe polish."

"I didn't realize you could do that."

"I use the liquid kind. It's the brand with a nurse's face on the label, if you ever need to know."

"*Accidental Tourist on Crutches,*" Julian said, and he rocked back happily in his chair.

Macon could tell he was about to start his Macon Leary act. He got hastily to his feet and said, "Well, I guess I'll be going."

"So soon? Why don't we have a drink?"

"No, thanks, I can't. My sister's picking me up as soon as she gets done with her errand."

"Ah," Julian said. "What kind of errand?"

Macon looked at him suspiciously.

"Well? Dry cleaner's? Shoe repair?"

"Just an ordinary errand, Julian. Nothing special."

"Hardware store? Pharmacy?"

"No."

"So what is it?"

"Uh . . . she had to buy Furniture Food."

Julian's chair rocked so far back, Macon thought he was going to tip over. He wished he would, in fact. "Macon, do me a favor," Julian said. "Couldn't you just once invite me to a family dinner?"

"We're really not much for socializing," Macon told him.

"It wouldn't have to be fancy. Just whatever you eat normally. What *do* you eat normally? Or I'll bring the meal myself. You could lock the dog up . . . what's his name again?"

"Edward."

"Edward. Ha! And I'll come spend the evening."

"Oh, well," Macon said vaguely. He arranged himself on his crutches.

"Why don't I step outside and wait with you."

"I'd really rather you didn't," Macon said.

He couldn't bear for Julian to see his sister's little basin hat.

He pegged out to the curb and stood there, gazing in the direction Rose should be coming from. He supposed she was lost again. The cold was already creeping through the stretched-out sock he wore over his cast.

The trouble was, he decided, Julian had never had anything happen to him. His ruddy, cheerful face was unscarred by anything but sunburn; his only interest was a ridiculously inefficient form of transportation. His brief marriage had ended amicably. He had no children. Macon didn't want to sound prejudiced, but he couldn't help feeling that people who had no children had never truly grown up. They weren't entirely . . . real, he felt.

Unexpectedly, he pictured Muriel after the Doberman had knocked her off the porch. Her arm hung lifeless; he knew the leaden look a broken limb takes on. But Muriel ignored it; she didn't even glance at it. Smudged and disheveled and battered, she held her other hand up. "Absolutely not," she said.

She arrived the next morning with a gauzy bouffant scarf swelling over her hair, her hands thrust deep in her coat pockets. Edward danced around her. She pointed to his rump. He sat, and she bent to pick up his leash.

"How's your little boy?" Macon asked her.

She looked over at him. "What?" she said.

"Wasn't he sick?"

"Who told you that?"

"Someone at the vet's, when I phoned."

She went on looking at him.

"What was it? The flu?" he asked.

"Oh, yes, probably," she said after a moment. "Some little stomach thing."

"It's that time of year, I guess."

"How come you phoned?" she asked him.

"I wanted to know why Edward wouldn't lie down."

She turned her gaze toward Edward. She wound the leash around her hand and considered him.

"I tap my foot but he never obeys me," Macon said. "Something's wrong."

"I told you he'd be stubborn about it."

"Yes, but I've been practicing two days now and he's not making any—"

"What do you expect? You think I'm magical or something? Why blame me?"

"Oh, I'm not blaming—"

"You most certainly are. You tell me something's wrong, you call me on the phone—"

"I just wanted to—"

"You think it's weird I didn't mention Alexander, don't you?"

"Alexander?"

"You think I'm some kind of unnatural mother."

"What? No, wait a minute—"

"You're not going to give me another thought, are you, now you know I've got a kid. You're like, 'Oh, forget it, no point getting involved in *that*,' and then you wonder why I didn't tell you about him right off. Well, isn't it obvious? Don't you see what happens when I do?"

Macon wasn't quite following her logic, perhaps because he was distracted by Edward. The shriller Muriel's voice grew, the stiffer Edward's hair stood up on the back of his neck. A bad sign. A very bad sign. Edward's lip was slowly curling. Gradually, at first almost soundlessly, he began a low growl.

Muriel glanced at him and stopped speaking. She didn't seem alarmed. She merely tapped her foot twice. But Edward not only failed to lie down; he rose from his sitting position. Now he had a distinct, electrified hump between his shoulders. He seemed to have altered his basic shape. His ears were flattened against his skull.

"Down," Muriel said levelly.

With a bellow, Edward sprang straight at her face. Every tooth was bare and gleaming. His lips were drawn back in a horrible grimace and flecks of white foam flew from his mouth. Muriel instantly raised the leash. She jerked it upward with both fists and lifted Edward completely off the floor. He stopped barking. He started making gargling sounds.

"He's choking," Macon said.

Edward's throat gave an odd sort of click.

"Stop it. It's enough! You're choking him!"

Still, she let him hang. Now Edward's eyes rolled back in their sockets. Macon grabbed at Muriel's shoulder but found himself with a handful of coat, bobbled and irregular like something alive. He shook it, anyhow. Muriel lowered Edward to the floor. He landed in a boneless heap, his legs crumpling beneath him and his head flopping over. Macon crouched at his side. "Edward? Edward? Oh, God, he's dead!"

Edward raised his head and feebly licked his lips.

"See that? When they lick their lips it's a sign they're giving in," Muriel said cheerfully. "Doggie, Do taught me that."

Macon stood up. He was shaking.

"When they lick their lips it's good but when they put a foot on top of your foot it's bad," Muriel said. "Sounds like a secret language, just about, doesn't it?"

"Don't you ever, ever do that again," Macon told her.

"Huh?"

"In fact, don't even bother coming again."

There was a startled silence.

"Well, fine," Muriel said, tightening her scarf. "If that's the way you feel, just fine and dandy." She stepped neatly around Edward and opened the front door. "You want a dog you can't handle? Fine with me."

"I'd rather a barking dog than a damaged, timid dog," Macon said.

"You want a dog that bites all your friends? Scars neighbor kids for life? Gets you into lawsuits? You want a dog that hates the whole world? Evil, nasty, *angry* dog? That kills the whole world?"

She slipped out the screen door and closed it behind her. Then she looked through the screen directly into Macon's eyes. "Why, yes, I guess you do," she said.

From the hall floor, Edward gave a moan and watched her walk away.

8

Now the days were shorter and colder, and the trees emptied oceans of leaves on the lawn but remained, somehow, as full as ever, so you'd finish raking and look upward to see a great wash of orange and yellow just waiting to cover the grass again the minute your back was turned. Charles and Porter drove over to Macon's house and raked there as well, and lit the pilot light in the furnace and repaired the basement window. They reported that everything seemed fine. Macon heard the news without much interest. Next week he'd be out of his cast, but no one asked when he was moving back home.

Each morning he and Edward practiced heeling. They would trudge the length of the block, with Edward matching Macon's gait so perfectly that he looked crippled himself. When they met passersby now he muttered but he didn't attack. "See there?" Macon wanted to tell someone. Bikers were another issue, but Macon had confidence they would solve that problem too, eventually.

He would make Edward sit and then he'd draw back, holding out a palm. Edward waited. Oh, he wasn't such a bad dog! Macon wished he could change the gestures of command—the palm, the pointed finger, all vestiges of that heartless trainer—but he supposed it was too late. He tapped his foot. Edward growled. "Dear one," Macon said, dropping heavily beside him. "Won't you please consider lying down?" Edward looked away. Macon stroked the soft wide space between his ears. "Ah, well, maybe tomorrow," he said.

His family was not so hopeful. "What about when you start traveling again?" Rose asked. "You're not leaving him with me. I wouldn't know how to handle him."

Macon told her they would get to that when they got to it.

It was hard for him to imagine resuming his travels. Sometimes he wished he could stay in his cast forever. In fact, he wished it covered him from head to foot. People would thump faintly on his chest. They'd peer through his eyeholes. "Macon? You in there?" Maybe he was, maybe he wasn't. No one would ever know.

One evening just after supper, Julian stopped by with a stack of papers. Macon had to slam Edward into the pantry before he opened the door. "Here you are!" Julian said, strolling past him. He wore corduroys and looked rugged and healthy. "I've been phoning you for three days straight. That dog sounds awfully close by, don't you think?"

"He's in the pantry," Macon said.

"Well, I've brought you some materials, Macon—mostly on New

York. We've got a lot of suggestions for New York."

Macon groaned. Julian set his papers on the couch and looked around him. "Where are the others?" he asked.

"Oh, here and there," Macon said vaguely, but just then Rose appeared, and Charles was close behind.

"I hope I'm not interfering with supper," Julian told them.

"No, no," Rose said.

"We've finished," Macon said triumphantly.

Julian's face fell. "Really?" he said. "What time do you eat, anyhow?"

Macon didn't answer that. (They ate at five thirty. Julian would laugh.)

Rose said, "But we haven't had our coffee. Wouldn't you like some coffee?"

"I'd love some."

"It seems a little silly," Macon said, "if you haven't eaten."

"Well, yes," Julian said, "I suppose it does, Macon, to someone like you. But for me, home-brewed coffee is a real treat. All the people in my apartment building eat out, and there's nothing in any of the kitchens but a couple cans of peanuts and some diet soda."

"What kind of place *is* that?" Rose asked.

"It's the Calvert Arms—a singles building. Everybody's single."

"Oh! What an interesting idea."

"Well, not really," Julian said gloomily. "Not after a while. I started out enjoying it but now I think it's getting me down. Sometimes I wish for the good old-fashioned way of doing things, with children and families and old people like normal buildings have."

"Well, of course you do," Rose told him. "I'm going to get you some nice hot coffee."

She left, and the others sat down. "So. Are you three all there is?" Julian asked.

Macon refused to answer, but Charles said, "Oh, no, there's Porter too."

"Porter? Where is Porter?"

"Um, we're not too sure."

"*Missing?*"

"He went to a hardware store and we think he got lost."

"Good grief, when did this happen?"

"A little while before supper."

"Supper. You mean today."

"He's just running an errand," Macon said. "Not lost in any permanent sense."

"Where was the store?"

"Someplace on Howard Street," Charles said. "Rose needed hinges."

"He got lost on Howard Street?"

Macon stood up. "I'll go help Rose," he said.

Rose was setting their grandmother's clear glass coffee mugs on a silver tray. "I hope he doesn't take sugar," she said. "The sugar bowl is empty and Edward's in the pantry where I keep the bag."

"I wouldn't worry about it."

"Maybe you could go to the pantry and get it for me."

"Oh, just give him his coffee straight and tell him to take it or leave it."

"Why, Macon! This is your employer!"

"He's only here because he hopes we'll do something eccentric," Macon told her. "He has this one-sided notion of us. I just pray none of us says anything unconventional around him, are you listening?"

"What would we say?" Rose asked. "We're the most conventional people I know."

This was perfectly true, and yet in some odd way it wasn't. Macon couldn't explain it. He sighed and followed her out of the kitchen.

In the living room, Charles was doggedly debating whether they should answer the phone in case it rang, in case it might be Porter, in case he needed them to consult a map. "Chances are, though, he wouldn't bother calling," he decided, "because he knows we wouldn't answer. Or he thinks we wouldn't answer. Or I don't know, maybe he figures we would answer even so, because we're worried."

"Do you always give this much thought to your phone calls?" Julian asked.

Macon said, "Have some coffee, Julian. Try it black."

"Why, thank you," Julian said. He accepted a mug and studied the inscription that arched across it. "CENTURY OF PROGRESS 1933," he read off. He grinned and raised the mug in a toast. "To progress," he said.

"Progress," Rose and Charles echoed. Macon scowled.

Julian said, "What do you do for a living, Charles?"

"I make bottle caps."

"Bottle caps! Is that a fact!"

"Oh, well, it's no big thing," Charles said. "I mean it's not half as exciting as it sounds, really."

"And Rose? Do you work?"

"Yes, I do," Rose said, in the brave, forthright style of someone being interviewed. "I work at home; I keep house for the boys. Also I take care of a lot of the neighbors. They're mostly old and they need me to read their prescriptions and repair their plumbing and such."

"You repair their plumbing?" Julian asked.

The telephone rang. The others stiffened.

"What do you think?" Rose asked Macon.

"Um . . ."

"But he knows we wouldn't answer," Charles told them.

"Yes, he'd surely call a neighbor instead."

"On the other hand . . ." Charles said.

"On the other hand," Macon said.

It was Julian's face that decided him—Julian's pleased, perked expression. Macon reached over to the end table and picked up the receiver. "Leary," he said.

"Macon?"

It was Sarah.

Macon shot a glance at the others and turned his back to them. "Yes," he said.

"Well, finally," she said. Her voice seemed oddly flat and concrete. All at once he saw her clearly: She wore one of his cast-off shirts and she sat hugging her bare knees. "I've been trying to get in touch with you at home," she said. "Then it occurred to me you might be having supper with your family."

"Is something wrong?" he asked.

He was nearly whispering. Maybe Rose understood, from that, who it was, for she suddenly began an animated conversation with the others. Sarah said, "What? I can't hear you."

"Is everything all right?"

"Who's that talking?"

"Julian's here."

"Oh, Julian! Give him my love. How's Sukie?"

"Sukie?"

"His boat, Macon."

"It's fine," he said. Or should he have said "she"? For all he knew, *Sukie* was at the bottom of the Chesapeake.

"I called because I thought we should talk," Sarah said. "I was hoping we could meet for supper some night."

"Oh. Well. Yes, we could do that," Macon said.

"Would tomorrow be all right?"

"Certainly."

"What restaurant?"

"Well, why not the Old Bay," Macon said.

"The Old Bay. Of course," Sarah said. She either sighed or laughed, he wasn't sure which.

"It's only because you could walk there," he told her. "That's the only reason I suggested it."

"Yes, well, let's see. You like to eat early; shall we say six o'clock?"

"Six will be fine," he said.

When he hung up, he found Rose embarked on a discussion of the English language. She pretended not to notice he had rejoined them. It was shocking, she was saying, how sloppy everyday speech had become. How the world seemed bound and determined to say "*the* hoi polloi," a clear redundancy in view of the fact that "hoi" was an article. How "chauvinist" had come to be a shorthand term for "male chauvinist," its original meaning sadly lost to common knowledge. It was incredible, Charles chimed in, that a female movie star traveled "incognito" when any fool should know she was "incognita" instead. Julian appeared to share their indignation. It was more incredible still, he said, how everyone slung around the word "incredible" when really there was very little on earth that truly defied credibility. "Credence," Macon corrected him, but Rose rushed in as if Macon hadn't spoken. "Oh, I know just what you mean," she told Julian. "Words are getting devalued, isn't that right?" She tugged handfuls of her gray tube skirt over her knees in a childlike gesture. You would think she had never been warned that outsiders were not to be trusted.

To enter the Old Bay Restaurant, Macon had to climb a set of steps. Before he broke his leg he hadn't even noticed those steps existed— let alone that they were made of smooth, unblemished marble, so that his crutches kept threatening to slide out from under him. Then he had to fight the heavy front door, hurrying a bit because Rose had taken a wrong turn driving him down and it was already five after six.

The foyer was dark as night. The dining room beyond was only slightly brighter, lit by netted candles on the tables. Macon peered into the gloom. "I'm meeting someone," he told the hostess. "Is she here yet?"

"Not as I know of, hon."

She led him past a tankful of sluggish lobsters, past two old ladies in churchy hats sipping pale pink drinks, past a whole field of empty tables. It was too early for anyone else to be eating; all the other customers were still in the bar. The tables stood very close together, their linens brushing the floor, and Macon had visions of catching a crutch on a tablecloth and dragging the whole thing after him, candle included. The maroon floral carpet would burst into flames. His grandfather's favorite restaurant—his great-grandfather's too, quite possibly— would be reduced to a heap of charred metal crab pots. "Miss! Slow down!" he called, but the hostess strode on, muscular and athletic in her off-the-shoulder square-dance dress and sturdy white crepe-soled shoes.

She put him in a corner, which was lucky because it gave him a place to lean his crutches. But just as he was matching them up and preparing to set them aside, she said, "I'll take those for you, darlin'."

"Oh, they'll be fine here."

"I need to check them up front, sweetheart. It's a rule."

"You have a rule about crutches?"

"They might trip the other customers, honeybunch."

This was unlikely, since the two other customers were clear across the room, but Macon handed his crutches over. Come to think of it, he might be better off without them. Then Sarah wouldn't get the impression (at least at first glance) that he'd fallen apart in her absence.

As soon as he was alone he tugged each shirt cuff till a quarter-inch of white showed. He was wearing his gray tweed suit coat with gray flannel trousers—an old pair of trousers, so it hadn't mattered if he cut one leg off. Charles had fetched them from home and Rose had hemmed them, and she'd also trimmed his hair. Porter had lent him his best striped tie. They had all been so discreetly helpful that Macon had felt sad, for some reason.

The hostess reappeared in the doorway, followed by Sarah. Macon had an instant of stunned recognition; it was something like accidentally glimpsing his own reflection in a mirror. Her halo of curls, the way her coat fell around her in soft folds, her firm, springy walk in trim pumps with wineglass heels—how had he forgotten all that?

He half stood. Would she kiss him? Or just, God forbid, coolly shake hands. But no, she did neither; she did something much worse. She came around the table and pressed her cheek to his briefly, as if they were mere acquaintances meeting at a cocktail party.

"Hello, Macon," she said.

He waved her speechlessly into the chair across from his. He sat again, with some effort.

"What happened to your leg?" she asked.

"I had a kind of . . . fall."

"Is it broken?"

He nodded.

"And what did you do to your hand?"

He held it up to examine it. "Well, it's sort of a dog bite. But it's nearly healed by now."

"I meant the other one."

The other one had a band of gauze around the knuckles. "Oh, that," he said. "It's just a scrape. I've been helping Rose build a cat door."

She studied him.

"But I'm all right!" he told her. "In fact the cast is almost comfortable. Almost familiar! I'm wondering if I broke a leg once before in some previous incarnation."

Their waitress asked, "Can I bring you something from the bar?"

She was standing over them, pad and pencil poised. Sarah started flipping hastily through the menu, so Macon said, "A dry sherry, please." Then he and the waitress turned back to Sarah. "Oh, my," Sarah said. "Let me see. Well, how about a Rob Roy. Yes, a Rob Roy would be nice, with extra cherries."

That was something else he'd forgotten—how she loved to order complicated drinks in restaurants. He felt the corners of his mouth twitching upward.

"So," Sarah said when the waitress had gone. "Why would Rose be building a cat door? I thought they didn't have any pets."

"No, this is for our cat. Helen. Helen and I have been staying there."

"What for?"

"Well, because of my leg."

Sarah said nothing.

"I mean, can you see me managing those steps at home?" Macon asked her. "Taking Edward for walks? Lugging the trash cans out?"

But she was busy shucking off her coat. Beneath it she wore a gathered wool dress in an indeterminate color. (The candlelight turned everything to shades of sepia, like an old-fashioned photograph.) Macon had time to wonder if he'd given her the wrong idea. It sounded, perhaps, as if he were complaining—as if he were reproaching her for leaving him alone.

"But really," he said, "I've been getting along wonderfully."

"Good," Sarah said, and she smiled at him and went back to her menu.

Their drinks were set before them on little cardboard disks embossed with crabs. The waitress said, "Ready to order, dearies?"

"Well," Sarah said, "I think I'll have the hot antipasto and the beef Pierre."

The waitress, looking startled, peered over Sarah's shoulder at the menu. (Sarah had never seemed to realize what the Old Bay Restaurant was all about.) "Here," Sarah said, pointing, "and here."

"If you say so," the waitress said, writing it down.

"I'll just have the, you know," Macon said. "Crab soup, shrimp salad platter . . ." He handed back his menu. "Sarah, do you want wine?"

"No, thank you."

When they were alone again, she said, "How long have you been at your family's?"

"Since September," Macon said.

"September! Your leg's been broken all that time?"

He nodded and took a sip of his drink. "Tomorrow I get the cast off," he said.

"And is Edward over there too?"

He nodded again.

"Was it Edward who bit your hand?"

"Well, yes."

He wondered if she'd act like the others, urge him to call the S.P.C.A.; but instead she meditatively plucked a cherry off the plastic sword from her drink. "I guess he's been upset," she said.

"Yes, he has, in fact," Macon said. "He's not himself at all."

"Poor Edward."

"He's getting kind of out of control, to tell the truth."

"He always did have a sensitivity to change," Sarah said.

Macon took heart. "Actually, he's been attacking right and left," he told her. "I had to hire a special trainer. But she was too harsh; let's face it, she was brutal. She nearly strangled him when he tried to bite her."

"Ridiculous," Sarah said. "He was only frightened. When Edward's frightened he attacks; that's just the way he is. There's no point scaring him more."

Macon felt a sudden rush of love.

Oh, he'd raged at her and hated her and entirely forgotten her, at different times. He'd had moments when he imagined he'd never cared for her to begin with; only went after her because everybody else had. But the fact was, she was his oldest friend. The two of them had been through things that no one else in the world knew of. She was embedded in his life. It was much too late to root her out.

"What he wants," she was saying, "is a sense of routine. That's all he needs: reassurance."

"Sarah," he said, "it's been awful living apart."

She looked at him. Some trick of light made her eyes appear a darker blue, almost black.

"Hasn't it?" he said.

She lowered her glass. She said, "I asked you here for a reason, Macon."

He could tell it was something he didn't want to hear.

She said, "We need to spell out the details of our separation."

"We've been separated; what's to spell out?" he asked.

"I meant in a legal way."

"Legal. I see."

"Now, according to the state of Maryland—"

"I think you ought to come home."

Their first course arrived, placed before them by a hand that, as far as Macon was concerned, was not attached to a body. Condiment bottles were shifted needlessly; a metal stand full of sugar packets was moved a half-inch over. "Anything else?" the waitress asked.

"No!" Macon said. "Thank you."

She left.

He said, "Sarah?"

"It's not possible," she told him.

She was sliding a single pearl up and down the chain at her throat. He had given her that pearl when they were courting. Was there any significance in her wearing it this evening? Or maybe she cared so little now, it hadn't even occurred to her to leave it off. Yes, that was more likely.

"Listen," he said. "Don't say no before you hear me out. Have you ever considered we might have another baby?"

He had shocked her, he saw; she drew in a breath. (He had shocked himself.)

"Why not?" he asked her. "We're not too old."

"Oh, Macon."

"This time, it would be easy," he said. "It wouldn't take us seven years again; I bet you'd get pregnant in no time!" He leaned toward her, straining to make her see it: Sarah blossoming in that luscious pink maternity smock she used to wear. But oddly enough, what flashed across his mind instead was the memory of those first seven years—their disappointment each month. It had seemed to Macon back then (though of course it was pure superstition) that their failures were a sign of something deeper, some essential incompatibility. They had missed connections in the most basic and literal sense. When she finally got pregnant, he had felt not only relieved but guilty, as if they had succeeded in putting something over on someone.

He pushed these thoughts back down. "I realize," he said, "that it wouldn't be Ethan. I realize we can't replace him. But—"

"No," Sarah said.

Her eyes were very steady. He knew that look. She'd never change her mind.

Macon started on his soup. It was the best crab soup in Baltimore, but unfortunately the spices had a tendency to make his nose run. He hoped Sarah wouldn't think he was crying.

"I'm sorry," she said more gently. "But it would never work."

He said, "All right, forget that. It was crazy, right? Crazy notion. By the time that baby was twenty we'd be . . . Aren't you going to eat?"

She glanced down at her plate. Then she picked up a fork.

"Suppose I did this," Macon said. "Suppose I packed a suitcase with your clothes and knocked on your door and said, 'Come on, we're going to Ocean City. We've wasted long enough.' "

She stared, an artichoke heart raised halfway to her mouth.

"Ocean City?" she said. "You hate Ocean City!"

"Yes, but I meant—"

"You always said it was way too crowded."

"Yes, but—"

"And what clothes could you be talking about? They're all in my apartment."

"It was only a manner of speaking," Macon said.

"Really, Macon," she told him. "You don't even communicate when you communicate."

"Oh, *communicate*," he said. (His least favorite word.) "All I'm saying is, I think we ought to start over."

"I am starting over," she said. She returned the artichoke heart to her plate. "I'm doing everything I can to start over," she said, "but that doesn't mean I want to live the same life twice. I'm trying to branch off in new directions. I'm taking some courses. I'm even dating, a little."

"Dating?"

"I've been going out with this physician."

There was a pause.

Macon said, "Why not just call him a doctor."

Sarah briefly closed her eyes.

"Look," she said. "I know this is hard for you. It's hard for both of us. But we really didn't have much left, don't you see? Look who you turned to when you broke your leg: your sister Rose! You didn't even let me know, and you do have my telephone number."

"If I'd turned to you instead," he said, "would you have come?"

"Well . . . but at least you could have asked. But no, you called on your family. You're closer to them than you ever were to me."

"That's not true," Macon said. "Or rather, it's true but it's not the point. I mean, in one sense, of course we're closer; we're blood relations."

"Playing that ridiculous card game no one else can fathom," Sarah said. "Plotting your little household projects, Rose with her crescent wrench and her soldering gun. Cruising hardware stores like other people cruise boutiques."

"As other people cruise boutiques," Macon said. And then regretted it.

"Picking apart people's English," Sarah said. "Hauling forth the dictionary at every opportunity. Quibbling over *method*. The kind of family that always fastens their seatbelts."

"For God's sake, Sarah, what's wrong with fastening your seatbelt?"

"They always go to one restaurant, the one their grandparents went to before them, and even there they have to rearrange the silver and set things up so they're sitting around the table the same way they sit at home. They dither and deliberate, can't so much as close a curtain without this group discussion back and forth, to and fro, all the pros and cons. 'Well if we leave it open it will be so hot but if we close it things will get musty . . .' They have to have their six glasses of water every day. Their precious baked potatoes every night. They don't believe in ballpoint pens or electric typewriters or automatic transmissions. They don't believe in hello and goodbye."

"Hello? Good-bye?" Macon said.

"Just watch yourself some time! People walk in and you just, oh, register it with your eyes; people leave and you just look away quickly. You don't admit to comings and goings. And the best house in the world might come on the market, but you can't buy it because you've ordered these address labels for the old house, a thousand five hundred gummed labels, and you have to use them up before you move."

"That wasn't me, it was Charles," Macon said.

"Yes, but it could have been you. And his wife divorced him for it, and I don't blame her."

"And now you're about to do the same damn thing," Macon said. "Ruin twenty years of marriage over whether I fasten my seatbelt."

"They were ruined long ago, believe me," Sarah said.

Macon laid down his spoon. He forced himself to take a deep breath.

"Sarah," he said. "We're getting away from the point."

After a silence, Sarah said, "Yes, I guess we are."

"It's what happened to Ethan that ruined us," Macon told her.

She set an elbow on the table and covered her eyes.

"But it wouldn't have to," he said. "Why, some people, a thing like this brings them closer together. How come we're letting it part us?"

The waitress said, "Is everything all right?"

Sarah sat up straighter and started rummaging through her purse.

"Yes, certainly," Macon said.

The waitress was carrying a tray with their main dishes. She cast a doubtful look at Sarah's antipasto. "Isn't she going to eat that, or what?" she asked Macon.

"No, I guess, um, maybe not."

"Didn't she like it?"

"She liked it fine. Take it away."

The waitress bustled around the table in an offended silence. Sarah put aside her purse. She looked down at her meal, which was something brown and gluey.

"You're welcome to half my shrimp salad," Macon told her when the waitress had gone.

She shook her head. Her eyes were deep with tears, but they hadn't spilled over.

"Macon," she said, "ever since Ethan died I've had to admit that people are basically bad. Evil, Macon. So evil they would take a twelve-year-old boy and shoot him through the skull for no reason. I read a paper now and I despair; I've given up watching the news on TV. There's so much wickedness, children setting other children on fire and grown men throwing babies out second-story windows, rape and torture and terrorism, old people beaten and robbed, men in our very own government willing to blow up the world, indifference and greed and instant anger on every street corner. I look at my students and they're so ordinary, but they're exactly like the boy who killed Ethan. If it hadn't said beneath that boy's picture what he'd been arrested for, wouldn't you think he was just anyone? Someone who'd made the basketball team or won a college scholarship? You can't believe in a soul. Last spring, Macon, I didn't tell you this, I was cutting back our hedge and I saw the bird feeder had been stolen out of the crape myrtle tree. Someone will even steal food from little birds! And I just, I don't know, went kind of crazy and attacked the crape myrtle. Cut it all up, ripped off branches, slashed it with my pruning shears . . ."

Tears were running down her face now. She leaned across the table and said, "There are times when I haven't been sure I could—I don't want to sound melodramatic but—Macon, I haven't been sure I could live in this kind of a world anymore."

Macon felt he had to be terribly careful. He had to choose exactly the right words. He cleared his throat and said, "Yes, um, I see what you mean but . . ." He cleared his throat again. "It's true," he said, "what you say about human beings. I'm not trying to argue. But tell me this, Sarah: Why would that cause you to leave me?"

She crumpled up her napkin and dabbed at her nose. She said, "Because I *knew* you wouldn't try to argue. You've believed all along they were evil."

"Well, so—"

"This whole last year I felt myself retreating. Withdrawing. I could feel myself shrinking. I stayed away from crowds, I didn't go to parties, I didn't ask our friends in. When you and I went to the beach in the summer I lay on my blanket with all those people around me, their squawking radios and their gossip and their quarrels, and I thought, 'Ugh, they're so depressing. They're so unlikable. So vile, really.' I felt myself shrinking away from them. Just like you do, Macon—just *as* you do; sorry. Just as you have always done. I felt I was turning into a Leary."

Macon tried for a lighter tone. He said, "Well, there are worse disasters than that, I guess."

She didn't smile. She said, "I can't afford it."

"Afford?"

"I'm forty-two years old. I don't have enough time left to waste it holing up in my shell. So I've taken action. I've cut myself loose. I live in this apartment you'd hate, all clutter. I've made a whole bunch of new friends, and you wouldn't like them much either, I guess. I'm studying with a sculptor. I always did want to be an artist, only teaching seemed more sensible. That's how you would think: sensible. You're so quick to be sensible, Macon, that you've given up on just about everything."

"What have I given up on?"

She refolded the napkin and blotted her eyes. An appealing blur of mascara shadowed the skin beneath them. She said, "Remember Betty Grand?"

"No."

"Betty Grand, she went to my school. You used to like her before you met me."

"I never liked anyone on earth before I met you," Macon said.

"You liked Betty Grand, Macon. You told me so when we first went out. You asked me if I knew her. You said you used to think she was pretty and you'd invited her to a ball game but she turned you down. You told me you'd changed your mind about her being pretty. Her gums showed any time she smiled, you said."

Macon still didn't remember, but he said, "Well? So?"

"Everything that might touch you or upset you or disrupt you, you've given up without a murmur and done without, said you never wanted it anyhow."

"I suppose I would have done better if I'd gone on pining for Betty Grand all my life."

"Well, you would have shown some feeling, at least."

"I do show feeling, Sarah. I'm sitting here with you, am I not? You don't see me giving up on *you*."

She chose not to hear this. "And when Ethan died," she said, "you peeled every single Wacky Pack sticker off his bedroom door. You emptied his closet and his bureau as if you couldn't be rid of him soon enough. You kept offering people his junk in the basement, stilts and sleds and skateboards, and you couldn't understand why they didn't accept them. 'I hate to see stuff sitting there useless,' you said. Macon, I know you loved him but I can't help thinking you didn't love him as much as I did, you're not so torn apart by his going. I know you mourned him but there's something so what-do-you-call, so muffled about the way you experience things, I mean love or grief or anything; it's like you're trying to slip through life unchanged. Don't you see why I had to get out?"

"Sarah, I'm not muffled. I . . . endure. I'm trying to endure, I'm standing fast, I'm holding steady."

"If you really think that," Sarah said, "then you're fooling yourself. You're not holding steady; you're ossified. You're encased. You're like something in a capsule. You're a dried-up kernal of a man that nothing really penetrates. Oh, Macon, it's not by chance you write those silly books telling people how to take trips without a jolt. That traveling armchair isn't just your logo; it's you."

"No, it's not," Macon said. "It's not!"

Sarah pulled her coat on, making a sloppy job of it. One corner of her collar was tucked inside. "So anyway," she said, "This is what I wanted to tell you: I'm having John Albright send you a letter."

"Who's John Albright?"

"He's an attorney."

"Oh," Macon said.

It was at least a full minute before he thought to say, "I guess you must mean a lawyer."

Sarah collected her purse, stood up, and walked out.

* * *

Macon made his way conscientiously through his shrimp salad. He ate his cole slaw for the vitamin C. Then he finished every last one of his potato chips, although he knew his tongue would feel shriveled the following morning.

Once when Ethan was little, not more than two or three, he had run out into the street after a ball. Macon had been too far away to stop him. All he could do was shout, "No!" and then watch, frozen with horror, as a pickup truck came barreling around the curve. In that instant, he released his claim. In one split second he adjusted to a future that held no Ethan—an immeasurably bleaker place but also, by way of compensation, plainer and simpler, free of the problems a small child trails along with him, the endless demands and the mess and the contests for his mother's attention. Then the truck stopped short and Ethan retrieved his ball, and Macon's knees went weak with relief. But he remembered forever after how quickly he had adjusted. He wondered, sometimes, if that first adjustment had somehow stuck, making what happened to Ethan later less of a shock than it might have been. But if people didn't adjust, how could they bear to go on?

He called for his bill and paid it. "Was there something wrong?" the waitress asked. "Did your friend not like her meal? She could always have sent it back, hon. We always let you send it back."

"I know that," Macon said.

"Maybe it was too spicy for her."

"It was fine," he said. "Could I have my crutches, please?"

She went off to get them, shaking her head.

He would have to locate a taxi. He'd made no arrangements for Rose to pick him up. Secretly, he'd been hoping to go home with Sarah. Now that hope seemed pathetic. He looked around the dining room and saw that most of the tables were filled, and that every person had someone else to eat with. Only Macon sat alone. He kept very erect and dignified but inside, he knew, he was crumbling. And when the waitress brought him his crutches and he stood to leave, it seemed appropriate that he had to walk nearly doubled, his chin sunk low on his chest and his elbows jutting out awkwardly like the wings of a baby bird. People stared at him as he passed. Some snickered. Was his foolishness so obvious? He passed the two churchy old ladies and one of them tugged at his sleeve. "Sir? Sir?"

He came to a stop.

"I suspect they may have given you my crutches," she said.

He looked down at the crutches. They were, of course, not his. They were diminutive—hardly more than child-sized. Any other time he would have grasped the situation right off, but today it had somehow escaped him. Any other time he would have swung into action—called for the manager, pointed out the restaurant's lack of concern for the

handicapped. Today he only stood hanging his head, waiting for someone to help him.

9

$$=$$

Back when Grandfather Leary's mind first began to wander, no one
had guessed what was happening. He was such an upright, firm old
man. He was all sharp edges. Definite. "Listen," he told Macon, "by
June the twelfth I'll need my passport from the safe deposit box. I'm
setting sail for Lassaque."

"Lassaque, Grandfather?"

"If I like it I may just stay there."

"But where is Lassaque?"

"It's an island off the coast of Bolivia."

"Ah," Macon said, And then, "Well, wait a minute . . ."

"It interests me because the Lassaquans have no written language.
In fact if you bring any reading matter they confiscate it. They say it's
black magic."

"But I don't think Bolivia *has* a coast," Macon said.

"They don't even allow, say, a checkbook with your name on it.
Before you go ashore you have to soak the label off your deodorant.
You have to get your money changed into little colored wafers."

"Grandfather, is this a joke?"

"A joke! Look it up if you don't believe me." Grandfather Leary
checked his steel pocket watch, then wound it with an assured, back-
and-forth motion. "An intriguing effect of their illiteracy," he said, "is
their reverence for the elderly. This is because the Lassaquans' knowledge doesn't come from books but from living; so they hang on every
word from those who have lived the longest."

"I see," Macon said, for now he thought he did see. "We hang on
your words, too," he said.

"That may be so," his grandfather told him, "but I still intend to
see Lassaque before it's corrupted."

Macon was silent a moment. Then he went over to the bookcase
and selected a volume from his grandfather's set of faded brown
encyclopedias. "Give it here," his grandfather said, holding out both
hands. He took the book greedily and started riffling through the pages.
A smell of mold floated up. "Laski," he muttered, "Lassalle, Lassaw
. . ." He lowered the book and frowned. "I don't . . ." he said. He
returned to the book. "Lassalle, Lassaw . . ."

He looked confused, almost frightened. His face all at once collapsed—a phenomenon that had startled Macon on several occasions lately. "I don't understand," he whispered to Macon. "I don't understand."

"Well," Macon said, "maybe it was a dream. Maybe it was one of those dreams that seem real."

"Macon, this was no dream. I *know* the place. I've bought my ticket. I'm sailing June the twelfth."

Macon felt a strange coldness creeping down his back.

Then his grandfather became an inventor—spoke of various projects he was tinkering with, he said, in his basement. He would sit in his red leather armchair, his suit and white shirt immaculate, his black dress shoes polished to a glare, his carefully kept hands folded in his lap, and he would announce that he'd just finished welding together a motorcycle that would pull a plow. He would earnestly discuss crankshafts and cotter pins, while Macon—though terribly distressed—had to fight down a bubble of laughter at the thought of some leather-booted Hell's Angel grinding away at a wheatfield. "If I could just get the kinks ironed out," his grandfather said, "I'd have my fortune made. We'll all be rich." For he seemed to believe he was poor again, struggling to earn his way in the world. His motorized radio that followed you from room to room, his floating telephone, his car that came when you called it—wouldn't there be some application for those? Wouldn't the right person pay an arm and a leg?

Having sat out on the porch for one entire June morning, studiously pinching the creases of his trousers, he announced that he had perfected a new type of hybrid: flowers that closed in the presence of tears. "Florists will be mobbing me," he said. "Think of the dramatic effect at funerals!" He was working next on a cross between basil and tomatoes. He said the spaghetti-sauce companies would make him a wealthy man.

By then, all three of his grandsons had left home and his wife had died; so Rose alone took care of him. Her brothers began to worry about her. They took to dropping by more and more often. Then Rose said, "You don't have to do this, you know."

They said, "What? Do what? What are you talking about?" And other such things.

"If you're coming so often on account of Grandfather, it's not necessary. I'm managing fine, and so is he. He's very happy."

"Happy!"

"I honestly believe," Rose said, "that he's having the richest and most . . . colorful, really, time of his life. I'll bet even when he was young, he never enjoyed himself this much."

They saw what she meant. Macon felt almost envious, once he thought about it. And later, when that period was over, he was sorry it had been so short. For their grandfather soon passed to pointless, disconnected mumbles, and then to a staring silence, and at last he died.

Early Wednesday morning, Macon dreamed Grandfather Leary woke him and asked where the center punch was. "What are you talking about?" Macon said. "I never had your center punch."

"Oh, Macon," his grandfather said sadly, "can't you tell that I'm not saying what I mean?"

"What do you mean, then?"

"You've lost the center of your *life*, Macon."

"Yes, I know that," Macon said, and it seemed that Ethan stood just slightly to the left, his bright head nearly level with the old man's.

But his grandfather said, "No, no," and made an impatient, shaking-off gesture and went over to the bureau. (In this dream, Macon was not in the sun porch but upstairs in his boyhood bedroom, with the bureau whose cut-glass knobs Rose had stolen long ago to use as dishes for her dolls.) "It's Sarah I mean," his grandfather said, picking up a hairbrush. "Where is Sarah?"

"She's left me, Grandfather."

"Why, Sarah's the best of all of us!" his grandfather said. "You want to sit in this old house and rot, boy? It's time we started digging out! How long are we going to stay fixed here?"

Macon opened his eyes. It wasn't morning yet. The sun porch was fuzzy as blotting paper.

There was still a sense of his grandfather in the air. His little shaking-off gesture was one that Macon had forgotten entirely; it had reappeared on its own. But Grandfather Leary would never have said in real life what he'd said in the dream. He had liked Sarah well enough, but he seemed to view wives as extraneous, and he'd attended each of his grandsons' weddings with a resigned and tolerant expression. He wouldn't have thought of any woman as a "center." Except, perhaps, Macon thought suddenly, his own wife, Grandmother Leary. After whose death—why, yes, immediately after—his mind had first begun to wander.

Macon lay awake till dawn. It was a relief to hear the first stirrings overhead. Then he got up and shaved and dressed and sent Edward out for the paper. By the time Rose came downstairs, he had started the coffee perking. This seemed to make her anxious. "Did you use the morning beans or the evening beans?" she asked.

"The morning beans," he assured her. "Everything's under control."

She moved around the kitchen raising shades, setting the table, opening a carton of eggs. "So today's the day you get your cast off," she said.

"Looks that way."

"And this afternoon's your New York trip."

"Oh, well . . ." he said vaguely, and then he asked if she wanted a bacon coupon he'd spotted in the paper.

She persisted: "Isn't it this afternoon you're going?"

"Well, yes."

The fact of the matter was, he was leaving for New York without having made any arrangements for Edward. The old place wouldn't accept him, the new place had that Muriel woman . . . and in Macon's opinion, Edward was best off at home with the family. Rose, no doubt, would disagree. He held his breath, but Rose started humming "Clementine" and breaking eggs into a skillet.

At nine o'clock, in an office down on St. Paul Street, the doctor removed Macon's cast with a tiny, purring electric saw. Macon's leg emerged dead-white and wrinkled and ugly. When he stood up, his ankle wobbled. He still had a limp. Also, he'd forgotten to bring different trousers and he was forced to parade back through the other patients in his one-legged summer khakis, exposing his repulsive-looking shin. He wondered if he'd ever return to his old, unbroken self.

Driving him home, Rose finally thought to ask where he planned to board Edward. "Why, I'm leaving him with you," Macon said, acting surprised.

"With me? Oh, Macon, you know how out of hand he gets."

"What could happen in such a short time? I'll be home by tomorrow night. If worst comes to worst you could lock him in the pantry; toss him some kibble now and then till I get back."

"I don't like this at all," Rose said.

"It's visitors that set him off. It's not as if you're expecting any visitors."

"Oh, no," she said, and then she let the subject drop, thank heaven. He'd been fearing more of a battle.

He took a shower, and he dressed in his traveling suit. Then he had an early lunch. Just before noon Rose drove him down to the railroad station, since he didn't yet trust his clutch foot. When he stepped from the car, his leg threatened to buckle. "Wait!" he said to Rose, who was handing his bag out after him. "Do you suppose I'm up to this?"

"I'm sure you are," she said, without giving it anywhere near enough thought. She pulled the passenger door shut, waved at him, and drove off.

In the period since Macon's last train trip, something wonderful had happened to the railroad station. A skylight in shades of watery blue arched gently overhead. Pale globe lamps hung from brass hooks. The carpenters' partitions that had divided the waiting room for so long had disappeared, revealing polished wooden benches. Macon stood bewildered at the brand-new, gleaming ticket window. Maybe, he thought, travel was not so bad. Maybe he'd got it all wrong. He felt a little sprig of hopefulness beginning.

But immediately afterward, limping toward his gate, he was overcome by the lost feeling that always plagued him on these trips. He envisioned himself as a stark Figure 1 in a throng of 2's and 3's. Look at that group at the Information counter, those confident young people with their knapsacks and sleeping bags. Look at the family occupying one entire bench, their four little daughters so dressed up, so stiff in new plaid coats and ribboned hats, you just knew they'd be met by grandparents at the other end of the line. Even those sitting alone— the old woman with the corsage, the blonde with her expensive leather luggage—gave the impression of belonging to someone.

He sat down on a bench. A southbound train was announced and half the crowd went off to catch it, followed by the inevitable breathless, disheveled woman galloping through some time later with far too many bags and parcels. Arriving passengers began to straggle up the stairs. They wore the dazed expressions of people who had been elsewhere till just this instant. A woman was greeted by a man holding a baby; he kissed her and passed her the baby at once, as if it were a package he'd been finding unusually heavy. A young girl in jeans, reaching the top of the stairs, caught sight of another girl in jeans and threw her arms around her and started crying. Macon watched, pretending not to, inventing explanations. (She was home for their mother's funeral? Her elopement hadn't worked out?)

Now his own train was called, so he picked up his bag and limped behind the family with all the daughters. At the bottom of the stairs a gust of cold, fresh air hit him. Wind always seemed to be howling down these platforms, no matter what the weather elsewhere. The smallest of the daughters had to have her coat buttoned. The train came into view, slowly assembling itself around a pinpoint of yellow light.

Most of the cars were full, it turned out. Macon gave up trying to find a completely empty seat and settled next to a plump young man with a briefcase. Just to be on the safe side, he unpacked *Miss MacIntosh*.

The train lurched forward and then changed its mind and then lurched forward again and took off. Macon imagined he could feel little scabs of rust on the tracks; it wasn't a very smooth ride. He watched the sights of home rush toward him and disappear—a tumble of row houses, faded vacant lots, laundry hanging rigid in the cold.

"Gum?" his seatmate asked.

Macon said, "No, thanks," and quickly opened his book.

When they'd been traveling an hour or so, he felt his lids grow heavy. He let his head fall back. He thought he was only resting his eyes, but he must have gone to sleep. The next thing he knew, the conductor was announcing Philadelphia. Macon jerked and sat up straight and caught his book just before it slid off his lap.

His seatmate was doing some kind of paperwork, using his briefcase as a desk. A businessman, obviously—one of the people Macon wrote his guides for. Funny, Macon never pictured his readers. What did businessmen do, exactly? This one was jotting notes on index cards, referring now and then to a booklet full of graphs. One graph showed little black trucks marching across the page—four trucks, seven trucks, three and a half trucks. Macon thought the half-truck looked deformed and pitiable.

Just before they arrived, he used the restroom at the rear of the car—not ideal, but more homey than anything he'd find in New York. He went back to his seat and packed *Miss MacIntosh.* "Going to be cold there," his seatmate told him.

"I imagine so," Macon said.

"Weather report says cold and windy."

Macon didn't answer.

He believed in traveling without an overcoat—just one more thing to carry—but he wore a thermal undershirt and long johns. Cold was the least of his worries.

In New York the passengers scattered instantly. Macon thought of a seed pod bursting open. He refused to be rushed and made his way methodically through the crowd, up a set of clanking, dark stairs, and through another crowd that seemed more extreme than the one he had left down below. Goodness, where did these women get their clothes? One wore a bushy fur tepee and leopardskin boots. One wore an olive-drab coverall exactly like an auto mechanic's except that it was made of leather. Macon took a firmer grip on his bag and pushed through the door to the street, where car horns blasted insistently and the air smelled gray and sharp, like the interior of a dead chimney. In his opinion, New York was a foreign city. He was forever taken aback by its pervasive atmosphere of purposefulness—the tight focus of its drivers, the brisk intensity of its pedestrians drilling their way through all obstacles without a glance to either side.

He hailed a cab, slid across the worn, slippery seat, and gave the address of his hotel. The driver started talking at once about his daughter. "I mean she's thirteen years old," he said, nosing out into traffic, "and got three sets of holes in her ears and an earring in each hole, and now she wants to get another set punched up toward the top. Thirteen years old!" He either had or had not heard the address. At any rate, he was driving along. "I wasn't even in favor of the first set of holes," he said. "I told her, 'What; you don't read Ann Landers?' Ann Landers says piercing your ears is mutilating your body. Was it Ann Landers? I think it was Ann Landers. You might as well wear a ring through your nose like the Africans, right? I told my daughter that. She says, 'So? What's wrong with a ring through my nose? Maybe that's what I'll get next.' I wouldn't put it past her, either. I would not put it past her. Now this fourth set goes through cartilage and most of these ear-piercing places won't do that; so you see how crazy it is. Cartilage is a whole different ball game. It's not like your earlobe, all spongy."

Macon had the feeling he wasn't fully visible. He was listening to a man who was talking to himself, who may have been talking before he got in and might possibly go on talking after he got out. Or was he present in this cab at all? Such thoughts often attacked while he was traveling. In desperation, he said, "Um—"

The driver stopped speaking, surprisingly enough. The back of his neck took on an alert look. Macon had to continue. He said, "Tell her something scary."

"Like what?"

"Like . . . tell her you know a girl whose ears dropped off."

"She'd never go for that."

"Make it scientific. Say if you puncture cartilage, it will wither right away."

"Hmm," the driver said. He honked his horn at a produce truck. " 'Imagine how you'd feel,' tell her, 'having to wear the same hairstyle forever. Covering up your withered ears.' "

"Think she'd believe me?"

"Why not?" Macon asked. And then, after a pause, "In fact, it may be true. Do you suppose I could have read it someplace?"

"Well, now, maybe you did," the driver said. "There's this sort of familiar ring to it."

"I might even have seen a photograph," Macon said. "Somebody's ears, shriveled. All shrunken."

"Wrinkly, like," the driver agreed.

Macon said, "Like two dried apricots."

"Christ! I'll tell her."

The taxi stopped in front of Macon's hotel. Macon paid the fare and said, as he slid out, "I hope it works."

"Sure it will," the driver said, "till next time. Till she wants a nose ring or something."

"Noses are cartilage too, remember! Noses can wither too!"

The driver waved and pulled into traffic again.

After Macon had claimed his room, he took a subway to the Buford Hotel. An electronics salesman had written to suggest it; the Buford rented small apartments, by the day or the week, to businessmen. The manager, a Mr. Aggers, turned out to be a short, round man who walked with a limp exactly like Macon's. Macon thought they must look very odd together, crossing the lobby to the elevators. "Most of our apartments are owned by corporations," Mr. Aggers said. He pressed the "Up" button. "Companies who send their men to the city regularly will often find it cheaper to buy their own places. Then those weeks the apartments are empty, they look to me to find other tenants, help defray the costs."

Macon made a note of this in the margin of his guidebook. Using an infinitesimal script, he also noted the decor of the lobby, which reminded him of some old-fashioned men's club. On the massive, claw-footed table between the two elevators stood a yard-high naked lady in brass, trailing brass draperies and standing on brass clouds, holding aloft a small, dusty light bulb with a frayed electric cord dangling from it. The elevator, when it arrived, had dim floral carpeting and paneled walls.

"May I ask," Mr. Aggers said, "whether you personally write the Accidental Tourist series?"

"Yes, I do," Macon told him.

"Well!" Mr. Aggers said. "This is a real honor, then. We keep your books in the lobby for our guests. But I don't know, I somehow pictured you looking a little different."

"How did you think I would look?" Macon asked.

"Well, maybe not quite so tall. Maybe a bit, well, heavier. More . . . upholstered."

"I see," Macon said.

The elevator had stopped by now but it took its time sliding open. Then Mr. Aggers led Macon down a hall. A woman with a laundry cart stood aside to let them pass. "Here we are," Mr. Aggers said. He unlocked a door and turned on a light.

Macon walked into an apartment that could have come straight from the 1950s. There was a square sofa with metallic threads in its fabric, a chrome-trimmed dinette set, and in the bedroom a double bed whose headboard was quilted in cream-colored vinyl. He tested the mattress. He took off his shoes, lay down, and thought a while. Mr. Aggers stood above him with his fingers laced. "Hmm," Macon said. He sat up and put his shoes back on. Then he went into the bathroom, where the toilet bore a white strip reading SANITIZED. "I've never understood these things," he said. "Why should it reassure me to know they've glued a paper band across my toilet seat?" Mr. Aggers made a helpless gesture with both hands. Macon drew aside a shower curtain printed with pink and blue fish, and he inspected the tub. It looked clean enough, although there was a rust stain leading down from the faucet.

In the kitchenette he found a single saucepan, two faded plastic plates and mugs, and an entire shelf of highball glasses. "Usually our guests don't cook much," Mr. Aggers explained, "but they might have their associates in for drinks." Macon nodded. He was faced with a familiar problem, here: the narrow line between "comfortable" and "tacky." In fact, sometimes comfortable *was* tacky. He opened the refrigerator, a little undercounter affair. The ice trays in the freezing compartment were exactly the same kind of trays—scummy aqua plastic, heavily scratched—that Rose had back in Baltimore.

"You have to admit it's well stocked," Mr. Aggers said. "See? An apron in the kitchen drawer. My wife's idea. Protects their suits."

"Yes, very nice," Macon said.

"It's just like home away from home; that's how I like to think of it."

"Oh, well, home," Macon said. "Nothing's *home*, really."

"Why? What's missing?" Mr. Aggers asked. He had very pale, fine-grained skin that took on a shine when he was anxious. "What more would you like to see added?"

"To tell the truth," Macon said, "I've always thought a hotel ought to offer optional small animals."

"Animals?"

"I mean a cat to sleep on your bed at night, or a dog of some kind to act pleased when you come in. You ever notice how a hotel room feels so lifeless?"

"Yes, but—well, I don't see how I could—there are surely health regulations or something . . . complications, paperwork, feeding all those different . . . and allergies, of course, many guests have—"

"Oh, I understand, I understand," Macon said. In the margin of his guidebook he was noting the number of wastebaskets: four. Excellent. "No," he said, "it doesn't seem that people ever take me up on that."

"Will you recommend us anyway?"

"Certainly," Macon said, and he closed his guidebook and asked for a list of the rates.

The rest of the afternoon he spent in hotels that he'd covered before. He visited managers in their offices, took brief guided tours to see that nothing had slid into ruin, and listened to talk of rising costs and remodeling plans and new, improved conference settings. Then he returned to his room and switched on the evening news. The world was doing poorly; but watching this unfamiliar TV set, propping his aching leg and braced in this chair that seemed designed for someone else's body, Macon had the feeling that none of the wars and famines he saw were real. They were more like, oh, staged. He turned off the set and went downstairs to hail a cab.

At Julian's suggestion, he was dining on the very top of an impossibly tall building. (Julian had a fondness for restaurants with gimmicks, Macon had noticed. He wasn't happy unless a place revolved, or floated, or could be reached only by catwalk.) "Imagine," Julian had said, "the effect on your out-of-town client. Yes, he'd have to be from out of town; I don't suppose a native New Yorker . . ." Macon had snorted. Now the cabdriver snorted, too. "Cup of coffee there will cost you five bucks," he told Macon.

"It figures."

"You're better off at one of those little Frenchy places."

"That's for tomorrow. *In*-town clients."

The taxi coasted down streets that grew darker and more silent, leading away from the crowds. Macon peered out of his window. He saw a lone man huddled in a doorway, wrapped in a long coat. Wisps of steam drifted up from manhold covers. All the shops were locked behind iron grilles.

At the end of the darkest street of all, the taxi stopped. The driver gave another snort, and Macon paid his fare and stepped out. He wasn't prepared for the wind, which rushed up against him like a great flat sheet of something. He hurried across the sidewalk, or was propelled, while his trousers twisted and flapped about his legs. Just before entering the building, he thought to look up. He looked up and up and up, and finally he saw a faint white pinnacle dwindling into a deep, black, starless sky eerily far away. He thought of once long ago when Ethan, visiting the zoo as a toddler, had paused in front of an elephant and raised his face in astonishment and fallen over backwards.

Inside, everything was streaky pink marble and acres of textureless carpeting. An elevator the size of a room stood open, half filled with people, and Macon stepped in and took his place between two women in silks and diamonds. Their perfume was almost visible. He imagined he could see it rippling the air.

Have chewing gum handy, he wrote in his guidebook as the elevator shot upward. His ears were popping. There was a dense, unresonant stillness that made the women's voices sound tinny. He tucked his guidebook in his pocket and glanced at the numbers flashing overhead. They progressed by tens: forty, fifty, sixty . . . One of the men said they'd have to bring Harold sometime—remember Harold when he got so scared on the ski lift?—and everyone laughed.

The elevator gave a sort of lilt and the door slid open without a sound. A girl in a white trouser suit directed them down a corridor, into a spacious darkness flickering with candles. Great black windows encircled the room from floor to ceiling, but Macon was taken to a table without a view. Lone diners, he supposed, were an embarrassment here. He might be the first they'd ever had. The array of silver at his single place could easily serve a family of four.

His waiter, far better dressed than Macon, handed him a menu and asked what he wanted to drink. "Dry sherry, please," Macon said. The minute the waiter left, Macon folded his menu in two and sat on it. Then he looked around at his neighbors. Everyone seemed to be celebrating something. A man and a pregnant woman held hands and smiled across the moony glow of their candle. A boisterous group to his left toasted the same man over and over.

The waiter returned, balancing a sherry neatly on a tray. "Very good," Macon said. "And now perhaps a menu."

"Menu? Didn't I give you one?"

"There could have been an oversight," he said, not exactly lying.

A second menu was brought and opened with a flourish before him. Macon sipped his sherry and considered the prices. Astronomical. He decided, as usual, to eat what he thought his readers might eat— not the quenelles or the sweetbreads but the steak, medium rare. After he'd given his order, he rose and slid his chair in and took his sherry over to a window.

All of a sudden, he thought he had died.

He saw the city spread far below like a glittering golden ocean, the streets tiny ribbons of light, the planet curving away at the edges, the sky a purple hollow extending to infinity. It wasn't the height; it was the distance. It was his vast, lonely distance from everyone who mattered. Ethan, with his bouncy walk—how would he ever know that his father had come to be trapped in this spire in the heavens? How would Sarah know, lazily tanning herself in the sunshine? For he did believe the sun could be shining wherever she was at this moment; she was so removed from him. He thought of his sister and brothers going about their business, playing their evening card game, unaware of how far behind he'd left them. He was too far gone to return. He would never, ever get back. He had somehow traveled to a point completely isolated from everyone else in the universe, and nothing was real but his own angular hand clenched around the sherry glass.

He dropped the glass, causing a meaningless little flurry of voices, and he spun around and ran lopsidedly across the room and out the door. But there was that endless corridor, and he couldn't manage the trip. He took a right turn instead. He passed a telephone alcove and stumbled into a restroom—yes, a men's room, luckily. More marble, mirrors, white enamel. He thought he was going to throw up, but when he entered one of the cubicles the sick feeling left his stomach and floated to his head. He noticed how light his brain felt. He stood above the toilet pressing his temples. It occurred to him to wonder how many feet of pipe a toilet at this altitude required.

He heard someone else come in, coughing. A cubicle door slammed shut. He opened his own door a crack and looked out. The impersonal lushness of the room made him think of science-fiction movies.

Well, this difficulty probably happened here often, didn't it? Or maybe not this difficulty exactly but others like it—people with a fear of heights, say, going into a panic, having to call upon . . . whom? The waiter? The girl who met the elevator?

He ventured cautiously out of the cubicle, then out of the restroom altogether, and he nearly bumped into a woman in the telephone alcove. She wore yards and yards of pale chiffon. She was just hanging up the phone, and she gathered her skirts around her and moved languidly, gracefully toward the dining room. *Excuse me, ma'am, I wonder if you would be so kind as to, um . . .* But the only request that came to mind rose up from his earliest childhood: *Carry me!*

The woman's little sequined evening purse was the last of her to go, trailed behind her in one white hand as she disappeared into the darkness of the restaurant.

He stepped over to the telephone and lifted the receiver. It was cool to the touch; she hadn't talked long. He fumbled through his pockets, found coins and dropped them in. But there was no one he could contact. He didn't know a soul in all New York. Instead he called home, miraculously summoning up his credit card number. He worried his family would let the phone ring—it was a habit, by now—but Charles answered. "Leary."

"Charles?"

"Macon!" Charles said, unusually animated.

"Charles, I'm up on top of this building and a sort of . . . silly thing has happened. Listen: You've got to get me out of here."

"*You* out! What are you talking about? You've got to get *me* out!"

"Pardon?"

"I'm shut in the pantry; your dog has me cornered."

"Oh. Well, I'm sorry, but . . . Charles, it's like some kind of illness. I don't think I can manage the elevator and I doubt I could manage a stairway either and—"

"Macon, do you hear that barking? That's Edward. Edward has me treed, I tell you, and you have to come home this instant."

"But I'm in New York! I'm up on top of this building and I can't get down!"

"Every time I open the door he comes roaring over and I slam the door and he attacks it, he must have clawed halfway through it by now."

Macon made himself take a deep breath. He said, "Charles, could I speak to Rose?"

"She's out."

"Oh."

"How do you think I got into this?" Charles asked. "Julian came to take her to dinner and—"

"Julian?"

"Isn't that his name?"

"Julian my *boss*?"

"Yes, and Edward went into one of his fits; so Rose said, 'Quick, shut him in the pantry.' So I grabbed his leash and he turned on me and nearly took my hand off. So I shut myself in the pantry instead and Rose must have left by then so—"

"Isn't Porter there?"

"It's his visitation night."

Macon imagined how safe the pantry must feel, with Rose's jams lined up in alphabetical order and the black dial telephone so ancient that the number on its face was still the old Tuxedo exchange. What he wouldn't give to be there!

Now he had a new symptom. His chest had developed a flutter that bore no resemblance to a normal heartbeat.

"If you don't get me out of this I'm going to call for the police to come shoot him," Charles said.

"No! Don't do that!"

"I can't just sit here waiting for him to break through."

"He won't break through. You could open the door and walk right past him. Believe me, Charles. Please: I'm up on top of this building and—"

"Maybe you don't know that I'm prone to claustrophobia," Charles said.

One possibility, Macon decided, was to tell the restaurant people he was having a coronary. A coronary was so respectable. They would send for an ambulance and he would be, yes, carried—just what he needed. Or he wouldn't have to be carried but only touched, a mere human touch upon his arm, a hand on his shoulder, something to put him back in connection with the rest of the world. He hadn't felt another person's touch in so long.

"I'll tell them about the key in the mailbox so they won't have to break down the door," Charles said.

"What? Who?"

"The police, and I'll tell them to—Macon, I'm sorry but you knew that dog would have to be done away with sooner or later."

"Don't do it!" Macon shouted.

A man emerging from the restroom glanced in his direction.

Macon lowered his voice and said, "He was Ethan's."

"Does that mean he's allowed to tear my throat out?"

"Listen. Let's not be hasty. Let's think this through. Now, I'm going to . . . I'm going to telephone Sarah. I'm going to ask her to come over and take charge of Edward. Are you listening, Charles?"

"But what if he attacks her too?" Charles asked.

"He won't, believe me. Now, don't do anything till she comes, you understand? Don't do anything hasty."

"Well . . ." Charles said doubtfully.

Macon hung up and took his wallet from his pocket. He rummaged through the business cards and torn-off snippets of paper, some of them yellow with age, that he kept in the secret compartment. When he found Sarah's number he punched it in with a trembling finger and held his breath. *Sarah*, he would say, *I'm up on top of this building and—*

She didn't answer.

That possibility hadn't occurred to him. He listened to her phone ring. What now? What on earth now?

Finally he hung up. He sifted despairingly through the other numbers in his wallet—dentist, pharmacist, animal trainer . . .

Animal trainer?

He thought at first of someone from a circus—a brawny man in satin tights. Then he saw the name: Muriel Pritchett. The card was handwritten, even hand-cut, crookedly snipped from a larger piece of paper.

He called her. She answered at once. "*Hel*-lo," roughly, like a weary barmaid.

"Muriel? It's Macon Leary," he told her.

"Oh! How you doing?"

"I'm fine. Or, rather . . . See, the trouble is, Edward's got my brother cornered in the pantry, overreacting, Charles I mean, he always overreacts, and here I am on top of this building in New York and I'm having this kind of, um, disturbance, you know? I was looking down at the city and it was miles away, miles, I can't describe to you how—"

"Let's make sure I've got this right," Muriel said. "Edward's in your pantry—"

Macon collected himself. He said, "Edward's *outside* the pantry, barking. My brother's inside. He says he's going to call the police and tell them to come shoot Edward."

"Well, what a dumb fool idea."

"Yes!" Macon said. "So I thought if you could go over and get the key from the mailbox, it's lying on the bottom of the mailbox—"

"I'll go right away."

"Oh, wonderful."

"So good-bye for now, Macon."

"Well, but also—" he said.

She waited.

"See, I'm up on top of this building," he said, "and I don't know what it is but something has scared the hell out of me."

"Oh, Lord, I'd be scared too after I went and saw *Towering Inferno*."

"No, no, it's nothing like that, fire or heights—"

"Did you see *Towering Inferno*? Boy, after that you couldn't get me past jumping level in any building. I think people who go up in skyscrapers are just plain brave. I mean if you think about it, Macon, you *have* to be brave to be standing where you are right now."

"Oh, well, not so brave as all that," Macon said.

"No, I'm serious."

"You're making too much out of it. It's nothing, really."

"You just say that because you don't realize what you went through before you stepped into the elevator. See, underneath you said, 'Okay. I'll trust it.' That's what everyone does; I bet it's what they do on airplanes, too. 'This is dangerous as all get-out but what the hay,' they say, 'let's fling ourselves out on thin air and trust it.' Why, you ought to be walking around that building so amazed and proud of yourself!"

Macon gave a small, dry laugh and gripped the receiver more tightly.

"Now, here's what I'm going to do," she said. "I'm going to go get Edward and take him to the Meow-Bow. It doesn't sound to me like your brother is much use with him. Then when you get back from your trip, we need to talk about his training. I mean, things just can't go on this way, Macon."

"No, they can't. You're right. They can't," Macon said.

"I mean this is ridiculous."

"You're absolutely right."

"See you, then. Bye."

"Well, wait!" he said.

But she was gone.

After he hung up, he turned and saw the latest arrivals just heading toward him from the elevator. First came three men, and then three women in long gowns. Behind them was a couple who couldn't be past their teens. The boy's wrist bones stuck out of the sleeves of his suit. The girl's dress was clumsy and touching, her small chin obscured by a monstrous orchid.

Halfway down the corridor, the boy and girl stopped to gaze around them. They looked at the ceiling, and then at the floor. Then they looked at each other. The boy said, "Hoo!" and grabbed both the girl's hands, and they stood there a moment, laughing, before they went into the restaurant.

Macon followed them. He felt soothed and tired and terribly hungry. It was good to find the waiter just setting his food in place when he sank back into his seat.

10

I'll be honest," Muriel said, "my baby was not exactly planned for. I mean we weren't exactly even married yet, if you want to know the truth. If you want to know the truth the baby was the reason we got married in the first place, but I did tell Norman he didn't have to go through with it if he didn't want to. It's not like I pushed him into it or anything."

She looked past Macon at Edward, who lay prone on the front hall rug. He'd had to be forced into position, but at least he was staying put.

"Notice I let him move around some, as long as he stays down," she said. "Now I'm going to turn my back, and you watch how he does."

She wandered into the living room. She lifted a vase from a table and examined its underside. "So anyhow," she said, "we went ahead and got married, with everybody acting like it was the world's biggest tragedy. My folks really never got over it. My mom said, 'Well, I always knew this was going to happen. Back when you were hanging out with Dana Scully and them, one or another of them no-count boys always honking out front for you, didn't I tell you this was going to happen?' We had a little bitty wedding at my folks' church, and we didn't take a honeymoon trip but went straight to our apartment and next day Norman started work at his uncle's. He just settled right into being married—shopping with me for groceries and picking out curtains and such. Oh, you know, sometimes I get to thinking what kids we were. It was almost like playing house! It was pretend! The candles I lit at suppertime, flowers on the table, Norman calling me 'hon' and bringing his plate to the sink for me to wash. And then all at once it turned serious. Here I've got this little boy now, this great big seven-year-old boy with his clompy leather shoes, and it wasn't playing house after all. It was for real, all along, and we just didn't know it."

She sat on the couch and raised one foot in front of her. She turned it admiringly this way and that. Her stocking bagged at the ankle.

"What is Edward up to?" she asked.

Macon said, "He's still lying down."

"Pretty soon he'll do that for three hours straight."

"Three *hours?*"

"Easy."

"Isn't that sort of cruel?"

"I thought you promised not to talk like that," she told him.

113

"Right. Sorry," Macon said.

"Maybe tomorrow he'll lie down on his own."

"You think so?"

"If you practice. If you don't give in. If you don't go all soft-hearted."

Then she stood up and came over to Macon. She patted his arm. "But never mind," she told him. "*I* think soft-hearted men are sweet." Macon backed away. He just missed stepping on Edward.

It was getting close to Thanksgiving, and the Learys were debating as usual about Thanksgiving dinner. The fact was, none of them cared for turkey. Still, Rose said, it didn't seem right to serve anything else. It would just feel wrong. Her brothers pointed out that she'd have to wake up at five a.m. to put a turkey in the oven. But it was she who'd be doing it, Rose said. It wouldn't be troubling *them* any.

Then it began to seem she had had an ulterior motive, for as soon as they settled on turkey she announced that she might just invite Julian Edge. Poor Julian, she said, had no close family living nearby, and he and his neighbors gathered forlornly at holidays, each bringing his or her specialty. Thanksgiving dinner last year had been a vegetarian pasta casserole and goat cheese on grape leaves and kiwi tarts. The least she could do was offer him a normal family dinner.

"What!" Macon said, acting surprised and disapproving, but unfortunately, it wasn't that much of a surprise. Oh, Julian was up to something, all right. But what could it be? Whenever Rose came down the stairs in her best dress and two spots of rouge, whenever she asked Macon to shut Edward in the pantry because Julian would be stopping by to take her this place or that—well, Macon had a very strong urge to let Edward accidentally break loose. He made a point of meeting Julian at the door, eyeing him for a long, silent moment before calling Rose. But Julian behaved; no glint of irony betrayed him. He was respectful with Rose, almost shy, and hovered clumsily when he ushered her out the door. Or was that the irony? His Rose Leary act. Macon didn't like the looks of this.

Then it turned out that Porter's children would be coming for Thanksgiving too. They usually came at Christmas instead, but wanted to trade off this year due to some complication with their grandparents on their stepfather's side. So really, Rose said, wasn't it good they were having turkey? Children were such traditionalists. She set to work baking pumpkin pies. "We gather together," she sang, "to ask the Lord's blessing . . ." Macon looked up from the sheaf of stolen menus he was spreading across the kitchen table. There was a note of gaiety in her voice that made him uneasy. He wondered if she had any mistaken ideas about Julian—if, for instance, she hoped for some kind of romance. But Rose was so plain and sensible in her long white apron. She reminded him of Emily Dickinson; hadn't Emily Dickinson also baked for her nieces and nephews? Surely there was no need for concern.

"My son's name is Alexander," Muriel said. "Did I tell you that? I named him Alexander because I thought it sounded high-class. He was never an easy baby. For starters something went wrong while I was carrying him and they had to do a Caesarean and take him out early and I got all these complications and can't ever have any more children. And then Alexander was so teeny he didn't even look like a human, more like a big-headed newborn kitten, and he had to stay in an incubator forever, just about, and nearly died. Norman said, 'When's it going to look like other babies?' He always called Alexander 'it.' I adjusted better; I mean pretty soon it seemed to me that that was what a baby *ought* to look like, and I hung around the hospital nursery but Norman wouldn't go near him, he said it made him too nervous."

Edward whimpered. He was just barely lying down—his haunches braced, his claws digging into the carpet. But Muriel gave no sign she had noticed.

"Maybe you and Alexander should get together some time," she told Macon.

"Oh, I, ah . . ." Macon said.

"He doesn't have enough men in his life."

"Well, but—"

"He's supposed to see men a lot; it's supposed to show him how to act. Maybe the three of us could go to a movie. Don't you ever go to movies?"

"No, I don't," Macon said truthfully. "I haven't been to a movie in months. I really don't care for movies. They make everything seem so close up."

"Or just out to a McDonald's, maybe."

"I don't think so," Macon said.

Porter's children arrived the evening before Thanksgiving, traveling by car because Danny, the oldest, had just got his driver's license. That worried Porter considerably. He paced the floor from the first moment they could be expected. "I don't know where June's brain is," he said. "Letting a sixteen-year-old boy drive all the way from Washington the first week he has his license! With his two little sisters in the car! I don't know how her mind works."

To make it worse, the children were almost an hour late. When Porter finally saw their headlights, he rushed out the door and down the steps well ahead of the others. "What kept you?" he cried.

Danny unfurled himself from the car with exaggerated nonchalance, yawning and stretching, and shook Porter's hand as a kind of after-thought while turning to study his tires. He was as tall as Porter now but very thin, with his mother's dark coloring. Behind him came Susan, fourteen—just a few months older than Ethan would have been. It was lucky she was so different from Ethan, with her cap of black curls and her rosy cheeks. This evening she wore jeans and hiking boots and one of those thick down jackets that made young people look so bulky and graceless. Then last came Liberty. What a name, Macon always thought. It was an invention of her mother's—a flighty woman who had run away from Porter with a hippie stereo salesman eight and a half years ago and discovered immediately afterward that she was two months pregnant. Ironically, Liberty was the one who looked most like Porter. She had fair, straight hair and a chiseled face and she was dressed in a little tailored coat. "Danny got lost," she said severely. "What a dummy." She kissed Porter and her aunt and uncles, but Susan wandered past them in a way that let everyone know she had outgrown all that.

"Oh, isn't this nice?" Rose said. "Aren't we going to have a wonderful Thanksgiving?" She stood on the sidewalk wrapping her hands in her apron, perhaps to stop herself from reaching out to Danny as he slouched toward the house. It was dusk, and Macon, happening to glance around, saw the grown-ups as pale gray wraiths—four middle-aged unmarried relatives yearning after the young folks.

For supper they had carry-out pizza, intended to please the children, but Macon kept smelling turkey. He thought at first it was his imagination. Then he noticed Danny sniffing the air. "Turkey? Already?" Danny asked his aunt.

"I'm trying this new method," she said. "It's supposed to save energy. You set your oven extremely low and cook your meat all night."

"Weird."

After supper they watched TV—the children had never seemed to warm to cards—and then they went to bed. But in the middle of the night, Macon woke with a start and gave serious thought to that turkey. She was cooking it till tomorrow? At an extremely low temperature? What temperature was that, exactly?

He was sleeping in his old room, now that his leg had mended. Eventually he nudged the cat off his chest and got up. He made his way downstairs in the dark, and he crossed the icy kitchen linoleum and turned on the little light above the stove. One hundred and forty degrees, the oven dial read. "Certain death," he told Edward, who had tagged along behind him. Then Charles walked in, wearing large, floppy pajamas. He peered at the dial and sighed. "Not only that," he said, "but this is a *stuffed* turkey."

"Wonderful."

"Two quarts of stuffing. I heard her say so."

"Two quarts of teeming, swarming bacteria."

"Unless there's something more to this method we don't understand."

"We'll ask her in the morning," Macon said, and they went back to bed.

In the morning, Macon came down to find Rose serving pancakes to the children. He said, "Rose, what exactly is it you're doing to this turkey?"

"I told you: slow heat. Jam, Danny, or syrup?"

"Is that *it?*" Macon asked.

"You're dripping," Rose said to Liberty. "What, Macon? See, I read an article about slow-cooked beef and I thought, well, if it works with beef it must work with turkey too so I—"

"It might work with beef but it will murder us with turkey," Macon told her.

"But at the end I'm going to raise the temperature!"

"You'd have to raise it mighty high. You'd have to autoclave the thing."

"You'd have to expose it to a nuclear flash," Danny said cheerfully.

Rose said, "Well, you're both just plain wrong. Who's the cook here, anyhow? I say it's going to be delicious."

Maybe it was, but it certainly didn't look it. By dinnertime the breast had caved in and the skin was all dry and dull. Rose entered the dining room holding the turkey high as if in triumph, but the only people who looked impressed were those who didn't know its history— Julian and Mrs. Barrett, one of Rose's old people. Julian said, "Ah!" and Mrs. Barrett beamed. "I just wish my neighbors could see this," Julian said. He wore a brass-buttoned navy blazer, and he seemed to have polished his face.

"Well, there may be a little problem here," Macon said.

Rose set the turkey down and glared at him.

"Of course, the rest of the meal is excellent," he said. "Why, we could fill up on the vegetables alone! In fact I think I'll do that. But the turkey . . ."

"It's pure poison," Danny finished for him.

Julian said, "Come again?" but Mrs. Barrett just smiled harder.

"We think it may have been cooked at a slightly inadequate temperature," Macon explained.

"It was not!" Rose said. "It's perfectly good."

"Maybe you'd rather just stick to the side dishes," Macon told Mrs. Barrett. He was worried she might be deaf.

But she must have heard, for she said, "Why, perhaps I will," never losing her smile. "I don't have much of an appetite anyhow," she said.

"And I'm a vegetarian," Susan said.

"So am I," Danny said suddenly.

"Oh, Macon, how could you do this?" Rose asked. "My lovely turkey! All that work!"

"I think it looks delicious," Julian said.

"Yes," Porter told him, "but you don't know about the other times."

"Other times?"

"Those were just bad luck," Rose said.

"Why, of course!" Porter said. "Or economy. You don't like to throw things away; I can understand that! Pork that's been sitting too long, or chicken salad left out all night . . ."

Rose sat down. Tears were glazing her eyes. "Oh," she said, "you're all so mean! You don't fool me for an instant; I know why you're doing this. You want to make me look bad in front of Julian."

"Julian?"

Julian seemed distressed. He took a handkerchief from his breast pocket but then went on holding it.

"You want to drive him off! You three wasted your chances and now you want me to waste mine, but I won't do it. I can see what's what! Just listen to any song on the radio; look at any soap opera. *Love* is what it's all about. On soap operas everything revolves around love. A new person comes to town and right away the question is, who's he going to love? Who's going to love him back? Who'll lose her mind with jealousy? Who's going to ruin her life? And you want to make me miss it!"

"Well, goodness," Macon said, trying to sort this out.

"You know perfectly well there's nothing wrong with that turkey. You just don't want me to stop cooking for you and taking care of this house, you don't want Julian to fall in love with me."

"Do what?"

But she scraped her chair back and ran from the room. Julian sat there with his mouth open.

"Don't you dare laugh," Macon told him.

Julian just went on gaping.

"Don't even consider it."

Julian swallowed. He said, "Do you think I ought to go after her?"

"No," Macon said.

"But she seems so—"

"She's fine! She's perfectly fine."

"Oh."

"Now, who wants a baked potato?"

There was a kind of murmur around the table; everyone looked unhappy. "That poor, dear girl," Mrs. Barrett said. "I feel just awful."

"Me too," Susan said.

"Julian?" Macon asked, clanging a spoon. "Potato?"

"I'll take the turkey," Julian said firmly.

At that moment, Macon almost liked the man.

"It was having the baby that broke our marriage up," Muriel said. "When you think about it, that's funny. First we got married on account of the baby and then we got divorced on account of the baby, and in between, the baby was what we argued about. Norman couldn't understand why I was all the time at the hospital visiting Alexander. 'It doesn't know you're there, so why go?' he said. I'd go early in the morning and just hang around, the nurses were as nice as could be about it, and I'd stay till night. Norman said, 'Muriel, won't we ever get our ordinary life back?' Well, you can see his point, I guess. It's like I only had room in my mind for Alexander. And he was in the hospital for months, for really months; there was everything in this world wrong with him. You should have seen our medical bills. We only had partial insurance and there were these bills running up, thousands and thousands of dollars. Finally I took a job at the hospital. I asked if I could work in the nursery but they said no, so I got a kind of, more like a maid's job, cleaning patients' rooms and so forth. Emptying trash cans, wet-mopping floors . . ."

She and Macon were walking along Dempsey Road with Edward, hoping to run into a biker. Muriel held the leash. If a biker came, she said, and Edward lunged or gave so much as the smallest yip, she was going to yank him so hard he wouldn't know what hit him. She warned Macon of that before they started out. She said he'd better not object because this was for Edward's own good. Macon hoped he'd be able to remember that when the time came.

It was the Friday after Thanksgiving and there'd been a light snow earlier, but the air didn't have a real bite to it yet and the sidewalks were merely damp. The sky seemed to begin about two feet above their heads.

"This one patient, Mrs. Brimm, she took a liking to me," Muriel said. "She said I was the only person who ever bothered talking to her. I'd come in and tell her about Alexander. I'd tell her what the doctors said, how they didn't give him much of a chance and some had even wondered if we *wanted* a chance, what with all that might be wrong with him. I'd tell her about me and Norman and the way he was acting, and she said it sounded exactly like a story in a magazine. When they let her go home she wanted me to come with her, take a job looking out for her, but I couldn't on account of Alexander."

A biker appeared at the end of the street, a girl with a Baskin-Robbins uniform bunching below her jacket. Edward perked his ears up. "Now, act like we expect no trouble," Muriel told Macon. "Just go along, go along, don't even look in Edward's direction."

The girl skimmed toward them—a little slip of a person with a tiny, serious face. When she passed, she gave off a definite smell of chocolate ice cream. Edward sniffed the breeze but marched on.

"Oh, Edward, that was wonderful!" Macon told him.

Muriel just clucked. She seemed to take his good behavior for granted.

"So anyhow," she said. "They finally did let Alexander come home. But he was still no bigger than a minute. All wrinkles like a little old man. Cried like a kitten would cry. Struggled for every breath. And *Norman* was no help. I think he was jealous. He got this kind of stubborn look whenever I had to do something, go warm a bottle or something. He'd say, 'Where you off to? Don't you want to watch the end of this program?' I'd be hanging over the crib watching Alexander fight for air, and Norman would call, 'Muriel? Commercial's just about over!' Then next thing I knew, there was his mother standing on my doorstep saying it wasn't his baby anyhow."

"What? Well, of all things!" Macon said.

"Can you believe it? Standing on my doorstep looking so pleased with herself. 'Not his baby!' I said. 'Whose, then?' 'Well, that I couldn't say,' she said, 'and I doubt if you could either. But I can tell you this much: If you don't give my son a divorce and release all financial claims on him, I will personally produce Dana Scully and his friends in a court of law and they will swear you're a known tramp and that baby could be any one of theirs. Clearly it's not Norman's; Norman was a *darling* baby.' Well. I waited till Norman got home from work and I said, 'Do you know what your mother told me?' Then I saw by his face that he did. I saw she must have been talking behind my back for who knows how long, putting these suspicions in his head. I said, 'Norman?' He just stuttered around. I said, 'Norman, she's lying, it's not true, I wasn't going with those boys when I met you! That's all in the past!' He said, 'I don't know what to think.' I said, 'Please!' He said, 'I don't know.' He went out to the kitchen and started fixing this screen I'd been nagging him about, window screen halfway out of its frame, even though supper was already on the table. I'd made him this special supper. I followed after him. I said, 'Norman, Dana and them are from way, way back. That baby couldn't be theirs.' He pushed up on one side of the screen and it wouldn't go, and he pushed up on the other side and it cut his hand, and all at once he started crying and wrenched the whole thing out of the window and threw it as far as he could. And next day his mother came to help him pack his clothes and he left me."

"Good Lord," Macon said. He felt shocked, as if he'd known Norman personally.

"So I thought about what to do. I knew I couldn't go back to my folks. Finally I phoned Mrs. Brimm and asked if she still wanted me to come take care of her, and she said yes, she did; the woman she had wasn't any use at all. So I said I would do it for room and board if I could bring the baby and she said yes, that would be fine. She had this little row house downtown and there was an extra bedroom where me and Alexander could sleep. And that's how I managed to keep us going."

They were several blocks from home now, but she didn't suggest turning back. She held the leash loosely and Edward strutted next to her, matching her pace. "I was lucky, wasn't I," she said. "If it wasn't for Mrs. Brimm I don't know what I'd have done. And it's not like it was all that much work. Just keeping the house straight, fixing her a bite to eat, helping her get around. She was crippled up with arthritis but just as spunky! It's not like I really had to nurse her."

She slowed and then came to a stop. Edward, with a martyred sigh, sat down at her left heel. "When you think about it, it's funny," she said. "All that time Alexander was in the hospital seemed so awful, seemed it would go on forever, but now when I look back, I almost miss it. I mean there was something cozy about it, now that I recall. I think about those nurses gossiping at the nurses' station and those rows of little babies sleeping. It was winter and sometimes I'd stand at a window and look out and I'd feel happy to be warm and safe. I'd look down at the emergency room entrance and watch the ambulances coming in. You ever wonder what a Martian might think if he happened to land near an emergency room? He'd see an ambulance whizzing in and everybody running out to meet it, tearing the doors open, grabbing up the stretcher, scurrying along with it. 'Why,' he'd say, 'what a helpful planet, what kind and helpful creatures.' He'd never guess we're not always that way; that we had to, oh, put aside our natural selves to do it. 'What a helpful race of beings,' a Martian would say. Don't you think so?"

She looked up at Macon then. Macon experienced a sudden twist in his chest. He felt there was something he needed to do, some kind of connection he wanted to make, and when she raised her face he bent and kissed her chapped, harsh lips even though that wasn't the connection he'd intended. Her fist with the leash in it was caught between them like a stone. There was something insistent about her—pressing. Macon drew back. "Well . . ." he said.

She went on looking up at him.

"Sorry," he said.

Then they turned around and walked Edward home.

Danny spent the holiday practicing his parallel parking, tirelessly wheeling his mother's car back and forth in front of the house. And Liberty baked cookies with Rose. But Susan had nothing to do, Rose said, and since Macon was planning a trip to Philadelphia, wouldn't he consider taking her along? "It's only hotels and restaurants," Macon said. "And

I'm cramming it into one day, leaving at crack of dawn and coming back late at night—"

"She'll be company for you," Rose told him.

However, Susan went to sleep when the train was hardly out of Baltimore, and she stayed asleep for the entire ride, sunk into her jacket like a little puffed-up bird roosting on a branch. Macon sat next to her with a rock magazine he'd found rolled up in one of her pockets. He saw that the Police were experiencing personality conflicts, that David Bowie worried about mental illness, that Billy Idol's black shirt appeared to have been ripped halfway off his body. Evidently these people led very difficult lives; he had no idea who they were. He rolled the magazine up again and replaced it in Susan's pocket.

If Ethan were alive, would he be sitting where Susan was? He hadn't traveled with Macon as a rule. The overseas trips were too expensive, the domestic trips too dull. Once he'd gone with Macon to New York, and he'd developed stomach pains that resembled appendicitis. Macon could still recall his frantic search for a doctor, his own stomach clenching in sympathy, and his relief when they were told it was nothing but too many breakfasts. He hadn't taken Ethan anywhere else after that. Only to Bethany Beach every summer, and that was not so much a trip as a kind of relocation of home base, with Sarah sunbathing and Ethan joining other Baltimore boys, also relocated, and Macon happily tightening all the doorknobs in their rented cottage or unsticking the windows or—one blissful year—solving a knotty problem he'd discovered in the plumbing.

In Philadelphia, Susan came grumpily awake and staggered off the train ahead of him. She complained about the railroad station. "It's way too big," she said. "The loudspeakers echo so you can't hear what they're saying. Baltimore's station is better."

"Yes, you're absolutely right," Macon said.

They went for breakfast to a café he knew well, which unfortunately seemed to have fallen upon hard times. Little chips of ceiling plaster kept dropping into his coffee. He crossed the name out of his guidebook. Next they went to a place that a reader had suggested, and Susan had walnut waffles. She said they were excellent. "Are you going to quote me on this?" she asked. "Will you put my name in your book and say I recommended the waffles?"

"It's not that kind of a book," he told her.

"Call me your companion. That's what restaurant critics do. 'My companion, Susan Leary, pronounced the waffles remarkable.' "

Macon laughed and signaled for their bill.

After their fourth breakfast, they started on hotels. Susan found these less enjoyable, though Macon kept trying to involve her. He told a manager, "My companion here is the expert on bathrooms." But

Susan just opened a medicine cabinet, yawned, and said, "All they have is Camay."

"What's wrong with that?"

"When Mama came back from her honeymoon she brought us perfumed designer soap from her hotel. One bar for me and one for Danny, in little plastic boxes with drainage racks."

"*I* think Camay is fine," Macon told the manager, who was looking worried.

Late in the afternoon Susan started feeling peckish again; so they had two more breakfasts. Then they went to Independence Hall. (Macon felt they should do something educational.) "You can tell your civics teacher," he said. She rolled her eyes and said, "Social studies."

"Whatever."

The weather was cold, and the interior of the hall was chilly and bleak. Macon noticed Susan gaping vacantly at the guide, who wasn't making his spiel very exciting; so he leaned over and whispered, "Imagine. George Washington sat in that very chair."

"I'm not really into George Washington, Uncle Macon."

"Human beings can only go 'into' houses, cars, and coffins, Susan."

"Huh?"

"Never mind."

They followed the crowd upstairs, through other rooms, but Susan had plainly exhausted her supply of good humor. "If it weren't for what was decided in this building," Macon told her, "you and I might very well be living under a dictatorship."

"We are anyhow," she said.

"Pardon?"

"You really think that you and me have any power?"

"You and I, honey."

"It's just free speech, that's all we've got. We can say whatever we like, then the government goes on and does exactly what it pleases. You call that democracy? It's like we're on a ship, headed someplace terrible, and somebody else is steering and the passengers can't jump off."

"Why don't we go get some supper," Macon said. He was feeling a little depressed.

He took her to an old-fashioned inn a few streets over. It wasn't even dark yet, and they were the first customers. A woman in a Colonial gown told them they'd have to wait a few minutes. She led them into a small, snug room with a fireplace, and a waitress offered them their choice of buttered rum or hot spiked cider. "I'll have buttered rum," Susan said, shucking off her jacket.

Macon said, "Uh, Susan."

She glared at him.

"Oh, well, make that two," he told the waitress. He supposed a little toddy couldn't do much harm.

But it must have been an exceptionally strong toddy—either that, or Susan had an exceptionally weak head for alcohol. At any rate, after two small sips she leaned toward him in an unbalanced way. "This is sort of fun!" she said. "You know, Uncle Macon, I like you much better than I thought I did."

"Why, thank you."

"I used to think you were kind of finicky. Ethan used to make us laugh, pointing to your artichoke plate."

"My artichoke plate."

She pressed her fingertips to her mouth. "I'm sorry," she said.

"For what?"

"I didn't mean to talk about him."

"You can talk about him."

"I don't want to," she said.

She gazed off across the room. Macon, following her eyes, found only a harpsichord. He looked back at her and saw her chin trembling.

It had never occurred to him that Ethan's cousins missed him too.

After a minute, Susan picked her mug up and took several large swallows. She wiped her nose with the back of her hand. "Hot," she explained. It was true she seemed to have recovered herself.

Macon said, "What was funny about my artichoke plate?"

"Oh, nothing."

"I won't be hurt. What was funny?"

"Well, it looked like geometry class. Every leaf laid out in such a perfect circle when you'd finished."

"I see."

"He was laughing *with* you, not at you," Susan said, peering anxiously into his face.

"Well, since I wasn't laughing myself, that statement seems inaccurate. But if you mean he wasn't laughing unkindly, I believe you."

She sighed and drank some more of her rum.

"Nobody talks about him," Macon said. "None of you mentions his name."

"We do when you're not around," Susan said.

"You do?"

"We talk about what he'd think, you know. Like when Danny got his license, or when I had a date for the Halloween Ball. I mean we used to make so much fun of the grown-ups. And Ethan was the funniest one; he could always get us to laugh. Then here we are, growing up ourselves. We wonder what Ethan would think of us, if he could come back and see us. We wonder if he'd laugh at *us*. Or if he'd feel . . . left out. Like we had moved on and left him behind."

The woman in the Colonial gown came to show them to their

table. Macon brought his drink; Susan had already finished hers. She was a bit unsteady on her feet. When their waitress asked them if they'd like a wine list, Susan gave Macon a bright-eyed look but Macon said, "No," very firmly. "I think we ought to start with soup," he said. He had some idea soup was sobering.

But Susan talked in a reckless, headlong way all through the soup course, and the main course, and the two desserts she hadn't been able to decide between, and the strong black coffee that he pressed upon her afterward. She talked about a boy she liked who either liked her back or else preferred someone named Sissy Pace. She talked about the Halloween Ball where this really juvenile eighth-grader had thrown up all over the stereo. She said that when Danny was eighteen, the three of them were moving to their own apartment because now that their mother was expecting (which Macon hadn't known), she wouldn't even realize they were gone. "That's not true," Macon told her. "Your mother would feel terrible if you left." Susan propped her cheek on her fist in a sort of slipshod manner and said that she wasn't born yesterday. Her hair had grown wilder through the evening, giving her an electrified appearance. Macon found it difficult to stuff her into her jacket, and he had to hold her up more or less by the back of her collar while they were waiting for a taxi.

In the railroad station she got a confused, squinty look, and once they were on the train she fell asleep with her head against the window. In Baltimore, when he woke her, she said, "You don't think he's mad at us, do you, Uncle Macon?"

"Who's that?"

"You think he's mad we're starting to forget him?"

"Oh, no, honey. I'm sure he's not."

She slept in the car all the way from the station, and he drove very gently so as not to wake her. When they got home, Rose said it looked as if he'd worn the poor child right down to a frazzle.

"You want your dog to mind you in every situation," Muriel said. "Even out in public. You want to leave him outside a public place and come back to find him waiting. That's what we'll work on this morning. We'll start with him waiting right on your own front porch. Then next lesson we'll go on to shops and things."

She picked up the leash and they stepped out the door. It was raining, but the porch roof kept them dry. Macon said, "Hold on a minute, I want to show you something."

"What's that?"

He tapped his foot twice. Edward looked uncomfortable; he gazed off toward the street and gave a sort of cough. Then slowly, slowly, one forepaw crumpled. Then the other. He lowered himself by degrees until he was lying down.

"Well! Good dog!" Muriel said. She clucked her tongue.

Edward flattened his ears back for a pat.

"I worked on him most of yesterday," Macon said. "It was Sunday and I had nothing to do. And then my brother's kids were getting ready to leave and Edward was growling the way he usually does; so I tapped my foot and down he went."

"I'm proud of both of you."

She told Edward, "Stay," holding out a hand. She backed into the house again. "Now, Macon, you come in too."

They closed the front door. Muriel tweaked the lace curtain and peered out. "Well, he's staying so far," she announced.

She turned her back to the door. She checked her fingernails and said, "Tsk!" Tiny beads of rain trickled down her raincoat, and her hair—reacting to the damp—stood out in corkscrews. "Someday I'm going to get me a professional manicure," she said.

Macon tried to see around her; he wasn't sure that Edward would stay put.

"Have you ever been to a manicurist?" she asked.

"Me? Goodness, no."

"Well, some men go."

"Not me."

"I'd like just once to get everything done professional. Nails, skin . . . My girlfriend goes to this place where they vacuum your skin. They just vacuum all your pores, she says. I'd like to go there sometime. And I'd like to have my colors done. What colors look good on me? What don't? What brings out the best in me?"

She looked up at him. All at once, Macon got the feeling she had not been talking about colors at all but something else. It seemed she used words as a sort of background music. He took a step away from her. She said, "You didn't have to apologize, the other day."

"Apologize?"

Although he knew exactly what she was referring to.

She seemed to guess that. She didn't explain herself.

"Um, I don't remember if I ever made this clear," Macon said, "but I'm not even legally divorced yet."

"So?"

"I'm just, what do you call. Separated."

"Well? So?"

He wanted to say, *Muriel, forgive me, but since my son died, sex has . . . turned.* (As milk turns; that was how he thought of it. As milk will alter its basic nature and turn sour.) *I really don't think of it anymore. I honestly don't. I can't imagine anymore what all that fuss was about. Now it seems pathetic.*

But what he said was, "I'm worried the mailman's going to come."

She looked at him for a moment longer, and then she opened the door for Edward.

Rose was knitting Julian a pullover sweater for Christmas. "Already?" Macon asked. "We've barely got past Thanksgiving."

"Yes, but this is a really hard pattern and I want to do it right."

Macon watched her needles flashing. "Actually," he said, "have you ever noticed that Julian wears cardigans?"

"Yes, I guess he does," she said.

But she went on knitting her pullover.

It was a heathery gray wool, what he believed they called Ragg wool. Macon and both his brothers had sweaters that color. But Julian wore crayon colors or navy blue. Julian dressed like a golfer. "He tends toward the V-necked look," Macon said to Rose.

"That doesn't mean he wouldn't wear a crew neck if he had one."

"Look," Macon said. "I guess what I'm getting at—"

Rose's needles clicked serenely.

"He's really kind of a playboy," he said. "I don't know if you realize that. And besides, he's younger."

"Two years," she said.

"But he's got a younger, I don't know, style of living. Singles apartments and so on."

"He says he's tired of all that."

"Oh, Lord."

"He says he likes homeyness. He appreciates my cooking. He can't believe I'm knitting him a sweater."

"No, I guess not," Macon said grimly.

"Don't try to spoil this, Macon."

"Sweetheart, I only want to protect you. It's wrong, you know, what you said at Thanksgiving. Love is *not* what it's all about. There are other things to consider besides, all kinds of other issues."

"He ate my turkey and did not get sick. Two big helpings," Rose said.

Macon groaned and tore at a handful of his hair.

"First we try him on a real quiet street," Muriel said. "Someplace public, but not too busy. Some out-of-the-way little store or something."

She was driving her long gray boat of a car. Macon sat in front beside her, and Edward sat in back, his ears out horizontal with joy. Edward was always happy to be invited for a car ride, though very soon he'd turn cranky. ("How much *longer?*" you could almost hear him whine.) It was lucky they weren't going far.

"I got this car on account of its big old trunk," Muriel said. She slung it dashingly around a corner. "I needed it for my errand business. Guess how much it cost?"

"Um . . ."

"Only two hundred dollars. That's because it needed work, but I took it to this boy down the street from where I live. I said, 'Here's the deal. You fix my car up, I let you have the use of it three nights a week and all day Sunday.' Wasn't that a good idea?"

"Very inventive," Macon said.

"I've *had* to be inventive. It's been scrape and scrounge, nail and knuckle, ever since Norman left me," she said. She had pulled into a space in front of a little shopping center, but she made no move to get out of the car. "I've lain awake, oh, many a night, thinking up ways to earn money. It was bad enough when room and board came free, but after Mrs. Brimm died it was worse; her house passed on to her son and I had to pay him rent. Her son's an old skinflint. Always wanting to jack up the price. I said, 'How's about this? You leave the rent where it is and I won't trouble you with maintenance. I'll tend to it all myself,' I said. 'Think of the headaches you'll save.' So he agreed and now you should see what I have to deal with, things go wrong and *I* can't fix them and so we just live with them. Leaky roof, stopped-up sink, faucet dripping hot water so my gas bill's out of this world, but at least I've kept the rent down. And I've got about fifty jobs, if you count them all up. You could say I'm lucky; I'm good at spotting a chance. Like those lessons at Doggie, Do, or another time a course in massage at the Y. The massage turned out to be a dud, seems you have to have a license and all like that, but I will say Doggie, Do paid off. And also I'm trying to start this research service; that's on account of all I picked up helping the school librarian. Wrote out these little pink cards I passed around at Towson State: We-Search Research. Xeroxed these flyers and mailed them to every Maryland name in the *Writer's Directory. Men and Women of Letters!* I said. *Do you want a long slow illness that will effectively kill off a character without unsightly disfigurement?* So far no one's answered but I'm still hoping. Twice now I've paid for an entire Ocean City vacation just by going up and down the beach offering folks these box lunches me and Alexander fixed in our motel room every morning. We lug them in Alexander's red wagon; I call out, 'Cold drinks! Sandwiches! Step right up!' And this is not even counting the regular jobs, like the Meow-Bow or before that the Rapid-Eze. Tiresome old Rapid-Eze; they did let me bring Alexander but it was nothing but copying documents and tedious things like that, canceled checks and invoices, little chits of things. I've never been so disinterested."

Macon stirred and said, "Don't you mean uninterested?"

"Exactly. Wouldn't you be? Copies of letters, copies of exams, copies of articles on how to shop for a mortgage. Knitting instructions, crochet instructions, all rolling out of the machine real slow and stately like they're such a big deal. Finally I quit. When I got my training at Doggie,

Do I said, 'I quit. I've had it!' Why don't we try the grocery."

Macon felt confused for a second. Then he said, "Oh. All right."

"You go into the grocery, put Edward on a down-stay outside. I'll wait here in the car and see if he behaves."

"All right."

He climbed from the car and opened the back door for Edward. He led him over to the grocery. He tapped his foot twice. Edward looked distressed, but he lay down. Was this humane, when the sidewalk was still so wet? Reluctantly, Macon stepped into the store. It had the old-fashioned smell of brown paper bags. When he looked back out, Edward's expression was heartbreaking. He wore a puzzled, anxious smile and he was watching the door intently.

Macon cruised an aisle full of fruits and vegetables. He picked up an apple and considered it and set it down again. Then he went back outside. Edward was still in place. Muriel had emerged from her car and was leaning against the fender, making faces into a brown plastic compact. "Give him lots of praise!" she called, snapping the compact shut. Macon clucked and patted Edward's head.

They went next door to the drugstore. "This time we'll both go in," Muriel said.

"Is that safe?"

"We'll have to try it sooner or later."

They strolled the length of the hair care aisle, all the way back to cosmetics, where Muriel stopped to try on a lipstick. Macon imagined Edward yawning and getting up and leaving. Muriel said, "Too pink." She took a tissue from her purse and rubbed the pink off. Her own lipstick stayed on, as if it were not merely a 1940s color but a 1940s formula—that glossless, cakey substance that used to cling to pillow-cases, napkins, and the rims of coffee cups. She said, "What are you doing for dinner tomorrow night?"

"For—?"

"Come and eat at my house."

He blinked.

"Come on. We'll have fun."

"Um . . ."

"Just for dinner, you and me and Alexander. Say six o'clock. Number Sixteen Singleton Street. Know where that is?"

"Oh, well, I don't believe I'm free then," Macon said.

"Think it over a while," she told him.

They went outside. Edward was still there but he was standing up, bristling in the direction of a Chesapeake Bay retriever almost a full block away. "Shoot," Muriel said. "Just when I thought we were getting someplace." She made him lie down again. Then she released him and the three of them walked on. Macon was wondering how soon he could decently say that he had thought it over now and remembered he definitely had an invitation elsewhere. They rounded a corner. "Oh, look, a thrift shop!" Muriel said. "My biggest weakness." She tapped her foot at Edward. "This time, I'll go in," she said. "I want to see what they have. You step back a bit and watch he doesn't stand up like before."

She went inside the thrift shop while Macon waited, skulking around the parking meters. Edward knew he was there, though. He kept turning his head and giving Macon beseeching looks.

Macon saw Muriel at the front of the shop, picking up and setting down little gilded cups without saucers, chipped green glass florists' vases, ugly tin brooches as big as ashtrays. Then he saw her dimly in the back where the clothes were. She drifted into sight and out again like a fish in dark water. She appeared all at once in the doorway, holding up a hat. "Macon? What do you think?" she called. It was a dusty beige turban with a jewel pinned to its center, a great false topaz like an eye.

"Very interesting," Macon said. He was starting to feel the cold.

Muriel vanished again, and Edward sighed and settled his chin on his paws.

A teenaged girl walked past—a gypsy kind of girl with layers of flouncy skirts and a purple satin knapsack plastered all over with Grateful Dead emblems. Edward tensed. He watched every step she took; he rearranged his position to watch after her as she left. But he said nothing, and Macon—tensed himself—felt relieved but also a little let down. He'd been prepared to leap into action. All at once the silence seemed unusually deep; no other people passed. He experienced one of those hallucinations of sound that he sometimes got on planes or trains. He heard Muriel's voice, gritty and thin, rattling along. "At the tone the time will be . . ." she said, and then she sang, "You will find your love in . . ." and then she shouted, "Cold drinks! Sandwiches! Step right up!" It seemed she had webbed his mind with her stories, wound him in slender steely threads from her life—her Shirley Temple childhood, unsavory girlhood, Norman flinging the screen out the window, Alexander mewing like a newborn kitten, Muriel wheeling on Doberman pinschers and scattering her salmon-pink business cards and galloping down the beach, all spiky limbs and flying hair, hauling a little red wagon full of lunches.

Then she stepped out of the thrift shop. "It was way too expensive," she told Macon. "Good dog," she said, and she snapped her fingers to let Edward up. "Now one more test." She was heading back toward her car. "We want to try both of us going in again. We'll do it down at the doctor's."

"What doctor's?"

"Dr. Snell's. I've got to pick up Alexander; I want to return him to school after I drop you off."

"Will that take long?"

"Oh, no."

They drove south, with the engine knocking in a way that Macon hadn't noticed the first time. In front of a building on Cold Spring Lane, Muriel parked and got out. Macon and Edward followed her. "Now, I don't know if he's ready or not," she said. "But all the better if he's not; gives Edward practice."

"I thought you said this wouldn't take long."

She didn't seem to hear him.

They left Edward on the stoop and went into the waiting room. The receptionist was a gray-haired woman with sequined glasses dangling from a chain of fake scarabs. Muriel asked her, "Is Alexander through yet?"

"Any minute, hon."

Muriel found a magazine and sat down but Macon remained standing. He raised one of the slats of the venetian blind to check on Edward. A man in a nearby chair glanced over at him suspiciously. Macon felt like someone from a gangster movie—one of those shady characters who twitches back a curtain to make sure the coast is clear. He dropped the blind. Muriel was reading an article called "Put on the New Sultry, Shadowed Eyes!" There were pictures of different models looking malevolent.

"How old did you say Alexander was?" Macon asked.

She glanced up. Her own eyes, untouched by cosmetics, were disquietingly naked compared to those in the magazine.

"He's seven," she said.

Seven.

Seven was when Ethan had learned to ride a bicycle.

Macon was visited by one of those memories that dent the skin, that strain the muscles. He felt the seat of Ethan's bike pressing into his hand—the curled-under edge at the rear that you hold onto when you're trying to keep a bicycle upright. He felt the sidewalk slapping against his soles as he ran. He felt himself let go, slow to a walk, stop with his hands on his hips to call out, "You've got her now! You've got her!" And Ethan rode away from him, strong and proud and straight-backed, his hair picking up the light till he passed beneath an oak tree.

Macon sat down next to Muriel. She looked over and said, "Have you thought?"

"Hmm?"

"Have you given any thought to coming to dinner?"

"Oh," he said. And then he said, "Well, I could come. If it's only for dinner."

"What else would it be for?" she asked. She smiled at him and tossed her hair back.

The receptionist said, "*Here* he is."

She was talking about a small, white, sickly boy with a shaved-looking skull. He didn't appear to have quite enough skin for his face; his skin was stretched, his mouth was stretched to an unattractive width, and every bone and blade of cartilage made its presence known. His eyes were light blue and lashless, bulging slightly, rimmed with pink, magnified behind large, watery spectacles whose clear frames had an unfortunate pinkish cast themselves. He wore a carefully coordinated shirt-and-slacks set such as only a mother would choose.

"How'd it go?" Muriel asked him.

"Okay."

"Sweetie, this is Macon. Can you say hi? I've been training his dog."

Macon stood up and held out his hand. After a moment, Alexander responded. His fingers felt like a collection of wilted stringbeans. He took his hand away again and told his mother, "You have to make another appointment."

"Sure thing."

She went over to the receptionist, leaving Macon and Alexander standing there. Macon felt there was nothing on earth he could talk about with this child. He brushed a leaf off his sleeve. He pulled his cuffs down. He said, "You're pretty young to be at the doctor's without your mother."

Alexander didn't answer, but Muriel—waiting for the receptionist to flip through her calendar—turned and answered for him. "He's used to it," she said, "because he's had to go so often. He's got these allergies."

"I see," Macon said.

Yes, he was just the type for allergies.

"He's allergic to shellfish, milk, fruits of all kinds, wheat, eggs, and most vegetables," Muriel said. She accepted a card from the receptionist and dropped it into her purse. She said as they were walking out, "He's allergic to dust and pollen and paint, and there's some belief he's allergic to air. Whenever he's outside a long time he gets these bumps on any uncovered parts of his body."

She clucked at Edward and snapped her fingers. Edward jumped up, barking. "Don't pat him," she told Alexander. "You don't know what dog fur will do to you."

They got into her car. Macon sat in back so Alexander could take the front seat, as far from Edward as possible. They had to drive with all the windows down so Alexander wouldn't start wheezing. Over the rush of wind, Muriel called, "He's subject to asthma, eczema, and nosebleeds. He has to get these shots all the time. If a bee ever stings him and he hasn't had his shots he could be dead in half an hour."

Alexander turned his head slowly and gazed at Macon. His expression was prim and censorious.

When they drew up in front of the house, Muriel said, "Well, let's see now. I'm on full time at the Meow-Bow tomorrow . . ." She ran a hand through her hair, which was scratchy, rough, disorganized. "So I guess I won't see you till dinner," she said.

Macon couldn't think of any way to tell her this, but the fact was that he would never be able to make that dinner. He missed his wife. He missed his son. They were the only people who seemed real to him. There was no point looking for substitutes.

11
=

Muriel Pritchett, was how she was listed. Brave and cocky: no timorous initials for Muriel. Macon circled the number. He figured now was the time to call. It was nine in the evening. Alexander would have gone to bed. He lifted the receiver.

But what would he say?

Best to be straightforward, of course, much less hurtful; hadn't Grandmother Leary always told them so? *Muriel, last year my son died and I don't seem to . . . Muriel, this has nothing to do with you personally but really I have no . . .*

Muriel, I can't. I just can't.

It seemed his voice had rusted over. He held the receiver to his ear but great, sharp clots of rust were sticking in his throat.

He had never actually said out loud that Ethan was dead. He hadn't needed to; it was in the papers (page three, page five), and then friends had told other friends, and Sarah got on the phone . . . So somehow, he had never spoken the words. How would he do it now? Or maybe he could make Muriel do it. *Finish this sentence, please: I did have a son but he _____.* "He what?" she would ask. "He went to live with your wife? He ran away? He died?" Macon would nod. "But *how* did he die? Was it cancer? Was it a car wreck? Was it a nineteen-year-old with a pistol in a Burger Bonanza restaurant?"

He hung up.

He went to ask Rose for notepaper and she gave him some from her desk. He took it to the dining room table, sat down, and uncapped his fountain pen. *Dear Muriel*, he wrote. And stared at the page a while.

Funny sort of name.

Who would think of calling a little newborn baby Muriel?

He examined his pen. It was a Parker, a swirly tortoiseshell lacquer with a complicated gold nib that he liked the looks of. He examined

Rose's stationery. Cream colored. Deckle edged. Deckle! What an odd word.

Well.

Dear Muriel.

I am very sorry, he wrote, *but I won't be able to have dinner with you after all. Something has come up.* He signed it, *Regretfully, Macon.*

Grandmother Leary would not have approved.

He sealed the envelope and tucked it in his shirt pocket. Then he went to the kitchen where Rose kept a giant city map thumbtacked to the wall.

Driving through the labyrinth of littered, cracked, dark streets in the south of the city, Macon wondered how Muriel could feel safe living here. There were too many murky alleys and stairwells full of rubbish and doorways lined with tattered shreds of posters. The gridded shops with their ineptly lettered signs offered services that had a sleazy ring to them: CHECKS CASHED NO QUESTIONS, TINY BUBBA'S INCOME TAX, SAME DAY AUTO RECOLORING. Even this late on a cold November night, clusters of people lurked in the shadows—young men drinking out of brown paper bags, middle-aged women arguing under a movie marquee that read CLOSED.

He turned onto Singleton and found a block of row houses that gave a sense of having been skimped on. The roofs were flat, the windows flush and lacking depth. There was nothing to spare, no excess material for overhangs or decorative moldings, no generosity. Most were covered in formstone, but the bricks of Number 16 had been painted a rubbery maroon. An orange bugproof bulb glowed dimly above the front stoop.

He got out of the car and climbed the steps. He opened the screen door, which was made of pitted aluminum. It clattered in a cheap way and the hinges shrieked. He winced. He took the letter from his pocket and bent down.

"I've got a double-barreled shotgun," Muriel said from inside the house, "and I'm aiming it exactly where your head is."

He straightened sharply. His heart started pounding. (Her voice sounded level and accurate—like her shotgun, he imagined.) He said, "It's Macon."

"Macon?"

The latch clicked and the inner door opened several inches. He saw a sliver of Muriel in a dark-colored robe. She said, "Macon! What are you doing here?"

He gave her the letter.

She took it and opened it, using both hands. (There wasn't a trace of a shotgun.) She read it and looked up at him.

He saw he had done it all wrong.

"Last year," he said, "I lost . . . I experienced a . . . loss, yes, I lost my . . ."

She went on looking into his face.

"I lost my son," Macon said. "He was just . . . he went to a hamburger joint and then . . . someone came up, a holdup man, and shot him. I can't go to dinner with people! I can't talk to their little boys! You have to stop asking me. I don't mean to hurt your feelings but I'm just not up to this, do you hear?"

She took one of his wrists very gently and she drew him into the house, still not fully opening the door, so that he had a sense of slipping through something, of narrowly evading something. She closed the door behind him. She put her arms around him and hugged him.

"Every day I tell myself it's time to be getting over this," he said into the space above her head. "I know that people expect it of me. They used to offer their sympathy but now they don't; they don't even mention his name. They think it's time my life moved on. But if anything, I'm getting worse. The first year was like a bad dream—I was clear to his bedroom door in the morning before I remembered he wasn't there to be wakened. But this second year is real. I've stopped going to his door. I've sometimes let a whole day pass by without thinking about him. That absence is more terrible than the first, in a way. And you'd suppose I would turn to Sarah but no, we only do each other harm. I believe that Sarah thinks I could have prevented what happened, somehow—she's so used to my arranging her life. I wonder if all this has only brought out the truth about us—how far apart we are. I'm afraid we got married *because* we were far apart. And now I'm far from everyone; I don't have any friends anymore and everyone looks trivial and foolish and not related to me."

She drew him through a living room where shadows loomed above a single beaded lamp, and a magazine lay face down on a lumpy couch. She led him up a stairway and across a hall and into a bedroom with an iron bedstead and a varnished orange bureau.

"No," he said, "wait. This is not what I want."

"Just sleep," she told him. "Lie down and sleep."

That seemed reasonable.

She removed his duffel coat and hung it on a hook in a closet curtained with a length of flowered sheeting. She knelt and untied his shoes. He stepped out of them obediently. She rose to unbutton his shirt and he stood passive with his hands at his sides. She hung his trousers over a chair back. He dropped onto the bed in his underwear and she covered him with a thin, withered quilt that smelled of bacon grease.

Next he heard her moving through the rest of the house, snapping off lights, running water, murmuring something in another room. She returned to the bedroom and stood in front of the bureau. Earrings clinked into a dish. Her robe was old, shattered silk, the color of sherry. It tied at the waist with a twisted cord and the elbows were clumsily darned. She switched off the lamp. Then she came over to the bed and lifted the quilt and slid under it. He wasn't surprised when she pressed against him. "I just want to sleep," he told her. But there were those folds of silk. He felt how cool and fluid the silk was. He put a hand on her hip and felt the two layers of her, cool over warm. He said, "Will you take this off?"

She shook her head. "I'm bashful," she whispered, but immediately afterward, as if to deny that, she put her mouth on his mouth and wound herself around him.

In the night he heard a child cough, and he swam up protestingly through layers of dreams to answer. But he was in a room with one tall blue window, and the child was not Ethan. He turned over and found Muriel. She sighed in her sleep and lifted his hand and placed it upon her stomach. The robe had fallen open; he felt smooth skin, and then a corrugated ridge of flesh jutting across her abdomen. The Caesarean, he thought. And it seemed to him, as he sank back into his dreams, that she had as good as spoken aloud. *About your son,* she seemed to be saying: *Just put your hand here. I'm scarred, too. We're all scarred. You are not the only one.*

12

I don't understand you," Rose told Macon. "First you say yes, you'll be here all afternoon, and then you say you won't. How can I plan when you're so disorganized?"

She was folding linen napkins and stacking them on the table, preparing her annual tea for the old people. Macon said, "Sorry, Rose, I didn't think it would matter that much."

"Last night you said you'd want supper and then you weren't here to eat it. Three separate mornings these past two weeks I go to call you for breakfast and I find you haven't slept in your bed. Don't you think I worry? Anything might have happened."

"Well, I said I was sorry."

Rose smoothed the stack of napkins.

"Time creeps up on me," he told her. "You know how it is. I mean I don't intend to go out at all, to begin with, but then I think, 'Oh, maybe for a little while,' and next thing I know it's so late, much too late to be driving, and I think to myself, 'Well . . .' "

Rose turned away quickly and went over to the buffet. She started counting spoons. "I'm not asking about your private life," she said.

"I thought in a sense you were."

"I just need to know how much food to cook, that's all."

"I wouldn't blame you for being curious," he said.

"I just need to know how many breakfasts to fix."

"You think I don't notice you three? Whenever she's here giving Edward his lesson, everyone starts coming out of the woodwork. Edging through the living room—'Just looking for the pliers! Don't mind me!' Sweeping the entire front porch the minute we take Edward out for a walk."

"Could I help it if the porch was dirty?"

"Well, I'll tell you what," he said. "Tomorrow night I'll definitely be here for supper. That's a promise. You can count on it."

"I'm not asking you to stay if you don't want to," she told him.

"Of course I want to! It's just this evening I'll be out," he said, "but not late, I'm sure of that. Why, I bet I'll be home before ten!"

Although even as he spoke, he heard how false and shallow he sounded, and he saw how Rose lowered her eyes.

He bought a large combination pizza and drove downtown with it. The smell made him so hungry that he kept snitching bits off the top at every stoplight—coins of pepperoni, crescents of mushroom. His fingers got all sticky and he couldn't find his handkerchief. Pretty soon the steering wheel was sticky too. Humming to himself, he drove past tire stores, liquor stores, discount shoe stores, the Hot-Tonight Novelty Company. He took a shortcut through an alley and jounced between a double row of backyards—tiny rectangles crammed with swing sets and rusted auto parts and stunted, frozen bushes. He turned onto Singleton and drew up behind a pickup truck full of moldy rolls of carpet.

The next-door neighbor's twin daughters were perched on their front stoop—flashy sixteen-year-olds in jeans as tight as sausage casings. It was too cold to sit outside, but that never stopped them. "Hey there, Macon," they singsonged.

"How are you, girls."

"You going to see Muriel?"

"I thought I might."

He climbed Muriel's steps, holding the pizza level, and knocked on the door. Debbie and Dorrie continued to watch him. He flashed them a broad smile. They sometimes baby-sat with Alexander; he had to be nice to them. Half the neighborhood sat with Alexander, it seemed. He still felt confused by Muriel's network of arrangements.

It was Alexander who opened the door. "Pizza man!" Macon told him.

"Mama's on the phone," Alexander said flatly. He turned away and wandered back to the couch, adjusting his glasses on his nose. Evidently he was watching TV.

"Extra-large combination, no anchovies," Macon said.

"I'm allergic to pizza."

"What part of it?"

"Huh?"

"What part are you allergic to? The pepperoni? Sausage? Mushrooms? We could take those off."

"All of it," Alexander said.

"You can't be allergic to all of it."

"Well, I am."

Macon went on into the kitchen. Muriel stood with her back to him, talking on the phone with her mother. He could tell it was her mother because of Muriel's high, sad, querulous tone. "Aren't you going to ask how Alexander is? Don't you want to know about his rash? I ask after *your* health, why don't you ask about ours?"

He stepped up behind her soundlessly. "You didn't even ask what happened with his eye doctor," she said, "and here I was so worried about it. I swear sometimes you'd think he wasn't your grandson! That time I sprained my ankle falling off my shoes and called to see if you'd look after him, what did you say? Said, 'Now let me get this straight. You want me to come all the way down to your house.' You'd think Alexander was nothing to do with you!"

Macon presented himself in front of her, holding out the pizza. "Ta-da!" he whispered. She looked up at him and gave that perky smile of hers—an ornate, Victorian V.

"Ma," she said, "I'm going now! Macon's here!"

It had been a long, long time since anyone made such an event of his arrival.

He went to Julian's office on a Monday afternoon and handed over what he'd done on the U.S. guidebook. "That wraps up the Northeast," he said. "I guess next I'll start on the South."

"Well, good," Julian told him. He was bent over behind his desk, rummaging through a drawer. "Excellent. Like to show you something, Macon. Now, where in hell—ah."

He straightened, with his face flushed. He gave Macon a tiny blue velvet box. "Your sister's Christmas present," he said.

Macon raised the lid. Inside, on a bed of white satin, was a diamond ring. He looked at Julian.

"What is it?" he asked.

"What *is* it?"

"I mean, is this a . . . what you would call, dinner ring? Or is it meant to be, rather . . ."

"It's an engagement ring, Macon."

"Engagement?"

"I want to marry her."

"You want to marry Rose?"

"What's so odd about that?"

"Well, I—" Macon said.

"If she'll agree to it, that is."

"What, you haven't asked her yet?"

"I'll ask her at Christmas, when I give her the ring. I want to do this properly. Old-fashioned. Do you think she'll have me?"

"Well, I really couldn't say," Macon said. Unfortunately, he was sure she would, but he'd be damned if he'd tell Julian that.

"She's got to," Julian said. "I am thirty-six years old, Macon, but I tell you, I feel like a schoolboy about that woman. She's everything those girls in my apartment building are not. She's so . . . true. Want to know something? I've never even slept with her."

"Well, I don't care to hear about that," Macon said hastily.

"I want us to have a real wedding night," Julian told him. "I want to do everything right. I want to join a real family. God, Macon, isn't it amazing how two separate lives can link up together? I mean two *differentnesses*? What do you think of the ring?"

Macon said, "It's okay." He looked down at it. Then he said, "It's very nice, Julian," and he closed the box gently and handed it back.

"Now, this is not your ordinary airplane," Macon told Muriel. "I wouldn't want you to get the wrong idea. This is what they call a commuter plane. It's something a businessman would take, say, to hop to the nearest city for a day and make a few sales and hop back again."

The plane he was referring to—a little fifteen-seater that resembled a mosquito or a gnat—stood just outside the door of the commuters' waiting room. A girl in a parka was loading it with baggage. A boy was checking something on the wings. This appeared to be an airline run by teenagers. Even the pilot was a teenager, it seemed to Macon. He entered the waiting room, carrying a clipboard. He read off a list of names. "Marshall? Noble? Albright?" One by one the passengers stepped forward—just eight or ten of them. To each the pilot said, "Hey, how you doing." He let his eyes rest longest on Muriel. Either he found her the most attractive or else he was struck by her outfit. She wore her highest heels, black stockings spattered with black net roses, and a flippy little fuchsia dress under a short fat coat that she referred to as her "fun fur." Her hair was caught all to one side in a great bloom of frizz, and there was a silvery dust of some kind on her eyelids. Macon knew she'd overdone it, but at the same time he liked her considering this such an occasion.

The pilot propped open the door and they followed him outside, across a stretch of concrete, and up two rickety steps into the plane. Macon had to bend almost double as he walked down the aisle. They threaded between two rows of single seats, each seat as spindly as a folding chair. They found spaces across from each other and settled in. Other passengers struggled through, puffing and bumping into things. Last came the copilot, who had round, soft, baby cheeks and carried a can of Diet Pepsi. He slammed the door shut behind him and went up front to the controls. Not so much as a curtain hid the cockpit. Macon could lean out into the aisle and see the banks of knobs and gauges, the pilot positioning his headset, the copilot taking a final swig and setting his empty can on the floor.

"Now, on a bigger plane," Macon called to Muriel as the engines roared up, "you'd hardly feel the takeoff. But here you'd better brace yourself."

Muriel nodded, wide-eyed, gripping the seat ahead of her. "What's that light that's blinking in front of the pilot?" she asked.

"I don't know."

"What's that little needle that keeps sweeping round and round?"

"I don't know."

He felt he'd disappointed her. "I'm used to jets, not these toys," he told her. She nodded again, accepting that. It occurred to Macon that he was really a very worldly and well-traveled man.

The plane started taxiing. Every pebble on the runway jolted it; every jolt sent a series of creaks through the framework. They gathered speed. The crew, suddenly grave and professional, made complicated adjustments to their instruments. The wheels left the ground. "Oh!" Muriel said, and she turned to Macon with her face all lit up.

"We're off," he told her.

"I'm flying!"

They rose—with some effort, Macon felt—over the fields surrounding the airport, over a stand of trees and a grid of houses. Above-ground swimming pools dotted backyards here and there like pale blue thumbtacks. Muriel pressed so close to her window that she left a circle of mist on the glass. "Oh, look!" she said to Macon, and then she said something else that he couldn't hear. The engines on this plane were loud and harsh, and the Pepsi can was rolling around with a clattering sound, and also the pilot was bellowing to the copilot, saying something about his refrigerator. "So I wake up in the middle of the night," he was shouting, "damn thing's thudding and thumping—"

Muriel said, "Wouldn't Alexander enjoy this!"

Macon hadn't seen Alexander enjoying anything yet, but he said dutifully, "We'll have to bring him sometime."

"We'll have to take just lots of trips! France and Spain and Switzerland . . ."

"Well," Macon said, "There's the little matter of money."

"Just America, then. California, Florida . . ."

California and Florida took money too, Macon should have said (and Florida wasn't even given space in his guidebook), but for the moment, he was borne along by her vision of things. "Look!" she said, and she pointed to something. Macon leaned across the aisle to see what she meant. This airplane flew so low that it might have been following road signs; he had an intimate view of farmlands, woodlands, roofs of houses. It came to him very suddenly that every little roof concealed actual lives. Well, of course he'd known that, but all at once it took his breath away. He saw how real those lives were to the people who lived them—how intense and private and absorbing. He stared past Muriel with his mouth open. Whatever she had wanted him to look at must be long past by now, but still he went on gazing out her window.

Porter and the others were talking money. Or Porter was talking money and the others were half listening. Porter was planning ahead for income taxes. He was interested in something called a chicken straddle. "The way it works," he said, "you invest in baby chicks right now, before the end of the year. Deduct the cost of feed and such. Then sell the grown hens in January and collect the profit."

Rose wrinkled her forehead. She said, "But chickens are so prone to colds. Or would you call it distemper. And December and January aren't usually all that warm here."

"They wouldn't be here in Baltimore, Rose. God knows where they'd be. I mean these are not chickens you actually see; they're a way to manage our taxes."

"Well, I don't know," Charles said. "I hate to get involved in things someone else would be handling. It's someone else's word those chickens even exist."

"You people have no imagination," Porter said.

The four of them stood around the card table in the sun porch, helping Rose with her Christmas present for Liberty. She had constructed an addition to Liberty's dollhouse—a garage with a guest apartment above it. The garage was convincingly untidy. Miniature wood chips littered the floor around a stack of twig-sized fire logs, and a coil of green wire made a perfect garden hose. Now they were working on the upstairs. Rose was stuffing an armchair cushion no bigger than an aspirin. Charles was cutting a sheet of wallpaper from a sample book. Porter was drilling holes for the curtain rods. There was hardly elbow room; so Macon, who had just come in with Edward, stood back and merely watched.

"Besides," Charles said, "chickens are really not, I don't know, very classy animals. I would hate to go round saying I'm a chicken magnate."

"You don't even have to mention the fact," Porter said.

"*Beef* magnate, now; that I wouldn't mind. Beef has more of a ring to it."

"They're not offering a straddle for beef, Charles."

Macon picked up some color photos that sat beside the wallpaper book. The top photo showed a window in a room he didn't recognize— a white-framed window with louvered shutters closed across its lower half. The next was a group portrait. Four people—blurry, out of focus— stood in a line in front of a couch. The woman wore an apron, the men wore black suits. There was something artificial about their posture. They were lined up too precisely; none of them touched the others. "Who *are* these people?" Macon asked.

Rose glanced over. "That's the family from Liberty's dollhouse," she said.

"Oh."

"Her mother sent me those pictures."

"It's a family with nothing but grown-ups?" he asked.

"One's a boy; you just can't tell. And one's a grandpa or a butler; June says Liberty switches him back and forth."

Macon laid the photos aside without looking at the rest of them. He knelt to pat Edward. "A cattle straddle," Charles was saying thoughtfully. Macon suddenly wished he were at Muriel's. He wrapped his arms around Edward and imagined he smelled her sharp perfume deep in Edward's fur.

Oh, above all else he was an orderly man. He was happiest with a regular scheme of things. He tended to eat the same meals over and over and to wear the same clothes; to drop off his cleaning on a certain set day and to pay all his bills on another. The teller who helped him on his first trip to a bank was the teller he went to forever after, even if she proved not to be efficient, even if the next teller's line was shorter. There was no room in his life for anyone as unpredictable as Muriel. Or as extreme. Or as . . . well, unlikable, sometimes.

Her youthfulness was not appealing but unsettling. She barely remembered Vietnam and had no idea where she'd been when Kennedy was shot. She made him anxious about his own age, which had not previously troubled him. He realized how stiffly he walked after he had been sitting in one position too long; how he favored his back, always expecting it to go out on him again; how once was plenty whenever they made love.

And she talked so much—almost ceaselessly; while Macon was the kind of man to whom silence was better than music. ("Listen! They're playing my song," he used to say when Sarah switched the radio off.) She talked about blushers, straighteners, cellulite, hemlines, winter skin. She was interested in the appearance of things, only the appearance: in lipstick shades and nail wrapping and facial masques and split ends. Once, on one of her more attractive days, he told her she was looking very nice, and she grew so flustered that she stumbled over a curb. She asked if that was because she had tied her hair back; and was it the hair itself or the ribbon; or rather the color of the ribbon, which she'd feared might be just a little too bright and set off the tone of her complexion wrong. And didn't he think her hair was hopeless, kerblamming out the way it did in the slightest bit of humidity? Till he was sorry he had ever brought it up. Well, not sorry, exactly, but tired. Exhausted.

Yet she could raise her chin sometimes and pierce his mind like a blade. Certain images of her at certain random, insignificant moments would flash before him: Muriel at her kitchen table, ankles twined around her chair rungs, filling out a contest form for an all-expense-paid tour of Hollywood. Muriel telling her mirror, "I look like the wrath of God"—a kind of ritual of leavetaking. Muriel doing the dishes in her big pink rubber gloves with the crimson fingernails, raising a soapy plate and trailing it airily over to the rinse water and belting out one of her favorite songs—"War Is Hell on the Home Front too" or "I Wonder If God Likes Country Music." (Certainly *she* liked country music—long, complaining ballads about the rocky road of life, the cold gray walls of prison, the sleazy, greasy heart of a two-faced man.) And Muriel at the hospital window, as he'd never actually seen her, holding a mop and gazing down at the injured coming in.

Then he knew that what mattered was the pattern of her life; that although he did not love her he loved the surprise of her, and also the surprise of himself when he was with her. In the foreign country that was Singleton Street he was an entirely different person. This person had never been suspected of narrowness, never been accused of chilliness; in fact, was mocked for his soft heart. And was anything but orderly.

"Why don't you come to my folks' house for Christmas dinner?" she asked him.

Macon was in her kitchen at the time. He was crouched beneath the sink, turning off a valve. For a moment he didn't answer; then he emerged and said, "Your folks?"

"For Christmas dinner."

"Oh, well, I don't know," he said.

"Come on, Macon, please say yes! I want you to meet them. Ma thinks I'm making you up. 'You made him up,' she says. You know how she is."

Yes, Macon did know, at least from second hand, and he could just imagine what that dinner would be like. Booby-trapped. Full of hidden digs and hurt feelings. The fact was, he just didn't want to get involved.

So instead of answering, he turned his attention to Alexander. He was trying to teach Alexander how to fix a faucet. "Now," he said, "you see I shut the valve off. What did I do that for?"

All he got was a glassy pale stare. This was Macon's idea, not Alexander's. Alexander had been hauled away from the TV like a sack of stones, plunked on a kitchen chair, and instructed to watch closely. "Oh," Muriel said, "I'm not so sure about this. He's not so very strong."

"You don't have to be Tarzan to fix a kitchen faucet, Muriel."

"Well, no, but I don't know . . ."

Sometimes Macon wondered if Alexander's ailments were all in Muriel's head.

"Why did I shut off the valve, Alexander?" he asked.

Alexander said, "Why."

"You tell me."

"You tell *me*."

"No, you," Macon said firmly.

There was a bad moment or two in which it seemed that Alexander might keep up that stare of his forever. He sat C-shaped in his chair, chin on one hand, eyes expressionless. The shins emerging from his trousers were thin as Tinkertoys, and his brown school shoes seemed very large and heavy. Finally he said, "So the water won't whoosh all over."

"Right."

Macon was careful not to make too much of his victory.

"Now, this leak is not from the spout, but from the handle," he said. "So you want to take the handle apart and replace the packing. First you unscrew the top screw. Let's see you do it."

"Me?"

Macon nodded and offered him the screwdriver.

"I don't want to," Alexander said.

"Let him just watch," Muriel suggested.

"If he just watches he won't know how to fix the one in the bathtub, and I'm going to ask him to manage that without me."

Alexander took the screwdriver, in one of those small, stingy gestures of his that occupied a minimum of space. He inched off the chair and came over to the sink. Macon pulled another chair up close and Alexander climbed onto it. Then there was the problem of fitting the screwdriver into the slot of the screw. It took him forever. He had tiny fingers, each tipped with a little pink pad above painfully bitten nails. He concentrated, his glasses slipping down on his nose. Always a mouth-breather, he was biting his tongue now and panting slightly.

"Wonderful," Macon said when the screwdriver finally connected.

At each infinitesimal turn, though, it slipped and had to be repositioned. Macon's stomach muscles felt tight. Muriel, for once, was silent, and her silence was strained and anxious.

Then, "Ah!" Macon said. The screw had loosened enough so that Alexander could twist it by hand. He managed that part fairly easily. He even removed the faucet without being told. "Very good," Macon said. "I believe you may have natural talents."

Muriel relaxed. Leaning back against the counter, she said, "My folks have their Christmas dinner in the daytime. I mean it's not at noon but it's not at night either, it's more like mid-afternoon, or this year it's really late afternoon because I've got the morning shift at the Meow-Bow and—"

"Look at this," Macon told Alexander. "See that gunk? That's old, rotted packing. So take it away. Right. Now here's the new packing. You wind it around, wind even a little more than you need. Let's see you wind it around."

Alexander wrapped the thread. His fingers turned white with the effort. Muriel said, "Usually we have a goose. My daddy brings a goose from the Eastern Shore. Or don't you care for goose. Would you rather just a turkey? A duck? What are you used to eating, Macon?"

Macon said, "Oh, well . . ." and was saved by Alexander. Alexander turned, having reassembled the faucet without any help, and said, "Now what?"

"Now make sure the screw is well in."

Alexander resumed his struggles with the screwdriver. Muriel said, "Maybe you'd rather a good hunk of beef. I know some men are like that. They think poultry is kind of pansy. Is that how you think too? You can tell me! I won't mind! My folks won't mind!"

"Oh, um, Muriel . . ."

"Now what," Alexander ordered.

"Why, now we turn the water back on and see what kind of job you've done."

Macon crouched beneath the sink and showed him where the valve was. Alexander reached past him and twisted it, grunting. Wasn't it odd, Macon thought, how little boys all had that same slightly green smell, like a cedar closet. He rose and turned on the faucet. No leak. "Look at that!" he told Alexander. "You've solved the problem."

Alexander fought to hold a grin back.

"Will you know how to do it the next time?"

He nodded.

"Now when you're grown," Macon said, "you can fix the faucets for your wife."

Alexander's face squinched up with amusement at the thought.

" 'Step back, dearie,' you can say. 'Just let me see to this.' "

Alexander said, "Tssh!"—his face like a little drawstring purse.
" 'Let a real *man* take care of this,' you can tell her."
"Tssh! Tssh!"
"Macon? Are you coming to my folks', or aren't you?" Muriel asked.
It seemed unreasonable to say he wasn't. Somehow or other, he had got himself involved already.

13

M uriel's parents lived out in Timonium, in a development called Foxhunt Acres. Muriel had to show Macon the way. It was the coldest Christmas Day either of them could remember, but they drove with the windows slightly open so that Alexander, riding in back, would not be bothered by the dog hair. The radio was tuned to Muriel's favorite station. Connie Francis was singing "Baby's First Christmas."
"You warm enough?" Muriel asked Alexander. "You doing okay?"
Alexander must have nodded.
"You feel like you're wheezing at all?"
"Nope."
"No, ma'am," she corrected him.
Sarah used to do that, too, Macon remembered—give their son a crash course in manners any time they set out to visit her mother.
Muriel said, "Once I was riding Alexander uptown on some errands for George? My company? And I'd had these two cats in the car just the day before? And I didn't think a thing about it, clean forgot to vacuum like I usually do, and all at once I turn around and Alexander's stretched across the seat, flat out."
"I wasn't flat *out*," Alexander said.
"You were just as good as."
"I was only laying down so I wouldn't need so much air."
"See there?" Muriel said to Macon.
They were traveling up York Road now, past body shops and fast food outlets all closed and bleak. Macon had never seen this road so empty. He overtook a van and then a taxicab; nothing else. Swags of Christmas greens hung stiffly above a used car lot.
"He can get shots, though," Muriel said.
"Shots?"
"He can get shots to keep him from wheezing."
"Then why doesn't he?"
"Well, if Edward was to move in I guess that's what we'd do."

"Edward?"

"I mean if, you know. If you moved in on a permanent basis and Edward came too."

"Oh," Macon said.

Brenda Lee was singing "I'm Gonna Lasso Santa Claus." Muriel hummed along, tipping her head perkily left and right to keep time.

"Would you ever think of doing that?" she asked him finally.

"Doing what?" he said, pretending not to know.

"Would you ever think of moving in with us?"

"Oh, um . . ."

"Or we could move in with you," she said. "Either way you preferred."

"With me? But my sister and my—"

"I'm talking about *your* house."

"Oh. My house."

His house swam up before him—small and dim and abandoned, hunkered beneath the oak trees like a woodchopper's cottage in a fairy tale. Muriel glanced at his face and then said, quickly, "I could understand if you didn't want to go back there."

"It's not that," he said. He cleared his throat. He said, "It's just that I haven't given it much thought."

"Oh, I understand!"

"Not yet, at least."

"You don't have to explain!"

She pointed out where to turn, and they started down a winding road. The eating places grew sparser and shabbier. There were scratchy little trees, frozen fields, a whole village of different-sized mailboxes bristling at the end of a driveway.

Every time the car jounced, something rattled on the backseat. That was Macon's Christmas present to Alexander—a kit full of tools that were undersized but real, with solid wooden handles. Macon had hunted those tools down one by one. He had rearranged them in their compartments a dozen times at least, like a miser counting his money.

They passed a segment of rickrack fence that was dissolving back into the ground. Muriel said, "What is *your* family doing today?"

"Oh, nothing much."

"Having a big Christmas dinner?"

"No, Rose has gone to Julian's. Charles and Porter are, I don't know, I think they said something about caulking the second-floor bathtub."

"Oh, the poor things! They should have come with us to my folks'."

Macon smiled, picturing that.

He turned where she directed, into a meadow dotted with houses. All were built to the same general plan—brick with half-stories of aluminum siding above. The streets were named for trees that weren't there, Birch Lane and Elm Court and Apple Blossom Way. Muriel had him make a right onto Apple Blossom Way. He pulled up behind a station wagon. A girl burst out of the house—a chunky, pretty teenager in blue jeans and a long yellow ponytail. "Claire!" Alexander shouted, bouncing in his seat.

"That's my sister," Muriel told Macon.

"Ah."

"Do you think she's good-looking?"

"Yes, she's very good-looking."

Claire had the car door open by now and was hoisting Alexander into her arms. "How's my fellow?" she was asking. "What did Santa Claus bring you?" She was so unlike Muriel that you'd never guess they were sisters. Her face was almost square, and her skin was golden, and by present-day standards she was probably ten pounds overweight. After she'd set Alexander down, she stuffed her hands awkwardly into the back pockets of her jeans. "So anyhow," she told Macon and Muriel. "Merry Christmas, and all that."

"Look," Muriel said, flashing a wristwatch. "See what Macon gave me."

"What'd you give him?"

"A key tag from a thrift shop. Antique."

"Oh."

With her house key attached, Muriel had neglected to say.

Macon unloaded things from the trunk—Muriel's presents for her family, along with his hostess gift—and Alexander took his toolbox from the backseat. They followed Claire across the yard. Muriel was anxiously feeling her hair as she walked. "You ought to see what Daddy gave Ma," Claire told her. "Gave her a microwave oven. Ma says she's scared to death of it. 'I just know I'll get radiation,' she says. We're worried she won't use it."

The door was held open for them by a small, skinny, gray woman in an aqua pantsuit. "Ma, this is Macon," Muriel said. "Macon, this is my mother."

Mrs. Dugan studied him, pursing her lips. Lines radiated from the corners of her mouth like cat whiskers. "Pleased to meet you," she said finally.

"Merry Christmas, Mrs. Dugan," Macon said. He handed her his gift—a bottle of cranberry liqueur with a ribbon tied around it. She studied that, too.

"Just put the rest of those things under the tree," Muriel told Macon. "Ma, aren't you going to say hello to your grandson?"

Mrs. Dugan glanced briefly at Alexander. He must not have expected anything more; he was already wandering over to the Christmas tree. Unrelated objects sat beneath it—a smoke detector, an electric drill, a makeup mirror encircled with light bulbs. Macon laid Muriel's packages next to them, and then he removed his coat and draped it across the arm of a white satin couch. Fully a third of the couch was occupied by the microwave oven, still jauntily decorated with a large red bow. "Look at my new microwave," Mrs. Dugan said. "If that's not just the weirdest durn thing I ever laid eyes on." She cleared a crumple of gift wrap off an armchair and waved Macon into it.

"Something certainly smells good," he said.

"Goose," she told him. "Boyd went and shot me a goose."

She sat down next to the oven. Claire was on the floor with Alexander, helping him open a package. Muriel, still in her coat, scanned a row of books on a shelf. "Ma—" she said. "No, never mind, I found it." She came over to Macon with a photo album, the modern kind with clear plastic pages. "Look here," she said, perching on the arm of his chair. "Pictures of me when I was little."

"Why not take off your coat and stay a while," Mrs. Dugan told her.

"Me at six months. Me in my stroller. Me and my first birthday cake."

They were color photos, shiny, the reds a little too blue. (Macon's own baby pictures were black-and-white, which was all that was generally available back then.) Each showed her to be a chubby, giggling blonde, usually with her hair fixed in some coquettish style—tied in a sprig at the top of her head, or in double ponytails so highly placed they looked like puppy ears. At first the stages of her life passed slowly—it took her three full pages to learn to walk—but then they speeded up. "Me at two. Me at five. Me when I was seven and a half." The chubby blonde turned thin and dark and sober and then vanished altogether, replaced by the infant Claire. Muriel said, "Oh, well," and snapped the album shut just midway through. "Wait," Macon told her. He had an urge to see her at her worst, at her most outlandish, hanging out with motorcycle gangs. But when he took the album away from her and flipped to the very last pages, they were blank.

Mr. Dugan wandered in—a fair, freckled man in a plaid flannel shirt—and gave Macon a callused hand to shake and then wandered out again, mumbling something about the basement. "He's fretting over the pipes," Mrs. Dugan explained. "Last night it got down below zero, did you know that? He's worried the pipes'll freeze."

"Oh, could I help?" Macon asked, perking up.

"Now, you just sit right where you are, Mr. Leary."

"Macon," he said.

"Macon. And you can call me Mother Dugan."

"Um . . ."

"Muriel tells me you're separated, Macon."

"Well, yes, I am."

"Do you think it's going to take?"

"Pardon?"

"I mean you're not just leading this child around Robin Hood's barn now, are you?"

"Ma, quit that," Muriel said.

"Well, I wouldn't have to ask, Muriel, if you had ever showed the least bit of common sense on your own. I mean face it, you don't have such a great track record."

"She's just worried for me," Muriel told Macon.

"Well, of course," he said.

"This girl was not but thirteen years old," Mrs. Dugan said, "when all at once it seemed boys of the very slipperiest character just came crawling out of the woodwork. I haven't had a good night's sleep since."

"Well, I don't know why not," Muriel told her. "That was years and years ago."

"Seemed every time we turned around, off she'd gone to the Surf'n'Turf or the Torch Club or the Hi-Times Lounge on Highway Forty."

"Ma, will you please open up you and Daddy's Christmas present?"

"Oh, did you bring us a present?"

Muriel rose to fetch it from under the tree, where Claire sat with Alexander. She was helping him set up some little cardboard figures. "This one goes on the green. This one goes on the blue," she said. Alexander jittered next to her, impatient to take over.

"Claire was the one who picked that game for him," Mrs. Dugan said, accepting the package Muriel handed her. "I thought it was too advanced, myself."

"It is not," Muriel said (although she hadn't even glanced at it). She returned to Macon's chair. "Alexander's just as smart as a tack. He'll catch on in no time."

"Nobody said he wasn't smart, Muriel. You don't have to take offense at every little thing a person says."

"Will you just open your present?"

But Mrs. Dugan proceeded at her own pace. She took off the ribbon and laid it in a box on the coffee table. "Your daddy has a bit of cash for your Christmas," she told Muriel. "Remind him before you go." She examined the wrapping. "Will you look at that! Teeny little Rudolph the Red-nosed Reindeers all over it. Real aluminum foil for their noses. I don't know why you couldn't just use tissue like I do."

"I wanted it to be special," Muriel told her.

Mrs. Dugan took off the paper, folded it, and laid it aside. Her gift was something in a gilded frame. "Well, isn't that nice," she said finally. She turned it toward Macon. It was a picture of Muriel and Alexander— a studio portrait in dreamy pastels, the lighting so even that it seemed to be coming from no particular place at all. Muriel was seated and

Alexander stood beside her, one hand resting delicately upon her shoulder. Neither of them smiled. They looked wary and uncertain, and very much alone.

Macon said, "It's beautiful."

Mrs. Dugan only grunted and leaned forward to lay the photo beside the box of ribbons.

Dinner was an industrious affair, with everyone working away at the food—goose, cranberry relish, two kinds of potatoes, and three kinds of vegetables. Mr. Dugan remained spookily quiet, although Macon offered him several openers about the basement plumbing. Muriel devoted herself to Alexander. "There's bread in that stuffing, Alexander. Put it back this instant. You want your allergy to start up? I wouldn't trust that relish, either."

"Oh, for Lord's sake, let him be," Mrs. Dugan said.

"You wouldn't say that if it was you he kept awake at night with itchy rashes."

"Half the time I believe you bring on those rashes yourself with all your talk," Mrs. Dugan said.

"That just shows how much you know about it."

Macon had a sudden feeling of dislocation. What would Sarah say if she could see him here? He imagined her amused, ironic expression. Rose and his brothers would just look baffled. Julian would say, "Ha! *Accidental Tourist in Timonium.*"

Mrs. Dugan brought out three different pies, and Claire scurried around with the coffeepot. Over her jeans now she wore an embroidered dirndl skirt—her gift from Muriel, purchased last week at Value Village. Her layers of clothing reminded Macon of some native costume. "What about the liqueur?" she asked her mother. "Shall I set out Macon's liqueur?"

"Maybe he wants you to call him Mr. Leary, hon."

"No, please, Macon's fine," he said.

He supposed there'd been a lot of discussion about his age. Oh, no doubt about it: He was too old, he was too tall, he was too dressed up in his suit and tie.

Mrs. Dugan said the liqueur was just about the best thing she'd ever drunk. Macon himself found it similar to the fluoride mixture his dentist coated his teeth with; he'd envisioned something different. Mr. Dugan said, "Well, these sweet-tasting, pretty-colored drinks are all very well for the ladies, but personally I favor a little sipping whiskey, don't you, Macon?" and he rose and brought back a fifth of Jack Daniel's and two shot glasses. The mere weight of the bottle in his hand seemed to loosen his tongue. "So!" he said, sitting down. "What you driving these days, Macon?"

"Driving? Oh, um, a Toyota."

Mr. Dugan frowned. Claire giggled. "Daddy hates and despises foreign cars," she told Macon.

"What is it, you don't believe in buying American?" Mr. Dugan asked him.

"Well, as a matter of fact—"

As a matter of fact his wife drove a Ford, he'd been going to say, but he changed his mind. He took the glass that Mr. Dugan held out to him. "I did once have a Rambler," he said.

"You want to try a Chevy, Macon. Want to come to the showroom sometime and let me show you a Chevy. What's your preference? Family-size? Compact?"

"Well, compact, I guess, but—"

"I'll tell you one thing: There is no way on earth you're going to get me to sell you a *sub*compact. No sir, you can beg and you can whine, you can get down on bended knee, I won't sell you one of those deathtraps folks are so set on buying nowadays. I tell my customers, I say, 'You think I got no principles? You're looking here before you at a man of principle,' I tell them, and I say, 'You want a subcompact you better go to Ed Mackenzie there. He'll sell you one without a thought. What does he care? But I'm a man of principle.' Why, Muriel here near about lost her life in one of them things."

"Oh, Daddy, I did not," Muriel said.

"Came a lot closer than *I'd* like to get."

"I walked away without a scratch."

"Car looked like a little stove-in sardine can."

"Worst thing I got was a run in my stocking."

"Muriel was taking a lift from Dr. Kane at the Meow-Bow," Mr. Dugan told Macon, "one day when her car was out of whack, and some durn fool woman driver swung directly into their path. See, she was hanging a left when—"

"Let me tell it," Mrs. Dugan said. She leaned toward Macon, gripping the wineglass that held her liqueur. "I was just coming in from the grocery store, carrying these few odds and ends I needed for Claire's school lunches. That child eats more than some grown men I know. Phone rings. I drop everything and go to answer. Man says, 'Mrs. Dugan?' I say, 'Yes.' Man says, 'Mrs. Dugan, this is the Baltimore City Police and I'm calling about your daughter Muriel.' I think, 'Oh, my God.' Right away my heart starts up and I have to find someplace to sit. Still have my coat on, rain scarf tied around my head so I couldn't even hear all that good but I never thought to take it off, that's how flustered I was. It was one of those hard rainy days like someone is purposely heaving buckets of water at you. I think, 'Oh, my God, now what has Muriel gone and—'"

"Lillian, you are getting way off the subject here," Mr. Dugan said.

"How can you say that? I'm telling him about Muriel's accident."

"He don't want to hear every little oh-my-God, he wants to know why he can't have a subcompact. Lady hangs a left smack in front of Dr. Kane's little car," Mr. Dugan told Macon, "and he has no choice but to ram her. He had the right of way. Want to know what happened? His little car is totaled. Little bitty Pinto. Lady's big old Chrysler barely dents its fender. Now tell me you still want a subcompact."

"But I didn't—"

"And the other thing is that Dr. Kane never, ever offered her another ride home, even after he got a new car," Mrs. Dugan said.

"Well, I don't exactly live in his neighborhood, Ma."

"He's a bachelor," Mrs. Dugan told Macon. "Have you met him? Real good-looking, Muriel says. First day on the job she says, 'Guess what, Ma.' Calls me on the phone. 'Guess what, my boss is single and he's real good-looking, a professional man, the other girls tell me he isn't even engaged.' Then he offers her that one lift home and they go and have an accident and he never offers again. Even when she lets him know she don't have her car some days, he never offers again."

"He does live clear up in Towson," Muriel said.

"I believe he thinks you're bad luck."

"He lives up in Towson and I live down on Singleton Street! What do you expect?"

"Next he got a Mercedes sports car," Claire put in.

"Well, sports cars," Mr. Dugan said. "We don't even talk about those."

Alexander said, "Can I be excused now?"

"I really had high hopes for Dr. Kane," Mrs. Dugan said sadly.

"Oh, quit it, Ma."

"You did, too! You said you did!"

"Why don't you just hush up and drink your drink."

Mrs. Dugan shook her head, but she took another sip of liqueur.

They left in the early evening, when the last light had faded and the air seemed crystallized with cold. Claire stood in the doorway singing out, "Come back soon! Thanks for the skirt! Merry Christmas!" Mrs. Dugan shivered next to her, a sweater draped over her shoulders. Mr. Dugan merely lifted an arm and disappeared—presumably to check on the basement again.

Traffic was heavier now. Headlights glowed like little white smudges. The radio—having given up on Christmas for another year—played "I Cut My Fingers on the Pieces of Your Broken Heart," and the toolbox rattled companionably in the backseat.

"Macon? Are you mad?" Muriel asked.

"Mad?"

"Are you mad at me?"

"Why, no."

She glanced back at Alexander and said no more.

It was night when they reached Singleton Street. The Butler twins, bundled into identical lavender jackets, stood talking with two boys on the curb. Macon parked and opened the back door for Alexander, who had fallen asleep with his chin on his chest. He gathered him up and carried him into the house. In the living room, Muriel set down her own burdens—the toolbox, Alexander's new game, and a pie Mrs. Dugan had pressed on them—and followed Macon up the stairs. Macon walked sideways to keep Alexander's feet from banging into the wall. They went into the smaller of the bedrooms and he laid Alexander on the bed. "I know what you must be thinking," Muriel said. She took Alexander's shoes off. "You're thinking, 'Oh, now I see, this Muriel was just on the lookout for anybody in trousers.' Aren't you."

Macon didn't answer. (He worried they'd wake Alexander.)

"I know what you're thinking!"

She tucked Alexander in. Turned off the light. They started back downstairs. "But that's not the way it was; I swear it," she said. "Oh, of course since he was single the possibility did cross my mind. Who would I be kidding if I said it didn't? I'm all alone, raising a kid. Scrounging for money. Of course it crossed my mind!"

"Well, of course," Macon said mildly.

"But it wasn't like she made it sound," Muriel told him.

She clattered after him across the living room. When he sat on the couch she sat next to him, still in her coat. "Are you going to stay?" she asked.

"If you're not too sleepy."

Instead of answering, she tipped her head back against the couch. "I meant are you giving up on me. I meant did you want to stop seeing me."

"Why would I want to stop seeing you?"

"After how bad she made me look."

"You didn't look bad."

"Oh, no?"

When she was tired, her skin seemed to tighten over her bones. She pressed her fingertips to her eyelids.

"Last Christmas," Macon said, "was the first one we had without Ethan. It was very hard to get through."

He often found himself talking with her about Ethan. It felt good to say his name out loud.

"We didn't know how to have a childless Christmas anymore," he said. "I thought, 'Well, after all, we managed before we had him, didn't we?' But in fact I couldn't remember how. It seemed to me we'd *always* had him; it's so unthinkable once you've got children that they ever didn't exist. I've noticed: I look back to when I was a boy, and it seems to me that Ethan was somehow there even then; just not yet visible, or something. So anyway. I decided what I should do was get Sarah a whole flood of presents, and I went out to Hutzler's the day before Christmas and bought all this junk—closet organizers and such. And Sarah: She went to the other extreme. She didn't buy anything. So there we were, each of us feeling we'd done it all wrong, acted inappropriately, but also that the other had done wrong; I don't know. It was a terrible Christmas."

He smoothed Muriel's hair off her forehead. "This one was better," he said.

She opened her eyes and studied him a moment. Then she slipped her hand in her pocket, came up with something and held it toward him—palming it, like a secret. "For you," she said.

"For me?"

"I'd like you to have it."

It was a snapshot stolen from her family album: Muriel as a toddler, clambering out of a wading pool.

She meant, he supposed, to give him the best of her. And so she had. But the best of her was not that child's Shirley Temple hairdo. It was her fierceness—her spiky, pugnacious fierceness as she fought her way toward the camera with her chin set awry and her eyes bright slits of determination. He thanked her. He said he would keep it forever.

14

You would have to say that he was living with her now. He began to spend all his time at her house, to contribute toward her rent and her groceries. He kept his shaving things in her bathroom and squeezed his clothes among the dresses in her closet. But there wasn't one particular point at which he made the shift. No, this was a matter of day by day. First there was that long Christmas vacation when Alexander was home alone; so why shouldn't Macon stay on with him once he'd spent the night there? And why not fetch his typewriter and work at the kitchen table? And then why not remain for supper, and after that for bed?

Though if you needed to put a date on it, you might say he truly moved in the afternoon he moved Edward in. He'd just got back from a business trip—an exhausting blitz of five southern cities, not one of which was any warmer than Baltimore—and he stopped by Rose's house to check the animals. The cat was fine, Rose said. (She had to speak above Edward's yelps; he was frantic with joy and relief.) The cat had probably not noticed Macon was missing. But Edward, well . . . "He spends a lot of time sitting in the hall," she said, "staring at the door. He keeps his head cocked and he waits for you to come back."

That did it. He brought Edward with him when he returned to Singleton Street.

"What do you think?" he asked Muriel. "Could we keep him just a day or two? See if Alexander can take it, without any shots?"

"I can take it!" Alexander said. "It's cats that get to me; not dogs."

Muriel looked doubtful, but she said they could give it a try.

Meanwhile, Edward darted madly all over the house snuffling into corners and under furniture. Then he sat in front of Muriel and grinned up at her. He reminded Macon of a schoolboy with a crush on his teacher; all his fantasies were realized, here he was at last.

For the first few hours they tried to keep him in a separate part of the house, which of course was hopeless. He had to follow Macon wherever he went, and also he developed an immediate interest in Alexander. Lacking a ball, he kept dropping small objects at Alexander's feet and then stepping back to look expectantly into his face. "He wants to play fetch," Macon explained. Alexander picked up a matchbook and tossed it, angling his arm behind him in a prissy way. While Edward went tearing after it, Macon made a mental note to buy a ball first thing in the morning and teach Alexander how to throw.

Alexander watched TV and Edward snoozed on the couch beside him, curled like a little blond cashew nut with a squinty, blissful expression on his face. Alexander hugged him and buried his face in Edward's ruff. "Watch it," Macon told him. He had no idea what to do if Alexander started wheezing. But Alexander didn't wheeze. By bedtime he just had a stuffy nose, and he usually had that anyhow.

Macon liked to believe that Alexander didn't know he and Muriel slept together. "Well, that's just plain ridiculous," Muriel said. "Where does he imagine you spend the night—on the living room couch?"

"Maybe," he said. "I'm sure he has some explanation. Or maybe he doesn't. All I'm saying is, we shouldn't hit him in the face with it. Let him think what he wants to think."

So every morning, Macon rose and dressed before Alexander woke. He started fixing breakfast and then roused him. "Seven o'clock! Time to get up! Go call your mother, will you?" In the past, he learned, Muriel had often stayed in bed while Alexander woke on his own and got ready for school. Sometimes he left the house while she was still asleep. Macon thought that was shocking. Now he made a full breakfast, and he insisted that Muriel sit at the table with them. Muriel claimed breakfast made her sick to her stomach. Alexander said it made him sick, too, but Macon said that was just too bad. "Ninety-eight percent of all A students eat eggs in the morning," he said (making it up as he went along). "Ninety-nine percent drink milk." He untied his apron and sat down. "Are you listening, Alexander?"

"I'll throw up if I drink milk."

"That's all in your head."

"Tell him, Mama!"

"He throws up," Muriel said gloomily. She sat hunched at the table in her long silk robe, resting her chin on one hand. "It's something to do with enzymes," she said. She yawned. Her hair, growing out of its permanent at last, hung down her back in even ripples like the crimps on a bobby pin.

Alexander walked to school with Buddy and Sissy Ebbetts, two tough-looking older children from across the street. Muriel either went back to bed or dressed and left for one or another of her jobs, depending on what day it was. Then Macon did the breakfast dishes and took Edward out. They didn't go far; it was much too cold. The few people they encountered walked rapidly, with jerky steps, like characters in a silent film. They knew Macon by sight now and would allow their eyes to flick over his face as they passed—a gesture like a nod—but they didn't speak. Edward ignored them. Other dogs could come up and sniff him and he wouldn't even break stride. Mr. Marcusi, unloading crates outside Marcusi's Grocery, would pause to say, "Well, hey there, stubby. Hey there, tub of lard." Edward, smugly oblivious, marched on. "Weirdest animal I ever saw," Mr. Marcusi called after Macon. "Looks like something that was badly drawn." Macon always laughed.

He was beginning to feel easier here. Singleton Street still unnerved him with its poverty and its ugliness, but it no longer seemed so dangerous. He saw that the hoodlums in front of the Cheery Moments Carry-Out were pathetically young and shabby—their lips chapped, their sparse whiskers ineptly shaved, an uncertain, unformed look around their eyes. He saw that once the men had gone off to work, the women emerged full of good intentions and swept their front walks, picked up the beer cans and potato chip bags, even rolled back their coat sleeves and scrubbed their stoops on the coldest days of the year. Children raced past like so many scraps of paper blowing in the wind— mittens mismatched, noses running—and some woman would brace herself on her broom to call, "You there! I see you! Don't think I don't know you're skipping school!" For this street was always backsliding, Macon saw, always falling behind, but was caught just in time by these women with their carrying voices and their pushy jaws.

Returning to Muriel's house, he would warm himself with a cup of coffee. He would set his typewriter on the kitchen table and sit down with his notes and brochures. The window next to the table had large, cloudy panes that rattled whenever the wind blew. Something about the rattling sound reminded him of train travel. *The airport in Atlanta must have ten miles of corridors,* he typed, and then a gust shook the panes and he had an eerie sensation of movement, as if the cracked linoleum floor were skating out from under him.

He would telephone hotels, motels, Departments of Commerce, and his travel agent, arranging future trips. He would note these arrangements in the datebook that Julian gave him every Christmas—a Businessman's Press product, spiralbound. In the back were various handy reference charts that he liked to thumb through. The birthstone for January was a garnet; for February, an amethyst. One square mile equaled 2.59 square kilometers. The proper gift for a first anniversary was paper. He would ponder these facts dreamily. It seemed to him that the world was full of equations; that there must be an answer for everything, if only you knew how to set forth the questions.

Then it was lunchtime, and he would put away his work and make himself a sandwich or heat a can of soup, let Edward have a quick run in the tiny backyard. After that he liked to putter around the house a bit. There was so much that needed fixing! And all of it somebody else's, not his concern, so he could approach it lightheartedly. He whistled while he probed the depth of a crack. He hummed as he toured the basement, shaking his head at the disarray. Upstairs he found a three-legged bureau leaning on a can of tomatoes, and he told Edward, "Scandalous!" in a tone of satisfaction.

It occurred to him—as he oiled a hinge, as he tightened a doorknob—that the house reflected amazingly little of Muriel. She must have lived here six or seven years by now, but still the place had an air of transience. Her belongings seemed hastily placed, superimposed, not really much to do with her. This was a disappointment, for Macon was conscious while he worked of his intense curiosity about her inner workings. Sanding a drawer, he cast a guilty eye upon its contents but found only fringed shawls and yellowed net gloves from the forties—clues to other people's lives, not hers.

But what was it he wanted to know? She was an open book, would tell him anything—more than he felt comfortable with. Nor did she attempt to hide her true nature, which was certainly far from perfect. It emerged that she had a nasty temper, a shrewish tongue, and a tendency to fall into spells of self-disgust from which no one could rouse her for hours. She was inconsistent with Alexander to the point of pure craziness—one minute overprotective, the next minute callous and offhand. She was obviously intelligent, but she counteracted that with the most global case of superstition Macon had ever witnessed. Hardly a day passed when she didn't tell him some dream in exhaustive detail and then sift through it for omens. (A dream of white ships on a purple sea came true the very next morning, she claimed, when a door-to-door salesman showed up in a purple sweater patterned with little white boats. "The very same purple! Same shape of ship!" Macon only wondered what kind of salesman would wear such clothing.) She believed in horoscopes and tarot cards and Ouija boards. Her magic number was seventeen. In a previous incarnation she'd been a fashion designer, and she swore she could recall at least one of her deaths. ("We think she's passed on," they told the doctor as he entered, and the doctor unwound his muffler.) She was religious in a blurry, non-denominational way and had no doubt whatsoever that God was looking after her personally—ironic, it seemed to Macon, in view of how she'd had to fight for every little thing she wanted.

He knew all this and yet, finding a folded sheet of paper on the counter, he opened it and devoured her lurching scrawl as if she were a stranger. *Pretzels. Pantyhose. Dentist,* he read. *Pick up Mrs. Arnold's laundry.*

No, not that. Not that.

Then it was three o'clock and Alexander was home from school, letting himself in with a key that he wore on a shoelace around his neck. "Macon?" he'd call tentatively. "Is that you out there?" He was scared of burglars. Macon said, "It's me." Edward leapt up and went running for his ball. "How was your day?" Macon always asked.

"Oh, okay."

But Macon had the feeling that school never went very well for Alexander. He came out of it with his face more pinched than ever, his glasses thick with fingerprints. He reminded Macon of a homework paper that had been erased and rewritten too many times. His clothes, on the other hand, were as neat as when he'd left in the morning. Oh, those clothes! Spotless polo shirts with a restrained brown pinstripe, matching brown trousers gathered bulkily around his waist with a heavy leather belt. Shiny brown shoes. Blinding white socks. Didn't he ever play? Didn't kids have recess anymore?

Macon gave him a snack: milk and cookies. (Alexander drank milk in the afternoons without complaint.) Then he helped him with his schoolwork. It was the simplest sort—arithmetic sums and reading questions. "Why did Joe need the dime? Where was Joe's daddy?"

"Umm . . ." Alexander said. Blue veins pulsed in his temples.

He was not a stupid child but he was limited, Macon felt. Limited. Even his walk was constricted. Even his smile never dared to venture beyond two invisible boundaries in the center of his face. Not that he was smiling now. He was wrinkling his forehead, raising his eyes fearfully to Macon.

"Take your time," Macon told him. "There's no hurry."

"But I can't! I don't know! I don't know!"

"You remember Joe," Macon said patiently.

"I don't think I do!"

Sometimes Macon stuck with it, sometimes he simply dropped it.

After all, Alexander had managed without him up till now, hadn't he? There was a peculiar kind of luxury here: Alexander was not his own child. Macon felt linked to him in all sorts of complicated ways, but not in that inseparable, inevitable way that he'd been linked to Ethan. He could still draw back from Alexander; he could still give up on him. "Oh, well," he could say, "talk it over with your teacher tomorrow." And then his thoughts could wander off again.

The difference was, he realized, that he was not held responsible here. It was a great relief to know that.

When Muriel came home she brought fresh air and bustle and excitement. "Is it ever cold! Is it ever windy! Radio says three below zero tonight. Edward, down, this minute. Who wants lemon pie for dessert? Here's what happened: I had to go shopping for Mrs. Quick. First I had to buy linens for her daughter who's getting married, then I had to take them back because they were all the wrong color, her daughter didn't want pastel but white and told her mother plain as day, she said . . . and then I had to pick up pastries for the bridesmaids' party and when Mrs. Quick sees the lemon pie she says, 'Oh, no, not lemon! Not that tacky lemon that always tastes like Kool-Aid!' I'm like, 'Mrs. Quick, you don't have any business telling me what is tacky. This is a fresh-baked, lemon meringue pie without a trace of artificial . . .' So anyway, to make a long story short, she said to take it home to my little boy. 'Well, for your information I'm certain he can't eat it,' I say. 'Chances are he's allergic.' But I took it."

She ranged around the kitchen putting together a supper—BLTs, usually, and vegetables from a can. Sometimes things were not where she expected (Macon's doing—he couldn't resist reorganizing), but she adapted cheerfully. While the bacon sputtered in the skillet she usually phoned her mother and went over all she'd just told Macon and Alexander. "But the daughter wanted white and . . . 'Oh, not that tacky lemon pie!' she says . . ."

If Mrs. Dugan couldn't come to the phone (which was often the case), Muriel talked to Claire instead. Evidently Claire was having troubles at home. "Tell them!" Muriel counseled her. "Just tell them! Tell them you won't stand for it." Cradling the receiver against her shoulder, she opened a drawer and took out knives and forks. "Why should they have to know every little thing you do? It doesn't *matter* that you're not up to anything, Claire. Tell them, 'I'm seventeen years old and it's none of your affair anymore if I'm up to anything or not. I'm just about a grown woman,' tell them."

But later, if Mrs. Dugan finally came to the phone, Muriel herself sounded like a child. "Ma? What kept you? You can't say a couple of words to your daughter just because your favorite song is playing on the radio? 'Lara's Theme' is more important than flesh and blood?"

Even after Muriel hung up, she seldom really focused on dinner.

Her girlfriend might drop by and stay to watch them eat—a fat young woman named Bernice who worked for the Gas and Electric Company. Or neighbors would knock on the kitchen door and walk right in. "Muriel, do you happen to have a coupon for support hose? Young and slim as *you* are, I know you wouldn't need it yourself." "Muriel, Saturday morning I got to go to the clinic for my teeth, any chance of you giving me a lift?" Muriel was an oddity on this street—a woman with a car of her own—and they knew by heart her elaborate arrangement with the boy who did her repairs. Sundays, when Dominick had the car all day, nobody troubled her; but as soon as Monday rolled around they'd be lining up with their requests. "Doctor wants me to come in and show him my . . ." "I promised I'd take my kids to the . . ."

If Muriel couldn't do it, they never thought to ask Macon instead. Macon was still an outsider; they shot him quick glances but pretended not to notice he was listening. Even Bernice was bashful with him, and she avoided using his name.

By the time the lottery number was announced on TV, everyone would have left. That was what mattered here, Macon had discovered: the television schedule. The news could be missed but the lottery drawing could not; nor could "Evening Magazine" or any of the action shows that followed. Alexander watched these shows but Muriel didn't, although she claimed to. She sat on the couch in front of the set and talked, or painted her nails, or read some article or other. "Look here! 'How to Increase Your Bustline.' "

"You don't want to increase your bustline," Macon told her.

" 'Thicker, More Luxurious Eyelashes in Just Sixty Days.' "

"You don't want thicker eyelashes."

He felt content with everything exactly the way it was. He seemed to be suspended, his life on hold.

And later, taking Edward for his final outing, he liked the feeling of the neighborhood at night. This far downtown the sky was too pale for stars; it was pearly and opaque. The buildings were muffled dark shapes. Faint sounds threaded out of them—music, rifle shots, the whinnying of horses. Macon looked up at Alexander's window and saw Muriel unfolding a blanket, as delicate and distinct as a silhouette cut from black paper.

One Wednesday there was a heavy snowstorm, starting in the morning and continuing through the day. Snow fell in clumps like white woolen mittens. It wiped out the dirty tatters of snow from earlier storms; it softened the street's harsh angles and hid the trash cans under cottony domes. Even the women who swept their stoops hourly could not keep pace with it, and toward evening they gave up and went inside. All night the city glowed lilac. It was absolutely silent.

The next morning, Macon woke late. Muriel's side of the bed was empty, but her radio was still playing. A tired-sounding announcer was reading out cancellations. Schools were closed, factories were closed, Meals on Wheels was not running. Macon was impressed by the number of activities that people had been planning for just this one day—the luncheons and lectures and protest meetings. What energy, what spirit! He felt almost proud, though he hadn't been going to attend any of these affairs himself.

Then he realized he was hearing voices downstairs. Alexander must be awake, and here he was, trapped in Muriel's bedroom.

He dressed stealthily, making sure the coast was clear before crossing the hall to the bathroom. He tried not to creak the floorboards as he descended the stairs. The living room was unnaturally bright, reflecting the snow outside. The couch was opened, a mass of sheets and blankets; Claire had slept over the last few nights. Macon followed the voices into the kitchen. He found Alexander eating pancakes, Claire at the stove making more, Muriel curled in her usual morning gloom above her coffee cup. Just inside the back door Bernice stood dripping snow, swathed in various enormous plaids. "So anyhow," Claire was telling Bernice, "Ma says, 'Claire, who was that boy you drove up with?' I said, 'That was no boy, that was Josie Tapp with her new punk haircut,' and Ma says, 'Expect me to believe a cock-and-bull story like that!' So I say, 'I've had enough of this! Grillings! Curfews! Suspicions!' And I leave and catch a bus down here."

"They're just worried you'll turn out like Muriel did," Bernice told her.

"But Josie Tapp! I mean God Almighty!"

There was a general shifting motion in Macon's direction. Claire said, "Hey there, Macon. Want some pancakes?"

"Just a glass of milk, thanks."

"They're nice and hot."

"Macon thinks sugar on an empty stomach causes ulcers," Muriel said. She wrapped both hands around her cup.

Bernice said, "Well, *I'm* not saying no," and she crossed the kitchen to pull out a chair. Her boots left pads of snow with each step. Edward toddled after her, licking them up. "You and me ought to build a snowman," Bernice told Alexander. "Snow must be four feet deep out there."

"Have the streets been cleared?" Macon asked.

"Are you kidding?"

"They couldn't even get through with the newspaper," Alexander told him. "Edward's about to lose his mind wondering where it's got to."

"And there's cars abandoned all over the city. Radio says nobody's going anywhere at all."

But Bernice had hardly spoken when Edward wheeled toward the back door and started barking. A figure loomed outside. "Who's that?" Bernice asked.

Muriel tapped her foot at Edward. He lay down but kept on barking, and Macon opened the door. He found himself face to face with his brother Charles—unusually rugged-looking in a visored cap with ear-flaps. "Charles?" Macon said. "What are you doing here?"

Charles stepped in, bringing with him the fresh, expectant smell of new snow. Edward's yelps changed to welcoming whines. "I came to pick you up," Charles said. "Couldn't reach you on the phone."

"Pick me up for what?"

"Your neighbor Garner Bolt called and said pipes or something have burst in your house, water all over everything. I've been trying to get you since early morning but your line was always busy."

"That was me," Claire said, setting down a platter of pancakes. "I took the receiver off the hook so my folks wouldn't call me up and nag me."

"This is Muriel's sister, Claire," Macon said, "and that's Alexander and that's Bernice Tilghman. My brother Charles."

Charles looked confused.

Come to think of it, this wasn't an easy group to sort out. Claire was her usual mingled self—rosebud bathrobe over faded jeans, fringed moccasin boots that laced to her knees. Bernice could have been a lumberjack. Alexander was neat and polished, while Muriel in her slinky silk robe was barely decent. Also, the kitchen was so small that there seemed to be more people than there actually were. And Claire was waving her spatula, spangling the air with drops of grease. "Pancakes?" she asked Charles. "Orange juice? Coffee?"

"No, thank you," Charles said. "I really have to be—"

"I bet you want milk," Muriel said. She got to her feet, fortunately remembering to clutch her robe together. "I bet you don't want sugar on an empty stomach."

"No, really I—"

"It won't be any trouble!" She was taking the carton from the refrigerator. "How'd you get here, anyways?"

"I drove."

"I thought the streets were blocked."

"They weren't so bad," Charles said, accepting a glass of milk. "*Finding* the place was the hard part." He told Macon, "I looked it up on the map but evidently I was mizzled."

"Mizzled?" Muriel asked.

"He was misled," Macon explained. "What did Garner say, exactly, Charles?"

"He said he saw water running down the inside of your living room window. He looked in and saw the ceiling dripping. Could have been that way for weeks, he said; you know that cold spell we had over Christmas."

"Doesn't sound good," Macon said.

He went to the closet for his coat. When he came back, Muriel was saying, "Now that you don't have an empty stomach, Charles, won't you try some of Claire's pancakes?"

"I've had half a dozen," Bernice told him. "They don't call me Big-Ass Bernice for nothing."

Charles said, "Uh, well—" and gave Macon a helpless look.

"We have to be going," Macon told the others. "Charles, are you parked in back?"

"No, in front. Then I went around back because I couldn't get the doorbell to work."

There was a reserved, disapproving note in Charles's voice when he said this, but Macon just said airily, "Oh, yes! Place is a wreck." He led the way toward the front of the house. He felt like someone demonstrating how well he got on with the natives.

They pushed open the door with some difficulty and floundered down steps so deeply buried that both men more or less fell the length of them, trusting that they would be cushioned. The sunlight sparked and flashed. They waded toward the street, Macon's shoes quickly filling with snow—a refreshing sharpness that almost instantly turned painful.

"I guess we'd better take both cars," he told Charles.

"How come?"

"Well, you don't want to have to drive all the way back down here."

"But if we take just one, then one of us can drive and one can push if we get stuck."

"Let's take mine, then."

"But mine's already cleared and dug out."

"But with mine I could drop you off home and save you the trip back down."

"But that leaves my car stranded on Singleton Street."

"We could get it to you after they plowed."

"And *my* car has its engine warmed!" Charles said.

Was this how they had sounded, all these years? Macon gave a short laugh, but Charles waited intently for his answer. "Fine, we'll take yours," Macon told him. They climbed into Charles's VW.

It was true there were a lot of abandoned cars. They sat in no particular pattern, featureless white mounds turned this way and that, so the street resembled a river of drifting boats. Charles dodged expertly between them. He kept a slow, steady speed and talked about Rose's wedding. "We told her April was too iffy. Better wait, we told her, if she's so set on an outdoor service. But Rose said no, she'll take her chances. She's sure the weather will be perfect."

A snow-covered jeep in front of them, the only moving vehicle they'd yet encountered, suddenly slurred to one side. Charles passed it smoothly in a long, shallow arc. Macon said, "Where will they live, anyhow?"

"Why, at Julian's, I suppose."

"In a singles building?"

"No, he's got another place now, an apartment near the Belvedere."

"I see," Macon said. But he had trouble picturing Rose in an apartment—or anywhere, for that matter, if it wasn't her grandparents' house with its egg-and-dart moldings and heavily draped windows.

All through the city people were digging out—tunneling toward their parked cars, scraping off their windshields, shoveling sidewalks. There was something holidaylike about them; they waved to each other and called back and forth. One man, having cleared not only his walk but a section of the street as well, was doing a little soft-shoe dance on the wet concrete, and when Charles and Macon drove through he stopped to shout, "What are you, crazy? Traveling around in this?"

"I must say you're remarkably calm in view of the situation," Charles told Macon.

"What situation?"

"Your house, I mean. Water pouring through the ceiling for who knows how long."

"Oh, that," Macon said. Yes, at one time he'd have been very upset about that.

By now they were high on North Charles Street, which the plows had already cleared. Macon was struck by the spaciousness here—the buildings set far apart, wide lawns sloping between them. He had never noticed that before. He sat forward to gaze at the side streets. They were still completely white. And just a few blocks over, when Charles turned into Macon's neighborhood, they saw a young girl on skis.

His house looked the same as ever, though slightly dingy in comparison with the snow. They sat in the car a moment studying it, and then Macon said, "Well, here goes, I guess," and they climbed out. They could see where Garner Bolt had waded through the yard; they saw the scalloping of footprints where he'd stepped closer to peer in a window. But the sidewalk bore no tracks at all, and Macon found it difficult in his smooth-soled shoes.

The instant he unlocked the door, they heard the water. The living room was filled with a cool, steady, dripping sound, like a greenhouse after the plants have been sprayed. Charles, who was the first to enter, said, "Oh, my God." Macon stopped dead in the hallway behind him.

Apparently an upstairs pipe (in that cold little bathroom off Ethan's old room, Macon would bet) had frozen and burst, heaven only knew how long ago, and the water had run and run until it saturated the ceiling and started coming through the plaster. All over the room it was raining. Chunks of plaster had fallen on the furniture, turning it white and splotchy. The floorboards were mottled. The rug, when Macon stepped on it, squelched beneath his feet. He marveled at the thoroughness of the destruction; not a detail had been overlooked. Every ashtray was full of wet flakes and every magazine was sodden. There was a gray smell rising from the upholstery.

"What are you going to *do?*" Charles breathed.

Macon pulled himself together. "Why, turn off the water main, of course," he said.

"But your living room!"

Macon didn't answer. His living room was . . . appropriate, was what he wanted to say. Even more appropriate if it had been washed away entirely. (He imagined the house under twelve feet of water, uncannily clear, like a castle at the bottom of a goldfish bowl.)

He went down to the basement and shut off the valve, and then he checked the laundry sink. It was dry. Ordinarily he let the tap run all winter long, a slender stream to keep the pipes from freezing, but this year he hadn't thought of it and neither had his brothers, evidently, when they came to light the furnace.

"Oh, this is terrible, just terrible," Charles was saying when Macon came back upstairs. But he was in the kitchen now, where there wasn't any problem. He was opening and shutting cabinet doors. "Terrible. Terrible."

Macon had no idea what he was going on about. He said, "Just let me find my boots and we can leave."

"Leave?"

He thought his boots must be in his closet. He went upstairs to the bedroom. Everything here was so dreary—the naked mattress with its body bag, the dusty mirror, the brittle yellow newspaper folded on the nightstand. He bent to root through the objects on the closet floor. There were his boots, all right, along with some wire hangers and a little booklet of some sort. *A Gardener's Diary, 1976.* He flipped through it. *First lawn-mowing of the spring,* Sarah had written in her compact script. *Forsythia still in bloom.* Macon closed the diary and smoothed the cover and laid it aside.

Boots in hand, he went back downstairs. Charles had returned to the living room; he was wringing out cushions. "Never mind those," Macon said. "They'll just get wet again."

"Will your insurance cover this?"

"I suppose so."

"What would they call it? Flood damage? Weather damage?"

"I don't know. Let's get going."

"You should phone our contractor, Macon. Remember the man who took care of our porch?"

"Nobody lives here anyhow," Macon said.

Charles straightened, still holding a cushion. "What's that supposed to mean?" he asked.

"Mean?"

"Are you saying you'll just let this stay?"

"Probably," Macon told him.

"All soaked and ruined? Nothing done?"

"Oh, well," Macon said, waving a hand. "Come along, Charles."

But Charles hung back, still gazing around the living room. "Terrible. Even the curtains are dripping. Sarah will feel just terrible."

"I doubt she'll give it a thought," Macon said.

He paused on the porch to pull his boots on. They were old and stiff, the kind with metal clasps. He tucked his wet trouser cuffs inside them and then led the way to the street.

Once they were settled in the car, Charles didn't start the engine but sat there, key in hand, and looked soberly at Macon. "I think it's time we had a talk," he said.

"What about?"

"I'd like to know what you think you're up to with this Muriel person."

"Is that what you call her? 'This Muriel person'?"

"No one else will tell you," Charles said. "They say it's none of their business. But I can't just stand by and watch, Macon. I have to say what I think. How old are you—forty-two? Forty-three now? And she is . . . but more than that, she's not your type of woman."

"You don't even know her!"

"I know her type."

"I have to be getting home now, Charles."

Charles looked down at his key. Then he started the car and pulled into the street, but he didn't drop the subject. "She's some kind of symptom, Macon! You're not yourself these days and this Muriel person's a symptom. Everybody says so."

"I'm more myself than I've been my whole life long," Macon told him.

"What kind of remark is that? It doesn't even make sense!"

"And who is 'everybody,' anyway?"

"Why, Porter, Rose, me . . ."

"All such experts."

"We're just worried for you, Macon."

"Could we switch to some other topic?"

"I had to tell you what I thought," Charles said.

"Well, fine. You've told me."

But Charles didn't look satisfied.

The car wallowed back through the slush, with ribbons of bright water trickling down the windshield from the roof. Then out on the main road, it picked up speed. "Hate to think what all that salt is doing to your underbody," Macon said.

Charles said, "I never told you this before, but it's my opinion sex is overrated."

Macon looked at him.

"Oh, when I was in my teens I was as interested as anyone," Charles said. "I mean it occupied my thoughts for every waking moment and all that. But that was just the *idea* of sex, you know? Somehow, the real thing was less . . . I don't mean I'm opposed to it, but it's just not all I expected. For one thing, it's rather messy. And then the weather is such a problem."

"Weather," Macon said.

"When it's cold you hate to take your clothes off. When it's hot you're both so sticky. And in Baltimore, it does always seem to be either too cold or too hot."

"Maybe you ought to consider a change of climate," Macon said. He was beginning to enjoy himself. "Do you suppose anyone's done a survey? City by city? Maybe the Businessman's Press could put out some sort of pamphlet."

"And besides it often leads to children," Charles said. "I never really cared much for children. They strike me as disruptive."

"Well, if that's why you brought this up, forget it," Macon said. "Muriel can't have any more."

Charles gave a little cough. "That's good to hear," he said, "but it's not why I brought it up. I believe what I was trying to say is, I just don't think sex is important enough to ruin your life for."

"So? Who's ruining his life?"

"Macon, face it. She's not worth it."

"How can you possibly know that?"

"Can you tell me one unique thing about her?" Charles asked. "I mean one really special quality, Macon, not something sloppy like 'She appreciates me' or 'She listens . . .' "

She looks out hospital windows and imagines how the Martians would see us, Macon wanted to say. But Charles wouldn't understand that, so instead he said, "I'm not such a bargain myself, in case you haven't noticed. I'm kind of, you could say, damaged merchandise. Somebody ought to warn *her* away from *me*, when you get right down to it."

"That's not true. That's not true at all. As a matter of fact, I imagine her people are congratulating her on her catch."

"Her catch!"

"Someone to support her. Anyone," Charles said. "She'd be lucky to find anyone. Why, she doesn't even speak proper English! She lives in that slummy house, she dresses like some kind of bag lady, she's got that little boy who appears to have hookworm or something—"

"Charles, just shut the hell up," Macon said.

Charles closed his mouth.

They had reached Muriel's neighborhood by now. They were driving past the stationery factory with its tangled wire fence like old bedsprings. Charles took a wrong turn. "Let's see, now," he said, "where do I . . ."

Macon didn't offer to help.

"Am I heading in the right direction? Or not. Somehow I don't seem to . . ."

They were two short blocks from Singleton Street, but Macon hoped Charles would drive in circles forever. "Lots of luck," he said, and he opened the door and hopped out.

"Macon?"

Macon waved and ducked down an alley.

Freedom! Sunlight glinting off blinding white drifts, and children riding sleds and TV trays. Cleared parking spaces guarded with lawn chairs. Throngs of hopeful boys with shovels. And then Muriel's house with its walk still deep in snow, its small rooms smelling of pancakes, its cozy mix of women lounging about in the kitchen. They were drinking cocoa now. Bernice was braiding Claire's hair. Alexander was painting a picture. Muriel kissed Macon hello and squealed at his cold cheeks. "Come in and get warm! Have some cocoa! Look at Alexander's picture," she said. "Don't you love it? Isn't he something? He's a regular da Vinci."

"Leonardo," Macon said.

"What?"

"Not da Vinci. For God's sake. It's Leonardo," he told her. Then he stamped upstairs to change out of his clammy trousers.

15

I'm sorry I'm so fat," Macon's seatmate said.

Macon said, "Oh, er, ah—"

"I know I'm using more than my share of space," the man told him. "Do you think I'm not aware of that? Every trip I take, I have to ask the stewardess for a seatbelt extender. I have to balance my lunch on my knees because the tray can't unfold in front of me. Really I ought to purchase two seats but I'm not a wealthy man. I ought to purchase two tickets and not spread all over my fellow passengers."

"Oh, you're not spreading all over me," Macon said.

This was because he was very nearly sitting in the aisle, with his knees jutting out to the side so that every passing stewardess ruffled

the pages of *Miss MacIntosh*. But he couldn't help feeling touched by
the man's great, shiny, despairing face, which was as round as a baby's.
"Name's Lucas Loomis," the man said, holding out a hand. When
Macon shook it, he was reminded of risen bread dough.

"Macon Leary," Macon told him.

"The stupid thing is," Lucas Loomis said, "I travel for a living."

"Do you."

"I demonstrate software to computer stores. I'm sitting in an airplane
seat six days out of seven sometimes."

"Well, none of us finds them all that roomy," Macon said.

"What do you do, Mr. Leary?"

"I write guidebooks," Macon said.

"Is that so? What kind?"

"Oh, guides for businessmen. People just like you, I guess."

"*Accidental Tourist*," Mr. Loomis said instantly.

"Why, yes."

"Really? Am I right? Well, what do you know," Mr. Loomis said.
"Look at this." He took hold of his own lapels, which sat so far in
front of him that his arms seemed too short to reach them. "Gray suit,"
he told Macon. "Just what you recommend. Appropriate for all occasions." He pointed to the bag at his feet. "See my luggage? Carry-on.
Change of underwear, clean shirt, packet of detergent powder."

"Well, good," Macon said. This had never happened to him before.

"You're my hero!" Mr. Loomis told him. "You've improved my
trips a hundred percent. You're the one who told me about those
springy items that turn into clotheslines."

"Oh, well, you could have run across those in any drug store,"
Macon said.

"I've stopped relying on hotel laundries; I hardly need to venture
into the streets anymore. I tell my wife, I say, you just ask her, I tell
her often, I say, 'Going with the *Accidental Tourist* is like going in a
capsule, a cocoon. Don't forget to pack my *Accidental Tourist!*' I tell
her."

"Well, this is very nice to hear," Macon said.

"Times I've flown clear to Oregon and hardly knew I'd left Baltimore."

"Excellent."

There was a pause.

"Although," Macon said, "lately I've been wondering."

Mr. Loomis had to turn his entire body to look at him, like someone
encased in a hooded parka.

"I mean," Macon said, "I've been out along the West Coast. Updating my U.S. edition. And of course I've covered the West Coast
before, Los Angeles and all that; Lord, yes, I knew the place as a child;
but this was the first I'd seen of San Francisco. My publisher wanted

me to add it in. Have you been to San Francisco?"

"That's where we just now got on the plane," Mr. Loomis reminded him.

"San Francisco is certainly, um, beautiful," Macon said.

Mr. Loomis thought that over.

"Well, so is Baltimore too, of course," Macon said hastily. "Oh, no place on earth like Baltimore! But San Francisco, well, I mean it struck me as, I don't know . . ."

"I was born and raised in Baltimore, myself," Mr. Loomis said. "Wouldn't live anywhere else for the world."

"No, of course not," Macon said. "I just meant—"

"Couldn't pay me to leave it."

"No, me either."

"You a Baltimore man?"

"Yes, certainly."

"No place like it."

"Certainly isn't," Macon said.

But a picture came to his mind of San Francisco floating on mist like the Emerald City, viewed from one of those streets so high and steep that you really could hang your head over and hear the wind blow.

He'd left Baltimore on a sleety day with ice coating the airport runways, and he hadn't been gone all that long; but when he returned it was spring. The sun was shining and the trees were tipped with green. It was still fairly cool but he drove with his windows down. The breeze smelled exactly like Vouvray—flowery, with a hint of mothballs underneath.

On Singleton Street, crocuses were poking through the hard squares of dirt in front of basement windows. Rugs and bedspreads flapped in backyards. A whole cache of babies had surfaced. They cruised imperiously in their strollers, propelled by their mothers or by pairs of grandmothers. Old people sat out on the sidewalk in beach chairs and wheelchairs, and groups of men stood about on corners, their hands in their pockets and their posture elaborately casual—the unemployed, Macon imagined, emerging from the darkened living rooms where they'd spent the winter watching TV. He caught snatches of their conversation:

"What's going down, man?"

"Nothing much."

"What you been up to?"

"Not a whole lot."

He parked in front of Muriel's house, where Dominick Saddler was working on Muriel's car. The hood was open and Dominick was deep in its innards; all Macon saw was his jeans and his gigantic, ragged sneakers, a band of bare flesh showing above his cowhide belt. On either side of him stood the Butler twins, talking away a mile a minute. "So she says to us we're grounded—"

"Can't go out with no one till Friday—"

"Takes away our fake i.d.'s—"

"We march upstairs and slam our bedroom door, like, just a little slam to let her know what we think of her—"

"And up she comes with a screwdriver and takes our door off its hinges!"

"Hmm," Dominick said.

Macon rested his bag on the hood and peered down into the engine. "Car acting up again?" he asked.

The Butler twins said, "Hey there, Macon," and Dominick straightened and wiped his forehead with the back of his hand. He was a dark, good-looking boy whose bulging muscles made Macon feel inadequate. "Damn thing keeps stalling out," he said.

"How'd Muriel get to work?"

"Had to take the bus."

Macon was hoping to hear she'd stayed home.

He climbed the steps and unlocked the front door. Just inside, Edward greeted him, squeaking and doing back flips and trying to hold still long enough to be petted. Macon walked through the rest of the house. Clearly, everyone had left in a hurry. The sofa was opened out. (Claire must have had another fight with her folks.) The kitchen table was littered with dishes and no one had put the cream away. Macon did that. Then he took his bag upstairs. Muriel's bed was unmade and her robe was slung across a chair. There was a snarl of hair in the pin tray on her bureau. He picked it up between thumb and index finger and dropped it into the wastebasket. It occurred to him (not for the first time) that the world was divided sharply down the middle: Some lived careful lives and some lived careless lives, and everything that happened could be explained by the difference between them. But he could not have said, not in a million years, why he was so moved by the sight of Muriel's thin quilt trailing across the floor where she must have dragged it when she rose in the morning.

It wasn't quite time for Alexander to come home from school, so he thought he would walk the dog. He put Edward on his leash and let himself out the front door. When he passed the Butler twins again they said, "Hey, there, Macon," singsong as ever, while Dominick cursed and reached for a wrench.

The men standing on the corner were discussing a rumor of jobs in Texas. Someone's brother-in-law had found work there. Macon passed with his head lowered, feeling uncomfortably privileged. He skirted a welcome mat that had been scrubbed and set out to dry on the pavement. The women here took spring cleaning seriously, he saw. They shook their dust mops out of upstairs windows; they sat on their sills to polish the panes with crumpled sheets of newspapers. They staggered between houses with borrowed vacuum cleaners, rug machines, and gallon jugs of upholstery shampoo. Macon rounded the block and started home, having paused to let Edward pee against a maple sapling.

Just as he was approaching Singleton Street, whom should he see but Alexander scurrying up ahead. There was no mistaking that stiff little figure with the clumsy backpack. "Wait!" Alexander was crying. "Wait for me!" The Ebbetts children, some distance away, turned and called something back. Macon couldn't hear what they said but he knew the tone, all right—that high, mocking chant. "Nyah-nyah-nyah-NYAH-nyah!" Alexander started running, stumbling over his own shoes. Behind him came another group, two older boys and a girl with red hair, and they began jeering too. Alexander wheeled and looked at them. His face was somehow smaller than usual. "Go," Macon told Edward, and he dropped the leash. Edward didn't need any urging. His ears had perked at the sound of Alexander's voice, and now he hurtled after him. The three older children scattered as he flew through them, barking. He drew up short in front of Alexander, and Alexander knelt to hug his neck.

When Macon arrived, he said, "Are you all right?"

Alexander nodded and got to his feet.

"What was that all about?" Macon asked him.

Alexander said, "Nothing."

But when they started walking again, he slipped his hand into Macon's.

Those cool little fingers were so distinct, so particular, so full of character. Macon tightened his grip and felt a pleasant kind of sorrow sweeping through him. Oh, his life had regained all its old perils. He was forced to worry once again about nuclear war and the future of the planet. He often had the same secret, guilty thought that had come to him after Ethan was born: *From this time on I can never be completely happy.*

Not that he was before, of course.

Macon's U.S. edition was going to be five separate pamphlets now, divided geographically, slipcased together so you had to buy all five even if you needed only one. Macon thought this was immoral. He said so when Julian stopped by for the West Coast material. "What's immoral about it?" Julian asked. He wasn't really paying attention; Macon could see that. He was filing mental notes on Muriel's household, no doubt the real purpose of this unannounced, unnecessary visit. Even though he'd already collected his material, he was wandering around the living room in an abstracted way, first examining a framed school photo of Alexander and then a beaded moccasin that Claire had left on the couch. It was Saturday and the others were in the kitchen, but

Macon had no intention of letting Julian meet them.

"It's always immoral to force a person to buy something he doesn't want," Macon said. "If he only wants the Midwest, he shouldn't have to buy New England too, for heaven's sake."

Julian said, "Is that your friend I hear out there? Is it Muriel?"

"Yes, I suppose it is," Macon said.

"Aren't you going to introduce us?"

"She's busy."

"I'd really like to meet her."

"Why? Hasn't Rose given you a full report?"

"Macon," Julian said, "I'm soon going to be a relative of yours."

"Ah, God."

"It's only natural I'm interested in knowing her."

Macon said nothing.

"Besides," Julian told him, "I want to invite her to the wedding."

"You do?"

"So can I talk to her?"

"Oh. Well. I guess so."

Macon led the way to the kitchen. He felt he'd made a mistake— that having acted so thorny, he'd caused this meeting to seem more important than it was. But Julian, as it happened, was breezy and offhand. "Hello, ladies," he said.

They looked up—Muriel, Claire, and Bernice, seated around a sheaf of notebook paper. Macon reeled their names off rapidly but got stuck on Julian's. "Julian, ah, Edge, my . . ."

"Future brother-in-law," Julian said.

"My boss."

"I've come to invite you to the wedding, Muriel. Also your little boy, if—where's your little boy?"

"He's out walking the dog," Muriel said. "But he's not too good in churches."

"This'll be a garden wedding."

"Well, maybe, then, I don't know . . ."

Muriel was wearing what she called her "paratrooper look"—a coverall from Sunny's Surplus—and her hair was concealed beneath a wildly patterned silk turban. A ballpoint pen mark slashed across one cheekbone. "We're entering this contest," she told Julian. "Write a country-music song and win a trip for two to Nashville. We're working on it all together. We're going to call it 'Happier Days.' "

"Hasn't that already been written?"

"Oh, I hope not. You know how they always have these photographs of couples in magazines? 'Mick Jagger and Bianca, in happier days.' 'Richard Burton and Liz Taylor, in—' "

"Yes, I get it."

"So this man is talking about his ex-wife. 'I knew her in another time and place . . .' "

She sang it right out, in her thin, scratchy voice that gave a sense of distance, like a used-up phonograph record:

> When we kissed in the rain,
> When we shared every pain,
> When we both enjoyed happier days.

"Very catchy," Julian said, "but I don't know about 'shared every pain.' "

"What's wrong with it?"

"I mean, in happier days they had pain?"

"He's right," Bernice told Muriel.

"Rain, brain, drain," Julian reflected. " 'When our lives were more sane,' 'When we used to raise Cain . . .' "

"Let it be, why don't you," Macon told him.

" 'When I hadn't met Jane,' 'When she didn't know Wayne . . .' "

"Wait!" Bernice said, scribbling furiously.

"I may have tapped some hidden talent here," Julian told Macon.

"I'll see you to the door," Macon said.

" 'When our love had no stain,' 'When she wasn't inane . . .' " Julian said, trailing Macon through the living room. "Don't forget the wedding!" he called back. He told Macon, "If she wins, you could cover Nashville free for your next U.S. edition."

"I think she's planning on taking Bernice," Macon told him.

" 'When we guzzled champagne . . .' " Julian mused.

"I'll be in touch," Macon said, "as soon as I start on the Canada guide."

"Canada! Aren't you coming to the wedding?"

"Well, that too, of course," Macon said, opening the door.

"Wait a minute, Macon. What's your hurry? Wait, I want to show you something."

Julian set down the West Coast material to search his pockets. He pulled out a shiny, colored advertisement. "Hawaii," he said.

"Well, I certainly see no point in covering—"

"Not for you; for me! For our honeymoon. I'm taking Rose."

"Oh, I see."

"Look," Julian said. He unfolded the ad. It turned out to be a map—one of those useless maps that Macon detested, with outsized, whimsical drawings of pineapples, palm trees, and hula dancers crowding the apple-green islands. "I got this from The Travel People Incorporated. Have you heard of them? Are they reliable? They suggested a hotel over here on . . ." He drew a forefinger across the page, hunting down the hotel.

"I know nothing at all about Hawaii," Macon said.

"Somewhere here . . ." Julian said. Then he gave up, perhaps just at that moment hearing what Macon had told him, and refolded the map. "She may be exactly what you need," he said.

"Pardon?"

"This Muriel person."

"Why does everyone call her—"

"She's not so bad! I don't think your family understands how you're feeling."

"No, they don't. They really don't," Macon said. He was surprised that it was Julian, of all people, who saw that.

Although Julian's parting words were, " 'When we stuffed on chow mein . . .' "

Macon shut the door firmly behind him.

He decided to buy Alexander some different clothes. "How would you like some blue jeans?" he asked. "How would you like some work shirts? How would you like a cowboy belt with 'Budweiser Beer' on the buckle?"

"You serious?"

"Would you wear that kind of thing?"

"Yes! I would! I promise!"

"Then let's go shopping."

"Is Mama coming?"

"We'll surprise her."

Alexander put on his spring jacket—a navy polyester blazer that Muriel had just paid a small fortune for. Macon didn't know if she would approve of jeans, which was why he'd waited till she was off buying curtains for a woman in Guilford.

The store he drove to was a Western-wear place where he used to take Ethan. It hadn't changed a bit. Its wooden floorboards creaked, its aisles smelled of leather and new denim. He steered Alexander to the boys' department, where he spun a rack of shirts. How many times had he done this before? It wasn't even painful. Only disorienting, in a way, to see that everything continued no matter what. The student jeans were still stacked according to waist and inseam. The horsey tie pins were still arrayed behind glass. Ethan was dead and gone but Macon was still holding up shirts and asking, "This one? This one? This one?"

"What I'd really like is T-shirts," Alexander said.

"T-shirts. Ah."

"The kind with a sort of stretched-out neck. And jeans with raggedy bottoms."

"Well, that you have to do for yourself," Macon said. "You have to break them in."

"I don't want to look new."

"Tell you what. Everything we buy, we'll wash about twenty times before you wear it."

"But nothing *pre*washed," Alexander said.

"No, no."

"Only nerds wear prewashed."

"Right."

Alexander chose several T-shirts, purposely too big, along with an assortment of jeans because he wasn't sure of his size. Then he went off to try everything on. "Shall I come with you?" Macon asked.

"I can do it myself."

"Oh. All right."

That was familiar, too.

Alexander disappeared into one of the stalls and Macon went on a tour of the men's department. He tried on a leather cowboy hat but took it off immediately. Then he went back to the stall. "Alexander?"

"Huh?"

"How's it going?"

"Okay."

In the space below the door, Macon saw Alexander's shoes and his trouser cuffs. Evidently he hadn't got around to putting on the jeans yet.

Someone said, "Macon?"

He turned and found a woman in a trim blond pageboy, her wrap skirt printed with little blue whales. "Yes," he said.

"Laurel Canfield. Scott's mother, remember?"

"Of course," Macon said, shaking her hand. Now he caught sight of Scott, who had been in Ethan's class at school—an unexpectedly tall, gawky boy lurking at his mother's elbow with an armload of athletic socks. "Why, Scott. Nice to see you," Macon said.

Scott flushed and said nothing. Laurel Canfield said, "It's nice to see *you*. Are you doing your spring shopping?"

"Oh, well, ah—"

He looked toward the stall. Now Alexander's trousers were slumped around his ankles. "I'm helping the son of a friend," he explained.

"We've just been buying out the sock department."

"Yes, I see you have."

"Seems every other week I find Scott's run through his socks again; you know how they are at this age—"

She stopped herself. She looked horrified. She said, "Or, rather . . ."

"Yes, certainly!" Macon said. "Amazing, isn't it?" He felt so embarrassed for her that he was pleased, at first, to see another familiar face behind her. Then he realized whose it was. There stood his mother-in-law. "Why!" he said. Was she still Mother Sidey? *Mrs.* Sidey? Who, for God's sake?

Luckily, it turned out that Laurel Canfield knew her too. "Paula Sidey," she said. "I haven't seen you since last year's Hunt Cup."

"Yes, I've been away," Mrs. Sidey told her, and then she dropped her lids somewhat, as if drawing a curtain, before saying, "Macon."

"How are you?" Macon said.

She was flawlessly groomed, industriously tended—a blue-haired woman in tailored slacks and a turtleneck. He used to worry that Sarah would age the same way, develop the same brittle carapace, but now he found himself admiring Mrs. Sidey's resolve. "You're looking well," he told her.

"Thank you," she said, touching her hairdo. "I suppose you're here for your spring wardrobe."

"Oh, Macon's helping a friend!" Laurel Canfield caroled. She was so chirpy, all of a sudden, that Macon suspected she'd just now recalled Mrs. Sidey's relationship to him. She looked toward Alexander's stall. Alexander was in his socks now. One sock rose and vanished, stepping into a flood of blue denim. "Isn't shopping for boys so difficult?" she said.

"I wouldn't know," Mrs. Sidey said. "I never had one. I'm here for the denim skirts."

"Oh, the skirts, well, I notice they're offering a—"

"What friend are you helping to buy for?" Mrs. Sidey asked Macon.

Macon didn't know what to tell her. He looked toward the stall. If only Alexander would just stay hidden forever, he thought. How to explain this scrawny little waif, this poor excuse of a child who could never hold a candle to the real child?

Contrary as always, Alexander chose that moment to step forth.

He wore an oversized T-shirt that slipped a bit off one shoulder, as if he'd just emerged from some rough-and-tumble game. His jeans were comfortably baggy. His face, Macon saw, had somehow filled out in the past few weeks without anybody's noticing; and his hair—which Macon had started cutting at home—had lost that shaved prickliness and grown thick and floppy.

"I look *wonderful!*" Alexander said.

Macon turned to the women and said, "Actually, I find shopping for boys is a pleasure."

16

There is no sound more peaceful than rain on the roof, if you're safe asleep in someone else's house. Macon heard the soft pattering; he heard Muriel get up to close a window. She crossed his vision like the gleam of headlights crossing a ceiling, white and slim and watery in a large plain slip from Goodwill Industries. She shut the window and the stillness dropped over him and he went back to sleep.

But in the morning his first thought was, *Oh, no! Rain! On Rose's wedding day!*

He got up, careful not to wake Muriel, and looked out. The sky was bright but flat, the color of oyster shells—not a good sign. The scrawny little dogwood in back was dripping from every twig and bud. Next door, Mr. Butler's ancient heap of scrap lumber had grown several shades darker.

Macon went downstairs, tiptoeing through the living room where Claire lay snoring in a tangle of blankets. He fixed a pot of coffee and then called Rose on the kitchen phone. She answered instantly, wide awake. "Are you moving the wedding indoors?" he asked her.

"We've got too many guests to move it indoors."

"Why? How many are coming?"

"Everyone we've ever known."

"Good grief, Rose."

"Never mind, it will clear."

"But the grass is all wet!"

"Wear galoshes," she told him. She hung up.

Since she'd met Julian she'd grown so airy, Macon thought. So flippant. Lacking in depth.

She was right about the weather, though. By afternoon there was a weak, pale sun. Muriel decided to wear the short-sleeved dress she'd planned on, but maybe with a shawl tossed over her shoulders. She wanted Alexander to put on a suit—he did have one, complete with waistcoat. He protested, though, and so did Macon. "Jeans and a good white shirt. That's plenty," Macon told her.

"Well, if you're sure."

Lately, she'd been deferring to him about Alexander. She had finally given in on the question of sneakers and she'd stopped policing his diet. Contrary to her predictions, Alexander's arches did not fall flat and he was not overtaken by raging eczema. At worst, he suffered a mild skin rash now and then.

The wedding was set for three o'clock. Around two thirty they started out, proceeding self-consciously toward Macon's car. It was a Saturday and no one else in the neighborhood was so dressed up. Mr. Butler was standing on a ladder with a hammer and a sack of nails. Rafe Daggett was taking his van apart. The Indian woman was hosing down a glowing threadbare carpet that she'd spread across the sidewalk, and then she turned off the water and lifted the hem of her sari and stamped around so the carpet radiated little bursts of droplets. Every passing car, it seemed, labored under a top-heavy burden of mattresses and patio furniture, reminding Macon of those ants who scuttle back to their nests with loads four times their own size.

"I think I'm supposed to be the best man," Macon told Muriel after he'd started driving.

"You didn't mention that!"

"And Charles is giving her away."

"It's a real wedding, then," Muriel said, "Not just two people standing up together."

"That's what Rose said she wanted."

"I wouldn't do it like that at all," Muriel said. She glanced toward the rear and said, "Alexander, quit kicking my seat. You're about to drive me crazy. No," she said, facing forward, "if I was to marry, know what I'd do? Never tell a soul. Act like I'd been married for years. Slip off somewheres to a justice of the peace and come back like nothing had happened and make out like I'd been married all along."

"This is Rose's first time, though," Macon told her.

"Yes, but even so, people can say, 'It sure *took* you long enough.' I can hear my mother now; that's what she'd say for certain. 'Sure *took* you long enough. I thought you'd never get around to it,' is what she'd say. If I was ever to marry."

Macon braked for a traffic light.

"If I was ever to decide to marry," Muriel said.

He glanced over at her and was struck by how pretty she looked, with the color high in her cheeks and the splashy shawl flung around her shoulders. Her spike-heeled shoes had narrow, shiny ankle straps. He never could figure out why ankle straps were so seductive.

The first person they saw when they arrived was Macon's mother. For some reason it hadn't occurred to Macon that Alicia would be invited to her daughter's wedding, and when she opened the front door it took him a second to place her. She was looking so different, for one thing. She had dyed her hair a dark tomato red. She wore a long white caftan trimmed with vibrant bands of satin, and when she reached up to hug him a whole culvert of metal bangles clattered and slid down her left arm. "Macon, dear!" she said. She smelled of bruised gardenias. "And who may this be?" she asked, peering past him.

"Oh, um, I'd like you to meet Muriel Pritchett. And Alexander, her son."

"Really?"

A politely inquisitive look remained on her face. Evidently no one had filled her in. (Or else she hadn't bothered to listen.) "Well, since I seem to be the maître d'," she said, "I'll show you out back where the bride and groom are."

"Rose is not in hiding?"

"No, she says she doesn't see the logic in missing her own wedding," Alicia said, leading them toward the rear of the house. "Muriel, have you known Macon long?"

"Oh, kind of."

"He's very stuffy," Alicia said confidingly. "All my children are. They get it from the Leary side."

"I think he's nice," Muriel said.

"Oh, *nice*, yes. All very well and good," Alicia said, throwing Macon a look he couldn't read. She had linked arms with Muriel; she was always so physical. The trim on her caftan nearly matched Muriel's shawl. Macon had a sudden appalling thought: Maybe in his middle age he was starting to choose his mother's style of person, as if concluding that Alicia—silly, vain, annoying woman—might have the right answers after all. But no. He put the thought away from him. And Muriel slipped free of Alicia's arm. "Alexander? Coming?" she asked.

They stepped through the double doors of the sun porch. The backyard was full of pastels—Rose's old ladies in pale dresses, daffodils set everywhere in buckets, forsythia in full bloom along the alley. Dr. Grauer, Rose's minister, stepped forward and shook Macon's hand. "Aha! The best man," he said, and behind him came Julian in black—not his color. His nose was peeling. It must be boating season again. He put a gold ring in Macon's palm and said, "Like for you to have this." For a moment Macon imagined he was really meant to *have* it. Then he said, "Oh, yes, the ring," and dropped it in his pocket.

"I can't believe I'm finally getting a son-in-law," Alicia told Julian. "All I've ever had is daughter-in-laws."

"Daughters," Macon said automatically.

"No, daughter-in-laws."

"*Daughters*-in-law, Mother."

"And didn't manage to keep them long, either," Alicia said.

When Macon was small, he used to worry that his mother was teaching him the wrong names for things. "They call this corduroy," she'd said, buttoning his new coat, and he had thought, *But do they really?* Funny word, in fact, corduroy. Very suspicious. How could he be sure that other people weren't speaking a whole different language out there? He'd examined his mother distrustfully—her foolish fluff of curls and her flickery, unsteady eyes.

Now here came Porter's children, the three of them sticking close together; and behind them June, their mother. Wasn't it unusual to invite your brother's ex-wife to your wedding? Particularly when she was big as a barn with another man's baby. But she seemed to be enjoying herself. She pecked Macon on the cheek and cocked her head appraisingly at Muriel. "Kids, this is Alexander," Macon said. He was hoping against hope that they'd all just fall in together somehow and be friends, which of course didn't happen. Porter's children eyed Alexander sullenly and said nothing. Alexander knotted his fists in his pockets. June told Julian, "Your bride is looking just radiant," and Julian said, "Yes, isn't she," but when Macon located Rose he thought she looked tense and frayed, as most brides do if people would only admit it. She wore a white dress, mid-calf length but very simple, and a little puff of lace or net or something on her head. She was talking to their hardware man. And yes, there was the girl who cashed their checks at the Mercantile Bank, and over next to Charles was the family dentist. Macon thought of *Mary Poppins*—those late-night adventures he used to read to Ethan, where all the tradespeople showed up behaving nothing like their daytime selves.

"I'm not sure if there's been any research on this," Charles was telling the dentist, "but have you ever tried polishing your teeth with a T-shirt after flossing?"

"Er . . ."

"A plain cotton T-shirt. One hundred percent cotton. I think you're going to be impressed when I have my next checkup. See, my theory is—"

Muriel and June were discussing Caesareans. Julian was asking Alicia if she'd ever sailed the Intracoastal Waterway. Mrs. Barrett was telling the mailman that Leary Metals used to make the handsomest stamped tin ceilings in Baltimore.

And Sarah was talking to Macon about the weather.

"Yes, I worried when it rained last night," Macon said. Or he said something; something or other . . .

He was looking at Sarah. Really he was consuming her: her burnished curls and her round, sweet face, and the dusting of powder on the down along her jawline.

"How have you been, Macon?" she asked him.

"I've been all right."

"Are you pleased about the wedding?"

"Well," he said, "I am if Rose is, I guess. Though I can't help feeling . . . well, Julian. You know."

"Yes, I know. But there's more to him than you think. He might be a very good choice."

When she stood in this kind of sunlight her eyes were so clear that it seemed you could see to the backs of them. He knew that from long ago. They might have been his own eyes; they were so familiar. He said, "How have *you* been?"

"I've been fine."

"Well. Good."

"I know that you're living with someone," she told him in a steady voice.

"Ah! Yes, actually I . . . yes. I am."

She knew who it was, too, because she looked past him then at Muriel and Alexander. But all she said was, "Rose told me when she invited me."

He said, "How about you?"

"Me?"

"Are you living with anyone?"

"Not really."

Rose came over and touched their arms, which was unlike her. "We're ready now," she said. She told Macon, "Sarah's my matron of honor, did I happen to mention that?"

"No, you didn't," Macon said.

Then he and Sarah followed her to a spot beneath a tulip tree, where Julian and Dr. Grauer were waiting. There was some kind of makeshift altar there—some little table or something covered with a cloth; Macon didn't pay much attention. He stood beside the minister and fingered the ring in his pocket. Sarah stood across from him, looking gravely into his face.

It all felt so natural.

17

Muriel said, "I never told you this, but a while before I met you I was dating somebody else."

"Oh? Who was that?" Macon asked.

"He was a customer at the Rapid-Eze Copy Center. He brought me his divorce papers to copy and we started having this conversation and ended up going out together. His divorce was awful. Really messy. His wife had been two-timing him. He said he didn't think he could ever trust a woman again. It was months before he would spend the night, even; he didn't like going to sleep when a woman was in the same room. But bit by bit I changed all that. He relaxed. He got to be a whole different man. Moved in with me and took over the bills, paid off all I still owed Alexander's doctor. We started talking about getting married. Then he met an airline stewardess and eloped with her within the week."

"I see," Macon said.

"It was like I had, you know, cured him, just so he could elope with another woman."

"Well," he said.

"You wouldn't do anything like that, would you, Macon?"

"Who, me?"

"Would you elope with someone else? Would you see someone else behind my back?"

"Oh, Muriel, of course not," he told her.

"Would you leave me and go home to your wife?"

"What are you talking about?"

"Would you?"

"Don't be silly," he said.

She cocked her head and considered him. Her eyes were alert and bright and knowing, like the eyes of some small animal.

It was a rainy Tuesday morning and Edward, who was squeamish about rain, insisted he didn't need to go out, but Macon took him anyway. While he was waiting in the backyard beneath his umbrella, he saw a young couple walking down the alley. They caught his attention because they walked so slowly, as if they didn't realize they were getting wet. The boy was tall and frail, in ragged jeans and a soft white shirt. The girl wore a flat straw hat with ribbons down the back and a longish, limp cotton dress. They swung hands, looking only at each other. They came upon a tricycle and they separated to walk around it; only instead of simply walking the girl did a little sort of dance step, spinning her skirt out, and the boy spun too and laughed and took her hand again.

Edward finally, finally peed, and Macon followed him back into the house. He set his umbrella in the kitchen sink and squatted to dry Edward off with an old beach towel. He rubbed briskly at first, and then more slowly. Then he stopped but remained on the floor, the towel bunched in his hands, the tin-can smell of wet dog rising all around him.

When he'd asked Sarah whether she was living with anyone, and Sarah had said, "Not really," what exactly had she meant by that?

The rain stopped and they put Edward on his leash and went out shopping. Muriel needed bedroom slippers with feathers on them. "Red. High-heeled. Pointy-toed," she said.

"Goodness. Whatever for?" Macon asked her.

"I want to clop around the house in them on Sunday mornings. Can't you just see it? I wish I smoked cigarettes. I wish Alexander wasn't allergic to smoke."

Yes, he could see it, as a matter of fact. "In your black-and-gold kimono," he said.

"Exactly."

"But I don't believe they sell those feathered slippers anymore."

"In thrift shops they do."

"Oh. Right."

Lately, Macon had begun to like thrift shops himself. In the usual sea of plastic he had found, so far, a folding boxwood carpenter's rule, an ingenious wheeled cookie cutter that left no waste space between cookies, and a miniature brass level for Alexander's toolbox.

The air outside was warm and watery. Mrs. Butler was propping up the squashed geraniums that flopped in the white-washed tire in her yard. Mrs. Patel—out of her luminous sari for once, clumsy and unromantic in tight, bulgy Calvin Klein jeans—was sweeping the puddles off her front steps. And Mrs. Saddler stood in front of the hardware store waiting for it to open. "I don't guess you'd have seen Dominick," she said to Muriel.

"Not lately."

"Last night he never came home," Mrs. Saddler said. "That boy just worries the daylights out of me. He's not what you would call bad," she told Macon, "but he's worrisome, know what I mean? When he's at home he's so much at home, those big noisy boots all over the place, but then when he's away he's so much away. You wouldn't believe how the house feels: just empty. Just echoing."

"He'll be back," Muriel said. "Tonight's his turn to have the car."

"Oh, and when he's out with the car it's worst of all," Mrs. Saddler said. "Then every siren I hear, I wonder if it's Dommie. I know how he screeches round corners! I know those fast girls he goes out with!"

They left her still standing there, distractedly fingering her coin purse, although the hardware-store owner had unlocked his door by now and was cranking down his awnings.

Outside a shop called Re-Runs, they ordered Edward to stay. He obeyed, looking put upon, while they went in. Muriel sifted through stacks of curled, brittle shoes that had hardened into the shapes of other people's feet. She shucked off her own shoes and stepped into a pair of silver evening sandals. "What do you think?" she asked Macon.

"I thought you were looking for slippers."

"But what do you think of these?"

"I can live without them," he said.

He was feeling bored because Re-Runs carried nothing but clothes.

Muriel abandoned the shoes and they went next door to Garage Sale Incorporated. Macon tried to invent a need for a rusty metal Rolodex file he found in a heap of tire chains. Could he use it for his guidebooks in some way? And make it tax-deductible. Muriel picked up a tan vinyl suitcase with rounded edges; it reminded Macon of a partly sucked caramel. "Should I get this?" she asked.

"I thought you wanted slippers."

"But for travel."

"Since when do you travel?"

"I know where you're going next," she said. She came closer to him, both hands clutching the suitcase handle. She looked like a very young girl at a bus stop, say, or out hitching a ride on the highway. "I wanted to ask if I could come with you."

"To Canada?"

"I mean the next place after that. France."

He set down the Rolodex. (Mention of France always depressed him.)

"Julian *said!*" she reminded him. "He said it's getting to be time to go to France again."

"You know I can't afford to bring you."

Muriel replaced the suitcase and they left the shop. "But just this once," she said, hurrying along beside him. "It wouldn't cost much!"

Macon retrieved Edward's leash and motioned him up. "It would cost a mint," he said, "not to mention that you'd have to miss work."

"No, I wouldn't. I've quit."

He looked over at her. "Quit?"

"Well, at the Meow-Bow. Then things like George and the dog training I'll just rearrange; if I was to travel I could just—"

"You quit the Meow-Bow?"

"So what?"

He couldn't explain the sudden weight that fell on him.

"It's not like it really paid much," Muriel said. "And you do buy most of the groceries now and help me with the rent and all; it's not like I needed the money. Besides, it took so much time! Time I could spend with you and Alexander! Why, I was coming home nights literally dead with exhaustion, Macon."

They passed Methylene's Beauty Salon, an insurance agency, a paint-stripping shop. Edward gave an interested glance at a large, jowly tomcat basking on the hood of a pickup.

"Figuratively," Macon said.

"Huh?"

"You were *figuratively* dead with exhaustion. Jesus, Muriel, you're so imprecise. You're so sloppy. And how could you quit your job like that? How could you just assume like that? You never even warned me!"

"Oh, don't make such a big deal about it," Muriel said.

They arrived at her favorite shop—a nameless little hole in the wall with a tumble of dusty hats in the window. Muriel started through the door but Macon stayed where he was. "Aren't you coming in?" she asked him.

"I'll wait here."

"But it's the place with all the gadgets!"

He said nothing. She sighed and disappeared.

Seeing her go was like shucking off a great, dragging burden.

He squatted to scratch behind Edward's ears, and then he rose and studied a sun-bleached election poster as if it held some fascinating coded message. Two black women passed him, pulling wire carts full of laundry. "It was just as warm as this selfsame day I'm speaking to you but she wore a very very fur coat . . ."

"May-con."

He turned toward the door of the shop.

"Oh, Maay-con!"

He saw a mitten, one of those children's mittens designed to look like a puppet. The palm was a red felt mouth that widened to squeak, "Macon, *please* don't be angry with Muriel."

Macon groaned.

"Come into this nice store with her," the puppet urged.

"Muriel, I think Edward's getting restless now."

"There's lots of things to buy here! Pliers and wrenches and T-squares . . . There's a silent hammer."

"What?"

"A hammer that doesn't make a sound. You can pound in nails in the dead of night."

"Listen—" Macon said.

"There's a magnifying glass all cracked and broken, and when you look at broken things through the lens you'd swear they'd turned whole again."

"Really, Muriel."

"I'm not Muriel! I'm Mitchell Mitten! Macon, don't you know Muriel can always take care of herself?" the puppet asked him. "Don't you know she could find another job tomorrow, if she wanted? So come inside! Come along! There's a pocketknife here with its own whetstone blade."

"Oh, for Lord's sake," Macon said.

But he gave a grudging little laugh.

And went on inside.

Over the next few days she kept bringing up France again and again. She sent him an anonymous letter pasted together from magazine print: *Don't FoRget tO BUY plANe Ticket for MuRiel.* (And the telltale magazine—with little blocks clipped out of its pages—still lay on the kitchen table.) She asked him to get her her keys from her purse and when he opened her purse he found photographs, two slick colored squares on thin paper showing Muriel's eyes at half mast. Passport photos, plainly. She must have meant for him to see them; she was watching him so intently. But all he did was drop her keys in her palm without comment.

He had to admire her. Had he ever known such a fighter? He went grocery shopping with her unusually late one evening, and just as they were crossing a shadowed area a boy stepped forth from a doorway. "Give over all what you have in your purse," he told Muriel. Macon was caught off guard; the boy was hardly more than a child. He froze, hugging the sack of groceries. But Muriel said, "The hell I will!" and swung her purse around by its strap and clipped the boy in the jaw. He lifted a hand to his face. "You get on home this instant or you'll be sorry you were ever born," Muriel told him. He slunk away, looking back at her with a puzzled expression.

When Macon had caught his breath again, he told Muriel she was a fool. "He might have had a gun, for all you knew," he said. "Anything might have happened! Kids show less mercy than grown-ups; you can see that any day in the papers."

"Well, it turned out fine, didn't it?" Muriel asked. "What are you so mad at?"

He wasn't sure. He supposed he might be mad at himself. He had done nothing to protect her, nothing strong or chivalrous. He hadn't thought as fast as she had or thought at all, in fact. While Muriel . . . why, Muriel hadn't even seemed surprised. She might have strolled down that street expecting a neighbor here, a stray dog there, a holdup just beyond—all equally part of life. He felt awed by her, and diminished. Muriel just walked on, humming "Great Speckled Bird" as if nothing particular had happened.

"I don't think Alexander's getting a proper education," he said to her one evening.

"Oh, he's okay."

"I asked him to figure what change they'd give back when we bought the milk today, and he didn't have the faintest idea. He didn't even know he'd have to subtract."

"Well, he's only in second grade," Muriel said.

"I think he ought to switch to a private school."

"Private schools cost money."

"So? I'll pay."

She stopped flipping the bacon and looked over at him. "What are you saying?" she asked.

"Pardon?"

"What are you saying, Macon? Are you saying you're committed?"

Macon cleared his throat. He said, "Committed."

"Alexander's got ten more years of school ahead of him. Are you saying you'll be around for all ten years?"

"Um . . ."

"I can't just put him in a school and take him out again with every passing whim of yours."

He was silent.

"Just tell me this much," she said. "Do you picture us getting married sometime? I mean when your divorce comes through?"

He said, "Oh, well, marriage, Muriel . . ."

"You don't, do you. You don't know *what* you want. One minute you like me and the next you don't. One minute you're ashamed to be seen with me and the next you think I'm the best thing that ever happened to you."

He stared at her. He had never guessed that she read him so clearly.

"You think you can just drift along like this, day by day, no plans," she said. "Maybe tomorrow you'll be here, maybe you won't. Maybe you'll just go on back to Sarah. Oh yes! I saw you at Rose's wedding. Don't think I didn't see how you and Sarah looked at each other."

Macon said, "All I'm saying is—"

"All *I'm* saying," Muriel told him, "is take care what you promise my son. Don't go making him promises you don't intend to keep."

"But I just want him to learn to subtract!" he said.

She didn't answer, and so the last word rang in the air for moments afterward. Subtract. A flat, sharp, empty sound that dampened Macon's spirits.

At supper she was too quiet; even Alexander was quiet, and excused himself the minute he'd finished his BLT. Macon, though, hung around the kitchen. Muriel was running a sinkful of water. He said, "Shall I dry?" Without any sort of warning, she whirled and flung a wet sponge in his face. Macon said, "Muriel?"

"Just get out!" she shouted, tears spiking her lashes, and she turned away again and plunged her hands into water so hot that it steamed. Macon retreated. He went into the living room where Alexander was watching TV, and Alexander moved over on the couch to give him space. He didn't say anything, but Macon could tell he'd heard from the way he tensed at each clatter in the kitchen. After a while the clatters died down. Macon and Alexander looked at each other. There was a silence; a single murmuring voice. Macon rose and returned to the kitchen, walking more quietly than usual and keeping a weather eye out, the way a cat creeps back after it's been dumped from someone's lap.

Muriel was talking on the phone with her mother. Her voice was gay and chirpy but just a shade thicker than usual, as if she were recovering from a cold. "So anyhow," she said, "I ask what kind of trouble her dog is giving her and the lady's like, 'Oh, no trouble,' so I ask her, 'Well, what's his problem, then?' and the lady's like, 'No real problem.' I say, 'Ma'am. You must have called me here for some reason.' She says, 'Oh. Well. That.' She says, 'Actually,' she says, 'I was wondering about when he makes.' I say, 'Makes?' She says, 'Yes, when he makes number one. He makes like little girl dogs do, he doesn't lift his leg.' I say to her, 'Now let me see if I've got this straight. You have called me here to teach your dog to lift his leg when he tinkles.' "

Her free hand kept flying out while she talked, as if she imagined her mother could see her. Macon came up behind her and put his arms around her, and she leaned back against him. "Oh, there's never a dull moment, I tell you," she said into the phone.

That night he dreamed he was traveling in a foreign country, only it seemed to be a medley of all the countries he'd ever been to and even some he hadn't. The sterile vast spaces of Charles de Gaulle airport chittered with those tiny birds he'd seen inside the terminal at Brussels; and when he stepped outdoors he was in Julian's green map of Hawaii with native dancers, oversized, swaying near the dots that marked various tourist attractions. Meanwhile his own voice, neutral and monotonous, murmured steadily: *In Germany the commercial traveler must be punctual for all appointments, in Switzerland he should be five minutes early, in Italy delays of several hours are not uncommon . . .*

He woke. It was pitch dark, but through the open window he heard distant laughter, a strain of music, faint cheers as if some sort of game were going on. He squinted at the clock radio: three thirty. Who would be playing a game at this hour? And on this street—this worn, sad street where nothing went right for anyone, where the men had dead-end jobs or none at all and the women were running to fat and the children were turning out badly. But another cheer went up, and someone sang a line from a song. Macon found himself smiling. He turned toward Muriel and closed his eyes; he slept dreamlessly the rest of the night.

The mailman rang the doorbell and presented a long, tube-shaped package addressed to Macon. "What's this?" Macon asked. He returned to the living room, frowning down at the label. Muriel was reading a paperback book called *Beauty Tips from the Stars*. She glanced up and said, "Why not open it and find out."

"Oh? Is this some of your doing?"

She only turned a page.

Another plea for the France trip, he supposed. He pulled off the tape on one end and shook the package till a cylinder of glossy paper slid out. When he unrolled it, he found a full-color photo of two puppies in a basket, with DR. MACK'S PET-VITES above it and a calendar for January below it.

"I don't understand," he said to Muriel.

She turned another page.

"Why would you send me a calendar for a year that's half gone?"

"Maybe there's something written on it," she told him.

He flipped through February, March, April. Nothing there. May. Then June: a scribble of red ink across a Saturday. *"Wedding,"* he read out. "Wedding? Whose wedding?"

"Ours?" she asked him.

"Oh, Muriel . . ."

"You'll be separated a year then, Macon. You'll be able to get your divorce."

"But, Muriel—"

"I always did want to have a June wedding."

"Muriel, please, I'm not ready for this! I don't think I ever will be. I mean I don't think marriage ought to be as common as it is; I really believe it ought to be the exception to the rule; oh, perfect couples could marry, maybe, but who's a perfect couple?"

"You and Sarah, I suppose," Muriel said.

The name brought Sarah's calm face, round as a daisy.

"No, no . . ." he said weakly.

"You're so selfish!" Muriel shouted. "You're so self-centered! You've got all these fancy reasons for never doing a single thing I want!"

Then she flung down her book and ran upstairs.

Macon heard the cautious, mouselike sounds of Alexander as he tiptoed around the kitchen fixing himself a snack.

Muriel's sister Claire arrived on the doorstep with a suitcase spilling clothes and her eyes pink with tears. "I'm never speaking to Ma again," she told them. She pushed past them into the house. "You want to know what happened? Well, I've been dating this guy, see: Claude McEwen. Only I didn't let on to Ma, you know how she's scared I'll turn out like Muriel did, and so last night when he came for me I jumped into his car and she happened to catch sight of me from the window, noticed he had a bumper sticker reading EDGEWOOD. That's because he used to go to a high school called Edgewood Prep in Delaware, but Ma thought it was Edgewood Arsenal and therefore he must be an Army man. So anyhow, this morning I get up and there she is fit to be tied, says, 'I know what you've been up to! Out all hours last night with the General!' and I say, 'Who? The what?' but there's never any stopping her once she gets started. She tells me I'm grounded for life and can't ever see the General again or she'll have him hauled up for court-martial and all his stars ripped off his uniform, so quick as a wink I pack up my clothes . . ."

Macon, listening absently while Edward sighed at his feet, had a sudden view of his life as rich and full and astonishing. He would have liked to show it off to someone. He wanted to sweep out an arm and say, "See?"

But the person he would have liked to show it to was Sarah.

Rose and Julian were back from their honeymoon; they were giving a family supper and Macon and Muriel were invited. Macon bought a bottle of very good wine as a hostess gift. He set the bottle on the counter, and Muriel came along and said, "What's this?"

"It's wine for Rose and Julian."

"Thirty-six dollars and ninety-nine cents!" she said, examining the sticker.

"Yes, well, it's French."

"I didn't know a wine *could* cost thirty-six ninety-nine."

"I figured since, you know, this'll be our first visit to their apartment . . ."

"You sure do think a lot of your family," Muriel said.

"Yes, of course."

"You never bought *me* any wine."

"I didn't know you wanted any; you told me it makes your teeth feel rough."

She didn't argue with that.

Later that day he happened to notice that the bottle had been moved. And was opened. And was half emptied. The cork lay beside it, still impaled on the corkscrew. A cloudy little juice glass gave off the smell of grapes. Macon called, "Muriel?"

"What," she answered from the living room.

He went to the living room doorway. She was watching a ball game with Alexander. He said, "Muriel, have you been drinking that wine I bought?"

"Yes."

He said, "Why, Muriel?"

"Oh, I just had this irresistible urge to try it out," she said.

Then she looked at him with slitted eyes, tilting her chin. He felt she was challenging him to take some action, but he said nothing. He picked up his car keys and went out to buy another bottle.

Macon felt shy about attending this dinner, as if Rose had turned into a stranger. He took longer than usual dressing, unable to decide between two shirts, and Muriel seemed to be having some trouble too. She kept putting on outfits and taking them off; brightly colored fabrics began to mount on the bed and on the floor all around it. "Oh, Lord, I wish I was just a totally nother person," she sighed. Macon, concentrating on tying his tie, said nothing. Her baby photo grinned out at him from the frame of the mirror. He happened to notice the date on the border: AUG 60. Nineteen sixty.

When Muriel was two years old, Macon and Sarah were already engaged to be married.

Downstairs, Dominick Saddler was sitting on the couch with Alexander. "Now this here is your paste wax," he was saying. He held up a can. "You never want to polish a car with anything but paste wax. And here we have a diaper. Diapers make real good rags because they don't shed hardly no lint. I generally buy a dozen at a time from Sears and Roebuck. And chamois skins: well, you know chamois skins. So what you do is, you get yourself these here supplies and a case of good beer and a girl, and you head on out to Loch Raven. Then you park in the sun and you take off your shirt and you and the girl start to polishing. Ain't no sweeter way that I know of to use up a spring afternoon."

Dominick's version of a bedtime story, Macon supposed. He was baby-sitting tonight. (The Butler twins had dates, and Claire was out with the General. As everybody referred to him now.) In payment, Muriel's car would be Dominick's to use for a week; mere money would never have persuaded him. He slouched next to Alexander with the diaper spread over one knee, muscles bulging under a T-shirt that read WEEKEND WARRIOR. A Greek sailor cap was tipped back on his head with a Judas Priest button pinned above the visor. Alexander looked enthralled.

Muriel came tapping down the stairs; she arrived craning her neck to see if her slip showed. "Is this outfit okay?" she asked Macon.

"It's very nice," he said, which was true, although it was also totally unlike her. Evidently, she had decided to take Rose for her model. She had pulled her hair back in a low bun and she wore a slim gray dress with shoulder pads. Only her spike-heeled sandals seemed her own; probably she didn't possess any shoes so sensible as Rose's schoolgirl flats. "I want you to tell me if there's anything not right," she said to Macon. "Anything you think is tacky."

"Not a thing," Macon assured her.

She kissed Alexander, leaving a dark red mark on his cheek. She made one last survey in the mirror beside the front door, meanwhile calling, "Don't let him stay up too late, now, Dommie; don't let him watch anything scary on TV—"

Macon said, *"Muriel."*

"I look like the wrath of God."

The Leary children had been raised to believe that when an invitation involved a meal, the guests should arrive exactly on time. Never mind that they often caught their hostess in curlers; they went on doing what they were taught. So Macon pressed the buzzer in the lobby at precisely six twenty-seven, and Porter and Charles joined them in front of the elevator. They both told Muriel it was nice to see her. Then they rode upward in a gloomy silence, eyes fixed on the numbers over the door. Charles carried a potted jade tree, Porter another bottle of wine.

"Isn't this exciting?" Muriel said. "We're their first invited guests."

"At home now we'd be watching the CBS Evening News," Charles told her.

Muriel couldn't seem to think of any answer to that.

By six thirty sharp they were ringing the doorbell, standing in a hushed corridor carpeted in off-white. Rose opened the door and called, "They're here!" and set her face lightly against each of theirs. She wore Grandmother Leary's lace-trimmed company apron and she smelled of lavender soap, the same as always.

But there was a strip of peeling sunburn across the bridge of her nose.

Julian, natty and casual in a navy turtleneck and white slacks (when it wasn't yet Memorial Day), fixed the drinks while Rose retreated to the kitchen. This was one of those ultra-modern apartments where the rooms all swam into each other, so they could see her flitting back and forth. Julian passed around snapshots of Hawaii. Either he had used inferior film or else Hawaii was a very different place from Baltimore, because some of the colors were wrong. The trees appeared to be blue. In most of the photos Rose stood in front of flower beds or flowering shrubs, wearing a white sleeveless dress Macon had never seen before, hugging her arms and smiling too broadly so that she looked older than she was. "I tell Rose you'd think she went on our honeymoon by herself," Julian said. "I'm the one who took the pictures because Rose never did learn how to work my camera."

"She didn't?" Macon asked.

"It was one of those German models with all the buttons."

"She couldn't figure out the buttons?"

"I tell her, 'People will think I wasn't even there.' "

"Why, Rose could have taken that camera apart and put it together twice over," Macon said.

"No, this was one of those German models with—"

"It wasn't very logically constructed," Rose called from the kitchen.

"Ah," Macon said, sitting back.

She entered the room with a tray and placed it on the glass coffee table. Then she knelt and began to spread pâté on little crackers. There was some change in the way she moved, Macon noticed. She was more graceful, but also more self-conscious. She offered the pâté first to Muriel, then to each of her brothers, last to Julian. "In Hawaii I started learning to sail," she said. She pronounced the two *i*'s in "Hawaii" separately; Macon thought it sounded affected. "Now I'm going to practice out on the Bay."

"She's trying to find her sea legs," Julian said. "She tends to feel motion-sick."

Macon bit into his cracker. The pâté was something familiar. It was rough in texture but delicate in taste; there was a kind of melting flavor that he believed came from adding a great amount of butter. The recipe was Sarah's. He sat very still, not chewing. He was flooded by a subtle blend of tarragon and cream and home.

"Oh, I know just what you're going through," Muriel said to Rose. "All I have to do is look at a boat and I get nauseous."

Macon swallowed and gazed down at the carpet between his feet. He waited for someone to correct her, but nobody did. That was even worse.

In bed she said, "You wouldn't ever leave me, would you? Would you ever think of leaving me? You won't be like the others, will you? Will you promise not to leave me?"

"Yes, yes," he said, floating in and out of dreams.

"You do take me seriously, don't you? Don't you?"

"Oh, Muriel, for pity's sake . . ." he said.

But later, when she turned in her sleep and moved away from him, his feet followed hers of their own accord to the other side of the bed.

18

Macon was sitting in a hotel room in Winnipeg, Manitoba, when the phone rang. Actually it took him a second to realize it was the phone. He happened to be having a very good time with a mysterious object he'd just discovered—an ivory-painted metal cylinder affixed to the wall above the bed. He'd never noticed such a thing before, although he'd stayed in this hotel on two previous trips. When he touched the cylinder to see what it was, it rotated, disappearing into the wall, while from within the wall a light bulb swung out already lit. At the same moment, the phone rang. Macon experienced an instant of confusion during which he imagined it was the cylinder that was ringing. Then he saw the telephone on the nightstand. Still he was confused. No one had his number, so far as he knew.

He picked up the receiver and said, "Yes?"

"Macon."

His heart lurched. He said, "Sarah?"

"Have I caught you at a bad time?"

"No, no . . . How did you know where I was?"

"Well, Julian thought you'd be in either Toronto or Winnipeg by now," she said, "so I looked in your last guidebook, and I knew the hotels where you discussed night noises were the ones where you stayed yourself, so . . ."

"Is anything wrong?" he asked.

"No, I just needed a favor. Would it be all right with you if I moved back into our house?"

"Um—"

"Just as a place to stay," she said hastily. "Just for a little while. My lease runs out at the end of the month and I can't find a new apartment."

"But the house is a mess," he told her.

"Oh, I'll take care of that."

"No, I mean something happened to it over the winter, pipes burst or something, ceiling came down—"

"Yes, I know."

"You do?"

"Your brothers told me."

"My brothers?"

"I went to ask them your whereabouts when they wouldn't answer their phone. And Rose said she'd been over to the house herself and—"

"You went to Rose's, too?"

"No, Rose was at your brothers'."

"Oh."

"She's living there for a while."

"I see," he said. Then he said, "She's what?"

"Well, June has had her baby," Sarah said, "so she asked Porter to keep the children a while."

"But what does that have to do with Rose?" he said. "Does Rose imagine Porter can't open a tin of soup for them? And how come June sent them away?"

"Oh, you know June, she always was kind of a birdbrain."

She sounded like her old self, when she said that. Up till now there'd been something careful about her voice, something wary and ready to retreat, but now a certain chuckly, confiding quality emerged. Macon leaned back against his pillow.

"She told the children she needs time to bond," Sarah said.

"Time to what?"

"She and her husband need to bond with the baby."

"Good grief," Macon said.

"When Rose heard that, she told Porter she was coming home. Anyhow she didn't think the boys were eating right, Porter and Charles;

and also there's a crack in the side of the house and she wanted to get it patched before it spreads."

"What kind of crack?" Macon asked.

"Some little crack in the masonry; I don't know. When the rain comes from a certain direction water seeps in above the kitchen ceiling, Rose says, and Porter and Charles were planning to fix it but they couldn't agree on the best way to do it."

Macon slipped out of his shoes and hoisted his feet up onto the bed. He said, "So is Julian living alone now, or what?"

"Yes, but she brings him casseroles," Sarah said. Then she said, "Have you thought about it, Macon?"

His heart gave another lurch. He said, "Have I thought about what?"

"About my using the house."

"Oh. Well. It's fine with me, but I don't believe you realize the extent of the damage."

"But we'd have to fix that anyway, if we were to sell it. So here's what I was thinking: I could pay for the repairs myself—anything the insurance doesn't cover—with what I'd ordinarily use for rent. Does that seem fair to you?"

"Yes, of course," Macon said.

"And maybe I'll get someone to clean the upholstery," she said.

"Yes."

"And the rugs."

"Yes."

After all these years, he knew when she was leading up to something. He recognized that distracted tone that meant she was bracing herself for what she really wanted to say.

"Incidentally," she said, "the papers came through from the lawyer."

"Ah."

"The final arrangements. You know. Things I have to sign."

"Yes."

"It was kind of a shock."

He said nothing.

"I mean of course I knew they were coming; it's been nearly a year; in fact he called ahead and told me they were coming, but when I saw them in black and white they just seemed so brisk. They didn't take into account the feelings of the thing. I guess I wasn't expecting that."

Macon had a sense of some danger approaching, something he couldn't handle. He said, "Ah! Yes! Certainly! That seems a natural reaction. So anyway, good luck with the house, Sarah."

He hung up quickly.

His seatmate on the flight to Edmonton was a woman who was scared of flying. He knew that before the plane had left the ground, before he'd looked in her direction. He was gazing out the window, keeping to himself as usual, and he heard her swallowing repeatedly. She kept tightening and releasing her grasp on the armrests and he could feel that, too. Finally he turned to see who this was. A pair of pouched eyes met his. A very old, baggy woman in a flowered dress was staring at him intently, had perhaps been willing him to turn. "Do you think this plane is safe," she said flatly, not exactly asking.

"It's perfectly safe," he told her.

"Then why have all these signs about. Oxygen. Life vests. Emergency exits. They're clearly expecting the worst."

"That's just federal regulations," Macon said.

Then he started thinking about the word "federal." In Canada, would it apply? He frowned at the seat ahead of him, considering. Finally he said, "*Government* regulations." When he checked the old woman's expression to see if this made any better sense to her, he discovered that she must have been staring at him all this time. Her face lunged toward him, gray and desperate. He began to worry about her. "Would you like a glass of sherry?" he asked.

"They don't give us sherry till we're airborne. By then it's much too late."

"Just a minute," he said.

He bent to unzip his bag, and from his shaving kit he took a plastic travel flask. This was something he always packed, in case of sleepless nights. He had never used it, though—not because he'd never had a sleepless night but because he'd gone on saving it for some occasion even worse than whatever the current one was, something that never quite arrived. Like his other emergency supplies (the matchbook-sized sewing kit, the tiny white Lomotil tablet), this flask was being hoarded for the *real* emergency. In fact, its metal lid had grown rusty inside, as he discovered when he unscrewed it. "I'm afraid this may have . . . turned a bit, or whatever sherry does," he told the old woman. She didn't answer but continued staring into his eyes. He poured the sherry into the lid, which was meant to double as a cup. Meanwhile the plane gave a creak and started moving down the runway. The old woman drank off the sherry and handed him the cup. He understood that she was not returning it for good. He refilled it. She drank that more slowly and then let her head tip back against her seat.

"Better?" he asked her.

"My name is Mrs. Daniel Bunn," she told him.

He thought it was her way of saying she was herself again—her formal, dignified self. "How do you do," he said. "I'm Macon Leary."

"I know it's foolish, Mr. Leary," she said, "but a drink does give the illusion one is doing something to cope, does it not."

"Absolutely," Macon said.

He wasn't convinced, though, that she was coping all that well.

As the plane gathered speed, her free hand tightened on the armrest. Her other hand—the one closest to him, clutching the cup—grew white around the nails. All at once the cup popped up in the air, squeezed out of her grip. Macon caught it nimbly and said, "Whoa there!" and screwed it onto the flask. Then he replaced the flask in his bag. "Once we're off the ground—" he said.

But a glance at her face stopped him. She was swallowing again. The plane was beginning to rise now—the nose was lifting off—and she was pressed back against her seat. She seemed flattened. "Mrs. Bunn?" Macon said. He was scared she was having a heart attack.

Instead of answering, she turned toward him and crumpled onto his shoulder. He put an arm around her. "Never mind," he said. "Goodness. You'll be all right. Never mind."

The plane continued slanting backward. When the landing gear retracted (groaning), Macon felt the shudder through Mrs. Bunn's body. Her hair smelled like freshly ironed tea cloths. Her back was large and boneless, a mounded shape like the back of a whale.

He was impressed that someone so old still wanted so fiercely to live.

Then the plane leveled off and she pulled herself together—straightening and drawing away from him, brushing at the teardrops that lay in the folds beneath her eyes. She was full of folds, wide and plain and sagging, but valiantly wore two pearl buttons in her long, spongy earlobes and maintained a coat of brave red lipstick on a mouth so wrinkled that it didn't even have a clear outline.

He asked, "Are you all right?"

"Yes, and I apologize a thousand times," she said. And she patted the brooch at her throat.

When the drink cart came he ordered her another sherry, which he insisted on paying for, and he ordered one for himself as well, even though he didn't plan to drink it. He thought it might be needed for Mrs. Bunn. He was right, as things turned out, because their flight was unusually rough. The seatbelt sign stayed lit the whole way, and the plane bounced and grated as if rolling over gravel. Every now and then it dropped sharply and Mrs. Bunn winced, but she went on taking tiny sips of sherry. "This is nothing," Macon told her. "I've been in much worse than this." He told her how to give with the bumps. "It's like traveling on a boat," he said. "Or on wheels, on roller skates. You keep your knees loose. You bend. Do you understand what I'm saying? You go along with it. You ride it out."

Mrs. Bunn said she'd certainly try.

Not only was the air unsteady, but also little things kept going wrong inside the plane. The drink cart raced away from the stewardess every time she let go of it. Mrs. Bunn's tray fell into her lap twice without warning. At each new mishap Macon laughed and said, "Ah, me," and shook his head. "Oh, not again," he said. Mrs. Bunn's eyes remained fixed on his face, as if Macon were her only hope. Once there was a bang and she jumped; the door to the cockpit had flung itself open for no good reason. "What? What?" she said, but Macon pointed out that now she could see for herself how unconcerned the pilot was. They were close enough to the front so she could even hear what the pilot was talking about; he was shouting some question to the copilot, asking why any ten-year-old girl with half a grain of sense would wear a metal nightbrace in a sauna room. "You call that a worried man?" Macon asked Mrs. Bunn. "You think a man about to bail out of his plane would be discussing orthodontia?"

"Bail out!" Mrs. Bunn said. "Oh, my, I never thought of that!"

Macon laughed again.

He was reminded of a trip he'd taken alone as a boy, touring colleges. Heady with his new independence, he had lied to the man sitting next to him and said he came from Kenya, where his father led safaris. In the same way he was lying now, presenting himself to Mrs. Bunn as this merry, tolerant person.

But after they had landed (with Mrs. Bunn hardly flinching, bolstered by all those sherries), and she had gone off with her grown daughter, a very small child ran headlong into Macon's kneecap. This child was followed by another and another, all more or less the same size—some kind of nursery school, Macon supposed, visiting the airport on a field trip—and each child, as if powerless to veer from the course the first had set, careened off Macon's knees and said, "Oops!" "Oops!" "Oops!"— while behind the children, a harassed-looking woman clapped a hand to her cheek. "Sorry," she said to Macon, and he said, "No harm done."

Only later, when he passed a mirror and noticed the grin on his face, did he realize that, in fact, he might not have been lying to Mrs. Bunn after all.

"The plumber says it won't be hard to fix," Sarah told him. "He says it *looks* bad but really just one pipe is cracked."

"Well, good," Macon said.

He was not as surprised this time by her call, of course, but he did feel there was something disconcerting about it—standing in an Edmonton hotel room on a weekday afternoon, listening to Sarah's voice at the other end of the line.

"I went over there this morning and straightened up a little," she said. "Everything's so disorganized."

"Disorganized?"

"Why are some of the sheets sewn in half? And the popcorn popper's in the bedroom. Were you eating popcorn in the bedroom?"

"I guess I must have been," he said.

He was near an open window, and he could look out upon a strangely beautiful landscape: an expanse of mathematical flatness, with straight-edged buildings rising in the distance like a child's toy blocks on a rug. It was difficult, in these surroundings, to remember why he'd had a popcorn popper in the bedroom.

"So how's the weather there?" Sarah asked.

"Kind of gray."

"Here it's sunny. Sunny and humid."

"Well, it's certainly not humid here," he told her. "The air's so dry that rain disappears before it hits the ground."

"Really? Then how can you tell it's raining?"

"You can see it above the plains," he said. "It looks like stripes that just fade away about halfway down from the sky."

"I wish I were there to watch it with you," Sarah said.

Macon swallowed.

Gazing out of the window, he all at once recalled Ethan as an infant. Ethan used to cry unless he was tightly wrapped in a blanket; the pediatrician had explained that new babies have a fear of flying apart. Macon had not been able to imagine that at the time, but now he had no trouble. He could picture himself separating, falling into pieces, his head floating away with terrifying swiftness in the eerie green air of Alberta.

In Vancouver she asked if the rain vanished there as well. "No," he said.

"No?"

"No, it rains in Vancouver."

It was raining this minute—a gentle night rain. He could hear it but not see it, except for the cone of illuminated drops spilling beneath a street lamp just outside his hotel room. You could almost suppose it was the lamp itself that was raining.

"Well, I've moved back into the house," she said. "Mostly I just stay upstairs. The cat and I: We camp in the bedroom. Creep downstairs for meals."

"What cat is that?" he asked.

"Helen."

"Oh, yes."

"I went and picked her up at Rose's. I needed company. You wouldn't believe how lonely it is."

Yes, he would believe it, he could have said. But didn't.

So here they were in their same old positions, he could have said: He had won her attention only by withdrawing. He wasn't surprised when she said, "Macon? Do you . . . What's her name? The person you live with?"

"Muriel," he said.

Which she knew before she asked, he suspected.

"Do you plan on staying with Muriel forever?"

"I really couldn't say," he said.

He was noticing how oddly the name hung in this starchy, old-fashioned hotel room. Muriel. Such a peculiar sound. So unfamiliar, suddenly.

On the flight back, his seatmate was an attractive young woman in a tailored suit. She spread the contents of her briefcase on her folding tray, and she riffled through computer printout sheets with her perfectly manicured hands. Then she asked Macon if he had a pen she might borrow. This struck him as amusing—her true colors shining out from beneath her businesslike exterior. However, his only pen was a fountain pen that he didn't like lending, so he said no. She seemed relieved; she cheerfully repacked all she'd taken from her briefcase. "I could have sworn I swiped a ballpoint from my last hotel," she said, "but maybe that was the one before this one; you know how they all run together in your mind."

"You must do a lot of traveling," Macon said politely.

"Do I! Some mornings when I wake up I have to check my hotel stationery just to find out what city I'm in."

"That's terrible."

"Oh, I like it," she said, bending to slip her briefcase under her seat. "It's the only time I can relax anymore. When I come home I'm all nervous, can't sit still. I prefer to be a . . . moving target, you could say."

Macon thought of something he'd once read about heroin: how it's not a pleasure, really, but it so completely alters the users' body chemistry that they're forced to go on once they've started.

He turned down drinks and dinner, and so did his seatmate; she rolled her suit jacket expertly into a pillow and went to sleep. Macon got out *Miss MacIntosh* and stared at a single page for a while. The top line began with *brows bristling, her hair streaked with white.* He studied the words so long that he almost wondered if they *were* words; the whole English language seemed chunky and brittle. "Ladies and gentlemen," the loudspeaker said, "we will be starting our descent . . ." and the word "descent" struck him as an invention, some new euphemism concocted by the airlines.

After they landed in Baltimore, he took a shuttle bus to the parking lot and retrieved his car. It was late evening here and the sky was pale and radiant above the city. As he drove he continued to see the words from *Miss MacIntosh.* He continued to hear the stewardess's gliding voice: *complimentary beverages* and *the captain has asked us* and *trays in an upright position.* He considered switching on the radio but he didn't know what station it was set to. Maybe it was Muriel's country music station. This possibility made him feel weary; he felt he wouldn't have the strength to press the buttons, and so he drove in silence.

He came to Singleton Street and flicked his signal on but didn't turn. After a while the signal clicked off on its own. He rode on through the city, up Charles Street, into his old neighborhood. He parked and cut the engine and sat looking at the house. The downstairs windows were dark. The upstairs windows were softly glowing. Evidently, he had come home.

19

Macon and Sarah needed to buy a new couch. They set aside a Saturday for it—actually just half a Saturday, because Sarah had a class to attend in the afternoon. At breakfast, she flipped through an interior decorating book so they could get a head start on their decision. "I'm beginning to think along the lines of something flowered," she told Macon. "We've never had a flowered couch before. Or would that be too frilly?"

"Well, I don't know. I wonder about winter," Macon said.

"Winter?"

"I mean right now in the middle of June a flowered couch looks fine, but it might seem out of place in December."

"So you prefer something in a solid," Sarah said.

"Well, I don't know."

"Or maybe stripes."

"I'm not sure."

"I know you don't like plaids."

"No."

"How do you feel about tweeds?"

"Tweeds," Macon said, considering.

Sarah handed over the book and started loading the dishwasher.

Macon studied pictures of angular modern couches, cozy chintz-covered couches, and period reproduction couches covered in complex fabrics. He took the book to the living room and squinted at the spot where the couch would be sitting. The old one, which had turned out to be too waterlogged to salvage, had been carted away, along with both armchairs. Now there was just a long blank wall, with the freshly plastered ceiling glaring above it. Macon observed that a room without furniture had a utilitarian feeling, as if it were merely a container. Or a vehicle. Yes, a vehicle: He had a sense of himself speeding through the universe as he stood there.

While Sarah got dressed, Macon took the dog out. It was a warm, golden morning. Neighbors were trimming their grass and weeding their flower beds. They nodded as Macon walked past. He had not been back long enough for them to feel at ease yet; there was something a little too formal about their greetings. Or maybe he was imagining that. He made an effort to remind them of how many years he had lived here: "I've always liked those tulips of yours!" and "Still got that nice hand mower, I see!" Edward marched beside him with a busybody waggle of his hind end.

In movies and such, people who made important changes in their lives accomplished them and were done with it. They walked out and never returned; or they married and lived happily ever after. In real life, things weren't so clean-cut. Macon, for instance, had had to go down to Muriel's and retrieve this dog, once he'd decided to move back home. He had had to collect his clothing and pack up his typewriter while Muriel watched in silence with her accusing, reproaching eyes. Then there were all kinds of other belongings that he discovered too late he'd forgotten—clothes that had been in the wash at the time, and his favorite dictionary, and the extra large pottery mug he liked to drink his coffee from. But of course he couldn't go back for them. He had to abandon them—messy, trailing strings of himself cluttering his leavetaking.

By the time he and Edward returned from their outing, Sarah was waiting in the front yard. She wore a yellow dress that made her tan glow; she looked very pretty. "I was just wondering about the azaleas," she told Macon. "Weren't we supposed to feed them in the spring?"

"Well, probably," Macon said, "but they seem all right to me."

"In April, I think," she said. "Or maybe May. No one was here to do it."

Macon veered away from that. He preferred to pretend that their lives had been going on as usual. "Never mind, Rose has whole sacks of fertilizer," he said. "We'll pick up some from her while we're out."

"No one was here to seed the lawn, either."

"The lawn looks fine," he said, more forcefully than he'd meant to.

They shut Edward in the house and climbed into Macon's car. Sarah had brought along a newspaper because there were several furniture ads. "Modern Homewares," she read off. "But that's all the way down on Pratt Street."

"Might as well give it a try," Macon said. Pratt was one of the few streets he knew how to find.

After they left their neighborhood, with its trees arching overhead, the car grew hotter and Macon rolled his window down. Sarah lifted her face to the sunlight. "Be a good day to go to the pool," she said.

"Well, if we have time. I was thinking of asking you to lunch."

"Oh, where?"

"Anywhere you like. Your choice."

"Aren't you nice," she said.

Macon drove past two unshaven men talking on a corner. Sarah locked her door. Macon thought of what the men would be saying: "What's coming down, man?" "Not all that much."

The sidewalks grew more crowded. Women lugged stringhandled shopping bags, an old man dragged a grocery cart, and a girl in a faded dress leaned her head against a bus stop sign.

At Modern Homewares, huge paper banners covered the plate glass windows. SPECIAL FOR FATHER'S DAY! they read. Sarah hadn't mentioned that this was a Father's Day sale. Macon made a point of mentioning it himself, to show it didn't bother him. Taking her arm as they entered, he said, "Isn't that typical. Father's Day! They'll capitalize on anything."

Sarah looked away from him and said, "All they seem to have is beds."

"I suppose it began with reclining chairs," Macon said. "A Barcalounger for Dad, and next thing you know it's a whole dinette set."

"Could we see your couches," Sarah told a salesman firmly.

The couches were all of the straight-backed, Danish sort, which was fine with Macon. He didn't really care. Sarah said, "What do you think? Legs? Or flush with the floor."

"It's all the same to me," he said. He sat down heavily on something covered in leather.

Sarah chose a long, low couch that opened into a queen-sized bed. "Macon? What do you say?" she asked. "Do you like what you're sitting on better?"

"No, no," he said.

"Well, what do you think of this one?"

"It's fine."

"Don't you have any opinion?"

"I just gave you my opinion, Sarah."

Sarah sighed and asked the salesman if he offered same-day delivery.

They'd been so efficient about picking out the couch that time remained for other errands as well. First they drove to Hutzler's and bought queen-sized sheets. Then they checked the furniture department for armchairs; there was a Father's Day sale there, too. "Maybe we're on a roll," Sarah told Macon. But they weren't as lucky with the armchairs; nothing looked just right. Not to Macon, at least. He gave up trying and stood watching a kiddie show on a row of television sets.

After Hutzler's they went to get fertilizer from Rose, but Macon braked on the way and said, "Wait! There's my bank." It had come upon him unexpectedly—the branch where he rented a safe deposit box. "I need my passport for the France trip," he told Sarah. "Might as well pick it up while I'm here."

Sarah said she'd just wait in the car.

He had to stand in line; two elderly women were ahead of him. They were checking out their jewels for Saturday night, he liked to imagine. Or clipping their coupons—whatever coupons were. While he stood there he kept feeling the presence of someone behind him. For some reason he didn't want to turn and find out who it was. He just kept staring ahead, every now and then glancing at his watch in a businesslike way. This person breathed very gently and smelled like flowers—bitter, real-life flowers, not the kind in perfume bottles. But when he finally squared his shoulders and looked around, he found only another stranger waiting for her jewels.

It wasn't true that Muriel had watched in silence as he packed. Actually, she had spoken. She had said, "Macon? Are you really doing this? Do you mean to tell me you can just use a person up and then move on? You think I'm some kind of . . . bottle of something you don't have any further need for? Is that how you see me, Macon?"

His turn for the vault had arrived, and he followed a girl in a miniskirt across a carpeted area, into the windowless cubicle lined with drawers. "I won't need to take my box to the other room," he told the girl. "I just want to get one thing."

She gave him his card to sign and accepted his key. After she had unlocked his box she stood back, scrutinizing her nails, while he rummaged through various papers for his passport. Then he turned to tell her he was finished, but all at once he was so moved by her tact in looking elsewhere, by the delicacy that people could come up with on their own (for surely it wouldn't have been written into the bank's instructions) . . . Well, he must be going soft in the head. It was the weather or something; it was the season or something; he had not been sleeping well. He said, "Thank you very much," and took back his key and left.

At his grandfather's house, Rose was out front pruning the hedge. Her gardening smock was an enormous gray workshirt inherited from Charles. When she saw their car pull up she straightened and waved. Then she went on pruning while they consulted her about fertilizers. "For azaleas and what else do you have, andromeda, acid-loving plants . . ." she mused.

Sarah said, "Where are the children today?"

"Children?"

"Your nephew and nieces."

"Oh, they went home to their mother."

Sarah said, "I just assumed, since you hadn't moved back with Julian . . ."

"Well, not yet, of course," Rose said.

Macon, anxious to guard her privacy, murmured, "No, of course not," practically at the same moment, but Sarah said, "Why? What's keeping you?"

"Oh, Sarah, you wouldn't believe what a state I found the boys in when I came back here," Rose said. "They were living in their pajamas so as not to have too much laundry. They were eating gorp for their suppers."

"I'm not even going to ask what gorp is," Sarah said.

"It's a mixture of wheat germ and nuts and dried—"

"But what about your apartment, Rose? What about Julian?"

"Oh, you know, I kept losing that apartment every time I turned around," Rose said vaguely. "I'd head one block east to the grocery store and then turn west to get back again and I'd always be wrong; always. The apartment building would have worked over to the east somehow; *I* don't know how."

There was a silence. Finally Macon said, "Well, if you could get us some of that fertilizer, Rose . . ."

"Certainly," she said. And she went off to the toolshed.

They had lunch at the Old Bay Restaurant—Sarah's idea. Macon said, "Are you sure?" and Sarah said, "Why wouldn't I be?"

"But you always tell me it's boring," Macon said.

"There are worse things than boring, I've decided."

He didn't think that was much of a recommendation, but he went along with it.

The restaurant was full, even though it was barely noon, and they had to wait a few minutes to be seated. Macon stood by the hostess's podium trying to adjust to the dimness. He surveyed the other diners and found something odd about them. They were not the usual Old Bay crowd—middle-aged, one face much like the next—but an assortment of particular and unusual individuals. He saw a priest offering a toast to a woman in a tennis dress, and a smartly suited woman with a young man in an orange gauze robe, and two cheerful schoolgirls loading all their potato chips onto the plate of a small boy. From where he stood Macon couldn't hear what any of these people were saying; he had to guess. "Maybe the woman wants to join a convent," he told Sarah, "and the priest is trying to discourage her."

"Pardon?"

"He's pointing out that sorting her husband's socks can be equally whatever-he'd-call-it, equally holy. And the young man in gauze, well . . ."

"The young man in gauze is Ashley Demming," Sarah said. "You know Ashley. Peter and Lindy Demming's son. My, he's aged poor

Lindy twenty years in the last six months, hasn't he? I don't think they're ever going to get over this."

"Ah, well," Macon said.

Then they were shown to a table.

Sarah ordered something called a White Lady and Macon ordered a sherry. With their meal they had a bottle of wine. Macon wasn't used to drinking in the daytime; he grew a little muzzy. So did Sarah, evidently, for she drifted off in the middle of a sentence about upholstery fabrics. She touched his hand, which was lying on the tablecloth. "We ought to do this more often," she said.

"Yes, we ought to."

"You know what I missed most when we were separated? The little, habitual things. The Saturday errands. Going to Eddie's for coffee beans. Even things that used to seem tiresome, like the way you'd take forever in the hardware store."

When he folded her hand into a fist it was round, like a bird. It had no sharp angles.

"I'm not sure if you know this," she said, "but for a while I was seeing another man."

"Well, fine; whatever; eat your salad," he told her.

"No, I want to say it, Macon. He was just getting over the death of his wife, and I was getting over things too so of course . . . Well, we started out very slowly, we started as friends, but then he began talking about getting married someday. After we'd given ourselves some time, he meant. In fact I think he really loved me. He took it hard when I told him you'd moved back."

She looked straight at Macon when she said that, her eyes a sudden blue flash. He nodded.

"But there were these things I had trouble with," she said. "I mean good things; qualities I'd always wished for. He was a very dashing driver, for instance. Not unsafe; just dashing. At first, I liked that. Then bit by bit it began to feel wrong. 'Double-check your rearview mirror!' I wanted to tell him. 'Fasten your seatbelt! Inch past stop signs the way my husband does!' He never examined a restaurant bill before he paid it—shoot, he didn't even take his credit card receipt when he walked away from a table—and I thought of all the times I sat stewing while you totted up every little item. I thought, 'Why do I miss that? It's perverse!' "

Like "eck cetera," Macon thought.

Like Muriel saying, "eck cetera." And Macon wincing.

And the emptiness now, the thinness, when he heard it pronounced correctly.

He stroked the dimpled peaks that were Sarah's knuckles.

"Macon, I think that after a certain age people just don't have a choice," Sarah said. "You're who I'm with. It's too late for me to change. I've used up too much of my life now."

You mean to tell me you can just use a person up and then move on?
Muriel had asked.

Evidently so, was the answer. For even if he had stayed with Muriel, then wouldn't Sarah have been left behind?

"After a certain age," he told Sarah, "it seems to me you can only choose what to lose."

"What?" she said.

"I mean there's going to be something you have to give up, whichever way you cut it."

"Well, of course," she said.

He supposed she'd always known that.

They finished their meal but they didn't order coffee because they were running late. Sarah had her class; she was studying with a sculptor on Saturdays. Macon called for the bill and paid it, self-consciously totaling it first. Then they stepped out into the sunshine. "What a pretty day," Sarah said. "It makes me want to play hooky."

"Why don't you?" Macon asked. If she didn't go to class, he wouldn't have to work on his guidebook.

But she said, "I can't disappoint Mr. Armistead."

They drove home, and she changed into a sweat suit and set off again. Macon carried in the fertilizer, which Rose had poured into a bucket. It was something shredded that had no smell—or only a harsh, chemical smell, nothing like the truckloads of manure the men used to bring for his grandmother's camellias. He set it on the pantry floor and then he took the dog out. Then he made himself a cup of coffee to clear his head. He drank it at the kitchen sink, staring into the yard. The cat rubbed against his ankles and purred. The clock over the stove ticked steadily. There was no other sound.

When the telephone rang, he was glad. He let it ring twice before he answered so as not to seem overeager. Then he picked up the receiver and said, "Hello?"

"Mr. Leary?"

"Yes!"

"This is Mrs. Morton calling, at Merkle Appliance Store. Are you aware that the maintenance policy on your hot water heater expires at the end of the month?"

"No, I hadn't realized," Macon said.

"You had a two-year policy at a cost of thirty-nine eighty-eight. Now to renew it for another two years the cost of course would be slightly higher since your hot water heater is older."

"Well, that makes sense," Macon said. "Gosh! How old *is* that thing by now?"

"Let's see. You purchased it three years ago this July."

"Well, I'd certainly like to keep the maintenance policy."

"Wonderful. I'll send you a new contract then, Mr. Leary, and thank you for—"

"And would that still include replacement of the tank?" Macon asked.

"Oh, yes. Every part is covered."

"And they'd still do the yearly checkups."

"Why, yes."

"I've always liked that. A lot of the other stores don't offer it; I remember from when I was shopping around."

"So I'll send you the contract, Mr.—"

"But I would have to arrange for the checkup myself, as I recall."

"Yes, the customer schedules the checkup."

"Maybe I'll just schedule it now. Could I do that?"

"That's a whole different department, Mr. Leary. I'll mail you out the contract and you can read all about it. Bye bye."

She hung up.

Macon hung up too.

He thought a while.

He had an urge to go on talking; anyone would do. But he couldn't think what number to dial. Finally he called the time lady. She answered before the first ring was completed. (*She* had no worries about seeming overeager.) "At the tone," she said, "the time will be one . . . forty-nine. And ten seconds." What a voice. So melodious, so well modulated. "At the tone the time will be one . . . forty-nine. And twenty seconds."

He listened for over a minute, and then the call was cut off. The line clicked and the dial tone started. This made him feel rebuffed, although he knew he was being foolish. He bent to pat the cat. The cat allowed it briefly before walking away.

There was nothing to do but sit down at his typewriter.

He was behind schedule with this guidebook. Next week he was supposed to start on France, and he still hadn't finished the conclusion to the Canada book. He blamed it on the season. Who could sit alone indoors when everything outside was blooming? *Travelers should be forewarned,* he typed, but then he fell to admiring a spray of white azaleas that trembled on the ledge of his open window. A bee crawled among the blossoms, buzzing. He hadn't known the bees were out yet. Did Muriel know? Would she recall what a single bee could do to Alexander?

. . . should be forewarned, he read over, but his concentration was shot now.

She was so careless, so unthinking; how could he have put up with her? That unsanitary habit she had of licking her finger before she turned a magazine page; her tendency to use the word "enormity" as if it referred to size. There wasn't a chance in this world that she'd remember about bee stings.

He reached for the phone on his desk and dialed her number. "Muriel?"

"What," she said flatly.

"This is Macon."

"Yes, I know."

He paused. He said, "Um, it's bee season, Muriel."

"So?"

"I wasn't sure you were aware. I mean summer just creeps up, *I* know how summer creeps up, and I was wondering if you'd thought about Alexander's shots."

"Don't you believe I can manage that much for myself?" she screeched.

"Oh. Well."

"What do you think I am, some sort of ninny? Don't you think I know the simplest dumbest thing?"

"Well, I wasn't sure, you see, that—"

"A fine one you are! Ditch that child without a word of farewell and then call me up on the telephone to see if I'm raising him right!"

"I just wanted to—"

"Criticize, criticize! Tell me Oodles of Noodles is not a balanced meal and then go off and desert him and then have the nerve to call me up and tell me I'm not a good mother!"

"No, wait, Muriel—"

"Dominick is dead," she said.

"What?"

"Not that you would care. He died."

Macon noticed how the sounds in the room had stopped. "Dominick Saddler?" he asked.

"It was his night to take my car and he went to a party in Cockeysville and coming home he crashed into a guardrail."

"Oh, no."

"The girl he had with him didn't get so much as a scratch."

"But Dominick . . ." Macon said, because he didn't believe it yet.

"But Dominick died instantly."

"Oh, my Lord."

He saw Dominick on the couch with Alexander, holding aloft a can of paste wax.

"Want to hear something awful? My car will be just fine," Muriel said. "Straighten the front end and it'll run good as ever."

Macon rested his head in his hand.

"I have to go now and sit with Mrs. Saddler in the funeral home," she said.

"Is there something I can do?"

"No," she said, and then, spitefully, "How could *you* be any help?"

"I could stay with Alexander, maybe."

"Alexander's got people of our own to stay with him," she said.

The doorbell rang, and Edward started barking. Macon heard him in the front hall.

"Well, I'll say good-bye now," Muriel said. "Sounds like you have company."

"Never mind that."

"I'll let you get back to your *life*," she said. "So long."

He kept the receiver to his ear a moment, but she had hung up.

He went out to the hall and tapped his foot at Edward. "Down!" he said. Edward lay down, the hump on his back still bristling. Macon opened the door and found a boy with a clipboard.

"Modern Homewares," the boy told him.

"Oh. The couch."

While the couch was being unloaded, Macon shut Edward in the kitchen. Then he returned to the hall and watched the couch lumbering toward him, borne by the first boy and another, just slightly older, who had an eagle tattooed on his forearm. Macon thought of Dominick Saddler's muscular, corded arms grappling beneath the hood of Muriel's car. The first boy spat as he approached the house, but Macon saw how young and benign his face was. "Aw, man," the second one said, stumbling over the doorstep.

Macon said, "That's all right," and gave them each a five-dollar bill when they'd placed the couch where he directed.

After they'd gone he sat down on the couch, which still had some sort of cellophane covering. He rubbed his hands on his knees. Edward barked in the kitchen. Helen padded in softly, stopped still, eyed the couch, and continued through the room with an offended air. Macon went on sitting.

When Ethan died, the police had asked Macon to identify the body. But Sarah, they suggested, might prefer to wait outside. Yes, Sarah had said; she would. She had taken a seat on a molded beige chair in the hallway. Then she'd looked up at Macon and said, "Can you do this?"

"Yes," he'd told her, evenly. He had felt he was barely breathing; he was keeping himself very level, with most of the air emptied out of his lungs.

He had followed a man into a room. It was not as bad as it could have been because someone had folded a wad of toweling under the back of Ethan's head to hide the damage. Also it wasn't Ethan. Not the real Ethan. Odd how clear it suddenly became, once a person had died, that the body was the very least of him. This was simply an untenanted shell, although it bore a distant resemblance to Ethan—the same groove down the upper lip, same cowlick over the forehead. Macon had a sensation like pressing against a blank wall, willing with all his being something that could never happen: *Please, please come back inside.* But finally he said, "Yes. That is my son."

He'd returned to Sarah and given her a nod. Sarah had risen and put her arms around him. Later, when they were alone in their motel, she'd asked him what he had seen. "Not really much of anything, sweetheart," he had told her. She kept at him. Was Ethan . . . well, hurt-looking? Scared? He said, "No, he was nothing." He said, "Let me get you some tea."

"I don't want tea, I want to hear!" she'd said. "What are you hiding?" He had the impression she was blaming him for something. Over the next few weeks it seemed she grew to hold him responsible, like a bearer of bad tidings—the only one who could say for a fact that Ethan had truly died. She made several references to Macon's chilliness, to his appalling calm that night in the hospital morgue. Twice she expressed some doubt as to whether, in fact, he was really capable of distinguishing Ethan from some similar boy. In fact, that may not have been Ethan at all. It may have been somebody else who had died. She should have ascertained for herself. She was the mother, after all; she knew her child far better; what did Macon know?

Macon said, "Sarah. Listen. I will tell you as much as I can. He was very pale and still. You wouldn't believe how still. He didn't have any expression. His eyes were closed. There was nothing bloody or gruesome, just a sense of . . . futility. I mean I wondered what the purpose had been. His arms were down by his sides and I thought about last spring when he started lifting weights. I thought, 'Is this what it comes to? Lift weights and take vitamins and build yourself up and then—nothing?'"

He hadn't been prepared for Sarah's response. "So what are you saying?" she asked him. "We die in the end, so why bother to live in the first place? Is that what you're saying?"

"No—" he said.

"It all comes down to a question of economy?" she asked.

"No, Sarah. Wait," he had said.

Thinking back on that conversation now, he began to believe that people could, in fact, be used up—could use each other up, could be of no further help to each other and maybe even do harm to each other. He began to think that who you are when you're with somebody may matter more than whether you love her.

Lord knows how long he sat there.

Edward had been barking in the kitchen all this time, but now he went into a frenzy. Somebody must have knocked. Macon rose and went to the front of the house, where he found Julian standing on the porch with a file folder. "Oh. It's you," Macon said.

"What's all that barking I hear?"

"Don't worry, he's shut in the kitchen. Come on in."

He held the screen door open and Julian stepped inside. "Thought I'd bring you the material for Paris," Julian said.

"I see," Macon said. But he suspected he was really here for some other reason. Probably hoping to hurry the Canada book. "Well, I was just this minute touching up my conclusion," he said, leading the way to the living room. And then, hastily, "Few details here and there I'm not entirely happy with; may be a little while yet . . ."

Julian didn't seem to be listening. He sat down on the cellophane that covered the couch. He tossed the folder aside and said, "Have you seen Rose lately?"

"Yes, we were over there just this morning."

"Do you think she's not coming back?"

Macon hadn't expected him to be so direct. In fact, Rose's situation had begun to look like one of those permanent irregularities that couples never refer to. "Oh, well," he told Julian, "you know how it is. She's worried about the boys. They're eating glop or something."

"Those are not boys, Macon. They're men in their forties."

Macon stroked his chin.

"I'm afraid she's left me," Julian said.

"Oh, now, you can't be sure of that."

"And not even for a decent reason!" Julian said. "Or for any reason. I mean our marriage was working out fine; that much I can swear to. But she'd worn herself a groove or something in that house of hers, and she couldn't help swerving back into it. At least, I can't think of any other explanation."

"Well, it sounds about right," Macon told him.

"I went to see her two days ago," Julian said, "but she was out. I was standing in the yard wondering where she'd got to when who should drive past but Rose in person, with her car stuffed full of old ladies. All the windows packed with these little old faces and feathered hats. I shouted after her, I said, 'Rose! Wait!' but she didn't hear me and she drove on by. Then just at the last minute she caught sight of me, I guess, and she turned and stared, and I got the funniest feeling, like the car was driving *her*—like she was just gliding past helpless and couldn't do a thing but send me one long look before she disappeared."

Macon said, "Why don't you give her a job, Julian."

"Job?"

"Why don't you show her that office of yours. That filing system you never get sorted, that secretary chewing her gum and forgetting whose appointment is when. Don't you think Rose could take all that in hand?"

"Well, sure, but—"

"Call her up and tell her your business is going to pieces. Ask if she could just come in and get things organized, get things under control. Put it that way. Use those words. *Get things under control*, tell her. Then sit back and wait."

Julian thought that over.

"But of course, what do I know," Macon said.

"No, you're right."

"Now let's see your folder."

"You're absolutely right," Julian said.

"Look at this!" Macon said. He held up the topmost letter. "Why do you bother me with this? *I just wanted to appraise you folks of a wonderful little hotel in . . .* A man who says he wants to 'appraise' us, do you really suppose he'd know a good hotel when he saw one?"

"Macon," Julian said.

"The whole damn language has been slaughtered," Macon said.

"Macon, I know you feel I'm crass and brash."

This took Macon a moment to answer, only partly because he first heard it as "crash and brass." "Oh," he said. "Why, no, Julian, not at—"

"But I just want to say this, Macon. I care about that sister of yours more than anything else in the world. It's not just Rose, it's the whole way she lives, that house and those turkey dinners and those evening card games. And I care about you, too, Macon. Why, you're my best friend! At least, I hope so."

"Oh, why, ah—" Macon said.

Julian rose and shook his hand, mangling all the bones inside, and clapped him on the shoulder and left.

Sarah came home at five thirty. She found Macon standing at the kitchen sink with yet another cup of coffee. "Did the couch get here?" she asked him.

"All safe and sound."

"Oh, good! Let's see it."

She went into the living room, leaving tracks of gray dust that Macon supposed was clay or granite. There was dust in her hair, even. She squinted at the couch and said, "What do you think?"

"Seems fine to me," he said.

"Honestly, Macon. I don't know what's come over you; you used to be downright finicky."

"It's fine, Sarah. It looks very nice."

She stripped off the cellophane and stood back, arms full of crackling light. "We ought to see how it opens out," she said.

While she was stuffing the cellophane into the wastebasket, Macon pulled at the canvas strap that turned the couch into a bed. It made him think of Muriel's house. The strap's familiar graininess reminded him of all the times Muriel's sister had slept over, and when the mattress slid forth he saw the gleam of Claire's tangled golden hair.

"Maybe we should put on the sheets, now that we've got it open," Sarah said. She brought the sack of linens from the front hall. With

Macon positioned at the other side of the couch, she floated a sheet above the mattress and then bustled up and down, tucking it in. Macon helped, but he wasn't as fast as Sarah. The clay dust or whatever it was had worked itself into the seams of her knuckles, he saw. There was something appealing about her small, brown, creased hands against the white percale. He said, "Let's give the bed a trial run."

Sarah didn't understand at first. She looked up from unfolding the second sheet and said, "Trial run?"

But she allowed him to take the sheet away and slip her sweat shirt over her head.

Making love to Sarah was comfortable and soothing. After all their years together, her body was so well known to him that he couldn't always tell the difference between what he was feeling and what she was feeling. But wasn't it sad that they hadn't the slightest uneasiness about anyone's walking in on them? They were so alone. He nestled his face in her warm, dusty neck and wondered if she shared that feeling as well—if she sensed all the empty air in the house. But he would never ask.

While Sarah took a shower, he shaved. They were supposed to go to Bob and Sue Carney's for supper. When he came out of the bathroom Sarah was standing in front of the bureau, screwing on little gold earrings. (She was the only woman Macon knew of who didn't have pierced ears.) He thought Renoir could have painted her: Sarah in her slip with her head cocked slightly, plump tanned arms upraised. "I'm really not in the mood to go out," she said.

"Me neither," Macon said, opening his closet door.

"I'd be just as content to stay home with a book."

He pulled a shirt off a hanger.

"Macon," she said.

"Hmm."

"You never asked me if I slept with anyone while we were separated."

Macon paused, halfway into one sleeve.

"Don't you want to know?" she asked him.

"No," he said.

He put on the shirt and buttoned the cuffs.

"I would think you'd wonder."

"Well, I don't," he said.

"The trouble with you is, Macon—"

It was astonishing, the instantaneous flare of anger he felt. "Sarah," he said, "don't even start. By God, if that doesn't sum up every single thing that's wrong with being married. 'The trouble with you is, Macon—' and, 'I know you better than you know yourself, Macon—' "

"The trouble with you is," she continued steadily, "you think people should stay in their own sealed packages. You don't believe in opening up. You don't believe in trading back and forth."

"I certainly don't," Macon said, buttoning his shirt front.

"You know what you remind me of? That telegram Harpo Marx sent his brothers: *No message. Harpo.*"

That made him grin. Sarah said, "You *would* think it was funny."

"Well? Isn't it?"

"It isn't at all! It's sad! It's infuriating! It would be infuriating to go to your door and sign for that telegram and tear it open and find no message!"

He took a tie from the rack in his closet.

"For your information," she said, "I didn't sleep with anyone the whole entire time."

He felt she'd won some kind of contest. He pretended he hadn't heard her.

Bob and Sue had invited just neighbors—the Bidwells and a new young couple Macon hadn't met before. Macon stuck mainly to the new couple because with them, he had no history. When they asked if he had children, he said, "No." He asked if they had any children.

"No," Brad Frederick said.

"Ah."

Brad's wife was in transit between girlhood and womanhood. She wore her stiff navy blue dress and large white shoes as if they belonged to her mother. Brad himself was still a boy. When they all went out back to watch the barbecue, Brad found a Frisbee in the bushes and flung it to little Delilah Carney. His white polo shirt pulled loose from his trousers. Dominick Saddler came to Macon's mind like a deep, hard punch. He remembered how, after his grandfather died, the sight of any old person could make his eyes fill with tears. Lord, if he wasn't careful he could end up feeling sorry for the whole human race. "Throw that thing here," he said briskly to Delilah, and he set aside his sherry and held out a hand for the Frisbee. Before long they had a real game going—all the guests joining in except Brad's wife, who was still too close to childhood to risk getting stuck there on a visit back.

At supper, Sue Carney seated Macon at her right. She put a hand on his and said it was wonderful that he and Sarah had worked things out. "Well, thank you," Macon said. "Gosh, you make a really good salad, Sue."

"We all have our ups and downs," she said. For a second, he thought she meant her salads weren't consistently successful. "I'll be honest," she told him, "there've been times when I have wondered if Bob and I would make it. There's times I feel we're just hanging in there, you know what I mean? Times I say, 'Hi, honey, how was your day?' but inside I'm feeling like a Gold Star mother."

Macon turned the stem of his glass and tried to think what step he'd missed in her logic.

"Like someone who's suffered a loss in a war," she said, "and then forever afterward she has to go on supporting the war; she has to support it louder than anyone else, because otherwise she'd be admitting the loss was for no purpose."

"Um . . ."

"But that's just a passing mood," she said.

"Well, naturally," Macon said.

He and Sarah walked home through air as heavy as water. It was eleven o'clock and the teenagers who had eleven o'clock curfews were just returning. These were the youngest ones, most of them too young to drive, and so they were chauffeured by grown-ups. They jumped out of cars shouting, "See you! Thanks! Call me tomorrow, hear?" Keys jingled. Front doors blinked open and blinked shut again. The cars moved on.

Sarah's skirt had the same whispery sound as the Tuckers' lawn sprinkler, which was still revolving slowly in a patch of ivy.

When they reached the house, Macon let Edward out for one last run. He tried to get the cat to come in, but she stayed hunched on the kitchen window ledge glaring down at him, owlish and stubborn; so he let her be. He moved through the rooms turning off lights. By the time he came upstairs Sarah was already in bed, propped against the headboard with a glass of club soda. "Have some," she said, holding out the glass. But he said no, he was tired; and he undressed and slid under the covers.

The tinkling of Sarah's ice cubes took on some meaning in his mind. It seemed that with every tinkle, he fell deeper. Finally he opened a door and traveled down an aisle and stepped into the witness stand. They asked him the simplest of questions. "What color were the wheels?" "Who brought the bread?" "Were the shutters closed or open?" He honestly couldn't remember. He tried but he couldn't remember. They took him to the scene of the crime, a winding road like something in a fairy tale. "Tell us all you know," they said. He didn't know a thing. By now it was clear from their faces that he wasn't merely a witness; they suspected him. So he racked his brain, but still he came up empty. "You have to see my side of this!" he cried. "I put it all out of my mind; I worked to put it out! Now I can't bring it back."

"Not even to defend yourself?" they asked.

He opened his eyes. The room was dark, and Sarah breathed softly next to him. The clock radio said it was midnight. The midnight-curfew group was just returning. Hoots and laughter rang out, tires scraped a curb, and a fanbelt whinnied as someone struggled to park. Then gradually the neighborhood fell silent. It would stay that way, Macon knew, till time for the one-o'clock group. He would first hear faint strands of their music and then more laughter, car doors slamming, house doors slamming. Porch lights would switch off all along the street, gradually dimming the ceiling as he watched. In the end, he would be the only one left awake.

20

The plane to New York was a little bird of a thing, but the plane to Paris was a monster, more like a building. Inside, great crowds were cramming coats and bags into overhead compartments, stuffing suitcases under seats, arguing, calling for stewardesses. Babies were crying and mothers were snapping at children. Steerage could not have been worse than this, Macon felt.

He took his place next to a window and was joined almost immediately by an elderly couple speaking French. The man sat next to Macon and gave him a deep, unsmiling nod. Then he said something to his wife, who passed him a canvas bag. He unzipped it and sorted through its contents. Playing cards, an entire tin of Band-aids, a stapler, a hammer, a light bulb . . . Macon was fascinated. He kept sliding his eyes to the right to try and see more. When a wooden mousetrap tumbled out, he began to wonder if the man might be some sort of lunatic; but of course even a mousetrap could be explained, given a little thought. Yes, what he was witnessing, Macon decided, was just one answer to the traveler's eternal choice: Which was better? Take all you own, and struggle to carry it? Or travel light, and spend half your trip combing the shops for what you've left behind? Either way had its drawbacks.

He glanced up the aisle, where more passengers were arriving. A Japanese man festooned with cameras, a nun, a young girl in braids. A woman with a little red vanity kit, her hair a dark tent, her face a thin triangle.

Muriel.

First he felt a kind of flush sweep through him—that flood of warmth that comes when someone familiar steps forth from a mass of strangers. And then: *Oh, my God,* he thought, and he actually looked around for some means of escape.

She walked toward him in a graceful, picky way, watching her feet, and then when she was next to him she raised her eyes and he saw that she'd known all along he was there. She wore a white suit that turned her into one of those black-white-and-red women he used to admire on movie screens as a child.

"I'm going to France," she told him.

"But you can't!" he said.

The French couple peered at him curiously, the wife sitting slightly forward so as to see him better.

More passengers arrived behind Muriel. They muttered and craned around her, trying to edge past. She stood in the aisle and said, "I'm going to walk along the Seine."

The wife made a little O with her mouth.

Then Muriel noticed the people behind her and moved on.

Macon wasn't even sure it was possible to walk along the Seine. As soon as the aisle was cleared he half stood and peered over the back of his seat, but she had vanished. The French couple turned to him, eyes expectant. Macon settled down again.

Sarah would find out about this. She would just somehow know. She had always said he had no feelings and this would confirm it— that he could tell her good-bye so fondly and then fly off to Paris with Muriel.

Well, it was none of his doing and he'd be damned if he'd assume the blame.

By the time it was dark they were airborne, and some kind of order had emerged inside the plane. It was one of those flights as fully programmed as a day in kindergarten. Safety film, drinks, headphones, dinner, movie. Macon turned down all he was offered and studied Julian's file folder instead. Most of the material was ridiculous. Sam'n'Joe's Hotel, indeed! He wondered if Julian had made it up to tease him.

A woman passed wearing white and he glanced at her surreptitiously, but it was no one he knew.

Just before the end of the movie, he got out his shaving kit and went to use one of the lavatories near the rear. Unfortunately other people had had the same idea. Both doors were locked, and he was forced to wait in the aisle. He felt someone arrive at his side. He looked and there was Muriel.

He said, "Muriel, what in—"

"You don't own this plane!" she told him.

Heads turned.

"And you don't own Paris, either," she said.

She was standing very close to him, face to face. She gave off a scent that barely eluded him; it was not just her perfume, no, but her house; yes, that was it—the smell inside her closet, the tantalizing, unsettling smell of other people's belongings. Macon pressed his left temple. He said, "I don't understand any of this. I don't see how you knew which flight to take, even."

"I called your travel agent."

"Becky? You called Becky? What must she have thought?"

"She thought I was your editorial assistant."

"And how could you afford the fare?"

"Oh, some I borrowed from Bernice and then some from my sister, she had this money she earned at . . . and I did everything economy-style, I took a train to New York instead of a plane—"

"Well, *that* wasn't smart," Macon said. "It probably cost you the same, in the long run, or maybe even more."

"No, what I did was—"

"But the point is, why, Muriel? Why are you doing this?"

She lifted her chin. (Her chin could get so sharp, sometimes.) "Because I felt like it," she said.

"You felt like spending five days alone in a Paris hotel? That's what it will be, Muriel."

"You need to have me around," she said.

"Need you!"

"You were falling to pieces before you had me."

A latch clicked and a man stepped out of one of the lavatories. Macon stepped inside and locked the door quickly behind him.

He wished he could just vanish. If there had been a window, he believed he would have pried it open and jumped—not because he wanted to commit any act so definite as suicide but because he wanted to erase it all; oh, Lord, just go back and erase all the untidy, unthinking things he'd been responsible for in his life.

If she had read even a one of his guidebooks, she'd have known not to travel in white.

When he emerged, she was gone. He went back to his seat. The French couple drew in their knees to let him slide past; they were transfixed by the movie screen, where a blonde wearing nothing but a bath towel was pounding on a front door. Macon got out *Miss MacIntosh* just for something to pin his mind to. It didn't work, though. Words flowed across his vision in a thin, transparent stream, mean-ingless. He was conscious only of Muriel somewhere behind him. He felt wired to her. He caught himself wondering what she made of this—the darkened plane, the invisible ocean beneath her, the murmur of half-real voices all around her. When he turned off his reading light and shut his eyes, he imagined he could sense that she was still awake. It was a feeling in the air—something alert, tense, almost vibrating.

By morning he was resolved. He used a different lavatory, toward the front. For once he was glad to be in such a large crowd. When they landed he was almost the first one off, and he cleared Immigration quickly and darted through the airport. The airport was Charles de Gaulle, with its space-age pods of seats. Muriel would be thoroughly lost. He exchanged his money in haste. Muriel must still be at Baggage

Claims. He knew she would carry lots of baggage.

There was no question of waiting for a bus. He hailed a cab and sped off, feeling wonderfully lightweight all of a sudden. The tangle of silvery highways struck him as actually pleasant. The city of Paris, when he entered, was as wide and pale and luminous as a cool gray stare, and he admired the haze that hung over it. His cab raced down misty boulevards, turned onto a cobbled street, lurched to a stop. Macon sifted through his envelopes of money.

Not till he was entering his hotel did he recall that his travel agent knew exactly where he was staying.

It wasn't a very luxurious hotel—a small brown place where mechanical things tended to go wrong, as Macon had discovered on past visits. This time, according to a sign in the lobby, one of the two elevators was not marching. The bellman led him into the other, then up to the third floor and down a carpeted corridor. He flung open a door, loudly exclaiming in French as if overcome by such magnificence. (A bed, a bureau, a chair, an antique TV.) Macon burrowed into one of his envelopes. "Thank you," he said, offering his tip.

Once he was alone, he unpacked and he hung up his suit coat. Then he went to the window. He stood looking out over the rooftops; the dust on the glass made them seem removed in time, part of some other age.

How would she manage alone in such an unaccustomed place?

He thought of the way she navigated a row of thrift shops—the way she cruised a street, deft and purposeful, greeting passersby by name. And the errands she took the neighbors on: chauffeuring Mr. Manion to the reflexologist who dissolved his kidney stones by massaging his toes; Mr. Runkle to the astrologer who told him when he'd win the million-dollar lottery; Mrs. Carpaccio to a certain tiny grocery near Johns Hopkins where the sausages hung from the ceiling like strips of flypaper. The places Muriel knew!

But she didn't know Paris. And she was entirely on her own. She didn't even have a credit card, probably carried very little money, might not have known to change what she did carry into francs. Might be wandering helpless, penniless, unable to speak a word of the language.

By the time he heard her knock, he was so relieved that he rushed to open the door.

"Your room is bigger than mine is," she said. She walked past him to the window. "I have a better view, though. Just think, we're really in Paris! The bus driver said it might rain but I told him I didn't care. Rain or shine, it's Paris."

"How did you know what bus to take?" he asked her.

"I brought along your guidebook."

She patted her pocket.

"Want to go to Chez Billy for breakfast?" she asked. "That's what your book recommends."

"No, I don't. I can't," he said. "You'd better leave, Muriel."

"Oh. Okay," she said. She left.

Sometimes she would do that. She'd press in till he felt trapped, then suddenly draw back. It was like a tug of war where the other person all at once drops the rope, Macon thought. You fall flat on the ground; you're so unprepared. You're so empty-feeling.

He decided to call Sarah. At home it was barely dawn, but it seemed important to get in touch with her. He went over to the phone on the bureau and picked up the receiver. It was dead. He pressed the button a few times. Typical. He dropped his key in his pocket and went down to the lobby.

The lobby telephone was housed in an ancient wooden booth, very genteel. There was a red leather bench to sit on. Macon hunched over and listened to the ringing at the other end, far away. "Hello?" Sarah said.

"Sarah?"

"Who is this?"

"It's Macon."

"Macon?"

She took a moment to absorb that. "Macon, where are you?" she asked. "What's the matter?"

"Nothing's the matter. I just felt like talking to you."

"What? What time is it?"

"I know it's early and I'm sorry I woke you but I wanted to hear your voice."

"There's some kind of static on the line," she said.

"It's clear at this end."

"You sound so thin."

"That's because it's an overseas call," he said. "How's the weather there?"

"How's who?"

"The weather! Is it sunny?"

"I don't know. All the shades are down. I don't think it's even light yet."

"Will you be gardening today?"

"What?"

"Gardening!"

"Well, I hadn't thought. It depends on whether it's sunny, I guess."

"I wish I were there," he said. "I could help you."

"You hate to garden!"

"Yes, but . . ."

"Macon, are you all right?"

"Yes, I'm fine," he said.

"How was the flight over?"

"Oh, the flight, well, goodness! Well, I don't know; I guess I was so busy reading I didn't really notice," he said.

"Reading?" she said. Then she said, "Maybe you've got jet lag."

"Yes, maybe I do," he told her.

Fried eggs, scrambled eggs, poached eggs, omelets. He walked blindly down the sidewalk, scribbling in the margins of his guidebook. He did not go near Chez Billy. *It's puzzling*, he wrote, *how the French are so tender in preparing their food but so rough in serving it.* In the window of a restaurant, a black cat closed her eyes at him. She seemed to be gloating. She was so much at home, so sure of her place.

Displays of crushed velvet, scattered with solid gold chains and watches no thicker than poker chips. Women dressed as if for the stage: elaborate hairdos, brilliant makeup, strangely shaped trousers that had nothing to do with the human anatomy. Old ladies in little-girl ruffles and white tights and Mary Janes. Macon descended the steps to the Métro; he ostentatiously dropped his canceled ticket into a tiny receptacle marked PAPIERS. Then he turned to glare at all the others who flung their tickets on the floor, and as he turned he thought he saw Muriel, her white face glimmering in the crowd, but he must have been mistaken.

In the evening he returned to his hotel—footsore, leg muscles aching—and collapsed on his bed. Not two minutes later he heard a knock. He groaned and rose to open the door. Muriel stood there with her arms full of clothes. "Look," she said, pushing past him. "See what-all I bought." She dumped the clothes on the bed. She held them up one by one: a shiny black cape, a pair of brown jodhpurs, a bouffant red net evening dress sprinkled with different-sized disks of glass like the reflectors on bicycles. "Have you lost your senses?" Macon asked. "What must all this have cost?"

"Nothing! Or next to nothing," she said. "I found a place that's like the granddaddy of all garage sales. A whole city of garage sales! This French girl was telling me about it where I went to have my breakfast. I complimented her hat and she told me where she got it. I took a subway train to find it; your book's really helpful about the subways; and sure enough, there's everything there. Tools and gadgets too, Macon. Old car batteries, fuse boxes . . . and if you say something's too expensive, they'll bring the price down till it's cheap enough. I saw this leather coat I would have killed for but that never did get cheap enough; the man wanted thirty-five francs."

"Thirty-five francs!" Macon said. "I don't know how you could get any cheaper than that. Thirty-five francs is four dollars or so."

"Oh, really? I thought francs and dollars were about the same."

"Lord, no."

"Well, then these things were *super* bargains," Muriel said. "Maybe I'll try again tomorrow."

"But how will you get all this stuff on the plane?"

"Oh, I'll figure out some way. Now let me take it back to my room so we can go eat."

He stiffened. He said, "No, I can't."

"What harm would it do to eat supper with me, Macon? I'm someone from home! You've run into me in Paris! Can't we have a bite together?"

When she put it that way, it seemed so simple.

They went to the Burger King on the Champs-Elysées; Macon wanted to recheck the place anyhow. He ordered two "Woppaires." "Careful," he warned Muriel, "these are not the Whoppers you're used to. You'll want to scrape the extra pickle and onion off." But Muriel, after trying hers, said she liked it the way it was. She sat next to him on a hard little seat and licked her fingers. Her shoulder touched his. He was amazed, all at once, that she really was here.

"Who's looking after Alexander?" he asked her.

"Oh, different people."

"What different people? I hope you haven't just parked him, Muriel. You know how insecure a child that age can—"

"Relax. He's fine. Claire has him in the daytime and then Bernice comes in and cooks supper and any time Claire has a date with the General the twins will keep him or if the twins can't do it then the General says Alexander can . . ."

Singleton Street rose up in front of Macon's eyes, all its color and confusion.

After supper Muriel suggested they take a walk, but Macon said he was tired. He was exhausted, in fact. They returned to their hotel. In the elevator Muriel asked, "Can I come to your room a while? My TV set only gets snow."

"We'd better say good night," he told her.

"Can't I just come in and keep you company?"

"No, Muriel."

"We wouldn't have to *do* anything," she said.

The elevator stopped at his floor. He said, "Muriel. Don't you understand my position? I've been married to her forever. Longer than you've been alive, almost. I can't change now. Don't you see?"

She just stood in her corner of the elevator with her eyes on his face. All her makeup had worn off and she looked young and sad and defenseless.

"Good night," he said.

He got out, and the elevator door slid shut.

He went to bed immediately but couldn't sleep after all, and ended up switching on the TV. They were showing an American western, dubbed. Rangy cowboys spoke a fluid, intricate French. Disaster followed disaster—tornadoes, Indians, droughts, stampedes. The hero stuck in there, though. Macon had long ago noticed that all adventure movies had the same moral: Perseverance pays. Just once he'd like to see a hero like himself—not a quitter, but a man who did face facts and give up gracefully when pushing onward was foolish.

He rose and switched the set off again. He tossed and turned a long time before he slept.

Large hotels, small hotels, dingy hotels with their wallpaper flaking, streamlined hotels with king-sized American beds and Formica-topped American bureaus. Dim café windows with the proprietors displayed like mannequins, clasping their hands behind their backs and rocking from heel to toe. *Don't fall for* prix fixe. *It's like a mother saying, "Eat, eat"—all those courses forced on you . . .*

In the late afternoon Macon headed wearily back to his own hotel. He was crossing the final intersection when he saw Muriel up ahead. Her arms were full of parcels, her hair was flying out, and her spike-heeled shoes were clipping along. "Muriel!" he called. She turned and he ran to catch up with her.

"Oh, Macon, I've had the nicest day," she said. "I met these people from Dijon and we ended up eating lunch together and they told me about . . . Here, can you take some of these? I think I overbought."

He accepted several of her parcels—crumpled, used-looking bags stuffed with fabrics. He helped her carry them into the hotel and up to her room, which seemed even smaller than it was because of the piles of clothing everywhere. She dumped her burdens on the bed and said, "Let me show you, now, where is it . . ."

"What's this?" Macon asked. He was referring to an oddly shaped soft drink bottle on the bureau.

"Oh, I found that in the fridge," she said. "They have this little fridge in the bathroom, Macon, and it's just full of soft drinks, and wine and liquor too."

"Muriel, don't you know those cost an arm and a leg? They'll put it on your bill, don't you know that? Now, that fridge is called a mini-bar, and here's what you use it for: In the morning, when they wheel in the continental breakfast, they bring a pitcher of hot milk for some strange reason and you just take that pitcher and stick it in the mini-bar so later you can have a glass of milk. Otherwise, Lord knows how you'd get your calcium in this country. And don't eat the rolls; you know that, don't you? Don't start your day with carbohydrates, especially under the strain of travel. You're better off taking the trouble to go to some café for eggs."

"Eggs, ugh," Muriel said. She was stepping out of her skirt and trying on another—one she'd just bought, with long fringes at the hem.

"I *like* the rolls," she said. "And I like the soft drinks, too."

"Well, I don't know how you can say that," he said. He picked up the bottle. "Just look at the brand name: Pschitt. If that's not the most suspicious-sounding . . . and there's another kind called Yukkie, Yukkery, something like that—"

"That's my favorite. I already finished those off," Muriel said. She was pinning her hair on top of her head. "Where we having dinner tonight?"

"Well, I don't know. I guess it's time to try someplace fancy."

"Oh, goody!"

He moved what appeared to be an antique satin bedjacket and sat down to watch her put her lipstick on.

They went to a restaurant lit with candles, although it wasn't quite dark yet, and were seated next to a tall, curtained window. The only other customers were American—four American business types, plainly enjoying themselves over four large platters of snails. (Sometimes Macon wondered if there really was any call for his books.)

"Now, what do I want?" Muriel said, studying the menu. "If I ask them what something is in English, do you think they'll be able to tell me?"

"Oh, you don't have to bother doing that," Macon said. "Just order Salade Niçoise."

"Order what?"

"I thought you said you'd read my guide! Salade Niçoise. It's the one safe dish. I've been all through France eating nothing but, day in and day out."

"Well, that sounds kind of monotonous," Muriel said.

"No, no. Some places put green beans in it, some don't. And at least it's low cholesterol, which is more than you can say for—"

"I think I'll just ask the waiter," Muriel told him. She laid her menu aside. "Do you suppose they call them French windows in France?"

"What? I wouldn't have the slightest idea," he said. He looked toward the window, which was paned with deep, greenish glass. Outside, in an overgrown courtyard, a pitted stone cherub was cavorting in a fountain.

The waiter spoke more English than Macon had expected. He directed Muriel toward a cream of sorrel soup and a special kind of fish. Macon decided to go for the soup as well, rather than sit idle while Muriel had hers. "There," Muriel said. "Wasn't he nice?"

"That was a rare exception," Macon said.

She batted at the hem of her skirt. "Durn fringe! I keep thinking something's crawling up my leg," she said. "Where you going tomorrow, Macon?"

"Out of Paris altogether. Tomorrow I start on the other cities."

"You're leaving me here alone?"

"This is high-speed travel, Muriel. Not fun. I'm waking up at crack of dawn."

"Take me anyway."

"I can't."

"I haven't been sleeping so good," she said. "I get bad dreams."

"Well, then you certainly don't want to go gallivanting off to more new places."

"Last night I dreamed about Dominick," she said. She leaned toward him across the table, two spots of color high on her cheekbones. "I dreamed he was mad at me."

"Mad?"

"He wouldn't talk to me. Wouldn't look at me. Kept kicking something on the sidewalk. Turned out he was mad because I wouldn't let him use the car anymore. I said, 'Dommie, you're dead. You *can't* use the car. I'd let you if I could, believe me.' "

"Well, don't worry about it," Macon said. "It was just a travel dream."

"I'm scared it means he's mad for real. Off wherever he's at."

"He's not," Macon told her. "He wouldn't be mad."

"I'm scared he is."

"He's happy as a lark."

"You really think so?"

"Sure! He's up there in some kind of motor heaven, polishing a car all his own. And it's always spring and the sun is always shining and there's always some blonde in a halter top to help him with the buffing."

"You really think that might be true?" Muriel asked.

"Yes, I do," he said. And the funny thing was that he did, just at that moment. He had a vivid image of Dominick in a sunlit meadow, a chamois skin in his hand and a big, pleased, cocky grin on his face.

She said at the end of the evening that she wished he would come to her room—couldn't he? to guard against bad dreams?—and he said no and told her good night. And then he felt how she drew at him, pulling deep strings from inside him, when the elevator creaked away with her.

In his sleep he conceived a plan to take her along tomorrow. What harm would it do? It was only a day trip. Over and over in his scattered, fitful sleep he picked up his phone and dialed her room. It was a surprise, when he woke in the morning, to find he hadn't invited her yet.

He sat up and reached for the phone and remembered only then—with the numb receiver pressed to his ear—that the phone was out of order and he'd forgotten to report it. He wondered if it were something he could repair himself, a cord unplugged or something. He rose and peered behind the bureau. He stooped to hunt for a jack of some kind.

And his back went out.

No doubt about it—that little twang! in a muscle to the left of his spine. The pain was so sharp it snagged his breath. Then it faded. Maybe it was gone for good. He straightened, a minimal movement. But it was enough to bring the pain zinging in again.

He lowered himself to the bed inch by inch. The hard part was getting his feet up, but he set his face and accomplished that too. Then he lay pondering what to do next.

Once he had had this happen and the pain had vanished in five minutes and not returned. It had been only a freaky thing like a foot cramp.

But then, once he'd stayed flat in bed for two weeks and crept around like a very old man for another month after that.

He lay rearranging his agenda in his mind. If he canceled one trip, postponed another . . . Yes, possibly what he'd planned for the next three days could be squeezed into two instead, if only he were able to get around by tomorrow.

He must have gone back to sleep. He didn't know for how long. He woke to a knock and thought it was breakfast, though he'd left instructions for none to be brought today. But then he heard Muriel. "Macon? You in there?" She was hoping he hadn't left Paris yet; she was here to beg again to go with him. He knew that as clearly as if she'd announced it. He was grateful now for the spasm that gripped him as he turned away from her voice. Somehow that short sleep had cleared his head, and he saw that he'd come perilously close to falling in with her again. *Falling in:* That was the way he put it to himself. What luck that his back had stopped him. Another minute—another few seconds—and he might have been lost.

He dropped into sleep so suddenly that he didn't even hear her walk away.

When he woke again it was much later, he felt, although he didn't want to go through the contortions necessary to look at his watch. A wheeled cart was passing his room and he heard voices—hotel employees, probably—laughing in the corridor. They must be so comfortable here; they must all know each other so well. There was a knock on his door, then a jingle of keys. A small, pale chambermaid poked her face in and said, *"Pardon, monsieur."* She started to retreat but then stopped and asked him something in French, and he gestured toward his back and winced. "Ah," she said, entering, and she said something else very rapidly. (She would be telling him about *her* back.) He said, "If you could just help me up, please," for he had decided he had no choice but to go call Julian. She seemed to understand what he meant and came over to the bed. He turned onto his stomach and then struggled up on one arm—the only way he could manage to rise without excruciating pain. The chambermaid took his other arm and braced herself beneath his weight as he stood. She was much shorter than he, and pretty in a fragile, meek way. He was conscious of his unshaven face and his rumpled pajamas. "My jacket," he told her, and they proceeded haltingly to the chair where his suit jacket hung. She draped it around his shoulders. Then he said, "Downstairs? To the telephone?" She looked over at the phone on the bureau, but he made a negative movement with the flat of his hand—a gesture that cost him. He grimaced. She clucked her tongue and led him out into the corridor.

Walking was not particularly difficult; he felt hardly a twinge. But the elevator jerked agonizingly and there was no way he could predict it. The chambermaid uttered soft sounds of sympathy. When they arrived in the lobby she led him to the telephone booth and started to seat him, but he said, "No, no, standing's easier. Thanks." She backed out and left him there. He saw her talking to the clerk at the desk, shaking her head in pity; the clerk shook his head, too.

Macon worried Julian wouldn't be in his office yet, and he didn't know his home number. But the phone was answered on the very first ring. "Businessman's Press." A woman's voice, confusingly familiar, threading beneath the hiss of long distance.

"Um—" he said. "This is Macon Leary. To whom am I—"

"Oh, Macon."

"Rose?"

"Yes, it's me."

"What are *you* doing there?"

"I work here now."

"Oh, I see."

"I'm putting things in order. You wouldn't believe the state this place is in."

"Rose, my back has gone out on me," Macon said.

"Oh, no, of all times! Are you still in Paris?"

"Yes, but I was just about to start my day trips and there are all these plans I have to change—appointments, travel reservations—and no telephone in my room. So I was wondering if Julian could do it from his end. Maybe he could get the reservations from Becky and—"

"I'll take care of it myself," Rose said. "Don't you bother with a thing."

"I don't know when I'm going to get to the other cities, tell him. I don't have any idea when I'll be—"

"We'll work it out. Have you seen a doctor?"

"Doctors don't help. Just bed rest."

"Well, rest then, Macon."

He gave her the name of his hotel, and she repeated it briskly and then told him to get on back to bed.

When he emerged from the phone booth the chambermaid had a bellboy there to help him, and between the two of them he made it to his room without much trouble. They were very solicitous. They seemed anxious about leaving him alone, but he assured them he would be all right.

All that afternoon he lay in bed, rising twice to go to the bathroom and once to get some milk from the mini-bar. He wasn't really hungry. He watched the brown flowers on the wallpaper; he thought he had never known a hotel room so intimately. The side of the bureau next to the bed had a streak in the woodgrain that looked like a bony man in a hat.

At suppertime he took a small bottle of wine from the mini-bar and inched himself into the armchair to drink it. Even the motion of raising the bottle to his lips caused him pain, but he thought the wine would help him sleep. While he was sitting there the chambermaid knocked and let herself in. She asked him, evidently, whether he wanted anything to eat, but he thanked her and said no. She must have been on her way home; she carried a battered little pocketbook.

Later there was another knock, after he had dragged himself back to bed, and Muriel said, "Macon? Macon?" He kept absolutely silent. She went away.

The air grew fuzzy and then dark. The man on the side of the bureau faded. Footsteps crossed the floor above him.

He had often wondered how many people died in hotels. The law of averages said some would, right? And some who had no close relatives—say one of his readers, a salesman without a family—well, what was done about such people? Was there some kind of potters' field for unknown travelers?

He could lie in only two positions—on his left side or on his back—and switching from one to the other meant waking up, consciously deciding to undertake the ordeal, plotting his strategy. Then he returned to a fretful semiconsciousness.

He dreamed he was seated on an airplane next to a woman dressed all in gray, a very narrow, starched, thin-lipped woman, and he tried to hold perfectly still because he sensed she disapproved of movement. It was a rule of hers; he knew that somehow. But he grew more and more uncomfortable, and so he decided to confront her. He said, "Ma'am?" She turned her eyes on him, mild, mournful eyes under finely arched brows. "Miss MacIntosh!" he said. He woke in a spasm of pain. He felt as if a tiny, cruel hand had snatched up part of his back and wrung it out.

When the waiter brought his breakfast in the morning, the chambermaid came along. She must keep grueling hours, Macon thought. But he was glad to see her. She and the waiter fussed over him, mixing his hot milk and coffee, and the waiter helped him into the bathroom while the chambermaid changed his sheets. He thanked them over and over; "*Merci,*" he said, clumsily. He wished he knew the French for, "I don't know why you're being so kind." After they left he ate all of his rolls, which the chambermaid had thoughtfully buttered and spread with strawberry jam. Then he turned on the TV for company and got back in bed.

He was sorry about the TV when he heard the knock on the door, because he thought it was Muriel and she would hear. But it seemed early for Muriel to be awake. And then a key turned in the lock, and in walked Sarah.

He said, "Sarah?"

She wore a beige suit, and she carried two pieces of matched luggage, and she brought a kind of breeze of efficiency with her. "Now, everything's taken care of," she told him. "I'm going to make your day trips for you." She set down her suitcases, kissed his forehead, and picked up a glass from his breakfast table. As she went off to the bathroom she said, "We've rescheduled the other cities and I start on them tomorrow."

"But how did you get here so soon?" he asked.

She came out of the bathroom; the glass was full of water. "You have Rose to thank for that," she said, switching off the TV. "Rose is just a wizard. She's revamped that entire office. Here's a pill from Dr. Levitt."

"You know I don't take pills," he said.

"This time you do," she told him. She helped him rise up on one elbow. "You're going to sleep as much as you can, so your back has a chance to heal. Swallow."

The pill was tiny and very bitter. He could taste it even after he'd lain down again.

"Is the pain bad?" she asked him.

"Kind of."

"How've you been getting your meals?"

"Well, breakfast comes anyway, of course. That's about it."

"I'll ask about room service," she told him, picking up the phone. "Since I'll be gone so . . . What's the matter with the telephone?"

"It's dead."

"I'll go tell the desk. Can I bring you anything while I'm out?"

"No, thank you."

When she left, he almost wondered if he'd imagined her. Except that her suitcases sat next to his bed, sleek and creamy—the same ones she kept on the closet shelf at home.

He thought about Muriel, about what would happen if she were to knock now. Then he thought about two nights ago, or was it three, when she had strolled in with all her purchases. He wondered if she'd left any traces. A belt lost under the bed, a glass disk fallen off her cocktail dress? He began to worry about it seriously. It seemed to him almost inevitable; of course she'd left something. The only question was, what. And where.

Groaning, he rolled over and pushed himself upright. He struggled off the bed and then sagged to his knees to peer beneath it. There didn't seem to be anything there. He got to his feet and tilted over the armchair to feel around the edges of the cushion. Nothing there either. Actually she hadn't gone anywhere near the armchair, to his recollection; nor had she gone to the bureau, but even so he slid out the drawers one by one to make sure. His own belongings—just a handful—occupied one drawer. The others were empty, but the second one down had a sprinkling of pink face powder. It wasn't Muriel's, of course, but it looked like hers. He decided to get rid of it. He tottered into the bathroom, dampened a towel, and came back to swab the drawer clean. Then he saw that the towel had developed a large pink smear, as if a woman wearing too much makeup had wiped her face with it. He folded the towel so the smear was concealed and laid it in the back of the drawer. No, too incriminating. He took it out again and hid it beneath the armchair cushion. That didn't seem right either. Finally he went into the bathroom and washed the towel by hand, scrubbing it with a bar of soap till the spot was completely gone. The pain in his back was constant, and beads of sweat stood out on his forehead. At some point he decided he was acting very peculiar; in fact it must be the pill; and he dropped the wet towel in a heap on the floor and crawled back into bed. He fell asleep at once. It wasn't a normal sleep; it was a kind of burial.

He knew Sarah came in but he couldn't wake up to greet her. And he knew she left again. He heard someone knock, he heard lunch being brought, he heard the chambermaid whisper, *"Monsieur?"* He remained in his stupor. The pain was muffled but still present—just covered up, he thought; the pill worked like those inferior room sprays in advertisements, the ones that only mask offending odors. Then Sarah came back for the second time and he opened his eyes. She was standing over the bed with a glass of water. "How do you feel?" she asked him.

"Okay," he said.

"Here's your next pill."

"Sarah, those things are deadly."

"They help, don't they?"

"They knock me out," he said. But he took the pill.

She sat down on the edge of the mattress, careful not to jar him.

She still wore her suit and looked freshly groomed, although she must be bushed by now. "Macon," she said quietly.

"Hmm."

"I saw that woman friend of yours."

He tensed. His back seized up.

"She saw me, too," she said. "She seemed very surprised."

"Sarah, this is not the way it looks," he told her.

"What is it then, Macon? I'd like to hear."

"She came over on her own. I didn't even know till just before the plane took off, I swear it! She followed me. I told her I didn't want her along. I told her it was no use."

She kept looking at him. "You didn't know till just before the plane took off," she said.

"I swear it," he said.

He wished he hadn't taken the pill. He felt he wasn't in full possession of his faculties.

"Do you believe me?" he asked her.

"Yes, I believe you," she said, and then she got up and started uncovering his lunch dishes.

He spent the afternoon in another stupor, but he was aware of the chambermaid's checking on him twice, and he was almost fully awake when Sarah came in with a bag of groceries. "I thought I'd make you supper myself," she told him. "Fresh fruit and things; you always complain you don't get enough fresh fruit when you travel."

"That's very nice of you, Sarah."

He worked himself around till he was half sitting, propped against a pillow. Sarah was unwrapping cheeses. "The phone's fixed," she said. "You'll be able to call for your meals and all while I'm out. Then I was thinking: After I've finished the trips, if your back is better, maybe we could do a little sightseeing on our own. Take some time for ourselves, since we're here. Visit a few museums and such."

"Fine," he said.

"Have a second honeymoon, sort of."

"Wonderful."

He watched her set the cheeses on a flattened paper bag. "We'll change your plane ticket for a later date," she said. "You're reserved to leave tomorrow morning; no chance you could manage that. I left my own ticket open-ended. Julian said I should. Did I tell you where Julian is living?"

"No, where?"

"He's moved in with Rose and your brothers."

"He's what?"

"I took Edward over to Rose's to stay while I was gone, and there was Julian. He sleeps in Rose's bedroom; he's started playing Vaccination every night after supper."

"Well, I'll be damned," Macon said.

"Have some cheese."

He accepted a slice, changing position as little as possible.

"Funny, sometimes Rose reminds me of a flounder," Sarah said. "Not in looks, of course . . . She's lain on the ocean floor so long, one eye has moved to the other side of her head."

He stopped chewing and stared at her. She was pouring two glasses of cloudy brown liquid. "Apple cider," she told him. "I figured you shouldn't drink wine with those pills."

"Oh. Right," he said.

She passed him a glass. "A toast to our second honeymoon," she said.

"Our second honeymoon," he echoed.

"Twenty-one more years together."

"Twenty-one!" he said. It sounded like such a lot.

"Or would you say twenty."

"No, it's twenty-one, all right. We were married in nineteen—"

"I mean because we skipped this past year."

"Oh," he said. "No, it would still be twenty-one."

"You think so?"

"I consider last year just another stage in our marriage," he said. "Don't worry: It's twenty-one."

She clinked her glass against his.

Their main dish was a potted meat that she spread on French bread, and their dessert was fruit. She washed the fruit in the bathroom, returning with handfuls of peaches and strawberries; and meanwhile she kept up a cozy patter that made him feel he was home again. "Did I mention we had a letter from the Averys? They might be passing through Baltimore later this summer. Oh, and the termite man came."

"Ah."

"He couldn't find anything wrong, he said."

"Well, that's a relief."

"And I've almost finished my sculpture and Mr. Armistead says it's the best thing I've done."

"Good for you," Macon said.

"Oh," she said, folding the last paper bag, "I know you don't think my sculptures are important, but—"

"Who says I don't?" he asked.

"I know you think I'm just this middle-aged lady playing artist—"

"Who says?"

"Oh, I know what you think! You don't have to pretend with me."

Macon started to slump against his pillow, but was brought up short by a muscle spasm.

She cut a peach into sections, and then she sat on the bed and passed him one of the sections. She said, "Macon. Just tell me this. Was the little boy the attraction?"

"Huh?"

"Was the fact that she had a child what attracted you to that woman?"

He said, "Sarah, I swear to you, I had no idea she was planning to follow me over here."

"Yes, I realize that," she said, "but I was wondering about the child question."

"What child question?"

"I was remembering the time you said we should have another baby."

"Oh, well, that was just . . . I don't know what that was," he said. He handed her back the peach; he wasn't hungry anymore.

"I was thinking maybe you were right," Sarah said.

"What? No, Sarah; Lord, that was a terrible idea."

"Oh, I know it's scary," she told him. "I admit I'd be scared to have another."

"Exactly," Macon said. "We're too old."

"No, I'm talking about the, you know, world we'd be bringing him into. So much evil and danger. I admit it: I'd be frantic any time we let him out on the street."

Macon saw Singleton Street in his mind, small and distant like Julian's little green map of Hawaii and full of gaily drawn people scrubbing their stoops, tinkering with their cars, splashing under fire hydrants.

"Oh, well, you're right," he said. "Though really it's kind of . . . heartening, isn't it? How most human beings do try. How they try to be as responsible and kind as they can manage."

"Are you saying yes, we can have a baby?" Sarah asked.

Macon swallowed. He said, "Well, no. It seems to me we're past the time for that, Sarah."

"So," she said, "her little boy wasn't the reason."

"Look, it's over with. Can't we close the lid on it? I don't cross-examine you, do I?"

"But I don't have someone following me to Paris!" she said.

"And what if you did? Do you think I'd hold you to blame if someone just climbed on a plane without your knowing?"

"Before it left the ground," she said.

"Pardon? Well, I should hope so!"

"Before it left the ground, you saw her. You could have walked up to her and said, 'No. Get off. Go this minute. I want nothing more to do with you and I never want to see you again.' "

"You think I own the airline, Sarah?"

"You could have stopped her if you'd really wanted," Sarah said. "You could have taken steps."

And then she rose and began to clear away their supper.

She gave him his next pill, but he let it stay in his fist a while because he didn't want to risk moving. He lay with his eyes closed, listening to Sarah undress. She ran water in the bathroom, slipped the chain on the door, turned off the lights. When she got into bed it stabbed his back, even though she settled carefully, but he gave no sign. He heard her breathing soften almost at once. She must have been exhausted.

He reflected that he had not taken steps very often in his life, come to think of it. Really never. His marriage, his two jobs, his time with Muriel, his return to Sarah—all seemed to have simply befallen him. He couldn't think of a single major act he had managed of his own accord.

Was it too late now to begin?

Was there any way he could learn to do things differently?

He opened his hand and let the pill fall among the bedclothes. It was going to be a restless, uncomfortable night, but anything was better than floating off on that stupor again.

In the morning, he negotiated the journey out of bed and into the bathroom. He shaved and dressed, spending long minutes on each task. Creeping around laboriously, he packed his bag. The heaviest thing he packed was *Miss MacIntosh, My Darling*, and after thinking that over a while, he took it out again and set it on the bureau.

Sarah said, "Macon?"

"Sarah. I'm glad you're awake," he said.

"What are you doing?"

"I'm packing to leave."

She sat up. Her face was creased down one side.

"But what about your back?" she asked. "And I've got all those appointments! And we were going to take a second honeymoon!"

"Sweetheart," he said. He lowered himself cautiously till he was sitting on the bed. He picked up her hand. It stayed lifeless while she watched his face.

"You're going back to that woman," she said.

"Yes, I am," he said.

"Why, Macon?"

"I just decided, Sarah. I thought about it most of last night. It wasn't easy. It's not the easy way out, believe me."

She sat staring at him. She wore no expression.

"Well, I don't want to miss the plane," he said.

He inched to a standing position and hobbled into the bathroom for his shaving kit.

"You know what this is? It's all due to that pill!" Sarah called after him. "You said yourself it knocks you out!"

"I didn't take the pill."

There was a silence.

She said, "Macon? Are you just trying to get even with me for the time I left you?"

He returned with the shaving kit and said, "No, sweetheart,"

"I suppose you realize what your life is going to be like," she said. She climbed out of bed. She stood next to him in her nightgown, hugging her bare arms. "You'll be one of those mismatched couples no one invites to parties. No one will know what to make of you. People will wonder whenever they meet you, 'My God, what does he see in her? Why choose someone so inappropriate? It's grotesque, how does he put up with her?' And her friends will no doubt be asking the same about you."

"That's probably true," Macon said. He felt a mild stirring of interest; he saw now how such couples evolved. They were not, as he'd always supposed, the result of some ludicrous lack of perception, but had come together for reasons that the rest of the world would never guess.

He zipped his overnight bag.

"I'm sorry, Sarah. I didn't want to decide this," he said.

He put his arm around her painfully, and after a pause she let her head rest against his shoulder. It struck him that even this moment was just another stage in their marriage. There would probably be still other stages in their thirtieth year, fortieth year—forever, no matter what separate paths they chose to travel.

He didn't take the elevator; he felt he couldn't bear the willynilliness of it. He went down the stairs instead. He managed the front door by backing through it, stiffly.

Out on the street he found the usual bustle of a weekday morning— shopgirls hurrying past, men with briefcases. No taxis in sight. He set off for the next block, where his chances were better. Walking was fairly easy but carrying his bag was torture. Lightweight though it was, it twisted his back out of line. He tried it in his left hand, then his right. And after all, what was inside it? Pajamas, a change of underwear, emergency supplies he never used . . . He stepped over to a building, a bank or office building with a low stone curb running around its base. He set the bag on the curb and hurried on.

Up ahead he saw a taxi with a boy just stepping out of it, but he discovered too late that hailing it was going to be a problem. Raising either arm was impossible. So he was forced to run in an absurd, scuttling fashion while shouting bits of French he'd never said aloud before: *"Attendez! Attendez, monsieur!"*

The taxi was already moving off and the boy was just slipping his wallet back into his jeans, but then he looked up and saw Macon. He acted fast; he spun and called out something and the taxi braked. *"Merci beaucoup,"* Macon panted, and the boy, who had a sweet, pure face and shaggy yellow hair, opened the taxi door for him and gently assisted him in. "Oof!" Macon said, seized by a spasm. The boy shut the door and then, to Macon's surprise, lifted a hand in a formal goodbye. The taxi moved off. Macon told the driver where he was going and sank back into his seat. He patted his inside pocket, checking passport, plane ticket. He unfolded his handkerchief and wiped his forehead.

Evidently his sense of direction had failed him, as usual. The driver was making a U-turn, heading back where Macon had just come from. They passed the boy once again. He had a jaunty, stiff-legged way of walking that seemed familiar.

If Ethan hadn't died, Macon thought, wouldn't he have grown into such a person?

He would have turned to give the boy another look, except that he couldn't manage the movement.

The taxi bounced over the cobblestones. The driver whistled a tune between his teeth. Macon found that bracing himself on one arm protected his back somewhat from the jolts. Every now and then, though, a pothole caught him off guard.

And if dead people aged, wouldn't it be a comfort? To think of Ethan growing up in heaven—fourteen years old now instead of twelve— eased the grief a little. Oh, it was their immunity to time that made the dead so heartbreaking. (Look at the husband who dies young, the wife aging on without him; how sad to imagine the husband coming back to find her so changed.) Macon gazed out the cab window, considering the notion in his mind. He felt a kind of inner rush, a racing forward. The real adventure, he thought, is the flow of time; it's as much adventure as anyone could wish. And if he pictured Ethan still part of that flow—in some other place, however unreachable—he believed he might be able to bear it after all.

The taxi passed Macon's hotel—brown and tidy, strangely homelike. A man was just emerging with a small anxious dog on his arm. And there on the curb stood Muriel, surrounded by suitcases and string-handled shopping bags and cardboard cartons overflowing with red velvet. She was frantically waving down taxis—first one ahead, then Macon's own. *"Arrêtez!"* Macon cried to the driver. The taxi lurched to a halt. A sudden flash of sunlight hit the windshield, and spangles flew across the glass. The spangles were old water spots, or maybe the markings of leaves, but for a moment Macon thought they were something else. They were so bright and festive, for a moment he thought they were confetti.

BREATHING
LESSONS

ONE

1

Maggie and Ira Moran had to go to a funeral in Deer Lick, Pennsylvania. Maggie's girlhood friend had lost her husband. Deer Lick lay on a narrow country road some ninety miles north of Baltimore, and the funeral was scheduled for ten-thirty Saturday morning; so Ira figured they should start around eight. This made him grumpy. (He was not an early-morning kind of man.) Also Saturday was his busiest day at work, and he had no one to cover for him. Also their car was in the body shop. It had needed extensive repairs and Saturday morning at opening time, eight o'clock exactly, was the soonest they could get it back. Ira said maybe they'd just better not go, but Maggie said they had to. She and Serena had been friends forever. Or nearly forever: forty-two years, beginning with Miss Kimmel's first grade.

They planned to wake up at seven, but Maggie must have set the alarm wrong and so they overslept. They had to dress in a hurry and rush through breakfast, making do with faucet coffee and cold cereal. Then Ira headed off for the store on foot to leave a note for his customers, and Maggie walked to the body shop. She was wearing her best dress—blue and white sprigged, with cape sleeves—and crisp black pumps, on account of the funeral. The pumps were only medium-heeled but slowed her down some anyway; she was more used to crepe soles. Another problem was that the crotch of her panty hose had somehow slipped to about the middle of her thighs, so she had to take shortened, unnaturally level steps like a chunky little wind-up toy wheeling along the sidewalk.

Luckily, the body shop was only a few blocks away. (In this part of town things were intermingled—small frame houses like theirs sitting among portrait photographers' studios, one-woman beauty parlors, driving schools, and podiatry clinics.) And the weather was perfect—a warm, sunny day in September, with just enough breeze to cool her face. She patted down her bangs where they tended to frizz out like a forelock. She hugged her dress-up purse under her arm. She turned left at the corner and there was Harbor Body and Fender, with the peeling green garage doors already hoisted up and the cavernous interior smelling of some sharp-scented paint that made her think of nail polish.

She had her check all ready and the manager said the keys were in the car, so in no time she was free to go. The car was parked toward the rear of the shop, an elderly gray-blue Dodge. It looked better than it had in years. They had straightened the rear bumper, replaced the mangled trunk lid, ironed out a half-dozen crimps here and there, and covered over the dapples of rust on the doors. Ira was right: no need to buy a new car after all. She slid behind the wheel. When she turned the ignition key, the radio came on—Mel Spruce's *AM Baltimore*, a call-in talk show. She let it run, for the moment. She adjusted the seat, which had been moved back for someone taller, and she tilted the rearview mirror downward. Her own face flashed toward her, round and slightly shiny, her blue eyes quirked at the inner corners as if she were worried about something when in fact she was only straining to see in the gloom. She shifted gears and sailed smoothly toward the front of the shop, where the manager stood frowning at a clipboard just outside his office door.

Today's question on *AM Baltimore* was: "What Makes an Ideal Marriage?" A woman was phoning in to say it was common interests. "Like if you both watch the same kind of programs on TV," she explained. Maggie couldn't care less what made an ideal marriage. (She'd been married twenty-eight years.) She rolled down her window and called, "Bye now!" and the manager glanced up from his clipboard. She glided past him—a woman in charge of herself, for once, lipsticked and medium-heeled and driving an undented car.

A soft voice on the radio said, "Well, I'm about to remarry? The first time was purely for love? It was genuine, true love and it didn't work at all. Next Saturday I'm marrying for security."

Maggie looked over at the dial and said, "Fiona?"

She meant to brake, but accelerated instead and shot out of the garage and directly into the street. A Pepsi truck approaching from the left smashed into her left front fender—the only spot that had never, up till now, had the slightest thing go wrong with it.

Back when Maggie played baseball with her brothers, she used to get hurt but say she was fine, for fear they would make her quit. She'd pick herself up and run on without a limp, even if her knee was killing her. Now she was reminded of that, for when the manager rushed over, shouting, "What the . . .? Are you all right?" she stared straight ahead in a dignified way and told him, "Certainly. Why do you ask?" and drove on before the Pepsi driver could climb out of his truck, which was probably just as well considering the look on his face. But in fact her fender was making a very upsetting noise, something like a piece of tin dragging over gravel, so as soon as she'd turned the corner and the two men—one scratching his head, one waving his arms—had disappeared from her rearview mirror, she came to a stop. Fiona was not on the radio anymore. Instead a woman with a raspy tenor was comparing her five husbands. Maggie cut the motor and got out. She could see what was causing the trouble. The fender was crumpled inward so the tire was hitting against it; she was surprised the wheel could turn, even. She squatted on the curb, grasped the rim of the fender in both hands, and tugged. (She remembered hunkering low in the tall grass of the outfield and stealthily, wincingly peeling her jeans leg away from the patch of blood on her knee.) Flakes of gray-blue paint fell into her lap. Someone passed on the sidewalk behind her but she pretended not to notice and tugged again. This time the fender moved, not far but enough to clear the tire, and she stood up and dusted off her hands. Then she climbed back inside the car but for a minute simply sat there. "Fiona!" she said again. When she restarted the engine, the radio was advertising bank loans and she switched it off.

Ira was waiting in front of his store, unfamiliar and oddly dashing in his navy suit. A shock of ropy black, gray-threaded hair hung over his forehead. Above him a metal sign swung in the breeze: SAM'S FRAME SHOP. PICTURE FRAMING. MATTING. YOUR NEEDLEWORK PROFESSIONALLY DISPLAYED. Sam was Ira's father, who had not had a thing to do with the business since coming down with a "weak heart" thirty years before. Maggie always put "weak heart" in quotation marks. She made a point of ignoring the apartment windows above the shop, where Sam spent his cramped, idle, querulous days with Ira's two sisters. He would probably be standing there watching. She parked next to the curb and slid over to the passenger seat.

Ira's expression was a study as he approached the car. Starting out pleased and approving, he rounded the hood and drew up short when he came upon the left fender. His long, bony, olive face grew longer.

His eyes, already so narrow you couldn't be sure if they were black or merely dark brown, turned to puzzled, downward-slanting slits. He opened the door and got in and gave her a sorrowful stare.

"There was an unexpected situation," Maggie told him.

"Just between here and the body shop?"

"I heard Fiona on the radio."

"That's five blocks! Just five or six blocks."

"Ira, Fiona's getting married."

He gave up thinking of the car, she was relieved to see. Something cleared on his forehead. He looked at her a moment and then said, "Fiona who?"

"Fiona your daughter-in-law, Ira. How many Fionas do we know? Fiona the mother of your only grandchild, and now she's up and marrying some total stranger purely for security."

Ira slid the seat farther back and then pulled away from the curb. He seemed to be listening for something—perhaps for the sound of the wheel hitting. But evidently her tug on the fender had done the trick. He said, "Where'd you hear this?"

"On the radio while I was driving."

"They'd announce a thing like that on the radio?"

"She telephoned it in."

"That seems kind of . . . self-important, if you want my honest opinion," Ira said.

"No, she was just—and she said that Jesse was the only one she'd ever truly loved."

"She said this on the *radio?*"

"It was a talk show, Ira."

"Well, I don't know why everyone has to go spilling their guts in public these days," Ira said.

"Do you suppose Jesse could have been listening?" Maggie asked. The thought had just occurred to her.

"Jesse? At this hour? He's doing well if he's up before noon."

Maggie didn't argue with that, although she could have. The fact was that Jesse was an early riser, and anyhow, he worked on Saturdays. What Ira was implying was that he was shiftless. (Ira was much harder on their son than Maggie was. He didn't see half as many good points to him.) She faced forward and watched the shops and houses sliding past, the few pedestrians out with their dogs. This had been the driest summer in memory and the sidewalks had a chalky look. The air hung like gauze. A boy in front of Poor Man's Grocery was tenderly dusting his bicycle spokes with a cloth.

"So you started out on Empry Street," Ira said.

"Hmm?"

"Where the body shop is."

"Yes, Empry Street."

"And then cut over to Daimler . . ."

He was back on the subject of the fender. She said, "I did it driving out of the garage."

"You mean right there? Right at the body shop?"

"I went to hit the brake but I hit the gas instead."

"How could that happen?"

"Well, Fiona came on the radio and I was startled."

"I mean the brake isn't something you have to think about, Maggie. You've been driving since you were sixteen years old. How could you mix up the brake with the gas pedal?"

"I just did, Ira. All right? I just got startled and I did. So let's drop it."

"I mean a brake is more or less *reflex*."

"If it means so much to you I'll pay for it out of my salary."

Now it was his turn to hold his tongue. She saw him start to speak and then change his mind. (Her salary was laughable. She tended old folks in a nursing home.)

If they'd had more warning, she thought, she would have cleaned the car's interior before they set out. The dashboard was littered with parking-lot stubs. Soft-drink cups and paper napkins covered the floor at her feet. Also there were loops of black and red wire sagging beneath the glove compartment; nudge them accidentally as you crossed your legs and you'd disconnect the radio. She considered that to be Ira's doing. Men just generated wires and cords and electrical tape everywhere they went, somehow. They might not even be aware of it.

They were traveling north on Belair Road now. The scenery grew choppy. Stretches of playgrounds and cemeteries were broken suddenly by clumps of small businesses—liquor stores, pizza parlors, dark little bars and taverns dwarfed by the giant dish antennas on their roofs. Then another playground would open out. And the traffic was heavier by the minute. Everyone else was going somewhere festive and Saturday-morningish, Maggie was certain. Most of the back seats were stuffed with children. It was the hour for gymnastics lessons and baseball practice.

"The other day," Maggie told Ira, "I forgot how to say 'car pool.' "

"Why would you need to remember?" Ira asked.

"Well, that's my point."

"Pardon?"

"It shows you how time has passed, is what I'm saying. I wanted to tell one of my patients her daughter wouldn't be visiting. I said, 'Today's her day for, um,' and I couldn't think of the words. I could not think of 'car pool.' But it seems like just last week that Jesse had a game or hockey camp, Daisy had a Brownie meeting . . . Why, I used to spend all Saturday behind the wheel!"

"Speaking of which," Ira said, "was it another vehicle you hit? Or just a telephone pole?"

Maggie dug in her purse for her sunglasses. "It was a truck," she said.

"Good grief. You do it any damage?"

"I didn't notice."

"You didn't notice."

"I didn't stop to look."

She put on her sunglasses and blinked. Everything turned muted and more elegant.

"You left the scene of an accident, Maggie?"

"It wasn't an accident! It was only one of those little, like, kind of things that just happen. Why make such a big deal of it?"

"Let me see if I've got this straight," Ira said. "You zoomed out of the body shop, slammed into a truck, and kept on going."

"No, the truck slammed into *me*."

"But you were the one at fault."

"Well, yes, I suppose I was, if you insist on holding someone to blame."

"And so then you just drove on away."

"Right."

He was silent. Not a good silence.

"It was a great big huge Pepsi truck," Maggie said. "It was practically an armored tank! I bet I didn't so much as scratch it."

"But you never checked to make sure."

"I was worried I'd be late," Maggie said. "You're the one who insisted on allowing extra travel time."

"You realize the body-shop people have your name and address, don't you? All that driver has to do is ask them. We're going to find a policeman waiting for us on our doorstep."

"Ira, will you drop it?" Maggie asked. "Don't you see I have a lot on my mind? I'm heading toward the funeral of my oldest, dearest friend's husband; no telling what Serena's dealing with right now, and here I am, a whole state away. And then on top of that I have to hear it on the radio that Fiona's getting married, when it's plain as the nose on your face she and Jesse still love each other. They've always loved each other; they never stopped; it's just that they can't, oh, connect, somehow. And besides that, my one and only grandchild is all at once going to have to adjust to a brand-new stepfather. I feel like we're just flying apart! All my friends and relatives just flying off from me like the . . . expanding universe or something! Now we'll never see that child, do you realize that?"

"We never see her anyhow," Ira said mildly. He braked for a red light.

"For all we know, this new husband could be a molester," Maggie said.

"I'm sure Fiona would choose better than that, Maggie."

She shot him a look. (It wasn't like him to say anything good about Fiona.) He was peering up at the traffic light. Squint lines radiated from the corners of his eyes. "Well, of course she would *try* to choose well," Maggie said carefully, "but even the most sensible person on God's earth can't predict every single problem, can she? Maybe he's somebody smooth and suave. Maybe he'll treat Leroy just fine till he's settled into the family."

The light changed. Ira drove on.

"Leroy," Maggie said reflectively. "Do you think we'll ever get used to that name? Sounds like a boy's name. Sounds like a football player. And the way they pronounce it: *Lee*-roy. Country."

"Did you bring that map I set out on the breakfast table?" Ira asked.

"Sometimes I think we should just start pronouncing it our way," Maggie said. "*Le-roy*." She considered.

"The map, Maggie. Did you bring it?"

"It's in my purse. Le *Rwah*," she said, gargling the *R* like a Frenchman.

"It's not as if we still had anything to do with her," Ira said.

"We could, though, Ira. We could visit her this very afternoon."

"Huh?"

"Look at where they live: Cartwheel, Pennsylvania. It's practically on the road to Deer Lick. What we could do," she said, digging through her purse, "is go to the funeral, see, and . . . Oh, where is that map? Go to the funeral and then head back down Route One to . . . You know, I don't think I brought that map after all."

"Great, Maggie."

"I think I left it on the table."

"I asked you when we were setting out, remember? I said, 'Are you going to bring the map, or am I?' You said, 'I am. I'll just stick it in my purse.' "

"Well, I don't know why you're making such a fuss about it," Maggie said. "All we've got to do is watch the road signs; anyone could manage that much."

"It's a little more complicated than that," Ira said.

"Besides, we have those directions Serena gave me over the phone."

"Maggie. Do you honestly believe any directions of Serena's could get us where we'd care to go? Ha! We'd find ourselves in Canada someplace. We'd be off in Arizona!"

"Well, you don't have to get so excited about it."

"We would never see home again," Ira said.

Maggie shook her billfold and a pack of Kleenex from her purse.

"Serena's the one who made us late for her own wedding reception, remember that?" Ira said. "At that crazy little banquet hall we spent an hour locating."

"Really, Ira. You always act like women are such flibbertigibbets," Maggie said. She gave up searching through her purse; evidently she had mislaid Serena's directions as well. She said, "It's Fiona's own good I'm thinking of. She'll need us to baby-sit."

"Baby-sit?"

"During the honeymoon."

He gave her a look that she couldn't quite read.

"She's getting married next Saturday," Maggie said. "You can't take a seven-year-old on a honeymoon."

He still said nothing.

They were out beyond the city limits now and the houses had thinned. They passed a used-car lot, a scratchy bit of woods, a shopping mall with a few scattered early-bird cars parked on a concrete wasteland. Ira started whistling. Maggie stopped fiddling with her purse straps and grew still.

There were times when Ira didn't say a dozen words all day, and even when he did talk you couldn't guess what he was feeling. He was a closed-in, isolated man—his most serious flaw. But what he failed to realize was, his whistling could tell the whole story. For instance—an unsettling example—after a terrible fight in the early days of their marriage they had more or less smoothed things over, patted them into place again, and then he'd gone off to work whistling a song she couldn't identify. It wasn't till later that the words occurred to her. *I wonder if I care as much,* was the way they went, *as I did before* . . .

But often the association was something trivial, something circumstantial—"This Old House" while he tackled a minor repair job, or "The Wichita Lineman" whenever he helped bring in the laundry. *Do, do, that voodoo . . .* he whistled, unknowingly, five minutes after circling a pile of dog-doo on the sidewalk. And of course there were times when Maggie had no idea what he was whistling. This piece right now, say: something sort of croony, something they might play on WLIF. Well, maybe he'd merely heard it while shaving, in which case it meant nothing at all.

A Patsy Cline song; that's what it was. Patsy Cline's "Crazy."

She sat up sharply and said, "Perfectly sane people baby-sit their grandchildren, Ira Moran."

He looked startled.

"They keep them for months. Whole summers," she told him.

He said, "They don't pay drop-in visits, though."

"Certainly they do!"

"Ann Landers claims drop-in visits are inconsiderate," he said.

Ann Landers, his personal heroine.

"And it's not like we're blood relatives," he said. "We're not even Fiona's in-laws anymore."

"We're Leroy's grandparents till the day we die," Maggie told him.

He didn't have any answer for that.

This stretch of road was such a mess. Things had been allowed to just happen—a barbecue joint sprouting here, a swim-pool display room there. A pickup parked on the shoulder overflowed with pumpkins: ALL U CAN CARRY $1.50, the hand-lettered sign read. The pumpkins reminded Maggie of fall, but in fact it was so warm now that a line of moisture stood out on her upper lip. She rolled down her window, recoiled from the hot air, and rolled it up again. Anyway, enough of a breeze came from Ira's side. He drove one-handed, with his left elbow jutting over the sill. The sleeves of his suit had rucked up to show his wristbones.

Serena used to say Ira was a mystery. That was a compliment, in those days. Maggie wasn't even dating Ira, she was engaged to someone else, but Serena kept saying, "How can you resist him? He's such a mystery. He's so mysterious." "I don't have to resist him. He's not after me," Maggie had said. Although she had wondered. (Serena was right. He was such a mystery.) But Serena herself had chosen the most open-faced boy in the world. Funny old Max! Not a secret in him. "This here is my happiest memory," Max had said once. (He'd been twenty at the time, just finishing his freshman year at UNC.) "Me and these two fraternity brothers, we go out partying. And I have a tad bit too much to drink, so coming home I pass out in the back seat and when I wake up they've driven clear to Carolina Beach and left me there on the sand. Big joke on me: Ha-ha. It's six o'clock in the morning and I sit up and all I can see is sky, layers and layers of hazy sky that just kind of turn into sea lower down, without the least dividing line. So I stand up and fling off my clothes and go racing into the surf, all by my lonesome. Happiest day of my life."

What if someone had told him then that thirty years later he'd be dead of cancer, with that ocean morning the clearest picture left of him in Maggie's mind? The haze, the feel of warm air on bare skin, the shock of the first cold, briny-smelling breaker—Maggie might as well have been there herself. She was grateful suddenly for the sunlit clutter of billboards jogging past; even for the sticky vinyl upholstery plastered to the backs of her arms.

Ira said, "Who would she be marrying, I wonder."

"What?" Maggie asked. She felt a little dislocated.

"Fiona."

"Oh," Maggie said. "She didn't say."

Ira was trying to pass an oil truck. He tilted his head to the left, peering for oncoming traffic. After a moment he said, "I'm surprised she didn't announce that too, while she was at it."

"All she said was, she was marrying for security. She said she'd married for love once before and it hadn't worked out."

"Love!" Ira said. "She was seventeen years old. She didn't know the first thing about love."

Maggie looked over at him. What *was* the first thing about love? she wanted to ask. But he was muttering at the oil truck now.

"Maybe this time it's an older man," she said. "Someone sort of fatherly. If she's marrying for security."

"This guy knows perfectly well I'm trying to pass and he keeps spreading over into my lane," Ira told her.

"Maybe she's just getting married so she won't have to go on working."

"I didn't know she worked."

"She got a job, Ira. You know that! She told us that! She got a job at a beauty parlor when Leroy started nursery school."

Ira honked at the oil truck.

"I don't know why you bother sitting in a room with people if you can't make an effort to listen," she said.

Ira said, "Maggie, is something wrong with you today?"

"What do you mean?"

"How come you're acting so irritable?"

"I'm not irritable," she said. She pushed her sunglasses higher. She could see her own nose—the small, rounded tip emerging below the nosepiece.

"It's Serena," he said.

"Serena?"

"You're upset about Serena and that's why you're snapping my head off."

"Well, of course I'm upset," Maggie said. "But I'm certainly not snapping your head off."

"Yes, you are, and it's also why you're going on and on about Fiona when you haven't given a thought to her in years."

"That's not true! How do you know how often I think about Fiona?"

Ira swung out around the oil truck at last.

By now, they had hit real country. Two men were splitting logs in a clearing, watched over by a gleaming black dog. The trees weren't changing color yet, but they had that slightly off look that meant they were just about to. Maggie gazed at a weathered wooden fence that girdled a field. Funny how a picture stayed in your mind without your knowing it. Then you see the original and you think, Why! It was there all along, like a dream that comes drifting back in pieces halfway through the morning. That fence, for instance. So far they were retracing the road to Cartwheel and she'd seen that fence on her spy trips and unconsciously made it her own. "Rickrack," she said to Ira.

"Hmm?"

"Don't they call that kind of fence 'rickrack'?"

He glanced over, but it was gone.

She had sat in her parked car some distance from Fiona's mother's house, watching for the teeniest, briefest glimpse of Leroy. Ira would have had a fit if he'd known what she was up to. This was back when Fiona first left, following a scene that Maggie never liked to recall. (She thought of it as That Awful Morning and made it vanish from her mind.) Oh, those days she'd been like a woman possessed; Leroy was not but a baby then, and what did Fiona know about babies? She'd always had Maggie to help her. So Maggie drove to Cartwheel on a free afternoon and parked the car and waited, and soon Fiona stepped forth with Leroy in her arms and set off in the other direction, walking briskly, her long blonde hair swinging in sheets and the baby's face a bright little button on her shoulder. Maggie's heart bounded upward, as if she were in love. In a way, she *was* in love—with Leroy and Fiona both, and even with her own son as he had looked while clumsily cradling his daughter against his black leather jacket. But she didn't dare show herself—not yet, at least. Instead she drove home and told Jesse, "I went to Cartwheel today."

His face flew open. His eyes rested on her for one startled, startling instant before he looked away and said, "So?"

"I didn't talk to her, but I could tell she misses you. She was walking all alone with Leroy. Nobody else."

"Do you think I care about that?" Jesse asked. "What do you think *I* care?"

The next morning, though, he borrowed the car. Maggie was relieved. (He was a loving, gentle, warmhearted boy, with an uncanny gift for drawing people toward him. This would be settled in no time.) He stayed gone all day—she phoned hourly from work to check—and returned as she was cooking supper. "Well?" she asked.

"Well, what?" he said, and he climbed the stairs and shut himself in his room.

She realized then that it would take a little longer than she had expected.

Three times—on Leroy's first three birthdays—she and Ira had made conventional visits, prearranged grandparent visits with presents; but in Maggie's mind the real visits were her spy trips, which continued without her planning them as if long, invisible threads were pulling her northward. She would think she was heading to the supermarket but she'd find herself on Route One instead, already clutching her coat collar close around her face so as not to be recognized. She would hang out in Cartwheel's one playground, idly inspecting her fingernails next to the sandbox. She would lurk in the alley, wearing Ira's sister Junie's bright-red wig. At moments she imagined growing old at this. Maybe she would hire on as a crossing guard when Leroy started school. Maybe she'd pose as a Girl Scout leader, renting a little Girl Scout of her own if that was what was required. Maybe she'd serve as a chaperon for Leroy's senior prom. Well. No point in getting carried away. She knew from Jesse's dark silences, from the listlessness with which Fiona pushed the baby swing in the playground, that they surely couldn't stay apart much longer. Could they?

Then one afternoon she shadowed Fiona's mother as she wheeled Leroy's stroller up to Main Street. Mrs. Stuckey was a slatternly, shapeless woman who smoked cigarettes. Maggie didn't trust her as far as she could throw her, and rightly so, for look at what she did: parked Leroy outside the Cure-Boy Pharmacy and left her there while she went in. Maggie was horrified. Leroy could be kidnapped! She could be kidnapped by any passerby. Maggie approached the stroller and squatted down in front of it. "Honey?" she said. "Want to come away with your granny?" The child stared at her. She was, oh, eighteen months or so by then, and her face had seemed surprisingly grown up. Her legs had lost their infant chubbiness. Her eyes were the same milky blue as Fiona's and slightly flat, blank, as if she didn't know who Maggie was. "It's Grandma," Maggie said, but Leroy began squirming and craning all around. "Mom-Mom?" she said. Unmistakably, she was looking toward the door where Mrs. Stuckey had disappeared. Maggie stood up and walked away quickly. The rejection felt like a physical pain, like an actual wound to the chest. She didn't make any more spy trips.

When she'd driven along here in springtime, the woods had been dotted with white dogwood blossoms. They had lightened the green hills the way a sprinkle of baby's breath lightens a bouquet. And once she'd seen a small animal that was something other than the usual— not a rabbit or a raccoon but something slimmer, sleeker—and she had braked sharply and adjusted the rearview mirror to study it as she left it behind. But it had already darted into the underbrush.

"Depend on Serena to make things difficult," Ira was saying now. "She could have phoned as soon as Max died, but no, she waits till the very last minute. He dies on Wednesday, she calls late Friday night. Too late to contact Triple A about auto routes." He frowned at the road ahead of him. "Um," he said. "You don't suppose she wants me to be a pallbearer or something, do you?"

"She didn't mention it."

"But she told you she needed our help."

"I think she meant moral support," Maggie said.

"Maybe pallbearing is moral support."

"Wouldn't that be physical support?"

"Well, maybe," Ira said.

They sailed through a small town where groups of little shops broke up the pastures. Several woman stood next to a mailbox, talking.

Maggie turned her head to watch them. She had a left-out, covetous feeling, as if they were people she knew.

"If she wants me to be a pallbearer I'm not dressed right," Ira said.

"Certainly you're dressed right."

"I'm not wearing a black suit," he said.

"You don't own a black suit."

"I'm in navy."

"Navy's fine."

"Also I've got that trick back."

She glanced at him.

"And it's not as if I was ever very close to him," he said.

Maggie reached over to the steering wheel and laid a hand on his. "Never mind," she told him. "I bet anything she wants us just to be sitting there."

He gave her a rueful grin, really no more than a tuck of the cheek.

How peculiar he was about death! He couldn't handle even minor illness and had found reasons to stay away from the hospital the time she had her appendix out; he claimed he'd caught a cold and might infect her. Whenever one of the children fell sick he'd pretended it wasn't happening. He'd told her she was imagining things. Any hint that he wouldn't live forever—when he had to deal with life insurance, for instance—made him grow set-faced and stubborn and resentful. Maggie, on the other hand, worried she *would* live forever—maybe because of all she'd seen at the home.

And if she were the one who died first, he would probably pretend that that hadn't happened, either. He would probably just go on about his business, whistling a tune the same as always.

What tune would he be whistling?

They were crossing the Susquehanna River now and the lacy, Victorian-looking superstructure of the Conowingo power plant soared on their right. Maggie rolled down her window and leaned out. She could hear the distant rush of water; she was almost breathing water, drinking in the spray that rose like smoke from far below the bridge.

"You know what just occurred to me," Ira said, raising his voice. "That artist woman, what's-her-name. She was bringing a bunch of paintings to the shop this morning."

Maggie closed her window again. She said, "Didn't you turn on your answering machine?"

"What good would that do? She'd already arranged to come in."

"Maybe we could stop off somewhere and phone her."

"I don't have her number with me," Ira said. Then he said, "Maybe we could phone Daisy and ask her to do it."

"Daisy would be at work by now," Maggie told him.

"Shoot."

Daisy floated into Maggie's mind, trim and pretty, with Ira's dark coloring and Maggie's small bones. "Oh, dear," Maggie said. "I hate to miss her last day at home."

"She isn't home anyhow; you just told me so."

"She will be later on, though."

"You'll see plenty of her tomorrow," Ira pointed out. "Good and plenty."

Tomorrow they were driving Daisy to college—her freshman year, her first year away. Ira said, "All day cooped up in a car, you'll be sick to death of her."

"No, I won't! I would never get sick of Daisy!"

"Tell me that tomorrow," Ira said.

"Here's a thought," Maggie said. "Skip the reception."

"What reception?"

"Or whatever they call it when you go to somebody's house after the funeral."

"Fine with me," Ira said.

"That way we could still get home early even if we stopped off at Fiona's."

"Lord God, Maggie, are you still on that Fiona crap?"

"If the funeral were over by noon, say, and we went straight from there to Cartwheel—"

Ira swerved to the right, careening onto gravel. For a moment she thought it was some kind of tantrum. (She often had a sense of inching closer and closer to the edge of his temper.) But no, he'd pulled up at a gas station, an old-fashioned kind of place, white clapboard, with two men in overalls sitting on a bench in front. "Map," he said briefly, getting out of the car.

Maggie rolled down her window and called after him, "See if they have a snack machine, will you?"

He waved and walked toward the bench.

Now that the car was stopped, the heat flowed through the roof like melting butter. She felt the top of her head grow hot; she imagined her hair turning from brown to some metallic color, brass or copper. She let her fingers dangle lazily out the window.

If she could just get Ira to Fiona's, the rest was easy. He was not immune, after all. He had held that child on his knee. He had answered Leroy's dovelike infant coos in the same respectful tone he'd used with his own babies. "Is that so. You don't say. Well, I believe now that you mention it I did hear something of the sort." Till Maggie (always so gullible) had had to ask, "What? What did she tell you?" Then he'd give her one of his wry, quizzical looks; and so would the baby, Maggie sometimes fancied.

No, he wasn't immune, and he would set eyes on Leroy and remember instantly how they were connected. People had to be reminded, that was all. The way the world was going now, it was so easy to forget. Fiona must have forgotten how much in love she had been at the start, how she had trailed after Jesse and that rock band of his. She must have put it out of her mind on purpose, for she was no more immune than Ira. Maggie had seen the way her face fell when they arrived for Leroy's first birthday and Jesse turned out not to be with them. It was pride at work now; injured pride. "But remember?" Maggie would ask her. "Remember those early days when all you cared about was being near each other? Remember how you'd walk everywhere together, each with a hand in the rear pocket of the other's jeans?" That had seemed sort of tacky at the time, but now it made her eyes fill with tears.

Oh, this whole day was so terribly sad, the kind of day when you realized that everyone eventually got lost from everyone else; and she had not written to Serena for over a year or even heard her voice till Serena phoned last night crying so hard she was garbling half her words. At this moment (letting a breeze ripple through her fingers like warm water), Maggie felt that the entire business of time's passing was more than she could bear. Serena, she wanted to say, just think: all those things we used to promise ourselves we'd never, ever do when we grew up. We promised we wouldn't mince when we walked barefoot. We promised we wouldn't lie out on the beach tanning instead of swimming, or swimming with our chins high so we wouldn't wet our hairdos. We promised we wouldn't wash the dishes right after supper because that would take us away from our husbands; remember that? How long since you saved the dishes till morning so you could be with Max? How long since Max even noticed that you didn't?

Ira came toward her, opening out a map. Maggie removed her sunglasses and blotted her eyes on her sleeves. "Find what you wanted?" she called, and he said, "Oh . . ." and disappeared behind the map, still walking. The back of the paper was covered with photos of scenic attractions. He reached his side of the car, refolded the map, and got in. "Wish I could've called Triple A," he told her. He started the engine.

"Well, I wouldn't worry," she said. "We've got loads of extra time."

"Not really, Maggie. And look how the traffic is picking up. Every little old lady taking her weekend drive."

A ridiculous remark; the traffic was mostly trucks. They pulled out in front of a moving van, behind a Buick and another oil truck, or perhaps the same truck they had passed a while back. Maggie replaced her sunglasses.

TRY JESUS, YOU WON'T REGRET IT, a billboard read. And BUBBA MCDUFF'S SCHOOL OF COSMETOLOGY. They entered Pennsylvania and the road grew smooth for a few hundred yards, like a good intention, before settling back to the same old scabby, stippled surface. The views were long and curved and green—a small child's drawing of farm country. Distinct black cows grazed on the hillsides. BENIGN ODOMETER TEST, Maggie read.

She sat up straighter. Almost immediately a tiny sign flashed by: 0.1 MI. She glanced at their odometer. "Point eight exactly," she told Ira.

"Hmm?"

"I'm testing our odometer."

Ira loosened the knot of his tie.

Two tenths of a mile. Three tenths. At four tenths, she felt they were falling behind. Maybe she was imagining things, but it seemed to her that the numeral lagged somewhat as it rolled upward. At five tenths, she was almost sure of it. "How long since you had this checked?" she asked Ira.

"Had what checked?"

"The odometer."

"Well, never," he said.

"Never! Not once? And you accuse *me* of poor auto maintenance!"

"Look at that," Ira said. "Some ninety-year-old lady they've let out loose on the highway. Can't even see above her steering wheel."

He veered around the Buick, which meant that he completely bypassed one of the mileage signs. "Darn," Maggie said. "You made me miss it."

He didn't respond. He didn't even look sorry. She pinned her eyes far ahead, preparing for the seven tenths marker. When it appeared she glanced at the odometer and the numeral was just *creeping* up. It made her feel itchy and edgy. Oddly enough, though, the next numeral came more quickly. It might even have been too quick. Maggie said, "Oh-oh."

"What's the matter?"

"This is making me a nervous wreck," she said. She was watching for the road sign and monitoring the odometer dial, both at once. The six rolled up on the dial several seconds ahead of the sign, she could swear. She tsked. Ira looked over at her. "Slow down," she told him.

"Huh?"

"Slow down! I'm not sure we're going to make it. See, here the seven comes, rolling up, up . . . and where's the sign? Where's the *sign*? Come on, sign! We're losing! We're too far ahead! We're—"

The sign popped into view. "Ah," she said. The seven settled into place at exactly the same instant, so precisely that she almost heard it click.

"Whew!" she said. She sank back in her seat. "That was too close for comfort."

"They do set all our gauges at the factory, you know," Ira said.

"Sure, years and years ago," she told him. "I'm exhausted."

Ira said, "I wonder how long we should keep to Route One?"

"I feel I've been wrung through a wringer," Maggie said.

She made little plucking motions at the front of her dress.

Now collections of parked trucks and RVs appeared in clearings at random intervals—no humans around, no visible explanation for anybody's stopping there. Maggie had noticed this on her earlier trips and never understood it. Were the drivers off fishing, or hunting, or what? Did country people have some kind of secret life?

"Another thing is their banks," she told Ira. "All these towns have banks that look like itty-bitty brick houses, have you noticed? With yards around them, and flower beds. Would you put your faith in such a bank?"

"No reason not to."

"I just wouldn't feel my money was secure."

"Your vast wealth," Ira teased her.

"I mean it doesn't seem professional."

"Now, according to the map," he said, "we could stay on Route One a good deal farther up than Oxford. Serena had us cutting off at Oxford, if I heard you right, but . . . Check it for me, will you?"

Maggie took the map from the seat between them and opened it, one square at a time. She was hoping not to have to spread it out completely. Ira would get after her for refolding it wrong. "Oxford," she said. "Is that in Maryland or Pennsylvania?"

"It's in Pennsylvania, Maggie. Where Highway Ten leads off to the north."

"Well, then! I distinctly remember she told us to take Highway Ten."

"Yes, but if we . . . Have you been listening to a word I say? If we stayed on Route One, see, we could make better time, and I think there's a cutoff further up that would bring us directly to Deer Lick."

"Well, she must have had a reason, Ira, for telling us Highway Ten."

"A reason? Serena? Serena Gill have a reason?"

She shook out the map with a crackle. He always talked like that about her girlfriends. He acted downright jealous of them. She suspected he thought women got together on the sly and gossiped about their husbands. Typical: He was so self-centered. Although sometimes it did happen, of course.

"Did that service station have a snack machine?" she asked him.

"Just candy bars. Stuff you don't like."

"I'm dying of hunger."

"I could have got you a candy bar, but I thought you wouldn't eat it."

"Didn't they have potato chips or anything? I'm starving."

"Baby Ruths, Fifth Avenues . . ."

She made a face and went back to the map.

"Well, I would say take Highway Ten," she told him.

"I could swear I saw a later cutoff."

"Not really," she said.

"Not really? What does that mean? Either there's a cutoff or there isn't."

"Well," she said, "to tell the truth, I haven't quite located Deer Lick yet."

He flicked on his turn signal. "We'll find you someplace to eat and I'll take another look at the map," he said.

"Eat? I don't want to eat!"

"You just said you were starving to death."

"Yes, but I'm on a diet! All I want is a snack!"

"Fine. We'll get you a snack, then," he said.

"Really, Ira, I hate how you always try to undermine my diets."

"Then order a cup of coffee or something. I need to look at the map."

He was driving down a paved road that was lined with identical new ranch houses, each with a metal toolshed out back in the shape of a tiny red barn trimmed in white. Maggie wouldn't have thought there'd be any place to eat in such a neighborhood, but sure enough, around the next bend they found a frame building with a few cars parked in front of it. A dusty neon sign glowed in the window: NELL'S GROCERY & CAFE. Ira parked next to a Jeep with a Judas Priest sticker on the bumper. Maggie opened her door and stepped out, surreptitiously hitching up the crotch of her panty hose.

The grocery smelled of store bread and waxed paper. It reminded her of a grade-school lunchroom. Here and there women stood gazing at canned goods. The café lay at the rear—one long counter, with faded color photos of orange scrambled eggs and beige link sausages lining the wall behind it. Maggie and Ira settled on adjacent stools and Ira flattened his map on the counter. Maggie watched the waitress cleaning a griddle. She sprayed it with something, scraped up thick gunk with a spatula, and sprayed again. From behind she was a large white rectangle, her gray bun tacked down with black bobby pins. "What you going to order?" she asked finally, not turning around.

Ira said, "Just coffee for me, please," without looking up from his map. Maggie had more trouble deciding. She took off her sunglasses and peered at the color photos. "Well, coffee too, I guess," she said, "and also, let me think, I ought to have a salad or something, but—"

"We don't serve any salads," the waitress said. She set aside her spray bottle and came over to Maggie, wiping her hands on her apron. Her eyes, netted with wrinkles, were an eerie light green, like old beach glass. "The onliest thing I could offer is the lettuce and tomato from a sandwich."

"Well, maybe just a sack of those taco chips from the rack, then," Maggie said happily. "Though I know I shouldn't." She watched the waitress pour two mugs of coffee. "I'm trying to lose ten pounds by

Thanksgiving. I've been working on the same ten pounds forever, but this time I'm determined."

"Shoot! *You* don't need to lose weight," the woman said, setting the mugs in front of them. The red stitching across her breast pocket read *Mabel*, a name Maggie had not heard since her childhood. What had become of all the Mabels? She tried to picture giving a new little baby that name. Meanwhile the woman was telling her, "I despise how everybody tries to look like a toothpick nowadays."

"That's what Ira says; he likes me the weight I am now," Maggie said. She glanced over at Ira but he was deep in his map, or else just pretending to be. It always embarrassed him when she took up with outsiders. "But then anytime I go to buy a dress it hangs wrong, you know? Like they don't expect me to have a bustline. I lack willpower is the problem. I crave salty things. Pickly things. Hot spices." She accepted the sack of taco chips and held it up, demonstrating.

"How about me?" Mabel asked. "Doctor says I'm so overweight my legs are going."

"Oh, you are not! Show me where you're overweight!"

"He says it wouldn't be so bad if I was in some other job but waitressing; it gets to my veins."

"Our daughter's been working as a waitress," Maggie said. She tore open the sack of taco chips and bit into one. "Sometimes she's on her feet for eight hours straight without a break. She started out in sandals but switched to crepe soles soon enough, I can tell you, even though she swore she wouldn't."

"You are surely not old enough to have a daughter that grown up," Mabel said.

"Oh, she's still a teenager; this was just a summer job. Tomorrow she leaves for college."

"College! A smarty," Mabel said.

"Oh, well, *I* don't know," Maggie said. "She did get a full scholarship, though." She held out the sack. "You want some?"

Mabel took a handful. "Mine are all boys," she told Maggie. "Studying came about as natural to them as flying."

"Yes, our boy was that way."

" 'Why aren't you doing your homework?' I'd ask them. They'd have a dozen excuses. Most often they claimed the teacher didn't assign them any, which of course was an out-and-out story."

"That's just exactly like Jesse," Maggie said.

"And their daddy!" Mabel said. "He was forever taking up for them. Seemed they were all in cahoots and I was left out in the cold. What I wouldn't give for a daughter, I tell you!"

"Well, daughters have their drawbacks too," Maggie said. She could see that Ira wanted to break in with a question (he'd placed a finger on the map and was looking at Mabel expectantly), but once he got his answer he'd be ready to leave, so she made him hold off a bit. "For instance, daughters have more secrets. I mean you think they're talking to you, but it's small talk. Daisy, for instance: She's always been so quiet and obedient. Then up she pops with this scheme to go away to school. I had no idea she was plotting that! I said, 'Daisy? Aren't you happy here at home?' I mean of course I knew she was planning on college, but I notice University of Maryland is good enough for other people's children. 'What's wrong with closer to Baltimore?' I asked her, but she said, 'Oh, Mom, you knew all along I was aiming for someplace Ivy League.' I knew no such thing! I had no idea! And since she got the scholarship, why, she's changed past recognition. Isn't that so, Ira. *Ira* says—" she said, rushing on (having regretted giving him the opening), "Ira says she's just growing up. He says it's just growing pains that make her so picky and critical, and only a fool would take it to heart so. But it's difficult! It's so difficult! It's like all at once, every little thing we do is wrong; like she's hunting up good reasons not to miss us when she goes. My hair's too curly and I talk too much and I eat too many fried foods. And Ira's suit is cut poorly and he doesn't know how to do business."

Mabel was nodding, all sympathy, but Ira of course thought Maggie was acting overemotional. He didn't say so, but he shifted in his seat; that was how she knew. She ignored him. "You know what she told me the other day?" she asked Mabel. "I was testing out this tuna casserole. I served it up for supper and I said, 'Isn't it delicious? Tell me honestly what you think.' And Daisy said—"

Tears pricked her eyelids. She took a deep breath. "Daisy just sat there and studied me for the longest time," she said, "with this kind of . . . fascinated expression on her face, and then she said, 'Mom? Was there a certain conscious point in your life when you decided to settle for being ordinary?' "

She meant to go on, but her lips were trembling. She laid aside her chips and fumbled in her purse for a Kleenex. Mabel clucked. Ira said, "For God's sake, Maggie."

"I'm sorry," she told Mabel. "It got to me."

"Well, sure it did," Mabel said soothingly. She slid Maggie's coffee mug a little closer to her. "Naturally it did!"

"I mean, to *me* I'm not ordinary," Maggie said.

"No indeedy!" Mabel said. "You tell her, honey! You tell her that. You tell her to stop thinking that way. Know what I said to Bobby, my oldest? This was over a tuna dish too, come to think of it; isn't that a coincidence. He announces he's sick to death of foods that are mingled together. I say to him, 'Young man,' I say, 'you can just get on up and leave this table. Leave this house, while you're at it. Find a place of your own,' I say, 'cook your own durn meals, see how you can afford prime rib of beef every night.' And I meant it, too. He thought I was only running my mouth, but he saw soon enough I was serious; I set all his clothes on the hood of his car. Now he lives across town with his girlfriend. He didn't believe I would really truly make him move out."

"But that's just it; I don't want her to move out," Maggie said. "I like to have her at home. I mean look at Jesse: He brought his wife and baby to live with us and I loved it! Ira thinks Jesse's a failure. He says Jesse's entire life was ruined by a single friendship, which is nonsense. All Don Burnham did was tell Jesse he had singing talent. Call that ruining a life? But you take a boy like Jesse, who doesn't do just brilliantly in school, and whose father's always at him about his shortcomings; and you tell him there's this one special field where he shines—well, what do you expect? Think he'll turn his back on that and forget it?"

"Well, of course not!" Mabel said indignantly.

"Of course not. He took up singing with a hard-rock band. He dropped out of high school and collected a whole following of girls and finally one particular girl and then he married her; nothing wrong with that. Brought her to live in our house because he wasn't making much money. I was thrilled. They had a darling little baby. Then his wife and baby moved out on account of this awful scene, just up and left. It was nothing but an argument really, but you know how those can escalate. I said, 'Ira, go after her; it's your fault she went.' (Ira was right in the thick of that scene and I blame him to this day.) But Ira said no, let her do what she liked. He said let them just go on and go, but I felt she had ripped that child from my flesh and left a big torn spot behind."

"Grandbabies," Mabel said. "Don't get me started."

Ira said, "Not to change the subject, but—"

"Oh, Ira," Maggie told him, "just take Highway Ten and shut up about it."

He gave her a long, icy stare. She buried her nose in her Kleenex, but she knew what kind of stare it was. Then he asked Mabel, "Have you ever been to Deer Lick?"

"Deer Lick," Mabel said. "Seems to me I've heard of it."

"I was wondering where we'd cut off from Route One to get there."

"Now, that I wouldn't know," Mabel told him. She asked Maggie, "Honey, can I pour you more coffee?"

"Oh, no, thank you," Maggie said. In fact, her mug was untouched. She took a little sip to show her appreciation.

Mabel tore the bill off a pad and handed it to Ira. He paid in loose change, standing up to root through his pockets. Maggie, meanwhile, placed her damp Kleenex in the empty chip sack and made a tidy package of it so as not to be any trouble. "Well, it was nice talking to you," she told Mabel.

"Take care, sweetheart," Mabel said.

Maggie had the feeling they ought to kiss cheeks, like women who'd had lunch together.

She wasn't crying anymore, but she could sense Ira's disgust as he led the way to the parking lot. It felt like a sheet of something glassy and flat, shutting her out. He ought to have married Ann Landers, she thought. She slid into the car. The seat was so hot it burned through the back of her dress. Ira got in too and slammed the door behind him. If he had married Ann Landers he'd have just the kind of hard-nosed, sensible wife he wanted. Sometimes, hearing his grunt of approval as he read one of Ann's snappy answers, Maggie felt an actual pang of jealousy.

They passed the ranch houses once again, jouncing along the little paved road. The map lay between them, crisply folded. She didn't ask what he'd decided about routes. She looked out the window, every now and then sniffing as quietly as possible.

"Six and half years," Ira said. "No, seven now, and you're still dragging up that Fiona business. Telling total strangers it was all my fault she left. You just have to blame someone for it, don't you, Maggie."

"If someone's to blame, why, yes, I do," Maggie told the scenery.

"Never occurred to you it might be your fault, did it."

"Are we going to go through this whole dumb argument again?" she asked, swinging around to confront him.

"Well, who brought it up, I'd like to know?"

"I was merely stating the facts, Ira."

"Who asked for the facts, Maggie? Why do you feel the need to pour out your soul to some waitress?"

"Now, there is nothing wrong with being a waitress," she told him. "It's a perfectly respectable occupation. Our own daughter's been working as a waitress, must I remind you."

"Oh, great, Maggie; another of your logical progressions."

"One thing about you that I really cannot stand," she said, "is how you act so superior. We can't have just a civilized back-and-forth discussion; oh, no. No, you have to make a point of how illogical I am, what a whifflehead I am, how you're so cool and above it all."

"Well, at least I don't spill my life story in public eating places," he told her.

"Oh, just let me out," she said. "I cannot bear your company another second."

"Gladly," he said, but he went on driving.

"Let me out, I tell you!"

He looked over at her. He slowed down. She picked up her purse and clutched it to her chest.

"Are you going to stop this car," she asked, "or do I have to jump from a moving vehicle?"

He stopped the car.

Maggie got out and slammed the door. She started walking back toward the café. For a moment it seemed that Ira planned just to sit there, but then she heard him shift gears and drive on.

The sun poured down a great wash of yellow light, and her shoes made little cluttery sounds on the gravel. Her heart was beating extra fast. She felt pleased, in a funny sort of way. She felt almost drunk with fury and elation.

She passed the first of the ranch houses, where weedy flowers waved along the edge of the front yard and a tricycle lay in the driveway. It certainly was quiet. All she could hear was the distant chirping of birds—their *chink! chink! chink!* and *video! video! video!* in the trees far across the fields. She'd lived her entire life with the hum of the city, she realized. You'd think Baltimore was kept running by some giant, ceaseless, underground machine. How had she stood it? Just like that, she gave up any plan for returning. She'd been heading toward the café with some vague notion of asking for the nearest Trailways stop, or maybe hitching a ride back home with a reliable-looking trucker; but what was the point of going home?

She passed the second ranch house, which had a mailbox out front shaped like a covered wagon. A fence surrounded the property—just whitewashed stumps linked by swags of whitewashed chain, purely ornamental—and she stopped next to one of the stumps and set her purse on it to take inventory. The trouble with dress-up purses was that they were so small. Her everyday purse, a canvas tote, could have kept her going for weeks. ("You give the line 'Who steals my purse steals trash' a whole new meaning," her mother had once remarked.) Still, she had the basics: a comb, a pack of Kleenex, and a lipstick. And in her wallet, thirty-four dollars and some change and a blank check. Also two credit cards, but the check was what mattered. She would go to the nearest bank and open the largest account the check would safely cover—say three hundred dollars. Why, three hundred dollars could last her a long time! Long enough to find work, at least. The credit cards, she supposed, Ira would very soon cancel. Although she might try using them just for this weekend.

She flipped through the rest of the plastic windows in her wallet, passing her driver's license, her library card, a school photo of Daisy, a folded coupon for Affinity shampoo, and a color snapshot of Jesse standing on the front steps at home. Daisy was double-exposed—it was all the rage last year—so her precise, chiseled profile loomed semi-transparent behind a full-face view of her with her chin raised haughtily. Jesse wore his mammoth black overcoat from Value Village and a very long red fringed neck scarf that dangled below his knees. She was struck—she was almost injured—by his handsomeness. He had taken Ira's one drop of Indian blood and transformed it into something rich and stunning: high polished cheekbones, straight black hair, long black lusterless eyes. But the look he gave her was veiled and impassive, as haughty as Daisy's. Neither one of them had any further need of her.

She replaced everything in her purse and snapped it shut. When she started walking again her shoes felt stiff and uncomfortable, as if her feet had changed shape while she was standing. Maybe they'd swollen; it was a very warm day. But even the weather suited her purposes. This way, she could camp out if she had to. She could sleep in a haystack. Providing haystacks still existed.

Tonight she'd phone Serena and apologize for missing the funeral. She would reverse the charges; she could do that, with Serena. Serena might not want to accept the call at first because Maggie had let her down—Serena was always so quick to take offense—but eventually she'd give in and Maggie would explain. "Listen," she would say, "right now I wouldn't mind going to *Ira's* funeral." Or maybe that was tactless, in view of the circumstances.

The café lay just ahead, and beyond that was a low cinderblock building of some sort and beyond that, she guessed, at least a semblance of a town. It would be one of those scrappy little Route One towns, with much attention given to the requirements of auto travel. She would register at a no-frills motel, the room scarcely larger than the bed, which she pictured, with some enjoyment, as sunken in the middle and covered with a worn chenille spread. She would shop at Nell's Grocery for foods that didn't need cooking. One thing most people failed to realize was that many varieties of canned soup could be eaten cold straight from the tin, and they made a fairly balanced meal, too. (A can opener: She mustn't forget to buy one at the grocery.)

As for employment, she didn't have much hope of finding a nursing home in such a town. Maybe something clerical, then. She knew how to type and keep books, although she wasn't wonderful at it. She'd had a little experience at the frame shop. Maybe an auto-parts store could use her, or she could be one of those women behind the grille at a service station, embossing credit card bills and handing people their keys. If worst came to worst she could punch a cash register. She could wait tables. She could scrub floors, for heaven's sake. She was only forty-eight and her health was perfect, and in spite of what some people might think, she was capable of anything she set her mind to.

She bent to pick a chicory flower. She stuck it in the curls above her left ear.

Ira thought she was a klutz. Everybody did. She had developed a sort of clownish, pratfalling reputation, somehow. In the nursing home once, there'd been a crash and a tinkle of glass, and the charge nurse had said, "Maggie?" Just like that! Not even checking first to make sure! And Maggie hadn't been anywhere near; it was someone else entirely. But that just went to show how people viewed her.

She had assumed when she married Ira that he would always look at her the way he'd looked at her that first night, when she stood in front of him in her trousseau negligee and the only light in the room was the filmy shaded lamp by the bed. She had unbuttoned her top button and then her next-to-top button, just enough to let the negligee slip from her shoulders and hesitate and fall around her ankles. He had looked directly into her eyes, and it seemed he wasn't even breathing. She had assumed that would go on forever.

In the parking lot in front of Nell's Grocery & Café two men stood next to a pickup, talking. One was fat and ham-faced and the other was thin and white and wilted. They were discussing someone named Doug who had come out all over in swelters. Maggie wondered what a swelter was. She pictured it as a combination of a sweat and a welt. She knew she must make an odd sight, arriving on foot out of nowhere so dressed up and citified. "Hello!" she cried, sounding like her mother. The men stopped talking and stared at her. The thin one took his cap off finally and looked inside it. Then he put it back on his head.

She could step into the café and speak to Mabel, ask if she knew of a job and a place to stay; or she could head straight for town and find something on her own. In a way, she preferred to fend for herself. It would be sort of embarrassing to confess she'd been abandoned by her husband. On the other hand, maybe Mabel knew of some marvelous job. Maybe she knew of the perfect boardinghouse, dirt cheap, with kitchen privileges, full of kindhearted people. Maggie supposed she ought to at least inquire.

She let the screen door slap shut behind her. The grocery was familiar now and she moved through its smells comfortably. At the lunch counter she found Mabel leaning on a wadded-up dishcloth and talking to a man in overalls. They were almost whispering. "Why, *you* can't do nothing about it," Mabel was saying. "What do they think *you* can do about it?"

Maggie felt she was intruding. She hadn't counted on having to share Mabel with someone else. She shrank back before she was seen; she skulked in the crackers-and-cookies aisle, hoping for her rival to depart.

"I been over it and over it," the man said creakily. "I still can't see what else I could have done."

"Good gracious, no."

Maggie picked up a box of Ritz crackers. There used to be a kind of apple pie people made that contained no apples whatsoever, just Ritz crackers. What would that taste like, she wondered. It didn't seem to her there was the remotest chance it could taste like apple pie. Maybe you soaked the crackers in cider or something first. She looked on the box for the recipe, but it wasn't mentioned.

Now Ira would be starting to realize she was gone. He would be noticing the empty rush of air that comes when a person you're accustomed to is all at once absent.

Would he go on to the funeral without her? She hadn't thought of that. No, Serena was more Maggie's friend than Ira's. And Max had been just an acquaintance. To tell the truth, Ira didn't have any friends. It was one of the things Maggie minded about him.

He'd be slowing down. He'd be trying to decide. Maybe he had already turned the car around.

He would be noticing how stark and upright a person feels when he's suddenly left on his own.

Maggie set down the Ritz crackers and drifted toward the fig newtons.

One time a number of years ago, Maggie had fallen in love, in a way, with a patient at the nursing home. The very notion was comical, of course. In love! With a man in his seventies! A man who had to ride in a wheelchair if he went any distance at all! But there you are. She was fascinated by his austere white face and courtly manners. She liked his stiff turns of speech, which gave her the feeling he was keeping his own words at a distance. And she knew what pain it caused him to dress so formally each morning, his expression magnificently disengaged as he worked his arthritic, clublike hands into the sleeves of his suit coat. Mr. Gabriel, his name was. "Ben" to everyone else, but "Mr. Gabriel" to Maggie, for she guessed how familiarity alarmed him. And she was diffident about helping him, always asking his permission first. She was careful not to touch him. It was a kind of reverse courtship, you might say. While the others treated him warmly and a little condescendingly, Maggie stood back and allowed him his reserve.

In the office files, she read that he owned a nationally prominent power-tool company. Yes, she could see him in that position. He had a businessman's crisp authority, a businessman's air of knowing what was what. She read that he was widowed and childless, without any close relations except for an unmarried sister in New Hampshire. Until recently he had lived by himself, but shortly after his cook started a minor grease fire in the kitchen he'd applied for admission to the home. His concern, he wrote, was that he was becoming too disabled to escape if his house burned down. Concern! You had to know the man to know what the word concealed: a morbid, obsessive dread of fire, which had taken root with that small kitchen blaze and grown till not even live-in help, and finally not even round-the-clock nursing care, could reassure him. (Maggie had observed his stony, fixed stare during fire drills—the only occasions on which he seemed truly to be a patient.)

Oh, why was she reading his file? She wasn't supposed to. Strictly speaking, she shouldn't read even his medical record. She was nothing but a geriatric nursing assistant, certified to bathe her charges and feed them and guide them to the toilet.

And even in her imagination, she had always been the most faithful of wives. She had never felt so much as tempted. But now thoughts of Mr. Gabriel consumed her, and she spent hours inventing new ways to be indispensable to him. He always noticed, and he always thanked her. "Imagine!" he told a nurse. "Maggie's brought me tomatoes from her own backyard." Maggie's tomatoes were subject to an unusual ailment: They were bulbous, like collections of little red rubber jack balls that had collided and mashed together. This problem had persisted for several years, through several varieties of hybrids. Maggie blamed the tiny plot of city soil she was forced to confine them to (or was it the lack of sun?), but often she sensed, from the amused and tolerant looks they drew, that other people thought it had something to do with Maggie herself—with the knobby, fumbling way she seemed to be progressing through her life. Yet Mr. Gabriel noticed nothing. He declared her tomatoes smelled like a summer's day in 1944. When she sliced them they resembled doilies—scalloped around the edges, full of holes between intersections—but all he said was: "I can't tell you how much this means to me." He wouldn't even let her salt them. He said they tasted glorious, just as they were.

Well, she wasn't stupid. She realized that what appealed to her was the image he had of her—an image that would have staggered Ira. It would have staggered anyone who knew her. Mr. Gabriel thought she was capable and skillful and efficient. He believed that everything she did was perfect. He said as much, in so many words. And this was during a very unsatisfactory period in her life, when Jesse was just turning adolescent and negative and Maggie seemed to be going through a quarrelsome spell with Ira. But Mr. Gabriel never guessed any of that. Mr. Gabriel saw someone collected, moving serenely around his room straightening his belongings.

At night she lay awake and concocted dialogues in which Mr. Gabriel confessed that he was besotted with her. He would say he knew that he was too old to attract her physically, but she would interrupt to tell him he was wrong. This was a fact. The mere thought of laying her head against his starched white shoulder could turn her all warm and melting. She would promise to go anywhere with him, anywhere on earth. Should they take Daisy too? (Daisy was five or six at the time.) Of course they couldn't take Jesse; Jesse was no longer a child. But then Jesse would think she loved Daisy better, and she certainly couldn't have that. She wandered off on a sidetrack, imagining what would happen if they did take Jesse. He would lag a few steps behind, wearing one of his all-black outfits, laboring under his entire stereo system and a stack of record albums. She started giggling. Ira stirred in his sleep and said, "Hmm?" She sobered and hugged herself— a competent, adventurous woman, with infinite possibilities.

Star-crossed, that's what they were; but she seemed to have found a way to be star-crossed differently from anyone else. How would she tend Mr. Gabriel and still go out to a job? He refused to be left alone. And what job would she go to? Her only employment in all her life had been with the Silver Threads Nursing Home. Fat chance they'd give her a letter of reference after she'd absconded with one of their patients.

Another sidetrack: What if she didn't abscond, but broke the news to Ira in a civilized manner and calmly made new arrangements? She could move into Mr. Gabriel's room. She could rise from his bed every morning and be right there at work; no commute. At night when the nurse came around with the pills, she'd find Maggie and Mr. Gabriel stretched out side by side, staring at the ceiling, with their roommate, Abner Scopes, in the bed along the opposite wall.

Maggie gave another snicker.

This was turning out all skewed, somehow.

Like anyone in love, she constantly found reasons to mention his name. She told Ira everything about him—his suits and ties, his gallantry, his stoicism. "I don't know why you can't act that keen about my father; he's family," Ira said, missing the point entirely. Ira's father was a whiner, a user. Mr. Gabriel was nothing like him.

Then one morning the home held another fire drill. The alarm bell jangled and the code blared over the loudspeaker: "Dr. Red in Room Two-twenty." This happened in the middle of activity hour—an inconvenient time because the patients were so scattered. Those with any manual dexterity were down in the Crafts Room, knotting colored silk flowers. Those too crippled—Mr. Gabriel, for instance—were taking an extra session of P.T. And of course the bedridden were still in their rooms. They were the easy ones.

The rule was that you cleared the halls of all obstructions, shut stray patients into any room available, and tied red cloths to the doorknobs to show which rooms were occupied. Maggie closed off 201 and 203, where her only bedridden patients lay. She attached red cloths from the broom closet. Then she coaxed one of Joelle Barrett's wandering old ladies into 202. There was an empty tray cart next to 202 and she set that inside as well, after which she dashed off to seize Lottie Stein, who was inching along in her walker and humming tunelessly. Maggie put her in 201 with Hepzibah Murray. Then Joelle arrived, wheeling Lawrence Dunn and calling, "Oops! Tillie's out!" Tillie was the one Maggie had just stashed in 202. That was the trouble with these drills. They reminded her of those pocket-sized games where you tried to get all the silver BBs into their nooks at once. She captured Tillie and slammed her back in 202. Disturbing sounds were coming from 201. That would be a fight between Lottie and Hepzibah; Hepzibah hated having outsiders in her room. Maggie should have dealt with it, and she should also have gone to the aid of Joelle, who was having quite a struggle with Lawrence, but there was something more important on her mind. She was thinking, of course, about Mr. Gabriel.

By now, he would be catatonic with fear.

She left her corridor. (You were never supposed to do that.) She zipped past the nurses' station, down the stairs, and made a right-angle turn. The P.T. room lay at the far end of the hall. Both of its swinging doors were shut. She raced toward them, rounding first a folding chair and then a canvas laundry cart, neither of which should have been there. But all at once she heard footsteps, the squeak of rubber soles. She stopped and looked around. Mrs. Willis! Almost certainly it was Mrs. Willis, her supervisor; and here Maggie was, miles from her proper station.

She did the first thing that came to mind. She vaulted into the laundry cart.

Absurd, she knew it instantly. She was cursing herself even as she sank among the crumpled linens. She might have got away with it, though, except that she'd set the cart to rolling. Somebody grabbed it and drew it to a halt. A growly voice said, "What in the world?"

Maggie opened her eyes, which she had closed the way small children do in one last desperate attempt to make herself invisible. Bertha Washington, from the kitchen, stood gaping down at her.

"Hi, there," Maggie said.

"Well, I never!" Bertha said. "Sateen, come look at who-all's waiting for the laundry man."

Sateen Bishop's face arrived next to Bertha's, breaking into a smile. "You goofball, Maggie! What will you get up to next? Most folks just takes baths," she said.

"This was a miscalculation," Maggie told them. She stood up, batting away a towel that draped one shoulder. "Ah, well, I guess I'd better be—"

But Sateen said, "Off we goes, girl."

"Sateen! No!" Maggie cried.

Sateen and Bertha took hold of the cart, chortling like maniacs, and tore down the hall. Maggie had to hang on tight or she would have toppled backward. She careened along, dodging as she approached the bend, but the women were quicker on their feet than they looked. They swung her around handily and started back the way they'd come. Maggie's bangs lifted off her forehead in the breeze. She felt like a figurehead on a ship. She clutched the sides of the cart and called, half laughing, "Stop! Please stop!" Bertha, who was overweight, snorted and thudded beside her. Sateen made a *sissing* sound through her teeth. They rattled toward the P.T. room just as the all-clear bell sounded—a hoarse burr over the loudspeaker. Instantly the doors swung open and Mr. Gabriel emerged in his wheelchair, propelled by Mrs. Inman. Not the physical therapist, not an assistant or a volunteer, but

Mrs. Inman herself, the director of nursing for the entire home. Sateen and Bertha pulled up short. Mr. Gabriel's jaw dropped.

Mrs. Inman said, "Ladies?"

Maggie laid a hand on Bertha's shoulder and climbed out of the cart. "Honestly," she told the two women. She batted down the hem of her skirt.

"Ladies, are you aware that we've been having a fire drill?"

"Yes, ma'am," Maggie said. She had always been scared to death of stern women.

"Are you aware of the seriousness of a fire drill in a nursing home?"

Maggie said, "I was just—"

"Take Ben to his room, please, Maggie. I'll speak with you in my office later."

"Yes, ma'am," Maggie said.

She wheeled Mr. Gabriel toward the elevator. When she leaned forward to press the button, her arm brushed his shoulder, and he jerked away from her. She said, "Excuse me." He didn't respond.

In the elevator he was silent, although that could have been because a doctor happened to be riding with them. But even after they arrived on the second floor and parted company with the doctor, Mr. Gabriel said nothing.

The hall had that hurricane-swept appearance it always took on after a drill. Every door was flung open and patients were roving distractedly and the staff was dragging forth the objects that didn't belong in the rooms. Maggie wheeled Mr. Gabriel into 206. His roommate hadn't returned yet. She parked the chair. Still he sat silent.

"Oh, land," she said, giving a little laugh.

His eyes slid slowly to her face.

Maybe he could view her as a sort of *I Love Lucy* type—madcap, fun-loving, full of irrepressible high spirits. That was one way to look at it. Actually, Maggie had never liked *I Love Lucy*. She thought the plots were so engineered—that dizzy woman's failures just built-in, just guaranteed. But maybe Mr. Gabriel felt differently.

"I came downstairs to find you," she said.

He watched her.

"I was worried," she told him.

So worried you took a joyride in a laundry cart, his glare said plainly.

Then Maggie, stooping to set the brake on his wheelchair, was struck by the most peculiar thought. It was the lines alongside his mouth that caused it—deep crevices that pulled the corners down. Ira had those lines. On Ira they were fainter, of course. They showed up only when he disapproved of something. (Usually Maggie.) And Ira would give her that same dark, sober, judging gaze.

Why, Mr. Gabriel was just another Ira, was all. He had Ira's craggy face and Ira's dignity, his aloofness, that could still to this day exert a physical pull on her. He was even supporting that unmarried sister, she would bet, just as Ira supported *his* sisters and his deadbeat father: a sign of a noble nature, some might say. All Mr. Gabriel was, in fact, was Maggie's attempt to find an earlier version of Ira. She'd wanted the version she had known at the start of their marriage, before she'd begun disappointing him.

She hadn't been courting Mr. Gabriel; she'd been courting Ira.

Well, she helped Mr. Gabriel out of his wheelchair and into the armchair next to his bed, and then she left to check the other patients, and life went on the same as ever. In fact, Mr. Gabriel still lived at the home, although they didn't talk as much as they used to. Nowadays he seemed to prefer Joelle. He was perfectly friendly, though. He'd probably forgotten all about Maggie's ride in the laundry cart.

But Maggie remembered, and sometimes, feeling the glassy sheet of Ira's disapproval, she grew numbly, wearily certain that there was no such thing on this earth as real change. You could change husbands, but not the situation. You could change *who*, but not *what*. We're all just spinning here, she thought, and she pictured the world as a little blue teacup, revolving like those rides at Kiddie Land where everyone is pinned to his place by centrifugal force.

She picked up a box of fig newtons and read the nutrition panel on the back. "Sixty calories each," she said out loud, and Ira said, "Ah, go ahead and splurge."

"Stop undermining my diet," she told him. She replaced the box on the shelf, not turning.

"Hey, babe," he said, "care to accompany me to a funeral?"

She shrugged and didn't answer, but when he hung an arm around her shoulders she let him lead her out to the car.

2

To find any place in Deer Lick, you just stopped at the one traffic light and looked in all four directions. Barbershop, two service stations, hardware, grocery, three churches—everything revealed itself at a glance. The buildings were set about as demurely as those in a model-railroad village. Trees were left standing, and the sidewalks ended after three blocks. Peer down any cross street; you'd see greenery and cornfields and even, in one case, a fat brown horse dipping his nose into a pasture.

Ira parked on the asphalt next to Fenway Memorial Church, a grayish-white frame cube with a stubby little steeple like a witch's hat. There were no other cars on the lot. He'd guessed right, as it turned out: Continuing on Route One had been quicker, which wasn't all that fortunate, since it meant they'd arrived in Deer Lick thirty minutes early. Still, Maggie had expected to find some sign of the other mourners.

"Maybe it's the wrong day," she said.

"It couldn't be. 'Tomorrow,' Serena told you. No way you could mix *that* up."

"You think we should go on in?"

"Sure, if it's not locked."

When they got out of the car, Maggie's dress stuck to the back of her legs. She felt shellacked. Her hair was knotted from the wind, and the waistband of her panty hose had folded over on itself so it was cutting into her stomach.

They climbed a set of wooden steps and tried the door. It swung open with a grudging sound. Immediately inside lay a long, dim room, uncarpeted, the raftered ceiling towering above dark pews. Massive floral arrangements stood on either side of the pulpit, which Maggie found reassuring. Only weddings and funerals called for such artificial-looking bouquets.

"Hello?" Ira tried.

His voice rang back.

They tiptoed up the aisle, creaking the floorboards. "Do you suppose there's a . . . side or something?" Maggie whispered.

"Side?"

"I mean a groom's side and a bride's side? Or rather—" Her mistake sent her into a little fit of giggles. To tell the truth, she hadn't had much experience with funerals. No one really close to her had died yet, knock on wood. "I mean," she said, "does it make any difference where we sit?"

"Just not in the front row," Ira told her.

"Well, of course not, Ira. I'm not a total fool."

She dropped into a right-hand pew midway up the aisle and slid over to make room for him. "You'd think at least some kind of music would be playing," she said.

Ira checked his watch.

Maggie said, "Maybe next time you should follow Serena's directions."

"What, and wander some cow path half the morning?"

"It's better than being the first people here."

"I don't mind being first," Ira said.

He reached into the left pocket of his suit coat. He brought out a deck of cards secured with a rubber band.

"Ira Moran! You're not playing cards in a house of worship!"

He reached into his right pocket and brought out another deck. "What if someone comes?" Maggie asked.

"Don't worry; I have lightning reflexes," he told her.

He removed the rubber bands and shuffled the two decks together. They rattled like machine-gun fire.

"Well," Maggie said, "I'm just going to pretend that I don't know you." She gathered the straps of her purse and slid out the other end of the pew.

Ira laid down cards where she'd been sitting.

She walked over to a stained-glass window. IN MEMORY OF VIVIAN DEWEY, BELOVED HUSBAND AND FATHER, a plaque beneath it read. A husband named Vivian! She stifled a laugh. She was reminded of a thought she'd often had back in the sixties when the young men wore their hair so long: Wouldn't it feel creepy to run your fingers through your lover's soft, trailing tresses?

Churches always put the most unseemly notions in her head.

She continued toward the front, her heels clicking sharply as if she knew where she was going. She stood on tiptoe beside the pulpit to smell a waxy white flower she couldn't identify. It didn't have any scent at all, and it gave off a definite chill. In fact, she was feeling a little chilly herself. She turned and walked back down the center aisle toward Ira.

Ira had his cards spread across half the length of the pew. He was shifting them around and whistling between his teeth. "The Gambler," that was the name of the song. Disappointingly obvious. *You've got to know when to hold them, know when to fold them* . . . The form of solitaire he played was so involved it could last for hours, but it started simply and he was rearranging the cards almost without hesitation. "This is the part that's dull," he told Maggie. "I ought to have an amateur work this part, the way the old masters had their students fill in the backgrounds of their paintings."

She shot him a glance; she hadn't known they'd done that. It sounded to her like cheating. "Can't you put that five on the six?" she asked.

"Butt out, Maggie."

She wandered on down the aisle, swinging her purse loosely from her fingers.

What kind of church was this? The sign outside hadn't said. Maggie and Serena had grown up Methodist, but Max was some other de-.nomination and after they married, Serena had switched over. She was married Methodist, though. Maggie had sung at her wedding; she'd sung a duet with Ira. (They were just starting to date then.) The wedding had been one of Serena's wilder inventions, a mishmash of popular songs and Kahlil Gibran in an era when everyone else was still clinging to "O Promise Me." Well, Serena had always been ahead of her time.

No telling what kind of funeral she would put on.

Maggie pivoted at the door and walked back toward Ira. He had left his pew and was leaning over it from the pew behind so he could study the full array of cards. He must have reached the interesting stage by now. Even his whistling was slower. *You never count your money when you're sitting at the table . . .* From here he looked like a scarecrow: coat-hanger shoulders, spriggy black cowlick, his arms set at wiry angles.

"Maggie! You came!" Serena called from the doorway.

Maggie turned, but all she saw was a silhouette against a blur of yellow light. She said, "Serena?"

Serena rushed toward her, arms outstretched. She wore a black shawl that completely enveloped her, with long satiny fringes swinging at the hem, and her hair was black too, untouched by gray. When Maggie hugged her she got tangled in the tail of hair that hung down straight between Serena's shoulder blades. She had to shake her fingers loose, laughing slightly, as she stepped back. Serena could have been a Spanish señora, Maggie always thought, with her center part and her full, oval face and vivid coloring.

"And Ira!" Serena was saying. "How are you, Ira?"

Ira stood up (having somehow spirited his cards out of sight), and she kissed his cheek, while he endured it. "Mighty sad to hear about Max," he told her.

"Well, thank you," Serena said. "I'm so grateful to you for making the trip; you have no idea. All Max's relatives are up at the house and I'm feeling outnumbered. Finally I slipped away; told them I had things to see to at the church ahead of time. Did you two eat breakfast?"

"Oh, yes," Maggie said. "But I wouldn't mind finding a bathroom."

"I'll take you. Ira?"

"No, thanks."

"We'll be back in a minute, then," Serena said. She hooked her arm through Maggie's and steered her down the aisle. "Max's cousins came from Virginia," she said, "and his brother George, of course, and George's wife and daughter, and Linda's been here since Thursday with the grandchildren. . . ."

Her breath smelled of peaches, or maybe that was her perfume. Her shoes were sandals with leather straps that wound halfway up her bare brown legs, and her dress (Maggie was not surprised to see) was a vibrant red chiffon with a rhinestone sunburst at the center of the V neckline. "Maybe it's a blessing," she was saying. "All this chaos keeps my mind off things."

"Oh, Serena, has it been just terrible?" Maggie asked.

"Well, yes and no," Serena said. She was leading Maggie through a little side door to the left of the entrance, and then down a flight of narrow stairs. "I mean it went on so long, Maggie; in an awful way it was kind of a relief, at first. He'd been sick since February, you know. Only back then we didn't realize. February is such a sick month anyhow: colds and flu and leaky roofs and the furnace breaking down. So we didn't put two and two together at the time. He was feeling off a little, was all he said. Touch of this, touch of that . . . Then he turned yellow. Then his upper lip disappeared. I mean, nothing you can report to a doctor. You can't exactly phone a doctor and say . . . but I looked at him one morning and I thought, 'My Lord, he's so old! His whole face is different.' And by that time it was April, when normal people feel wonderful."

They were crossing an unlit, linoleum-floored basement overhung with pipes and ducts. They picked their way between long metal tables and folding chairs. Maggie felt right at home. How often had she and Serena traded secrets in one or another Sunday-school classroom? She thought she could smell the coated paper that was used for Bible-study leaflets.

"One day I came back from the grocery store," Serena said, "and Max wasn't there. It was a Saturday, and when I'd left he was working in the yard. Well, I didn't think much about it, started putting away the groceries—"

She ushered Maggie into a bathroom tiled in white. Her voice took on an echo. "Then all at once I look out the window and there's this totally unknown woman leading him by the hand. She was sort of . . . hovering; you could tell she thought he was handicapped or something. I went running out. She said, 'Oh! Is he yours?' "

Serena leaned back against a sink, arms folded, while Maggie entered a booth. "Was he mine!" Serena said. "Like when a neighbor comes dragging your dog who's dripping garbage from every whisker and she asks, 'Is he yours?' But I said yes. Turns out this woman found him wandering Dunmore Road with a pair of pruning shears, and he didn't seem to know where he was headed. She asked if she could help and all he said was: 'I'm not certain. I'm not certain.' But he recognized me when he saw me. His face lit up and he told her, 'There's Serena.' So I took him inside and sat him down. I asked him what had happened and he said it was the oddest feeling. He said that out of the blue, he just seemed to be walking on Dunmore Road. Then when the woman turned him back toward where he'd come from he said he saw our house, and he knew it was ours, but at the same time it was like it had nothing to do with him. He said it was like he had stepped outside his own life for a minute."

MARCY + DAVE, read the chalked words above the toilet paper dispenser. SUE HARDY WEARS A PADDED BRA. Maggie tried to adjust to this new version of Max—vague and bewildered and buckling at the knees, no doubt, like one of her patients at the home. But what she came up with was the Max she'd always known, a hefty football-player type with a prickle of glinting blond hair and a broad, good-natured, freckled face; the Max who'd run naked into the surf at Carolina Beach. She'd seen him only a few times in the past ten years, after all; he was not the world's best at holding down a job and had moved his family often. But he had struck her as the type who stays boyish forever. It was hard to imagine him aging.

She flushed the toilet and emerged to find Serena considering one of her sandals, twisting her foot this way and that. "Have you ever done such a thing?" Serena asked her. "Stepped outside your own life?"

Maggie said, "Well, not that I can recall," and turned on the hot water.

"What would it be like, I wonder," Serena said. "Just to look around you one day and have it all amaze you—where you'd arrived at, who you'd married, what kind of person you'd grown into. Say you suddenly came to while you were—oh, say, out shopping with your daughter— but it was your seven- or eight-year-old self observing all you did. 'Why!' you'd say. 'Can this be me? Driving a car? Taking charge? Nagging some young woman like I knew what I was doing?' You'd walk into your house and say, 'Well, I don't think all that much of my taste.' You'd go to a mirror and say, 'Goodness, my chin is starting to slope just the way my mother's did.' I mean you'd be looking at things without their curtains. You'd say, 'My husband isn't any Einstein, is he?' You'd say, 'My daughter certainly could stand to lose some weight.' "

Maggie cleared her throat. (All those observations were disconcertingly true. Serena's daughter, for instance, could stand to lose a *lot* of weight.) She reached for a paper towel and said, "I thought on the phone you said he died of cancer."

"He did," Serena said. "But it was everywhere before we knew about it. Every part of him, even his brain."

"Oh, Serena."

"One day he was out selling radio ads the same as always, and next day he was flat on his back. Couldn't walk right, couldn't see right; everything he did was one-sided. He kept saying he smelled cookies. He'd say, 'Serena, when will those cookies be done?' I haven't baked cookies in years! He'd say, 'Bring me one, Serena, as soon as they're out of the oven.' So I would make a batch and then he'd look surprised and tell me he wasn't hungry."

"I wish you'd called me," Maggie said.

"What could you have done?"

Well, nothing, really, Maggie thought. She couldn't even say for certain that she knew what Serena was going through. Every stage of their lives, it seemed, Serena had experienced slightly ahead of Maggie; and every stage she'd reported on in her truthful, startling, bald-faced way, like some foreigner who didn't know the etiquette. Talk about stripping the curtains off! It was Serena who'd told Maggie that marriage was not a Rock Hudson-Doris Day movie. It was Serena who'd said that motherhood was much too hard and, when you got right down to it, perhaps not worth the effort. Now this: to have your husband die. It made Maggie nervous, although she knew it wasn't catching.

She frowned into the mirror and caught sight of the squinched blue chicory flower lolling above one ear. She plucked it off and dropped it in the wastebasket. Serena hadn't mentioned it—sure proof of her distracted state of mind.

"At first I wondered, 'How are we going to do this?' " Serena said. " 'How will the two of us manage?' Then I saw that it was only me who would manage. Max was just assuming that I would see him through it. Did the tax people threaten to audit us; did the car need a new transmission? That was *my* affair; Max had left it all behind him. He'd be dead by the time the audit rolled around, and he didn't have any further use for a car. Really it's laughable, when you stop to think. Isn't there some warning about your wishes coming true? 'Be careful what you set your heart on'—isn't there some such warning? Here I'd vowed since I was a child that I wouldn't be dependent on a man. You'd never find *me* waiting around for some man to give me the time of day! I wanted a husband who'd dote on me and stick to me like glue, and that's exactly what I got. Exactly. Max hanging on to the sight of me and following me with his eyes around the room. When he had to go to the hospital finally, he begged me not to leave him and so I stayed there day and night. But I started feeling mad at him. I remembered how I'd always been after him to exercise and take better care of his health, and he'd said exercise was nothing but a fad. Claimed jogging gave people coronaries. To hear him talk, the sidewalks were just littered with the piled-up corpses of joggers. I'd look at him in his bed and I'd say, 'Well, which do you prefer, Max: sudden death in a snazzy red warm-up suit or lying here stuck full of needles and tubes?' I said that, right out loud! I acted horrible to him."

"Oh, well," Maggie said unhappily, "I'm sure you didn't intend—"

"I intended every word," Serena said. "Why do you always have to gloss things over, Maggie? I acted horrible. Then he died."

"Oh, dear," Maggie said.

"It was nighttime, Wednesday night. I felt someone had lifted a weight off my chest, and I went home and slept twelve hours straight. Then Thursday Linda came down from New Jersey and that was nice; her and our son-in-law and the kids. But I kept feeling I ought to be doing something. There was something I was forgetting. I ought to be over at the hospital; that was it. I felt so restless. It was like that trick we used to try as children, remember? Where we'd stand in a doorway and press the backs of both hands against the frame and then when we stepped forward our hands floated up on their own as if all that pressure had been, oh, stored for future use; operating retroactively. And then Linda's kids started teasing the cat. They dressed the cat in their teddy bear's pajamas and Linda didn't even notice. She's never kept them properly in line. Max and I used to bite our tongues not to point that out. Anytime they'd come we wouldn't say a word but we'd give each other this look across the room: just trade a look, you know how you do? And all at once I had no one to trade looks with. It was the first I'd understood that I'd truly lost him."

She drew her tail of hair over one shoulder and examined it. The skin beneath her eyes was shiny. In fact, she was crying, but she didn't seem to realize that. "So I drank a whole bottle of wine," she said, "and then I phoned everyone I ever used to know, all the friends we had when Max and I were courting. You, and Sissy Parton, and the Barley twins—"

"The Barley twins! Are they coming?"

"Sure, and Jo Ann Dermott and Nat Abrams, whom she finally did end up marrying, you'll be interested to hear—"

"I haven't thought of Jo Ann in years!"

"She's going to read from *The Prophet*. You and Ira are singing."

"We're what?"

"You're singing 'Love Is a Many Splendored Thing.' "

"Oh, have mercy, Serena! Not 'Love Is a Many Splendored Thing.' "

"You sang it at our wedding, didn't you?"

"Yes, but—"

"That was what they were playing when Max first told me how he felt about me," Serena said. She lifted a corner of her shawl and delicately blotted the shiny places beneath her eyes. "October twenty-second, nineteen fifty-five. Remember? The Harvest Home Ball. I came with Terry Simpson, but Max cut in."

"But this is a funeral!" Maggie said.

"So?"

"It's not a . . . request program," Maggie said.

Over their heads, a piano began thrumming the floorboards. Chord, chord, chord was plunked forth like so many place settings. Serena flung her shawl across her bosom and said, "We'd better get back up there."

"Serena," Maggie said, following her out of the bathroom, "Ira and I haven't sung in public since your wedding!"

"That's all right. I don't expect anything professional," Serena said. "All I want is a kind of rerun, like people sometimes have on their golden anniversaries. I thought it would make a nice touch."

"Nice touch! But you know how songs, well, age," Maggie said, winding after her among the tables. "Why not just some consoling hymns? Doesn't your church have a choir?"

At the foot of the stairs, Serena turned. "Look," she said. "All I'm asking is the smallest, simplest favor, from the closest friend I've had in this world. Why, you and I have been through everything together! Miss Kimmel's first grade! Miss van Deeter! Long division! Our weddings and our babies! You helped me put my mother in the nursing home. I sat up with you that time that Jesse got arrested."

"Yes, but—"

"Last night I started thinking and I said to myself, 'What am I holding this funeral for? Hardly anyone will come; we haven't lived here long enough. Why, we're not even burying him; I'm flinging his ashes on the Chesapeake next summer. We're not even going to have his casket at the service. What's the point of sitting in that church,' I said, 'listening to Mrs. Filbert tinkle out gospel hymns on the piano? "Stumbling up the Path of Righteousness" and "Death Is Like a Good Night's Sleep." I don't even know Mrs. Filbert! I'd rather have Sissy Parton. I'd rather have "My Prayer" as played by Sissy Parton at our wedding.' So then I thought, Why not all of it? Kahlil Gibran? 'Love Is a Many Splendored Thing'?"

"Not everyone would understand, though," Maggie said. "People who weren't at the wedding, for instance."

Or even people who *were* at the wedding, she thought privately. Some of those guests had worn fairly puzzled expressions.

"Let them wonder, then," Serena said. "It's not for them I'm doing it." And she spun away and started up the stairs.

"Also there's Ira," Maggie called, following her. The fringe of Serena's shawl swatted her in the face. "Of course I'd move the earth for you, Serena, but I don't think Ira would feel comfortable singing that song."

"Ira has a nice tenor voice," Serena said. She turned at the top of the stairs. "And yours is like a silver bell; remember how people always told you that? High time you stopped keeping it a secret."

Maggie sighed and followed her up the aisle. No use pointing out, she supposed, that that bell was nearly half a century old by now.

Several other guests had arrived in Maggie's absence. They dotted the pews here and there. Serena bent to speak to a hatted woman in a slim black suit. "Sugar?" she said.

Maggie stopped short behind her and said, "Sugar Tilghman?"

Sugar turned. She had been the class beauty and was beautiful still, Maggie supposed, although it was hard to tell through the heavy black veil descending from her hat. She looked more like a widow than the widow herself. Well, she always had viewed clothes as costumes. "There you are!" she said. She rose to press her cheek against

Serena's. "I am so, so sorry for your loss," she said. "Except they call me Elizabeth now."

"Sugar, you remember Maggie," Serena said.

"Maggie Daley! What a surprise."

Sugar's cheek was smooth and taut beneath the veil. It felt like one of those netted onions in a grocery store.

"If this is not the saddest thing," she said. "Robert would have come with me but he had a meeting in Houston. He said to send you his condolences, though. He said, 'Seems like only yesterday we were trying to find our way to their wedding reception.'"

"Yes, well, that's what I want to discuss with you," Serena said. "Remember at our wedding? Where you sang a solo after the vows?"

"'Born to Be with You,'" Sugar said. She laughed. "You two marched out to it; I can see you still. The march took longer than the song, and at the finish all we heard was your high heels."

"Well," Serena said, "I'd like you to sing it again today."

Shock made Sugar's face appear to emerge from the netting. She was older-looking than Maggie had first realized. "Do what?" she said.

"Sing."

Sugar raised her eyebrows at Maggie. Maggie looked away, refusing to conspire. It was true the pianist was playing "My Prayer." But that couldn't be Sissy Parton, could it? That plump-backed woman with dimpled elbows like upside-down valentines? Why, she resembled any ordinary church lady.

"I haven't sung for twenty years or more," Sugar said. "I couldn't sing even then! All I was doing was showing off."

"Sugar, it's the last favor I'll ever ask of you," Serena said.

"Elizabeth."

"Elizabeth, one song! Among friends! Maggie and Ira are singing."

"No, wait—" Maggie said.

Sugar said, "And besides: 'Born to Be with You.'"

"What's wrong with it, I'd like to know?" Serena asked.

"Have you thought about the lyrics? *By your side, satisfied?* You want to hear that at a funeral?"

"Memorial service," Serena said, though she'd been calling it a funeral herself up till now.

"What's the difference?" Sugar asked.

"Well, it's not like there was a coffin present."

"What's the *difference*, Serena?"

"It's not like I'm by his side in the coffin or anything! It's not like I'm being ghoulish or anything! I'm by his side in a spiritual sense, is all I'm saying."

Sugar looked at Maggie. Maggie was trying to remember the words to "My Prayer." In a funeral context, she thought (or in a memorial-service context), even the blandest lines could take on a different aspect.

"You'd be the laughingstock of this congregation," Sugar said flatly.

"What do I care about that?"

Maggie left them and walked on up the aisle. She was alert to the people she passed now; they could be old-time friends. But no one looked familiar. She stopped at Ira's pew and gave him a nudge. "I'm back," she told him. He moved over. He was reading his pocket calendar—the part that listed birthstones and signs of the zodiac.

"Am I imagining things," he asked when she'd settled next to him, "or is that 'My Prayer' I'm hearing?"

"It's 'My Prayer,' all right," Maggie said. "And it's not just any old pianist, either. It's Sissy Parton."

"Who's Sissy Parton?"

"Honestly, Ira! You remember Sissy. She played at Serena's wedding."

"Oh, yes."

"Where you and I sang 'Love Is a Many Splendored Thing,'" Maggie said.

"How could I forget *that*," he said.

"Which Serena wants us to sing again today."

Ira didn't even change expression. He said, "Too bad we can't oblige her."

"Sugar Tilghman won't sing, either, and Serena's giving her fits. I don't think she'll let us out of this, Ira."

"Sugar Tilghman's here?" Ira said. He turned and looked over his shoulder.

Boys had always been fascinated by Sugar.

"She's sitting back there in the hat," Maggie told him.

"Did Sugar sing at their wedding?"

"She sang 'Born to Be with You.'"

Ira faced forward again and thought a moment. He must have been reviewing the lyrics. Eventually, he gave a little snort.

Maggie said, "Do you recall the words to 'Love Is a Many Splendored Thing'?"

"No, and I don't intend to," Ira said.

A man paused in the aisle next to Maggie. He said, "How you doing, Morans?"

"Oh, Durwood," Maggie said. She told Ira, "Move over and let Durwood have a seat."

"Durwood. Hi, there," Ira said. He slid down a foot.

"If I'd known you were coming too, I'd have hitched a ride," Durwood said, settling next to Maggie. "Peg had to take the bus to work."

"Oh, I'm sorry; we should have thought," Maggie said. "Serena must have phoned everyone in Baltimore."

"Yes, I noticed old Sugar back there," Durwood said. He slipped a ballpoint pen from his breast pocket. He was a rumpled, quiet man, with wavy gray hair that he wore just a little too long. It trailed thinly over the tops of his ears and lay in wisps on the back of his collar, giving him the look of someone down on his luck. In high school Maggie had not much liked him, but over the years he'd stayed on in the neighborhood and married a Glen Burnie girl and raised a family, and now she saw more of him than anyone else she'd grown up with. Wasn't it funny how that happened, she thought. She couldn't remember now why they hadn't been close to begin with.

Durwood was patting all his pockets, hunting something. "You wouldn't have a piece of paper, would you?" he said.

All she found was her shampoo coupon. She gave him that and he laid it on a hymnbook. Clicking his pen point, he frowned into space. "What are you writing?" Maggie asked.

"I'm trying to think of the words to 'I Want You, I Need You, I Love You.'"

Ira groaned.

The church was filling now. A family settled in the pew just in front of theirs, the children arranged by height so that the line of round blond heads slanted upward like a question. Serena flitted from guest to guest, no doubt pleading and cajoling. The fringes of her shawl had gathered a row of dust mice from somewhere. "My Prayer" played over and over, turning dogged.

Now that she knew how many people from her past were sitting here, Maggie wished she'd given more thought to her appearance. She could have worn powder, for instance, or foundation of some kind— something to make her face less rosy. Maybe she'd have tried painting brown hollows on her cheeks, the way the magazines were always recommending. Also she'd have chosen a younger dress, an eye-catching dress like Serena's. Except that she didn't own such a dress. Serena had always been more flamboyant—the only girl in their school with pierced ears. She had teetered on the edge of downright gaudy, but had somehow brought it off.

How gloriously Serena had defied the stodgy times they'd grown up in! In third grade she'd worn ballet-style shoes, paper-thin, with a stunning spray of sequins across each toe, and the other girls (in their sensible brown tie oxfords and thick wool knee socks) had bitterly envied the tripping way she walked and the dancer-like grace of her bare legs, which came out in goose bumps and purple splotches at every recess period. She had brought adventurous lunches to the stewy-smelling cafeteria: one time, tiny silver sardines still in their flat silver tin. (She ate the tails. She ate the little bones. "Mm-mm! Crunch, crunch," she said, licking off each finger.) Every year on Parents' Day she proudly, officiously ushered around her scandalous mother, Anita, who wore bright-red, skin-tight toreador pants and worked in a bar.

And she never hesitated to admit that she had no father. Or no father who was married, at any rate. Not married to her mother, at any rate.

In high school she had evolved her own personal fashion statement—rayon and machine embroidery and slinky blouses from the Philippines, when the other girls were wearing crinolines. You'd see the other girls wafting through the corridors, their skirts standing out like frilled lampshades; and then in their midst Serena's sultry, come-hither, plum-colored sheath handed down from Anita.

But wasn't it odd that the boys she went out with were never the sultry types themselves? They were not the dark Lotharios you would expect but the sunny innocents like Max. The plaid-shirt boys, the gym-sneaker boys: Those were the ones she'd gravitated toward. Maybe she'd coveted everydayness, more than she ever let on. Was that possible? Well, of course it was, but Maggie hadn't guessed it at the time. Serena had made such a point of being different. She was so thorny and spiky, so quick to get her hackles up and order you out of her sight forever. (How many times had she and Maggie stopped speaking—Serena swishing past as grandly as a duchess?) Even now, enfolding a funeral guest in her dramatic shawl, she gave off a rich, dark glow that made the people around her seem faded.

Maggie looked down at her hands. Lately, when she took a pinch of skin from the back of a hand and released it, she noticed the skin would stay pleated for moments afterward.

Durwood muttered to himself and scribbled phrases on her coupon. Then he muttered something else, staring at the hymnal rack in front of him. Maggie felt a clutch of anxiety. She placed her fingertips together and whispered, " 'Love is a many splendored thing, it's the April rose that only grows in the—' "

"I am not going to sing that song, I tell you," Ira said.

Maggie wasn't, either, but she had a sense of being borne along by something. All through this church, she imagined, middle-aged people were mumbling sentimental phrases from the fifties. *Wondrously, love can see . . .* and *More than the buds on the May-apple tree . . .*

Why did popular songs always focus on romantic love? Why this preoccupation with first meetings, sad partings, honeyed kisses, heartbreak, when life was also full of children's births and trips to the shore and longtime jokes with friends? Once Maggie had seen on TV where archaeologists had just unearthed a fragment of music from who knows how many centuries B.C., and it was a boy's lament for a girl who didn't love him back. Then besides the songs there were the magazine stories and the novels and the movies, even the hair-spray ads and the panty-hose ads. It struck Maggie as disproportionate. Misleading, in fact.

A slim blade of black knelt at Durwood's elbow. It was Sugar Tilghman, blowing at a swatch of net to free it from her lipstick. "If

I'd known I was expected to provide the entertainment I never would have come," she said. "Oh, Ira. I didn't see you there."

"How you doing, Sugar," Ira said.

"Elizabeth."

"Pardon?"

"The Barley twins have the right idea," Sugar said. "They flat-out refuse to go along with this."

"Isn't that just like them," Maggie said. The Barley twins had always acted so snobbish, preferring each other to anybody else.

"And Nick Bourne wouldn't even come to the funeral."

"Nick Bourne?"

"Said it was too long a drive."

"*I* don't recall Nick at the wedding," Maggie said.

"Well, he was in the chorus, right?"

"Oh, yes, I guess he was."

"And the chorus sang 'True Love,' remember? But if the Barley twins won't join in and Nick Bourne's not coming, there wouldn't be but the four of us, so she's going to skip the chorus part."

"You know," Durwood said, "I never understood why 'True Love' went so high on the charts. That was a really boring tune, when you think about it."

"And then 'Born to Be with You,' " Sugar said. "Wasn't it funny about Serena? Sometimes she kind of overdid. She'd take some run-of-the-mill pop song like 'Born to Be with You' that all the rest of us liked okay, and she would make so much of it, it would start to look weird. It would start to look bizarre. Things always got so exaggerated, with Serena."

"Like her wedding reception," Durwood said.

"Oh, her wedding reception! Her receiving line with just that mother of hers and one fat twelve-year-old girl cousin and Max's parents."

"Max's parents looked miserable."

"They never did approve of her."

"They thought she was sort of cheap."

"They kept asking who her people were."

"Better not to have a receiving line at all," Durwood said. "Shoot, better just to elope. I don't know why she went to so much trouble."

"Well, anyhow," Sugar said, "I told Serena I'd sing today if she insisted, but she'd have to make it some other piece. Something more appropriate. I mean I know we're supposed to be humoring the bereaved, but there are limits. And Serena said, well, all right, so long as it came from the time when they were first dating. Nineteen fifty-five, fifty-six, she said; nothing later."

" 'The Great Pretender,' " Durwood said suddenly. "Now, there was a song. Remember, Ira? Remember 'The Great Pretender'?"

Ira put on a soulful look and crooned, "O-o-o-o-o-o-oh, yes . . ."

BREATHING LESSONS   *287*

"Why not sing that?" Durwood asked Sugar.

"Oh, be serious," Sugar said.

"Sing 'Davy Crockett,' " Ira suggested.

He and Durwood started competing: "Sing 'Yellow Rose of Texas.' "

"Sing 'Hound Dog.' "

"Sing 'Papa Loves Mambo.' "

"Will you be serious for a minute?" Sugar said. "I'm going to get up there and open my mouth and nothing's going to come out."

"Or how about 'Heartbreak Hotel'?" Ira asked.

"Ssh, everybody. They're starting," Maggie said. She had glimpsed the family approaching from the rear. Sugar rose hastily and returned to her seat, while Serena, who was bending over two women who could only be the Barley twins, settled next to them in a pew that was nowhere near the front and went on whispering. No doubt she still hoped to talk them into singing. Both twins wore their yellow hair in the short, curly, caplike style they'd favored in high school, Maggie saw, but the backs of their necks were scrawny as chicken necks and their fussy pink ruffles gave them a Minnie Pearl look.

An usher led the family up the aisle: Serena's daughter, Linda, fat and freckled, and Linda's bearded husband and two little boys in grownup suits, their expressions self-consciously solemn. Behind them came a fair-haired man, most likely the brother, and various other people, severely, somberly dressed. Several had Max's wide face, which gave Maggie a start. She seemed to have drifted away from the reason for this ceremony, and now all at once she remembered: Max Gill had actually gone and died. The striking thing about death, she thought, was its eventfulness. It made you see you were leading a real life. Real life at last! you could say. Was that why she read the obituaries each morning, hunting familiar names? Was that why she carried on those hushed, awed conversations with the other workers when one of the nursing home patients was carted away in a hearse?

The family settled in the frontmost pew. Linda glanced back at Serena, but Serena was too busy arguing with the Barley twins to notice. Then the piano fell silent, and a door near the altar opened and a lean, bald-headed minister appeared in a long black robe. He crossed behind the pulpit. He seated himself in a dark wooden armchair and arranged the skirt of his robe fastidiously over his trousers.

"That's not Reverend Connors, is it?" Ira whispered.

"Reverend Connors is *dead*," Maggie told him.

She was louder than she'd meant to be. The row of blond heads in front of her swiveled.

Now the piano trudged off on "True Love." Evidently Sissy was filling in for the chorus. Serena was giving the Barley twins a pointed, accusing glare, but they faced stubbornly forward and pretended not to notice.

Maggie remembered Grace Kelly and Bing Crosby singing "True Love" in a movie. They'd been perched on a yacht or a sailboat or something. Both of them were dead too, come to think of it.

If the minister found the music surprising, he gave no sign. He waited till the last note had faded and then he stood and said, "Turning now to the Holy Word . . ." His voice was high-pitched and stringy. Maggie wished he were Reverend Connors. Reverend Connors had shaken the rafters. And she didn't think he'd read any Holy Word at Serena's wedding, at least not that she could recollect.

This man read a psalm, something about a lovely dwelling place, which came as a relief to Maggie because in her experience, most of the Book of Psalms tended to go on in a sort of paranoid way about enemies and evil plots. She pictured Max reclining in a lovely dwelling place with Grace Kelly and Bing Crosby, his crew cut glinting against the sunlit sails. He would be telling them one of his jokes. He could tell jokes for hours, one after the other. Serena used to say, "All right already, Gill, enough." They'd often called each other by their last names—Max using Serena's maiden name even after they were married. "Watch it there, Palermo." Maggie could hear him now. It had made the two of them look more amiable than other married couples. They'd seemed like easygoing buddies, unaware of that dark, helpless, angry, confined feeling that Maggie's own marriage descended to from time to time.

In fact, if Serena believed that marriage was not a Doris Day movie, she had certainly never proved it in public, for her grownup life had looked from outside like the cheeriest of domestic comedies: Serena ironic and indulgent and Max the merry good-time guy. They had appeared to remain focused exclusively upon each other even after becoming parents; Linda had seemed more or less extraneous. Maggie envied that. So what if Max was a bit of a failure in the outside world? "If I just didn't feel I had to *carry* him; always be the one to carry the household," Serena had confided once. But then she had turned breezy and waved a hand, clanging her bangle bracelets. "Oh, well! But he's my sweetie, right?" she'd said, and Maggie had agreed. He was as sweet as they came.

(And she remembered, if Serena didn't, how she and Serena had spent the summer after fifth grade spying on the gracious Guilford home of the man who was Serena's father, and how they had cunningly shadowed his teenaged sons and his ladylike wife. "I could bring that woman's world crashing around her ears," Serena had said. "I could knock on her door and she would go, 'Why, hello, dear, whose little girl are you?' and I could tell her." But she had said this while hidden behind one of the two complacent stone lions that guarded the front walk, and she had made no move to show herself. And then she had whispered, "I will *never* be like her, I tell you." A stranger would think she meant the wife, but Maggie knew better: She meant her mother. "Mrs." Palermo—love's victim. A woman whose every trait—even the tilted, off-center way she carried her waterfall of black curls—hinted at permanent injuries.)

The minister seated himself, orchestrating his robe. Sissy Parton weighed in with a few ominous notes. She looked toward the congregation and Durwood said, "Me?" right out loud. The blond heads swiveled again. Durwood rose and headed up the aisle. Apparently you were expected to remember on your own when your song was due. Never mind that you had to cast your thoughts back twenty-nine years.

Durwood struck a pose beside the piano, resting one arm on the lid. He nodded at Sissy. Then he started off in a throbbing bass: "Hold me close. Hold me tight . . ."

A lot of parents had forbidden that song in their houses. All this wanting and needing really didn't sound very nice, they had said. So Maggie and her classmates had had to go to Serena's, or to Oriole Hi Fidelity, where you could still, in those days, pile into a listening booth and play records all afternoon without making a purchase.

And now she recalled why she hadn't liked Durwood; his operatic tremolo brought it all back. Once upon a time he'd been considered quite a catch, with his wavy dark hair and his deep-brown eyes and that habit he had of beseechingly crinkling his brow. He'd sung "Believe Me if All Those Endearing Young Charms" in the high school auditorium on every conceivable occasion, always the same song, the same theatrical gestures, the same fifties crooner style, where the voice breaks with feeling. Sometimes Durwood's voice broke so extremely that the first syllable of a line was silent, and even on the second syllable he kicked in a touch late, while the plump, bespectacled music teacher gazed up at him mistily from her piano. "Dreamboat," his entry in the yearbook had read. "Man I'd Most Like to Be Shipwrecked With," he'd been voted in the school paper. He'd asked Maggie for a date and Maggie had said no and her girlfriends had told her she was crazy. "You turned down Durwood? Durwood Clegg?"

"He's too soft," she'd said, and they had repeated the word and passed it among themselves for consideration. "Soft," they'd murmured tentatively.

He was too pliant, she meant; too supplicating. She failed to see the appeal. For if Serena had made her resolutions about who not to be, why, so had Maggie; and in order not to be her mother, she planned to avoid any man remotely like her father—the person she loved best in the world. No one mild and clumsy for Maggie, thank you; no one bumbling and well-meaning and sentimental, who would force her to play the heavy. You'd never find *her* sitting icily erect while her husband, flushed with merriment, sang nonsense songs at the dinner table.

So Maggie had refused Durwood Clegg and had watched with no regrets as he went on to date Lu Beth Parsons instead. She could see Lu Beth as clear as day this very minute, clearer than Peg, whom he'd ended up marrying. She could see Durwood's khaki trousers with the Ivy League buckle in back buckled up ("attached," that signified; "going steady") and his button-down shirt and natty brown loafers decorated with bobbing leather acorns. But of course this morning he was wearing a suit—baggy and unfashionable, inexpensive, husbandly. For a moment he shifted back and forth like those trick portraits that change expression according to where you're standing: the old lady-killer Durwood meaningfully lingering on *darling, you're all that I'm living for*, with his eyebrows quirked, but then the present-day, shabby Durwood searching for the next stanza on Maggie's shampoo coupon, which he held at arm's length, with his forehead wrinkled, as he tried to make out the words.

The blond children in front were tittering. They probably found this whole event hilarious. Maggie had an urge to slam the nearest one flat over the head with a hymnbook.

When Durwood finished singing, someone mistakenly clapped—just two sharp explosions—and Durwood nodded in a grimly relieved way and returned to his seat. He settled next to Maggie with a sigh. His face was filmed with sweat and he fanned himself with the coupon. Would it seem mercenary if she asked for it back? Twenty-five cents off, at double-coupon rates . . .

Jo Ann Dermott stepped up to the pulpit with a small book covered in tooled leather. She had been a gawky girl, but middle age had filled out her corners or something. Now she was willowy and attractive in a fluid, pastel dress and subtle makeup. "At Max's and Serena's wedding," she announced, "I read Kahlil Gibran on marriage. Today, at this sadder occasion, I'll read what he says about death."

At the wedding, she had pronounced Gibran with a hard G. Today the G was soft. Maggie had no idea which was correct.

Jo Ann started reading in a level, teacher-like voice, and immediately Maggie was overcome by nervousness. It took her a moment to realize why: She and Ira were next on the program. Just the cadence of *The Prophet* had reminded her.

At the wedding they'd sat on folding chairs behind the altar, and Jo Ann had sat in front of the altar with Reverend Connors. When Jo Ann began reading, Maggie had felt that breathless flutter high in her chest that foretold stage fright. She had taken a deep, trembly breath, and then Ira had unobtrusively set a hand at the small of her back. That had steadied her. When it was time for them to sing, they had begun at the same split second, on exactly the same note, as if they were meant for each other. Or so Maggie had viewed it at the time.

Jo Ann closed her book and returned to her pew. Sissy flipped pages of sheet music, the puffed flesh swinging from her valentine elbows. She flounced a bit on the bench, and then she played the opening bars of "Love Is a Many Splendored Thing."

Maybe if Maggie and Ira stayed seated, Sissy would just go on playing. She would cover for them as she had covered for the chorus.

But the piano notes died away and Sissy glanced back toward the congregation. Her hands remained on the keys. Serena turned too and, knowing exactly where to find Maggie, gave her a fond, expectant look in which there was not the slightest suspicion that Maggie would let her down.

Maggie stood up. Ira just sat there. He might be anyone—a total stranger, someone who merely happened to have chosen the same pew.

So Maggie, who had never sung a solo in her life, clutched the seat ahead of her and called out, " 'Love!' "

A bit squeakily.

The piano sailed into it. The blond children pivoted and stared up into her face.

" '. . . is a many splendored thing,' " she quavered.

She felt like an orphaned, abandoned child, with her back held very straight and her round-toed pumps set resolutely together.

Then there was a stirring at her side, not her right side, where Ira sat, but her left, where Durwood sat. Durwood hastily unfolded himself as if all at once reminded of something. " 'It's the April rose,' " he sang, " 'that only grows . . .' " This near, his voice had a resonant sound. She thought of sheets of vibrating metal.

" 'Love is Nature's way of giving . . .' " they sang together.

They knew all the words straight through, which Maggie found surprising, because earlier she had forgotten what it was that makes a man a king. " 'It's the golden crown,' " she sang confidently. You had to sort of *step forth*, she decided, and trust that the words would follow. Durwood carried the melody and Maggie went along with it, less quavery now although she could have used a little more volume. It was true that her voice had once been compared to a bell. She had sung in the choir for years, at least till the children came along and things got complicated; and she had taken real joy in rounding out a note just right, like a pearl or a piece of fruit that hung in the air a moment before it fell away. Though age had certainly not helped. Did anyone else hear the thread of a crack running through her high notes? Hard to tell; the congregation faced decorously forward, except for those confounded little blonds.

She thought time had gone into one of its long, slow, taffy-like stretches. She was acutely conscious of each detail of her surroundings. She felt the fabric of Durwood's sleeve just brushing her arm, and she heard Ira absentmindedly twanging a rubber band. She saw how accepting and uninterested her audience was, taking it for granted that this song would of course be sung and then some other song after that. " 'Then your fingers touched my silent heart,' " she sang, and she remembered how she and Serena had giggled over that line when they sang it themselves—oh, long before that fateful Harvest Home Ball—because where else was your heart but in your chest? Weren't they saying the lover had touched their *chests*? Serena was facing the pulpit but her head had a listening stillness to it. Her tail of hair was gathered into one of those elastic arrangements secured by two red plastic marbles, the kind of thing very young girls wore. Like a very young girl, she had summoned all her high-school friends around her—no one from a later time, no one from the dozen small towns Max had lugged her to during their marriage, for they hadn't stayed in any of those places long enough. Maggie decided that that was the saddest thing about this whole event.

The song came to an end. Maggie and Durwood sat down.

Sissy Parton moved directly into "Friendly Persuasion," but the Barley twins, who used to harmonize as closely as the Lennon Sisters, stayed seated. Serena seemed resigned by now; she didn't even give them a look. Sissy played just one stanza, and then the minister rose and said, "We are gathered here today to mourn a grievous loss."

Maggie felt she had turned to liquid. She was so exhausted that her knees were shaking.

The minister had a lot to say about Max's work for the Furnace Fund. He didn't seem to know him personally, however. Or maybe that was all Max had amounted to, in the end: a walking business suit, a firm handshake. Maggie switched her attention to Ira. She wondered how he could sit there, so impervious. He'd have let her slog through that entire song alone; she knew that. She could have stumbled and stuttered and broken down; he would have watched as coolly as if she had nothing to do with him. Why not? he would say. What obligated him to sing some corny fifties song at a semi-stranger's funeral? As usual, he'd be right. As usual, he'd be forcing Maggie to do the giving in.

She made up her mind that when the funeral was over, she would stride off in her own direction. She would certainly not drive back with him to Baltimore. Maybe she'd hitch a ride with Durwood. Gratitude rushed over her at the thought of Durwood's kindness. Not many people would have done what he had done. He was a gentle, sympathetic, softhearted man, as she should have realized from the start.

Why, if she had accepted that date with Durwood she'd be a whole different person now. It was all a matter of comparison. Compared to Ira she looked silly and emotional; anybody would have. Compared to Ira she talked too much and laughed too much and cried too much. Even ate too much! Drank too much! Behaved so sloppily and mawkishly!

She'd been so intent on not turning into her mother, she had gone and turned into her father.

The minister sat down with an audible groan. There was a rustle of linen a few pews back and then here came Sugar Tilghman, bearing her black straw hat as smoothly as a loaded tray. She tip-tapped up front to Sissy and bent over her, conferring. They murmured together. Then Sugar straightened and took a stance beside the piano with her hands held just the way their choir leader used to insist—loosely clasped at waist level, no higher—and Sissy played a bar of music that Maggie couldn't immediately name. An usher approached Serena and she rose and accepted his arm and let him escort her down the aisle, eyes lowered.

Sugar sang, " 'When I was just a little girl . . .' "

Another usher crooked his arm toward Serena's daughter, and one by one the family members filed out. Up front, Sugar gathered heart and swung gustily into the chorus:

> Que sera sera,
> Whatever will be will be.
> The future's not ours to see,
> Que sera sera.

3

When they stepped out of the church it was like stepping out of a daytime movie—that sudden shock of sunshine and birdsong and ordinary life that had been going on without them. Serena was hugging Linda. Linda's husband stood awkwardly by with the children, looking like a visitor who hoped to be invited in. And all around the churchyard, members of the class of '56 were recognizing each other. "Is that you?" they asked. And, "How long has it been?" And, "Can you believe this?" The Barley twins told Maggie she hadn't changed a bit. Jo Ann Dermott announced that everyone had changed, but only for the better. Wasn't it odd, she said, how much younger they were than their parents had been at the very same age. Then Sugar Tilghman appeared in the doorway and asked the crowd at large what other song she possibly could have sung. "I mean I know it wasn't perfect," she said, "but look what I had to choose from! Was it just too absolutely inappropriate?"

They all swore it wasn't.

Maggie said, "Durwood, I owe you the world for coming to my rescue."

"My pleasure," he told her. "Here's your coupon, by the way. None the worse for wear."

This wasn't quite true; it was limp around the edges and slightly damp. Maggie dropped it into her purse.

Ira stood near the parking lot with Nat Abrams. He and Nat had been a couple of classes ahead of the others; they were the outsiders. Not that Ira seemed to mind. He looked perfectly at ease, in fact. He was discussing auto routes. Maggie overheard snatches of "Triple A" and "Highway Ten." You would think the man was obsessed.

"Funny little place, isn't it?" Durwood said, gazing around him.

"Funny?"

"You couldn't even call it a town."

"Well, it is kind of small," Maggie said.

"I wonder if Serena will be staying on here."

They both looked over at Serena, who seemed to be trying to put her daughter back together. Linda's face was streaming with tears, and Serena had set her at a distance and was patting down various parts of her clothes. "Doesn't she still have relatives in Baltimore?" Durwood asked.

"None that claim her," Maggie said.

"I thought she had that mother."

"Her mother died a few years ago."

"Aw, really?" Durwood said.

"She got one of those diseases, some muscular something."

"Us boys were all just, like, fixated on her, once upon a time," Durwood said.

This startled Maggie, but before she could comment she saw Serena heading toward them. She had her shawl clasped tightly around her. "I want to thank you both for singing," she said. "It meant a lot to me."

"That Ira is just so stubborn I could spit," Maggie said, and Durwood said, "Beautiful service, Serena."

"Oh, be honest, you thought it was crazy," Serena said. "But you were nice to humor me. Everyone's been so nice!" Her lips took on a blurred look. She drew a knot of Kleenex from her V neckline and pressed it first to one eye and then to the other. "Sorry," she said. "I keep changing moods. I feel like, I don't know, a TV screen in a windstorm. I'm so changeable."

"Most natural thing in the world," Durwood assured her.

Serena blew her nose and then tucked the Kleenex away again. "Anyhow," she said. "A neighbor's setting out some refreshments back at the house. Can you all come? I need to have people around me right now."

"Well, certainly," Maggie told her, and Durwood said, "Wouldn't miss it, Serena," both at the same time. "Just let me get my car," Durwood said.

"Oh, never mind that; we're all walking. It's just over there through the trees, and anyway there's not a lot of parking space."

She took Maggie's elbow, leaning slightly. "It did go well, didn't it?" she said. She steered her toward the road, while Durwood dropped behind with Sugar Tilghman. "I'm so glad I had the idea. Reverend Orbison threw a fit, but I said, 'Isn't this for me? Isn't a memorial service meant to comfort the living?' So he said yes, he guessed it was. And that's not the end of it, either! Wait till you see the surprise I've got up at the house."

"Surprise? What kind?" Maggie asked.

"I'm not telling," Serena said.

Maggie started chewing her lower lip.

They turned onto a smaller street, keeping to the shoulder because there wasn't a sidewalk. The houses here had a distinctly Pennsylvanian air, Maggie thought. They were mostly tall stone rectangles, flat-faced, set close to the road, with a meager supply of narrow windows. She imagined spare wooden furniture inside, no cushions or frills or modern conveniences, which of course was silly because a television antenna was strapped to every chimney.

The other guests were following in a leisurely parade—the women tiptoeing through the gravel in their high heels, the men strolling with their hands in their pockets. Ira brought up the rear between Nat and Jo Ann. He gave no sign of minding this change in plans; or if he had at some earlier point, Maggie had luckily missed it.

"Durwood was wondering if you'd be staying on here," she told Serena. "Any chance you might move back to Baltimore?"

"Oh," Serena said, "Baltimore seems so far away by now. Who would I know anymore?"

"Me and Ira, for one thing," Maggie said. "Durwood Clegg. The Barley twins."

The Barley twins were walking just behind them, clinging to each other's arms. Both wore clip-on sunglasses over their regular glasses.

"Linda has been after me to move to New Jersey," Serena said. "Get an apartment close to her and Jeff."

"That would be nice."

"Well, I'm not so sure," Serena said. "Seems anytime we spend a few days together I begin to realize we haven't got a thing in common."

"But if you lived close by you wouldn't be spending days together," Maggie said. "You'd be dropping in and out. You'd be leaving when the conversation ran down. And besides, you'd see more of your grandchildren."

"Oh, well, grandchildren. I've never felt they had all that much to do with me."

"You wouldn't say that if someone kept them away from you," Maggie told her.

"How's *your* grandchild, Maggie?"

"I have no idea," Maggie said. "Nobody tells me a thing. And Fiona's getting married again; I found that out purely by accident."

"Is that so! Well, it'll be good for Larue to have a man around."

"Leroy," Maggie said. "But see, Fiona's true love is still Jesse. She's said as much, in so many words. There's just something gone wrong between them temporarily. It would be a terrible mistake for her to marry someone else! And then poor little Leroy . . . oh, I hate to think of all that child has been through. Living in that run-down house, secondhand smoking—"

"Smoking! A six-year-old?"

"Seven-year-old. But it's her grandmother who smokes."

"Well, then," Serena said.

"But it's Leroy's lungs getting coated with tar."

"Oh, Maggie, let her go," Serena said. "Let it all go! That's what I say. I was watching Linda's boys this morning, climbing our back fence, and first I thought, Oh-oh, better call them in; they're bound to rip those sissy little suits, and then I thought, Nah, forget it. It's not *my* affair, I thought. Let them go."

"But I don't want to let go," Maggie said. "What kind of talk is that?"

"You don't have any choice," Serena told her. She stepped over a branch that lay across their path. "That's what it comes down to in the end, willy-nilly: just pruning and disposing. Why, you've been doing that all along, right? You start shucking off your children from the day you give birth; that's the whole point. A big, big moment is when you can look at them and say, 'Now if I died they could get along without me. I'm free to die,' you say. 'What a relief!' Discard, discard! Throw out the toys in the basement. Move to a smaller house. Menopause delighted me."

"Menopause!" Maggie said. "You've been through menopause?"

"Gladly," Serena told her.

"Oh, Serena!" Maggie said, and she stopped short, nearly causing the Barley twins to bump into her.

"Well, goodness," Serena said, "why should that bother you?"

"But I remember when we first got our periods," Maggie said. "Remember how we all waited? Remember," she said, turning to the Barley twins, "how that was once the only thing we talked about? Who had started and who had not? What it must feel like? How on earth we'd keep it secret from our husbands when we married?"

The Barley twins nodded, smiling. Their eyes were invisible behind their dark glasses.

"And now she's gone and stopped," Maggie told them.

"*We* haven't stopped," Jeannie Barley caroled.

"She's gone through change of life!" Maggie cried.

"Wonderful; announce it to the world," Serena said. She linked arms with Maggie and they resumed walking. "Believe me, I barely gave it a thought. 'Well, good,' I told myself. 'Just one more thing to let go of.'"

Maggie said, "I don't feel I'm letting go; I feel they're taking things away from me. My son's grown up and my daughter's leaving for college and they're talking at the nursing home about laying off some of the workers. It's something to do with the new state regulations— they're going to hire on more professionals and lay off people like me."

"So? That job was always beneath you anyway," Serena said. "You were a straight-A student, remember? Or near about."

"It is not beneath me, Serena; I love it. You sound just like my mother. I love that job!"

"Then go back to school and get to be a professional yourself," Serena said.

Maggie gave up on her. She was too tired, all at once, to argue.

They turned in through a little gate, onto a flagstone path. Serena's house was newer than the others—raw brick, one story, modern and compact. Someone stood at the front window, drawing back a curtain to gaze out, but when the guests approached she dropped the curtain and vanished. She reappeared at the door, a buttressed and corseted woman in a stiff navy dress. "Oh, you poor thing!" she cried to Serena. "You come right on in. Everybody, come in! There's lots to eat and drink. Anyone want to freshen up?"

Maggie did. She followed the woman's directions and passed through the living room, which was filled with heavy furniture in a wagon-wheel motif, and down a short hall to the bedroom. The decor seemed purely Max's doing: a bedspread patterned with multicolored license plates, a beer stein collection lining the bookshelf. On the bureau, a photo of Linda in cap and gown stood next to a bronze cowboy boot stuffed with pencils and gnawed plastic swizzle sticks. But someone had hung guest towels in the bathroom and set out a bowl of rosette-shaped soaps. Maggie washed up, using the bar of Ivory she found in a cabinet beneath the sink. She dried her hands on a grayish bath towel draped behind the shower curtain, and then she peered into the mirror. The walk had not done anything for her appearance. She tried to flatten her bangs down. She stood sideways to the mirror and sucked in her stomach. Meanwhile the Barley twins were discussing Linda's photograph: "Isn't it a pity she got Max's looks and not Serena's." Nat

Abrams said, "Would this be the line for the john?" and Maggie called, "Just coming out."

She emerged to find Ira waiting with Nat; now their topic was gas mileage. She returned to the living room. The guests were gathered in the dining alcove, where platters of food covered a table—sandwiches and cakes and drinks. Sissy Parton's husband was serving as bartender. Maggie recognized him by his violent pink hair, the color of freshly cut cedarwood. It hadn't dimmed in the slightest. She went over to him and said, "Hello, Michael."

"Maggie Daley! Nice singing," he said. "But what became of Ira?"

"Oh, well . . ." she said vaguely. "Could I have a gin and tonic, please?"

He made her one, pouring the gin with a flourish. "I hate these affairs," he told her. "This is my second funeral this week."

"Who else died?" Maggie asked.

"Oh, an old poker buddy. And last month my Aunt Linette, and the month before that . . . I tell you, first I went to all my kids' school plays, and no sooner was I done with those than we start on this."

A stranger came up and asked him for a Scotch. Maggie started circulating through the living room. She didn't hear much talk of Max. People were discussing the World Series, the prevalence of crime, the proper death for tulip bulbs. Two women Maggie had never seen before were assembling a composite portrait of some couple they both knew. "*He* was a bit of a drinker," one said.

"Yes, but he adored her."

"Oh, he'd never have managed without her."

"Were you at that Easter brunch they gave?"

"Was I there! The one with the chocolate centerpiece?"

"It was a present from him to her, she said. He'd surprised her with it that morning."

"A hollow chocolate rabbit. He'd filled it with rum."

"*She* didn't know he'd filled it with rum."

"He said he'd wanted it to be like those Swiss candies they fill with liqueurs."

"Rum seeped out the bottom."

"Little melty holes in the chocolate."

"Worst mess you ever saw, all across the tablecloth."

"Lucky it was only one of those Hallmark paper tablecloths for holidays."

Back in the dining alcove, the Barley twins were talking with Michael. They had flipped up their clip-on shades, which stuck out above their glasses like the perky antennas of some sharp-faced, cute little creatures from outer space, and they were nodding earnestly, in unison. Jo Ann and Sugar were discussing mixed marriages—the consuming interest of Jo Ann's life for years before her wedding to Nat and evidently afterward as well. "But tell me the truth," Sugar was saying. "Doesn't it sometimes seem to you like *every* marriage is mixed?" And Serena's two little grandsons were surreptitiously bombarding each other with bits of cake. It looked good: angel food. Maggie thought about trying a slice but then she remembered her diet. She had a virtuous, empty feeling in the center of her rib cage. She traveled around the table surveying what was offered, resisting even the bowl of Fritos. "The dump salad is mine," Serena's neighbor said at her elbow.

"Dump salad?"

"You take a packet of orange Jell-O powder, a can of crushed pineapple, a carton of Cool Whip . . ."

Some woman in a bouffant hairdo said hello and the neighbor turned to greet her, leaving Maggie with the gritty feeling of Jell-O powder on her teeth.

Serena was over by the buffet, beneath an oil painting of a dead bird with a basket of olive-drab fruit. Linda and her husband stood next to her. "When all these people leave, Mom," Linda was saying, "we're taking you out to dinner, anyplace your heart desires." She spoke a little above normal volume, as if Serena were hard of hearing. "We're going to buy you a real meal," she said.

"Oh, well, there's so much food right here in the house," Serena said. "And I'm honestly not all that hungry anyhow."

Her son-in-law said, "Now, Mother Gill, just tell us your favorite restaurant." Jeff, that was it. Maggie couldn't think of his last name.

Serena said, "Um . . ." She glanced around, as if hoping for a suggestion. Her eyes brushed Maggie and traveled on. Finally she said, "Oh, well, maybe the Golden Chopsticks. That's a good place."

"What kind is it, Chinese?"

"Well, yes, but they also have—"

"Oh, I just don't care for Chinese food," Linda said. "Not Chinese or Japanese, either one, I'm sorry to say."

"Or any other Oriental," Jeff pointed out. "You don't like Thai food either."

"No, that's true. Or Filipino or Burmese."

Serena said, "But—"

"And you can't eat Indian; don't forget Indian," Jeff said.

"No; Indian has those spices."

"Spices affect her digestion," Jeff told Serena.

"I guess I'm just sensitive or something," Linda said.

"Same goes for Mexican."

"But we don't have any Mexican," Serena said. "We don't have any of those places."

Linda said, "What I'd like to know is how the Mexicans themselves can stand all those spicy seasonings."

"They can't," Jeff told her. "They come down with this awful condition that coats the insides of their mouths like plates of armor."

Serena blinked. "Well," she said, "what kind of restaurant did you two have in mind?"

"We thought maybe that steak house off of Route One," Jeff told her.

"MacMann's? Oh."

"That is, if it's all right with you."

"Well, MacMann's is kind of . . . noisy, isn't it?" Serena asked.

"I never thought it was noisy," Linda said.

"I mean it's always so noisy and crowded."

"Just take it or leave it, Mom," Linda told her, raising her chin. "We were only trying to be nice, for God's sake."

Maggie, standing just outside their little circle, waited for Serena to toss her one of her wry, eye-rolling expressions. But Serena didn't even glance at her. She seemed shrunken, somehow; she had lost her dash. She lifted her drink to her lips and sipped reflectively.

Then Max's brother called, "Serena? You ready for this?"

He was gesturing toward a mildewed black leatherette case that stood on the coffee table. It looked familiar; Maggie couldn't think why. Serena brightened. She turned to Maggie and said, "That there is my surprise."

"What is it?" Maggie asked.

"We're going to show a movie of my wedding."

Of course: a film projector. Maggie hadn't seen one of those in years. She watched as Max's brother unsnapped the silver clasps. Meanwhile Serena moved away to lower the window shades. "We'll use this biggest shade for the screen," she called. "Oh, I hope the film hasn't just disintegrated or bleached out or whatever it is that old film does."

"You mean your and *Max's* wedding?" Maggie asked, following her.

"His uncle Oswald took it."

"I don't remember a camera at the wedding."

"I was thinking back over the songs last night and I all at once remembered. 'If it's still in one piece,' I said to myself, 'wouldn't it be fun to watch?' "

Fun? Maggie wasn't so sure. But she wouldn't have missed it, all the same; so she found herself a seat on the rug. She set down her glass and curled her legs to one side. A very old lady was sitting in a chair next to her, but at this level all Maggie saw were her thick beige cotton ankles melting over the tops of her shoes.

Now the guests had got wind of what was about to take place. Serena's classmates were settling around the projector, while the others started flowing distractedly in different directions, like something under a microscope. A few edged toward the door, mentioning baby-sitters and appointments elsewhere, promising Serena they would keep in touch. Several returned to the bar, and since Michael had deserted, they began mixing their own drinks. Michael was in the living room now, and so was Nat. Ira wasn't anywhere that Maggie could see. Nat was asking Sugar, "Am I in this, do you think?"

"You are if you sang at the wedding."

"Well, I didn't," he said glumly.

With just a little stretch of the imagination, Maggie thought, this could be Mr. Alden's civics class. (You had to overlook the old lady, who had remained contentedly seated with her tinkling cup of tea.) She glanced around and saw a semicircle of graying men and women, and there was something so worn down about them, so benign and unassuming, that she felt at that moment they were as close to her as family. She wondered how she could have failed to realize that they would have been aging along with her all these years, going through more or less the same stages—rearing their children and saying goodbye to them, marveling at the wrinkles they discovered in the mirror, watching their parents turn fragile and uncertain. Somehow, she had pictured them still fretting over Prom Night.

Even the sound of the projector came straight from Mr. Alden's class—the clickety-click as the reels started spinning and a square of flawed, crackled light was cast upon the window shade. What would Mr. Alden say if he could see them all together again? He was probably dead by now. And anyway, this movie wasn't showing how democracy worked or how laws were born, but—

Why, Sissy! Sissy Parton! Young and slender and prim, wearing a tight chignon encircled with artificial daisies like a French maid's frill. She was playing the piano, her wrists so gracefully arched that you could believe it was only the delicacy of her touch that caused the film to remain soundless. Above the white choir robe, the Peter Pan collar of her blouse was just visible, a pale salmon pink (in real life a deep rose, Maggie recalled). She lifted her head and looked purposefully toward a certain point, and the camera followed her gaze and the screen was suddenly filled with a double row of ridiculously clean-cut young people in pleated robes. They sang silently, their mouths perfect ovals. They resembled the carolers on a Christmas card. It was Serena who identified the tune. " 'True love,' " she sang, " 'true—' " And then she broke off to say, "Oh! Would you look? Mary Jean Bennett! I never even thought to invite her. I forgot all about her. Does anybody know where Mary Jean lives now?"

No one answered, although several, in low, dreamy murmurs, carried on with " '. . . for you and I have a guardian angel . . .' "

"There's Nick Bourne, the rat," Serena said. "He claimed it was too far to come to the funeral."

She was sitting on the arm of a chair, craning her neck toward the movie. In profile she looked commanding, almost glorious, Maggie thought, with that silver line of light from the screen running down her large, straight nose and the curve of her lips.

Maggie herself stood in the front row of the chorus, next to Sugar Tilghman. Her hair was in tiny squiggles all over her head; it made her face look too big. Oh, this was humiliating. But no doubt the others felt the same way. She distinctly heard Sugar groan. And when the camera switched to Durwood, with his wet, black, towering pompadour like the crest on the top of a Dairy Queen cone, he gave a sharp bark of laughter. This younger Durwood strode over to the piano with his robe flapping behind him. He assumed his position and paused importantly. Then he embarked on a silent "I Want You, I Need You, I Love You" with his eyes closed more often than open, his left arm gesturing so passionately that once he swatted a lily in a papier-mâché vase. Maggie wanted to laugh but she held it in. So did everyone else, although the old lady said, "Well! My goodness," and rattled her teacup. A couple of people were humming along with this song too, which Maggie thought was charitable of them.

Next the camera swung dizzyingly to Jo Ann Dermott at the front of the church. She gripped the edges of the pulpit and read from a book that the audience couldn't see. Since she wasn't in the chorus, her dress was completely exposed—stiff, square-shouldered, full-skirted, more matronly than anything she would ever wear again. Her lowered eyes looked naked. No one could hum along with *The Prophet*, so the reading just went on and on in total silence. Out in the dining alcove the other guests talked and laughed and clinked ice cubes. "Good Lord, fast-forward it, someone," Jo Ann said, but evidently Max's brother didn't know how (if you *could* fast-forward these old films), and so they had to sit through it.

Then the camera swooped again and there was Sissy playing the piano, with one damp curl plastered to her forehead. Maggie and Ira, side by side, stood watching Sissy gravely. (Ira was a boy, a mere child.) They drew a breath. They started singing. Maggie was slightly bunchy in her robe—she'd been fighting her extra ten pounds even then—and Ira had a plucked, fledgling look. Had he really worn his hair that short? In those days, he'd seemed totally unreadable. His unreadability was his greatest attraction. He'd reminded her of those math geniuses who don't need to write out the process but simply arrive at the answer.

He was twenty-one when that movie was filmed. Maggie was nineteen. Where they'd met, she had no idea, because at the time it hadn't mattered. They had probably passed each other in the halls in high school, maybe even elementary school. He might have visited her house, hanging out with her brothers. (He and her brother Josh were nearly the same age.) Certainly he'd sung with her at church; she knew that much. His family were members there, and Mr. Nichols, always short on male voices, had somehow talked Ira into joining the choir. But he hadn't lasted long. About the time he graduated from high school, he quit. Or maybe it was the year after. Maggie hadn't noticed exactly when it was he'd stopped appearing.

Her boyfriend in high school had been a classmate named Boris Drumm. He was short and dark, with rough skin and a frizz of cropped black hair—manly even at that age, everything she'd been looking for. It was Boris who taught Maggie to drive, and one of his exercises involved her speeding alone across the Sears, Roebuck parking lot till he loomed suddenly in front of the car to test her braking skills. Her clearest picture of him, to this day, was the determined stance he had taken in her path: arms straight out, feet wide apart, jaw set. Rock-hard, he'd seemed. Indestructible. She had had the feeling she could run him over, even, and he'd have bobbed up again untouched, like one of those plastic toy men weighted with lead at the base.

He planned on attending a college in the Midwest after graduation, but it was understood that as soon as he got his degree he and Maggie would marry. Meanwhile Maggie would live at home and go to Goucher. She wasn't much looking forward to it; it was her mother's idea. Her mother, who had taught English before she married, filled out all the application forms and even wrote Maggie's essay for her. It was very important to her that her children should rise in the world. (Maggie's father installed garage doors and had not had any college at all.) So Maggie resigned herself to four years at Goucher. In the meantime, to help with tuition, she took a summer job washing windows.

This was at the Silver Threads Nursing Home, which hadn't yet officially opened. It was a brand-new, modern building off Erdman Avenue, with three long wings and one hundred and eighty-two windows. Each of the larger windows had twelve panes of glass; the smaller windows had six. And in the left-hand corner of each pane was a white paper snowflake reading KRYSTAL KLEER MFG. CO. These snowflakes clung to the glass with a force that Maggie had never seen before or since. Whatever substance held them on, she thought later, should have been adopted by NASA. If you peeled off the top layer of paper a lower, fuzzy layer remained, and if you soaked that in hot water and then scraped it with a razor blade there were still gray shreds of rubbery glue, and after those were gone the whole pane, of course, was a mess, fingerprinted and streaky, so it had to be sprayed with Windex and buffed with a chamois skin. For one whole summer, from nine in the morning till four in the afternoon, Maggie scraped and soaked and scraped again. The tips of her fingers were continually sore. She felt her nails had been driven back into their roots. She didn't have anyone to talk to while she worked, because she was the only window washer they'd hired. Her sole company was the radio, playing "Moonglow" and "I Almost Lost My Mind."

In August the home started admitting a few patients, although not all the work was finished yet. Of course they were settled in those rooms where the windows were fully scraped, but Maggie got in the habit of taking a break from time to time and going visiting. She would stop at one bed or another to see how people were doing. "Could you move my water pitcher a little closer, doll?" a woman would ask, or, "Would you mind pulling that curtain?" While performing these tasks, Maggie felt valuable and competent. She began attracting a following of those patients who were mobile. Someone in a wheelchair would discover which room she was working in and suddenly there'd be three or four patients sitting around her talking. Their style of conversation was to ignore her presence and argue heatedly among themselves. (Was it the blizzard of '88 or the blizzard of '89? And which number counted more in the blood pressure reading?) But they conveyed an acute awareness of their audience; she knew it was all for her benefit. She would laugh at appropriate moments or make sounds of sympathy, and the old people would take on gratified expressions.

No one in her family understood when she announced that she wanted to forget about college and become an aide in the nursing home instead. Why, an aide was no better than a servant, her mother pointed out; no better than a chambermaid. And here Maggie had such a fine mind and had graduated at the top of her class. Did she want to be just ordinary? Her brothers, who had made the same kind of choice themselves (three were involved in some phase of the construction business, while the fourth welded locomotives at the Mount Clare railyards), claimed they had been looking to her to go further. Even her father wondered half audibly whether she knew what she was doing. But Maggie remained firm. What did she want with college? What did she want with those pointless, high-flown bits of information like the ones she'd learned in high school—*Ontogeny recapitulates phylogeny* and *Synecdoche is the use of the part to symbolize the whole*? She enrolled in a Red Cross training program, which in those days was all that was needed, and took a job at Silver Threads.

So there she was, eighteen and a half years old, working among old people and living with two elderly parents and her one unmarried brother, who was elderly himself, in a way. Boris Drumm had to earn his own school expenses, so he came back to Baltimore only at Christmas and spent the other holidays selling menswear in a shop near his campus. He wrote lengthy letters describing how his studies were altering his perceptions of the universe. The world was so full of injustice! he wrote. He had never realized. Writing back was hard because Maggie had very little to report. She didn't run into many of their friends anymore. Some had gone away to college, and when they returned they had changed. Some had married, which caused an even bigger change. Pretty soon the only people she saw regularly were Sugar and the Barley twins—just because they still sang in the choir—and, of course, Serena, her best friend. But Boris had never thought much of Serena, so Maggie seldom mentioned her in her letters.

Serena worked in a lingerie shop, clerking. She brought home translucent, lacy underwear in colors that made no sense. (Wouldn't a bright-red bra advertise itself through almost any piece of clothing you owned?) Modeling a black nightgown with a see-through bodice, she announced that she and Max were marrying in June, after he had finished his freshman year at UNC. UNC was a deal he had made with his parents. He had promised to try one year of college and then if he really, truly hated it they would let him drop out. What they were hoping, of course, was that he would meet a nice Southern girl and get over his infatuation with Serena. Not that they would admit it.

Max said that after they were married she could quit her job at the lingerie shop and never work again, Serena said; and also, she said (languorously lowering a black lace strap and admiring her own creamy shoulder), he was pleading with her to accompany him to the Blue Hen Motel the next time he came home. They wouldn't *do* anything, he said; just be together. Maggie was impressed and envious. It sounded very romantic to her. "You're going, aren't you?" she asked, but Serena said, "What do you think: I'm insane? I'd have to be out of my mind."

"But, Serena—" Maggie began. She was about to say that this was nothing like Anita's situation, nothing whatsoever, but Serena's fierce expression stopped her.

"*I'm* no sucker," Serena said.

Maggie wondered what she herself would do if Boris ever invited her to the Blue Hen Motel. She didn't think that would occur to him, though. Maybe it was just because she was forced to rely on his long, stuffy letters for any sense of him these days, but lately Boris had begun to seem less . . . crisp, you might say; less hard-edged. In his letters now he was talking about entering law school after college and then going into politics. Only in politics, he said, did you have the power to right the world's wrongs. But it was funny: Maggie had never seen politicians as powerful. She saw them as beggars. They were always begging for votes, altering themselves to satisfy their public, behaving spinelessly and falsely in a pathetic bid for popularity. She hated to think that Boris was that way.

She wondered if Serena ever had second thoughts about Max. No, probably not. Serena and Max seemed perfectly suited. Serena was so lucky.

Maggie's nineteenth birthday—Valentine's Day, 1957—fell on a Thursday, which was choir practice night. Serena brought a cake and after practice she passed out slices, along with paper cups of ginger ale, and everyone sang "Happy Birthday." Old Mrs. Britt, who really should have retired from singing years before but no one had the heart to suggest it, looked around her and sighed. "Isn't it sad," she said, "how the young folks are drifting away. Why, Sissy hardly comes at all since she married, and Louisa's moving to Montgomery County, and now I hear the Moran boy's gone and got himself killed."

"Killed?" Serena said. "How did that happen?"

"Oh, one of those freak training accidents," Mrs. Britt said. "I don't know the details."

Sugar, whose fiancé was at Camp Lejeune, said, "Lord, Lord, all I want is for Robert to come back safe and in one piece"—as if he were off waging hand-to-hand combat someplace, which of course he wasn't. (It happened to be one of those rare half-minutes in history when the country was not engaged in any serious hostilities.) Then Serena offered seconds on the birthday cake, but everyone had to go home.

That night in bed Maggie started thinking about the Moran boy, for some reason. Although she hadn't known him well, she found she had a clear mental picture of him: a sloucher, tall and high-cheekboned, with straight, oily black hair. She should have guessed he was doomed to die young. He'd been the only boy in the choir who didn't horse around while Mr. Nichols was talking to them. He had had an air of self-possession. She remembered too that he drove a car that ran on pure know-how, on junkyard parts and friction tape. Now that she thought of it, she believed she could envision his hands on the steering wheel. They were tanned and leathery, unusually wide across the base of the thumb, and the creases of his knuckles were deeply ingrained with mechanic's grease. She saw him in an army uniform with knife-sharp creases down the front of the trousers—a man who drove headlong to his death without even changing expression.

It was her first inkling that her generation was part of the stream of time. Just like the others ahead of them, they would grow up and grow old and die. Already there was a younger generation prodding them from behind.

Boris wrote and said he would try his very best to come home for spring vacation. Maggie wished he wouldn't sound so effortful. He had none of Ira Moran's calm assurance.

Serena got an engagement ring with a diamond shaped like a heart. It was dazzling. She began to plan and replan a great involved wedding production scheduled for the eighth of June, a date toward which she moved majestically, like a ship, with all her girlfriends fluttering in her wake. Maggie's mother said it was absurd to make such a fuss about a wedding. She said that people who lived for their weddings experienced a big letdown afterward, and then she said, changing her tone,

"That poor, sad child, going to such lengths; I have to say I pity her."
Maggie was shocked. (Pity! It seemed to her that Serena was already
beginning her life, while she, Maggie, waited on a side rail.) Meanwhile
Serena chose an ivory lace wedding dress but then changed her mind
and decided white satin would be better, and she selected first an
assortment of sacred music and then an assortment of secular music,
and she notified all her friends that her kitchen would have a strawberry
motif.

Maggie tried to remember what she knew of Ira Moran's family.
They must be devastated by their loss. His mother, she seemed to
recall, was dead. His father was a vague, seedy man with Ira's stooped
posture, and there had been some sisters—two or three, perhaps. She
could point exactly to which pew they'd always occupied in church,
but now that she thought to look, she found they weren't there anymore.
She watched for them all the rest of February and most of March, but
they never showed up.

Boris Drumm came home for spring break and accompanied her
to church that Sunday. Maggie stood in the choir section looking down
at where he sat, between her father and her brother Elmer, and it
occurred to her that he fit in very well. Too well. Like all the men in
her family, he assumed a sort of hangdog expression during hymns
and muttered them rather than sang them, or perhaps merely mouthed
the words, letting his eyes skate to one side as if hoping not to be
noticed. Only Maggie's mother actually sang, jutting her chin forward
and enunciating clearly.

After Sunday dinner with her family, Maggie and Boris went out
on the porch. Maggie lazily toed the porch swing back and forth while
Boris discussed his political aspirations. He said he figured he would
start small, maybe just get on the school board or something. Then he
would work up to senator. "Hmm," Maggie said. She swallowed a
yawn.

Then Boris gave a little cough and asked if she had ever thought
of going to nursing school. That might be a good plan, he said, if she
was so all fired up about taking care of old people. Probably this too
had some connection with his career; senators' wives didn't empty
bedpans. She said, "But I don't want to be a nurse."

"You were always so smart at your studies, though," he told her.

"I don't want to stand at a nursing station filling out forms; I want
to deal with folks!" Maggie said.

Her voice was sharper than she had intended. He drew away.

"Sorry," she said.

She felt too big. She was taller than he when they were seated,
especially when he hunkered down, as he was doing now.

He said, "Is something troubling you, Maggie? You haven't seemed
yourself all spring vacation."

"Well, I'm sorry," she said, "but I've had a . . . loss. A very close friend of mine has passed away."

She didn't feel she was exaggerating. It did seem, by now, that she and Ira had been close. They just hadn't consciously understood that.

"Well, why didn't you say so?" Boris asked. "Who was it?"

"No one you knew."

"You can't be sure of that! Who was it?"

"Oh, well," she said, "his name was Ira."

"Ira," Boris said. "You mean Ira Moran?"

She nodded, keeping her eyes down.

"Skinny guy? Couple of classes ahead of us?"

She nodded.

"Wasn't he part Indian or something?"

She hadn't been aware of this but it sounded right. It sounded perfect.

"Of course I knew him," Boris said. "Just to say hello to, I mean. I mean, he wasn't actually a friend or anything. I didn't realize he was your friend, either."

Where does she *get* these characters, his beetled expression was saying. First Serena Palermo and now a red Indian.

"He was one of my favorite people," she said.

"He was? Oh. Is that right. Well. Well, you have my condolences, Maggie," Boris said. "I just wish you'd told me earlier." He considered a minute. He said, "How did it happen, anyway?"

"It was a training accident," Maggie said.

"Training?"

"In boot camp."

"I didn't even know he'd enlisted," Boris said. "I thought he worked in his father's frame shop. Isn't that where I got our prom photo framed? Sam's Frame Shop? Seems to me Ira was the one who waited on me."

"Really?" Maggie said, and she thought of Ira behind a counter, another image to add to her small collection. "Well, he did," she said. "Enlist, I mean. And then he had this accident."

"I'm sorry to hear that," Boris said.

A few minutes later she told him she'd prefer to spend the rest of the day alone, and Boris said that of course he understood.

That night in bed she started crying. Speaking of Ira's death out loud was what had done it. She hadn't mentioned it before, not even to Serena, who would say, "What are you talking about? You barely knew the guy."

She and Serena were growing apart, Maggie realized. She cried harder, blotting her tears on the hem of her sheet.

The next day Boris went back to school. Maggie had the morning off and so she was the one who drove him to the bus station. She felt

lonesome after she had said goodbye. It suddenly seemed very sad
that he had come all this way just to see her. She wished she had
been nicer to him.

At home, her mother was spring cleaning. She had already rolled
up the carpets and laid down the sisal mats for summer, and now she
stripped the curtains from the windows with a snapping sound. A bleak
white light gradually filled the house. Maggie climbed the stairs to her
room and flung herself on her bed. For the rest of her life, probably,
she was doomed to live on unmarried in this tedious, predictable family.

After a few minutes, she got up and went to her parents' room.
She took the yellow pages from under the telephone. *Frames*, no. *Picture
frames*, yes. *Sam's Frame Shop*. She had thought she just wanted to see
it in print, but eventually she scribbled the address on a memo pad
and took it back to her room.

She owned no black-bordered stationery, so she chose the plainest
of what she'd been given for graduation—white with a single green
fern in one corner. *Dear Mr. Moran*, she wrote.

*I used to sing in the choir with your son and I had to let you
know how sad I am to hear of his death. I'm not writing just out
of politeness. I thought Ira was the most wonderful person I've
ever met. There was something special about him and I wanted to
tell you that as long as I live, I'm going to remember him fondly.*

With deepest sympathy,
Margaret M. Daley

She sealed and addressed the envelope and then, before she could
change her mind, she walked to the corner and dropped it in the
mailbox.

At first she didn't think about Mr. Moran's answering, but later
on, at work, it occurred to her that he might. Of course: People were
supposed to answer sympathy notes. Maybe he would say something
personal about Ira that she could store up and treasure. Maybe he
would say that Ira had mentioned her name. That wasn't completely
impossible. Or, seeing how she had been one of the few who had
properly valued his son, he might even send her some little memento—
maybe an old photo. She would love a photo. She wished now she
had thought to ask for one.

Since she'd mailed the letter Monday, it would probably reach Ira's
father Tuesday. So his answer could come on Thursday. She hurried
through her work Thursday morning in a fever of impatience. At lunch
hour she phoned home, but her mother said the mail hadn't arrived
yet. (She also said, "Why? What are you expecting?" which was the
kind of thing that made Maggie long to get married and move out.)

At two she phoned again, but her mother said there'd been nothing for her.

That evening, walking to choir practice, she counted up the days once more and realized that Mr. Moran might not have received her letter on Tuesday after all. She hadn't mailed it till nearly noon, she remembered. This made her feel better. She started walking faster, waving at Serena when she spotted her on the steps of the church.

Mr. Nichols was late, and the choir members joked and gossiped while they waited for him. They were all a little heady now that spring was here—even old Mrs. Britt. The church windows were open and they could hear the neighborhood children playing out on the sidewalk. The night air smelled of newly cut grass. Mr. Nichols, when he arrived, wore a sprig of lavender in his buttonhole. He must have bought it from the street vendor, who had only that morning appeared with his cart for the first time that year. "Sorry, ladies and gentlemen," Mr. Nichols said. He set his briefcase on a pew and rooted through it for his notes.

The church door opened again and in walked Ira Moran.

He was very tall and somber, in a white shirt with the sleeves rolled up and slim black trousers. He wore a stern expression that lengthened his chin, as if there were something lumpy in his mouth. Maggie felt her heart stop. She felt icy at first and then overheated, but she stared through him blankly with dry, wide eyes, keeping her thumb in place in the hymnbook. Even in that first moment, she knew he wasn't a ghost or a mirage. He was as real as the gummy varnished pews, not so flawlessly assembled as she had pictured but more intricately textured—more physical, somehow; more complicated.

Mr. Nichols said, "Oh, Ira. Glad to see you."

"Thanks," Ira said. Then he filed through the folding chairs toward the rear, where the men sat, and he took a seat. But Maggie saw how his gaze first skimmed the women in front, resting finally on her. She could tell he knew about the letter. She felt a flush pass over her face. Ordinarily graceful out of pure caution, pure timidity, she had been caught in an error so clumsy that she didn't believe she could ever again meet another person's eyes.

She sang numbly, standing and sitting as ordered. She sang "Once to Every Man and Nation" and "Shall We Gather at the River." Then Mr. Nichols had the men do "Shall We Gather at the River" on their own, and then he asked the accompanist to repeat a certain passage. While this was going on, Maggie leaned toward Mrs. Britt and whispered, "Wasn't that the Moran boy? The one who came in late?"

"Why, yes, I believe it was," Mrs. Britt said pleasantly.

"Didn't you tell us he'd been killed?"

"I did?" Mrs. Britt asked. She looked surprised and sat back in her

chair. A moment later, she sat forward again and said, "That was the
Rand boy who was killed. Monty Rand."

"Oh," Maggie said.

Monty Rand had been a little pale dishcloth of a person with an
incongruously deep bass voice. Maggie had never much liked him.

After choir practice she gathered her belongings as quickly as
possible and was first out the door, scuttling down the sidewalk with
her purse hugged to her chest, but she hadn't even reached the corner
when she heard Ira behind her. "Maggie?" he called.

She slowed beneath a streetlight and then stopped, not looking
around. He came up next to her. His legs made a shadow like scissors
on the sidewalk.

"Mind if I walk your way?" he said.

"Do what you like," she told him shortly. He fell into step beside her.

"So how've you been?" he asked.

"I'm okay."

"You're out of school now, right?"

She nodded. They crossed a street.

"Got a job?" he asked.

"I work at the Silver Threads Nursing Home."

"Oh. Well, good."

He started whistling the last hymn they had practiced: "Just a Closer
Walk with Thee." He sauntered beside her with his hands in his pockets.
They passed a couple kissing at a bus stop. Maggie cleared her throat
and said, "Silly me! I mixed you up with the Rand boy."

"Rand?"

"Monty Rand; he got killed in boot camp and I thought they said
it was you."

She still didn't look at him, although he was near enough so she
could smell his fresh-ironed shirt. She wondered who had ironed it.
One of his sisters, probably. What did that have to do with anything?
She tightened her hold on her purse and walked faster, but Ira kept
up with her. She was conscious of his dark, hooked presence at her
elbow.

"So now will you write to *Monty's* father?" he asked her.

When she risked a sidelong glance she saw the humorous pleat at
the corner of his mouth.

"Go ahead and laugh," she told him.

"I'm not laughing."

"Go ahead! Tell me I made a fool of myself."

"Do you hear me laughing?"

They had reached her block now. She could see her house up
ahead, part of a string of row houses, the porch glowing orange beneath
the bugproof light. This time when she stopped she looked directly

into his face, and he returned the look without a hint of a smile, keeping his hands shoved in his pockets. She hadn't expected his eyes to be so narrow. He could have been Asian, rather than Indian.

"Your father must have split his sides," she said.

"No, he was just . . . he just asked me what it could mean."

She tried to think what words she had used in the letter. Special, she'd written. Oh, Lord. And worse yet: wonderful. She wished she could disappear.

"I remember you from choir practice," Ira said. "You're Josh's sister, right? But I guess we never really knew each other."

"No, of course not," she said. "Goodness! We were total strangers." She tried to sound brusque and sensible.

He studied her a moment. Then he said, "So do you think we might get to know each other now?"

"Well," she said, "I do go out with someone."

"Really? Who?"

"Boris Drumm," she said.

"Oh, yes."

She looked off toward her house. She said, "We'll probably get married."

"I see," he said.

"Well, goodbye," she told him.

He lifted a hand in silence, thought a moment, and then turned and walked away.

That Sunday, though, he came to sing with the choir at the morning service. Maggie felt relieved, almost lightweight with relief, as if she'd been given a second chance, and then her heart sank when he just melted into the crowd again after church. But Thursday night he was at choir practice again and he walked her home when it was over. They talked about trivial subjects—Mrs. Britt's splintery voice, for instance. Maggie grew more comfortable. When they reached her house she saw her neighbor's dog out front, peeing on Maggie's mother's one rosebush, with the neighbor standing there watching; so she called, "Hey, lady! Get your dog out of our yard, you hear?" She was joking; it was the rough style of humor she had picked up from her brothers. But Ira didn't know that and he looked taken aback. Then Mrs. Wright laughed and said, "You and who else going to make me, kid?" and Ira relaxed. But Maggie felt she'd been clumsy once again, and she murmured a hasty good night and went inside.

Soon enough it became a pattern—Thursday nights and Sunday mornings. People started to notice. Maggie's mother said, "Maggie? Does Boris know about this new friendship of yours?" and Maggie snapped, "Of course he knows"—a lie, or at best a half-truth. (Maggie's mother thought Boris was God's gift to women.) But Serena said, "Good for you! High time you dumped Mr. Holier-than-Thou."

"I haven't dumped him!"

"Why not?" Serena asked. "When you compare him to Ira! Ira's so mysterious."

"Well, he *is* part Indian, of course," Maggie said.

"And you have to admit he's attractive."

Oh, Jesse was not the only one who'd been swayed by a single friend! Certainly Serena had more than a little to do with all that happened afterward.

She asked Maggie and Ira to sing a duet at her wedding, for instance. Out of the blue (for Ira had never been thought to have a particularly striking voice), she took it into her head that they should sing "Love is a Many Splendored Thing" before the exchange of vows. So of course they had to practice; so of course he had to come to her house. They commiserated with each other and they clucked over Serena's musical taste, but it never occurred to them to refuse her. Maggie's mother kept tip-tapping in and out with folded laundry that had no business in the living room. " 'Once,' " they sang, " 'on a high and windy hill,' " and then Maggie sputtered into laughter, but Ira remained sober. Maggie seemed to be turning into someone else, those days—someone giddy and unstable and accident-prone. Sometimes she imagined that that sympathy note had thrown her permanently off balance.

She knew by then that Ira ran his father's frame shop single-handed—Sam's "weak heart" had got to him the day after Ira's high-school graduation—and that he lived above the shop with his father and his two much older sisters, one of whom was a little slow and the other just shy or retiring or something. He wanted to go to college, though, if he could ever scrape together the money. He'd had hopes since childhood of becoming a doctor. He told her this in a neutral tone; he didn't seem discouraged about the way his life was turning out. Then he said maybe she'd like to come home with him sometime and meet his sisters; they didn't get to talk to very many people. But Maggie said, "No!" and then flushed and said, "Oh, I guess I'd better not," and pretended not to notice his amusement. She was afraid she'd run into his father. She wondered if his sisters knew about the letter too, but she didn't want to ask.

Never, not once in all this time, did he act any more than mildly friendly. When necessary he would take her arm—just to steer her through a crowd, say—and his hand felt firm and warm on her bare skin; but as soon as they'd passed the crowd he would release her. She wasn't even sure what he thought of her. She wasn't sure what she thought of him, either. And after all, there was Boris to consider. She went on writing Boris regularly—if anything, a little more often than usual.

Serena's wedding rehearsal was a Friday evening. It wasn't a very formal rehearsal. Max's parents, for instance, didn't even bother attending, although Serena's mother showed up with her hair in a million pink rollers. And events happened out of order, with Maggie (standing in for the bride, for good luck) coming down the aisle ahead of all the musical selections because Max had a trainload of relatives to meet in half an hour. She walked alongside Anita, which was one of Serena's more peculiar innovations. "Who else could give me away?" Serena asked. "You surely don't imagine my father would do it." Anita herself, however, didn't seem so happy with this arrangement. She teetered and staggered in her spike-heeled shoes and dug her long red nails into Maggie's wrist in order to keep her balance. At the altar Max slung an arm around Maggie and said, shoot, maybe he'd just settle for her instead; and Serena, sitting in a center pew, called. "That'll be quite enough of that, Max Gill!" Max was the same freckled, friendly, overgrown boy he'd always been. It was hard for Maggie to picture him married.

After the vows Max left for Penn Station and the rest of them practiced the music. They all performed in a fairly amateurish style, Maggie thought, which was fine with her because she and Ira didn't sound their best that night. They started off raggedly, and Maggie forgot that they had planned to split up the middle verse. She sailed right into the first two lines along with Ira, then stopped in confusion, then missed her own cue and fell into a fit of giggles. At that moment, the laughter not yet faded from her face, she saw Boris Drumm in the foremost pew. He wore a baffled, rumpled frown, as if someone had just awakened him.

Well, she'd known he was due home for the summer, but he hadn't told her which day. She pretended not to recognize him. She and Ira finished their song, and then she reverted to Serena's role and marched back up the aisle, minus Max, so Sugar could practice the timing on "Born to Be with You." After that Serena clapped her hands and shouted, "Okay, gang!" and they prepared to leave, all talking at once. They were thinking of going out for pizza. They swarmed toward Maggie, who waited at the rear of the church, but Boris stayed where he was, facing forward. He would be expecting Maggie to join him. She studied the back of his head, which was block-like and immobile. Serena handed her her purse and said, "You've got company, I see." Right behind Serena was Ira. He stopped in front of Maggie and looked down at her. He said, "Will you be going for pizza?"

Maggie said, "I guess not."

He nodded, blank-faced, and left. But he walked in a different direction from the others, as if he didn't feel they would welcome him without Maggie. Which of course was nonsense.

Maggie went back up the aisle and sat next to Boris, and they kissed. She said, "How was your trip?" and he said, "Who was that you were singing with?" at exactly the same instant. She pretended she hadn't heard. "How was your trip?" she asked again, and he said, "Wasn't that Ira Moran?"

"Who, the one singing?" she asked.

"That was Ira Moran! You told me he was dead!"

"It was a misunderstanding," she said.

"I heard you say it, Maggie."

"I mean I misunderstood that he was dead. He was only, um, wounded."

"Ah," Boris said. He turned that over in his mind.

"It was only a flesh wound, was all," Maggie told him. "A scalp wound." She wondered if the two terms contradicted each other. She riffled quickly through various movies she had seen.

"So then what? He just comes walking in one day?" Boris asked. "I mean he just pops up, like some kind of ghost? How did it happen, exactly?"

"Boris," Maggie said, "I fail to comprehend why you keep dwelling on this in such a tiresome fashion."

"Oh. Well. Sorry," Boris said.

(Had she really sounded so authoritative? She found it hard to imagine, looking back.)

On the morning of the wedding, Maggie got up early and walked to Serena's apartment—the second floor of a formstone row house—to help her dress. Serena seemed unruffled but her mother was all in a dither. Anita's habit when she was nervous was to speak very fast and with practically no punctuation, like someone in a hard-sell commercial. "Why she won't roll her hair like everybody else when I told her way last week I said hon nobody wears long hair anymore you ought to go to the beauty shop and get you a nice little flip to peek out under your veil . . ." She was rushing around the shabby, sparsely equipped kitchen in a dirty pink satin bathrobe, with a cigarette dangling from her lips. She was making a great clatter but not much was getting accomplished. Serena, lazy and nonchalant in one of Max's big shirts, said, "Take it easy, Mom, will you?" She told Maggie, "Mom thinks we ought to change the whole ceremony."

"Change it how?" Maggie asked.

"She doesn't have any bridesmaids!" Anita said. "She doesn't have a maid of honor even and what's worse there's no kind of masculine person to walk her down the aisle!"

"She's upset she has to walk me down the aisle," Serena told Maggie.

"Oh if only your uncle Maynard would come and do it instead!" Anita cried. "Maybe we should move the wedding up a week and give him another chance because the way you have it now is all cockeyed it's too oddball I can just picture how those hoity-toity Gills will be scrupulizing me and smirking amongst themselves and besides that last perm I got scorched the tip-ends of my hair *I* can't walk down the aisle."

"Let's go get me dressed," Serena told Maggie, and she led her away.

In Serena's room, which was really just half of Anita's room curtained off with a draggled aqua bed sheet, Serena sat down at her vanity table. She said, "I thought of giving her a belt of whiskey, but I worried it might backfire."

Maggie said, "Serena, are you sure you ought to be marrying Max?"

Serena squawked and wheeled to face her. She said, "Maggie Daley, don't you start with me! I've already got my wedding cake frosted."

"But I mean how do you know? How can you be certain you chose the right man?"

"I can be certain because I've come to the end of the line," Serena said, turning back to the mirror. Her voice was at normal level now. She patted on liquid foundation, expertly dotting her chin and forehead and cheeks. "It's just *time* to marry, that's all," she said. "I'm so tired of dating! I'm so tired of keeping up a good front! I want to sit on the couch with a regular, normal husband and watch TV for a thousand years. It's going to be like getting out of a girdle; that's exactly how I picture it."

"What are you saying?" Maggie asked. She was almost afraid of the answer. "Are you telling me you don't really love Max?"

"Of course I love him," Serena said. She blended the dots into her skin. "But I've loved other people as much. I loved Terry Simpson our sophomore year—remember him? But it wasn't time to get married then, so Terry is not the one I'm marrying."

Maggie didn't know what to think. Did everybody feel that way? Had the grownups been spreading fairy tales? "The minute I saw Eleanor," her oldest brother had told her once, "I said, 'That girl is going to be my wife someday.'" It hadn't occurred to Maggie that he might simply have been ready for a wife, and therefore had his eye out for the likeliest prospect.

So there again, Serena had managed to color Maggie's view of things. "We're not in the hands of fate after all," she seemed to be saying. "Or if we are, we can wrest ourselves free any time we care to."

Maggie sat down on the bed and watched Serena applying her rouge. In Max's shirt, Serena looked casual and sporty, like anybody's girl next door. "When this is over," she told Maggie, "I'm going to dye my wedding dress purple. Might as well get some use out of it."

Maggie gazed at her thoughtfully.

The wedding was due to start at eleven, but Anita wanted to get to the church much earlier, she said, in case of mishaps. Maggie rode with them in Anita's ancient Chevrolet. Serena drove because Anita said she was too nervous, and since Serena's skirt billowed over so much of the seat, Maggie and Anita sat in back. Anita was talking nonstop and sprinkling cigarette ashes across the lap of her shiny peach mother-of-the-bride dress. "Now that I think of it Serena I can't imagine why you're holding your reception in the Angels of Charity building which is so damn far away and every time I've tried to find it I've gotten all turned around and had to ask directions from passing strangers . . ."

They came to the Alluring Lingerie Shop, and Serena double-parked and heaved her cascades of satin out of the car in order to go model her dress for Mrs. Knowlton, her employer. While they waited for her, Anita said, "Honestly you'd suppose if you can rent a man to come tend your bar or fix your toilet or check on why your door won't lock it wouldn't be any problem at all to engage one for the five eentsy minutes it takes to walk your daughter down the aisle don't you agree?"

"Yes, ma'am," Maggie said, and she dug absently into a hole in the vinyl seat and pulled out a wad of cotton batting.

"Sometimes I think she's trying to show me up," Anita said.

Maggie didn't know how to answer that.

Finally Serena returned to the car, bearing a wrapped gift. "Mrs. Knowlton told me not to open this till our wedding night," she said. Maggie blushed and slid her eyes toward Anita. Anita merely gazed out the window, sending two long streamers of smoke from her nostrils.

In the church, Reverend Connors led Serena and her mother to a side room. Maggie went to wait for the other singers. Mary Jean was already there, and soon Sissy arrived with her husband and her mother-in-law. No Ira, though. Well, there was plenty of time. Maggie took her long white choir robe from its hanger and slipped it over her head, losing herself in its folds, and then of course she emerged all tousled and had to go off to comb her hair. But even when she returned, Ira was not to be seen.

The first of the guests had arrived. Boris sat in one of the pews, uncomfortably close. He was listening to a lady in a spotted veil and he was nodding intelligently, respectfully, but Maggie felt there was something tense about the set of his head. She looked toward the entrance. Other people were straggling in now, her parents and the Wrights next door and Serena's old baton teacher. No sign of the long, dark shape that was Ira Moran.

After she had let him walk off alone the night before, he must have decided to vanish altogether.

"Excuse me," she said. She bumped down the row of folding chairs and hurried through the vestibule. One of her full sleeves caught on the knob of the open door and yanked her up short in a foolish way, but she shook herself loose before anybody noticed, she thought. She paused on the front steps. "Well, hi!" an old classmate said. "Um . . ." Maggie murmured, and she shaded her eyes and looked up and down the street. All she saw were more guests. She felt a moment's impatience with them; they seemed so frivolous. They were smiling and greeting each other in that gracious style they used only at church, and the women turned their toes out fastidiously as they walked, and their white gloves glinted in the sunlight.

In the doorway, Boris said, "Maggie?"

She didn't turn around. She ran down the steps with her robe flowing behind her. The steps were the wide, exceptionally shallow sort unsuited for any normal human stride; she was forced to adopt a limping, uneven rhythm. "Maggie!" Boris cried, so she had to run on after reaching the sidewalk. She shouldered her way between guests and then was past them, skimming down the street, ballooning white linen like a sailboat in a wind.

Sam's Frame Shop was only two blocks from the church, but they were long blocks and it was a warm June morning. She was damp and breathless when she arrived. She pulled open the plate-glass door and stepped into a close, cheerless interior with a worn linoleum floor. L-shaped samples of moldings hung from hooks on a yellowing pegboard wall, and the counter was painted a thick, cold gray. Behind this counter stood a bent old man in a visor, with shocks of white hair poking every which way. Ira's father.

She was surprised to find him there. The way she'd heard it, he never set foot in the shop anymore. She hesitated, and he said, "Can I help you, miss?"

She had always thought Ira had the darkest eyes she'd ever seen, but this man's eyes were darker. She couldn't even tell where they were focused; she had the fleeting notion that he might be blind.

"I was looking for Ira," she told him.

"Ira's not working today. He's got some kind of event."

"Yes, a wedding; he's singing at a wedding," she said. "But he hasn't shown up yet, so I came to get him."

"Oh?" Sam said. He moved his head closer to her, leading with his nose, not lessening in the least his impression of a blind man. "You wouldn't be Margaret, would you?" he asked.

"Yes, sir," she said.

He thought that over. He gave an abrupt, wheezy chuckle.

"Margaret M. Daley," he said.

She stood her ground.

"So you assumed Ira was dead," he said.

"Is he here?" she asked.

"He's upstairs, dressing."

"Could you call him, please?"

"How did you suppose he'd died?" he asked her.

"I mistook him for someone else. Monty Rand," she said, mumbling the words. "Monty got killed in boot camp."

"Boot camp!"

"Could you call Ira for me, please?"

"You'd never find Ira in boot camp," Sam told her. "Ira's got dependents, just as much as if he was married. Not that he ever could be married in view of our situation. My heart has been acting up on me for years and one of his sisters is not quite right in the head. Why, I don't believe the army would have him even if he volunteered! Then me and the girls would have to go on welfare; we'd be a burden on the government. 'Get along with you,' those army folks would tell him. 'Go on back to them that need you. We've got no use for you here.' "

Maggie heard feet running down a set of stairs somewhere—a muffled, drumming sound. A door opened in the pegboard wall behind the counter and Ira said, "Pop—"

He stopped and looked at her. He wore a dark, ill-fitting suit and a stiff white shirt, with a navy tie dangling unknotted from his collar.

"We'll be late for the wedding," she told him.

He shot back a cuff and checked his watch.

"Come on!" she said. It wasn't only the wedding she was thinking of. She felt there was something dangerous about staying around Ira's father.

And sure enough, Sam said, "Me and your little friend here was just discussing you going into the army."

"Army?"

"*Ira* couldn't join the army, I told her. He's got us."

Ira said, "Well, anyhow, Pop, I ought to be back from this thing in a couple of hours."

"You really have to take that long? That's most of the morning!" Sam turned to Maggie and said, "Saturday's our busiest day at work."

Maggie wondered why, in that case, the shop was empty. She said, "Yes, well, we should be—"

"In fact, if Ira joined the army we'd just have to close this place up," Sam said. "Sell it off lock, stock, and barrel, when it's been in the family for forty-two years come October."

"What are you talking about?" Ira asked him. "Why would I want to join the army?"

"Your little friend here thought you'd gone into the army and got yourself killed," Sam told him.

"Oh," Ira said. Now the danger must have dawned on him too, for this time it was he who said, "We should be going."

"She thought you'd blown yourself up in boot camp," Sam told him. He gave another of his wheezy chuckles. There was something mole-like and relentless about that way he led with his nose, Maggie felt. "Ups and writes me a letter of condolence," he said. "Ha!" He told Maggie, "Gave me quite a start. I had this half-second or so where I thought, Wait a minute. Has Ira *passed?* First I knew of it, if so. And first I'd heard of you. First I'd heard of any girl, matter of fact, in years. I mean it's not like he has any friends anymore. His chums at school were that brainy crowd that went away to college and by now they've all lost touch with him and he doesn't see a soul his own age. 'Look here!' I told him. 'A girl at last!' After I'd withstood the shock. 'Better grab her while you got the chance,' I told him."

"Let's go," Ira said to Maggie.

He lifted a hinged section of the counter and stepped through it, but Sam went on talking. "Trouble is, now you know she can manage fine without you," he said.

Ira paused, still holding up the hinged section.

"She writes a little note of condolence and then continues with her life, as merry as pie," Sam told him.

"What did you expect her to do, throw herself in my grave?"

"Well, you got to admit she bore up under her grief mighty well. Writes me a nice little note, sticks a postage stamp in one corner, then carries on with her girlfriend's wedding arrangements."

"Right," Ira said, and he lowered the counter and came over to Maggie. Was he totally impenetrable? His eyes were flat, and his hand, when he took her arm, was perfectly steady.

"You're wrong," Maggie told Sam.

"Huh?"

"I wasn't doing fine without him! I was barely existing."

"No need to get all het up about it," Sam said.

"And for your information, there's any number of girls who think he's perfectly wonderful and I am not the only one and also it's ridiculous to say he can't get married. You have no right; anyone can get married if they want to."

"He wouldn't dare!" Sam told her. "He's got me and his sisters to think of. You want us all in the poorhouse? Ira? Ira, you wouldn't dare to get married!"

"Why not?" Ira asked calmly.

"You've got to think of me and your sisters!"

"I'm marrying her anyhow," Ira said.

Then he opened the door and stood back to let Maggie walk through it.

On the stoop outside, they stopped and he put his arms around her and drew her close. She could feel the narrow bones of his chest against her cheek and she heard his heart beating in her ear. His father must have been able to see everything through the plate-glass door, but even so Ira bent his head and kissed her on the lips, a long, warm, searching kiss that turned her knees weak.

Then they started off toward the church, although first there was a minor delay because the hem of her choir robe caught her up short. Ira had to open the door once again (not even glancing at his father) and set her loose.

But to look at Serena's movie, would you guess what had come just before? They seemed an ordinary couple, maybe a bit mismatched as to height. He was too tall and thin and she was too short and plump. Their expressions were grave but they certainly didn't look as if anything earth-shattering had recently taken place. They opened and closed their mouths in silence while the audience sang for them, poking gentle fun, intoning melodramatically. " 'Love is Nature's way of giving, a reason to be living . . .' " Only Maggie knew how Ira's hand had braced the small of her back.

Then the Barley twins leaned into each other and sang the processional, their faces raised like baby birds' faces; and the camera swung from them to Serena all in white. Serena sailed down the aisle with her mother hanging on to her. Funny: From this vantage neither one of them seemed particularly unconventional. Serena stared straight ahead, intent. Anita's makeup was a little too heavy but she could have been anybody's mother, really, anxious-looking and outdated in her tight dress. "Look at you!" someone told Serena, laughing. Meanwhile the audience sang, " 'Though I don't know many words to say . . .' "

But then the camera jerked and swooped and there was Max, waiting next to Reverend Connors in front of the altar. One by one, the singers trailed off. Sweet Max, pursing his chapped lips and squinting his blue eyes in an attempt to seem fittingly dignified as he watched Serena approaching. Everything about him had faded except for his freckles, which stood out like metal spangles across his broad cheeks.

Maggie felt tears welling up. Several people blew their noses.

No one, she thought, had suspected back then that it would all turn out to be so serious.

But of course the mood brightened again, because the song went on too long and the couple had to stand in position, with Reverend Connors beaming at them, while the Barley twins wound down. And by the time the vows were exchanged and Sugar rose to sing the recessional, most of the people in the audience were nudging each other expectantly. For who could forget what came next?

Max escorted Serena back down the aisle far too slowly, employing a measured, hitching gait that he must have thought appropriate. Sugar's song was over and done with before they had finished exiting. Serena tugged at Max's elbow, spoke urgently in his ear, traveled almost backward for the last few feet as she towed him into the vestibule. And then once they were out of sight, what a battle there'd been! The whispers, rising to hisses, rising to shouts! "If you'd stayed through the goddamn rehearsal," Serena had cried, "instead of tearing off to

Penn Station for your never-ending relatives and leaving me to practice on my own so you had no idea how fast to walk me—" The congregation had remained seated, not knowing where to look. They'd grinned sheepishly at their laps, and finally broke into laughter.

"Serena, honey," Max had said, "pipe down. For Lord's sake, Serena, everyone can hear you, Serena, honey pie . . ."

Naturally none of this was apparent from the movie, which was finished anyhow except for a few scarred numerals flashing by. But all around the room people were refreshing other people's recollections, bringing the scene back to life. "And then she stalked out—"

"Slammed the church door—"

"Shook the whole building, remember?"

"Us just staring back toward the vestibule wondering how to behave—"

Someone flipped a window shade up: Serena herself. The room was filled with light. Serena was smiling but her cheeks were wet. People were saying, "And then, Serena . . ." and, "Remember, Serena?" and she was nodding and smiling and crying. The old lady next to Maggie said, "Dear, dear Maxwell," and sighed, perhaps not even aware of the others' merriment.

Maggie rose and collected her purse. She wanted Ira; she felt lost without Ira. She looked around for him but saw only the others, meaningless and bland. She threaded her way to the dining alcove, but he wasn't among the guests who stood picking over the platters of food. She walked down the hall and peeked into Serena's bedroom.

And there he was, seated at the bureau. He'd pulled a chair up close and moved Linda's graduation picture out of the way so he could spread a solitaire layout clear across the polished surface. One angular brown hand was poised above a jack, preparing to strike. Maggie stepped inside and shut the door. She set her purse down and wrapped her arms around him from behind. "You missed a good movie," she said into his hair. "Serena showed a film of her wedding."

"Isn't that just like her," Ira said. He placed the jack on a queen. His hair smelled like coconut—its natural scent, which always came through sooner or later no matter what shampoo he used.

"You and I were singing our duet," she said.

"And I suppose you got all teary and nostalgic."

"Yes, I did," she told him.

"Isn't that just like *you*," he said.

"Yes, it is," she said, and she smiled into the mirror in front of them. She felt she was almost boasting, that she'd made a kind of proclamation. If she was easily swayed, she thought, at least she had chosen who would sway her. If she was locked in a pattern, at least she had chosen what that pattern would be. She felt strong and free and definite. She watched Ira scoop up a whole row of diamonds, ace through ten, and lay them on the jack. "We looked like children," she told him. "Like infants. We were hardly older than Daisy is now; just imagine. And thought nothing of deciding then and there who we'd spend the next sixty years with."

"Mmhmm," Ira said.

He pondered a king, while Maggie laid her cheek on the top of his head. She seemed to have fallen in love again. In love with her own husband! The convenience of it pleased her—like finding right in her pantry all the fixings she needed for a new recipe.

"Remember the first year we were married?" she asked him. "It was awful. We fought every minute."

"Worst year of my life," he agreed, and when she moved around to the front he sat back slightly so she could settle on his lap. His thighs beneath her were long and bony—two planks of lumber. "Careful of my cards," he told her, but she could feel he was getting interested. She laid her head on his shoulder and traced the stitching of his shirt pocket with one finger.

"That Sunday we invited Max and Serena to dinner, remember? Our very first guests. We rearranged the furniture five times before they got there," she said. "I'd go out in the kitchen and come back to find you'd shifted all the chairs into corners, and I'd say, 'What have you *done*?' and shift them all some other way, and by the time the Gills arrived, the coffee table was upside down on the couch and you and I were having a shouting quarrel."

"We were scared to death, is what it was," Ira said. He had his arms around her now; she felt his amused, dry voice vibrating through his chest. "We were trying to act like grownups but we didn't know if we could pull it off."

"And then our first anniversary," Maggie said. "What a fiasco! Mother's etiquette book said it was either the paper anniversary or the clock anniversary, whichever I preferred. So I got this bright idea to construct your gift from a kit I saw advertised in a magazine: a working clock made out of paper."

"*I* don't remember that."

"That's because I never gave it to you," Maggie said.

"What happened to it?"

"Well, I must have put it together wrong," Maggie said. "I mean I followed all the directions, but it never really acted like it was supposed to. It dragged, it stopped and started, one edge curled over, there was a ripple under the twelve where I'd used too much glue. It was . . . makeshift, amateur. I was so ashamed of it, I threw it in the trash."

"Why, sweetheart," he said.

"I was afraid it was a symbol or something, I mean a symbol of our marriage. We were makeshift ourselves, is what I was afraid of."

He said, "Shoot, we were just learning back then. We didn't know what to do with each other."

"We know now," she whispered. Then she pressed her mouth into one of her favorite places, that nice warm nook where his jaw met his neck.

Meanwhile her fingers started traveling down to his belt buckle.

Ira said, "Maggie?" but he made no move to stop her. She straightened up to loosen his belt and unzip his fly.

"We can sit right here in this chair," she whispered. "No one will ever guess."

Ira groaned and pulled her against him. When he kissed her his lips felt smooth and very firm. She thought she could hear her own blood flooding through her veins; it made a rushing sound, like a seashell.

"Maggie Daley!" Serena said.

Ira started violently and Maggie jumped up from his lap. Serena stood frozen with one hand on the doorknob. She was gaping at Ira, at his open zipper and his shirttail flaring out.

Well, it could have gone in either direction, Maggie figured. You never knew with Serena. Serena could have just laughed it off. But maybe the funeral had been too much for her, or the movie afterward, or just widowhood in general. At any rate, she said, "I don't believe this. I do not believe it."

Maggie said, "Serena—"

"In my own house! My bedroom!"

"I'm sorry; please, we're both so sorry . . ." Maggie said, and Ira, hastily righting his clothes, said, "Yes, we honestly didn't—"

"You always were impossible," Serena told Maggie. "I suspect it's deliberate. No one could act so goofy purely by chance. I haven't forgotten what happened with my mother at the nursing home. And now this! At a funeral gathering! In the bedroom I shared with my husband!"

"It was an accident, Serena. We never meant to—"

"An accident!" Serena said. "Oh, just go."

"What?"

"Just leave," she said, and she wheeled and walked away.

Maggie picked up her purse, not looking at Ira. Ira collected his cards. She went through the doorway ahead of him and they walked down the hall to the living room. People stood back a little to let them pass. She had no idea how much they had heard. Probably everything; there was something hushed and thrilled about them. She opened the front door and then turned around and said, "Well, bye now!"

"Goodbye," they murmured. "Bye, Maggie, bye, Ira . . ."

Outside, the sunlight was blinding. She wished they'd driven over from the church. She took hold of Ira's hand when he offered it and picked her way along the gravel next to the road, fixing her eyes on her pumps, which had developed a thin film of dust.

"Well," Ira said finally, "we certainly livened up *that* little gathering."

"I feel just terrible," Maggie said.

"Oh, it'll blow over," Ira told her. "You know how she is." Then he gave a snort and said, "Just look on the bright side. As class reunions go—"

"But it wasn't a class reunion; it was a funeral," Maggie said. "A memorial service. I went and ruined a memorial service! She probably thinks we were showing off or something, taunting her now that she's a widow. I feel terrible."

"She'll forgive us," he told her.

A car swished by and he changed places with her, setting her to the inside away from the traffic. Now they walked slightly apart, not touching. They were back to their normal selves. Or almost back. Not entirely. Some trick of light or heat blurred Maggie's vision, and the stony old house they were passing seemed to shimmer for a moment. It dissolved in a gentle, radiant haze, and then it regrouped itself and grew solid again.

TWO

For the past several months now, Ira had been noticing the human race's wastefulness. People were squandering their lives, it seemed to him. They were splurging their energies on petty jealousies or vain ambitions or long-standing, bitter grudges. It was a theme that emerged wherever he turned, as if someone were trying to tell him something. Not that he needed to be told. Didn't he know well enough all he himself had wasted?

He was fifty years old and had never accomplished one single act of consequence. Once he had planned to find a cure for some major disease and now he was framing petit point instead.

His son, who couldn't carry a tune, had dropped out of high school in hopes of becoming a rock star. His daughter was one of those people who fritter themselves away on unnecessary worries; she chewed her fingernails to nubbins and developed blinding headaches before exams and agonized so over her grades that their doctor had warned of ulcers.

And his wife! He loved her, but he couldn't stand how she refused to take her own life seriously. She seemed to believe it was a sort of practice life, something she could afford to play around with as if they offered second and third chances to get it right. She was always making clumsy, impetuous rushes toward nowhere in particular—side trips, random detours.

Like today, for instance: this Fiona business. Fiona was no longer any relation, not their daughter-in-law and not even an acquaintance, in Ira's opinion. But here Maggie sat, trailing a hand out the window as they whizzed down Route One toward home, and what did she return to (just when he was hoping she'd forgotten) but her whim to pay Fiona a visit. Bad enough they'd lost their Saturday to Max Gill's funeral—a kind of side trip in itself—but now she wanted to plunge off in a whole new direction. She wanted to swing by Cartwheel, Pennsylvania, just so she could offer to baby-sit while Fiona went on her honeymoon. A completely pointless proposal; for Fiona did have a mother, didn't she, who'd been tending Leroy all along and surely could be counted on for the next little bit as well. Ira pointed that out. He said, "What's the matter with what's-her-name? Mrs. Stuckey?"

"Oh, Mrs. *Stuckey*," Maggie said, as if that were answer enough. She brought in her hand and rolled up the window. Her face glowed in the sunlight, round and pretty and intense. The breeze had ruffled her hair so it stood out in loops all over her head. It was a hot, gasoline-smelling breeze and Ira wasn't sorry to have lost it. However, this constant opening and shutting of the window was getting on his nerves. She operated from second to second, he thought. She never looked any distance ahead. A spasm of irritation darted raggedly through his temples.

Here was a woman who had once let a wrong number consume an entire evening. "Hello?" she'd said into the phone, and a man had said, "Laverne, stay right there safe in your house. I just talked to Dennis and he's coming to fetch you." And then had hung up. Maggie cried, "Wait!"—speaking into a dead receiver; typical. Whoever it was, Ira had told her, deserved what he got. If Dennis and Laverne never managed to connect, why, that was their problem, not hers. But Maggie had gone on and on about it. " 'Safe,' " she moaned. " 'Safe in the house,' he told me. Lord only knows what that poor Laverne is going through." And she had spent the evening dialing all possible variations of their own number, every permutation of every digit, hoping to find Laverne. But never did, of course.

Cartwheel, Pennsylvania, was so close it could practically reach out and grab them, to hear her talk. "It's on that cutoff right above the state line. I forget the name," she was saying. "But I couldn't see it anywhere on that map you got at the service station."

No wonder she'd been so little help navigating; she'd been hunting Cartwheel instead.

Traffic was surprisingly sparse for a Saturday. Mostly it was trucks—

small, rusty trucks carrying logs or used tires, not the sleek monsters you'd see on I-95. They were traveling through farm country at this point, and each truck as it passed left another layer of dust on the wan, parched, yellowing fields that lined the road.

"Here's what we'll do," Maggie told him. "Stop by Fiona's just for an instant. A teeny, eeny instant. Not accept even a glass of iced tea. Make her our offer and go."

"That much you could handle by telephone," Ira said.

"No, I couldn't!"

"Telephone when we get back to Baltimore, if you're so set on baby-sitting."

"That child is not but seven years old," Maggie told him, "and she must just barely remember us. We can't take her on for a week just cold! We have to let her get reacquainted first."

"How do you know it's a week?" Ira asked.

She was riffling through her purse now. She said, "Hmm?"

"How do you know the honeymoon will last a week, Maggie?"

"Well, I *don't* know. Maybe it's two weeks. Maybe even a month, I don't know."

He wondered, all at once, if this whole wedding was a myth—something she'd invented for her own peculiar reasons. He wouldn't put it past her.

"And besides!" he said. "We could never stay away that long. We've got jobs."

"Not away: in Baltimore. We'd take her back down to Baltimore."

"But then she'd be missing school," he said.

"Oh, that's no problem. We'll let her go to school near us," Maggie said. "Second grade is second grade, after all, the same all over."

Ira had so many different arguments against that that he was struck speechless.

Now she dumped her purse upside down in her lap. "Oh, dear," she said, studying her billfold, her lipstick, her comb, and her pack of Kleenex. "I wish I'd brought that map from home."

It was another form of wastefulness, Ira thought, to search yet again through a purse whose contents she already knew by heart. Even Ira knew those contents by heart. And it was wasteful to continue caring about Fiona when Fiona obviously had no feeling for them, when she had made it very clear that she just wanted to get on with her life. Hadn't she stated that, even? "I just want to get on with my life"—it had a familiar ring. Maybe she had shouted it during that scene before she left, or maybe later during one of those pathetic visits they used to pay after the divorce, with Leroy bashful and strange and Mrs. Stuckey a single accusatory eye glaring around the edge of the living room door. Ira winced. Waste, waste, and more waste, all for nothing. The long drive and the forced conversation and the long drive home again, for absolutely nothing.

And it was wasteful to devote your working life to people who forgot you the instant you left their bedsides, as Ira was forever pointing out. Oh, it was also admirably selfless, he supposed. But he didn't know how Maggie endured the impermanence, the lack of permanent results—those feeble, senile patients who confused her with a long-dead mother or a sister who'd insulted them back in 1928.

It was wasteful too to fret so over the children. (Who were no longer children anyhow—not even Daisy.) Consider, for instance, the cigarette papers that Maggie had found last spring on Daisy's bureau. She had picked them up while she was dusting and come running to Ira. "What'll we do? What are we going to do?" she had wailed. "Our daughter's smoking marijuana; this is one of the telltale clues they mention in that pamphlet that the school gives out." She'd got Ira all involved and distressed; that happened more often than he liked to admit. Together they had sat up far into the night, discussing ways of dealing with the problem. "Where did we go wrong?" Maggie cried, and Ira hugged her and said, "There now, dear heart. I promise you we'll see this thing through." All for nothing yet again, it turned out. Turned out the cigarette papers were for Daisy's flute. You slid them under the keys whenever they started sticking, Daisy explained off-handedly. She hadn't even bothered to take umbrage.

Ira had felt ridiculous. He'd felt he had spent something scarce and real—hard currency.

Then he thought of how a thief had once stolen Maggie's pocketbook, marched right into the kitchen where she was shelving groceries and stolen it off the counter as bold-faced as you please; and she took after him. She could have been killed! (The efficient, the streamlined thing to do was to shrug and decide she was better off without that pocketbook—had never cared for it anyhow, and surely could spare the few limp dollars in the billfold.) It was February and the sidewalks were sheets of glare ice, so running was impossible. Ira, returning from work, had been astonished to see a young boy shuffling toward him at a snail's pace with Maggie's red pocketbook dangling from his shoulder, and behind him Maggie herself came jogging along inch by inch with her tongue between her teeth as she concentrated on her footing. The two of them had resembled those mimes who can portray a speedy stride while making no progress at all. In fact, it had looked sort of comical, Ira reflected now. His lips twitched. He smiled.

"What," Maggie ordered.

"You were crazy to go after that pocketbook thief," he told her.

"Honestly, Ira. How does your mind work?"

Exactly the question he might have asked her.

"Anyhow, I did get it back," she said.

"Only by chance. What if he'd been armed? Or a little bigger? What if he hadn't panicked when he saw me?"

"You know, come to think of it, I believe I dreamed about that boy just a couple of nights ago," Maggie said. "He was sitting in this kitchen that was kind of our kitchen and kind of not our kitchen, if you know what I mean . . ."

Ira wished she wouldn't keep telling her dreams. It made him feel fidgety and restless.

Maybe if he hadn't gotten married. Or at least had not had children. But that was too great a price to pay; even in his darkest moods he realized that. Well, if he had put his sister Dorrie in an institution, then—something state-run that wouldn't cost too much. And told his father, "I will no longer provide your support. Weak heart or not, take over this goddamn shop of yours and let me get on with my original plan if I can cast my mind back far enough to remember what it was." And made his other sister venture into the world to find employment. "You think we're not *all* scared?" he would ask her. "But we go out anyway and earn our keep, and so will you."

But she would die of terror.

He used to lie in bed at night when he was a little boy and pretend he was seeing patients. His drawn-up knees were his desk and he'd look across his desk and ask, kindly, "What seems to be the trouble, Mrs. Brown?" At one point he had figured he might be an orthopedist, because bonesetting was so immediate. Like furniture repair, he had thought. He had imagined that the bone would make a clicking sound as it returned to its rightful place, and the patient's pain would vanish utterly in that very instant.

"Hoosegow," Maggie said.

"Pardon?"

She scooped up her belongings and poured them back in her purse. She set the purse on the floor at her feet. "The cutoff to Cartwheel," she told him. "Wasn't it something like Hoosegow?"

"I wouldn't have the faintest idea."

"Moose Cow. Moose Lump."

"I'm not going there, whatever it's called," Ira told her.

"Goose Bump."

"I would just like to remind you," he said, "about those other visits. Remember how they turned out? Leroy's second birthday, when you phoned ahead to arrange things, *telephoned,* and still Fiona somehow forgot you were coming. They went off to Hershey Park and we had to wait on the doorstep forever and finally turn around and come home."

Carrying Leroy's gift, he didn't say: a gigantic, blankly smiling Raggedy Ann that broke his heart.

"And her third birthday, when you brought her that kitten unannounced even though I warned you to check with Fiona beforehand, and Leroy started sneezing and Fiona said she couldn't keep it. Leroy cried all afternoon, remember? When we left, she was still crying."

"She could have taken shots for that," Maggie said, stubbornly missing the point. "Lots of children take allergy shots and they have whole housefuls of pets."

"Yes, but Fiona didn't want her to. She didn't want us interfering, and she really didn't want us visiting, either, which is why I said we shouldn't go there anymore."

Maggie cut her eyes over at him in a quick, surmising way. Probably she was wondering if he knew about those other trips, the ones she had made on her own. But if she had cared about keeping them secret you'd think she would have filled the gas tank afterward.

"What I'm saying is—" he said.

"I know what you're saying!" she cried. "You don't have to keep hammering at it!"

He drove in silence for a while. A row of dotted lines stitched down the highway ahead of him. Dozens of tiny birds billowed up from a grove of trees and turned the blue sky cindery, and he watched them till they disappeared.

"My Grandma Daley used to have a picture in her parlor," Maggie said. "A little scene carved in something yellowish like ivory, or more likely celluloid. It showed this old couple sitting by the fireplace in their rocking chairs, and the title was etched across the bottom of the frame: 'Old Folks at Home.' The woman was knitting and the man was reading an enormous book that you just knew was the Bible. And you knew there must be grown children away someplace; I mean that was the whole idea, that the old folks were left at home while the children went away. But they were so *extremely* old! They had those withered-apple faces and potato-sack bodies; they were people you would classify in an instant and dismiss. I never imagined that I would be an Old Folk at Home."

"You're plotting to have that child come live with us," Ira said. It hit him with a thump, as clearly as if she had spoken the words. "That's what you've been leading to. Now that you're losing Daisy you're plotting for Leroy to come and fill her place."

"I have no such intention!" Maggie said—too quickly, it seemed to him.

"Don't think I don't see through you," he told her. "I suspected all along there was something fishy about this baby-sitting business. You're counting on Fiona to agree to it, now that she's all caught up with a brand-new husband."

"Well, that just shows how little you know, then, because I have no earthly intention of keeping Leroy for good. All I want to do is drop in on them this afternoon and make my offer, which might just incidentally cause Fiona to reconsider a bit about Jesse."

"Jesse?"

"Jesse our son, Ira."

"Yes, Maggie, I know Jesse's our son, but I can't imagine what you think she could reconsider. They're finished. She walked out on him. Her lawyer sent him those papers to sign and he signed them every one and sent them back."

"And has never, ever been the same since," Maggie said. "He or Fiona, either. But anytime he makes a move to reconcile, she is passing through a stage where she won't speak to him, and then when *she* makes a move he has slammed off somewhere with hurt feelings and doesn't know she's trying. It's like some awful kind of dance, some out-of-sync dance where every step's a mistake."

"Well? So?" Ira said. "I would think that ought to tell you something."

"Tell me what?"

"Tell you those two are a lost cause, Maggie."

"Oh, Ira, you just don't give enough credit to luck," Maggie said. "Good luck or bad luck, either one. Watch out for that car in front of you."

She meant the red Chevy—an outdated model, big as a barge, its finish worn down to the color of a dull red rubber eraser. Ira was already watching it. He didn't like the way it kept drifting from side to side and changing speeds.

"Honk," Maggie instructed him.

Ira said, "Oh, I'll just—"

He would just get past the fellow, he was going to say. Some incompetent idiot; best to put such people far behind you. He pressed the accelerator and checked the rearview mirror, but at the same time Maggie reached over to jab his horn. The long, insistent blare startled him. He seized Maggie's hand and returned it firmly to her lap. Only then did he realize that the Chevy driver, no doubt equally startled, had slowed sharply just feet ahead. Maggie made a grab for the dashboard. Ira had no choice; he swerved right and plowed off the side of the road.

Dust rose around them like smoke. The Chevy picked up speed and rounded a curve and vanished.

"Jesus," Ira said.

Somehow their car had come to a stop, although he couldn't recall braking. In fact, the engine had died. Ira was still gripping the wheel, and the keys were still swinging from the ignition, softly jingling against each other.

"You just had to butt in, Maggie, didn't you," he said.

"Me? You're blaming this on me? What did I do?"

"Oh, nothing. Only honked the horn when I was the one driving.

Only scared that fellow so he lost what last few wits he had. Just once in your life, Maggie, I wish you would manage not to stick your nose in what doesn't concern you."

"And if I didn't, who would?" she asked him. "And how can you say it doesn't concern me when here I sit in what's known far and wide as the death seat? And also, it wasn't my honking that caused the trouble; it was that crazy driver, slowing down for no apparent reason."

Ira sighed. "Anyway," he said. "Are you all right?"

"I could just strangle him!" she said.

He supposed that meant she was fine.

He restarted the engine. It coughed a couple of times and then took hold. He checked for traffic and pulled out onto the highway again. After the gravelly roadside, the pavement felt too frictionless, too easy. He noticed how his hands were shaking on the steering wheel.

"That man was a maniac," Maggie said.

"Good thing we had our seat belts fastened."

"We ought to report him."

"Oh, well. So long as no one was hurt."

"Go faster, will you, Ira?"

He glanced over at her.

"I want to get his license number," she said. Her tangled curls gave her the look of a wild woman.

Ira said, "Now, Maggie. When you think about it, it was really as much our doing as his."

"How can you say that? When he was driving by fits and starts and wandering every which way; have you forgotten?"

Where did she find the energy? he wondered. How come she had so much to expend? He was hot and his left shoulder ached where he'd slammed against his seat belt. He shifted position, relieving the pressure of the belt across his chest.

"You don't want him causing a serious accident, do you?" Maggie asked.

"Well, no."

"Probably he's been drinking. Remember that public-service message on TV? We have a civic duty to report him. Speed up, Ira."

He obeyed, mostly out of exhaustion.

They passed an electrician's van that had passed them earlier and then, as they crested a hill, they caught sight of the Chevy just ahead. It was whipping right along as if nothing had happened. Ira was surprised by a flash of anger. Damn fool driver. And who said it had to be a man? More likely a woman, strewing chaos everywhere without a thought. He pressed harder on the accelerator. Maggie said, "Good," and rolled down her window.

"What are you doing?" he asked.

"Go faster."

"What did you open your window for?"

"Hurry, Ira! We're losing him."

"Be funny if we got a ticket for this," Ira said.

But he let the speedometer inch up to sixty-five, to sixty-eight. They drew close behind the Chevy. Its rear window was so dusty that Ira had trouble seeing inside. All he could tell was that the driver wore a hat of some kind and sat very low in the seat. There didn't seem to be any passengers. The license plate was dusty too—a Pennsylvania plate, navy and yellow, the yellow mottled with gray as if mildewed.

"Y two eight—" Ira read out.

"Yes, yes, I have it," Maggie said. (She was the type who could still reel off her childhood telephone number.) "Now let's pass him," she told Ira.

"Oh, well . . ."

"You see what kind of driver he is. I think we ought to pass."

Well, that made sense. Ira veered left.

Just as they came alongside the Chevy, Maggie leaned out her window and pointed downward with her index finger. "Your wheel!" she shouted. "Your wheel! Your front wheel is falling off!"

"Good grief," Ira said.

He checked the mirror. Sure enough, the Chevy had slowed and was moving toward the shoulder.

"Well, he believed you," he said.

He had to admit it was sort of a satisfaction.

Maggie twisted around in her seat, gazing out the rear window. Then she turned to Ira. There was a stricken look on her face that he couldn't account for. "Oh, Ira," she said.

"Now what."

"He was old, Ira."

Ira said, "These goddamn senior-citizen drivers . . ."

"Not only was he old," she said. "He was black."

"So?"

"I didn't see him clearly till I'd said that about the wheel," she said. "He didn't mean to run us off the road! I bet he doesn't even know it happened. He had this wrinkled, dignified face and when I told him about the wheel his mouth dropped open but still he remembered to touch the brim of his hat. His hat! His gray felt hat like my grandfather wore!"

Ira groaned.

Maggie said, "Now he thinks we played a trick on him. He thinks we're racist or something and lied about his wheel to be cruel."

"He doesn't think any such thing," Ira said. "As a matter of fact, he has no way of knowing his wheel *isn't* falling off. How would he check it? He'd have to watch it in motion."

"You mean he's still sitting there?"

"No, no," Ira said hastily. "I mean he's probably back on the road by now but he's traveling a little slower, just to make sure it's all right."

"*I* wouldn't do that," Maggie said.

"Well, you're not him."

"He wouldn't do that, either. He's old and confused and alone and he's sitting there in his car, too scared to drive another inch."

"Oh, Lord," Ira said.

"We have to go back and tell him."

Somehow, he'd known that was coming.

"We won't say we deliberately lied," Maggie said. "We'll tell him we just weren't sure. We'll ask him to make a test drive while we watch, and then we'll say, 'Oops! Our mistake. Your wheel is fine; we must have misjudged.' "

"Where'd you get this 'we' business?" Ira asked. "I never told him it was loose in the first place."

"Ira, I'm begging you on bended knee, please turn around and go rescue that man."

"It is now one-thirty in the afternoon," Ira said. "With luck we could be home by three. Maybe even two-thirty. I could open the shop for a couple of hours, which may not be much but it's better than nothing."

"That poor old man is sitting in his car staring straight in front of him not knowing what to do," Maggie said. "He's still hanging on to the steering wheel. I can see him as plain as day."

So could Ira.

He slowed as they came to a large, prosperous-looking farm. A grassy lane led toward the barn, and he veered onto that without signaling first, in order to make the turn seem more sudden and more exasperated. Maggie's sunglasses scooted the length of the dashboard. Ira backed up, waited for a stream of traffic that all at once materialized, and then spun out onto Route One again, this time heading north.

Maggie said, "I knew you couldn't be heartless."

"Just imagine," Ira told her. "All up and down this highway, other couples are taking weekend drives together. They're traveling from Point A to Point B. They're holding civilized discussions about, I don't know, current events. Disarmament. Apartheid."

"He probably thinks we belong to the Ku Klux Klan," Maggie said. She started chewing her lip the way she always did when she was worried.

"No stops, no detours," Ira said. "If they take any break at all, it's for lunch in some classy old inn. Someplace they researched ahead of time, where they even made reservations."

He was starving, come to think of it. He hadn't eaten a thing at Serena's.

"It was right about here," Maggie said, perking up. "I recognize those silos. It was just before those mesh-looking silos. There he is."

Yes, there he was, not sitting in his car after all but walking around it in a wavery circle—a stoop-shouldered man the color of a rolltop desk, wearing one of those elderly suits than seem longer in front than in back. He was studying the tires of the Chevy, which might have been abandoned years ago; it had a settled, resigned appearance. Ira signaled and made a U-turn, arriving neatly behind so the two cars' bumpers almost touched. He opened the door and stepped out. "Can we help?" he called.

Maggie got out too but seemed willing for once to let Ira do the talking.

"It's my wheel," the old man said. "Lady back up the road a ways pointed out my wheel was falling off."

"That was us," Ira told him. "Or my wife, at least. But you know, I believe she might have been wrong. That wheel seems fine to me."

The old man looked at him directly now. He had a skull-like, deeply lined face, and the whites of his eyes were so yellow they were almost brown. "Oh, well, surely, *seems* fine," he said. "When the car is setting stark still like it is."

"But I mean even before," Ira told him. "Back when you were still on the road."

The old man appeared unconvinced. He prodded the tire with the toe of his shoe. "Anyhow," he said. "Mighty nice of you folks to stop."

Maggie said, "Nice! It's the least we could do." She stepped forward. "I'm Maggie Moran," she said. "This is my husband, Ira."

"My name's Mr. Daniel Otis," the old man said, touching the brim of his hat.

"Mr. Otis, see, I had this sort of, like, mirage as we were driving past your car," Maggie said. "I thought I noticed your wheel wobbling. But then the very next instant I said, 'No, I believe I imagined it.' Didn't I, Ira? Just ask Ira. 'I believe I made that driver stop for no good reason,' I told him."

"They's all kindly explanations why you might have seen it wobble," Mr. Otis said.

"Why, certainly!" Maggie cried. "Heat waves, maybe, rippling above the pavement. Or maybe, I don't know—"

"Might have been a sign, too," Mr. Otis said.

"Sign?"

"Might have been the Lord was trying to warn me."

"Warn you about what?"

"Warn me my left front wheel was fixing to drop off."

Maggie said, "Well, but—"

"Mr. Otis," Ira said. "I think it's more likely my wife just made a mistake."

"Now, you can't know that."

"An understandable mistake," Ira said, "but all the same, a mistake. So what we ought to do is, you get into your car and drive it just a few yards down the shoulder. Maggie and I will watch. If your wheel's not loose, you're free and clear. If it is, we'll take you to a service station."

"Oh, why, I appreciate that," Mr. Otis said. "Maybe Buford, if it ain't too much trouble."

"Pardon?"

"Buford Texaco. It's up ahead a piece; my nephew works there."

"Sure, anywhere," Ira said, "but I'm willing to bet—"

"In fact, if it ain't too much trouble you might just go on and carry me there right now," Mr. Otis said.

"Now?"

"I don't relish driving a car with a wheel about to drop off."

"Mr. Otis," Ira said. "We'll test the wheel. That's what I've been telling you."

"I'll test it," Maggie said.

"Yes, Maggie will test it. Maggie? Honey, maybe I should be the one."

"Shoot, yes; it's way too risky for a lady," Mr. Otis told her.

Ira had been thinking of the risk to the Chevy, but he said, "Right. You and Mr. Otis watch; I'll drive."

"No, sir, I can't allow you to do that," Mr. Otis said. "I appreciate it, but I can't allow it. Too much danger. You folks just carry me to the Texaco, please, and my nephew will come fetch the car with the tow truck."

Ira looked at Maggie. Maggie looked back at him helplessly. The sounds of traffic whizzing past reminded him of those TV thrillers where spies rendezvoused in modern wastelands, on the edges of superhighways or roaring industrial complexes.

"Listen," Ira said. "I'll just come right out with this—"

"Or don't carry me! Don't," Mr. Otis cried. "I already inconvenienced you-all enough, I know that."

"The fact is, we feel responsible," Ira told him. "What we said about your wheel wasn't so much a mistake as a plain and simple, um, exaggeration."

"Yes, we made it up," Maggie said.

"Aw, no," Mr. Otis said, shaking his head, "you just trying to stop me from worrying."

"A while back you kind of, like, more or less, slowed down too suddenly in front of us," Maggie said, "and caused us to run off the road. Not intending to, I realize, but—"

"I did that?"

"Not intending to," Maggie assured him.

"And besides," Ira said, "you probably slowed because we accidentally honked. So it's not as if—"

"Oh, I declare. Florence, that's my niece, she is all the time after me to turn in my driver's license, but I surely never expected—"

"Anyhow, I did a very inconsiderate thing," Maggie told him. "I said your wheel was falling off when really it was fine."

"Why, I call that a very *Christian* thing," Mr. Otis said. "When I had caused you to run off the road! You folks been awful nice about this."

"No, see, really the wheel was—"

"Many would've let me ride on to my death," Mr. Otis said.

"The wheel was fine!" Maggie told him. "It wasn't wobbling in the slightest."

Mr. Otis tipped his head back and studied her. His lowered eyelids gave him such a haughty, hooded expression that it seemed he might finally have grasped her meaning. But then he said, "Naw, that can't be right. Can it? Naw. I tell you: Now that I recollect, that car was driving funny all this morning. I knew it and yet *didn't* know it, you know? And I reckon it must've hit you-all the same way—kindly like you half glimpsed it out of the corner of your vision so you were moved to say what you did, not understanding just why."

That settled it; Ira took action. "Well, then," he said, "nothing to do but test it. Keys inside?" And he strode briskly to the Chevy and opened the door and slid in.

"Aw, now!" Mr. Otis cried. "Don't you go risking your neck for *me*, mister!"

"He'll be all right," Maggie told him.

Ira gave Mr. Otis a reassuring wave.

Even though the window was open, the Chevy was pulsing with heat. The clear plastic seat cover seemed to have partially melted, and there was a strong smell of overripe banana. No wonder: The remains of a bag lunch sat on the passenger seat—a crumpled sack, a banana peel, and a screw of cellophane.

Ira turned the key in the ignition. When the engine roared up he leaned out toward Maggie and Mr. Otis and said, "Watch carefully."

They said nothing. For two people who looked so little alike, they wore oddly similar expressions: wary and guarded, as if braced for the worst.

Ira put the car in gear and started rolling along the shoulder. He felt he was driving something that stood out too far on all sides—a double bed, for instance. Also, there was a rattle in the exhaust system.

After a few yards, he braked and cocked his head out the window. The others had not moved from where they stood; they'd merely turned their faces in his direction.

"Well?" he called.

There was a pause. Then Mr. Otis said, "Yessir, seem like I did see a bit of a jiggling motion to it."

"You did?" Ira asked.

He quirked an eyebrow at Maggie.

"But you didn't," he said.

"Well, I'm not certain," Maggie told him.

"Excuse me?"

"Maybe I just imagined it," she said, "but I thought there was a little, sort of, I don't know . . ."

Ira shifted gears and backed up with a jolt. When he was alongside them once more he said, "Now I want you both to watch very, very closely."

He drove farther this time, a dozen yards or so. They were forced to follow him. He glanced in the side-view mirror and saw Maggie scurrying along with her arms folded beneath her bosom. He stopped the car and climbed out to face them.

"Oh, that wheel is loose, all right," Mr. Otis called as he arrived.

Ira said, "Maggie?"

"It reminded me of a top, just before it stops spinning and falls over," Maggie said.

"Now listen here, Maggie—"

"I know! I know!" she said. "But I can't help it, Ira; I really saw it wobble. And also it looked kind of squashy."

"Well, that's a whole different problem," Ira said. "The tire may be underinflated. But that wheel is on tight as a drum, I swear it. I could feel it. I can't believe you're doing this, Maggie."

"Well, I'm sorry," she said stubbornly, "but I refuse to say I didn't see what I saw with my own two eyes. I just think we're going to have to take him to that Texaco."

Ira looked at Mr. Otis. "You got a lug wrench?" he asked.

"A . . . sir?"

"If you've got a lug wrench, I could tighten that wheel myself."

"Oh, why . . . Is a lug wrench like a ordinary wrench?"

"You probably have one in your trunk," Ira told him, "where you keep your jack."

"Oh! But where do I keep my jack, I wonder," Mr. Otis said.

"In your trunk," Ira repeated doggedly, and he reached inside the car for the keys and handed them over. He was keeping his face as impassive as possible, but inwardly he felt the way he felt anytime he stopped by Maggie's nursing home: utterly despairing. He couldn't see how this Mr. Otis fellow made it from day to day, bumbling along as he did.

"Lug wrench, lug wrench," Mr. Otis was murmuring. He unlocked the trunk and flung the lid up. "Now let me just . . ."

At first glance, the trunk's interior seemed a solid block of fabric. Blankets, clothes, and pillows had been packed inside so tightly that they had congealed together. "Oh, me," Mr. Otis said, and he plucked at a corner of a graying quilt, which didn't budge.

"Never mind," Ira told him. "I'll get mine."

He walked back to the Dodge. It suddenly seemed very well kept, if you overlooked what Maggie had done to the left front fender. He took his keys from the ignition and unlocked the trunk and opened it.

Nothing.

Where once there'd been a spare tire, tucked into the well beneath the floor mat, now there was an empty space. And not a sign of the gray vinyl pouch in which he kept his tools.

He called, "Maggie?"

She turned lazily from her position by the Chevy and tilted her head in his direction.

"What happened to my spare tire?" he asked.

"It's on the car."

"*On* the car?"

She nodded vigorously.

"You mean it's in use?"

"Right."

"Then where's the original tire?"

"It's getting patched at the Exxon back home."

"Well, how did . . .?"

No, never mind; better not get sidetracked. "So where are the tools, then?" he called.

"What tools?"

He slammed the lid down and walked back to the Chevy. There was no point shouting; he could see his lug wrench was not going to be anywhere within reach. "The tools you changed the tire with," he told her.

"Oh, I didn't change the tire. A man stopped and helped me."

"Did he use the tools in the trunk?"

"I guess so, yes."

"Did he put them back?"

"Well, he must have," Maggie said. She frowned, evidently trying to recall.

"They're not there, Maggie."

"Well, I'm sure he didn't steal them, if that's what you're thinking. He was a very nice man. He wouldn't even accept any money; he said he had a wife of his own and—"

"I'm not saying he stole them; I'm just asking where they are."

Maggie said, "Maybe on the . . ." and then mumbled something further, he wasn't sure what.

"Pardon?"

"I said, maybe on the corner of Charles Street and Northern Parkway!" she shouted.

Ira turned to Mr. Otis. The old man was watching him with his eyes half closed; he appeared to be falling asleep on his feet.

"I guess we'll have to unpack your trunk," Ira told him.

Mr. Otis nodded several times but made no move to begin.

"Shall we just unload it?" Ira asked.

"Well, we could do that," Mr. Otis said doubtfully.

There was a pause.

Ira said, "Well? Shall we start?"

"We could start if you like," Mr. Otis told him, "but I'd be very much surprised if we was to find a wheel wrench."

"Everybody has a wheel wrench. Lug wrench," Ira said. "It comes with the car."

"I never saw it."

"Oh, Ira," Maggie said. "Can't we just drive him to the Texaco and get his nephew to fix it properly?"

"And how do you think he would do that, Maggie? He'd take a wrench and tighten the lug nuts, not that they need it."

Mr. Otis, meanwhile, had managed to remove a single item from the trunk: a pair of flannel pajama bottoms. He held them up and considered them.

Maybe it was the dubious expression on his face, or maybe it was the pajamas themselves—crinkled and withered, trailing a frazzled drawstring—but at any rate, Ira all at once gave in. "Oh, what the hell," he said. "Let's just go to the Texaco."

"Thank you, Ira," Maggie told him sweetly.

And Mr. Otis said, "Well, if you sure it ain't too much trouble."

"No, no . . ." Ira passed a hand across his forehead. "So I guess we'd better lock up the Chevy," he said.

Maggie said, "What Chevy?"

"That's what kind of car this is, Maggie."

"Ain't hardly no point locking it with a wheel about to fly off," Mr. Otis said.

Ira had a brief moment when he wondered if this whole situation might be Mr. Otis's particularly passive, devilish way of getting even.

He turned and walked back to his own car. Behind him he heard the Chevy's trunk lid clanging shut and the sound of their feet on the gravel, but he didn't wait for them to catch up.

Now the Dodge was as hot as the Chevy, and the chrome shaft of the gearshift burned his fingers. He sat there with the motor idling while Maggie helped Mr. Otis settle in the back seat. She seemed to know by instinct that he would require assistance; he had to be folded across the middle in some complicated fashion. The last of him to enter was his feet, which he gathered to him by lifting both knees with his hands. Then he let out a sigh and took his hat off. In the mirror Ira saw a bony, plated-looking scalp, with two cottony puffs of white hair snarling above his ears.

"I surely do appreciate this," Mr. Otis said.

"Oh, no trouble!" Maggie told him, flouncing onto the front seat.

Speak for yourself, Ira thought sourly.

He waited for a cavalcade of motorcyclists to pass (all male, un-helmeted, swooping by in long S-curves, as free as birds), and then he pulled onto the highway. "So whereabouts are we headed?" he asked.

"Oh, why, you just drive on past the dairy farm and make a right," Mr. Otis told him. "It ain't but three, four miles."

Maggie craned around in her seat and said, "You must live in this area."

"Back-air a ways on Dead Crow Road," Mr. Otis told her. "Or used to, till last week. Lately I been staying with my sister Lurene."

Then he started telling her about his sister Lurene, who worked off and on at the K Mart when her arthritis wasn't too bad; and that of course led to a discussion of Mr. Otis's own arthritis, the sneaky slow manner it had crept up on him and the other things he had thought it was first and how the doctor had marveled and made over his condition when Mr. Otis finally thought to consult him.

"Oh, if you had seen what I have seen," Maggie said. "People in the nursing home where I work just knotted over; don't I know it." She had a tendency to fall into other people's rhythms of speech while she was talking to them. Close your eyes and you could almost fancy she was black herself, Ira thought.

"It's a evil, mean-spirited ailment; no two ways about it," Mr. Otis said. "This here is the dairy farm, mister. You want to take your next right."

Ira slowed down. They passed a small clump of cows moonily chomping and staring, and then they turned onto a road not two full lanes wide. The pavement was patchy, with hand-painted signs tilting off the grassy embankment: DANGER LIVESTOCK MAY BE LOOSE and SLOW THIS MEANS YOU and HOUNDS AND HORSES CROSSING.

Now Mr. Otis was explaining how arthritis had forced him to retire. He used to be a roofer, he said, down home in North Carolina. He used to walk those ridgepoles as nimble as a squirrel and now he couldn't manage the lowest rung of a ladder.

Maggie made a clucking sound.

Ira wondered why Maggie always had to be inviting other people into their lives. She didn't feel a mere husband was enough, he suspected. Two was not a satisfactory number for her. He remembered all the strays she had welcomed over the years—her brother who spent a winter on their couch when his wife fell in love with her dentist, and Serena that time that Max was in Virginia hunting work, and of course Fiona with her baby and her mountains of baby equipment, her stroller and her playpen and her wind-up infant swing. In his present mood, Ira thought he might include their own children as well, for weren't Jesse and Daisy also outsiders—interrupting their most private moments, wedging between the two of them? (Hard to believe that some people had children to hold a marriage *together*.) And neither one had been planned for, at least not quite so soon. In the days before Jesse was born, Ira had still had hopes of going back to school. It was supposed to be the next thing in line, after paying off his sister's medical bills and his father's new furnace. Maggie would keep on working full time. But then she found out she was pregnant, and she had to take leave from her job. And after that Ira's sister developed a whole new symptom, some kind of seizures that required hospitalization; and a moving van crashed into the shop one Christmas Eve and damaged the building. Then Maggie got pregnant with Daisy, another surprise. (Had it been unwise, perhaps, to leave matters of contraception to someone so accident-prone?) But that was eight years after Jesse, and Ira had more or less abandoned his plans by then anyhow.

Sometimes—on a day like today, say, this long, hot day in this dusty car—he experienced the most crushing kind of tiredness. It was an actual weight on his head, as if the ceiling had been lowered. But he supposed that everybody felt that way, now and again.

Maggie was telling Mr. Otis the purpose of their trip. "My oldest, closest friend just lost her husband," she was saying, "and we had to go to his funeral. It was the saddest occasion."

"Oh, gracious. Well, now, I want to offer my sincere condolences," Mr. Otis said.

Ira slowed behind a round-shouldered, humble-looking car from the forties, driven by an old lady so hunched that her head was barely visible above the steering wheel. Route One, the nursing home of highways. Then he remembered that this wasn't Route One anymore, that they had drifted sideward or maybe even backward, and he had a dreamy, floating sensation. It was like that old spell during a change of seasons when you momentarily forget what stage the year is going through. Is it spring, or is it fall? Is the summer just beginning, or is it coming to an end?

They passed a modern, split-level house with two plaster statues in the yard: a Dutch boy and girl bobbing delicately toward each other so their lips were almost touching. Then a trailer park and assorted signs for churches, civic organizations, Al's Lawn and Patio Furnishings.

Mr. Otis sat forward with a grunt, clutching the back of the seat. "Right up-air is the Texaco," he said. "See it?"

Ira saw it: a small white rectangle set very close to the road. Mylar balloons hovered high above the pumps—three to each pump, red, silver, and blue, twining lazily about one another.

He turned onto the concrete apron, carefully avoiding the signal cord that stretched across it, and braked and looked back at Mr. Otis. But Mr. Otis stayed where he was; it was Maggie who got out. She opened the rear door and set a hand beneath the old man's elbow while he uncurled himself. "Now, just where is your nephew?" she asked.

Mr. Otis said, *"Somewheres* about."

"Are you sure of that? What if he's not working today?"

"Why, he must be working. Ain't he?"

Oh, Lord, they were going to prolong this situation forever. Ira cut the engine and watched the two of them walking across the apron.

Over by the full-service island, a white boy with a stringy brown ponytail listened to what they asked and then shook his head. He said something, waving an arm vaguely eastward. Ira groaned and slid down lower in his seat.

Then here came Maggie, clicking along, and Ira took heart; but when she reached the car all she did was lean in through the passenger window. "We have to wait a minute," she told him.

"What for?"

"His nephew's out on a call but he's expected back in no time."

"Then why can't we just leave?" Ira asked.

"I couldn't do that! I wouldn't rest easy. I wouldn't know how it came out."

"What do you mean, how it came out? His wheel is perfectly fine, remember?"

"It wobbled, Ira. I saw it wobble."

He sighed.

"And maybe his nephew won't show up for some reason," she said, "so Mr. Otis will be stranded here. Or maybe it will cost money. I want to make sure he's not out any money."

"Look here, Maggie—"

"Why don't you fill the tank? Surely we could use some gas."

"We don't have a Texaco credit card," he told her.

"Pay cash. Fill the tank and by then I bet Lamont will be pulling into the station."

"Lamont," already. Next thing you knew, she'd have adopted the boy.

He restarted the engine, muttering, and drew up next to the self-serve island and got out. They had an older style of pump here that Baltimore no longer used—printed flip-over numerals instead of LED, and a simple pivot arrangement to trip the switch. Ira had to readjust, cast his mind back a couple of years in order to get the thing going. Then while the gas flowed into the tank he watched Maggie settle Mr. Otis on a low, whitewashed wall that separated the Texaco from someone's vegetable garden. Mr. Otis had his hat back on and he was hunkered under it like a cat under a table, peering forth reflectively, chewing on a mouthful of air, as old men were known to do. He was ancient, and yet probably not so many years older than Ira himself. It was a thought to give you pause. Ira heard the jolt as the gas cut off, and he turned back to the car. Overhead, the balloons rustled against each other with a sound that made him think of raincoats.

While he was paying inside the station he noticed a snack machine, so he walked over to the others to see if they wanted something. They were deep in conversation, Mr. Otis going on and on about someone named Duluth. "Maggie, they've got potato chips," Ira said. "The kind you like: barbecue."

Maggie waved a hand at him. "I think you were absolutely justified," she told Mr. Otis.

"And bacon rinds!" Ira said. "You hardly ever find bacon rinds these days."

She gave him a distant, abstracted look and said, "Have you forgotten I'm on a diet?"

"How about you, then, Mr. Otis?"

"Oh, why, no, thank you, sir; thank you kindly, sir," Mr. Otis said. He turned to Maggie and went on: "So anyways, I axes her, 'Duluth, how can you hold me to count for that, woman?' "

"Mr. Otis's wife is mad at him for something he did in her dream," Maggie told Ira.

Mr. Otis said, "Here I am just as unaware as a babe and I come down into the kitchen, I axes, 'Where my breakfast?' She say, 'Fix it yourself.' I say, 'Huh?' "

"That is just so unfair," Maggie told him.

Ira said, "Well, I believe I'll have a snack," and he walked back toward the station, hands stuffed into his pockets, feeling left out.

Dieting too, he thought; dieting was another example of Maggie's wastefulness. The water diet and the protein diet and the grapefruit diet. Depriving herself meal after meal when in Ira's opinion she was just exactly right as she was—not even what you'd call plump; just a satisfying series of handfuls, soft, silky breasts and a creamy swell of bottom. But since when had she ever listened to Ira? He dropped coins glumly into the snack machine and punched the key beneath a sack of pretzels.

When he got back, Maggie was saying, "I mean think if we all did that! Mistook our dreams for real life. Look at me: Two or three times a year, near-about, I dream this neighbor and I are kissing. This totally bland neighbor named Mr. Simmons who looks like a salesman of something, I don't know, insurance or real estate or something. In the daytime I don't give him a thought, but at night I dream we're kissing and I long for him to unbutton my blouse, and in the morning at the bus stop I'm so embarrassed I can't even meet his eyes but then I see he's just the same as ever, bland-faced man in a business suit."

"For God's sake, Maggie," Ira said. He tried to picture this Simmons character, but he had no idea who she could be talking about.

"I mean what if I was held to blame for that?" Maggie asked. "Some thirty-year-old . . . kid I don't have the faintest interest in! I'm not the one who designed that dream!"

"No, indeed," Mr. Otis said. "And anyways, this here of Duluth's was Duluth's dream. It weren't even me that dreamed it. She claim I was standing on her needlepoint chair, her chair seat she worked forever on, so she order me off but when I stepped down I was walking on her crocheted shawl and her embroidered petticoat, my shoes was dragging lace and ruffles and bits of ribbon. 'If that ain't just like you,' she tell me in the morning, and I say, 'What did I do? Show me what I did. Show me where I ever tromped on a one of them things.' She say, 'You are just a mowing-down type of man, Daniel Otis, and if I knew I'd have to put up with you so long I'd have made a more thoughtful selection when I married.' So I say, 'Well, if that's how you feel, I'm leaving,' and she say, 'Don't forget your things,' and off I go."

"Mr. Otis has been living in his car these last few days and moving around among relatives," Maggie told Ira.

"Is that right," Ira said.

"So it matters quite a heap to me that my wheel not pop off," Mr. Otis added.

Ira sighed and sat down on the wall next to Maggie. The pretzels were the varnished kind that stuck in his teeth, but he was so hungry that he went on eating them.

Now the ponytailed boy walked toward them, so direct and purposeful in his tap-heeled leather boots that Ira stood up again, imagining they had some business to discuss. But all the boy did was coil the air hose that had been hissing on the concrete all this time without their noticing. In order not to look indecisive, Ira went on over to him anyhow. "So!" he said. "What's the story on this Lamont?"

"He's out," the boy told him.

"No chance we could get you to come, I guess. Run you over to the highway in our car and get you to look at Mr. Otis here's wheel for us."

"Nope," the boy said, hanging the hose on its hook.

Ira said, "I see."

He returned to the wall, and the boy walked back to the station.

"I think it might be Moose Run," Maggie was telling Mr. Otis. "Is that the name? This cutoff that leads into Cartwheel."

"Now, I don't know about no Moose Run," Mr. Otis said, "but I have heard tell of Cartwheel. Just can't say right off exactly how you'd get there. See, they's so many places hereabouts that sound like towns, call theyselves towns, but really they ain't much more than a grocery store and a gas pump."

"That's Cartwheel, all right," Maggie said. "One main street. No traffic lights. Fiona lives on a skinny little road that doesn't even have a sidewalk. Fiona's our daughter-in-law. Ex-daughter-in-law, I suppose I should say. She used to be our son Jesse's wife, but now they're divorced."

"Yes, that is how they do nowadays," Mr. Otis said. "Lamont is divorced too, and my sister Florence' girl Sally. I don't know why they bother getting married."

Just as if his own marriage were in perfect health.

"Have a pretzel," Ira said. Mr. Otis shook his head absently but Maggie dug down deep in the bag and came up with half a dozen.

"Really it was all a misunderstanding," she told Mr. Otis. She bit into a pretzel. "They were perfect for each other. They even looked perfect: Jesse so dark and Fiona so blond. It's just that Jesse was working musician's hours and his life was sort of, I don't know, unsteady. And Fiona was so young, and inclined to fly off the handle. Oh, I used to just ache for them. It broke Jesse's heart when she left him; she took their little daughter and went back home to her mother. And Fiona's heart was broken too, I know, but do you think she would say so? And now they're so neatly divorced you would think they had never been married."

All true, as far as it went, Ira reflected; but there was a lot she'd left out. Or not left out so much as slicked over, somehow, like that image of their son—the "musician" plying his trade so busily that he was forced to neglect his "wife" and his "daughter." Ira had never thought of Jesse as a musician; he'd thought of him as a high-school dropout in need of permanent employment. And he had never thought of Fiona as a wife but rather as Jesse's teenaged sidekick—her veil of gleaming blond hair incongruous above a skimpy T-shirt and tight jeans—while poor little Leroy had not been much more than their pet, their stuffed animal won at a carnival booth.

He had a vivid memory of Jesse as he'd looked the night he was arrested, back when he was sixteen. He'd been picked up for public drunkenness with several of his friends—a onetime occurrence, as it turned out, but Ira had wanted to make sure of that and so, intending to be hard on him, he had insisted Maggie stay home while he went down alone to post bail. He had sat on a bench in a public waiting area and finally there came Jesse, walking doubled over between two officers. Evidently his wrists had been handcuffed behind his back and he had attempted, at some point, to step through the circle of his own arms so as to bring his hands in front of him. But he had given up or been interrupted halfway through the maneuver, and so he hobbled out lopsided, twisted like a sideshow freak with his wrists trapped between his legs. Ira had experienced the most complicated mingling of emotions at the sight: anger at his son and anger at the authorities too, for exhibiting Jesse's humiliation, and a wild impulse to laugh and an aching, flooding sense of pity. Jesse's jacket sleeves had been pushed up his forearms in the modern style (something boys never did in Ira's day) and that had made him seem even more vulnerable, and so had his expression, once he was unlocked and could stand upright, although it was a fiercely defiant expression and he wouldn't acknowledge Ira's presence. Now when Ira thought of Jesse he always pictured him as he'd been that night, that same combination of infuriating and pathetic. He wondered how Maggie pictured him. Maybe she delved even farther into the past. Maybe she saw him at age four or age six, a handsome, uncommonly engaging little kid with no more than the average kid's problems. At any rate, she surely didn't view him as he really was.

No, nor their daughter, either, he thought. Maggie saw Daisy as a version of Maggie's mother—accomplished, efficient—and she fluttered around her, looking inadequate. She had fluttered ever since Daisy was a little girl with an uncannily well-ordered room and a sheaf of color-coded notebooks for her homework. But Daisy was pitiable too, in her way. Ira saw that clearly, even though she was the one he felt closer to. She seemed to be missing out on her own youth—had never even had a boyfriend, so far as Ira could tell. Whenever Jesse got into mischief as a child Daisy had taken on a pinch-faced expression of disapproval, but Ira would almost rather she had joined in the mischief herself. Wasn't that how it was supposed to work? Wasn't that how it worked in other families, those jolly, noisy families Ira used to watch wistfully when he was a little boy? Now she was packed for college— had been packed for weeks—and had no clothes left but the throwaways that she wasn't taking with her; and she walked around the house looking bleak and joyless as a nun in her limp, frayed blouses and faded skirts. But Maggie thought she was admirable. "When I was her age I hadn't even begun to decide what I wanted to be," she said. Daisy wanted to be a quantum physicist. "I'm just so impressed with that," Maggie said, till Ira said, "Maggie, just what is a quantum physicist?"—honestly wanting to know. "Do you have the foggiest inkling?" he asked. Then Maggie thought he was belittling her and she said, "Oh, I admit I'm not scientific! I never said I was scientific! I'm just a geriatric nursing assistant, I admit it!" and Ira said, "All I meant was—Jesus! All I meant was—" and Daisy poked her head in the door and said, "Would you please, please not have another one of your blowups; I'm trying to read."

"Blowup!" Maggie cried. "I make the simplest little remark—"

And Ira told Daisy, "Listen here, miss, if you're so easily disturbed as all that, you can just go read in the library."

So Daisy had withdrawn, pinch-faced once again, and Maggie had buried her head in her hands.

"Same old song and dance"—that was how Jesse had once referred to marriage. This was one morning when Fiona had left the breakfast table in tears, and Ira had asked Jesse what was wrong. "You know how it is," Jesse had answered. "Same old song and dance as always." Then Ira (who had asked not out of empty curiosity but as a means of implying *This matters, son; pay her some heed*) had wondered what that "you know" signified. Was Jesse saying that Ira's marriage and his own had anything in common? Because if so, he was way out of line. They were two entirely different institutions. Ira's marriage was as steady as a tree; not even he could tell how wide and deep the roots went.

Still, Jesse's phrase had stuck in his memory: same old song and dance. Same old arguments, same recriminations. The same jokes and affectionate passwords, yes, and abiding loyalty and gestures of support and consolations no one else knew how to offer; but also the same old resentments dragged up year after year, with nothing ever totally forgotten: the time Ira didn't act happy to hear Maggie was pregnant, the time Maggie failed to defend Ira in front of her mother, the time Ira refused to visit Maggie in the hospital, the time Maggie forgot to invite Ira's family to Christmas dinner.

And the unvaryingness—ah, Lord; who could blame Jesse for chafing against that? Probably the boy had been watching his parents sideways all the years of his childhood, swearing *he* would never put up with such a life: plugging along day after day, Ira heading to his shop every morning, Maggie to the nursing home. Probably those afternoons that Jesse had spent helping out at the shop had been a kind of object lesson. He must have recoiled from it—Ira sitting endlessly on his high wooden stool, whistling along with his easy-listening radio station as he measured a mat or sawed away at his miter box. Women came in asking him to frame their cross-stitched homilies and their amateur seascapes and their wedding photos (two serious people in profile gazing solely at each other). They brought in illustrations torn from magazines—a litter of puppies or a duckling in a basket. Like a tailor measuring a half-dressed client, Ira remained discreetly sightless, appearing to form no judgment about a picture of a sad-faced kitten tangled in a ball of yarn. "He wants a pastel-colored mat of some kind, wouldn't you say?" the women might ask. (They often used personal pronouns, as if the pictures were animate.)

"Yes, ma'am," Ira would answer.

"Maybe a pale blue that would pick up the blue of his ribbon."

"Yes, we could do that."

And through Jesse's eyes he would see himself all at once as a generic figure called The Shopkeeper: a drab and obsequious man of indeterminate age.

Above the shop he could usually hear the creak, pause, creak of his father's rocking chair, and the hesitant footsteps of one of his sisters crossing the living room floor. Their voices, of course, weren't audible, and for this reason Ira had fallen into the habit of imagining that his family never spoke during the day—that they were keeping very still till Ira came. He was the backbone of their lives; he knew that. They depended on him utterly.

In his childhood he had been extraneous—a kind of afterthought, half a generation younger than his sisters. He had been so much the baby that he'd called every family member "honey," because that was how all those grownups or almost-grownups addressed him and he'd assumed it was a universal term. "I need my shoes tied, honey," he would tell his father. He didn't have the usual baby's privileges, though; he was never the center of attention. If any of them could be said to occupy that position it was his sister Dorrie—mentally handicapped, frail and jerky, bucktoothed, awkward—although even Dorrie had a neglected air and tended to sit by herself on the outskirts of a room. Their mother suffered from a progressive disease that killed her when Ira was fourteen, that left him forever afterward edgy and frightened in the presence of illness; and anyhow she had never shown much of a talent for mothering. She devoted herself instead to religion, to radio evangelists and inspirational pamphlets left by door-to-door missionaries. Her idea of a meal was saltines and tea, for all of them. She never got hungry like ordinary mortals or realized that others could be hungry, but simply took in sustenance when the clock reminded her. If they wanted real food it was up to their father, for Dorrie was not capable of anything complicated and Junie was subject to some kind of phobia that worsened over the years till she refused to leave the house for so much as a quart of milk. Their father had to see to that when he was finished down at the shop. He would trudge upstairs for the grocery list, trudge out again, return with a few tin cans, and putter around the kitchen with the girls. Even after Ira was old enough, his assistance was not required. He was the interloper, the one rude splash of color in a sepia photograph. His family gave him a wide berth while addressing him remotely and kindly. "You finish your homework, honey?" they would ask, and they asked this even in the summer and over the Christmas holidays.

Then Ira graduated—had already paid his deposit at the University of Maryland, with dreams of going on to medical school—and his father suddenly abdicated. He just . . . imploded, was how Ira saw it. Declared he had a weak heart and could not continue. Sat down in his platform rocker and stayed there. Ira took over the business, which wasn't easy because he'd never played the smallest part in it up till then. All at once he was the one his family turned to. They relied on him for money and errands and advice, for transportation to the doctor and news of the outside world. It was, "Honey, is this dress out of style?" and, "Honey, can we afford a new rug?" In a way, Ira felt gratified, especially at the beginning, when this seemed to be just a temporary, summer-vacation state of affairs. He was no longer on the sidelines; he was central. He rooted through Dorrie's bureau drawers for the mate to her favorite red sock; he barbered Junie's graying hair; he dumped the month's receipts into his father's lap, all in the knowledge that he, Ira, was the only one they could turn to.

But summer stretched into fall, and first the university granted him a semester's postponement and then a year's postponement, and then after a while the subject no longer came up.

Well, face it, there were worse careers than cutting forty-five-degree angles in strips of gilded molding. And he did have Maggie, eventually— dropping into his lap like a wonderful gift out of nowhere. He did have two normal, healthy children. Maybe his life wasn't exactly what he had pictured when he was eighteen, but whose was? That was how things worked, most often.

Although he knew that Jesse didn't see it that way.

No compromises for Jesse Moran, no, sir. No modifications, no lowering of sights for Jesse. "I refuse to believe that I will die unknown," he had said to Ira once, and Ira, instead of smiling tolerantly as he should have, had felt slapped in the face.

Unknown.

Maggie said, "Ira, did you happen to notice a soft-drink machine inside the station?"

He looked at her.

"Ira?"

He pulled himself together and said, "Why, yes, I think so."

"With diet soft drinks?"

"Um . . ."

"I'll go check," Maggie said. "Those pretzels made me thirsty. Mr. Otis? Want something to drink?"

"Oh, no, I'm doing all right," Mr. Otis told her.

She tripped off toward the building, her skirt swinging. Both men watched her go.

"A fine, fine lady," Mr. Otis said.

Ira let his eyes close briefly and rubbed the ache in his forehead.

"A real angel of mercy." Mr. Otis said.

In stores sometimes Maggie would bring her selections to a clerk

and say, "I suppose you expect me to pay for these," in the fake-tough
tone that her brothers used when they were joking. Ira always worried
she had overstepped, but the clerk would laugh and say something
like: "Well, that thought had occurred to me." So the world was not
as Ira had perceived it, evidently. It was more the way Maggie perceived
it. She was the one who got along in it better, collecting strays who
stuck to her like lint and falling into heart-to-heart talks with total
strangers. This Mr. Otis, for instance: his face alight with enthusiasm,
his eyes stretched into crepe-edged triangles. "She puts me in mind of
the lady with the chimney," he was telling Ira. "I knew it was someone;
just couldn't think who."

"Chimney?"

"White lady I did not know from Adam," Mr. Otis said. "She was
leaking round her chimney she say and she call me to come give a
estimate. But I misstepped somehow and fell right off her roof while
I was walking about. Only knocked the wind out as it happened, but
Lordy, for a while there I thought I was a goner, laid there on the
ground not able to catch my breath, and this lady she insist on driving
me to the hospital. On the way, though, my breath come back to me
and so I say, 'Mrs., let's not go after all, they'll only take my life
savings to say I got nothing wrong with me,' so she say fine but then
has to buy me a cup of coffee and some hash browns at McDonald's,
which happen to lie next to a Toys R Us, so she axes would I mind
if we run in afterwards and bought a little red wagon for her nephew
whose birthday it was tomorrow? And I say no and in fact she buy
two, one for my niece's son Elbert also, and next to that is this gardening
place—"

"Yes, that is Maggie, all right," Ira said.

"Not a straight-line kind of person."

"No indeedy," Ira said.

That seemed to use up all their topics of conversation. They fell
silent and focused on Maggie, who was returning with a soft-drink can
held at arm's length. "Darn thing just bubbled up all over me," she
called cheerfully. "Ira? Want a sip?"

"No, thanks."

"Mr. Otis?"

"Oh, why, no, I don't believe I do, thanks anyhow."

She settled between them and tipped her head back for a long,
noisy swig.

Ira started wishing for a game of solitaire. All this idleness was
getting to him. Judging from the way those balloons were bobbing
about, though, he guessed his cards might blow away, and so he tucked
his hands in his armpits and slouched lower on the wall.

They sold balloons like that at Harborplace, or next to it. Lone,
grim men stood on street corners with trees of Mylar lozenges floating

overhead. He remembered how entranced his sister Junie had been when she first saw them. Poor Junie: in a way more seriously handicapped than Dorrie, even—more limited, more imprisoned. Her fears confounded them all, because nothing very dreadful had ever befallen her in the outside world, at least not so far as anyone knew. In the beginning they tried to point that out. They said useless things like: "What's the worst that could happen?" and "I'll be with you." Then gradually they stopped. They gave up on her and let her stay where she was.

Except for Maggie, that is. Maggie was too obstinate to give up. And after years of failed attempts, one day she conceived the notion that Junie might be persuaded to go out if she could go in costume. She bought Junie a bright-red wig and a skin-tight dress covered with poppies and a pair of spike-heeled pattent-leather shoes with ankle straps. She plastered Junie's face with heavy makeup. To everyone's astonishment, it worked. Giggling in a terrified, unhappy way, Junie allowed Maggie and Ira to lead her to the front stoop. The next day, slightly farther. Then finally to the end of the block. Never without Ira, though. She wouldn't do it with just Maggie; Maggie was not a blood relation. (Ira's father, in fact, wouldn't even call Maggie by name but referred to her as "Madam." "Will Madam be coming too, Ira?"— a title that exactly reflected the mocking, skeptical attitude he had assumed toward her from the start.)

"You see what's at work here," Maggie said of Junie. "When she's in costume it's not she who's going out; it's someone else. Her real self is safe at home."

Evidently she was right. Clinging to Ira's arm with both hands, Junie walked to the pharmacy and requested a copy of *Soap Opera Digest*. She walked to the grocery store and placed an order for chicken livers in an imperious, brazen manner as if she were another kind of woman entirely—a flamboyant, maybe even trampish woman who didn't care what people thought of her. Then she collapsed into giggles again and asked Ira how she was doing. Well, Ira was pleased at her progress, of course, but after a while the whole thing got to be a nuisance. She wanted to venture this place and that, and always it was such a production—the preparations, the dress and the makeup, the assurances he was forced to offer. And those ridiculous heels hampered her so. She walked like someone navigating a freshly mopped floor. Really it would have been simpler if she'd gone on staying home, he reflected. But he was ashamed of himself for the thought.

Then she got this urge to visit Harborplace. She had watched on TV when Harborplace first opened and she had somehow come to the conclusion that it was one of the wonders of the world. So naturally, after she'd gained some confidence, nothing would do but that she must see it in person. Only Ira didn't want to take her. To put it mildly, he was not a fan of Harborplace. He felt it was un-Baltimorean—in fact, a glorified shopping mall. And parking would be bound to cost an arm and a leg. Couldn't she settle for somewhere else? No, she couldn't, she said. Couldn't just Maggie take her, then? No, she needed Ira. He knew she needed him; how could he suggest otherwise? And then their father wanted to come too, and then Dorrie, who was so excited that she already had her "suitcase" (a Hutzler's coat box) packed for the occasion. Ira had to set his teeth and agree to it.

They scheduled the trip for a Sunday—Ira's only day off. Unfortunately, it turned out to be a misty, lukewarm morning, with showers predicted for afternoon. Ira suggested a postponement but no one would hear of it, not even Maggie, who had become as fired up as the others. So he drove them all downtown, where by some miracle he found a parking spot on the street, and they got out and started walking. It was so foggy that buildings just a few yards away were invisible. When they reached the corner of Pratt and Light streets and looked across to Harborplace they couldn't even see the pavilions; they were merely denser patches of gray. The traffic signal, turning green, was the one little pinprick of color. And nobody else was in sight except for a single balloon man, who took shape eerily on the opposite corner as they approached.

It was the balloons that snagged Junie's attention. They seemed made of liquid metal; they were silver-toned and crushy, puckered around the edges like sofa cushions. Junie cried, "Oh!" She stepped up onto the curb, gaping all the while. "What *are* those?" she cried.

"Balloons, of course," Ira said. But when he tried to lead her past, she craned back to look at them and so did Dorrie, who was hanging on his other arm.

He could see what the problem was. TV had kept Junie informed of the world's important developments but not the trivial ones, like Mylar; so those were what stopped her in her tracks. It was perfectly understandable. At that moment, though, Ira just didn't feel like catering to her. He didn't want to be there at all, and so he rushed them forward and around the first pavilion. Junie's hand was like a claw on his arm. Dorrie, whose left leg had been partially paralyzed after her latest seizure, leaned on his other arm and hobbled grotesquely, her Hutzler's coat box slamming against her hip at every step. And behind them, Maggie murmured encouragement to his father, whose breathing was growing louder and more effortful.

"But those are not any balloons *I* have had experience of!" Junie said. "What material is that? What do they call it?"

By then they had reached the promenade around the water's edge, and instead of answering, Ira gazed pointedly toward the view. "Isn't this what you were dying to see?" he reminded her.

But the view was nothing but opaque white sheets and a fuzzy-edged *U.S.S. Constellation* riding on a cloud, and Harborplace was a hulking, silent concentration of vapors.

Well, the whole trip ended in disaster, of course. Junie said everything had looked better on TV, and Ira's father said his heart was flapping in his chest, and then Dorrie somehow got her feelings hurt and started crying and had to be taken home before they'd set foot inside a pavilion. Ira couldn't remember now what had hurt her feelings, but what he did remember, so vividly that it darkened even this glaringly sunlit Texaco, was the sensation that had come over him as he stood there between his two sisters. He'd felt suffocated. The fog had made a tiny room surrounding them, an airless, steamy room such as those that house indoor swimming pools. It had muffled every sound but his family's close, oppressively familiar voices. It had wrapped them together, locked them in, while his sisters' hands dragged him down the way drowning victims drag down whoever tries to rescue them. And Ira had thought, *Ah, God, I have been trapped with these people all my life and I am never going to be free.* And he had known then what a failure he'd been, ever since the day he took over his father's business.

Was it any wonder he was so sensitive to waste? He had given up the only serious dream he'd ever had. You can't get more wasteful than that.

"Lamont!" Maggie said.

She was looking toward a revolving yellow light over by the gas pumps—a tow truck, towing nothing. It stopped with a painful screeching sound and the engine died. A black man in a denim jacket swung out of the cab.

"That's him, all right," Mr. Otis said, rising by inches from his seat.

Lamont walked to the rear of the truck and examined something. He kicked a tire and then started toward the cab. He was not as young as Ira had expected—no mere boy but a solidly built, glowering man with plum-black skin and a heavy way of walking.

"Well, hey there!" Mr. Otis called.

Lamont halted and looked over at him. "Uncle Daniel?" he said.

"How you been, son?"

"What *you* doing here?" Lamont asked, approaching.

When he reached the wall, Maggie and Ira stood up, but Lamont didn't glance in their direction. "Ain't you gone back to Aunt Duluth yet?" he asked Mr. Otis.

"Lamont, I'm going to need that truck of yourn," Mr. Otis said.

"What for?"

"Believe my left front wheel is loose."

"What? Where's it at?"

"Out on Route One. This here fellow kindly give me a lift."

Lamont briefly skimmed Ira with his eyes.

"We just happened to be driving past," Ira told him.

"Hmm," Lamont said in an unfriendly tone, and then, turning again to his uncle, "Now let's see what you telling me. Your car is out on the highway someplace . . ."

"It was Mrs. here caught on to it," Mr. Otis said, and he gestured toward Maggie, who beamed up at Lamont trustfully. A slender thread of soft-drink foam traced her upper lip; it made Ira feel protective.

"I won't offer you my hand," she told Lamont. "This Pepsi has just fizzed all over me."

Lamont merely studied her, with the corners of his mouth pulled down.

"She lean out her window and call, 'Your wheel!'" Mr. Otis said. "'Your front wheel is falling off!'"

"Really that was a fabrication," Maggie told Lamont. "I made it up."

Sweet Jesus.

Lamont said, "Say what?"

"I fibbed," Maggie said blithely. "We admitted as much to your uncle, but I don't know, it was kind of hard to convince him."

"You saying you told him a lie?" Lamont asked.

"Right."

Mr. Otis smiled self-consciously down at his shoes.

"Well, actually—" Ira began.

"It was after he almost stopped dead in front of us," Maggie said. "We had to veer off the road, and I was so mad that as soon as we caught up with him I said that about his wheel. But I didn't know he was old! I didn't know he was helpless!"

"Helpless?" Mr. Otis asked, his smile growing less certain.

"And besides, then it did seem his wheel was acting kind of funny," Maggie told Lamont. "So we brought him here to the Texaco."

Lamont looked no more threatening than he'd seemed all along, Ira was relieved to see. In fact, he dismissed the two of them entirely. He turned instead to his uncle. "Hear that?" he asked. "See there? Now it comes to you running folks off the road."

"Lamont, I'll tell you the truth," Mr. Otis said. "I do believe when I think back on it that wheel has not been acting properly for some days now."

"Didn't I say you ought to give up driving? Didn't we all say that? Didn't Florence beg you to hand in your license? Next time you might not be so lucky. Some crazy white man going to shoot your head off next time."

Mr. Otis appeared to shrink, standing there quietly with his hat brim shielding his face.

"If you'd've stayed home with Aunt Duluth where you belong, none of this wouldn't be happening," Lamont told him. "Cruising about on the interstate! Sleeping here and there like some hippie!"

"Well, I had thought I was driving real cautious and careful," Mr. Otis said.

Ira cleared his throat. "So about the wheel—" he said.

"You just got to go on back home and make up," Lamont told Mr. Otis. "Quit drawing this thing out and apologize to Aunt Duluth and get that rust heap out of folkses' way."

"I can't apologize! I ain't done nothing to be sorry for," Mr. Otis said.

"What's the difference, man? Apologize even so."

"See, I *couldn't* have done it; it was only in her dream. Duluth went and had this dream, see—"

"You been married fifty-some years to that woman," Lamont said, "and half of those years the two of you been in a snit about something. She ain't speaking to you or you ain't speaking to her or she moves out or you moves out. Shoot, man, one time you both moves out and leaves your house standing empty. Plenty would give their right arms for a nice little house like you-all's, and what do you do? Leave it stand empty while you off careening about in your Chevy and Aunt Duluth's sleeping on Florence's couch discommoding her family."

A reminiscent smile crossed Mr. Otis's face. "It's true," he said. "I had thought I was leaving her, that time, and she thought she was leaving me."

"You two act like quarrelsome children," Lamont told him.

"Well, at least I'm still married, you notice!" Mr. Otis said. "At least I'm still married, unlike some certain others I could name!"

Ira said, "Well, at any rate—"

"Even worse than children," Lamont went on, as if he hadn't heard. "Children at least got the time to spare, but you two are old and coming to the end of your lives. Pretty soon one or the other of you going to die and the one that's left behind will say, 'Why did I act so ugly? That was who it *was;* that person was who I was with; and here we threw ourselves away on spitefulness,' you'll say."

"Well, it's probably going to be me that dies first," Mr. Otis said, "so I just ain't going to worry about that."

"I'm serious, Uncle."

"*I'm* serious. Could be what you throw away is all that really counts; could be that's the whole point of things, wouldn't that be something? Spill it! Spill it all, I say! No way *not* to spill it. And anyhow, just look at the times we had. Maybe that's what I'll end up thinking. 'My, we surely did have us a time. We were a real knock-down, drag-out, heart-and-soul type of couple,' I'll say. Something to reflect on in the nursing home."

Lamont rolled his eyes heavenward.

Ira said, "Well, not to change the subject, but is this wheel business under control now?"

Both men looked over at him. "Oh," Mr. Otis said finally. "I reckon you two will want to be moving on."

"Only if you're sure you're all right," Maggie told him.

"He'll be fine," Lamont said. "Get on and go."

"Yes, don't you give me another thought," Mr. Otis said. "Let me squire you to your car." And he walked off between the two of them. Lamont stayed behind, looking disgusted.

"That boy is just so cranky," Mr. Otis told Ira. "I don't know who he takes after."

"You think he'll be willing to help you?"

"Oh, surely. He just want to rant and carry on some first."

They reached the Dodge, and Mr. Otis insisted on opening Maggie's door for her. It took longer than if she had done it herself; he had to get positioned just right and gain some leverage. Meanwhile he was saying to Ira, "And it ain't like he had room to criticize. A divorced man! Handing out advice like a expert!"

He closed the door after Maggie with a loose, ineffectual sound so that she had to reopen it and give it a good slam. "A man who ups and splits at the first little setback," he told Ira. "Lives alone all pruned and puckerish, drying out like a raisin. Sets alone in front of the TV, night after night, and won't go courting nobody new for fear she'll do him like his wife did."

"Tsk!" Maggie said, looking up at him through her window. "That is always so sad to see."

"But do you think *he* sees it?" Mr. Otis asked. "Naw." He followed Ira around to the driver's side of the car. "He believe that's just a regular life," he told Ira.

"Well, listen," Ira said as he slid behind the wheel. "If there's any kind of expense with the tow truck I want to hear about it, understand?" He shut the door and leaned out the window to say, "I'd better give you our address."

"There won't be no expense," Mr. Otis said, "but I appreciate the thought." He tipped his hat back slightly and scratched his head. "You know I used to have this dog," he said. "Smartest dog I ever owned. Bessie. She just loved to chase a rubber ball. I would throw it for her and she would chase it. Anytime the ball landed on a kitchen chair, though, Bessie would poke her nose through the spindles of the chair-back and whine and moan and whimper, never dreaming she could just walk around and grab the ball from in front."

Ira said, "Um . . ."

"Puts me in mind of Lamont," Mr. Otis said.

"Lamont."

"Blind in spots."

"Oh! Yes, Lamont!" Ira said. He was relieved to find the connection.

"Well, I don't want to hold you up," Mr. Otis told him, and he offered Ira his hand. It felt very light and fragile, like the skeleton of a bird. "You-all take care driving now, hear?" He bent forward to tell Maggie, "Take care!"

"You too," she told him. "And I hope things work out with Duluth."

"Oh, they will, they will. Sooner or later." He chuckled and stepped back as Ira started the engine. Like a host seeing off his guests, he stood there gazing after them till they pulled out onto the road and he disappeared from Ira's rearview mirror.

"Well!" Maggie said, bouncing into a more comfortable position in her seat. "So anyhow . . ."

As if that whole excursion had been only a little hiccup in the midst of some long story she was telling.

Ira turned on the radio but all he could find was the most local kind of news—crop prices, a fire in a Knights of Columbus building. He turned it off. Maggie was rooting through her purse. "Now, where on earth?" she said.

"What're you looking for?"

"My sunglasses."

"On the dashboard."

"Oh, right."

She reached for them and perched them on the end of her nose. Then she rotated her face, staring all around as if testing their effectiveness. "Doesn't the sunlight bother your eyes?" she asked him finally.

"No, I'm fine."

"Maybe *I* should drive."

"No, no . . ."

"I haven't taken a single turn this whole day," she said.

"That's all right. Thanks anyhow, sweetheart."

"Well, you just let me know if you change your mind," she told him, and she sank back in her seat and gazed out at the view.

Ira cocked an elbow on the window ledge. He started whistling a tune.

Maggie stiffened and looked over at him.

"You just think I'm some sort of harum-scarum lady driver," she told him.

"Huh?" he said.

"You're just wondering what kind of fool you are even to consider allowing me behind the wheel."

He blinked. He had assumed the subject was concluded. "Lord, Maggie," he said, "why do you always take things so personally?"

"I just do, that's why," she told him, but she spoke without heat, as if uninterested in her own words, and then returned to studying the scenery.

Once they were back on Route One, Ira picked up speed. Traffic had grown heavier, but it was moving briskly. The farms gave way to patches of commercial land—a mountain of bald tires, a stepped, angular cliff of cinder blocks, a field of those windowed enclosures that fit over the beds of pickup trucks and turn them into campers. Ira wasn't sure what those were called. It bothered him; he liked to know the names of things, the specific, accurate term that would sum an object up.

"Spruce Gum," Maggie said.

"Pardon?"

She was twisted around in her seat, gazing behind her. She said, "Spruce Gum! That was the cutoff to Fiona's! We just now passed it."

"Oh, yes, Spruce Gum," he said. It did ring a bell.

"Ira," Maggie said.

"Hmm?"

"It's not so far out of the way."

He glanced at her. She had her hands pressed together, her face set toward him, her mouth bunched up a little as if she were willing certain words from him (the way she used to will the right answer out of Jesse when she was drilling him on his multiplication tables).

"Is it?" she said.

"No," he said.

She misunderstood him; she drew in a breath to start arguing. But he said, "No, I guess it's not."

"What: You mean you'll take me there?"

"Well," he said. And then he said, "Oh, well, we've already pretty much shot the day, right?" And he flicked his blinker on and looked for a place to turn the car around.

"Thank you, Ira," she told him, and she slid over as far as her seat belt allowed and planted a little brush stroke of a kiss below his ear.

Ira said, "Hmf," but he sounded more grudging than he really felt.

After he'd reversed the car in a lumberyard, he headed back up Route One and took a left onto Spruce Gum Road. They were facing into the sun now. Dusty shafts of light filmed the windshield. Maggie pushed her glasses higher on her nose, and Ira flipped his visor down.

Was it the haze on the windshield that made him think again of their trip to Harborplace? At any rate, for some reason he suddenly remembered why Dorrie had started crying that day.

Standing at the water's edge, hemmed in by fog, she had been moved to open her suitcase and show him its contents. None of what she'd brought was much different from any other time. There were the usual two or three comic books, he recalled, and probably a snack for her sweet tooth—a squashed Hostess cupcake perhaps, with the frosting smashed into the cellophane—and of course the rhinestone hatband that had once belonged to their mother. And finally her greatest treasure:

a fan magazine with Elvis Presley on the cover. *King of Rock*, the title read. Dorrie worshiped Elvis Presley. Ordinarily Ira humored her, even bought her posters whenever he came across them, but on that particular morning he was feeling so burdened, he just hadn't had the patience. "Elvis," Dorrie said happily, and Ira said, "For God's sake, Dorrie, don't you know the guy is dead and buried?"

Then she had stopped smiling and her eyes had filled with tears, and Ira had felt pierced. Everything about her all at once saddened him—her skimpy haircut and her chapped lips and her thin face that was so homely and so sweet, if only people would see. He put an arm around her. He hugged her bony little body close and gazed over her head at the *Constellation* floating in the fog. The tops of the masts had dwindled away and the ropes and chains had dissolved and the old ship had looked its age for once, swathed in clouds of mist you could mistake for the blurring of time. And Junie had pressed close to his other side and Maggie and Sam had watched steadfastly, waiting for him to say what to do next. He had known then what the true waste was; Lord, yes. It was not his having to support these people but his failure to notice how he loved them. He loved even his worn-down, defeated father, even the memory of his poor mother who had always been so pretty and never realized it because anytime she approached a mirror she had her mouth drawn up lopsided with shyness.

But then the feeling had faded (probably the very next instant, when Junie started begging to leave) and he forgot what he had learned. And no doubt he would forget again, just as Dorrie had forgotten, by the time they reached home, that Elvis Presley was no longer King of Rock.

THREE

|
=

Maggie had a song that she liked to sing with Ira when they were traveling. "On the Road Again," it was called—not the Willie Nelson chestnut but a blues-sounding piece from one of Jesse's old Canned Heat albums, stomping and hard-driving. Ira did the beat: "Boom-da-da, boom-da-da, boom-da-da, boom! boom!" Maggie sang the melody. " 'Take a hint from me, Mama, please! don't you cry no more,' " she sang. The telephone poles appeared to be flashing by in rhythm. Maggie felt rangy and freewheeling. She tipped her head back against the seat and swirled one ankle, keeping time.

In the old days, when she'd driven this road alone, the countryside had seemed unwelcoming—enemy territory. Among these woods and stony pastures her only grandchild was being held hostage, and Maggie (smothered in scarves, or swathed in an anonymous trench coat, or half obscured by Junie's bubbly red wig) had driven as if slipping between something. She'd had a sense of slithering, evading. She had fixed her mind on that child and held her face firmly before her: a bright baby face as round as a penny, eyes that widened with enthusiasm whenever Maggie walked into the room, dimpled fists revving up at the sight of her. I'm coming, Leroy! Don't forget me! But then over and over again those trips had proved so unsatisfactory, ending with that last awful time, when Leroy had twisted in her stroller and called, "Mom-Mom?"—hunting her other grandmother, her lesser grandmother, her *pretender* grandmother; and Maggie had finally given up and limited herself thereafter to the rare official visits with Ira. And even those had stopped soon enough. Leroy had begun to fade and dwindle, till one day she was no larger than somebody at the wrong end of a telescope—still dear, but very far removed.

Maggie thought of last summer when her old cat, Pumpkin, had died. His absence had struck her so intensely that it had amounted to a presence—the lack of his furry body twining between her ankles whenever she opened the refrigerator door, the lack of his motorboat purr in her bed whenever she woke up at night. Stupidly, she had been reminded of the time Leroy and Fiona had left, although of course there was no comparison. But here was something even stupider: A month or so later, when cold weather set in, Maggie switched off the basement dehumidifier as she did every year and even *that* absence had struck her. She had mourned in the most personal way the silencing of the steady, faithful whir that used to thrum the floorboards. What on earth was wrong with her? she had wondered. Would she spend the rest of her days grieving for every loss equally—a daughter-in-law, a baby, a cat, a machine that dries the air out?

Was this how it felt to grow old?

Now the fields were a brassy color, as pretty as a picture on a calendar. They held no particular significance. Maybe it helped that Ira was with her—an ally. Maybe it was just that sooner or later, even the sharpest pain became flattened.

" 'But I ain't going down that long old lonesome road all by myself,' " she sang automatically, and Ira sang, "Boom-da-da, boom-da-da—"

If Fiona remarried she would most likely acquire a new mother-in-law. Maggie hadn't considered that. She wondered if Fiona and this woman would be close. Would they spend their every free moment together, as cozy as two girlfriends?

"And suppose she has another baby!" Maggie said.

Ira broke off his boom-das to ask, "Huh?"

"I saw her through that whole nine months! What will she do without me?"

"Who're you talking about?"

"Fiona, of course. Who do you think?"

"Well, I'm sure she'll manage somehow," Ira said.

Maggie said, "Maybe, and maybe not." She turned away from him to look out at the fields again. They seemed unnaturally textureless. "I drove her to her childbirth classes," she said. "I drilled her in her exercises. I was her official labor coach."

"So now she knows all about it," Ira said.

"But it's something you have to repeat with each pregnancy," Maggie told him. "You have to keep at it."

She thought of how she had kept at Fiona, whom pregnancy had turned lackadaisical and vague, so that if it hadn't been for Maggie she'd have spent her entire third trimester on the couch in front of the TV. Maggie would clap her hands briskly—"Okay!"—and snap off the *Love Boat* rerun and fling open the curtains, letting sunshine flood the dim air of the living room and the turmoil of rock magazines and Fresca bottles. "Time for your pelvic squats!" she would cry, and Fiona would shrink and raise one arm to shield her eyes from the light.

"Pelvic squats, good grief," she would say. "Abdominal humps. It all sounds so gross." But she would heave to her feet, sighing. Even in pregnancy, her body was a teenager's—slender and almost rubbery, reminding Maggie of those scantily clad girls she'd glimpsed on beaches who seemed to belong to a completely different species from her own. The mound of the baby was a separate burden, a kind of package jutting out in front of her. "Breathing lessons—really," she said, dropping to the floor with a thud. "Don't they reckon I must know how to breathe by now?"

"Oh, honey, you're just lucky they offer such things," Maggie told her. "*My* first pregnancy, there wasn't a course to be found, and I was scared to death. I'd have loved to take lessons! And afterward: I remember leaving the hospital with Jesse and thinking, 'Wait. Are they going to let me just walk off with him? I don't know beans about babies! I don't have a license to do this. Ira and I are just amateurs.' I mean you're given all these lessons for the unimportant things— piano-playing, typing. You're given years and years of lessons in how to balance equations, which Lord knows you will never have to do in normal life. But how about parenthood? Or marriage, either, come to think of it. Before you can drive a car you need a state-approved course of instruction, but driving a car is nothing, nothing, compared to living day in and day out with a husband and raising up a new human being."

Which had not been the most reassuring notion, perhaps; for Fiona had said, "Jiminy," and dropped her head in her hands.

"Though I'm certain you'll do fine," Maggie said in a hurry, "And of course you have me here to help you."

"Oh, jiminy," Fiona said.

Ira turned down a little side road called Elm Lane—a double string of tacky one-story cottages with RVs in most of the driveways and sometimes a sloping tin trailer out back. Maggie asked him, "Who will wake up in the night now and bring her the baby to nurse?"

"Her husband, one would hope," Ira said. "Or maybe she'll keep the baby in *her* room this time, the way you should have had her do last time." Then he gave his shoulders a slight shake, as if ridding himself of something, and said, "What baby? Fiona's not having a baby; she's just getting married, or so you claim. Let's put first things first here."

Well, but first things weren't put first the time before; Fiona had been two months pregnant when she married Jesse. Not that Maggie wanted to remind him of that. Besides, her thoughts were on something else now. She was caught by an unexpected, piercingly physical memory of bringing the infant Leroy in to Fiona for her 2 a.m. feeding—that downy soft head wavering on Maggie's shoulder, that birdlike mouth searching the bend of Maggie's neck inside her bathrobe collar, and then the close, sleep-smelling warmth of Jesse's and Fiona's bedroom. "Oh," she said without meaning to, and then, "Oh!" For there in Mrs. Stuckey's yard (hard-packed earth, not really a yard at all) stood a wiry little girl with white-blond hair that stopped short squarely at her jawline. She had just let go of a yellow Frisbee, which sailed shuddering toward their car and landed with a thump on the hood as Ira swung into the driveway.

"That's not—" Maggie said. "Is that—?"

"Must be Leroy," Ira told her.

"It's not!"

But of course, it had to be. Maggie was forced to make such a leap across time, though—from the infant on her shoulder to this gawky child, all in two seconds. She was experiencing some difficulty. The child dropped her hands to her sides and stared at them. Frowning gave her forehead a netted look. She wore a pink tank top with some kind of red stain down the front, berry juice or Kool-Aid, and baggy shorts in a blinding Hawaiian print. Her face was so thin it was triangular, a cat's face, and her arms and legs were narrow white stems.

"Maybe it's a neighbor girl," Maggie told Ira—a last-ditch effort.

He didn't bother replying.

As soon as he switched the ignition off, Maggie opened the door and stepped out. She called "Leroy?"

"What."

"Are you Leroy?"

The child deliberated a moment, as if uncertain, and then nodded.

"So," Maggie said. "Well, hi there!" she cried.

Leroy went on staring. She didn't seem one grain less suspicious.

Actually, Maggie reflected (already adjusting to new developments), this was one of the most interesting ages. Seven and a half—old enough to converse with but not yet past willing to admire a grownup, provided the grownup played her cards right. Cagily, Maggie rounded the car and approached the child with her purse in both hands, resisting the urge to fling out her arms for a hug. "I guess you must not remember me," she said, stopping a measured distance away.

Leroy shook her head.

"Why, sweetie, I'm your grandma!"

"You are?" Leroy said. She reminded Maggie of someone peering through a veil.

"Your other grandma. Your Grandma Moran."

It was crazy to have to introduce herself to her own flesh and blood. And crazier still, Maggie thought, that Jesse would have needed to do the same thing. He had not laid eyes on his daughter since— when? Since just after he and Fiona split up—before Leroy was a year old, even. What a sad, partitioned life they all seemed to be living!

"I'm from your father's side of the family," she told Leroy, and Leroy said, "Oh."

So at least she did know she had a father.

"And this is your grandpa," Maggie said.

Leroy shifted her gaze to Ira. In profile, her nose was seen to be tiny and extremely pointed. Maggie could have loved her for her nose alone.

Ira was out of the car by now, but he didn't come over to Leroy immediately. Instead he reached for the Frisbee on the hood. Then he crossed the yard to them, meanwhile studying the Frisbee and turning it around and around in his hands as if he'd never seen one before. (Wasn't this just like him? Allowing Maggie to rush in while he hung back all reserved, but you notice he did tag along, and would share the benefit of anything she accomplished.) When he arrived in front of Leroy he tossed the Frisbee toward her lightly, and both her hands came up like two skinny spiders to grab it.

"Thanks," she said.

Maggie wished *she* had thought of the Frisbee.

"We don't seem familiar at all?" she asked Leroy.

Leroy shook her head.

"Why! I was standing by when you were born, I'll have you know. I was waiting in the hospital for you to be delivered. You stayed with us the first eight or nine months of your life."

"I did?"

"You don't remember staying with us?"

"How could she, Maggie?" Ira asked.

"Well, she might," Maggie said, for she herself had a very clear memory of a scratchy-collared dress she used to hate being stuffed into as an infant. And besides, you would think all that loving care had to have left some mark, wouldn't you? She said, "Or Fiona might have told her about it."

"She told me I lived in Baltimore," Leroy said.

"That was us," Maggie said. "Your parents lived with us in your daddy's old boyhood room in Baltimore."

"Oh."

"Then you and your mother moved away."

Leroy rubbed her calf with the instep of her bare foot. She was standing very straight, militarily straight, giving the impression she was held there only by a sense of duty.

"We visited on your birthdays afterward, remember that?"

"Nope."

"She was just a little thing, Maggie," Ira said.

"We came for your first three birthdays," Maggie persisted. (Sometimes you could snag a memory and reel it in out of nowhere, if you used the proper hook.) "But your second birthday you were off at Hershey Park, and so we didn't get to see you."

"I've been to Hershey Park six times," Leroy said. "Mindy Brant has only been twice."

"Your third birthday, we brought you a kitten."

Leroy tilted her head. Her hair wafted to one side—corn silk, lighter than air. "A tiger kitten," she said.

"Right."

"Stripy all over, even on its tummy."

"You do remember!"

"That was you-all brought me that kitten?"

"That was us," Maggie said.

Leroy looked back and forth between the two of them. Her skin was delicately freckled, as if dusted with those sugar sprinkles people put on cakes. That must come from the Stuckey side. Maggie's family never freckled, and certainly Ira's didn't, with their Indian connections. "And then what happened?" she was asking.

"What happened when?"

"What happened to the kitten! You must've took it back."

"Oh, no, honey, we didn't take it back. Or rather, we did but only because you turned out to be allergic. You started sneezing and your eyes got teary."

"And after that, what?" Leroy asked.

"Well, I wanted to visit again," Maggie said, "but your grandpa told me we shouldn't. I wanted to with all my heart, but your grandpa told me—"

"I meant, what did you do with the kitten," Leroy said.

"Oh. The kitten. Well. We gave it to your grandpa's two sisters, your . . . great-aunts, I suppose they'd be; goodness."

"So have they still got it?"

"No, actually it was hit by a car," Maggie said.

"Oh."

"It wasn't used to traffic and somehow it slipped out when someone left the door open."

Leroy stared ahead, fixedly. Maggie hoped she hadn't upset her. She said, "So tell me! Is your mother home?"

"My mother? Sure."

"Could we see her, maybe?"

Ira said, "Maybe she's busy."

"No, she's not busy," Leroy said, and she turned and started toward the house. Maggie didn't know if they were supposed to follow or not. She looked over at Ira. He was standing there slouched with his hands in his trouser pockets, so she took her cue from him and stayed where she was.

"Ma!" Leroy called, climbing the two front steps. Her voice had a certain mosquito quality that went with her thin face. "Ma? You in there?" She opened the screen door. "Hey, Ma!"

Then all at once there was Fiona leaning in the doorway, one arm outstretched to keep the screen door from banging shut again. She wore cut-off denim shorts and a T-shirt with some kind of writing across it. "No need to shout," she said. At that moment she saw Maggie and Ira. She stood up straighter.

Maggie moved forward, clutching her purse. She said, "How are you, Fiona?"

"Well . . . fine," Fiona said.

And then she looked beyond them. Oh, Maggie was not mistaken about that. Her eyes swept the yard furtively and alighted on the car for just the briefest instant. She was wondering if Jesse had come too. She still cared enough to wonder.

Her eyes returned to Maggie.

"I hope we're not disturbing you," Maggie said.

"Oh, um, no, . . ."

"We were just passing through and thought we'd stop by and say hello."

Fiona lifted her free arm and smoothed her hair off her forehead with the back of her hand—a gesture that exposed the satiny white inner surface of her wrist, that made her seem distracted, at a loss. Her hair was still fairly long but she had done something to it that bushed it out more; it didn't hang in sheets now. And she had gained a bit of weight. Her face was slightly broader across the cheekbones, the hollow of her collarbone was less pronounced, and although she was translucently pale, as always, she must have started using makeup, for Maggie detected a half-moon of powdered shadow on each eyelid—that rose-colored shadow that seemed to be so popular lately, that made women look as if they were suffering from a serious cold.

Maggie climbed the steps and stood next to Leroy, continuing to hold her purse in a way that implied she wasn't expecting so much as a handshake. She was able now to read the writing on Fiona's shirt: LIME SPIDERS, it said—whatever that meant. "I heard you on the radio this morning." she said.

"Radio," Fiona said, still distracted.

"On *AM Baltimore*."

"Baltimore," Fiona said.

Leroy, meanwhile, had ducked under her mother's arm and then turned so she was facing Maggie, side by side with Fiona, gazing up with the same unearthly clear-aqua eyes. There wasn't a trace of Jesse in that child's appearance. You'd think at least his coloring would have won out.

"I told Ira, 'Why not just stop off and visit,' " Maggie said. "We were up this way anyhow, for Max Gill's funeral. Remember Max Gill? My friend Serena's husband? He died of cancer. So I said, 'Why not stop off and visit Fiona. We wouldn't stay but a minute.' "

"It feels funny to see you," Fiona said.

"Funny?"

"I mean . . . Come inside, why don't you?"

"Oh, I know you must be busy," Maggie said.

"No, I'm not busy. Come on in."

Fiona turned and led the way into the house. Leroy followed, with Maggie close behind. Ira took a little longer. When Maggie looked over her shoulder she found him kneeling in the yard to tie his shoe, a slant of hair falling over his forehead. "Well, come on, Ira," she told him.

He rose in silence and started toward her. Her annoyance changed to something softer. Sometimes Ira took on a gangling aspect, she thought, like a bashful young boy not yet comfortable in public.

The front door opened directly into the living room, where the sun slipping through the venetian blinds striped the green shag rug. Heaps of crocheted cushions tumbled across a couch upholstered in a fading tropical print. The coffee table bore sliding stacks of magazines and comic books, and a green ceramic ashtray shaped like a rowboat. Maggie remembered the ashtray from earlier visits. She remembered staring at it during awkward pauses and wondering if it could float, in which case it would make a perfect bathtub toy for Leroy. Now that came back to her, evidently having lurked all these years within some cupboard in her brain.

"Have a seat," Fiona said, plumping a cushion. She asked Ira, "So how're you doing?" as he ducked his head in the doorway.

"Oh, passably," he told her.

Maggie chose the couch, hoping Leroy would sit there too. But Leroy dropped to the rug and stretched her reedy legs out in front of her. Fiona settled in an armchair, and Ira remained standing. He circled the room, pausing at a picture of two basset puppies nestled together in a hatbox. With the tip of one finger, he traced the gilded molding that lined the frame.

"Would you like some refreshments?" Fiona asked.

Maggie said, "No, thank you."

"Maybe a soda or something."

"We're not thirsty, honestly."

Leroy said, "*I* could use a soda."

"You're not who I was asking." Fiona told her.

Maggie wished she'd brought Leroy some sort of present. They had so little time to make connections; she felt pushed and anxious. "Leroy," she said too brightly, "is Frisbee a big interest of yours?"

"Not really," Leroy told her bare feet.

"Oh."

"I'm still just learning," Leroy said. "I can't make it go where I want yet."

"Yes, that's the tricky part, all right," Maggie said.

Unfortunately, she had no experience with Frisbees herself. She looked hopefully at Ira, but he had moved on to some kind of brown metal appliance that stood in the corner—a box fan, perhaps, or a heater. She turned back to Leroy. "Does it glow in the dark?" she asked after a pause.

Leroy said, "Huh?"

"Excuse me," Fiona reminded her.

"Excuse me?"

"Does your Frisbee glow in the dark? Some do, I believe."

"Not this one," Leroy said.

"Ah!" Maggie cried. "Then maybe we should buy you one that does."

Leroy thought about that. Finally she asked, "Why would I want to play Frisbee in the dark?"

"Good question," Maggie said.

She sat back, spent, wondering where to go from there. She looked again at Ira. He was hunkered over the appliance now, inspecting the controls with total concentration.

Well, no point avoiding this forever. Maggie made herself smile. She tilted her head receptively and said, "Fiona, we were so surprised to hear about your wedding plans."

"My what?"

"Wedding plans."

"Is that supposed to be a joke?"

"Joke?" Maggie asked. She faltered. "Aren't you getting married?"

"Not that I'm aware of."

"But I heard it on the radio!"

Fiona said, "What is this radio business? I don't know what you're talking about."

"On WNTK," Maggie said. "You called in and said—"

"The station I listen to is WXLR," Fiona told her.

"No, this was—"

"*Excellent Rock Around the Clock*. A Brittstown station."

"This was WNTK," Maggie said.

"And they claimed I was getting married?"

"*You* claimed it. You called in and claimed your wedding was next Saturday."

"Not me," Fiona said.

There was a kind of alteration of rhythm in the room.

Maggie experienced a surge of relief, followed by acute embarrassment. How could she have been so sure? What on earth had got into her, not even to question that the voice she'd heard was Fiona's? And on such a staticky, inadequate radio; she'd known perfectly well how inadequate it was, with those dinky little auto speakers that didn't begin to approach high fidelity.

She braced herself for Ira's I-told-you-so. He still seemed absorbed in the appliance, though, which was nice of him.

"I guess I made a mistake," she said finally.

"I guess you did," Fiona said.

And Leroy said, "Married!" and uttered a little hiss of amusement and wiggled her toes. Each toenail, Maggie saw, bore the tiniest dot of red polish, almost completely chipped off.

"So who was the lucky guy?" Fiona asked.

"You didn't say," Maggie told her.

"What: I just came on the air and announced my engagement?"

"It was a call-in talk show," Maggie said. She spoke slowly; she was rearranging her thoughts. All at once Fiona was not getting married. There was still a chance, then! Things could still be worked out! And yet in some illogical way Maggie continued to believe the wedding really had been planned, so that she wondered at the girl's inconsistency. "People called in to discuss their marriages with the host," she said.

Fiona knit her pale brows, as if considering the possibility that she might have been one of them.

She was so pretty, and Leroy was so endearingly spiky and unusual; Maggie felt how thirsty her eyes were, drinking them in. It was like the early days with her children, when every neck-crease, every knuckle-dent, could send her into a reverie. Look at Fiona's hair shining like ribbons, like bands of crinkle gift ribbon! Look at the darling little gold studs in Leroy's earlobes!

Ira, speaking into the grille of the appliance, said, "This thing really do much good?" His voice rang back at them tinnily.

"So far as I know," Fiona said.

"Fairly energy-efficient?"

She lifted both hands, palms up. "Beats me."

"How many BTUs does it give off?"

"That's just something Mom runs in the wintertime to keep her feet warm," Fiona said. "I never have paid it much heed, to tell the truth."

Ira leaned farther forward to read a decal on the appliance's rear.

Maggie seized on a change of subject. She said, "How *is* your mother, Fiona?"

"Oh, she's fine. Right now she's at the grocery store."

"Wonderful," Maggie said. Wonderful that she was fine, she meant. But it was also wonderful that she was out. She said, "And you're looking well too. You're wearing your hair a little fuller, aren't you?"

"It's crimped," Fiona said. "I use this special iron, like; you know bigger hair has a slimming effect."

"Slimming! You don't need slimming."

"I most certainly do. I put on seven pounds over this past summer."

"Oh, you didn't, either. You couldn't have! Why you're just a—"

Just a twig, she was going to say; or just a stick. But she got mixed up and combined the two words: "You're just a twick!"

Fiona glanced at her sharply, and no wonder; it had sounded vaguely insulting. "Just skin and bones, I mean," Maggie said, fighting back a giggle. She remembered now how fragile their relationship had been, how edgy and defensive Fiona had often seemed. She folded her hands and placed her feet carefully together on the green shag rug.

So Fiona was not getting married after all.

"How's Daisy?" Fiona asked.

"She's doing well."

Leroy said, "Daisy who?"

"Daisy Moran," Fiona said. Without further explanation, she turned back to Maggie. "All grown up by now, I bet."

"Daisy is your aunt. Your daddy's little sister," Maggie told Leroy. "Yes; tomorrow she leaves for college," she said to Fiona.

"College! Well, she always was a brain."

"Oh, no . . . but it's true she won a full scholarship."

"Little bitty Daisy," Fiona said. "Just think."

Ira had finished with the appliance, finally. He moved on to the coffee table. The Frisbee rested on a pile of comic books, and he picked it up and examined it all over again. Maggie stole a peek at him. He still had not said, "I told you so," but she thought she detected something noble and forebearing in the set of his spine.

"You know, I'm in school myself, in a way," Fiona said.

"Oh? What kind of school?"

"I'm studying electrolysis."

"Why, that's lovely, Fiona," Maggie said.

She wished she could shake off this fulsome tone of voice. It seemed to belong to someone else entirely—some elderly, matronly, honey-sweet woman endlessly marveling and exclaiming.

"The beauty parlor where I'm a shampoo girl is paying for my course," Fiona said. "They want their own licensed operator. They say I'm sure to make heaps of money."

"That's just lovely!" Maggie said. "Then maybe you can move out and find a place of your own."

And leave the pretender grandma behind, was what she was thinking. But Fiona gave her a blank look.

Leroy said, "Show them your practice kit, Ma."

"Yes, show us," Maggie said.

"Oh, you don't want to see that," Fiona said.

"Yes, we do. Don't we, Ira?"

Ira said, "Hmm? Oh, absolutely." He held the Frisbee up level, like a tea tray, and gave it a meditative spin.

"Well, then, wait a sec," Fiona said, and she got up and left the room. Her sandals made a dainty slapping sound on the wooden floor of the hallway.

"They're going to hang a sign in the beauty parlor window," Leroy told Maggie. "Professionally painted with Ma's name."

"Isn't that something!"

"It's a genuine science, Ma says. You've got to have trained experts to teach you how to do it."

Leroy's expression was cocky and triumphant. Maggie resisted the urge to reach down and cup the complicated small bones of her knee.

Fiona returned, carrying a rectangular yellow kitchen sponge and a short metal rod the size of a ballpoint pen. "First we practice with a dummy instrument," she said. She dropped onto the couch beside Maggie. "We're supposed to work at getting the angle exactly, perfectly right."

She set the sponge on her lap and gripped the rod between her fingers. There was a needle at its tip, Maggie saw. For some reason she had always thought of electrolysis as, oh, not quite socially mentionable, but Fiona was so matter-of-fact and so skilled, targeting one of the sponge's pores and guiding the needle into it at a precisely monitored slant; Maggie couldn't help feeling impressed. This was a highly technical field, she realized—maybe something like dental hygiene. Fiona said, "We travel into the follicle, see, easy, easy . . ." and then she said, "Oops!" and raised the heel of her hand an inch or two. "If this was a real person I'd have been leaning on her eyeball," she said. "Pardon me, lady," she told the sponge. "I didn't mean to smush you." Mottled black lettering was stamped across the sponge's surface: STABLER'S DARK BEER. MADE WITH MOUNTAIN SPRING WATER.

Ira stood over them now, with the Frisbee dangling from his fingers. He asked, "Does the school provide the sponge?"

"Yes, it's included in the tuition," Fiona said.

"They must get it free," he reflected. "Courtesy of Stabler's. Interesting."

"Stabler's? Anyhow, first we practice with the dummy and then with the real thing. Us students all work on each other: eyebrows and mustache and such. This girl that's my partner, Hilary, she wants me to do her bikini line."

Ira pondered that for a moment and then backed off in a hurry.

"You know these high-cut swimsuits nowadays, they show everything you've got," Fiona told Maggie.

"Oh, it's becoming impossible!" Maggie cried. "I'm just making do with my old suit till the fashions change."

Ira cleared his throat and said, "Leroy, what would you say to a game of Frisbee."

Leroy looked up at him.

"I could show you how to make it go where you want," he told her.

She took so long deciding that Maggie felt a pang for Ira's sake, but finally she said, "Well, okay," and unfolded herself from the floor. "Tell about the professionally painted sign," she told Fiona. Then she followed Ira out of the room. The screen door made a sound like a harmonica chord before it banged shut.

So.

This was the first time Maggie had been alone with Fiona since that awful morning. For once the two of them were free of Ira's hampering influence and the hostile, suspicious presence of Mrs. Stuckey. Maggie edged forward on the couch. She clasped her hands tightly; she pointed her knees intimately in Fiona's direction.

"The sign's going to read FIONA MORAN," Fiona was saying. "LICENSED ELECTROLOGIST. PAINLESS REMOVAL OF SUPERFLUOUS HAIR."

"I can't wait to see it," Maggie said.

She thought about that last name: Moran. If Fiona really hated Jesse, would she have kept his name all these years?

"On the radio," she said, "you told the man you were marrying for security."

"Maggie, I swear to you, the station I listen to is—"

"WXLR," Maggie said. "Yes, I know. But I just had it in my head that that was you, and so I . . ."

She watched Fiona set the sponge and needle in the rowboat ashtray.

"Anyway," she said. "Whoever it was who called, she said the first time she'd married for love and it hadn't worked out. So this time she was aiming purely for security."

"Well, what a ninny," Fiona said. "If marriage was such a drag when she loved the guy, what would it be like when she didn't?"

"Exactly," Maggie said. "Oh, Fiona, I'm so glad that wasn't you!"

"Shoot, I don't even have a steady boyfriend," Fiona said.

"You don't?"

But Maggie found the phrasing of that a bit worrisome. She said, "Does that mean . . . you have someone not steady?"

"I just barely get to date at all," Fiona said.

"Well! What a pity," Maggie said. She put on a sympathetic expression.

"This one guy? Mark Derby? I went out with him for about three months, but then we had a fight. I bashed his car in after I had borrowed it, was the reason. But it really wasn't my fault. I was starting to make a left turn, when these teenage boys came up from behind and passed me on the left and so of course I hit them. Then they had the nerve to claim it was all my doing; they claimed I had my right-turn signal on instead of my left."

"Well, anyone who'd get mad about *that* you don't want to date anyhow," Maggie told her.

"I said, 'I had my left-turn signal on. Don't you think I know my left from my right?' "

"Of course you do," Maggie said soothingly. She lifted her left hand and flicked an imaginary turn signal, testing. "Yes, left is down and right is . . . or maybe it's the not the same in every model of car."

"It's exactly the same," Fiona told her. "At least, I think it is."

"Then maybe it was the windshield wipers," Maggie said. "I've done that, lots of times: switched on my wipers instead of my blinkers."

Fiona considered. Then she said, "No, because *something* was lit up. Otherwise they wouldn't say I was signaling a right turn."

"One time I had my mind elsewhere and I went for my blinkers and shifted gears instead," Maggie said. She started laughing. "Going along about sixty miles an hour and shifted into reverse. Oh, Lord." She pulled the corners of her mouth down, recollecting herself. "Well," she told Fiona, "I'd say you're better off without the man."

"What man? Oh. Mark," Fiona said. "Yes, it's not like we were in love or anything. I only went out with him because he asked me. Plus my mom is friends with his mom. He has the nicest mother; real sweet-faced woman with a little bit of a stammer. I always feel a stammer shows sincerity of feeling, don't you?"

Maggie said, "Why, c-c-certainly I do."

It took Fiona a second to catch on. Then she laughed. "Oh, you're such a card," she said, and she tapped Maggie's wrist. "I'd forgotten what a card you are."

"So is that the end of it?" Maggie asked.

"End of what?"

"This . . . thing with Mark Derby. I mean suppose he asks you out again?"

"No way," Fiona said. "Him and his precious Subaru; no way would I go out with him."

"That's very wise of you," Maggie told her.

"Shoot! I'd have to be a moron."

"*He* was a moron, not to appreciate you," Maggie said.

Fiona said, "Hey. How's about a beer."

"Oh, I'd love a beer!"

Fiona jumped up, tugging down her shorts, and left the room. Maggie sank lower on the couch and listened to the sounds drifting in through the window—a car swishing past and Leroy's throaty chuckle. If this house were hers, she thought, she would get rid of all this clutter. You couldn't see the surface of the coffee table, and the layers of sofa cushions nudged her lower back uncomfortably.

"Only thing we've got is Bud Light—is that okay?" Fiona asked when she returned. She was carrying two cans and a sack of potato chips.

"It's perfect; I'm on a diet," Maggie said.

She accepted one of the cans and popped the tab, while Fiona settled next to her on the couch. "*I* ought to go on a diet," Fiona said. She ripped open the cellophane sack. "Snack foods are my biggest downfall."

"Oh, mine too," Maggie said. She took a sip of her beer. It was crisp-tasting and bitter; it brought memories flooding in the way the smell of a certain perfume will. How long had it been since she'd last had a beer? Maybe not since Leroy was a baby. Back then (she recalled as she waved away the potato chips), she sometimes drank as many as two or three cans a day, keeping Fiona company because beer was good for her milk supply, they'd heard. Now that would probably be frowned upon, but at the time they had felt dutiful and virtuous, sipping their Miller High Lifes while the baby drowsily nursed. Fiona used to say she could feel the beer zinging directly to her breasts. She and Maggie would start drinking when Maggie came home from work— midafternoon or so, just the two of them. They would grow all warm and confiding together. By the time Maggie got around to fixing supper she would be feeling, oh, not drunk or anything but filled with optimism, and then later at the table she might act a bit more talkative than usual. It was nothing the others would notice, though. Except perhaps for Daisy. "Really, Mom. Honestly," Daisy would say. But then, she was always saying that.

As was Maggie's mother, come to think of it. "Honestly, Maggie." She had stopped by late one afternoon and caught Maggie lounging on the couch, a beer balanced on her midriff, while Fiona sat next to her singing "Dust in the Wind" to the baby. "How have you let things get so *common*?" Mrs. Daley had asked, and Maggie, looking around her, had all at once wondered too. The cheap, pulpy magazines scattered everywhere, the wadded wet diapers, the live-in daughter-in-law—it did look common. How had it happened?

"I wonder if Claudine and Peter ever married," Maggie said now, and she took another sip of her beer.

"Claudine? Peter?" Fiona asked.

"On that soap opera we used to watch. Remember? His sister Natasha was trying to split them up."

"Oh, Lord, Natasha. She was one mean lady," Fiona said. She dug deep into the sack of potato chips.

"They had just got engaged when you left us," Maggie said. "They were planning to throw a big party and then Natasha found out about it—remember?"

"She looked kind of like this girl I always detested in elementary school," Fiona said.

"Then you left us," Maggie said.

Fiona said, "Actually, now that you mention it she must not have managed to split them up after all, because a couple of years later they had this baby that was kidnapped by a demented airline stewardess."

"At first I couldn't believe you had really gone for good," Maggie said. "Whole months passed by when I'd come home and switch on the TV and check what was happening with Claudine and Peter, just so I could fill you in when you got back."

"Anyhow," Fiona said. She set her beer on the coffee table.

"Silly of me, wasn't it? Wherever you had gone, you surely would have been near a TV. It's not like you had abandoned civilization. But I don't know; maybe I just wanted to keep up with the story for my own sake, so that after you came back we could carry on like before. I was positive you'd be coming back."

"Well, anyhow. What's past is past," Fiona said.

"No, it's not! People are always saying that, but what's past is never past; not entirely," Maggie told her. "Fiona, this is a marriage we're talking about. You two had so much sunk into it; such an exhausting amount was sunk in. And then one day you quarreled over nothing whatsoever, no worse than any other time, and off you went. As easy as that! Shrugged your shoulders and walked away from it! How could that be possible?"

"It just was, all right?" Fiona said. "Jiminy! Do we have to keep rehashing this?" And she reached for her beer can and drank, tipping her head far back. She wore rings on every one of her fingers, Maggie saw—some plain silver, some set with turquoise stones. That was new. But her nails were still painted the pearly pink that had always seemed her special color, that could bring her instantly to mind whenever Maggie caught sight of it somewhere.

Maggie rotated her own can thoughtfully, meanwhile stealing sideways peeks at Fiona.

"I wonder where Leroy's got to," Fiona said.

Another evasion. It was obvious where she'd got to; she was right outside the window. "Give her a little more spin, now," Ira was saying, and Leroy called, "Watch out, here comes a killer!"

"On the radio you said your first marriage was real, true love," Maggie told Fiona.

"Look. How many times—"

"Yes, yes," Maggie said hastily, "that wasn't you; I understand. But still, something about what the girl on the radio was saying . . . I mean it's like she was speaking for more than just herself. It's like she was talking about what the whole *world* was doing. 'Next Saturday I'm marrying for security,' she said, and I just suddenly had this sense that the world was sort of drying up or withering away or something, getting small and narrow and pinched. I felt so—I don't know—so unhopeful, all of a sudden. Fiona, maybe I shouldn't mention this, but last spring Jesse brought this young woman he'd met to supper—oh, no one important! not anybody important!—and I thought to myself, Well, she's all very well and good, I suppose, but she's not the real thing. I mean she's only second best, I thought. We're only making do here. Oh, why is everyone settling for less? is what I thought. And I feel the same way about what's-his-name, Mark Derby. Why bother dating someone merely because he asks you, when you and Jesse love each other so much?"

"You call it love when he signed that lawyer's papers without a word and sent them back, not putting up the slightest token of a fight?" Fiona asked. "When he's two or three or even four months late with his support check and then mails it without a letter or a note, not even my full name on the envelope but only F. Moran?"

"Well, that's pure pride, Fiona. Both of you are way too—"

"And when he hasn't laid eyes on his daughter since her fifth birthday? Try explaining that to a child. 'Oh, he's just proud, Leroy, honey—' "

"Fifth birthday?" Maggie said.

"Here she keeps wondering why all the other kids have fathers. Even the kids whose parents are divorced—at least they get to see their fathers on weekends."

"He visited on her fifth birthday?" Maggie asked.

"Look at that! He didn't even bother telling you."

"What: He just showed up? Or what?"

"He showed up out of the blue in a car packed to the teeth with the most unsuitable presents you ever saw," Fiona said. "Stuffed animals and dolls, and a teddy bear so big he had to strap it in the front seat like a human because it wouldn't fit through the rear door. It was much too big for a child to cuddle, not that Leroy would have wanted to. She isn't a cuddly type of person. She's more the sporty type. He should have brought her athletic equipment; he should have brought her—"

"But, Fiona, how was he to know that?" Maggie asked. She felt an ache beginning inside her; she grieved for her son with his carful of wrongheaded gifts that he must have spent his last penny on, because heaven knows he wasn't well off. She said, "He was trying his best, after all. He just didn't realize."

"Of course he didn't realize! He didn't have the faintest idea; the last time he visited, she was still a baby. So here he comes with this drink-and-wet doll that cries 'Mama,' and when he catches sight of Leroy in her dungarees he stops short; you can see he's not pleased. He says, 'Who *is* that?' He says, 'But she's so—' I had had to run fetch her from the neighbor's and quick smooth down her hair on the way through the alley. In the alley I told her, 'Tuck your shirt in, honey. Here, let me lend you my barrette,' and Leroy stood still for it, which she wouldn't do ordinarily, believe me. And when I had fastened the barrette I said, 'Stand back and let me look at you,' and she stood back and licked her lips and said, 'Am I okay? Or not.' I said, 'Oh, honey, you're beautiful,' and then she walks into the house and Jesse says, 'But she's so—' "

"He was surprised she had grown, that's all it was," Maggie said.

"I could have cried for her," Fiona said.

"Yes," Maggie said gently. She knew how that felt.

Fiona said, " 'She's so what, Jesse?' I ask him. 'She's so what? How dare you come tromping in here telling me she's so something or other when the last time you sent us a check was December? And instead you waste your money on this trash, this junk,' I tell him, 'this poochy-faced baby doll when the only doll she'll bother with is G.I. Joe.' "

"Oh, Fiona," Maggie said.

"Well, what did he expect?"

"Oh, why does this always happen between you two? He loves you, Fiona. He loves you both. He's just the world's most inept at showing it. If you knew what it must have cost him to make that trip! I can't tell you how often I've asked him, I've said, 'Are you planning to let your daughter just drift on out of your life? Because that's what she's bound to do, Jesse; I'm warning you,' and he said, 'No, but I don't . . . but I can't figure how to . . . I can't stand to be one of those artificial fathers,' he said, 'with those busywork visits to zoos and smalltalk suppers at McDonald's.' And I said, 'Well, it's better than nothing, isn't it?' and he said, 'No, it is not better than nothing. It's not at all. And what do *you* know about the subject, anyhow?'—that way he does, you've seen how he does, where he acts so furious but if you look at his eyes you'll notice these sudden dark rings beneath them that he used to get when he was just a little fellow trying not to cry."

Fiona ducked her head. She started tracing the rim of her beer can with one finger.

"On Leroy's first birthday," Maggie said, "he was all set to come with us and visit, I told you that. I said, 'Jesse, I really feel it would mean a lot to Fiona if you came,' and he said, 'Well, maybe I will, then. Yes,' he said, 'I could do that, I guess,' and he asked me about fifty times what kind of present a year-old baby might enjoy. Then he went shopping all Saturday and brought back one of those shape-sorter boxes, but Monday after work he exchanged it for a woolen lamb because, he said, he didn't want to seem like he was pushing her intellectually or anything. 'I don't want to be like Grandma Daley, always popping up with these educational toys,' he said, and then on Thursday—her birthday was a Friday that year, remember?—he asked me exactly how you had phrased your invitation. 'I mean,' he said, 'did it sound to you like maybe she was expecting me to stay on over the weekend? Because if so then I might borrow Dave's van and drive up separately from you and Dad.' And I said, 'Well, you could do that, Jesse. Yes, what a good idea; why don't you.' He said, 'But how did she word it, is what I'm asking,' and I said, 'Oh, I forget,' and he said, 'Think.' I said, 'Well, as a matter of fact . . .' I said, 'Um, in fact, she didn't actually word it any way, Jesse, not directly straight out,' and he said, 'Wait. I thought she told you it would mean a lot to her if I came.' I said, 'No, it was me who said that, but I know it's true. I know it would mean a great deal to her.' He said, 'What's going on here? You told me clearly that it was Fiona who said that.' I said, 'I never told you any such thing! Or at least I don't think I did; unless maybe perhaps by accident I—' He said, 'Are you saying she didn't ask for me?' 'Well, I just know she would have,' I told him, 'if the two of you were not so all-fired careful of your dignity. I just know she wanted to, Jesse—' But by then he was gone. Slammed out of the house and vanished, did not come home all Thursday night, and Friday we had to set off without him. I was so disappointed."

"You were disappointed!" Fiona said. "You had promised you would be bringing him. I waited, I dressed up, I got myself a make-over at the beauty parlor. Then you turn into the driveway and he's not with you."

"Well, I told him when we got home," Maggie said, "I told him, 'We tried our best, Jesse, but it wasn't us Fiona dressed up for, you can be certain. It was you, and you should have seen her face when you didn't get out of the car.' "

Fiona slapped a sofa cushion with the flat of her palm. She said, "I might have known you would do that."

"Do what?"

"Oh, make me look pitiful in front of Jesse."

"I didn't make you look pitiful! I merely said—"

"So then he calls me on the phone. I knew that was why he called me. Says, 'Fiona? Hon?' I could hear it in his voice that he was sorry for me. I knew what you must have told him. I say, 'What do you want? Are you calling for a reason?' He says, 'No, um, no reason . . .' I say, 'Well, then, you're wasting your money, aren't you?' and I hang up."

"Fiona, for Lord's sake," Maggie said. "Didn't it occur to you he might have called because he missed you?"

Fiona said, "Ha!" and took another swig of beer.

"I wish you could have seen him the way I saw him," Maggie said. "After you left, I mean. He was a wreck! A shambles. His most cherished belonging was your tortoiseshell soapbox."

"My what?"

"Don't you remember your soapbox, the one with the tortoiseshell lid?"

"Well, yes."

"He would open it sometimes and draw a breath of it," Maggie said. "I saw him! I promise! The day you left, that evening, I found Jesse in the bedroom with his nose buried deep in your soapbox and his eyes closed."

"Well, what in the world?" Fiona said.

"I believe he must have inherited some of my sense of smell," Maggie told her.

"You're talking about that little plastic box. The one I used to keep my face soap in."

"Then as soon as he saw me he hid it behind his back," Maggie said. "He was embarrassed I had caught him. He always liked to act so devil-may-care; you know how he acted. But a few days later, when your sister came for your things, I couldn't find your soapbox anywhere. She was packing up your cosmetic case, is how I happened to think of it, so I said, 'Let's see, now, somewhere around . . .' but that soapbox seemed to have vanished. And I couldn't ask Jesse because he had walked out as soon as your sister walked in, so I started opening his bureau drawers and that's where I found it, in his treasure drawer among the things he never throws away—his old-time baseball cards and the clippings about his band. But I didn't give it to your sister. I just shut the drawer again. In fact, I believe he has kept that soapbox to this day, Fiona, and you can't tell me it's because he feels sorry for you. He wants to remember you. He goes by smell, just the way I do; smell is what brings a person most clearly to his mind."

Fiona gazed down at her beer can. That eye shadow was oddly attractive, Maggie realized. Sort of peach-like. It gave her lids a peach's pink blush.

"Does he still look the same?" Fiona asked finally.

"The same?"

"Does he still look like he used to?"

"Why, yes."

Fiona gave a sharp sigh.

There was a moment of quiet, during which Leroy said, "Durn! Missed." A car passed, trailing threads of country music. *I've had some bad times, lived through some sad times* . . .

"You know," Fiona said, "there's nights when I wake up and think, How could things have gotten so twisted? They started out perfectly simple. He was just this boy I was crazy about and followed anyplace his band played, and everything was so straightforward. When he didn't notice me at first, I sent him a telegram, did he ever mention that? *Fiona Stuckey would like to go with you to Deep Creek Lake,* that's what it said, because I knew he was planning to drive there with his friends. And so he took me along, and that's where it all began. Wasn't that straightforward? But then, I don't know, everything sort of folded over on itself and knotted up, and I'm not even sure how it happened. There's times I think, Shoot, maybe I ought to just fire off another telegram. *Jesse,* I'd say, *I love you still, and it begins to seem I always will.* He wouldn't even have to answer; it's just something I want him to know. Or I'll be down in Baltimore at my sister's and I'll think, Why not drop by and visit him? Just walk in on him? Just see what happens?"

"Oh, you ought to," Maggie said.

"But he'd say, 'What are *you* doing here?' Or some such thing. I mean it's bound and determined to go wrong. The whole cycle would just start over again."

"Oh, Fiona, isn't it time somebody broke that cycle?" Maggie asked. "Suppose he did say that; not that I think he would. Couldn't you for once stand your ground and say, 'I'm here because I want to see you, Jesse'? Cut through all this to-and-fro, these hurt feelings and these misunderstandings. Say, 'I'm here because I've missed you. So there!' "

"Well, maybe I should do that," Fiona said slowly.

"Of course you should."

"Maybe I should ride back down with you."

"With us?"

"Or maybe not."

"You're talking about . . . this afternoon?"

"No, maybe not; what am I saying? Oh, Lord. I knew I shouldn't drink in the daytime; it always makes my head so muzzy—"

"But that's a wonderful idea!" Maggie said.

"Well, if Leroy came with me, for instance; if we just made a little visit. I mean visiting you two, not Jesse. After all, you're Leroy's grandparents, right? What could be more natural? And then spent the night at my sister's place—"

"No, not at your sister's. Why there? We have plenty of room at our house."

There was a crunch of gravel outside—the sound of a car rolling up. Maggie tensed, but Fiona didn't seem to hear. "And then tomorrow after lunch we could catch the Greyhound bus," she was saying, "or let's see, midafternoon at the latest. The next day's a working day and Leroy has school, of course—"

A car door clunked shut. A high, complaining voice called, "Leroy?"

Fiona straightened. "Mom," she said, looking uneasy.

The voice said, "Who's that you got with you, Leroy?" And then, "Why. Mr. Moran."

What Ira answered, Maggie had no idea. All that filtered through the venetian blinds was a brief rumble.

"My, my," Mrs. Stuckey said. "Isn't this . . ." something or other.

"It's Mom," Fiona told Maggie.

"Oh, how nice; we'll get to see her after all," Maggie said unhappily.

"She is going to have a fit."

"A fit?"

"She would kill me if I was to go and visit you."

Maggie didn't like the uncertain sound of that verb construction.

The screen door opened and Mrs. Stuckey plodded in—a gray, scratchy-haired woman wearing a ruffled sundress. She was lugging two beige plastic shopping bags, and a cigarette drooped from her colorless, cracked lips. Oh, Maggie had never understood how such a woman could have given birth to Fiona—finespun Fiona. Mrs. Stuckey set the bags in the center of the shag rug. Even then, she didn't glance up. "One thing I despise," she said, removing her cigarette, "is these new-style plastic grocery bags with the handles that cut your fingers in half."

"How are you, Mrs. Stuckey?" Maggie asked.

"Also they fall over in the car trunk and spill their guts out," Mrs. Stuckey said. "I'm all right, I suppose."

"We just stopped by for a second," Maggie said. "We had to go to a funeral in Deer Lick."

"Hmm," Mrs. Stuckey said. She took a drag of her cigarette. She held it like a foreigner, pinched between her thumb and her index finger. If she had calculated outright, she could not have chosen a more unbecoming dress. It completely exposed her upper arms, which were splotched and doughy.

Maggie waited for Fiona to mention the trip to Baltimore, but Fiona was fiddling with her largest turquoise ring. She slid it up past her first knuckle, twisted it, and slid it down again. So Maggie had to be the one. She said, "I've been trying to talk Fiona into coming home with us for a visit."

"Fat chance of that," Mrs. Stuckey said.

Maggie looked over at Fiona. Fiona went on fiddling with her ring. "Well, she's thinking she might do it," Maggie said finally.

Mrs. Stuckey drew back from her cigarette to glare at the long tube of ash at its tip. Then she stubbed it out in the rowboat, perilously close to the yellow sponge. A strand of smoke wound toward Maggie.

"Me and Leroy might go just for the weekend," Fiona said faintly.

"For the what?"

"For the weekend."

Mrs. Stuckey stooped for the grocery bags and started wading out of the room, bending slightly at the knees so her arms looked too long for her body. At the door she said, "I'd sooner see you lying in your casket."

"But, Mom!"

Fiona was on her feet now, following her into the hallway. She said, "Mom, the weekend's half finished anyhow. We're talking about just one single night! One night at Leroy's grandparents' house."

"And Jesse Moran would be nowhere about, I suppose," Mrs. Stuckey said at a distance. There was a crash—presumably the grocery bags being dumped on a counter.

"Oh, Jesse might be *around* maybe, but—"

"Yah, yah," Mrs. Stuckey said on an outward breath.

"Besides, so what if he is? Don't you think Leroy should get to know her daddy?"

Mrs. Stuckey's answer to that was just a mutter, but Maggie heard it clearly. "Anyone whose daddy is Jesse Moran is better off staying strangers."

Well! Maggie felt her face grow hot. She had half a mind to march out to the kitchen and give Mrs. Stuckey what for. "Listen," she would say. "You think there haven't been times I've cursed your daughter? She hurt my son to the bone. There were times I could have wrung her neck, but have you ever heard me speak a word against her?"

In fact, she even stood up, with a sudden, violent motion that creaked the sofa springs, but then she paused. She smoothed down the front of her dress. The gesture served to smooth her thoughts as well, and instead of heading for the kitchen she collected her purse and went off to find a bathroom, clamping her lips very tightly. Please, God, don't let the bathroom lie on the other side of the kitchen. No, there it was—the one open door at the end of the hall. She caught the watery green of a shower curtain.

After she had used the toilet, she turned on the sink faucet and patted her cheeks with cool water. She bent closer to the mirror. Yes, definitely she had a flustered look. She would have to get hold of herself. She hadn't finished even that one beer, but she thought it might be affecting her. And it was essential just now to play her cards right.

For instance, about Jesse. Although she had failed to mention it to Fiona, Jesse lived in an apartment uptown now, and therefore they couldn't merely assume that he would happen by while Fiona was visiting. He would have to be expressly invited. Maggie hoped he hadn't made other plans. Saturday: That could mean trouble. She checked her watch. Saturday night he might very well be singing with his band, or just going out with his friends. Sometimes he even dated—no one important, but still . . .

She flushed the toilet, and under cover of the sound she slipped out of the bathroom and opened the door next to it. This room must be Leroy's. Dirty clothes and comic books lay everywhere. She closed the door again and tried the one opposite. Ah, a grownup's room. A decorous white candlewick bedspread, and a telephone on the nightstand.

"After all you done to free yourself, you want to go back to that boy and get snaggled up messy as ever," Mrs. Stuckey said, clattering tin cans.

"Who says I'm getting snaggled? I'm just paying a weekend visit."

"He'll have you running circles around him just like you was before."

"Mom, I'm twenty-five years old. I'm not that same little snippet I used to be."

Maggie closed the door soundlessly behind her and went over to lift the receiver. Oh, dear, no push buttons. She winced each time the dial made its noisy, rasping return to home base. The voices in the kitchen continued, though. She relaxed and pressed the receiver to her ear.

One ring. Two rings.

It was a good thing Jesse was working today. For the last couple of weeks, the phone in his apartment had not been ringing properly. He could call other people all right, but he never knew when someone might be calling him. "Why don't you get it fixed? Or buy a new one; they're dirt cheap these days," Maggie had said, but he said, "Oh, I don't know, it's kind of a gas. Anytime I pass the phone I just pick it up at random. I say, 'Hello?' Twice I've actually found a person on the other end." Maggie had to smile now, remembering that. There was something so . . . oh, so *lucky* about Jesse. He was so fortunate and funny and haphazard.

"Chick's Cycle Shop," a boy said.

"Could I speak to Jesse, please?"

The receiver at the other end clattered unceremoniously against a hard surface. "Jess!" the boy called, moving off. There was a silence, overlaid by the hissing sound of long distance.

Of course this was stealing, if you wanted to get picky about it— using someone else's phone to call out of state. Maybe she ought to leave a couple of quarters on the nightstand. Or would that be considered an insult? With Mrs. Stuckey, there was no right way to do a thing.

Jesse said, "Hello."

"Jesse?"

"Ma?"

His voice was Ira's voice, but years younger.

"Jesse, I can't talk long," she whispered.

"What? Speak up, I can barely hear you."

"I can't," she said.

"What?"

She cupped the mouthpiece with her free hand. "I was wondering," she said. "Do you think you could come to supper tonight?"

"Tonight? Well, I was sort of planning on—"

"It's important," she said.

"How come?"

"Well, it just is," she said, playing for time.

She had a decision to make, here. She could pretend it was on Daisy's account, for Daisy's going away. (That was safe enough. In spite of their childhood squabbles he was fond of Daisy, and had asked her only last week whether she would forget him after she left.) Or she could tell him the truth, in which case she might set in motion another of those ridiculous scenes.

But hadn't she just been saying it was time to cut through all that?

She took a deep breath. She said, "I'm having Fiona and Leroy to dinner."

"You're what?"

"Don't hang up! Don't say no! This is your only daughter!" she cried in a rush.

And then glanced anxiously toward the door, fearing she'd been too loud.

"Now, slow down, Ma," Jesse said.

"Well, we're up here in Pennsylvania," she said more quietly, "because we happened to be going to a funeral. Max Gill died—I don't know if Daisy's had a chance to tell you. And considering that we were in the neighborhood . . . and Fiona told me in so many words that she wanted very much to see you."

"Oh, Ma. Is this going to be like those other times?"

"What other times?"

"Is this like when you said she phoned and I believed you and phoned her back—"

"She did phone then! I swear it!"

"*Some*body phoned, but you had no way of knowing who. An anonymous call. You didn't tell me that part, did you?"

Maggie said, "The telephone rang, I picked it up. I said, 'Hello?' No answer. It was just a few months after she left; who else could it have been? I said, 'Fiona?' She hung up. If it wasn't Fiona, why did she hang up?"

"Then all you tell me is: 'Jesse, Fiona called today,' and I break my neck getting to the phone and make a total fool of myself. I say, 'Fiona? What did you want?' and she says, 'To whom am I speaking, please?' I say, 'Goddamn it, Fiona, you know perfectly well this is Jesse,' and she says, 'Don't you use that language with me, Jesse Moran,' and I say, 'Now, look here. It wasn't me who called *you*, may I remind you,' and she says, 'But it was you, Jesse, because here you are on the line, aren't you,' and I say, 'But goddamn it—' "

"Jesse," Maggie said, "Fiona says she sometimes thinks of sending you another telegram."

"Telegram?"

"Like the first one. You remember the first one."

"Yes," Jesse said. "I remember."

"You never told me about that. But at any rate," she hurried on, "the telegram would read, *Jesse, I love you still, and it begins to seem I always will.*"

A moment passed.

Then he said, "You just don't quit, do you?"

"You think I'd make such a thing up?"

"If she really wanted to send it, then what stopped her?" he asked. "Why didn't I ever get it? Hmm?"

"How could I make it up when I didn't even know about the first one, Jesse? Answer me that! And I'm quoting her exactly; for once I'm able to tell you exactly how she worded it. I remember because it was one of those unintentional rhymes. You know the way things can rhyme when you don't want them to. It's so ironic, because if you did want them to, you'd have to rack your brain for days and comb through special dictionaries. . . ."

She was babbling whatever came to mind, just to give Jesse time to assemble a response. Was there ever anyone so scared of losing face? Not counting Fiona, of course.

Then she imagined she heard some change in the tone of his silence—a progression from flat disbelief to something less certain. She let her voice trail off. She waited.

"If I did happen to come," he said finally, "what time would you be serving supper?"

"You'll do it? You will? Oh, Jesse, I'm so glad! Let's say six-thirty," she told him. "Bye!" and she hung up before he could proceed to some further, more resistant stage.

She stood beside the bed a moment. In the front yard, Ira called, "Whoa, there!"

She picked up her purse and left the room.

Fiona was kneeling in the hallway, rooting through the bottom of a closet. She pulled out a pair of galoshes and threw them aside. She reached in again and pulled out a canvas tote bag.

"Well, I talked to Jesse," Maggie told her.

Fiona froze. The tote bag was suspended in midair.

"He's really pleased you're coming," Maggie said.

"Did he say that?" Fiona asked.

"He certainly did."

"I mean in so many words?"

Maggie swallowed. "No," she said, because if there was a cycle to be broken here, she herself had had some part in it; she knew that. She said, "He just told me he'd be there for supper. But anyone could hear how pleased he was."

Fiona studied her doubtfully.

"He said, 'I'll be there!' " Maggie told her.

Silence.

" 'I'll be there right after work, Ma! You can count on me!' " Maggie said. " 'Goddamn! I wouldn't miss it for the world!' "

"Well," Fiona said finally.

Then she unzipped the tote bag.

"If I were traveling alone I'd make do with just a toothbrush," she told Maggie. "But once you've got a kid, you know how it is. Pajamas, comics, storybooks, coloring books for the car . . . and she has to have her baseball glove, her everlasting baseball glove. You never know when you might rustle up a game, she says."

"No, that's true, you never do," Maggie said, and she laughed out loud for sheet happiness.

2

Ira had a way, when he was truly astonished, of getting his face sort of locked in one position. Here Maggie had worried he'd be angry, but no, he just took a step backward and stared at her and then his face locked, blank and flat like something carved of hardwood.

He said, "Fiona's what?"

"She's coming for a visit," Maggie said. "Won't that be nice?"

No reaction.

"Fiona and Leroy, both," Maggie told him.

Still no reaction.

Maybe it would have been better if he'd got angry.

She moved past him, keeping her smile. "Leroy, honey, your mother wants you," she called. "She needs you to help her pack."

Leroy was less easily surprised than Ira, evidently. She said, "Oh. Okay," and give the Frisbee an expert flip in Ira's direction before skipping toward the house. The Frisbee ricocheted off Ira's left knee and landed in the dirt. He gazed down at it absently.

"We should have cleaned the car out," Maggie told him. "If I'd known we would be riding so many passengers today . . ."

She went over to the Dodge, which was blocked now by a red Maverick that must be Mrs. Stuckey's. You could tell the Dodge had recently traveled some distance. It had a beaten-down, dusty look. She opened a rear door and tsked. A stack of library books slumped across the back seat, and a crocheted sweater that she had been hunting for days lay there all squinched and creased, no doubt from being sat upon by Otis. The floor was cobbled with cloudy plastic lids from soft-drink cups. She reached in to gather the books—major, important novels by Dostoevsky and Thomas Mann. She had checked them out in a surge of good intentions at the start of the summer and was returning them unread and seriously overdue. "Open the trunk, will you?" she asked Ira.

He moved slowly toward the trunk and opened it, not changing his expression. She dumped in the books and went back for the sweater.

"How could this happen?" Ira asked her.

"Well, we were discussing her soapbox, see, and—"

"Her what? I mean it came about so quickly. So all of a sudden. I leave you alone for a little game of Frisbee and the next thing I know you're out here with beer on your breath and a whole bunch of unexpected houseguests."

"Why, Ira, I would think you'd be glad," she told him. She folded the sweater and laid it in the trunk.

"But it's like the second I shut the door behind me, you two got down to business," he said. "How do you accomplish these things?"

Maggie started collecting soft-drink lids from the floor of the car. "You can close the trunk now," she told him.

She carried a fistful of lids around to the rear of the house and dropped them in a crumpled garbage can. The cover was only a token cover, a battered metal beret that she replaced crookedly on top. And the house's siding was speckled with mildew, and rust stains trailed from a fuel tank affixed beneath the window.

"How long will they be staying?" Ira asked when she returned.

"Just till tomorrow."

"We have to take Daisy to college tomorrow, did you forget?"

"No, I didn't forget."

"Aha," he said. "Your fiendish plot: Throw Jesse and Fiona together on their own. I know you, Maggie Moran."

"You don't necessarily know me at all," she told him.

If things went the way she hoped they would this evening, she would have no need of plots for tomorrow.

She opened the front door on her side of the Dodge and sank onto the seat. Inside, the car was stifling. She blotted her upper lip on the hem of her skirt.

"So how do we present this?" Ira asked. " 'Surprise, surprise, Jesse boy! Here's your ex-wife, here's your long-lost daughter. Never mind that you legally parted company years ago; *we've* decided you're getting back together now.' "

"Well, for your information," she said, "I've already told him they're coming, and he'll be at our house for supper."

Ira bent to look in on her. He said, "You told him?"

"Right."

"How?" he asked.

"By phone, of course."

"You phoned him? You mean just now?"

"Right."

"And he'll be there for supper?"

"Right."

He straightened up and leaned against the car. "I don't get it," he said finally.

"What's to get?"

"There's something too simple about it."

All she could see of him was his midsection—a hollow-looking white shirt wilting over a belt. Wouldn't he be baking? This metal must radiate heat like a flatiron. Although it was true that the air had grown cooler now and the sun was slightly less direct, already starting to slip behind a faraway scribble of trees.

"I'm worried about that Maverick," she said, speaking to Ira's belt buckle.

"Hmm?"

"Mrs. Stuckey's Maverick. I'd hate to ask her to move it, and I'm not sure we have room to get around it."

That caught him, as she'd guessed it would—a question of logistics. He left, abruptly; she felt the car rock. He wandered off to check the Maverick's position, and Maggie tipped her head back against the seat and closed her eyes.

Why was Ira so negative about Jesse? Why did he always have that skeptical twist to his voice when he discussed him? Oh, Jesse wasn't perfect—good heavens, no—but he had all kinds of endearing qualities. He was so generous and affectionate. And if he lost his temper easily, why, he regained it easily too, and had never been known to bear a grudge, which was more than you could say for Ira.

Was it plain old envy—a burdened, restrained man's envy of someone who was constitutionally carefree?

When Jesse was just a baby Ira was always saying, "Don't pick him up every time he cries. Don't feed him every time he's hungry. You'll spoil him."

"Spoil him?" Maggie had asked. "Feeding him when he's hungry is spoiling him? That's nonsense."

But she had sounded more confident than she'd felt. *Was* she spoiling him? This was her very first experience with an infant. She had been the youngest in her family and never had the casual contact with babies that some of her friends had had. And Jesse was such a puzzling baby—colicky, at the start, giving no hint of the merry little boy he would later turn out to be. He had flown into tiny, red-faced rages for no apparent reason in the middle of the night. Maggie had had to walk him endlessly, wearing an actual path in the rug around the dining room table. Was it possible, she had wondered, that this baby just plain didn't like her? Where was it written that a child was always compatible with his parents? When you thought about it, it was amazing that so many families got along as well as they did. All they had to rely on was luck—the proper personality genes turning up like dice. And in Jesse's case, maybe the luck had been poor. She felt he was chafing against his parents. They were too narrow, too sedate, too conservative.

Once, carrying a squalling Jesse down the aisle of a city bus, Maggie had been surprised to feel him suddenly relax in her arms. He had hushed, and she had looked at his face. He was staring at a dressed-up blonde in one of the seats. He started smiling at her. He held out his arms. His kind of person, at last! Unfortunately, though, the blonde was reading a magazine and she never gave him so much as a glance.

And then the minute he discovered other children—all of whom instantly loved him—why, he hit the streets running and was hardly seen at home anymore. But that, too, Ira found fault with, for Jesse missed his curfews, forgot to appear for dinner, neglected his schoolwork in favor of a pickup basketball game in the alley. Mr. Moment-by-Moment, Ira used to call him. And Maggie had to admit the name was justified. Were some people simply born without the ability to link one moment to the next? If so, then Jesse was one of them: a disbeliever in consequences, mystified by others' habit of holding against him things that had happened, why, hours ago! days ago! way last week, even! He was genuinely perplexed that someone could stay angry at something he himself had immediately forgotten.

Once when he was eleven or twelve he'd been horsing around with Maggie in the kitchen, punching his catcher's mitt while he teased her about her cooking, and the telephone rang and he answered and said, "Huh? Mr. Bunch?" Mr. Bunch was his sixth-grade teacher, so Maggie assumed the call was for Jesse and she turned back to her work. Jesse said, "Huh?" He said, "Wait a minute! You can't blame *me* for that!" Then he slammed the phone down, and Maggie, glancing over, saw those telltale dark rings beneath his eyes. "Jesse? Honey? What's the matter?" she had asked. "Nothing," he told her roughly, and he walked out. He left his catcher's mitt on the table, worn and deeply pocketed and curiously alive. The kitchen echoed.

But not ten minutes later she noticed him in the front yard with Herbie Albright, laughing uproariously, crashing through the little box-wood hedge as he'd been told not to a hundred times.

Yes, it was his laughter that she pictured when she thought of him—his eyes lit up and dancing, his teeth very white, his head thrown back to show the clean brown line of his throat. (And why was it that Maggie remembered the laughter while Ira remembered the tantrums?) In a family very nearly without a social life, Jesse was intensely, almost ridiculously social, knee-deep in friends. Classmates came home with him from school every afternoon, and sometimes as many as seven or eight stayed over on weekends, their sleeping bags taking up all the floor space in his room, their cast-off jackets and six-guns and model airplane parts spilling out into the hallway. In the morning when Maggie went to wake them for pancakes the musky, wild smell of boy hung in the doorway like curtains, and she would blink and back off and return to the safety of the kitchen, where little Daisy, swathed to her toes in one of Maggie's aprons, stood on a chair earnestly stirring batter.

He took up running one spring and ran like a maniac, throwing himself into it the way he did with everything that interested him, however briefly. This was when he was fifteen and not yet licensed to drive, so he sometimes asked Maggie for a lift to his favorite track, the Ralston School's cedar-chip-carpeted oval in the woods out in Baltimore County. Maggie would wait for him in the car, reading a library book and glancing up from time to time to check his progress. She could always spot him, even when the track was crowded with middle-aged ladies in sweat suits and Ralston boys in numbered uniforms. Jesse wore tattered jeans and a black T-shirt with the sleeves ripped off, but it wasn't only his clothes that identified him; it was his distinctive style of running. His gait was free and open, as if he were holding nothing in reserve for the next lap. His legs flew out and his arms made long reaching motions, pulling in handfuls of the air in front of him. Every time Maggie located him, her heart would pinch with love. Then he would vanish into the forested end of the track and she would go back to her book.

But one day he didn't come out of the forest. She waited but he didn't appear. And yet the others came, even the slowest, even the silly-looking Swedish-walker people with their elbows pumping like chicken wings. She got out of the car finally and went over to the track, shading her eyes. No Jesse. She followed the bend of the oval into the woods, her crepe-soled work shoes sinking into the cedar chips so her calf muscles felt weighted. People pounded past her, glancing over momentarily, giving her the impression they were leaving their faces behind. In the woods to her left, she noticed a flash of white. It was a girl in a white shirt and shorts, lying on her back in the leaves, and Jesse was lying on top of her. He was fully clothed but, yes, smack on top of her, and the girl's white arms were twined around his neck. "Jesse, I have to be getting home soon," Maggie called. Then she turned and walked back toward the car, feeling plain and clumsy. A moment later cedar chips crunched behind her and Jesse overtook her and sped past, his amazingly long gym shoes landing deftly, plop-plop, and his muscular brown arms scooping the air.

So then it was girls, girls, girls—a jostling parade of girls, all of them fair and slender and pretty, with soft, unformed faces and a tidy style of dressing. They called him on the phone and sent letters reeking of perfume and sometimes simply arrived on the doorstep, treating Maggie with a deference that made her feel ancient. They paid her vivacious compliments—"Oh, Mrs. Moran, I love that blouse!"—meanwhile searching behind her for Jesse. Maggie had to fight down the urge to bristle, to bar their entrance. Who would know better than she how deviously girls could behave? Why, a boy didn't stand a chance! But then Jesse would saunter out, not even rearranging his face at the sight of them, making no effort whatsoever, his T-shirt giving off the yeasty smell of fresh sweat and his hair obscuring his eyes. The girls would grow positively swaybacked with perkiness, and Maggie knew it was they who didn't stand a chance. She felt rueful and proud, both. She was ashamed of herself for feeling proud, and to make up for it she acted especially kind to every girl who came. Sometimes she acted so kind that the girls continued to visit her for months after Jesse had dropped them. They'd sit in the kitchen and confide in her, not just about Jesse but about other things as well, problems with their parents and such. Maggie enjoyed that. Usually Daisy would be sitting there too, her head bent over her homework, and Maggie had the feeling they were all three part of a warm community of females, a community she had missed out on when she was growing up with her brothers.

Was it about that time that the music began? Loud music, with a hammering beat. One day it just flooded the house, as if Jesse's turning adolescent had opened a door through which the drums and electric guitars suddenly poured in. Let him merely duck into the kitchen for a sandwich and the clock radio would start blaring out "Lyin' Eyes." Let him dash up to his room for his catcher's mitt and his stereo would swing into "Afternoon Delight." And of course he never turned anything off again, so long after he'd left the house the music would still be playing. Maybe he intended it that way. It was his signature, his footprint on their lives. "I'll be out in the world now, but don't forget me," he was saying, and there they sat, two stodgy grownups and a prim little girl, while "When Will I Be Loved" jangled through the emptiness he left behind him.

Then he stopped liking what his classmates liked and he claimed the Top Forty was dentist music, elevator music. ("Oh," Maggie said sadly, for she had enjoyed that music—or some of it, at least.) The songs that filled the house grew whining and slippery or downright ill-tempered, and they were sung by scroungy, beatnik-looking groups dressed in rags and tags and bits of military uniforms. (Meanwhile the old albums filtered downstairs to line the shelf beneath the living room hi-fi, each new stage Jesse entered adding to Maggie's collection of castoffs, which she sometimes played secretly when she was all alone in the house.)

And then he started writing his own songs, with peculiar modern names like "Microwave Quartet" and "Cassette Recorder Blues." A few of these he sang for Maggie when Ira wasn't around. He had a nasal, deadpan style of singing that was more like talking. To Maggie it sounded very professional, very much like what you might hear on the radio, but then, of course, she was only his mother. Although his friends were impressed, too; she knew that. His friend Don Burnham, whose second cousin had come this close to being hired as a roadie for the Ramones, said Jesse was good enough to form a group of his own and sing in public.

This Don Burnham was a perfectly nice, well-raised boy who had transferred to Jesse's school at the start of eleventh grade. When Jesse first brought him home, Don had made conversation with Maggie (not something you would take for granted, in a boy that age) and sat politely through Daisy's exhibit of her state-capitals postcard collection. "Next time I come," he'd told Maggie out of the blue, "I'll bring you my *Doonesbury* scrapbook." Maggie had said, "Oh, why, I'll look forward to that." But the next time he came he had his acoustic guitar along, and Jesse sang one of his songs for him while Don strummed beneath it. *Seems like this old world is on fast forward nowadays . . .* Then Don told Jesse he ought to sing in public, and from that moment ever afterward (or so it seemed in retrospect), Jesse was gone.

He formed a band called Spin the Cat—he and a bunch of older boys, high-school dropouts mostly. Maggie had no idea where he'd found them. He began to dress more heavily, as if for combat; he wore black denim shirts and black jeans and crumpled leather motorcycle boots. He came in at all hours smelling of beer and tobacco or, who knows, maybe worse than tobacco. He developed a following of a whole new type of girl, crisper and flashier, who didn't bother making up to Maggie or sitting in her kitchen. And in the spring it emerged that he hadn't attended school in some time, and would not be promoted from junior year to senior.

Seventeen and a half years old and he'd thrown away his future, Ira said, all for a single friendship. Never mind that Don Burnham wasn't even part of Jesse's band, and had passed smoothly on to senior year himself. In Ira's version of things, Don's one piece of advice had landed with a *ping!* and life had never been the same again. Don was some kind of providential instrument, fate's messenger. In Ira's version of things.

Shape up or ship out, Ira told Jesse. Earn the missing credits in summer school, or otherwise find a job and move to his own apartment. Jesse said he'd had a bellyful of school. He would be glad to get a job, he said, and he couldn't wait to move to his own apartment, where he could come and go as he pleased, with nobody breathing down his neck. Ira said, "Good riddance," and went upstairs without another word. Jesse left the house, tramping across the porch in his motorcycle boots. Maggie started crying.

How could Ira imagine Jesse's life? Ira was one of those people who are born competent. Everything came easy to him. There was no way he could fully realize how Jesse used to feel plodding off to school every morning—his shoulders already hunched against defeat, his jacket collar standing up crooked, and his hands shoved deep in his pockets. What it must be like to be Jesse! To have a perfectly behaved younger sister, and a father so seamless and infallible! Really his only saving grace was his mother, his harum-scarum klutzy mother, Maggie said to herself. She was making one of her wry private jokes but she meant it, all the same. And she wished he'd taken more from her. Her ability to see the best in things, for instance. Her knack for accepting, for adapting.

But no. Slit-eyed and wary, all his old light-heartedness gone, Jesse prowled the city in search of work. He was hoping for a job in a record store. He didn't even have pocket money (at this point that band of his still played for free—for the "exposure," was how they put it) and was forced to borrow bus fare from Maggie. And each day he came back glummer than the day before, and each evening he and Ira fought. "If you showed up for your interviews dressed like a normal person—" Ira told him.

"A place puts that much stock in appearance, I wouldn't want to work there anyhow," Jesse said.

"Fine, then you'd better learn how to dig ditches, because that's the only job where they *don't* put stock in appearance."

Then Jesse would slam out of the house once again, and how flat things seemed after he left! How shallow, how lacking in spirit! Maggie and Ira gazed at each other bleakly across the living room. Maggie blamed Ira; he was too harsh. Ira blamed Maggie; she was too soft.

Sometimes, deep down inside, Maggie blamed herself too. She saw now that there was a single theme to every decision she had made as a parent: The mere fact that her children were children, condemned for years to feel powerless and bewildered and confined, filled her with such pity that to add any further hardship to their lives seemed unthinkable. She could excuse anything in them, forgive them everything. She would have made a better mother, perhaps, if she hadn't remembered so well how it felt to be a child.

She dreamed that Jesse was dead—that in fact he had died years ago, back when he was still a sunny, prankish little boy, and she had somehow failed to realize it. She dreamed she was sobbing uncontrollably; there was no way to survive such a loss. Then she saw in the crowd on deck (for she was taking a boat trip, all at once) a child who resembled Jesse, standing with his parents, whom she had never seen before. He glanced over at her and looked quickly away, but she could tell that he thought she seemed familiar. She smiled at him. He glanced at her again and then looked away again. She edged a few inches closer, meanwhile pretending to study the horizon. He had come back to life in another family; that was how she explained it to herself. He wasn't hers now, but never mind, she would start over. She would win him to her side. She felt his eyes alight on her once more and she sensed how puzzled he was, half remembering her and half not; and she knew it meant that underneath, he and she would always love each other.

Now, at this point Daisy was nine years old, or just about to turn nine—enough of a child still, you would think, to keep Maggie fully occupied. But the fact was that at that very moment, Daisy took it into her head to start growing away too. She had always been a bit precocious. In her infancy Ira had called her Lady-Baby, because she was so mature and reserved, her small face a knot of opinion. At thirteen months she had undertaken her own toilet training. In first grade she had set her alarm for an hour earlier than anyone else in the household and slipped downstairs each morning to sort through the laundered clothes for a proper outfit. (She could iron better than Maggie even then, and liked to look neat as a pin and color-coordinated.) And now she seemed to have leapt ahead to that stage where the outside world took precedence over family. She had four very serious, like-minded friends, including one, Lavinia Murphy, whose mother was perfect. Perfect Mrs. Murphy headed the PTA and the Bake Sale and (since she didn't work) was free to drive the little girls to every kind of cultural event, and she hosted wonderful slumber parties, with treasure hunts. The spring of '78, Daisy practically lived with the Murphys. Maggie would come home from work and call, "Daisy?" but all she found was a silent house and a note on the front-hall bookshelf.

Then one afternoon the house wasn't silent after all but murmury and conspiratorial, she could sense it the moment she entered, and upstairs, Jesse's bedroom door was closed. She knocked. After a startled pause, Jesse called, "Just a second." She heard rustles and whispers. When he came out he had a girl in tow. Her long blond hair was rumpled and her lips had a bruised look. She sidled past Maggie with her eyes downcast and descended the stairs behind Jesse. Maggie heard the front door open; she heard Jesse saying goodbye in a low voice. As soon as he came back upstairs (unashamedly heading straight to Maggie), she told him that the mother of that girl, whoever she was, would be horrified to know her daughter had been alone with a boy in his bedroom. Jesse said, "Oh, no, her mom lives in Pennsylvania somewhere. Fiona stays with her sister, and her sister doesn't mind."

"Well, I do," Maggie said.

Jesse didn't argue with that, and the girl stopped coming around. Or at least she was out of sight when Maggie returned from work each day. Though Maggie had a feeling; she picked up certain clues. She noticed that Jesse was gone more than ever, that he returned abstracted, that his brief spells at home were marked by long private conversations on the upstairs telephone and it was always the same girl's voice— soft and questioning—when Maggie happened to lift the receiver.

He found a job in an envelope factory, finally, something to do with shipping, and started looking for an apartment. The only trouble was, the rents were so high and his paycheck was so puny. Good, Ira said. Now maybe he would have to face a few hard facts. Maggie wished Ira would just shut up. "Don't worry," she told Jesse. "Something will come along." That was toward the end of June. In July he was still living at home. And one Wednesday evening in August, he caught Maggie alone in the kitchen and informed her, very calmly and directly, that he seemed to have got this girl he knew in trouble.

The air in the room grew oddly still. Maggie wiped her hands on her apron.

She said, "Is it that Fiona person?"

He nodded.

"So now what?" Maggie asked. She was as cool as he was; she surprised herself. This seemed to be happening to someone else. Or maybe she had expected it without knowing. Maybe it was something that had been heading their way all along, like a glacier bearing down on them.

"Well," Jesse said, "that's what I needed to discuss with you. I mean, what I want and what she wants are two different things."

"What is it you want?" Maggie asked, thinking she knew.

"I want her to keep the baby."

For a moment, that didn't register. Even the word itself—"baby"— seemed incongruous on Jesse's lips. It seemed almost, in an awful way, cute.

She said, "Keep it?"

"I thought I'd start hunting an apartment for the three of us."

"You mean get married?"

"Right."

"But you're not even eighteen years old," Maggie said. "And I bet the girl isn't, either. You're too young."

"My birthday's in two weeks, Ma, and Fiona's is not long after. And she doesn't like school anyway; half the time she skips class and hangs out with me instead. Besides, I've always looked forward to having a kid. It's exactly what I've been needing: something of my own."

"Something of your own?"

"I'll just have to find a better-paying job, is all."

"Jesse, you've got a whole family of your own! What are you talking about?"

"But it's not the same," Jesse said. "I've just never felt . . . I don't know. So anyhow, I've been looking for a job that pays more money. See, a baby takes a lot of equipment and such. I've written down a list from Dr. Spock."

Maggie stared at him. The only question she could come up with was: "Where on earth did you get hold of a Dr. Spock?"

"At the bookstore; where else?"

"You went into a bookstore and bought a baby-care book?"

"Sure."

That seemed the biggest surprise of all. She couldn't picture it.

"I've learned a lot," he told her. "I think Fiona ought to breast-feed."

"Jesse—"

"I found these plans in *Home Hobby Journal* for building a cradle."

"Honey, you don't know how hard it is. You're children yourselves! You can't take on a baby."

"I'm asking you, Ma. I'm serious," Jesse said. And he did have that sharply etched look to his lips that he always got when he felt strongly about something.

"But just what are you asking me?" Maggie said.

"I want you to go and talk to Fiona."

"What? Talk about what?"

"Tell her you think she should keep it."

"You mean she wants to put it up for adoption," Maggie said. "Or else . . . um . . . stop the pregnancy."

"Well, that's what she says, but—"

"Which?" Maggie asked.

"The second thing."

"Ah."

"But she doesn't really want that. I know she doesn't," he said. "It's just that she's so stubborn. She expects the worst of me, seems like. She takes it for granted I'm going to, like, ditch her or something.

Well, first off, she didn't even tell me about it—can you believe it? Hid it from me! Went through weeks of worrying and never breathed a hint of it even though she saw me every day, near about. And then when the test came out positive, what does she do? Asks me for the money to get rid of the baby. I say, 'Huh? To do what? Now, hold on a sec,' I tell her. 'Aren't you skipping over a few of the usual steps here? Whatever happened to "What do *you* think, Jesse?" and "Which decision are we two going to settle on?" Aren't you going to offer me a chance?' I ask her. She says, 'Chance for what?' 'Well, what about marriage?' I ask her. 'What about me taking on my proper responsibilities, for God's sake?' She says, 'Don't do me any favors, Jesse Moran.' I say, 'Favors? You're talking about my son, here.' She says, 'Oh, I have no illusions'—that is how she talks when she gets on her high horse. 'I have no illusions,' she says. 'I knew what you were when I first laid eyes on you. Footloose and fancy-free,' she says, 'lead singer in a hard-rock band. You don't have to explain yourself to me.' I felt I'd been, like, stenciled or something. I mean where did she get this picture of me? Not from anything that happened in real life, I can tell you. So I say, 'No, I will *not* give you the money; no, sir, no way,' and she says, 'I might have known to expect that'—purposely misunderstanding. I hate when people do that, purposely acting so wronged and martyred. 'I might have figured,' she says, 'that I couldn't count on you for the simplest little abortion fee.' Says the word right out, kind of like she cracked the air with it; I honestly couldn't speak for a second. I say, 'Goddammit, Fiona—' and she says, 'Oh, fine, great, just cuss at me too on top of everything else,' and I say—"

"Jesse. Honey," Maggie said. She rubbed her left temple. She had a sense that she was losing track of some important thread here. "I really think that if Fiona has made up her mind—" she said.

"She's got an appointment the first thing Monday morning, at this clinic over on Whitside Avenue. Monday is her sister's day off; her sister's going with her. See there? She doesn't invite *me* to go with her. And I have talked to her till I'm blue in the face. There's nothing more I can say. So here's what I'm asking: You be the one. You go to the clinic and stop her."

"Me?"

"You always get along so well with my girlfriends. You can do it; I know you can. Tell her about my job. I'm quitting at the envelope factory. I've applied at this computer store, where they'll train me to fix computers, pay me while I'm learning. They said I have a good chance of getting hired. And also Dave in the band, his mother owns a house in Waverly near the stadium and the whole top floor's an apartment that'll be vacant by November, cheap as dirt, Dave says, with a little room for the baby. You're supposed to let the baby sleep in a separate room from its parents; I've been reading up on that.

You'd be amazed how much I know! I've decided I'm for pacifiers. Some people don't like the looks of them, but if you give a baby a pacifier he won't suck his thumb later on. Also, it is absolutely not true that pacifiers push their front teeth out of line."

He hadn't talked so much in months, but the sad part was that the more he talked, the younger he seemed. His hair was tangled where he'd run his fingers through it, and his body was all sharp angles as he tore around the kitchen. Maggie said, "Jesse, honey, I know you're going to make a wonderful father someday, but the fact of the matter is, this really has to be the girl's decision. It's the girl who has to go through the pregnancy."

"Not alone, though. I would support her. I would comfort her. I would take care of her. I want to do this, Ma."

She didn't know what more to say, and Jesse must have realized that. He stopped his pacing. He stood squarely in front of her. He said, "Look. You're my only hope. All I'm asking is, you let her know how I feel. Then she can decide whichever way she likes. What could be the harm in that?"

"But why can't *you* let her know how you feel?" Maggie said.

"Don't you think I've tried? I've talked till I'm blue in the face. But everything I say seems to come out wrong. She takes offense, I take offense; we just get all tangled in knots, somehow. By now we're used up. We're worn down into the ground."

Well, she certainly knew what that felt like.

"Couldn't you just consider it?" he asked.

She tilted her head.

"Just consider the possibility?"

"Oh," she said, "the *possibility*, maybe . . ."

He said, "Yes! That's all I'm asking! Thanks, Ma. Thanks a million."

"But, Jesse—"

"And you won't tell Dad yet, will you?"

"Well, not for the time being," she said lamely.

"You can picture what *he* would say," he said.

Then he gave her one of his quick hugs, and he was gone.

For the next few days she felt troubled, indecisive. Examples came to mind of Jesse's fickleness—how (like most boys his age) he kept moving on to new stages and new enthusiasms, leaving the old ones behind. You couldn't leave a wife and baby behind! But then other pictures came too: for instance, the year they'd all got the flu except for Jesse, and he had had to take care of them. She had glimpsed him blurrily through a haze of fever; he had sat on the edge of the bed and fed her a bowl of chicken soup, spoonful by spoonful, and when she fell asleep between swallows he had waited without complaint until she jerked awake, and then he fed her another spoonful.

"You haven't forgotten, have you?" Jesse asked now whenever he met up with her. And, "You won't go back on your promise, will you?"

"No, no . . ." she would say. And then, "What promise?" What had she let herself in for, exactly? He tucked a slip of paper into her palm one evening—an address on Whitside Avenue. The clinic, she supposed. She dropped it in her skirt pocket. She said, "Now you realize I can't—" But Jesse had already evaporated, dexterous as a cat burglar.

Ira was in a good mood those days, because he'd heard about the computer job. It had come through, as Jesse had foreseen, and he was due to start training in September. "This is more like it," Ira told Maggie. "This is something with a future. And who knows? Maybe after a bit he'll decide to go back to school. I'm sure they'll want him to finish school before they promote him."

Maggie was quiet, thinking.

She had to work on Saturday, so that kept her mind off things, but Sunday she sat a long time on the porch. It was a golden hot day and everyone seemed to be out walking infants. Carriages and strollers wheeled past, and men lunged by with babies in backpacks. Maggie wondered if a backpack was one of the pieces of equipment Jesse considered essential. She would bet it was. She cocked her head toward the house, listening. Ira was watching a ball game on TV and Daisy was away at Mrs. Perfect's. Jesse was still asleep, having come in late from playing at a dance in Howard County. She'd heard him climb the stairs a little after three, singing underneath his breath. *Girlie if I could, I would put you on defrost . . .*

"Music is so different now," she had said to Jesse once. "It used to be 'Love Me Forever' and now it's 'Help Me Make It Through the Night.' "

"Aw, Ma," he had said, "don't you get it? In the old days they just hid it better. It was always 'Help Me Make It Through the Night.' "

A line came to her from a song that was popular back when Jesse was a little boy. *I must think of a way*, it went, tactfully, tentatively, *into your heart . . .*

When Jesse was a little boy he liked to tell her stories while she cooked; he seemed to believe she needed entertaining. "Once there was a lady who never fed her children anything but doughnuts," he might begin, or, "Once there was a man who lived on top of a Ferris wheel." All of his stories were whimsical and inventive, and now that she considered, she saw that they had had in common the theme of joyousness, of the triumph of sheer fun over practicality. He strung one particular story out for weeks, something about a retarded father who bought an electric organ with the grocery money. The retarded part came from his Aunt Dorrie, she supposed. But the way he told it, the father's handicap was a kind of virtue. The father said, "What do we need food for anyhow? I like better for my children to hear nice music." Maggie laughed when she repeated the story to Ira, but Ira hadn't seen the humor. He took offense first on Dorrie's account (he didn't like the word "retarded") and then on his own. Why was it the father who was retarded? Why not the mother, was probably what he meant—much more realistic, given Maggie's shortcomings. Or maybe he didn't mean that at all, but Maggie imagined he did, and it developed into a quarrel.

They had quarreled over Jesse ever since he was born, it seemed now, always taking the same stances. Ira criticized, Maggie excused. Ira claimed that Jesse wouldn't keep a civil tongue in his head, refused to wipe that obstinate expression off his face, acted hopelessly inept when helping out at the shop. He just had to come into his own, Maggie said. For some it took longer than for others. "Decades longer?" Ira asked. She said, "Have a little patience, Ira." (A switch. Ira was the one with the patience. Maggie was the rusher-in.)

How was it that she had never realized the power of the young back when she was young herself? She saw it now as a missed opportunity. In her girlhood she'd been so easily cowed; she hadn't dreamed that children were capable of setting up such storms in a family.

She and Ira tried to keep their own storms private, but no doubt Jesse overheard at least a little. Or maybe he just sensed how they felt; for more and more, as he entered his teens, it was to Maggie that he offered his few crumbs of conversation, while he grew steadily more distant from Ira. By the time he told her about the baby, Maggie felt fairly distant from Ira herself. They'd been through too many arguments, rehashed the subject of Jesse too many thousand times. It wasn't merely her promise that kept Maggie from telling Ira about the baby; it was battle fatigue. Ira would hit the roof! And rightly so, of course.

But she thought of how Jesse had nudged her lips with the soup spoon, coaxing her to eat. Sometimes, at the height of her fever, she had wakened to hear thin, sad, faraway music emerging from the earphones on his head, and she had been convinced that they were the sounds of his innermost thoughts made clear to her at long last.

Monday morning she went to work as usual at seven but begged off sick at a quarter till nine and drove to Whitside Avenue. The clinic was a remodeled store of some kind, with a curtained plate-glass window. She spotted it first not by its street number but by the knot of picketers outside. There were three women, several children, and a small, dapper man. THIS CLINIC MURDERS THE INNOCENT, one sign said, and another showed a blown-up photo of a beautiful smiling baby with GIVE HER A CHANCE printed in white across her mop of black curls. Maggie parked in front of an insurance agency next door. The picketers glanced over at her and then went back to watching the clinic.

A car drew up and a girl in jeans got out, followed by a young boy. The girl bent to say something to the driver, after which she waved and the car moved on. The couple walked briskly toward the clinic, while the picketers swarmed around them. "God sees what you're about to do!" one woman called, and another blocked the girl's path, but she veered away. "Where is your conscience?" the man shouted after her. She and the boy vanished behind the door. The picketers straggled back to their places. They were discussing something heatedly; they appeared to be disagreeing. Maggie had the impression that some of them felt they should have been more forceful.

A few minutes later, a woman alighted from a taxi. She was maybe Maggie's age, very well dressed and all by herself. The picketers seemed to feel they had to make up for past defeats. They circled her; they had so much to say that it came to Maggie's ears as a garble of bee sounds. They pressed pamphlets on her. The largest of the women put an arm around her shoulders. The patient, if that was what she was, cried, "Let go of me!" and jabbed an elbow into the picketer's rib cage. Then she was gone too. The picketer bent over—in pain, Maggie thought at first, but she was merely lifting one of the children. They returned to their original positions. In this heat, they moved so slowly that their indignation looked striven-for and counterfeit.

Maggie rooted through her purse for a piece of paper to fan herself with. She would have liked to get out of the car, but then where would she stand? Alongside the picketers?

Footsteps approached, a double set, and she glanced up to see Fiona and a slightly older girl, who must have been her sister.

She had worried she wouldn't recognize Fiona, having caught sight of her only the once. But she knew her right off—the long fair hair, the pale face with nothing yet written upon it. She wore jeans and a bright, shrimp-pink T-shirt. As it happened, Maggie had a prejudice against shrimp pink. She thought it was lower-class. (Oh, how strange it was to remember now that she had once viewed Fiona as lower-class! She had imagined there was something cheap and gimcrack about her; she had mistrusted the bland pallor of her face, and she had suspected that her sister's too-heavy makeup concealed the same unhealthy complexion. Pure narrow-mindedness! Maggie could admit that now, having come to see Fiona's good points.)

At any rate, she got out of the car. She walked over to them and said, "Fiona?"

The sister murmured, "Told you they'd try something." She must have thought Maggie was a picketer. And Fiona walked on, eyelids lowered so they were two white crescents.

"Fiona, I'm Jesse's mother," Maggie said.

Fiona slowed and looked at her. The sister came to a stop.

"I won't interfere if you're certain you know what you're doing,"

Maggie said, "but, Fiona, have you considered every angle?"

"Not all that many *to* consider," the sister said bluntly. "She's seventeen years old."

Fiona allowed herself to be led away then, still gazing at Maggie over her shoulder.

"Have you talked about it with Jesse?" Maggie asked. She ran after them. "Jesse wants this baby! He told me so."

The sister called back, "Is he going to bear it? Is he going to walk it at night and change its diapers?"

"Yes, he is!" Maggie said. "Well, not bear it, of course . . ."

They had reached the picketers by now. A woman held out one of the pamphlets. On the front was a color photo of an unborn baby who seemed a good deal past the embryo stage, in fact almost ready to be delivered. Fiona shrank away. "Leave her alone," Maggie told the woman. She said, "Fiona, Jesse really cares about you. You have to believe me."

"I have seen enough of Jesse Moran to last me a lifetime," the sister said. She shoved past a fat woman with two toddlers and an infant in a sling.

"You're just saying that because you have him cast in this certain role," Maggie told her, "this rock-band member who got your little sister pregnant. But it's not so simple! It's not so cut-and-dried! He bought a Dr. Spock book—did he mention that, Fiona? He's already researched pacifiers and he thinks you ought to breast-feed."

The fat woman said to Fiona, "All the angels in heaven are crying over you."

"Listen," Maggie told the woman. "Just because *you've* got too many children is no reason to wish the same trouble on other people."

"The angels call it murder," the woman said.

Fiona flinched. Maggie said, "Can't you see you're upsetting her?" They had reached the door of the clinic now, but the dapper little man was barring their way. "Get out of here," Maggie told him. "Fiona! Just think it over! That's all I ask of you."

The man held his ground, which gave Fiona time to turn to Maggie. She looked a little teary. "Jesse doesn't care," she said.

"Of course he cares!"

"He says to me, 'Don't worry, Fiona, I won't let you down.' Like I am some kind of obligation! Some charitable cause!"

"He didn't mean it that way. You're misreading him. He honestly wants to marry you."

"And live on what money?" the sister asked. She had a braying, unpleasant voice, much deeper than Fiona's. "He doesn't even have a decent-paying job."

"He's getting one! Computers! Opportunity for advancement!" Maggie said. She was forced to speak so telegraphically because Fiona's sister had somehow cleared the door of picketers and was tugging it open. A woman held a postcard in front of Fiona's face: the curly-haired baby again. Maggie batted it aside. "At least come home with me so you and Jesse can talk it over," she told Fiona. "That won't commit you to anything."

Fiona hesitated. Her sister said, "For God's sake, Fiona," but Maggie seized her advantage. She took Fiona by the wrist and led her back through the crowd, keeping up a steady stream of encouragement. "He says he's building a cradle; he's already got the plans. It's enough to break your heart. Leave her alone, dammit! Do I have to call the police? Who gave you the right to pester us?"

"Who gave her the right to murder her baby?" a woman called.

"She has every right in the world! Fiona, this is a natural-born caretaker we're talking about here. You should have seen him during the Hong Kong flu."

"The what?"

"Or Bangkok, or Sing Sing, or one of those flus . . . Anyway, it's nothing to do with charity. He wants this baby more than anything."

Fiona peered into her face. She said, "And he's building a . . . ?"

"He's building a cradle. A beautiful one, with a hood," Maggie said. If it turned out not to have a hood she could always say she had been mistaken.

Fiona's sister scurried alongside them, her heels clicking busily. She said, "Fiona, if you don't get back in there this instant I am washing my hands of this whole affair, I tell you. Fiona, they have scheduled you!" And the picketers milled uncertainly a few feet behind. Fiona's wrist was smooth and impossibly thin, like a stalk of bamboo. Maggie released it, reluctantly, in order to open the car door. "Climb in," she said. "Buzz off," she told the picketers. And to the sister she said, "Nice meeting you."

The picketers dropped back. One said, "Now look, uh . . ."

"We have constitutional permission to do this, I'll have you know," Maggie said. The woman looked confused.

"I hunt up a clinic," Fiona's sister said, "I take her to be tested. I make the appointment, I sacrifice a perfectly good day off when I could have gone to Ocean City with my boyfriend—"

"You could still do that," Maggie said, checking her watch.

She hurried around to the driver's side, fearful that Fiona would try to escape, but when she got in, Fiona was sitting there limply with her head tipped back and her eyes closed. Her sister bent in through the open window. "Fiona, just tell me this much," she said. "If Jesse Moran was so hot for this baby, how come it wasn't him who came down here to fetch you?"

Fiona raised her lids and looked over at Maggie. "Well, he tried,"

Maggie told her. "He's been trying for days, you know he has, but somehow you're always at cross-purposes."

Fiona closed her eyes again. Maggie started the car and drove off.

The strange part was that having won—at least temporarily—she didn't feel a bit triumphant. Just worn out. And slightly confused, to tell the truth. How was it things had ended up this way, when all along she'd been telling Jesse he was nowhere near old enough? Oh, Lord. What had she gone and done? She glanced secretly at Fiona. Fiona's skin seemed slick, almost glazed. "Are you feeling ill?" Maggie asked her.

"I believe I might upchuck," Fiona said, barely moving her lips.

"You want me to stop the car?"

"Let's just get there."

Maggie drove more carefully, as if transporting a basket of eggs.

In front of the house she parked, got out, and came around to help Fiona from her seat. Fiona was a dead weight. She leaned heavily against Maggie. But she had a young smell—fresh-ironed cotton and those sugary beginner cosmetics you find in dime stores—and that gave Maggie some reassurance. Oh, this girl was not bad at heart! She was barely older than Daisy; she was an ordinary, open-faced child bewildered by what had happened to her.

They crossed the sidewalk slowly and climbed the steps to the porch. Their shoes made a hollow sound on the floorboards. "Sit here," Maggie said, and she helped Fiona into the chair where she herself had sat all yesterday afternoon. "You need the air," she said. "Take deep, deep breaths. I'm going to go find Jesse."

Fiona closed her eyes.

Inside, the rooms were cool and dark. Maggie climbed the stairs to Jesse's room and knocked on his door. She poked her head in. "Jesse?" she said.

"Mmf."

His window shades were lowered so she could barely make out the shapes of the furniture. His bed was a tangle of twisted sheets. "Jesse, I've brought Fiona," she said. "Could you come down to the porch?"

"Huh?"

"Could you come down to the porch and talk with Fiona?"

He stirred a little and raised his head, so she knew she could leave him. She went back downstairs and into the kitchen, where she poured a glass of iced tea from a pitcher in the refrigerator. She put the glass on a china plate, encircled it with saltine crackers, and carried it out to Fiona. "Here," she said. "Take little bites of these saltines. Take tiny sips of tea."

Fiona was already looking better, sitting upright now in her chair, and she said, "Thank you," when Maggie laid the plate on her knees.

She nibbled at a corner of a cracker. Maggie settled in a rocker next to her.

"When I was expecting Daisy," Maggie said, "I lived on tea and saltines for two solid months. It's a wonder we didn't both get malnutrition. I was so sick with Daisy I thought I would die, but with Jesse I never had a moment's discomfort. Isn't that funny? You'd think it would have been the other way around."

Fiona set down her cracker. "I should've stayed at the clinic," she said.

"Oh, honey," Maggie said. She felt suddenly depressed. She had an instantaneous, chillingly clear vision of how Ira's face would look when he learned what she had done. "Fiona, it's not too late," she said. "You're only here to discuss it all, right? You're not committed to a thing." Although even as she spoke she saw the clinic receding steadily. This was something like rushing toward a jump rope, she imagined. Miss that split second where entry is possible and you've flubbed up everything. She reached out and touched Fiona's arm. "And after all," she said, "you do love each other, don't you? Don't you love each other?"

"Yes, but maybe if we got married he would start to hold it against me," Fiona said. "I mean, he's a lead singer! He'll probably want to go to England or Australia or some such after he gets famous. And meanwhile, his band has just barely started earning any money. Where would we live? How would we work this?"

"At first you could live here with us," Maggie said. "Then in November you can move to an apartment Jesse knows about in Waverly. Jesse has it all figured out."

Fiona stared toward the street. "If I had stayed on at the clinic everything would be over by now," she said after a minute.

"Oh, Fiona. Please. Oh, tell me I didn't do wrong!" Maggie said. She looked around for Jesse. What was keeping him? It shouldn't be up to her to carry on this courtship. "Wait here," she said. She got up and hurried into the house. "Jesse!" she cried. But he didn't answer, and she heard the shower running. That boy would insist on showering first if the house were on fire, she thought. She ran upstairs and pounded on the bathroom door. "Jesse, are you coming?" she called.

He cut the water off. "What?" he said.

"Come out, I tell you!"

No answer. But she heard the shower curtain screech across the rod.

She went into his bedroom and snapped up both window shades. She wanted to find his Dr. Spock book. It would serve as a kind of selling point till he came downstairs; or at least it would provide a topic of conversation. But she couldn't find it—just dirty clothes, French-fry cartons, records left out of their jackets. She looked for the cradle plans then. What would they be—blueprints? Not a sign of them. Well, of course, he'd have taken them to the basement, where Ira kept his tools. She tore back down the stairs, calling toward the porch as she passed, "He's on his way!" (She could picture Fiona getting up and leaving.) Through the kitchen, down a set of narrow wooden steps, over to Ira's workbench. No plans there, either. Ira's tools hung neatly on the backboard, each matching its own painted outline—a sure sign Jesse had not been near them. On the workbench itself were two squares of sandpaper and a sheaf of doweling rods still bound together by rubber bands, part of a drying rack that Ira had promised to build into a corner of the back porch. She seized the doweling rods and raced back up the basement steps. "Look," she told Fiona, slamming out the screen door. "Jesse's cradle."

Fiona lowered her glass. She accepted the rods and gazed at them. "Cradle?" she said doubtfully.

"It's going to have . . . spindles; that's what they are," Maggie said. "Antique style."

You would think those rods could be read, the way Fiona studied them.

Then Jesse came out, bringing with him the fragrance of shampoo. His hair was wet and tousled and his skin was radiant. He said, "Fiona? You didn't go through with it?" and she lifted her face, still holding the rods like a kind of scepter, and said, "Well, all right, Jesse, if you want. I guess we could get married if you want."

Then Jesse wrapped his arms around her and dropped his head to her shoulder, and something about that picture—his dark head next to her blond one—reminded Maggie of the way she used to envision marriage before she was married herself. She had thought of it as more different than it really was, somehow, more of an alteration in people's lives—two opposites drawn together with a dramatic crashing sound. She had supposed that when she was married all her old problems would fall away, something like when you go on vacation and leave a few knotty tasks incomplete as if you'd never have to come back and face them. And of course, she had been wrong. But watching Jesse and Fiona, she could almost believe that that early vision was the right one. She slipped into the house, shutting the screen door very softly behind her, and she decided everything was going to work out after all.

They were married in Cartwheel, in Mrs. Stuckey's living room. Just family attended. Ira was grim-faced and silent, Maggie's mother sat stiff with outrage, and Maggie's father seemed befuddled. Only Mrs. Stuckey showed the proper festive attitude. She wore a fuchsia corduroy pantsuit and a corsage as big as her head, and before the ceremony she told everybody that her one regret was that Mr. Stuckey had not lived to see this day. Although maybe, she said, he was here in spirit; and then she went on at some length about her personal theory of ghosts. (They were the completions of the dead's intended gestures, their unfinished plans still hanging in the air—something like when you can't remember what it was you went to the kitchen for and so you pantomime the motion, a twist of the wrist perhaps, and that reminds you you had come out to turn the dripping faucet off. So wasn't there a chance that Mr. Stuckey was right here in the living room, having dreamed of walking both his precious daughters down the aisle someday?) Then she said that to her mind, marriage was just as educational as high school and maybe more so. "I mean I dropped out of school myself," she said, "and have never once regretted it." Fiona's sister rolled her eyes. But it was a good thing Mrs. Stuckey felt that way, since Fiona wouldn't turn eighteen till January and required parental permission for a marriage license.

Fiona herself wore a beige, loose-waisted dress that she and Maggie had gone shopping for together, and Jesse looked very distinguished in a suit and tie. He looked like a grownup, in fact. Daisy acted shy around him, and kept hanging on to Maggie's arm and looking over at him. "What's the matter with you? Straighten up," Maggie told her. She was feeling very irritable, for some reason. She worried that Ira was going to be angry at her forever. He seemed to be holding her solely accountable for this entire situation.

After the wedding, Jesse and Fiona went to Ocean City for a week. Then they came home to Jesse's room, where Maggie had moved in an extra bureau and exchanged his old bunks for a double bed from J. C. Penney. The house grew more crowded, of course, but it was a pleasant sort of crowdedness, cheerful and expectant. Fiona seemed to fit right in; she was so agreeable, so ready to let Maggie take charge—more so than Maggie's own children had ever been. Jesse set off happily every morning for his computer job, and returned every evening with some new baby-care gadget—a pack of bunny-shaped diaper pins or an ingenious spouted training cup. He was reading up on childbirth and kept embracing different theories, each more peculiar than the last. (For instance, at one point he proposed that the delivery take place underwater, but he couldn't find a doctor who would agree to it.)

Daisy and her friends forgot Mrs. Perfect entirely and camped in Maggie's living room—five dumbstruck, enchanted little girls reverently eyeing Fiona's stomach. And Fiona played up to them, sometimes inviting them to her room to admire her growing layette, after which she might seat them one by one at the mirror and experiment with their hair. (Her sister was a beautician and had taught Fiona everything she knew, Fiona said.) Then in the evening, if Jesse's band had an engagement somewhere, he and Fiona would go out together and not return till 2 or 3 a.m., and Maggie, half waking, would hear their

whispers on the stairs. The lock on their bedroom door would click
stealthily and Maggie would sink back into sleep, contented.

Even Ira seemed resigned, after he'd got over the shock. Oh, at
first he was so disgusted that Maggie had feared he would walk out
of the house forever. For days he had not spoken, and when Jesse
entered the room he would leave. But gradually he came around. He
was most comfortable, Maggie thought, when he could act tolerant and
long-suffering, and surely he had the opportunity for that now. Here
all his apprehensions had been confirmed: His son had got a girl in
trouble and his wife had meddled unforgivably and now the girl was
living in Jesse's bedroom among the Iggy Pop posters. He could sigh
and say, "Didn't I tell you? Didn't I always warn you?" (Or at least
he could give that impression; not that he said it aloud.) Fiona drifted
past him into the bathroom every morning, wearing her fluffy pink
robe and her big pink powder-puff slippers and carrying her tortoiseshell
soapbox, and Ira flattened himself against the wall as if she were twice
as big as she was. But he treated her with unfailing courtesy. He even
taught her his complicated brand of solitaire, when the boredom of
sitting at home got to be too much for her, and he lent her his Mariner's
Library books—a whole row of memoirs by people who had sailed
alone around the world and such. He had been trying to press them
on his children for years. ("As far as I'm concerned," Fiona told Maggie,
"those books are just more of that 'How I took Route So-and-so' that
men always think is so fascinating." But she didn't let on to Ira.) And
by November, when the Waverly apartment was supposed to become
available, Ira didn't ask why they weren't moving out.

Nor did Maggie; she carefully avoided the subject. In fact, for all
she knew, the apartment had fallen through somehow. Maybe the
current tenants had changed their plans. At any rate, Jesse and Fiona
said nothing about leaving. Fiona followed Maggie around now the
way the children had followed her when they were tiny. She trailed
her from room to room, asking fractious questions. "Why do I feel so
logy?" she asked, and, "Am I ever going to have anklebones again?"
She had started attending childbirth classes and wanted Maggie to go
with her to the labor room. Jesse, she said, might pass out or something.
Maggie said, "Why, Jesse's dying to go with you," but Fiona said, "I
don't want him to see me like that! He isn't even kin."

Nor was Maggie, Maggie could have said. Although it seemed she
really was, in some ways.

In Jesse's company, Fiona began to take on an aggrieved and nagging
tone. She complained about the unfairness—how Jesse got to go off
to work every day while she sat home growing fatter. She should have
stayed in school after all, she said, at least through fall semester; but
no, no, Jesse had to have things his way: homebody wife, the Little
Mother act. When she spoke like this there was something old-ladyish

in her voice, and Jesse when he answered sounded sullen. "Have you heard one word I've been saying?" Fiona would ask, and Jesse would say, "I heard, I heard." What was it that struck Maggie as so familiar? It was a tune, almost. It was the tune of the arguments Jesse used to have with his parents; that was it. Jesse and Fiona were more like a boy and his mother than husband and wife.

But Fiona wasn't feeling well; no wonder she was snappish. That early-pregnancy sleepiness never left her, even in her seventh and eighth months, when most women were bundles of energy. Jesse would say, "Put on your clothes! We're booked at the Granite Tavern tonight and they're paying us real money," and she would say, "Oh, I don't know; maybe I'll let you go on without me."

"Without you?" he would ask. "You mean alone?" And his face would get all hurt and surprised. But he would go. Once, he didn't even eat supper—just left the minute she told him she wasn't coming with him, although it was barely 6 p.m. Then Fiona didn't eat, either, but sat there at the table playing with her food, a tear slipping down her cheek from time to time, and afterward she put on the hooded windbreaker that didn't button over her stomach anymore and she went for a long, long walk. Or she might have gone to visit her sister; Maggie had no idea. At eight or so Jesse phoned and Maggie had to tell him she was out someplace. "What do you mean, out?" he asked.

"Just out, Jesse. I'm sure she'll be coming back soon."

"She said she was too tired to go out. She couldn't come to the Granite Tavern because she was too tired."

"Oh, maybe she—"

But he had already hung up, a metalic clunk in her ear.

Well, these things happened. (Didn't Maggie know they happened?) And the next morning Jesse and Fiona were fine—had reconciled at some point and acted more loving than ever. Maggie had been anxious for no reason, it turned out.

The baby was due in early March, but on February first Fiona woke up with a backache. Maggie was excited the instant she heard. "This is it, I bet," she told Fiona.

"It can't be!" Fiona said. "I'm not ready."

"Of course you're ready. You've got your layette; your suitcase is packed—"

"But Jesse hasn't built the cradle yet."

It was true. Whatever other equipment he'd laid in, that cradle had not materialized. Maggie said, "Never mind; he can do it while you're in the hospital."

"This is a plain old backache anyhow," Fiona said. "I've had this feeling often, before I was pregnant, even."

At noon, though, when Maggie phoned from work, Fiona sounded less certain. "I'm getting these cramps, like, in my stomach," she said. "Can you please come home early?"

"I'll be there," Maggie told her. "Have you called Jesse yet?"

"Jesse? No."

"Why don't you call him."

"Okay, but promise you'll come home? Start right now."

"I'm on my way."

She arrived to find Jesse timing Fiona's contractions, using an official-looking stopwatch he'd bought especially for this occasion. He was jubilant. "We're moving right along!" he told Maggie.

Fiona looked scared. She kept giving little moans, not during the contractions but between them. "Hon, I don't think you're breathing right," Jesse told her.

Fiona said, "Lay off about my breathing! I'll breathe any way I choose."

"Well, I just want you to be comfortable. Are you comfortable? Is the baby moving?"

"I don't know."

"Is he moving or isn't he? Fiona? You must have some idea."

"I don't know, I tell you. No. He's not."

"The baby isn't moving," Jesse told Maggie.

"Don't worry. He's just getting ready," Maggie said.

"Something must be wrong."

"Nothing's wrong, Jesse. Believe me."

But he didn't believe her, which is why they ended up leaving for the hospital far too early. Maggie drove. Jesse said he might crash the car if he drove, but then he spent the whole trip protesting every move Maggie made. "What possessed you to get behind a bus? Switch lanes. Not now, for God's sake! Check your rearview mirror. Oh, God, we'll all be killed and they'll have to cut the baby out of her stomach in the middle of Franklin Street."

Fiona shrieked at this, which so unnerved Maggie that she slammed on the brakes and threw all three of them against the windshield. Jesse said, "Let us out! Better we go by foot! Let her give birth on the sidewalk!"

"Fine," Maggie said. "Get out of the car."

Fiona said, "What?"

"Now, Ma, just cool it," Jesse said. "No need to get hysterical. Depend on Ma to fall apart in any little emergency," he told Fiona.

They rode the rest of the way in silence, and Maggie left them at the hospital entrance and went off to park.

When she located them in Admissions, Fiona was just settling into a wheelchair. "I want my mother-in-law to come with me," she told the nurse.

"Only Daddy can come with you," the nurse said. "Grandma has to stay in the waiting room."

Grandma?

"I don't want Daddy, I want Grandma!" Fiona cried, sounding about six years old.

"Here we go now," the nurse said. She wheeled her away. Jesse followed, wearing that hurt, undefended expression Maggie had seen so often lately.

Maggie went to the waiting room, which was the size of a football field. A vast expanse of beige carpeting was broken up by clustered arrangements of beige vinyl couches and chairs. She settled on an empty couch and chose a ruffle-edged magazine from the beige wooden end table. "How to Keep the Zing! in Your Marriage," the first article was called. It instructed her to be unpredictable; greet her husband after work wearing nothing but a black lace apron. Ira would think she had lost her mind. Not to mention Jesse and Fiona and the five enchanted little girls. She wished she had thought to bring her knitting. She wasn't that much of a knitter—her stitches had a way of galloping along for a few inches and then squinching up in tight little puckers, reminding her of a car that bucks and stalls—but lately she had thrown herself into a purple football jersey for the baby. (It was going to be a boy; everybody assumed so, and only boys' names had been considered.)

She set the magazine aside and went over to the flank of pay phones that lined one wall. First she dialed the number at home. When no one answered—not even Daisy, who was usually back from school by three—she checked her watch and discovered it was barely two o'clock. She had thought it was much later. She dialed Ira's work number. "Sam's Frame Shop," he answered.

"Ira?" she said. "Guess what—I'm at the hospital."

"You are? What's wrong?"

"Nothing's wrong. Fiona's having her baby."

"Oh," he said. "I thought you'd crashed the car or something."

"You want to come wait with me? It's going to be a while yet."

"Well, maybe I should go home to watch Daisy," Ira said.

Maggie sighed. "Daisy's at school," she told him. "And anyhow, she hasn't needed watching in years."

"You'll want someone to put supper on, though."

She gave up on him. (Lord forbid her deathbed should be in a hospital; he would probably not attend it.) She said, "Well, suit yourself, Ira, but I would think you'd want to see your own grandchild."

"I'll see him soon enough, won't I?" Ira asked.

Maggie glimpsed Jesse across the waiting room. "I have to go now," she said, and she hung up. "Jesse?" she said, hurrying toward him. "What's the news?"

"Everything's fine. Or so they claim."

"How's Fiona?"

"She's scared," he said, "and I try to calm her down, but those hospital people keep shooing me out. Anytime someone official comes they ask me to leave."

So much for modern developments, Maggie thought. Men were still being shielded from everything truly important.

Jesse went back to Fiona but kept Maggie posted, reappearing every half hour or so to speak knowingly of stages and centimeters. "It's going pretty fast now," he said once, and another time, "Many people believe that an eight-months baby is more at risk than a seven-months baby, but that's an old wives' tale. It's just a superstition." His hair stood up in thick tufts, like wind-tossed grass. Maggie restrained herself from reaching out to smooth it. Unexpectedly, he reminded her of Ira. However different the two might be in other ways, they both had this notion that reading up on something, getting equipped for something, would put them in control.

She considered going home for a while (it was nearly five o'clock) but she knew she would only fret and pace, so she stayed where she was and kept in touch by telephone. Daisy reported that Ira was fixing a pancake supper. "No green vegetable?" Maggie asked. "Where's the green vegetable?" Ira got on the phone to assure her that he was serving spiced crab-apple rings on the side. "Spiced crab-apple rings are not green, Ira," Maggie said. She felt herself growing weepy. She ought to be at home supervising her family's nutrition; she ought to be storming the labor room to comfort Fiona; she ought to take Jesse in her arms and rock him because he was nothing but a child still, much too young for what was happening to him. But here she stood, clutching a salty-smelling receiver in a public phone hutch. Her stomach felt all knotted and tight. It hadn't been so long since she was a patient in the labor room herself, and her muscles recalled it exactly.

She told Ira goodbye and went through the doors where Jesse kept disappearing. She traveled down a corridor, hoping for, oh, at least a nursery full of newborns to cheer her up. She passed another, smaller waiting room, perhaps leading to some lab or private office. An elderly couple sat there on two molded plastic chairs, and across from them sat a burly man in paint-spattered coveralls. As Maggie slowed to glance in, a nurse called, "Mr. Plum?" and the elderly man rose and went toward a back room, leaving behind a brand new magazine. Maggie breezed in as if she had a perfect right to be there and scooped up the magazine, at the same time performing a clumsy half-curtsy to show the old woman she meant no intrusion. She settled beside the man in coveralls. Never mind that this was just another ladies' magazine; at least the pages still gave off a shellacked, unused smell and the movie stars spilling their secrets were wearing up-to-date hairdos. She skimmed an article about a new kind of diet. You picked one favorite food and ate all you wanted, three times a day, nothing else besides. Maggie would have chosen beef-and-bean burritos from Lexington Market.

In the back room, the nurse said, "Now, Mr. Plum, I'm giving you this jar for urine."

"My what?"

"Urine."

"How's that?"

"It's for urine!"

"Speak up—I can't hear you."

"*Urine*, I said! You take this jar home! You collect all your urine! For twenty-four hours! You bring the jar back!"

In the chair across from Maggie, the wife gave an embarrassed titter. "He's deaf as a doorknob," she told Maggie. "Has to have everything shouted out for all and sundry to hear."

Maggie smiled and shook her head, not knowing how else to respond. Then the man in coveralls stirred. He placed his great, furry fists on his knees. He cleared his throat. "You know," he said, "it's the funniest thing. I can catch that nurse's voice all right but I don't understand a single word she's saying."

Maggie's eyes filled with tears. She dropped her magazine and groped in her purse for a Kleenex, and the man said, "Lady? You okay?"

She couldn't tell him it was his kindness that had undone her— such delicacy, in such an unlikely-looking person—and so she said, "It's my son, he's having a baby. I mean my son's wife is."

The man and the older woman waited, their faces prepared to take on the proper look of shock and pity as soon as they heard the bad part. And she couldn't tell them, "It's all my fault, I set everything pell-mell in motion not once considering the consequences," so instead she said, "It's months and months too early, it's nowhere near her due date . . ."

The man clicked his tongue. His forehead furrowed upon itself like cloth. The old woman said, "Oh, my stars, you must be worried sick. But don't you give up hope, because my nephew Brady's wife, Angela . . ."

And that was why, when Jesse passed down the corridor from the delivery room a few minutes later, he found his mother in a little side cubicle surrounded by a huddle of strangers. They were patting her and murmuring consolations—an old woman, a workman of some sort, a nurse with a clipboard, and a stooped old man clutching a gigantic empty jar. "Ma?" Jesse said, stepping in. "The baby's here, and both of them are fine."

"Praise Jesus!" the old woman shouted, flinging her hands toward the ceiling.

"The only trouble is," Jesse said, eyeing the woman dubiously, "it's a girl. I wasn't counting on a girl, somehow."

"You would let a thing like that bother you?" the old woman demanded. "At a moment such as this? That child was snatched from the jaws of death!"

"From . . .?" Jesse said. Then he said, "No, it's just a superstition that an eight-months—"

"Let's get out of here," Maggie said, and she fought her way free of the huddle to grab his arm and steer him away.

How that baby took over the house! Her cries of fury and her mourning-dove coos, her mingled smells of powder and ammonia, her wheeling arms and legs. She had Fiona's coloring but Jesse's spirit and his feistiness (no Lady-Baby this time). Her small, fine features were scrunched very close together low down in her face, so when Fiona combed her bit of hair into a sprout on top of her head she resembled a Kewpie doll; and like a doll she was trundled everywhere by the enchanted little girls, who would have cut school if permitted, just to lug her about by the armpits and shake her rattle too close to her eyes and hang over her, breathing heavily, while Maggie bathed her. Even Ira showed some interest, although he pretended not to. "Let me know when she's big enough to play baseball," he said, but as early as the second week, Maggie caught him taking sidelong peeks into the bureau drawer where Leroy slept, and by the time she had learned to sit up, the two of them were deep in those exclusive conversations of theirs.

And Jesse? He was devoted—always offering to help out, sometimes making a nuisance of himself, to hear Fiona tell it. He walked Leroy during her fussy spells, and he left his warm bed to burp her and then carry her back to Maggie's room after the two o'clock feeding. And once, when Maggie took Fiona shopping, he spent a whole Saturday morning solely in charge, returning Leroy none the worse for wear, although the careful way he had dressed her—with her overall straps mistakenly clamping down her collar, severely mashing the double row of ruffles—made Maggie feel sad, for some reason. He claimed that he had never wanted a boy at all; or if he had, he couldn't remember why. "Girls are perfect," he said. "Leroy is perfect. Except, you know . . ."

"Except?" Maggie asked.

"Well, it's just that . . . shoot, before she was born I had this sort of, like, anticipation. And now I've got nothing to anticipate, you know?"

"Oh, that'll pass," Maggie said. "Don't worry."

But later, to Ira, she said, "I never heard of a father getting postpartum blues."

Maybe if the mother didn't, the father did; was that the way it worked? For Fiona herself was cheerful and oblivious. Often as she flitted around the baby she seemed more like one of the enchanted little girls than like a mother. She paid too much heed to Leroy's appurtenances, Maggie felt—to her frilly clothes, her ribboned sprout of hair. Or maybe it just seemed so. Maybe Maggie was jealous. It was true that she hated to relinquish the baby when she went off to work every morning. "How can I leave her?" she wailed to Ira. "Fiona doesn't know the first little bit about child care."

"Well, only one way she's ever going to learn," Ira said. And so Maggie left, hanging back internally, and called home several times a day to see how things were going. But they were always going fine.

In the nursing home one afternoon she heard a middle-aged visitor talking to his mother—a vacant, slack-jawed woman in a wheelchair. He told her how his wife was, how the kids were. His mother smoothed her lap robe. He told her how his job was. His mother plucked a bit of lint and flicked it onto the floor. He told her about a postcard that had come for her at the house. The church was holding an Easter bazaar and they wanted her to check off which task she would volunteer for. This struck the son as comical, in view of his mother's disabilities. "They offered you your choice," he said, chuckling. "You could clerk at the needlework booth or you could tend the babies." His mother's hands grew still. She raised her head. Her face lit up and flowered. "Oh!" she cried softly. "I'll tend the babies!"

Maggie knew just how she felt.

Leroy was a long, thin infant, and Fiona worried she was outgrowing the bureau drawer she slept in. "When are you going to get started on that cradle?" she asked Jesse, and Jesse said, "Any day now."

Maggie said, "Maybe we should just buy a crib. A cradle's for a newborn; she wouldn't fit it for long."

But Fiona said, "No, I set my heart on a cradle." She told Jesse. "You promised."

"I don't remember promising."

"Well, you did," she said.

"All right! I'll get to it! Didn't I tell you I would?"

"You don't have to shout at me," she said.

"I'm not shouting."

"Yes, you are."

"Am not."

"Are too."

"Children! Children!" Maggie said, pretending she was joking.

But only pretending.

Once, Fiona spent the night at her sister's, snatching up the baby and stomping out after a fight. Or not a fight exactly but a little misunderstanding: The band was playing at a club in downtown Baltimore and Fiona planned to come along, as usual, till Jesse worried aloud that Leroy had a cold and shouldn't be left. Fiona said Maggie would tend her just fine and Jesse said a baby with a cold needed her mother and then Fiona said it was amazing how he was so considerate of that baby but so inconsiderate of his wife and then Jesse said . . .

Well.

Fiona left and did not come back until morning; Maggie feared she was gone for good, endangering that poor sick baby, who needed much more nursing than Fiona could provide. She must have been planning to desert them all along, in fact. Why, just look at her soapbox! Wasn't it odd that for almost a year now she had borne off to the bathroom twice daily a tortoiseshell soapbox, a tube of Aim toothpaste (*not* the Moran's brand), and a toothbrush in a plastic cylinder? And that her toilet supplies were continually stored in a clear vinyl travel case on the bureau? She might as well be a guest. She had never meant to settle in permanently.

"Go after her," Maggie told Jesse, but Jesse asked, "Why should I? She's the one who walked out." He was at work when Fiona returned the next day, wan and puffy-eyed. Strands of her uncombed hair mingled with the fake-fur trim of her windbreaker hood, and Leroy was wrapped clumsily in a garish daisy-square afghan that must have belonged to the sister.

What Maggie's mother said was true: The generations were sliding downhill in this family. They were descending in every respect, not just in their professions and their educations but in the way they reared their children and the way they ran their households. ("How have you let things get so *common?*" Maggie heard again in her memory.) Mrs. Daley stood over the sleeping Leroy and pleated her lips in disapproval. "They would put an infant in a bureau drawer? They would let her stay in here with you and Ira? What can they be thinking of? It must be that Fiona person. Really, Maggie, that Fiona is so . . . Why, she isn't even a Baltimore girl! Anyone who would pronounce Wicomico as Weeko-Meeko! And what is that racket I'm hearing?"

Maggie tilted her head to listen. "It's Canned Heat," she decided.

"Candide? I'm not asking the name of it; I mean why is it playing? When you children were small I played Beethoven and Brahms, I played all of Wagner's operas!"

Yes, and Maggie could still recall her itch of boredom as Wagner's grandiose weight crashed through the house. And her frustration when, beginning some important story with "Me and Emma went to—" she had been cut short by her mother. ("'Emma and I,' if you please.") She had sworn never to do that to her own children, preferring to hear what it was they had to say and let the grammar take care of itself. Not that it had done so, at least not in Jesse's case.

Maybe her own downhill slide was deliberate. If so, she owed Jesse an apology. Maybe he was just carrying out her secret scheme for revolution, and would otherwise—who knows?—have gone on to be a lawyer like Mrs. Daley's father.

Well, too late now.

Leroy learned to crawl and she crawled right out of her bureau drawer, and the next day Ira came home with a crib. He assembled it, without comment, in his and Maggie's bedroom. Without comment, Fiona watched from the doorway. The skin beneath her eyes had a sallow, soiled look.

On a Saturday in September, they celebrated Ira's father's birthday. Maggie had made it a tradition to spend his birthday at the Pimlico Race Track—all of them together, even though it meant closing the frame shop. They would take a huge picnic lunch and a ten-dollar bill for each person to bet with. In times past the whole family had squeezed into Ira's car, but of course that was no longer possible. This year they had Jesse and Fiona (who had been away on their honeymoon the year before), and Leroy too, and even Ira's sister Junie decided she might brave the trip. So Jesse borrowed the van that his band used to transport their instruments. SPIN THE CAT was lettered across its side, the S and the C striped like tigers' tails. They loaded the back with picnic hampers and baby supplies, and then they drove to the shop to pick up Ira's father and sisters. Junie wore her usual going-out costume, everything cut on the bias, and carried a parasol that wouldn't collapse, which caused some trouble when she climbed in. And Dorrie was hugging her Hutzler's coat box, which caused even more trouble. But everyone acted good-natured about it—even Ira's father, who always said he was way too old to make a fuss over birthdays.

It was a beautiful day, the kind that starts out cool until sunlight gently warms your outer layers and then your inner layers. Daisy was trying to get them to sing "Camptown Races," and Ira's father wore a grudging, self-conscious smile. This was how families ought to be, Maggie thought. And in the bus that carried them in from the parking lot—a bus they half filled, if you counted the picnic hampers balanced on empty seats and the diaper bag and folded stroller blocking the aisle—she felt sorry for their fellow passengers who sat alone or in pairs. Most of them had a workaday attitude. They wore sensible clothes and stern, purposeful expressions, and they were here to win. The Morans were here to celebrate.

They spread out over one whole row of bleachers, parking Leroy alongside in her stroller. Then Mr. Moran, who prided himself on his knowledge of horseflesh, went off to the paddocks to size things up, and Ira went too, to keep him company. Jesse found a couple he knew—a man in motorcycle gear and a slip of a girl in fringed buckskin pants—and disappeared with them; he wasn't much of a gambler. The women settled down to select their horses by the ring of their names, which was a method that seemed to work about as well as any other. Maggie favored one called Infinite Mercy, but Junie disagreed. She said that didn't sound to her like a horse with enough fight to it.

Because of the baby, who was teething or something and acted a little fretful, they staggered their trips to the betting windows. Fiona went first with Ira's sisters, while Maggie stayed behind with Leroy and Daisy. Then the others came back and Maggie and Daisy went, Daisy bristling with good advice. "What you do," she said, "is put two dollars to show. That's safest." But Maggie said, "If I'd wanted *safe* I'd be sitting at home," and bet all ten dollars on Number Four to win. (In the past she'd argued for the family to pool every bit of their money and head straight for the fifty-dollar-minimum window, a dangerous and exciting spot she'd never so much as approached, but she knew by now not to bother trying.) Along the way they ran into Ira and his father, who were discussing statistics. The jockeys' weights, their previous records, the horses' fastest times and what kind of turf they did best on—there was plenty to consider, if you cared. Maggie bet her ten dollars and left, while Daisy joined the men, and the three of them stood deliberating.

"This kid is wearing me out," Fiona said when Maggie got back. Leroy evidently didn't want to be carried and she kept straining toward the ground, which was littered with beer-can tabs and cigarette butts. Dorrie, who was supposed to be helping, had opened her coat box instead and was laying an orderly row of marshmallows from one end of the bleacher to the other. Maggie said, "Here, I'll take her, poor lamb," and she bore Leroy off to the railing to admire the horses, which were just assembling at the starting gate with skittery, mincing steps. "What do horses say?" Maggie asked. "*Nicker*-nicker-nicker!" she supplied. Ira and his father returned, still arguing. Their subject now was the sheet of racing tips that Mr. Moran had purchased from a man with no teeth. "Which ones did you vote for?" Maggie asked them.

"You don't *vote*, Maggie," Ira told her. The horses took off, looking somehow quaint and toylike. They galloped past with a sound that reminded her of a flag ruffling in the wind. Then, just like that, the race was finished. "So soon!" Maggie lamented. She never could get over how quickly it all happened; there was hardly anything to watch. "Really baseball gives a better sense of time," she told the baby.

The results lit up the electric billboard: Number Four was nowhere to be seen. That struck Maggie as a relief, in a way. She wouldn't need to make any more choices. In fact, the only person who came out ahead was Mr. Moran. He had won six dollars on Number Eight, a horse his tip sheet had recommended. "See there?" he asked Ira. Daisy hadn't bet at all; she was saving for a race she felt surer of.

Maggie gave the baby to Daisy and started unpacking their lunch.

"There's ham on rye, turkey on white, roast beef on whole wheat," she announced. "There's chicken salad, deviled eggs, potato salad, and cole slaw. Peaches, fresh strawberries, and melon balls. Don't forget to save room for the birthday cake." The people nearby were munching on junk food bought right there at the track. They stared curiously at the hampers, each one of which Daisy had lined with a starched checkered cloth tucked into little pleats around the edges. Maggie passed out napkins. "Where's Jesse?" she asked, searching the crowd.

"I have no idea," Fiona said. Somehow, she had ended up with Leroy again. She jiggled her sharply against her shoulder, while Leroy screwed up her face and made fussing noises. Well, Maggie could have predicted as much. You don't use such a rapid rhythm with a baby; shouldn't Fiona have learned that by now? Wouldn't simple instinct have informed her? Maggie felt an edgy little poke of irritation in the small of her back. To be fair, it wasn't Fiona who annoyed her so much as the fussing—Leroy's jagged "eh, eh." If Maggie weren't loading paper plates she could have taken over herself, but as it was, all she could do was make suggestions. "Try putting her in the stroller, Fiona. Maybe she'll fall asleep."

"She won't fall asleep; she'll just climb out again," Fiona said. "Oh, where is Jesse?"

"Daisy, go look for your brother," Maggie commanded.

"I can't; I'm eating."

"Go anyway. For goodness' sake, I can't do everything."

"Is it my fault he went off with his dumb friends somewhere?" Daisy asked. "I just got started on my sandwich."

"Now listen, young lady . . . Ira?"

But Ira and his father had left again for the betting windows. Maggie said, "Oh, for—Dorrie, could you please go and hunt Jesse for me?"

"Well, but I am dealing out these here marshmallows," Dorrie said.

The marshmallows traveled in a perfect, unbroken row the length of their bleacher, like a dotted line. As a result, none of them could sit down. People kept pausing at the far end, meaning to take a seat, but then they saw the marshmallows and moved on. Maggie sighed. Behind her back, a bugle call floated on the clear, still air, but Maggie, facing the bleachers, went on searching the crowd for Jesse. Then Junie nudged a few of Dorrie's marshmallows out of line and sat down very suddenly, clutching her parasol with both hands. "Maggie," she murmured, "I am feeling just so, I don't know, all at once . . ."

"Take a deep breath," Maggie said briskly. This happened, from time to time. "Remind yourself you're here as someone else."

"I believe I'm going to faint," Junie said, and without warning she swung her spike-heeled sandals up and lay down flat upon the bleacher. The parasol remained in both her hands, rising from her chest as if planted there. Dorrie rushed distractedly around her, trying to retrieve as many marshmallows as possible.

"Daisy, is that your brother up there with those people?" Maggie asked.

Daisy said, "Where?" but Fiona was quicker. She wheeled and said, "It most certainly is." Then she shrieked, "Jesse Moran! You get your ass on down here!"

Her voice was that stringy, piercing kind. Everybody stared. Maggie said, "Oh, well, I wouldn't—"

"You hear me?" Fiona shrieked, and Leroy started crying in earnest.

"There's no need to shout, Fiona," Maggie said.

Fiona said, "What?"

She glared at Maggie, ignoring the squalling baby. It was one of those moments when Maggie just wanted to back up and start over. (She had always felt paralyzed in the presence of an angry woman.) Meanwhile Jesse, who couldn't have missed hearing his name, began to thread his way toward them. Maggie said, "Oh, here he comes!"

"You're telling me not to shout at my own husband?" Fiona asked.

She was shouting even now. She had to, over the cries of the baby. Leroy's face was red, and spikes of damp hair were plastered to her forehead. She looked sort of homely, to be frank. Maggie felt an urge to walk off from this whole group, pretend they had nothing to do with her; but instead she made her voice go light and she said, "No, I only meant he wasn't that far from us, you see—"

"You meant nothing of the sort," Fiona said, squeezing the baby too tightly. "You're trying to *run* us, just like always; trying to run our lives."

"No, really, Fiona—"

"What's up?" Jesse asked breezily, arriving among them.

"Ma and Fiona are having a fight," Daisy said. She took a dainty nibble from her sandwich.

"We are not!" Maggie cried. "I merely suggested—"

"A fight?" Ira said. "What?"

He and Mr. Moran were all at once standing in the aisle behind Jesse. "What's going on here?" he asked above Leroy's cries.

Maggie told him, "Nothing's going on! For Lord's sake, all I said was—"

"Can't you folks be left to your own devices for even a minute?" Ira asked. "And why is Junie lying down like that? How do these things happen so *fast*?"

Unfair, unfair. To hear him talk, you would think they had such scenes every day. You would think that Ira himself was in line for the Nobel Peace Prize. "For your information," Maggie told him, "I was just standing here minding my own business—"

"You have never once in all the time I've known you managed to mind your own business," Fiona said.

"Now cool it, Fiona," Jesse said.

"And you!" Fiona screeched, turning on him. "You think this baby is just mine? How come I always get stuck with her while you go off with your buddies, answer me that!"

"Those weren't my buddies; they were only—"

"He was drinking with them too," Daisy murmured, with her eyes on her sandwich.

"Well, big deal," Jesse told her.

"Drinking from this silver flat kind of bottle that belonged to that girl."

"So what if I was, Miss Goody-Goody?"

"Now listen," Ira said. "Let's just all sit down a minute and get ahold of ourselves. We're blocking people's view."

He sat, setting an example. Then he looked behind him.

"My marshmallows!" Dorrie squawked.

"You can't leave your marshmallows here, Dorrie. No one has room to sit."

"You messed up my marshmallows!"

"I believe I'm going to be ill," Junie said, speaking upward into the spokes of her parasol.

Leroy's crying had reached the stage where she had to fight for each breath.

Ira stood up again, dusting off the seat of his pants. He said, "Now listen, folks—"

"Will you stop calling us *folks*?" Fiona demanded.

Ira halted, looking startled.

Maggie felt a tug on her sleeve and turned. It was Mr. Moran, who had at some point worked around behind her. He held up a ticket. "What?" she asked.

"I won."

"Won what?"

"I won that last race! My horse came in first."

"Oh, the race," she said. "Well, isn't that . . ."

But her attention veered toward Fiona, who was reeling off a list of wrongs that she seemed to have been saving up for Jesse all these months. ". . . knew from the start I'd be a fool to marry you; didn't I say so? But you were so gung-ho, you and your pacifiers and your Dr. Spock . . ."

The people in the bleachers behind them were gazing pointedly in different directions, but they sent each other meaningful glances and small, secret smiles. The Morans had turned into spectacles. Maggie couldn't bear it. She said, "Please! Can't we just sit down?"

"You and your famous cradle," Fiona told Jesse, "that you didn't build one stick of after you promised, you swore to me—"

"I never swore to you! Where do you keep coming up with this cradle business from?"

"You swore on the Bible," Fiona told him.

"Well, good God Almighty! I mean, maybe it crossed my mind once to build one, but I'd have had to be crazy to go through with it. I can see it now: Dad standing there criticizing every little hammer blow, letting me know what a hopeless clod I am, and you'd be agreeing with him just like always, I bet, by the time I was finished. No way would I let myself in for that!"

"Well, you bought the wood, didn't you?"

"What wood?"

"You bought those long wooden rods."

"Rods? For a cradle? I never bought any rods."

"Your mother told me—"

"How would I use rods to build a cradle?"

"Spindles, she told me."

They both looked at Maggie. Coincidentally, the baby paused just then for a deep, hiccuping breath. A bass voice rumbled over the loudspeaker, announcing that Misappropriation had been scratched.

Ira cleared his throat and said, "Are you talking about doweling rods? Those were mine."

"Ira, no," Maggie wailed, because there was still a chance they could smooth things over, if only he wouldn't insist on spelling out every boring little fact. "They were the spindles for your cradle," she told Jesse. "You already had the blueprints. Right?"

"What blueprints? All I said was—"

"If I remember correctly," Ira interrupted in his stuffy way, "those rods were purchased for the drying rack I built on the back porch. You've all seen that drying rack."

"Drying rack," Fiona said. She continued looking at Maggie.

"Oh, well," Maggie said, "this cradle business is so silly, isn't it? I mean, it's like the dime-store necklace that relatives start quarreling over after the funeral. It's just a . . . And besides, Leroy couldn't even use a cradle anymore! She's got that nice crib Ira bought."

Leroy remained quiet, still hiccuping, gazing at Maggie intently.

"I married you for that cradle," Fiona told Jesse.

"Well, that's just plain ridiculous!" Maggie said. "For a cradle! I never heard such a—"

"Maggie, enough," Ira said.

She stopped, with her mouth open.

"If you married Jesse for a cradle," Ira told Fiona, "you were sadly mistaken."

"Oh, Ira!" Maggie cried.

"Shut up, Maggie. She had no business telling you that," Ira said to Fiona. "It's Maggie's weakness: She believes it's all right to alter people's lives. She thinks the people she loves are better than they really are, and so then she starts changing things around to suit her view of them."

"That's not one bit true," Maggie said.

"But the fact is," Ira told Fiona calmly, "Jesse is not capable of following through with *anything*, not even a simple cradle. He's got some lack; I know he's my son, but he's got some lack, and you might as well face up to it. He's not a persevering kind of person. He lost that job of his a month ago and he hangs out every day with his pals instead of looking for work."

Maggie and Fiona, together, said, "What?"

"They found out he wasn't a high school graduate," Ira told them. And then, as an afterthought: "He's seeing another girl too."

Jesse said, "What are you talking about? That girl is just a friend."

"I don't know her name," Ira said, "but she belongs to a rock group called Babies in Trouble."

"We're just good friends, I tell you! That girl is Dave's girl!"

Fiona seemed to be made of china. Her face was dead white and still; her pupils were black pinpoints.

"If you knew this all along," Maggie demanded of Ira, "why didn't you say something?"

"I didn't feel right about it. I for one don't hold with changing people's worlds around," Ira said. And then (just as Maggie was getting ready to hate him) his face sagged and he dropped wearily onto the bleacher. "I shouldn't have done it now, either," he said.

He had dislodged a whole section of marshmallows, but Dorrie, who could be sensitive to atmospheres, merely bent in silence to collect them.

Fiona held out her palm. "Give me the keys," she told Jesse.

"Huh?"

"The keys to the van. Hand them over."

"Where are you going?" Jesse asked her.

"I don't know! How would I know? I just have to get out of here."

"Fiona, I only ever talked to that girl because she didn't think I was some kind of clod like everyone else seems to do. You've got to believe me, Fiona."

"The keys," Fiona said.

Ira said, "Let her have them, Jesse."

"But—"

"We'll take a bus."

Jesse reached into the rear pocket of his jeans. He brought out a cluster of keys attached to a miniature black rubber gym shoe. "So will you be at the house? Or what," he said.

"I have no idea," Fiona told him, and she snapped the keys out of his grasp.

"Well, where will you be? At your sister's?"

"Anywhere. None of your business. *I* don't know where. I just want to get on with my life," she said.

And she hoisted the baby higher on her hip and stalked off, leaving behind the diaper bag and the stroller and her paper plate of lunch with the potato salad turning a pathetic shade of ivory.

"She'll come around," Maggie told Jesse. Then she said, "I will never forgive you for this, Ira Moran."

She felt another tug on her sleeve and she turned. Ira's father was still holding up his ticket. "I was right to buy that tip sheet," he said. "What does Ira know about tip sheets?"

"Nothing," Maggie said furiously, and she started rewrapping Fiona's sandwich.

All around her she heard murmuring, like ripples widening across a pond:

"What'd he say?"

"Tip sheet."

"What'd she say?"

"Nothing."

"She did say something, I saw her lips move."

"She said, 'Nothing.' "

"But I thought I saw—"

Maggie straightened and faced the rows of people on the bleachers. "I said, 'Nothing,' is what I said," she called out clearly.

Somebody sucked in a breath. They all looked elsewhere.

It was amazing, Ira often said, how people fooled themselves into believing what they wanted to. (How Maggie fooled herself, he meant.) He said it when Maggie threatened to sue the Police Department that time they charged Jesse with Drunk and Disorderly. He said it when she swore that Spin the Cat sounded better than the Beatles. And he said it again when she refused to accept that Fiona was gone for good.

That evening after the races Maggie sat up late with Jesse, pretending to be knitting although she ripped out as much as she added. Jesse drummed his fingers on the arm of his chair. "Can't you sit still for once?" Maggie asked him, and then she said, "Maybe you should try calling her sister again."

"I already tried three times, for God's sake. They must be just letting it ring."

"Maybe you should go in person."

"That would be worse," Jesse said. "Pounding on the door while they hid inside and listened. I bet they'd be laughing and looking over at each other and making these goggly eyes."

"They wouldn't do that!"

"I guess I'll take the van back to Dave," Jesse said.

He rose to leave. Maggie didn't try to stop him, because she figured he was secretly going to the sister's place after all.

The van had been parked out front when they returned from Pimlico. For one relieved moment, everyone assumed Fiona was in the house. And the keys were on top of the bookcase just inside the door, where the family always left keys and stray gloves and notes saying when they'd be back. But there wasn't any note from Fiona. In the room she shared with Jesse, the unmade bed had a frozen look. Every hillock of the sheets appeared to have hardened. In Maggie's and Ira's room the crib was empty and desolate. However, this couldn't be a permanent absence. Nothing was packed; nothing was missing. Even Fiona's toilet articles still sat on the bureau in their travel case. "See there?" Maggie told Jesse, because he was worried too, she could tell; and she pointed to the travel case. "Oh. Right," he said, reassured. She crossed the hall to the bathroom and found the usual fleet of rubber ducks and tugboats. "*You* people," she said happily. Emerging, passing Jesse's room once more, she found him standing in front of the bureau with his eyes half shut and his nose buried deep in Fiona's soapbox. She understood him perfectly. Smells could bring a person back clearer than pictures, even; didn't she know that?

When the night stretched on and Jesse didn't return, she told herself that he must have found Fiona. They must be having a nice long talk. She ripped out all her garbled rows of knitting and rewound her ball of yarn and went to bed. In the dark, Ira mumbled, "Jesse back yet?"

"No, nor Fiona, either one," she said.

"Oh, well, Fiona," he said. "Fiona's gone for good."

There was a sudden clarity to his voice. It was the voice of someone talking in his sleep, which made his words seem oracular and final. Maggie felt a clean jolt of anger. Easy for *him* to say! He could toss off people without a thought.

It struck her as very significant that Ira's idea of entertainment was those interminable books about men who sailed the Atlantic absolutely alone.

He was right, though: In the morning, Fiona was still missing. Jesse came down to breakfast with that same stunned expression on his face. Maggie hated to ask, but finally she said, "Honey? You didn't find her?"

"No," he said shortly, and then he requested the marmalade in a way that shut off all further questions.

Not till that afternoon did the notion of foul play occur to her. How could they have missed it? Of course: No one traveling with an infant would leave behind all Fiona had left—the diaper bag, the stroller, the pink plastic training cup Leroy liked to drink her juice from. Someone must have kidnapped them, or worse: shot them during a street crime. The police would have to be notified this instant. She said as much to Ira, who was reading the Sunday paper in the living room. Ira didn't even look up. "Spare yourself the embarrassment, Maggie," he said quietly.

"Embarrassment?"

"She's walked out of her own free will. Don't bother the police with this."

"Ira, young mothers do not walk out with just their purses. They pack. They have to! Think," she said. "Remember all she took with her on a simple trip to Pimlico. You know what I suspect? I suspect she came back here, parked the van, carried Leroy to the grocery store for teething biscuits—I heard her say yesterday morning she was low on teething biscuits—and stepped smack into a holdup scene. You've read how robbers always choose women and children for hostages! It's more effective that way. It gets results."

Ira regarded her almost absently over the top of his paper, as if he found her just marginally interesting.

"Why, she's even left behind her soap! Her toothbrush!" she told Ira.

"Her travel case," Ira pointed out.

"Yes, and if she'd gone of her own free will—"

"Her travel case, Maggie, like she'd use in a hotel. But now she's back at, I don't know, her sister's or her mother's, where her real belongings are, and she doesn't need a travel case."

"Oh, that's nonsense," Maggie said. "And just look at her closet. It's full of clothes."

"Are you sure of that?"

"Of course. It's the first thing I checked."

"Are you sure there's nothing missing? Her favorite sweater? That jacket she's so keen on?"

Maggie considered a moment. Then she stood up and went down the hall to Jesse's room.

Jesse lay on the bed, fully dressed, with his arms folded behind his head. He glanced over at her as she entered. "Excuse me a moment," she told him, and she opened the door of his closet.

Fiona's clothes hung inside, all right, but not her windbreaker or that big striped duster she liked to wear around the house. There were only two or three skirts (she hardly ever wore skirts), a few blouses, and a ruffled dress that she'd always claimed made her look fat. Maggie spun around and went to Fiona's bureau. Jesse watched from the bed. She jerked open a drawer and found a single pair of blue jeans (artificially whitened with bleach, a process that was no longer stylish) and below them two turtlenecks from last winter and below those a pair of maternity slacks with an elastic panel in front. It was like the layers in an archaeological dig. Maggie had the fleeting fantasy that if she delved farther she would find cheerleader sweaters, then grade-school pinafores, then Fiona's baby clothes. She smoothed the layers down again and shut the drawer.

"But where would she be?" she asked Jesse.

It seemed for a long while that he wasn't going to answer. Finally, though, he said, "I guess her sister's."

"You said you didn't find her there."

"I didn't go there."

She thought that over. Then she said, "Oh, Jesse."

"I'll be damned if I make a fool of myself."

"Jesse, honey—"

"If I have to beg her then I'd sooner not have her," he said.

And he turned over with his face to the wall, ending the conversation.

It was two or three days afterward that Fiona's sister called. She said, "Mrs. Moran?" in that braying voice that Maggie instantly recognized. "This is Crystal Stuckey," she said. "Fiona's sister?"

"Oh, yes!"

"And I want to know if you'll be home for the next little bit so we can come by and pick up her things."

"Yes, of course, come right away," Maggie said. Because Jesse was home too, as it happened—lying on his bed again. She went to find him as soon as she'd hung up. "That was Fiona's sister," she said. "Christina?"

He slid his eyes toward her. "Crystal," he said.

"Crystal. They're coming to get her things."

He sat up slowly and swung his boots over the side of the bed.

"I'll go out and do some shopping," Maggie told him.

"What? No, wait."

"You'll have the place to yourselves."

"Wait, don't go. How will I—? Maybe we'll need you."

"Need me? What for?"

"I don't want to say the wrong thing to her," he said.

"Honey, I'm sure you won't say the wrong thing."

"Ma. Please," he said.

So she stayed, but she went to her own room, out of the way. Her room was at the front of the house, which was why, when a car drove up, she was able to draw aside the curtain and see who was coming. It was Crystal and a beefy young man, no doubt the famous boyfriend Fiona was always referring to. That was whom Crystal had meant by "we"; Fiona was nowhere in evidence. Maggie dropped the curtain. She heard the doorbell ring; she heard Jesse shout, "Coming!" and clatter down the stairs two at a time. Then, after a pause, she heard a brief mumble. The door slammed shut again. Had he kicked them out, or what? She lifted the curtain once more and peered down, but it was Jesse she saw, not the guests—Jesse tearing off down the sidewalk, shrugging himself into his black leather jacket as he went. In the downstairs hall, Crystal called, "Mrs. Moran?"—her voice less braying now, more tentative.

"Just a minute," Maggie said.

Crystal and her boyfriend had brought cartons from the liquor store, and Maggie helped fill them. Or tried to help. She slid a blouse from a hanger and folded it slowly, regretfully, but Crystal said, "You can just give those blouses to the veterans. Don't bother with nothing synthetic, Fiona told me. She's living back at home now and she hasn't got much closet room."

Maggie said, "Ah," and laid the blouse aside. She felt a twinge of envy. Wouldn't it be wonderful to save only what was first-class and genuine and pure, and walk out on everything else! When Crystal and the boyfriend drove off, all they left behind was the chaff.

Then Jesse found a job at a record store and stopped lying around on his bed so much of the time; and Daisy and the enchanted little girls returned to Mrs. Perfect. Maggie was on her own again. Just like that, she was deprived of all the gossip and eventfulness and the peeks into other households that children can provide. It was then she started making her spy trips to Cartwheel, not that those were ever very satisfying; or sometimes after work she would choose to walk to the frame shop rather than continue sitting in an empty house. But then she would wonder why she had come, for Ira was usually too busy to talk with her and anyhow, he said, he'd be home in just a couple of hours, wouldn't he? What was it she was hanging about for?

So she would climb the stairs to his family's apartment, and she'd pass a bit of time listening to his sisters recount the latest soap opera or his father list his aches and pains. In addition to his so-called weak heart, Mr. Moran suffered from arthritis and his vision was failing. He was over eighty, after all. The men in that family had traditionally fathered their children so late in life that when Mr. Moran talked about his great-grandfather, he was referring to a man who'd been born in the 1700s. That had never struck Maggie before, but now it seemed positively creepy. What an elderly, faltering atmosphere she lived in! Her mornings at the nursing home, her afternoons at the Morans', her evenings with Ira's solitaire games . . . She drew her sweater more tightly around her and clucked at news of her father-in-law's indigestion. "Used to be I could eat anything," he told her. "What has happened here?" He peered at her with his glintless eyes, as if expecting an answer. Lately his upper lids had developed heavy, pouched folds; his Cherokee grandmother emerged more clearly year by year. "Rona never had the remotest inkling," he told Maggie. Rona was Ira's mother. "She died before she went through all this," he said. "Wrinkles and gnarls and creaky joints and heartburn—she missed out on it."

"Well, but she had other pains," Maggie reminded him. "Maybe worse ones."

"It's like she didn't live a real life," he said, not listening. "I mean all of life, the whole messy kit and caboodle that comes at the end."

He sounded peevish; he seemed to think his wife had got away with something. Maggie clucked again and patted his hand. It felt the way she imagined an eagle's foot would feel.

Eventually she would go back downstairs to Ira, coax him to close shop a few minutes early and walk her home. He would slouch along in a kind of dark fog, something inward-turned in his gaze. When they passed the Larkin sisters' house, Maggie always glanced toward it and then looked quickly away. In the old days, wheeling Leroy homeward in her stroller, they would find a rocking horse waiting hopefully on the Larkins's front porch. It would have appeared by magic at the top of the steps where earlier there'd been nothing: a tiny, faded wooden animal with a bashful smile and long black lowered lashes. But now there was no sign of it; even those two ancient ladies knew somehow that the Morans hadn't managed to keep their family together.

Oh, how would Fiona summon the constant vigilance that child required? It wasn't merely a matter of feeding her and changing her. Leroy was one of those dauntless babies who fling themselves brazenly off stair landings and chair edges, trusting someone will be there to catch them. Fiona was nowhere near alert enough. And she had hardly any sense of smell, Maggie had noticed. Why, Maggie could scent a fire before it started, almost. Maggie could walk through a mall and unerringly detect the smell of foods improperly handled—a musty, etherish sharpness not unlike the smell of a child with a fever. Everybody else would be oblivious, but, "Stop!" Maggie would call, holding up a palm as the others drifted toward a sandwich stand. "Not there! Anywhere but there!"

She had so much to offer, if only someone would take it.

It seemed pointless to cook a real supper now. Jesse was always out and Daisy most often ate at Mrs. Perfect's, or if forced to eat at home would sulk so that it wasn't worth having her around. So Maggie just heated a couple of frozen dinners or a can of soup. Sometimes she didn't even do that. One evening, when she had sat two hours at the kitchen table staring into space instead of making the trip to the frame shop, Ira walked in and said, "What's for supper?" and she said, "I can't deal with supper! I mean look at this!" and she waved at the can of soup in front of her. "Two and three quarters servings," she read out. "What do they expect, I have two and three quarters people to feed? Or three, and I'll just give one of them less? Or maybe I'm supposed to save the rest for another meal, but do you know how long it would take me to come out even? First I'd have an extra three quarters of a serving and then six quarters and then nine. I'd have to open four cans of soup before I had leftovers that weren't in fractions. Four cans, I tell you! Four cans of the same single flavor!"

She started crying, letting the tears roll down her cheeks luxuriously. She felt the way she had felt as a child when she knew she was behaving unreasonably, knew she was shocking the grownups and acting like a perfect horror, but all at once *wanted* to behave unreasonably and even took some pleasure in it.

Ira might have turned on his heel and walked out; she was half expecting that. Instead, he sank into the chair across from her. He put his elbows on the table and lowered his head into his hands.

Maggie stopped crying. She said, "Ira?"

He didn't answer.

"Ira, what is it?" she asked him.

She rose and bent over him and hugged him. She squatted next to him and tried to peer up into his face. Had something happened to his father? To one of his sisters? Was he just so disgusted with Maggie that he couldn't endure it? What *was* it?

The answer seemed to arrive through his back—through the ripple of knobby vertebrae down his C-shaped, warm, thin back. Her fingers felt the answer first.

He was just as sad as Maggie was, and for just the same reasons. He was lonely and tired and lacking in hope and his son had not turned out well and his daughter didn't think much of him, and he still couldn't figure where he had gone wrong.

He let his head fall against her shoulder. His hair was thick and rough, strung through with threads of gray that she had never noticed before, that pierced her heart in a way that her own few gray hairs never had. She hugged him tightly and nuzzled her face against his cheekbone. She said, "It will be all right. It will be all right."

And it was, eventually. Don't ask her why. Well, for one thing, Jesse really liked his new job, and he seemed bit by bit to recover some of his old spirit. And then Daisy announced at last that Mrs. Perfect was "too tennis-y" and returned to her place in the family. And Maggie gave up her spy trips, as if Leroy and Fiona had been put to rest in her mind somehow. But none of those reasons was the most important one. It was more to do with Ira, she believed—that moment with Ira in the kitchen. Although they never referred to it afterward, and Ira didn't act any different, and life continued just the same as always.

She straightened in her seat and peered through the windshield, looking for the others. They should be about ready by now. Yes, here came Leroy, just backing out of the house with a suitcase bigger than she was. Ira thudded among things in the trunk and whistled a cheerful tune. "King of the Road," that's what he was whistling. Maggie got out to open the rear door. It seemed to her now that unknowingly, she'd been aiming ever since she woke up this morning toward this single purpose: bringing Leroy and Fiona home at last.

3
=

The way Mrs. Stuckey's car was parked behind theirs, they had just enough room to maneuver around it. Or so Ira claimed. Maggie thought he was wrong. "You could manage if the mailbox wasn't there," she said, "but it is there, and you are going to hit it when you veer out."

"Only if I were deaf, dumb, and blind," Ira said.

In the back seat, Fiona gave a small sigh.

"Look," Ira told Maggie. "You go stand beside the mailbox. Let me know when I come close. All I have to do is swing into the yard a few feet, take a sharp right back onto the driveway—"

"I'm not going to be responsible for that! You'll hit the mailbox and blame me."

"Maybe we should just ask Mom to move the Maverick," Fiona suggested.

Maggie said, "Oh, well," and Ira said, "No, I'm sure we can make it."

Neither one of them wanted Mrs. Stuckey marching out all put-upon.

"All right, then you get behind the wheel," Ira told Maggie, "and I'll direct you."

"Then I'll be the one to hit the mailbox, and I'll still get blamed."

"Maggie. There's a good ten feet between the mailbox and the Maverick. So once you're past the Maverick you just nip back onto the driveway and you're free and clear. I'll tell you when."

Maggie thought that over. She said, "Promise you won't yell if I hit the mailbox?"

"You won't hit the mailbox."

"Promise, Ira."

"Lord above! Fine, I promise."

"And you won't look up at the heavens, or make that hissing noise through your teeth—"

"Maybe I should just go get Mom," Fiona said.

"No, no, this is a cinch," Ira told her. "Any imbecile could handle it; believe me."

Maggie didn't like the sound of that.

Ira climbed out of the car and went to stand by the mailbox. Maggie slid over on the seat. She gripped the steering wheel with both hands and checked the rearview mirror. It was angled wrong, set for Ira's height instead of hers, and she reached up to adjust it. The top of Leroy's head flashed toward her, gleaming dully like the back of a watch case, followed by Ira's lean figure with his elbows cocked and his hands jammed into his rear pockets. The mailbox was a little Quonset hut beside him.

The driver's seat had been set for Ira also, way too far back, but Maggie figured it wouldn't matter for such a short distance. She shifted into reverse. Ira called, "Okay, bring her hard to your left . . ."

How come he always referred to difficult tasks as feminine? This car was not a she until it had to perform some complicated maneuver. It was the same for stubborn screws and tight jar lids, and for bulky pieces of furniture as they were being moved.

She swung onto the packed dirt yard and around the Maverick, proceeding perhaps a bit too fast but still in control. Then she reached with her foot for the brake. There wasn't one. Or there was, but it was positioned wrong, closer than she had expected considering that the seat was moved back. Her foot hit the shaft instead of the pedal and the car raced on unimpeded. Ira shouted, "What the—?" Maggie, with her gaze still fixed on the rearview mirror, saw the blur as he dove for cover. *Whap!* the mailbox said when she hit it. Leroy said, "Golly," in an awed tone of voice.

Maggie shifted into Park and poked her head out the window. Ira was hauling himself up from the dirt. He dusted off his hands. He said, "You just had to prove you were right about that mailbox, Maggie, didn't you."

"You promised, Ira!"

"Left taillight is smashed all to hell," he said, bending to examine it. He prodded something. There was a clinking sound. Maggie pulled her head in and faced forward.

"He promised he wouldn't say a word," she told Fiona and Leroy. "Watch how he goes back on that."

Fiona absently patted Leroy's bare knee.

"Smashed to smithereens," Ira called.

"You promised you wouldn't make a fuss!"

He grunted; she saw that he was righting the mailbox. From here, it didn't even look dented. "I don't suppose we need to tell your mother about this," Maggie said to Fiona.

"She already knows," Leroy said. "She's watching from the house."

It was true there was a suspicious slant to one of the venetian blind slats. Maggie said, "Oh, this day has seemed just so . . . I don't know . . ." and she slid down in her seat till she was more or less sitting on her shoulder blades.

Then Ira appeared in the window. "Try your lights," he told her.

"Hmm?"

"Your lights. I want to see if she works or not."

There he went with that "she" again. Maggie reached out wearily, not bothering to sit up straight, and pulled the knob.

"Just as I thought," Ira called from the rear. "No left taillight."

"I don't want to hear about it," Maggie told the ceiling.

Ira reappeared at the window and motioned for her to move over. "We'll be ticketed for this—what do you bet?" he said, opening the door and getting in.

"I really couldn't care less," she said.

"Late as we're running now," he said (another reproach), "it'll be dark before we're halfway home, and the state police are going to nail us for driving without a taillight."

"Stop off and get it fixed, then," Maggie said.

"Oh, well, you know those highway service stations," Ira told her. He shifted gears, pulled forward a little, and then backed smoothly out of the driveway. It didn't seem to cause him any difficulty whatsoever. "They charge an arm and a leg for something I could pick up almost free at Rudy's Auto Supply," he said. "I'm just going to take my chances."

"You could always explain your wife was a blithering idiot."

He didn't argue with that.

As they started down the road, Maggie glanced at the mailbox, which was standing at a slight tilt but otherwise seemed fine. She twisted in her seat till she was looking at Fiona and Leroy—their pale, staring faces unsettlingly alike. "You two all right?" she asked them.

"Sure," Leroy answered for both of them. She was hugging her baseball glove to her chest.

Ira said, "Bet you didn't expect us to have a wreck before we'd left your driveway, did you?"

"Didn't expect you to go asking for a wreck, either," Fiona told him.

Ira glanced over at Maggie with his eyebrows raised.

By now the sun had dropped out of sight and the sky had lost its color. All the pastures were turning up their undersides in a sudden breeze. Leroy said, "How long is this trip going to take us anyhow?"

"Just an hour or so," Fiona told her. "You remember how far it is to Baltimore."

Maggie said, "Leroy remembers Baltimore?"

"From visiting my sister."

"Oh. Of course," Maggie said.

She watched the scenery for a while. Something about the fading light gave the little houses a meek, defeated look. Finally she forced herself to ask, "How *is* your sister, Fiona?"

"She's fine, considering," Fiona said. "You knew she lost her husband."

"I didn't realize she was married, even."

"Well, no, I guess you wouldn't," Fiona said. "She married her boyfriend? Avery? And he died not six weeks later in a construction accident."

"Oh, poor Crystal," Maggie said. "What is happening here? Everyone's losing their husbands. Did I tell you we've just come from Max Gill's funeral?"

"Yes, but I don't think I knew him," Fiona said.

"You must have known him! He was married to my friend Serena that I went to school with. The Gills. I'm positive you met them."

"Well, those people were old, though," Fiona said. "Or not old, maybe, but you know. Crystal and Avery, they were barely back from their honeymoon. When you've been married only six weeks everything is still perfect."

And later it is not, was her implication. Which Maggie couldn't argue with. Still, it saddened her to realize they all took such a thing for granted.

A stop sign loomed ahead and Ira slowed and then turned onto Route One. After the country roads they had been traveling, Route One seemed more impressive. Trucks were streaming toward them, a few with their headlights already on. Someone had set a hand-lettered signboard on the porch of a little café: SUPPER NOW BEING SERVED. Good farm food, no doubt—corn on the cob and biscuits. Maggie said, "I suppose we should stop for groceries on the way home. Leroy, are you starved?"

Leroy nodded emphatically.

"I haven't had a thing but chips and pretzels since morning," Maggie said.

"That and a beer in broad daylight," Ira reminded her.

Maggie pretended not to hear him. "Leroy," she said, "tell me what your favorite food is."

Leroy said, "Oh, I don't know."

"There must be something."

Leroy poked a fist into the palm of her baseball glove.

"Hamburgers? Hot dogs?" Maggie asked. "Charcoaled steaks? Or how about crabs?"

Leroy said, "Crabs in their shells, you mean? Ick!"

Maggie felt suddenly at a loss.

"She's partial to fried chicken," Fiona said. "She asks Mom to fix that all the time. Don't you, Leroy?"

"Fried chicken! Perfect," Maggie said. "We'll pick up the makings on our way into town. Won't that be nice?"

Leroy remained silent, and no wonder; Maggie knew how chirpy and artificial she sounded. An old person, trying too hard. But if only Leroy could see that Maggie was still young underneath, just peering out from behind an older face mask!

Now all at once Ira cleared his throat. Maggie tensed. Ira said, "Um, Fiona, Leroy . . . you heard we're taking Daisy to college tomorrow."

"Yes, Maggie told me," Fiona said. "I can't believe it: eentsy little Daisy."

"I mean, we two are going to be driving her. We're starting early in the morning."

"Not *that* early," Maggie said quickly.

"Well, eight or nine o'clock, Maggie."

"What's your point?" Fiona asked Ira. "You don't think we ought to be visiting?"

Maggie said, "Good heavens, no! He didn't mean that at all."

"Well, it sounded to me like he did," Fiona said.

Ira said, "I just wanted to be sure you knew what you were getting into. That it would have to be such a short stay, I mean."

"That's no problem, Ira," Maggie told him. "If she wants she can go on over to her sister's in the morning."

"Well, fine then, but it's getting dark and we're not even halfway home. I would think—"

"Maybe we better just stop right here and go on back where we came from," Fiona said.

"Oh, no, Fiona!" Maggie cried. "We had this all settled!"

"I can't remember now why I said we'd come in the first place," Fiona said. "Lord! What must I have been thinking of?"

Maggie unbuckled her seat belt and twisted around so she was facing Fiona. "Fiona, please," she said. "It's only for a little while, and it's been so long since we've seen Leroy. I've got all these things I want to show her. I want her to meet Daisy and I was planning to take her by the Larkin sisters'; they won't believe how she's grown."

"Who're the Larkin sisters?" Leroy asked.

"These two old ladies; they used to set out their rocking horse for you to ride on."

Fiona said, "I don't remember that."

"We'd pass by their porch and it would be empty, and then when we turned around to come home the horse would be sitting there waiting."

"I don't remember a thing about it," Fiona said.

Leroy said, "Me neither."

"Well, of course *you* wouldn't," Fiona told her. "You were just a baby. You didn't live there hardly any time at all."

This struck Maggie as unfair. She said, "Well, goodness, she was nearly a year old when you left, Fiona."

"She was not! She was barely seven months."

"That's not right; she had to have been, oh, eight months at least. If you left in September—"

"Seven months, eight months, what's the difference?" Ira asked. "Why make a federal case of it?" He found Leroy's face in the mirror and said, "I bet you don't remember how your grandma tried to teach you to say 'Daddy,' either."

"I did?" Maggie asked.

"It was going to be a surprise for his birthday," Ira told Leroy. "She would clap her hands and you were supposed to say 'Daddy' on cue. But when she clapped her hands all you'd do was laugh. You thought it was some kind of game."

Maggie tried to picture that. Why did her memories never coincide with Ira's? Instead they seemed to dovetail—one moment his to recall and the next hers, as if they had agreed to split their joint life between them. (Illogically, she always worried about whether she had behaved right during those moments she had forgotten.)

"So did it work, or not?" Leroy was asking Ira.

"Work?"

"Did I learn to say 'Daddy'?"

"Well, no, actually," Ira said. "You were way too little to be talking yet."

"Oh."

Leroy seemed to be digesting that. Then she sat forward so she was practically nose to nose with Maggie. Her eyes had darker blue specks in them, as if even they were freckled. "I am going to get to see him, aren't I?" she said. "He's not giving a concert or anything, is he?"

"Who?" Maggie asked, although of course she knew.

"My . . . Jesse."

"Well, certainly you are. You'll see him at supper after he gets off work. He loves fried chicken, just like you. It must be genetic."

"The thing of it is—" Ira began.

Maggie said, "What do you like for dessert, Leroy?"

"The thing of it is," Ira said, "this is Saturday night. What if Jesse has other plans and he can't make supper?"

"But he *can* make supper, Ira; I already told you that."

"Or if he has to leave right after. I mean what are we doing here, Maggie? We don't have any toys anymore or any sports equipment and our TV is on the blink. We don't have anything to keep a child occupied. And would you please face forward and fasten your seat belt? You're making me nervous."

"I'm just trying to figure out what to buy for dessert," Maggie said. But she turned around and reached for her seat belt. "Your daddy's favorite dessert is mint chocolate chip ice cream," she told Leroy.

"Oh, mine too," Leroy said.

Fiona said, "What are you talking about? You hate mint chocolate chip."

"I love it," Leroy told her.

"You absolutely do not!"

"Yes, I do, Ma. It was only when I was little I didn't like it."

"Well, you must have been little just last week, then, missy."

Maggie said hastily, "What other flavors do you like, Leroy?"

"Well, fudge ripple, for instance," Leroy said.

"Oh, what a coincidence! Jesse is crazy about fudge ripple."

Fiona rolled her eyes. Leroy said, "Really? I think fudge ripple is just excellent."

"I have seen you go without any dessert whatsoever if the only choice was mint chocolate chip ice cream," Fiona told Leroy.

"You don't know every little thing about me!" Leroy cried.

Fiona said, "Geeze, Leroy," and slumped down low in her seat with her arms tightly folded.

They were in Maryland now, and Maggie imagined that the country here looked different—more luxurious. The hillsides, emptied of live-stock, had turned a deep, perfect green, and in the faded light the long white fences gave off a moony glimmer. Ira was whistling "Sleepytime Gal." Maggie couldn't think why, for a second. Did it signify he was tired, or what? But then she realized he must still have his mind on Leroy's baby days. That was the song they used to sing her to sleep with—he and Maggie, harmonizing. Maggie leaned her head against the back of the seat and silently followed the lyrics as he whistled.

> When you're a stay-at-home, play-at-home, eight-o'clock
> Sleepytime gal . . .

All at once she looked down at her wrist and saw that she wore two watches. One was her regular watch, a little Timex, and the other was a big old chunky man's watch with a wide leather band. In fact, it belonged to her father, but it had been lost or broken years ago. The face was a rectangle, pinkish, and the numerals were a pale blue that would glow in the dark. She cupped her hand over her wrist and bent close, making a little cave of darkness so she could see the numbers light up. Her fingers smelled of bubble gum. Beside her, Serena said, "Just another five minutes, that's all I ask. If nothing happens by then, I promise we can go."

Maggie raised her head and stared through the leaves at the two stone lions across the street. Between them lay a white sidewalk, curving across an immaculate lawn and arriving finally at a stately brick colonial house, and within that house lived the man who was Serena's father. The front door was the kind without a window, without even those tiny glass panes that are placed too high to be useful. Maggie wondered how Serena could stare so intently at something so blank and ungiving. They were crouched uncomfortably among the twisted branches of a rhododendron bush. Maggie said, "That's what you told me half an hour ago. No one's going to come."

Serena laid a hand on her arm, hushing her. The door was swinging open. Mr. Barrett stepped out and then turned back to say something. His wife appeared, tugging at her gloves. She wore a slim brown dress with long sleeves, and Mr. Barrett's suit was almost the same shade of brown. Neither Maggie nor Serena had ever seen him in anything but a suit, not even on weekends. He was like a dollhouse doll, Maggie thought—one of those jointed plastic figures with the clothes painted on, nonremovable, and a clean-cut, anonymous face. He shut the door and took his wife's elbow and they moved down the sidewalk, their heels gritty-sounding. When they passed between the stone lions they seemed to be looking directly at Maggie and Serena; Maggie could see the needles of silver in Mr. Barrett's crew cut. But his expression told her nothing, and neither did his wife's. They turned sharply to their left and headed toward a long blue Cadillac parked at the curb. Serena let her breath out. Maggie felt a sense of frustration that was almost suffocating. How sealed off these people were! You could study them all day and still not know them. (Or any other married couple either, maybe.) There were moments—the first time they had made love, say, or say a conversation they'd once had when one of them woke up frightened in the middle of the night—that nobody else in the world had any inkling of.

Maggie turned to Serena and said, "Oh, Serena, I'm so sorry for your loss." Serena wore her red funeral dress and she was blotting her tears on the fringe of her black shawl. "Dear heart, I am so sorry," Maggie said, and when she woke up, she was crying too. She thought she was home in bed and Ira was asleep beside her, his breath as steady as tires hissing past on a pavement and his warm bare arm supporting her head, but that was the back of the car seat she felt. She sat up and brushed at her eyes with her fingertips.

The light had slipped yet another notch downward into dusk and they had reached that long, tangled commercial stretch just above Baltimore. Blazing signs streaked by, HI-Q PLUMBING SUPPLIES and CECIL'S GRILL and EAT EAT EAT. Ira was just a gray profile, and when Maggie turned to see Leroy and Fiona she found all the color washed out of them except for what flashed across their faces from the neon. "I must have been asleep," she told them, and they nodded. She asked Ira, "How much further?"

"Oh, another fifteen minutes or so. We're already inside the Beltway."

"Don't forget we need to stop at a grocery store."

She was cross with herself for missing out on part of the conversation. (Or hadn't there been any? That would be worse.) Her head felt cottony and nothing seemed completely real. They passed a house with a lighted, glassed-in porch on which drum sets were displayed, smaller drums stacked on top of larger, some gold-spangled like a woman's lamé evening gown and all of them glittering with chrome, and she wondered if she were dreaming again. She turned to follow the house with her eyes. The drums grew smaller but stayed eerily bright, like fish in an aquarium.

"I had the weirdest dream," she said after a moment.

"Was I in it?" Leroy wanted to know.

"Not that I can remember. But you might have been."

"Last week my friend Valerie dreamed I had died," Leroy said.

"Ooh, don't even say such a thing!"

"She dreamed I got run over by a tractor trailer," Leroy said with satisfaction.

Maggie swiveled to catch Fiona's eye. She wanted to assure her that such a dream meant nothing, or maybe she wanted the assurance for herself. But Fiona wasn't listening. She was gazing at the clutter of convenience stores and pizza parlors.

"Mighty Value Supermarket," Ira said. He flicked his left turn signal on.

Maggie said, "Mighty what? I never heard of it."

"It's handy, is what counts," Ira told her. He was delayed by a stream of oncoming traffic, but finally he found an opening and darted across the street and into a lot littered with abandoned shopping carts. He parked beside a panel truck and switched off the engine.

Leroy said she wanted to come too. Maggie said, "Well, of course," and then Ira, who had just started to slouch down behind the wheel, straightened and opened his door as if he'd been planning to go with them all along. This made Maggie smile. (Don't try and tell *her* he didn't care about his grandchild!) Fiona said, "Well, I certainly don't want to sit here by myself," and she stepped out of the car to follow them. She had never been fond of grocery shopping, as Maggie recalled.

The Mighty Value turned out to be one of those vast, cold, white, shiny places with rank upon rank of checkout counters, most of them closed. Some syrupy love song was playing over the loudspeaker. Against her will, Maggie slowed down, keeping time with the music. She drifted past the fruits and vegetables, dreamily swinging her pocketbook, while the others went ahead. Leroy took a run with an empty cart and then hopped on the back and coasted until she caught up with Ira, who had already reached the poultry counter. He turned and smiled at her. From Maggie's angle his profile looked sharp and wolfish—

hungry, really. It was something about the way he jutted his face toward Leroy. Maggie bypassed Fiona and arrived next to him. She slipped her arm through his and lightly brushed her cheek against his shoulder.

"Dark meat or white?" Ira was asking Leroy.

"Dark," Leroy said promptly. "Me and Ma like drumsticks."

"Us too," Ira told her, and he picked out a pack and dropped it into her cart.

"And sometimes me and Ma eat thighs, but we don't think wings are worth the bother," Leroy said.

"Me and Ma" this, "me and Ma" that—how long had it been since Maggie herself was so central to anyone's world? And this "Ma" was only Fiona, fragile-boned Fiona sashaying up the aisle in her cut-off shorts.

Humming along with the loudspeaker music, Ira placed a pack of thighs on top of the drumsticks in the cart. "Now for the ice cream," he said. Leroy coasted away on the cart and Maggie and Ira followed. Maggie still had her arm linked through Ira's. Fiona trailed behind.

In the freezer section they had no trouble deciding on fudge ripple, but then there were so many different fudge ripples to choose from: Mighty Value's house brand and the standard brands and then the fancy, foreign-sounding brands that Ira called "designer desserts." He was opposed to designer desserts on principle; he wanted to get the Mighty Value. Fiona, who had discovered the Hair Care section, offered no opinion, but Leroy said that she and Ma had always favored Breyer's. And Maggie voted to go all out and choose something foreign. They could have discussed it forever, except that by now the loudspeaker was playing "Tonight You Belong to Me," and halfway through the song Ira began muttering along with it. " 'Way down,' " he rumbled absently, " 'by the stream . . .' " So then Maggie couldn't resist chiming in on that airy little soprano part: " 'How sweet, it will seem . . .' "

It started as a spoof, but it developed into a real production. " 'Once more, just to dream, in the moonlight!' " Their voices braided together on the chorus and then sailed apart, only to reunite and twine around each other once again. Fiona forgot the box of hair dye she was studying; Leroy clasped her hands admiringly under her chin; an old woman paused in the aisle to smile at them. It was the old woman who brought Maggie back to earth. All at once she imagined some deception in this scene, some lie that she and Ira were collaborating in with their compliant harmonizing and the romantic gaze they trained upon each other. She broke off in the middle of a solo line. "Patience and Prudence," she informed Leroy briskly. "Nineteen fifty-seven."

"Fifty-six," Ira said.

Maggie said, "Whatever."

They turned their attention back to the ice cream.

In the end they decided on Breyer's, with chocolate sauce from the shelf above the freezer. "Hershey's chocolate sauce, or Nestlé's?" Ira asked.

"I'll leave it up to you two."

"Or here's a Mighty Value brand. What do you say we go for that?"

"Just not Brown Cow," Leroy told him. "I can't abide Brown Cow."

"Definitely not Brown Cow," Ira said.

"Brown Cow smells like candle wax," Leroy told Maggie.

Maggie said, "Ah." She looked down at Leroy's pointy little face and smiled.

Fiona asked Maggie, "Have you ever considered using a mousse?"

"A what?"

"A styling mousse. On your hair."

"Oh, on my hair," Maggie said. She had thought they were talking about some kind of ice-cream sauce. "Why, no, I don't believe I have."

"A lot of our beauticians recommend it."

Was Fiona recommending it to Maggie? Or maybe she was only speaking generally. "Just what would it do for a person?" Maggie asked.

"Well, in your case it would give your hair a little, I don't know, a little shape or something. It would kind of organize it."

"I'll buy some," Maggie decided.

She picked up a silvery container, along with a bottle of Affinity shampoo since she still had that coupon. (*Brings back the fullness that time has taken away*, a display card promised.) Then they all went to the express lane, rushed along by Maggie because it was after six, according to her watch, and she had told Jesse six-thirty. Ira said, "Do you have enough money? I could go get the car while you're paying."

She nodded, and he left them. Leroy laid their purchases neatly on the counter. The customer in front of them was buying nothing but breads. Rye bread, white bread, biscuits, whole wheat rolls. Maybe he was trying to fatten up his wife. Say he was the jealous type, and his wife was very thin and beautiful. The customer departed, taking his breads with him. Leroy said, "Double bags, please," in a bossy, experienced voice. The boy at the cash register grunted without looking. He was muscular and good-looking, deeply tanned, and he wore a gold razor blade on a chain inside the open collar of his shirt. What on earth could that mean? He rang up their items swiftly, his fingers stabbing the keys. Last came the shampoo. Maggie dug through her purse for the coupon and handed it to him. "Here," she said, "this is for you."

He took it and turned it over. He read it narrowly, not quite moving his lips. Then he gave it back to her. He said, "Well, uh, thanks," and then, "That'll be sixteen forty-three."

Maggie felt confused, but she counted out the money and picked up the bag. As they left the register she asked Fiona, "Does Mighty Value not accept coupons, or what?"

"Coupons? I wouldn't know," Fiona said.

"Maybe it's expired," Maggie said. She shifted her grocery bag in order to peer at the expiration date. But the print was covered over at right angles by Durwood Clegg's heavy blue script: *Hold me close, hold me tight, make me thrill with delight* . . .

Maggie's face grew hot. She said, "Well! Of all the conceit!"

"Pardon?" Fiona asked, but Maggie didn't answer. She screwed up the coupon and dropped it into the grocery bag.

Outside, it was much darker now. The air was a deep, transparent blue and insects were flitting around the lights high above the parking lot. Ira leaned against the car by the curb. "You want to put the groceries in the trunk?" he asked Maggie, but she said, "No, I'll just hold them." She suddenly felt old and weary. It seemed they would never reach home. She got into the car and sat down hard, with the grocery bag slumped any which way on her knees.

St. Michael the Archangel. Charlie's Fine Liquors. Used-car dealers, one after the other. Gatch Memorial Church. Dead Man's Fingers Crab House. HAPPY HOUR NITELY, with red and blue neon bubbles fizzing above a neon cocktail glass. Cemeteries and shabby frame houses and fast-food restaurants and empty playgrounds. They took a right off Belair Road—finally, finally leaving Route One—and headed down their own street. The frame houses grew more numerous. Their windows were squares of yellow light, some gauzy with curtains and some fully exposed, revealing ornate decorative lamps or china figurines meticulously centered on the sills. For no good reason, Maggie was reminded of rides she had taken with Ira during their courtship, driving past houses where every other couple in the world, it seemed, had a space to be alone in. What she would have given, back then, for even the smallest of those houses, even just four walls and a bed! She felt a sweet, sad fullness in her chest now, remembering that long-ago ache.

They passed the Seeing Eye Palmistry Parlor, really just a private home with a sign propped in the living room window. A girl was sitting out on the steps, maybe waiting her turn; she had a small, heart-shaped face and she was dressed all in black except for her purple suede shoes, which showed up clearly in the light from the porch. A man trudged down the sidewalk with a little girl riding his shoulders and clutching two handfuls of his hair. It seemed the scenery had grown more intimate, more specific. Maggie turned toward Leroy and said, "I don't suppose any of this is familiar."

"Oh, I've seen it," Leroy said.

"You have?"

"Only in passing," Fiona corrected her quickly.

"When was that?"

Leroy looked at Fiona, who said, "We might have driven by here once or twice."

Maggie said, "Is that so."

In front of their own house, Ira parked. It was one of those houses that appear to be mostly front porch, at least from the street—squat and low-browed, not at all impressive, as Maggie was the first to admit. She wished at least the lights were on. That would have made it seem more welcoming. But every window was dark. "Well!" she said, too heartily. She opened her door and got out of the car, clutching the groceries. "Come on in, everyone!"

There was something befuddled about the way they milled around on the sidewalk. They had been traveling for too long. When Ira started up the steps, he accidentally banged Fiona's suitcase against the railing, and he fumbled awhile with the key before he got the door unlocked.

They entered the musty, close darkness of the front hallway. Ira flipped on the light. Maggie called, "Daisy?" without a hope that Daisy would answer. Clearly the house was deserted. She shifted the grocery bag to her left hip and picked up the notepad that lay on top of the bookcase. *Gone to say goodbye to Lavinia*, Daisy's precise italics read. "She's at Mrs. Perfect's," Maggie told Ira. "Well, she'll be back! How long can it take to say goodbye? She'll be back in no time!"

This was all for Leroy's benefit, to show that Daisy really existed—that there was more to this house than old people.

Leroy was circling the hallway, with her baseball glove tucked under one arm. She was squinting up at the photographs that covered the walls. "Who's that?" she asked, pointing to one.

Ira as a young father stood in dappled sunlight, awkwardly holding a baby. "That's your grandpa, holding your daddy," Maggie told her.

Leroy said, "Oh," and moved on at once. Probably she had hoped it was Jesse holding Leroy. Maggie cast her eyes around the room to see if she could locate such a picture. You could hardly make out the wallpaper pattern for all the photos that hung here, each framed professionally by Ira and each mat and molding different, like a sample of something. There was Jesse as a toddler, as a little boy on a scooter, as a thumbtack-sized face among rows of other faces in fifth grade. But no picture of Jesse as a grownup, Maggie realized; not even as a teenager. And certainly not as a father. They had run out of wall space by then. Besides, Maggie's mother was always saying how trashy it was to display one's family photographs anywhere but a bedroom.

Fiona was pushing her suitcase toward the stairs, leaving two long thin scratches on the floorboards behind her. "Oh, don't bother with that," Maggie told her. "Ira will carry it up for you later."

How must Fiona feel, returning after so long—walking across the porch where she'd decided to keep her baby, passing through the front door that she had so often slammed out of in a huff? She looked drawn and dispirited. The sudden light had crumpled the skin around her eyes. She abandoned her suitcase and pointed to a photo high on the wall. "There *I* happen to be," she told Leroy. "In case you're interested."

She meant her bridal photo. Maggie had forgotten that. A wedding present from Crystal, who had brought a camera to the ceremony, it showed a coltish young girl in a wrinkled dress. The frame was a black plastic diploma frame that must have come from Woolworth's. Leroy studied the photo without expression. Then she moved into the living room, where Ira was switching on lamps.

Maggie took the groceries out to the kitchen, with Fiona close behind. "So where is he?" Fiona asked in a low voice.

"Well, he's probably . . ." Maggie said. She flicked on the overhead light and glanced at the clock. "I told him we'd eat at six-thirty and it's barely that now and you know how he loses track of time, so don't worry—"

Fiona said, "I'm not worried! Who says I'm worried? I don't care if he comes or he doesn't."

"No, of course not," Maggie said soothingly.

"I just brought Leroy to visit you two. I don't care if he comes."

"Well, of course you don't."

Fiona sat down heavily in a kitchen chair and threw her purse on the table. Like the most formal of guests, she was carrying that purse with her from room to room; some things never changed. Maggie sighed and began unpacking the groceries. She put the ice cream in the freezer, and then she slit open both packs of chicken and dumped them into a bowl. "What kind of vegetables does Leroy like?" she asked.

Fiona said, "Hmm? Vegetables?" She didn't seem to have her mind on the question. She was gazing at the wall calendar, which still showed the month of August. Oh, this wasn't a very organized house, not that Fiona had any right to complain. The counters seemed to collect stray objects on their own. The cupboards were filled with dusty spice bottles and cereal boxes and mismatched dishes. Drawers sagged open, exposing a jumble of belongings. One drawer caught Maggie's eye, and she went over to riffle through the layers of papers stuffed inside. "Now, somewhere here," she said, "I could almost swear . . ."

She came across a PTA announcement. A torn-out recipe for something called Amazin' Raisin Pie. A packet of get-well cards that she'd been hunting since the day she bought them. And then, "Aha," she said, holding up a flier.

"What is it?"

"Picture of Jesse as a grownup. For Leroy."

She brought it over to Fiona: a darkly photocopied photo of the band. Lorimer was sitting in front with his drums and Jesse stood behind, his arms draped loosely around the necks of the other two, Dave and what's-his-name. All wore black. Jesse had his eyebrows knitted in a deliberate scowl. SPIN THE CAT was printed in furry, tiger-striped letters beneath their picture, and a blank space at the bottom allowed for a specific time and place to be written in by hand.

"Of course it doesn't do him justice," Maggie said. "These rock groups always try to look so, I don't know, so surly; have you noticed? Maybe I should just show her the snapshot I carry in my wallet. He isn't smiling there, either, but at least he's not frowning."

Fiona took the flier to study it more closely. "How funny," she said. "Everyone's just the same."

"Same?"

"I mean they were always going to be *going* somewhere; didn't you always think so? They had such high-and-mighty plans. And they used to keep changing so, changing their views of music. Why, one time Leroy asked me just what kind of songs her daddy played, new wave or punk or heavy metal or what, exactly—I think she wanted to impress her friends—and I said, 'Lordy, by now it could be anything; I wouldn't have the foggiest notion.' But just look at them."

"Well? So?" Maggie said. "What's to look at?"

"Lorimer's still got his hair fixed in that silly shag haircut with the tail down the back of his neck that I was always dying to chop off," Fiona said. "They're still wearing the same style of clothes, even. Same old-fashioned Hell's Angels style of clothing."

"Old-fashioned?" Maggie asked.

"You could picture how they'll get to be forty and still playing together on weekends when their wives will let them, playing for Rotary Club get-togethers and such."

It bothered Maggie to hear this, but she didn't let on. She turned back to her bowl of chicken.

Fiona said, "Who was it he brought to dinner?"

"Pardon?"

"You said he brought this woman to dinner one time."

Maggie glanced over at her. Fiona was still holding the photo, gazing at it with a bemused expression. "Nobody important," Maggie said.

"Well, who?"

"Just some woman he'd met someplace; we've been through a lot of those. Nobody long-term."

Fiona set the photo down on the table, but she went on looking at it.

Out in the living room, ragged music started thrumming forth from the hi-fi. Evidently Leroy had found one of Jesse's castoffs. Maggie heard *Hey hey* and *Every day* and a familiar twanging of strings, although she couldn't say who was playing. She took a carton of buttermilk from the refrigerator and poured it over the chicken. A headache was tightening the skin of her forehead. Now that she thought of it, she realized it had been nagging at her for some time.

"I'm going to call Jesse," she told Fiona suddenly.

She went over to the wall telephone and lifted the receiver. There wasn't any dial tone. Instead she heard a ringing at the other end. "Ira must be using the extension," she said, and she hung up again. "Well, so anyhow. Vegetables. Which vegetables will Leroy eat?"

"She likes tossed salad," Fiona said.

"Oh, dear, I should've bought lettuce."

"Maggie," Ira said, entering the kitchen, "what did you do to my answering machine?"

"Me? I didn't do anything."

"You most certainly did."

"I did not! I already told you about that little mishap last evening, but then I put a new message on."

He crooked his finger, beckoning her to the telephone. "Try it," he told her.

"What for?"

"Try dialing the shop."

She shrugged and came over to the phone. After she dialed, the phone at the other end rang three times. Something clicked. "Well, here goes," Maggie's own voice said, faraway and tinny. "Let's see: Press Button A, wait for the red . . . oh, shoot."

Maggie blinked.

"I must be doing something wrong," her voice continued. Then, in the falsetto she often used when she was clowning around with her children: "Who, me? Do something wrong? Little old perfect me? I'm shocked at the very suggestion!"

There was a ribbony shriek, like a tape on fast forward, followed by a beep. Maggie hung up. She said, "Well . . . um . . ."

"God knows what my customers thought," Ira told her.

"Maybe no one called," she said hopefully.

"I don't even know how you managed it! That machine is supposed to be foolproof."

"Well, it only goes to show: You can't trust the simplest product nowadays," she told him. She lifted the receiver again and started dialing Jesse's number. While his telephone rang and rang, she twined the cord nervously between her fingers. She was conscious of Fiona watching them, seated at the table with her chin resting on her cupped hand.

"Who're you calling?" Ira asked.

She pretended not to hear.

"Who's she calling, Fiona?"

"Well, Jesse, I think," Fiona told him.

"Did you forget his phone won't ring?"

Maggie looked up at him. "Oh!" she said.

She replaced the receiver and then gazed at it regretfully.

"Oh, well," Fiona said, "maybe he's on his way. It's Saturday night, after all; how late does he work?"

"Not late at all," Ira told her.

"*Where* does he work, come to think of it?"

"Chick's Cycle Shop. He sells motorcycles."

"Wouldn't they be closed by now?"

"Of course they're closed. They close at five."

"Then why bother calling?"

"No, no, she was calling his apartment," Ira said.

Fiona said, "His—"

Maggie went back to the bowl of chicken. She stirred it around in the buttermilk. She took a flattened brown paper bag from one of the drawers and poured some flour into it.

"Jesse has an apartment?" Fiona asked Ira.

"Why, yes."

Maggie measured in baking powder, salt, and pepper.

"An apartment away from here?"

"Up on Calvert Street."

Fiona thought that over.

Maggie said, "Here's something I always wanted to ask you, Fiona!" Her voice had somehow taken on that chirpy tone again. "Remember just a few months after you left?" she asked. "When Jesse phoned you and said you'd phoned him first and you said you hadn't? Well, had you, or hadn't you? Was it you who phoned our house and I said, 'Fiona?' and you hung up?"

"Oh, goodness . . ." Fiona said vaguely.

"I mean it had to be, or why else would the person hang up when I said your name?"

"I really don't recollect," Fiona said, and then she reached for her purse and rose. Walking in an airy, aimless way, as if she hardly noticed she was leaving, she wandered out of the kitchen, calling, "Leroy? Where'd you get to?"

"See there?" Maggie told Ira.

"Hmm?"

"It was her. I knew it all along."

"She didn't say it was."

"Oh, Ira, you are so obtuse sometimes," she said.

She closed the brown paper bag and shook it, mixing the seasonings. You can't have things both ways, she should have told Fiona. You can't laugh at him for staying the same and also object when he changes. Why, of course he had moved! Did Fiona imagine he had sat here waiting for her all these years?

And yet Maggie knew how she felt, somehow. You have this picture of a person; you have him tucked away in your mind in this certain fixed position.

She looked again at the band photo on the table. They had all been so enthusiastic once, she thought. So much energy had been invested. She remembered those early rehearsals in Lorimer's parents' garage, and the months and months when they'd been thrilled to perform for free, even, and the night that Jesse had come home triumphantly waving a ten-dollar bill—his share of their first paycheck.

"Is that Daisy?" Ira asked.

"What?"

"I thought I heard the front door."

"Oh!" Maggie said. "Maybe it's Jesse."

"Don't count on it," he told her.

But only Jesse would sling the door back against the bookcase that way. Maggie dusted off her hands. "Jesse?" she called.

"Here I am."

She hurried out to the hall, and Ira followed more slowly. Jesse stood just inside the door. He was looking toward the living room, where Leroy was poised like some startled small animal with her hands pressed together in front of her and one foot drawn up behind her. Jesse said, "Well, hi."

"Hi," Leroy said.

"How're you doing?"

"I'm okay."

He looked over at Maggie. Maggie said, "Hasn't she grown?"

His long black eyes returned to Leroy.

Now Maggie moved toward him, willing him further into the house. (He always seemed on the verge of leaving.) She took his arm and said, "I'm frying up some chicken; it'll be a few more minutes. You two can sit in here and get acquainted."

But he had never been easily led. He was wearing a knitted jersey, and beneath the thin cloth she felt his resistance—the steely muscle above his elbow. His boots remained rooted to the floor. He was going to take his own sweet time at this.

"So what're you listening to?" he asked Leroy.

"Oh, just some record."

"You a Dead fan?"

"Dead? Um, sure."

"You want some better album, then," he said. "This one here is too popular with the masses."

"Oh, yeah, well," she said. "I was just thinking that myself."

He glanced at Maggie again. He was holding his face in a way that caused his chin to lengthen, just as Ira always did when he was trying to keep back a smile.

"She's athletic too," Maggie told him. "Brought along her baseball glove."

"That so?" he asked Leroy.

She nodded. The toe of her raised foot pointed daintily downward, ballet style.

Then something clattered upstairs and Fiona called, "Maggie, where—?"

She arrived on the landing. They all looked up at her.

"Oh," she said.

And she began to descend the stairs very smoothly and quietly, with one hand trailing along the banister. The only sound was the slapping of her sandals against her bare heels.

Jesse said, "Good to see you, Fiona."

She reached the hall and looked up at him. "It's good to see you too," she said.

"Done something new to your hair, haven't you?"

She lifted a hand, with her eyes still on his face, and touched the ends of her hair. "Oh! Maybe so," she told him.

Maggie said, "Well, I guess I'd better get back to—"

And Ira said, "Need help in the kitchen, Maggie?"

"Yes, please!" she sang out happily.

Fiona told Jesse, "I was just upstairs hunting my soapbox."

Maggie hesitated.

"Soapbox?" Jesse asked.

"I tried your bureau drawer, but it's empty. All I found was mothballs. Did you take my soapbox with you when you moved to your apartment?"

"What soapbox are you talking about?"

"My tortoiseshell soapbox! The one you kept."

Jesse looked over at Maggie. Maggie said, "You remember her soapbox."

"Well, no, I can't say as I do," Jesse said, and he grabbed hold of his forelock the way he always did when he was puzzled.

"You kept it after she left," Maggie told him. "I saw you with it. There was a bar of soap inside, remember? That clear kind of soap you can see through."

"*Oh*, yes," Jesse said, letting go of his forelock.

"You remember it?"

"Sure."

Maggie relaxed. She flashed a bracing smile at Leroy, who had lowered her foot to the floor now and was looking uncertain.

"So where is it?" Fiona asked. "Where's my soapbox, Jesse?"

"Well, uh, didn't your sister take it?"

"No."

"I thought she packed it up along with your other things."

"No," Fiona said. "You had it in your bureau."

Jesse said, "Gosh, Fiona. In that case maybe it's thrown out by now. But look, if it means so much to you, then I'd be glad to—"

"But you kept it, because it reminded you of me," Fiona told him. "It smelled like me! You closed your eyes and held my soapbox to your nose."

Jesse's gaze swiveled to Maggie again. He said, "Ma? Is that what you told her?"

"You mean it's not true?" Fiona asked him.

"You said I went around sniffing soapboxes, Ma?"

"You did!" Maggie said. Although she hated having to repeat it to his face. She had never meant to shame him. She turned to Ira (who was wearing exactly the shocked, reproachful expression she had expected) and said, "He kept it in his top drawer."

"Your treasure drawer," Fiona told Jesse. "Do you suppose I'd come all the way down here like any ordinary . . . groupie if your mother hadn't told me that? I didn't have to come! I was getting along just fine! But your mother says you hung on to my soapbox and wouldn't let Crystal pack it, you closed your eyes and took this big whiff, you've kept it to this day, she said, you've never let it go, you sleep with it under your pillow at night."

Maggie cried, "I never said—!"

"What do you think I am? Some kind of loser?" Jesse asked Fiona.

"Now, listen," Ira said.

Everyone seemed glad to turn to him.

"Let me get this straight," he said. "You're talking about a plastic soapbox."

"*My* plastic soapbox," Fiona told him, "that Jesse sleeps every night with."

"Well, there seems to be some mistake," Ira said. "How would Maggie even know such a thing? Jesse has his own apartment now. All he sleeps with that *I've* ever heard of is an auto greeter."

"A what?"

"Oh, never mind."

"What's an auto greeter?"

There was a pause. Then Ira said, "You know: the person who stands at the door when you go in to buy a car. She makes you give your name and address before she'll call a salesman."

"She? You mean a woman?"

"Right."

"Jesse sleeps with a woman?"

"Right."

Maggie said, "You just had to spoil things, Ira, didn't you."

"No," Ira told her, "it's the simple truth that's spoiled things, Maggie, and the truth is, Jesse's involved with somebody else now."

"But that woman's no one important! I mean they're not engaged or married or anything! She's no one he really cares about!"

She looked to Jesse to back her up, but he was studiously examining the toe of his left boot.

"Oh, Maggie, admit it," Ira said. "This is the way things *are*. This is how he's going to be. He never was fit husband material! He passes from girlfriend to girlfriend and he can't seem to hold the same job for longer than a few months; and every job he loses, it's somebody else's fault. The boss is a jerk, or the customers are jerks, or the other workers are—"

"Now, hold on," Jesse began, while Maggie said, "Oh, why do you always, always exaggerate, Ira! He worked in the record shop a full year, have you forgotten that?"

"Everyone in Jesse's acquaintance," Ira finished calmly, "by some magical coincidence ends up being a jerk."

Jesse turned and walked out of the house.

It made things more disturbing, somehow, that he didn't slam the door but let it click shut very gently behind him.

Maggie said, "He'll be back." She was speaking to Fiona, but when Fiona didn't respond (her face was almost wooden; she was staring after Jesse), she told Leroy instead. "You saw how glad he was to see you, didn't you?"

Leroy just gaped.

"He's upset at what Ira said about him, is all," Maggie told her. And then she said, "Ira, I will never forgive you for this."

"Me!" Ira said.

Fiona said, "Stop it."

They turned.

"Just stop, both of you," she said. "I'm tired to death of it. I'm tired of Jesse Moran and I'm tired of the two of you, repeating your same dumb arguments and niggling and bickering, Ira forever so righteous and Maggie so willing to be wrong."

"Why . . . Fiona?" Maggie said. Her feelings were hurt. Maybe it was silly of her, but she had always secretly believed that outsiders regarded her marriage with envy. "We're not bickering; we're just discussing," she said. "We're compiling our two views of things."

Fiona said, "Oh, forget it. I don't know why I thought anything would be any different here." And she stepped into the living room and hugged Leroy, whose eyes were wide and startled. She said, "There, there, honey," and she buried her face in the crook of Leroy's neck. Plainly, Fiona herself was the one who needed consoling.

Maggie glanced at Ira. She looked elsewhere.

"Soapbox?" Ira asked. "How could you invent such a story?"

She didn't answer. (Anything she said might look like bickering.) Instead she walked away from him. She headed toward the kitchen in what she hoped was a dignified silence, but Ira followed, saying, "Look here, Maggie, you can't keep engineering other people's lives this way. Face facts! Wake up and smell the coffee!"

Ann Landers's favorite expression: Wake up and smell the coffee. She hated it when he quoted Ann Landers. She went over to the counter and started dropping chicken parts into the paper bag.

"Soapbox!" Ira marveled to himself.

"You want peas with your chicken?" she asked. "Or green beans."

But Ira said, "I'm going to go wash up." And he left.

So here she was alone. Well! She brushed a tear from her lashes. She was in trouble with everybody in this house, and she deserved to be; as usual she had acted pushy and meddlesome. And yet it hadn't seemed like meddling while she was doing it. She had simply felt as if the world were the tiniest bit out of focus, the colors not quite within the lines—something like a poorly printed newspaper ad—and if she made the smallest adjustment then everything would settle perfectly into place.

"Stupid!" she told herself, rattling the chicken parts in the bag. "Stupid old nosy-bones!" She slammed a skillet onto the stove and poured in too much oil. She twisted a knob savagely and then stood back and waited for the burner to heat. Now look: Droplets of oil were dotted across the front of her best dress, over the mound of her stomach. She was clumsy and fat-stomached and she didn't even have the sense to wear an apron while she was cooking. Also she had paid way too much for this dress, sixty-four dollars at Hecht's, which would scandalize Ira if he knew. How could she have been so greedy? She dabbed at her nose with the back of her hand. Took a deep breath. Well. Anyhow.

The oil wasn't hot enough yet, but she started adding the chicken. Unfortunately, there was quite a lot of it. Too much, it appeared now. (Unless they could coax Jesse back before suppertime.) She had to push the pieces too close together in order to fit in the last few drumsticks.

Peas, or green beans? That still hadn't been settled. She wiped her hands on a dishtowel and went out to the living room to check. "Leroy," she said, "what would—?"

But the living room was empty. Leroy's record had a worn sound now, as if it were playing for the second or third time. "Truckin', got my chips cashed in . . ." an assortment of men sang doggedly. No one sat on the sofa or in either of the armchairs.

Maggie crossed the hallway to the front porch and called, "Leroy? Fiona?"

No answer. Four vacant rockers faced out toward the streetlight. "Ira?"

"Upstairs," he called, his voice muffled-sounding.

She turned away from the door. Fiona's suitcase, thank goodness, still stood at the foot of the stairs; so she couldn't have gone far. "Ira, is Leroy with you?" Maggie called.

He appeared on the landing with a towel draped around his neck. Still drying his face, he looked down at her.

"I can't find her," she told him. "I can't find either one of them."

"Did you look on the porch?"

"Yes."

He came downstairs, carrying the towel. "Well, maybe they went out back," he said.

She followed him through the front door and around the side of the house. The night air was warm and humid. A gnat or mosquito whined in her ear and she waved it away. Who would want to be out here at this hour? Not Leroy or Fiona, evidently. The backyard, when they reached it, was a small, empty square of darkness.

"They've gone," Ira told her.

"Gone? You mean for good?"

"They must have."

"But their suitcase is still in the hall."

"Well, it was pretty heavy," he said, and he took her arm and steered her up the back porch steps. "If they were traveling on foot, they most likely didn't want to carry it."

"On foot," she said.

In the kitchen, the chicken was crackling away. Maggie paid no attention, but Ira turned the burner down.

"If they're on foot, we can catch them," Maggie said.

"Wait, Maggie—"

Too late; she was off. She sped through the hall again, out the door, down the steps to the street. Fiona's sister lived somewhere west of here, near Broadway. They would have turned left, therefore. Shading her eyes beneath the glare of the streetlight, Maggie peered up the stretch of deserted sidewalk. She saw a white cat walking alone in that high-bottomed, hesitant manner that cats take on in unfamiliar surroundings. A moment later a girl with long dark hair flew out of an alley and scooped it up, crying "Turkey! *There* you are!" She vanished with a flounce of her skirt. A car passed, leaving behind a scrap of a ball game: ". . . no outs and the bases loaded and it's hot times on Thirty-third Street tonight, folks . . ." The sky glowed a grayish pink over the industrial park.

Ira came up and set a hand on her shoulder. "Maggie, honey," he said.

But she shook him off and started back toward the house.

When she was upset she lost all sense of direction, and she concentrated now on her path like a blind man, reaching out falteringly to touch the little boxwood hedge by the walk, stumbling twice as she climbed the steps to the porch. "Sweetheart," Ira said behind her. She crossed the hallway to the foot of the stairs. She laid Fiona's suitcase flat and knelt to unfasten the latches.

Inside she found a pink cotton nightgown and a pair of child's pajamas and some lacy bikini underpants—none of these folded but scrunched instead like wrung-out dishcloths. And beneath those, a zippered cosmetics case, two stacks of tattered comic books, half a dozen beauty magazines, a box of dominoes, and a giant, faded volume of horse stories. All objects Fiona and Leroy could easily do without. What they couldn't do without—Fiona's purse and Leroy's baseball glove—had gone with them.

Sifting through these layers of belongings while Ira stood mute behind her, Maggie had a sudden view of her life as circular. It forever repeated itself, and it was entirely lacking in hope.

4

There was an old man in Maggie's nursing home who believed that once he reached heaven, all he had lost in his lifetime would be given back to him. "Oh, yes, what a good idea!" Maggie had said when he told her about it. She had assumed he meant intangibles—youthful energy, for instance, or that ability young people have to get swept away and impassioned. But then as he went on talking she saw that he had something more concrete in mind. At the Pearly Gates, he said, Saint Peter would hand everything to him in a gunnysack: The little red sweater his mother had knit him just before she died, that he had left on a bus in fourth grade and missed with all his heart ever since. The special pocketknife his older brother had flung into a cornfield out of spite. The diamond ring his first sweetheart had failed to return to him when she broke off their engagement and ran away with the minister's son.

Then Maggie thought of what she might find in her own gunnysack—the misplaced compacts, single earrings, and umbrellas, some of which she hadn't noticed losing at the time but recollected weeks or months afterward. ("Didn't I used to have a . . .?" "Whatever became of my . . .?") Objects freely given up, even, which later she wished back again—for example, those 1950s skirts she had donated to Goodwill, now that lower hemlines were once more in fashion. And she had said, "Oh, yes," again, but a shade less certainly, for it didn't seem that she had suffered losses quite as bitter as the old man's.

Now, though (sorting leftover fried chicken into plastic containers for Ira's lunches), she reconsidered that gunnysack, and this time it bulged much fuller. She remembered a green dress that her brother Josh's wife, Natalie, had admired one day. Maggie had said, "Take it, it matches your eyes," for it truly did, and she had been glad for Natalie to have it; she had loved her like a sister. But then Josh and Natalie had divorced and Natalie moved away and didn't keep in touch anymore, as if she'd divorced Maggie as well, and now Maggie wanted that dress returned. It used to move so fluidly when she walked! It was one of those dresses that go anywhere, that feel right for every occasion.

And she would like that funny little kitten, Thistledown, who'd been Ira's very first present to her in their courting days. She was a jokey, mischievous creature, forever battling imaginary enemies with her needle teeth and soft gray paws, and Maggie and Ira used to spend hours playing with her. But then Maggie had unintentionally murdered the poor thing by running her mother's dryer without checking inside first, and when she'd gone to pull the clothes out there was Thistle, as limp and frowsy and boneless as her namesake, and Maggie had cried and cried. After that there had been a whole string of other cats—Lucy and Chester and Pumpkin—but now all at once Maggie wanted Thistle back again. Surely Saint Peter allowed animals in that gunnysack, didn't he? Would he allow all the lean, unassuming dogs of Mulraney Street, those part-this-part-thats whose distant voices had barked her to sleep every night of her childhood? Would he allow the children's little gerbil, tirelessly plodding the years away on his wire treadmill till Maggie set him free out of pity and Pumpkin caught him and ate him?

And that corny key chain she used to have, a metal disk that rotated on an axle, with LOVES ME on one side and LOVES ME NOT on the other. Boris Drumm had given her that, and when Jesse got his license she had sentimentally passed it on to him. She had dropped it into his palm after chauffeuring him home from his driver's test, but unfortunately the car was still in gear and it had started rolling as she climbed out. "Oh, great going, Ma," Jesse had said, reaching for the brake; and something about his lofty amusement had made her see him for the first time as a man. But now he carried his keys in a little leather case—snakeskin, she believed. She would like that key chain back again. She could actually feel it between her fingers—the lightweight, cheap metal and the raised lettering, the absentminded spin she used to give it as she stood talking with Boris: Loves me, loves me not. And once again she saw Boris rising up before her car as she practiced braking. Why, all he'd been trying to say was: Here I am! Pay me some notice!

Also, her clear brown bead necklace that looked something like dark amber. Antique plastic, the girl at the thrift shop had called it. A contradiction in terms, you would think; but Maggie had loved that necklace. So had Daisy, who in her childhood often borrowed it, along with a pair of Maggie's high-heeled shoes, and finally lost it in the alley out back of the house. She had worn it jumping rope on a summer evening and come home in tears because it had vanished. Definitely that would be in the gunnysack. And the summer evening as well, why not—the children smelling of sweat and fireflies, the warm porch floorboards sticking slightly to your chair rockers, the voices ringing from the alley: "Call *that* a strike?" and "Miss Mary Mack, Mack, Mack, dressed all in black, black, black . . ."

She stowed the containers of chicken at the front of the refrigerator, where Ira couldn't overlook them, and she pictured Saint Peter's astonishment as he watched what spilled forth: a bottle of wind, a box of fresh snow, and one of those looming moonlit clouds that used to float overhead like dirigibles as Ira walked her home from choir practice.

The dishes in the draining rack were dry by now and she stacked them and put them in the cupboard. Then she fixed herself a big bowl of ice cream. She wished they had bought mint chocolate chip. Fudge ripple was too white-tasting. She climbed the stairs, digging her spoon in. At the door to Daisy's room, she paused. Daisy was kneeling on the floor, fitting books into a carton. "Want some ice cream?" Maggie asked her.

Daisy glanced up and said, "No, thanks."

"All you had for supper was a drumstick."

"I'm not hungry," Daisy said, and she pushed a lock of hair off her forehead. She was wearing clothes that she wouldn't be taking with her—baggy jeans and a blouse with a torn buttonhole. Her room already seemed uninhabited; the knickknacks that usually sat on her shelves had been packed for weeks.

"Where are your stuffed animals?" Maggie said.

"In my suitcase."

"I thought you were leaving them home."

"I was, but I changed my mind," Daisy said.

She had been quiet all through supper. Maggie could tell she was anxious about tomorrow. It was like her not to talk about it, though. You had to read the signs—her lack of appetite and her decision to bring her stuffed animals after all. Maggie said, "Well, honey, you let me know if you want any help."

"Thanks, Mom."

Maggie went on down the hall to the bedroom she shared with Ira. Ira was sitting tailor-fashion on the bed, laying out a game of solitaire. He had taken off his shoes and rolled his shirt sleeves up. "Care for some ice cream?" Maggie asked him.

"No, thanks."

"I shouldn't have any, either," she said. "But travel is such a strain, somehow. I feel I've burned a million calories just sitting in that car."

In the mirror above the bureau, though, she was positively obese. She set her ice cream on the dresser scarf and leaned forward to study her face, sucking in her cheeks to give herself a hollow look. It didn't work. She sighed and moved away. She went into the bathroom for her nightgown. "Ira," she called, her voice echoing off the tiles, "do you suppose Serena is still mad at us?"

She had to peer around the door to catch his answer: a shrug.

"I was thinking I might phone to see how she's doing," she told him, "but I'd hate for her to hang up on me."

She unbuttoned her dress and pulled it over her head and tossed it onto the toilet lid. Then she stepped out of her shoes. "Remember when I helped her put her mother in the nursing home?" she asked. "That time, she didn't speak for months and whenever I tried to call she'd bang the receiver down. I hated when she did that. That thunk on the other end of the line. It made me feel so small. It made me feel we were back in third grade."

"That's because she was *behaving* like a third-grader," Ira said.

Maggie came out in her slip to take another spoonful of ice cream. "And I don't even know why she got so upset," she told Ira's reflection in the mirror. "It was a perfectly honest mistake! I had the best intentions in the world! I said to her mother, 'Listen,' I said, 'you want to make a hit with the other residents? Want to show the staff right off that you're not just another bland old lady?' I mean this was Anita! Who used to wear the red toreador pants! I couldn't have them underestimating her, could I? That's why I told Serena we shouldn't take her in till Sunday evening, Halloween, and that's why I sewed that clown suit on my own machine and went all the way out Eastern Avenue to a what-do-you-call-it. What's it called?"

"Theatrical supply house," Ira said, dealing out another row of cards.

"Theatrical supply house, for white greasepaint. How was I to know they'd thrown the costume party on Saturday that year?"

She brought her ice cream over to the bed and settled down, propping her pillow against the headboard. Ira was frowning at his layout. "You would think I had deliberately plotted to make her a laughingstock," Maggie told him, "the way Serena carried on."

Whom she was picturing in her mind, though, was not Serena just then but Anita: her painted face, her red yarn hair, the triangles Maggie had lipsticked beneath her eyes which made them seem unnaturally bright or even teary, just like a real circus clown's. And then her chin quivering and denting inward as she sat in her wheelchair, watching Maggie leave.

"I was a coward," Maggie said suddenly, setting down her bowl. "I should have stayed and helped Serena get her changed. But I felt so foolish; I felt I'd made such a mess of things. I just said, 'Bye now!' and walked out, and the last I saw of her she was sitting there in a fright wig like somebody . . . inappropriate and senile and pathetic, with everyone around her dressed in normal clothing."

"Oh, honey, she adjusted to the place just fine, in the end," Ira said. "Why make such a big deal of it?"

"Because you didn't see how she looked, Ira. And also she was wearing one of those Poseys, you know? One of those Posey restraining devices because she couldn't sit upright on her own anymore. A clown suit and a Posey! I was dumb, I tell you."

She was hoping Ira would continue contradicting her, but all he did was lay a jack of clubs on a queen.

"I don't know why I kid myself that I'm going to heaven," Maggie told him.

Silence.

"So shall I call her, or not?"

"Call who?"

"Serena, Ira. Who have we been talking about here?"

"Sure, if you like," he said.

"But suppose she hangs up on me?"

"Then think of all you'll save on the phone bill."

She made a face at him.

She took the telephone from the nightstand and set it in her lap. Pondered it for a moment. Lifted the receiver. Tactfully, Ira bent lower over his cards and started whistling. (He was so polite about privacy, although as Maggie knew from experience you could overhear quite a lot while pretending to be absorbed in your song.) She punched in Serena's number very slowly and deliberately, as if that would help their conversation.

Serena's telephone gave two short rings instead of one long. Maggie thought of that as rural and slightly backward. *Breep-breep*, it said. *Breep-breep.*

Serena said, "Hello?"

"Serena?"

"Yes?"

"It's me."

"Oh, hi."

Maybe she hadn't realized yet who "me" was. Maggie cleared her throat. She said, "It's Maggie."

"Hi, Maggie."

Maggie relaxed against her pillow and stretched her legs out. She said, "I called to see how you were doing."

"Just fine!" Serena said. "Or, well, I don't know. Not so hot, to tell the truth. I keep walking up and down, walking from one room to another. Can't seem to stay in one place."

"Isn't Linda there?"

"I sent her away."

"What for?"

"She got on my nerves."

"On your nerves! How?"

"Oh, this way and that. I forget. They took me out to dinner and . . . I admit it was partly my fault. I was acting sort of contrary. I didn't like the restaurant and I couldn't stand the people who were eating there. I kept thinking how good it would feel to be alone, to have the house to myself. But now here I am and it's so quiet. It's like I'm wrapped in cotton or something. I was thrilled to hear the phone ring."

"I wish you lived closer," Maggie said.

Serena said, "I don't have anyone to tell about the trivia, what the plumbing's up to and how the red ants have come back in the kitchen."

"You can tell *me*," Maggie said.

"Well, but they're not your red ants too, don't you see? I mean you and I are not in this together."

"Oh," Maggie said.

There was a pause.

What was it Ira was whistling? Something from that record Leroy had played this evening; the lyrics were on the tip of Maggie's tongue. He scooped up a run of diamonds and shifted them to a king.

"You know," Serena said, "whenever Max went on a business trip we'd have so much to tell each other when he came home. He would talk and talk, and *I* would talk and talk, and then, you know what we'd do?"

"What?"

"We'd have a great big horrible fight."

Maggie laughed.

"And then we'd patch it up, and then we'd go to bed together," Serena said. "Crazy, wasn't it? And now I keep thinking: If Max were resurrected this minute, hale and hearty, would we still have our horrible fight just the same?"

"Well, I guess you would," Maggie said.

She wondered how it would feel to know she had seen Ira for the very last time on this earth. She supposed she would have trouble believing it. For several months, maybe, she would half expect him to come sauntering in again just as he had sauntered into choir practice that first spring evening thirty years ago.

"Um, also, Serena," she said, "I want to apologize for what happened after the funeral."

"Oh, forget it."

"No, really, both of us feel just terrible."

She hoped Serena couldn't hear Ira in the background; it made her apology seem insincere. *Lately it occurs to me*, he was whistling cheerily, *what a long, strange trip it's been* . . .

"Forget it; I flew off the handle," Serena told her. "Widow's nerves, or something. Pure silliness. I'm past the stage now where I can discard old friends without a thought; I can't afford it."

"Oh, don't say that!"

"What, you *want* me to discard you?"

"No, no . . ."

"Just joking," Serena told her. "Maggie, thanks for calling. I mean it. It was good to hear your voice."

"Anytime," Maggie said.

"Bye."

"Bye."

Serena hung up. A moment later, so did Maggie.

This ice cream wasn't even edible anymore. She had let it turn to soup. Also she was feeling overstuffed. She looked down at herself— at the bodice of her slip stretched tight across her breasts. "I'm an elephant," she told Ira.

He said, "Not again."

"Seriously."

He tapped his upper lip with a forefinger and studied his cards.

Well. She rose and went into the bathroom, stripping as she walked, and took her nightgown from its hook. When she dropped it over her head it shook itself out around her, loose and cool and weightless. "Whew!" she said. She washed her face and brushed her teeth. A trail of underclothes led from bedroom to bathroom; she picked them up and stuffed them into the hamper.

Sometimes, after an especially trying day, she felt an urge to burn everything she had worn.

Then while she was arranging her dress on a hanger, she was struck by a thought. She looked over at Ira. She looked away. She hung the dress in her closet, next to her one silk blouse.

"Goodness," she said, turning toward him again. "Wasn't Cartwheel dinky."

"Mm."

"I'd forgotten how dinky," she said.

"Mmhmm."

"I bet their school is dinky too."

No response.

"Do you suppose the Cartwheel school offers a good education?"

"I really couldn't say," Ira said.

She closed the closet door firmly. "Well, *I* can say," she told him. "It must be a full year behind the schools in Baltimore. Maybe two."

"And naturally Baltimore's schools are superb," Ira said.

"Well, at least they're better than Cartwheel's."

He raised an eyebrow at her.

"I mean most likely," Maggie said.

He picked up a card, moved it onto another, then changed his mind and moved it back again.

"Here's what we could do," Maggie said. "Write and ask Fiona if she's given any thought to Leroy's education. Offer to enroll her down here in Baltimore and let Leroy live with us nine months of the year."

"No," Ira said.

"Or even twelve months, if it works out that way. You know how attached children get to their classmates and such. She might not want to leave."

"Maggie, look at me."

She faced him, hands on her hips.

"No," he said.

There were a lot of arguments she could have mentioned. All kinds of arguments!

But she didn't, somehow. She dropped her hands and wandered over to the window.

It was a warm, deep, quiet night, with just enough breeze to set the shade-pull swinging. She raised the shade higher and leaned out, pressing her forehead against the gritty screen. The air smelled of rubber tires and grass. Snatches of adventure music drifted up from the Lockes' TV next door. Across the street, the Simmonses were climbing their front steps, the husband jingling his house keys. *They* would not be going to bed yet; no chance of that. They were one of those happily childless young couples with eyes for only each other, and no doubt they were returning from dinner in a restaurant and now would . . . do what? Put on some romantic music, maybe, something with violins, and sit conversing graciously on their spotless white love seat, each raising a wineglass made of that thin, extra-breakable crystal that doesn't even have a lip around the rim. Or maybe they would dance. She had seen them dancing on their front porch once—the wife in spike heels, with her hair swept up in an igloo shape, the husband holding her slightly apart in a formal, admiring way.

Maggie spun around and returned to the bed. "Oh, Ira," she said, dropping down beside him, "what are we two going to live for, all the rest of our lives?"

She had dislodged a stack of his cards, but he kindly refrained from straightening them and instead reached out one arm and drew her in. "There, now, sweetheart," he said, and he settled her next to him. Still holding her close, he transferred a four of spades to a five, and Maggie rested her head against his chest and watched. He had arrived at the interesting part of the game by now, she saw. He had passed that early, superficial stage when any number of moves seemed possible, and now his choices were narrower and he had to show real skill and judgment. She felt a little stir of something that came over her like a flush, a sort of inner buoyancy, and she lifted her face to kiss the warm blade of his cheekbone. Then she slipped free and moved to her side of the bed, because tomorrow they had a long car trip to make and she knew she would need a good night's sleep before they started.

SEARCHING
FOR CALEB

1
=

The fortune teller and her grandfather went to New York City on an Amtrak train, racketing along with their identical, peaky white faces set due north. The grandfather had left his hearing aid at home on the bureau. He wore a black suit, pearl-gray suspenders, and a very old-fashioned, expensive-looking pinstriped collarless shirt. No matter what happened he kept his deep-socketed eyes fixed upon the seat in front of him, he continued sliding a thumb over the news clipping he held in his hand. Either the train had turned his deafness absolute or else he had something very serious on his mind, it was hard to tell which. In any case, he would not answer the few things the fortune teller said to him.

Past his downy white head, outside the scummy window, factories and warehouses streamed along. Occasionally a leftover forest would coast into view and then out again—twisted bare trees, trunks ripped by lightning, logs covered with vines, tangled raspy bushes and beer cans, whisky bottles, rusted carburetors, sewing machines, and arm-chairs. Then some town or other would take over. Men wearing several layers of jackets struggled with crates and barrels on loading docks, their breaths trailing out of their mouths in white tatters. It was January, and cold enough to make the brick buildings appear to darken and condense.

The fortune teller, who was not a gypsy or even Spanish but a lanky, weedy blond woman in a Breton hat and a faded shift, took a *National Geographic* from a straw bag on the floor and started reading it from back to front. She flicked the pages after barely a glance, rapidly swinging one crossed foot. Halfway through the magazine she bent to rummage through the bag again. She felt her grandfather slide his eyes over to see what she was keeping there. Tarot cards? A crystal ball? Some other tool of her mysterious, disreputable profession? But all she showed was a spill of multicolored kerchief and then a box of Luden's cough drops, which she took out and offered him. He refused. She put one in her mouth, giving him a sudden smile that completely upturned every one of her pale, straight features. Her grandfather absorbed it but forgot to smile back. He returned to his view of the seat ahead, a button-on antimacassar with an old lady's netted hat just beyond.

In his hand, stroked by his puckered thumb, the newspaper clipping first rustled and then wilted and drooped, but the fortune teller knew it by heart anyway.

TABOR

    Suddenly on December 18, 1972, Paul Jeffrey, Sr., of
New York City, formerly of Baltimore. Beloved husband of
Deborah Palmer Tabor. Father of Paul J. Tabor, Jr., of
Chicago and Theresa T. Hanes of Springline,
Massachusetts. Also survived by five grandchildren and
seven great-grandchildren.
    Services will be held Thursday at the . . .

"My throat is dry, Justine," her grandfather said.

"I'll get you a soda."

"What?"

"A *soda.*"

He drew back, offended. No telling what he thought she had said. Justine patted his hand and told him, "Never mind, Grandfather. I'll just be gone a minute."

She left, sidling between shopping bags and weekend cases along the narrow aisle, holding tight to her saucer-like hat. Three cars up, she paid for two root beers and a sack of Cheez Doodles. She returned walking carefully, opening doors with her elbows and frowning at the plastic cups, which were filled to the brim. Just inside her own car, the Cheez Doodles fell and a man in a business suit had to pick them up for her. "Oh! Thank you!" she said, and smiled at him, her cheeks grown suddenly pink. At first glance she could be taken for a young girl, but then people saw the fine lines beginning to show in her skin, and the faded blue of her eyes and the veined, parched, forty-year-old hands with the scratched wedding band looking three sizes too large below one knobby knuckle. She had a ramshackle way of walking and a sharp, merry voice. "*Root* beer, Grandfather!" she sang out. If he didn't hear her, all the rest of the car did.

She put a cup in his hand, and he took a sip. "Ah yes," he said. He liked herby things, root beer and horehound drops and sassafras tea. But when she tore open the cellophane bag and presented him with a Cheez Doodle—a fat orange worm that left crystals on his fingertips—he frowned at it from beneath a tangle of white eyebrows. He had once been a judge. He still gave the impression of judging everything that came his way. "What *is* this," he said, but that was a verdict, not a question.

"It's a Cheez Doodle, Grandfather, try it and see."

"What's that you say?"

She held out the bag, showing him the lettering on the side. First he replaced the Cheez Doodle and then he wiped his fingers on a handkerchief he took from his pocket. Then he went back to drinking root beer and studying the clipping, which he had laid flat on one narrow, triangular knee. "Theresa," he said. "I never cared for that name."

Justine nodded, chewing.

"I don't like *difficult* names. I don't like foreignness."

"Perhaps they're Catholic," Justine said.

"How's that?"

"Perhaps they're Catholic."

"I didn't quite hear."

"*Catholic!*"

Faces spun around.

"Don't be ridiculous," her grandfather said. "Paul Tabor went to the same church I did, he was in my brother's Sunday school class. The two of them graduated from the Salter Academy together. Then this—dissatisfaction set in. This, this *newness.* I can't tell you how many times I've seen it come to pass. A young man goes to a distant city instead of staying close to home, he gets a job, switches friends, widens his circle of acquaintances. Marries a girl from a family no one knows, lives in a house of unusual architecture, names his children foreign names that never were in his family in any preceding generation. He takes to traveling, buys winter homes and summer homes and vacation cottages in godforsaken states like Florida where none of us has ever been. Meanwhile his parents die and all his people just seem to vanish, there's no one you can ask any more, 'Now, what is Paul up to these days?' Then he dies himself, most likely in a very large city where there's nobody to notice, only his wife and his barber and his tailor and maybe not even the last two, and what's it for? What's it all about? Now in Paul's case I just couldn't say for certain, of course. He was my brother's friend, not mine. However I will hazard a guess: he had no *stamina.* He couldn't endure, he wouldn't stay around to fight it out or live it down or sit it through, whatever was required. He hadn't the patience. He wanted something new, something different, he couldn't quite name it. He thought things would be better somewhere else. Anywhere else. And what did it get him? Watch, next time I'm in Baltimore I'll tell the family, 'Paul Tabor died.' 'Paul *who?*' they'll say. 'Paul Tabor, it was in the Baltimore *Sun.* Don't you read it any more? Don't you know?' Well, of course they do read it and would catch any familiar name in a flash but not Paul Tabor's. Forgotten, all forgotten. He discarded us, now he's dead and forgotten. Hear what I say, Justine. Do you hear?"

Justine smiled at him. "I hear," she said.

She had moved away from Baltimore herself. She and her husband and daughter now lived in Semple, Virginia; in another place last year and another the year before that. (Her husband was a restless man.) Next week they were moving to Caro Mill, Maryland. Was it Caro Mill? Caro Mills? Sometimes all these places would run together in her mind. She would mentally locate friends in towns those friends had never set foot in, she would await a visit from a client whom she had left two years ago without a forwarding address. She would ransack the telephone book for a doctor or a dentist or a plumber who was actually three hundred miles away and three or four or fourteen years in the past. Her grandfather didn't guess that, probably. Or care. He had scarcely bothered to learn the towns' names in the first place. Although he lived with Justine and made all those moves with her he called it visiting; he considered himself a citizen still of Baltimore, his birthplace. All other towns were ephemeral, no-account; he shuffled through them absent-mindedly like a man passing a string of shanties on the way to his own sturdy house. When he arrived in Baltimore (for Thanksgiving or Christmas or the Fourth of July) he would heave a sigh and lower the sharp narrow shoulders that he held, at all other times, so tightly hunched. The brackets around his mouth would relax somewhat. He would set his old leather suitcase down with finality, as if it held all his earthly goods and not just a shirt and a change of underwear and a scruffy toothbrush. "There's no place in the world like Baltimore, Maryland," he would say.

He said it now.

This morning they had passed through the Baltimore railroad station, even stopping a moment to let other, luckier passengers alight. The thought of having come so near must have made him melancholy. He looked down at his clipping now and shook his head, maybe even regretting this trip, which had been entirely his own idea. But when Justine said, "Are you tired, Grandfather?"—thinning her voice to that special, carrying tone he would be certain to hear—he only looked at her blankly. It seemed that his mind was on Paul Tabor again.

"They don't say a word about where they buried him," he said.

"Oh well, I imagine—"

"If you died in New York City, where would you be buried?"

"I'm sure they have—"

"No doubt they ship you someplace else," he said. He turned his face to the window. Without his hearing aid he gave an impression of rudeness. He interrupted people and changed the subject willfully and spoke in a particularly loud, flat voice, although normally he was so well-mannered that he caused others to feel awkward. "I never made the acquaintance of Paul's wife," he said, while Justine was still considering cemeteries. "I don't recollect even hearing when he got married. But then he was younger than I of course and moved in different circles. Or perhaps he married late in life. Now if I had known the wife I would have gone up for the funeral, then asked my questions afterwards. But as it is, I hesitated to barge in upon a family affair and immediately put my case. It would look so—it would seem so self-serving. Do you think I did right to wait?"

He had asked her this before. He didn't listen for the answer.

"By now she will be calmer," he said. "Not so likely to break down at any mention of his name."

He folded the clipping suddenly, as if he had decided something. He creased it with one broad yellow thumbnail.

"Justine," he said.

"Hmm?"

"Am I going to be successful?"

She stopped swirling the ice in her cup and looked at him. "Oh," she said. "Why—I'm certain you are. Certainly, Grandfather. Maybe not *this* time, maybe not right away, but—"

"Truly. Tell me."

"Certainly you will."

He was looking too closely into her face. Possibly he hadn't heard her. She set her voice to the proper tone and said, "I'm sure that—"

"Justine, how much do you know?"

"What?"

"This telling fortunes. This bunk. This—*piffle*," said her grandfather, and he brushed something violently off his sleeve. "I hate the very thought of it."

"You've told me all that, Grandfather."

"It's not respectable. Your aunts go into a state whenever we speak of it. You know what people call you? 'The fortune teller.' Like 'the cleaner,' 'the greengrocer.' 'How's that granddaughter of yours, Judge

Peck, the fortune teller. How's she doing?' Ah, it turns my stomach."

Justine picked up her magazine and opened to a page, any page.

"But, Justine," her grandfather said, "I ask you this. Is there anything to it at all?"

Her eyes snagged on a line of print.

"Do you really have some inkling of the future?"

She shut the magazine. He locked her in a fierce, steady frown; his intensity made everything around him seem pale.

"I want to know if I will find my brother," he said.

Yet immediately afterward he turned away, watching the train's descent into the blackness beneath Manhattan. And Justine repacked her straw bag and brushed cheese crumbs off her lap and put her coat on, her expression calm and cheerful. Neither one of them appeared to be waiting for anything more to be said.

Because they were trying to save money, they took the subway from Penn Station. Justine loved subways. She enjoyed standing on them, gripping a warm, oily metal pole, feet planted slightly apart and knees dipping with the roll of the train as they careened through the darkness. But her grandfather distrusted them, and once they were off the shuttle and onto the IRT, he made her sit down. He continually rotated his face, scanning the car for enemies. Silent young people returned his stare. "I don't know, Justine, I don't know what's happening. I don't like this city at all any more," her grandfather said. But Justine was enjoying herself too much to answer. She watched each station as they drew into it, the murky light and bathroom-tile walls and those mysterious, grimy men who sat on benches, one or two at every stop, watching trains come and go without ever boarding one. Then when they were moving again she drank in the sensation of speed. *Getting* somewhere. She loved going fast in any kind of vehicle. She particularly liked the rickety sound of these tracks, on which something unexpected might happen at any moment. She hoped the wheels would howl in that eerie way they had while heading through the deepest stretch of darkeess. Once the lights went out and when they came on again her face was surprised and joyous, open-mouthed; everybody noticed. Her grandfather touched her wrist.

"Are you watching for the proper station?" he asked.

"Oh yes."

Although she hadn't been.

Clutched in her hand was Mrs. Tabor's address, which she had copied from a telephone book. She had suggested calling ahead from Penn Station, but her grandfather refused. He was too impatient, or he wanted to hold onto his hopes just a little bit longer, or he was afraid of being turned away. Also he might have been anxious to reach Mrs. Tabor's bathroom. He preferred not to use any public facilities.

When they were above ground again—Justine taking gulps of the ashy, foreign air, the old man limp with relief—they walked a block and a half west and entered a gray building with a revolving door. "Look," her grandfather said. "Wood for the door and polished handles. Marble floor. I like old buildings. I like places like this." And he nodded to a lady just stepping out of the elevator—the first person in all New York whose existence he had recognized. He was disappointed, however, that the elevator was self-service. "*Once* upon a time they would have had a boy to do this," he said, watching Justine jab a button. The elevator toiled upward, creaking and sighing. Its walls were fine oak but on one panel there was a concentration of four-letter words that the old man covered immediately, stepping square in front of them without appearing to notice and then staring upward. Justine smiled at him. He pursed his lips and studied an inspection certificate.

On the eighth floor, at the end of a long dark hall, they pressed another button. Bolts slithered and locks rattled, as if connected somehow to the button. The door opened three inches and a rouged, seamed face peered out from behind a police chain. "Yes?" she asked.

"Mrs. Tabor?" said Justine.

Puffy eyes took her in from top to toe, her streaky ribbons of hair and her brown coat with the uneven hemline. "What is this," Mrs. Tabor said, "are you selling something? I don't need a thing and I already have religion."

So the grandfather had to step up and take over. There was no mistaking the elegance of his bow, or the way he raised one hand to his head even though he wore no hat. He presented her with his card. Not his business card, oh no, but his calling card, cream-colored, aged yellow around the edges. He slipped it beneath the police chain into her jeweled hand. "Daniel Peck," he said, as if she could not read, and she looked up into his face while one finger tested the engraving. "Peck," she said.

"I knew your husband. Paul? Back in Baltimore."

"Why didn't you *say* so?" she asked, and she unhooked the chain and stood back to let them in. They entered a room that Justine might have grown up in, all wine-colored and velvety, giving off a scent of dust although every piece of furniture gleamed. Mrs. Tabor's white hair was precisely finger-waved, webby with beauty parlor hairspray. She wore black wool and ropes and ropes of pearls. Her focus was on the old man and she barely looked at Justine even when he remembered to introduce her. "Of course you do know about his passing, Mr. Peck," she said.

"I beg your pardon?"

"You'll have to speak up," said Justine. "He left his hearing aid at home."

"You know he *passed*, Mr. Peck."

"Oh. Passed. Oh yes. Yes, naturally, I read it in the paper. You see we hadn't heard of Paul for many many years, we—" He followed, absently, to the couch where she led him. He sat down beside Justine, pinching the creases in his trousers. "We had no idea where he might be until that death notice, Mrs. Tabor. Why, I've made several trips to New York in my life and never even knew he was here! Never guessed! We could have talked over old times together."

"Oh, it's sad how people lose track," said Mrs. Tabor.

"Well, I wanted to offer my condolences. Our family thought highly of Paul and my brother Caleb in particular was very close to him."

"Why, thank you, Mr. Peck. It was painless, I'm happy to say, sudden and painless, just the way he would have wished it. All the more shock to *me*, therefore, but—"

"What was that?"

"*Thank* you."

"My brother's name was Caleb Peck."

"What a fine old-fashioned name," said Mrs. Tabor.

The old man looked at her for a minute, perhaps wondering whether it was worthwhile asking her to repeat herself. Then he sighed and shook his head. "I don't suppose you knew him, did you?" he said.

"Why, not that I remember, no. I don't believe so. Because of Paul's work we moved about so, you see. It was difficult to—"

"What? What?"

"*No*, Grandfather," Justine said, and laid one hand on top of his. He looked at her dimly for a moment, as if he didn't recognize her.

"I assumed he might have kept in touch with Paul," he told Mrs. Tabor. "Written, or sent Christmas cards. Or visited, even. You know they were very close. Perhaps he stopped to see you on his way to someplace else."

"We never had many visitors, Mr. Peck."

"Pardon?"

He looked at Justine. Justine shook her head.

"Or possibly Paul just mentioned his *name* on some occasion," he said.

"Possibly, yes, but—"

"Yes?"

He snatched his hand from Justine's and sat forward. "When would that have been?" he asked.

"But—no, Mr. Peck, I can't say I remember it. I'm sorry."

"Look here," he said. He searched a pocket and came up with something—a small brown photograph framed in gold. He leaned over to jab it in her face. "Don't you know him? Doesn't he look familiar in any way? Take your time. Don't be in a hurry to say no."

Mrs. Tabor seemed a little startled by the picture, but it took her only a second to make up her mind. "I'm sorry," she said. Then she looked at Justine. "I don't understand. Is this important in some way?"

"Well—" said Justine.

"We've lost track of Caleb too, you see," her grandfather said. He shoved the photograph back in his pocket. He turned down the corners of his mouth in a bitter smile. "You must think we're very careless people."

Mrs. Tabor did not smile back.

"However it was no more our fault in this case than in Paul's; he left us."

"Oh, what a pity," Mrs. Tabor said.

"Our family is very close knit, a *fine* family, we have always stuck together, but I don't know, periodically some . . . *explorer* sets out on his own." He scowled suddenly at Justine. "The last time I saw Caleb was in nineteen twelve. I have never heard of him since."

"Nineteen twelve!" Mrs. Tabor said. She sank back in her chair. Wheels seemed to be clicking in her head. When she spoke next her voice had become softer and sadder. "Mr. Peck, I'm so very sorry that I can't help you. I *wish* I could. Might I offer you some tea?"

"How's that?" he said.

"*Tea,* Grandfather."

"Tea. Oh. Well . . ."

This time when he looked at Justine he was handing the rest of the visit to her, and she straightened and clutched her carry-all. "Thank you, but I don't think so," she said. Phrases her mother had taught her thirty years ago came wisping back to her. "It's kind of you to . . . but we really must be . . . however, I wonder if my grandfather might freshen up first? He just got off the train and he . . ."

"Surely," said Mrs. Tabor. "Mr. Peck, may I show you the way?"

She beckoned to him and he rose without question, either guessing at where she was leading him or no longer caring. He followed her through a polished door that swept open with a hushing sound across the carpet. He went down a short hall with his hands by his sides, like a child being sent to his room. When she pointed him toward another door he stepped through it and vanished, not looking around. Mrs. Tabor returned to the living room with careful, outward-turned steps.

"That poor, poor man," she said.

Justine would not answer.

"And will you be in New York long?"

"Just till we find a train home again."

Mrs. Tabor stopped patting her pearls. "You mean you only came for this?"

"Oh, we're used to it, we do it often," Justine said.

"Often! You go looking for his *brother* often?"

"Whenever we have some kind of lead," said Justine. "Some name or letter or something. We've been at this several years now. Grandfather takes it very seriously."

"He'll never find him, of course," said Mrs. Tabor.

Justine was silent.

"Will he?"

"Maybe he will."

"But—nineteen *twelve!* I mean—"

"Our family tends to live a long time," Justine said.

"But even so! And of course, dear," she said, leaning forward suddenly, "it must be hard on *you.*"

"Oh no."

"All that wandering around? I'd lose my mind. And he can't be so easy to travel with, his handicap and all. It must be a terrible burden for you."

"I love him very much," said Justine.

"Oh, well yes. Naturally!"

But the mention of love had turned Mrs. Tabor breathless, and she seemed delighted to hear the bathroom door clicking open. "Well, now!" she said, turning to Justine's grandfather.

He came into the room searching all his pockets, a sign he was preparing to leave a place. Justine rose and hoisted her straw bag. "Thank you, Mrs. Tabor," she said. "I'm sorry about your husband. I hope we haven't put you to any trouble."

"No, no."

The grandfather ducked his head in the doorway. "If you should recollect at some later date . . ." he said.

"I'll let you know."

"I wrote my Baltimore number on my calling card. Justine has no phone. If you should chance to think of something, anything at all . . ."

"Will do, Mr. Peck," she said, suddenly jaunty.

"You do?"

"What?"

"She *will* do, Grandfather," Justine said, and led him into the hall. But he did not hear and was still turned to Mrs. Tabor, puzzled and unhappy, when the door swung shut and the locks began tumbling into place again.

In the railroad station they sat on a wooden bench, waiting for the next train home. Justine ate a sack of Fritos, a Baby Ruth, and two hot dogs; her grandfather would not take anything. Neither of them liked Cokes and they could not find any root beer so they drank warm, bleachy New York water begged from a concession stand. Justine finished the last of her cough drops. She had to go buy more, paying too much for them at a vending machine. When she came back she found that her grandfather had fallen asleep with his head tipped back and his mouth open, his empty hands curled at his sides. She moved some sailor's unattended seabag over next to him and adjusted his head to rest upon it. Then she opened her carry-all and took out magazines, scarves, a coin purse, road maps and unmailed letters and a snaggle-toothed comb and a clutch of candy wrappers, until at the very bottom she came upon a deck of playing cards wrapped in a square of old, old silk. She unwrapped them and laid them out on the bench one by one, choosing places for them as surely and delicately as a cat chooses where to set its paws. When she had formed a cross she sat still for a moment, holding the remaining cards in her left hand. Then her grandfather stirred and she gathered the cards quickly and without a sound. They were back in their silk before he was fully awake again, and Justine was sitting motionless on the bench with her hands folded neatly over her straw bag.

$$\underset{=}{2}$$

On moving day they were up at five, not because there was any rush but because the house was so uncomfortable now with everything packed, the walls bare and the furniture gone, no place to sleep but mattresses laid upon newspapers. All night long one person or another had been coughing or rearranging blankets or padding across the moonlit floor to the bathroom. People fell out of dreams and into them again, jerking awake and then spiraling back to sleep. The hollow walls creaked almost as steadily as the ticking of a clock.

Then Justine rose and stalked around the mattress, working a cramp out of one long, narrow foot. And Duncan opened his eyes to watch her fling on her bathrobe, all flurry and rustling and sleight-of-hand. Darkness swirled around her, but that was only chenille. "What time is it?" he asked. "Is it morning yet?"

"I don't know," she said.

Neither of them wore watches. On them, watches broke or lost themselves or speeded up to keep some lawless schedule of their own so you could almost see the minute hand racing around the dial.

Duncan sat up and felt for his clothing, while Justine sailed through the living room. Her gritty bare feet whispered on the floor and her bathrobe sash galloped behind. "Coming through! Excuse me! Coming through!" Her daughter's bedclothes stirred and rumpled. In the kitchen, Justine switched on the light and went to the sink to make tap-water coffee. The room gave off an icy chill. Everything was bare, scraped and smudged by the past—four bald spots on the linoleum where the table had once stood, and dimples where Duncan had tipped back in his chair, scorches and chips on the countertop, the uncurtained window filmed with cooking grease, the rickety wooden shelves empty but still bearing rings of molasses and catsup. Justine made the coffee in paper cups and stirred it with a screwdriver. When she had set the cups on the counter she turned to find her grandfather teetering in the doorway. Noise could not wake him, but light could. He wore withered silk pajamas and held his snaptop pocket watch open in his hand. "It's five ten a.m.," he said.

"Good morning, Grandfather."

"Yesterday you slept till noon. *Regularity* is what we want to aim for here."

"Would you like some coffee?"

But he hadn't heard. He pursed his lips and snapped the watch shut and went back to his bedroom for his clothes.

Now throughout the house came the sounds of people dressing, doors opening and closing, teeth being brushed. Nobody spoke. They were struggling free of their dreams still—all but Justine, who hummed a polka as she darted around the kitchen. In her flimsy robe, flushed with heat when anyone else would be shivering, she gave an impression of energy burning and wasting. She moved very fast and accomplished very little. She opened drawers for no reason and slammed them shut, pulled down the yellowed windowshade and let it snap up again. Then she called, "Duncan? Meg? Am I the only one *doing* anything?"

Duncan came in with his oldest clothes on: a white shirt worn soft and translucent and a shrunken pair of dungarees. His arms and legs gawked out like a growing boy's. He had a boy's face still, the expression trustful and the corners of his mouth pulled upward. With his hair and skin a single color and his long-boned, awkward body he might have been Justine's brother, except that he seemed to be continually turning over some mysterious private thought that set him apart. Also he moved differently; he was slower and more deliberate. Justine ran circles around him with his cup of coffee until he stopped her and took it from her hands.

"I could be dressed and gone by now, the rest of you would still be lolling in bed," she told him.

He swallowed a mouthful of coffee, looked down into the cup and raised his eyebrows.

Justine went back through the living room, where Meg's mattress lay empty with her blanket already folded in a neat, flat square. She knocked on the bathroom door. "Meg? Meggie? Is that you? We're not going to *wait* all day for you."

Water ran on and on.

"If you set up housekeeping there the way you did yesterday we'll leave you, we'll walk right out and leave you, hear?"

She tapped the door once more and returned to the kitchen. "Meg is crying again," she told Duncan.

"How can you tell?"

"She's shut up in the bathroom running the faucet. If today's like yesterday, what are we going to do?" she asked, but she was already trailing off, heading toward her bedroom with her mind switched to something else, and Duncan didn't bother answering.

In the bedroom, Justine dressed and then gathered up heaps of cast-off clothing, a coffee cup and a half-empty bottle of bourbon and a *Scientific American*. She tried to fold her blanket as neatly as Meg's. Then she straightened and looked around her. The room swooped with shadows from the swinging lightbulb. Without furniture it showed itself for what it was: a paper box with sagging walls. In every corner were empty matchbooks, safety pins, dustballs, Kleenexes, but she was not a careful housekeeper and she left them for whoever came after.

When she returned to the kitchen her grandfather and Duncan were standing side by side drinking their coffee like medicine. Her grandfather wore his deerskin slippers: otherwise, he was ready to leave. No one was going to accuse him of holding things up. "One of the trials I expect to see in hell," he said, "is paper cups, where your thumbnail is forever tempted to scrape off a strip of wax. And plastic spoons, and pulpy paper plates."

"That's for sure," Duncan told him.

"What say?"

"Where's your *hearing* aid?" Justine asked.

"Not so very well," said her grandfather. He held one hand out level, palm down. "I'm experiencing some discomfort in my fingers and both knees, I believe because of the cold. I was cold all night. I haven't been so cold since the blizzard of eighty-eight. Why are there not enough blankets, all of a sudden?"

Duncan flashed Justine a wide, quick smile, which she returned with the corners tucked in. There were not enough blankets because she had used most of them yesterday to pad the furniture, shielding claw feet and bureau tops and peeling veneer from the splintery walls of the U-Haul truck, although Duncan had told her, several times, that it might be best to save the blankets out. This was still January, the nights were cold. What was her hurry? But Justine was *always* in a hurry. "I want to get things done, I want to get going," she had said. Duncan gave up. There had been no system to their previous moves either; it seemed pointless to start now.

Meg came into the kitchen and claimed her coffee without looking to left or right—a neat, pretty girl in a shirtwaist dress, with short hair held in place by a sterling silver barrette. She was scrubbed and shining, buttoned, combed, smelling of toothpaste, but her eyes were pink. "Oh, honey!" Justine cried, but Meg ducked out from between her hands. She was seventeen years old. This move was the worst thing that had ever happened to her. Justine said, "Would you like some bread? It's all we've got out."

"No, thank you, Mama."

"I thought we'd have breakfast when we get to what's-its-name, if it's not too long to wait."

"I'm not hungry anyway."

She said nothing to her father. It was plain what she thought: If it weren't for Duncan they would never have to move at all. He had gone and grown tired of another business and chosen yet another town to drag them off to, seemingly picked it out of a hat, or might as well have.

"Your father will be driving the truck all alone," Justine said, "since last time it made Grandfather sick. Would you like to ride with him?" She never would let a quarrel wind on its natural way. She knew it herself, she had no tact or subtlety. She always had to be interfering. "Why not go, he could use the company."

But Meg's tears were back and she wouldn't speak, even to say no. She bent her head. The two short wings of her hair swung forward to hide her cheeks. And Duncan, of course, was off on some tangent of his own. His mind had started up again; he was finally awake. His mind was an intricate, multigeared machine, or perhaps some little animal with skittery paws. "I am fascinated by randomness," he said. "Do you realize that there is no possible permutation of four fingers that could be called absolutely random?"

"Duncan, it's time to roll the mattresses," Justine said.

"Mattresses. Yes."

"Would you?"

"Hold up your hand," Duncan told the grandfather, leading him through the living room. "Then take away two fingers. The first and third elements, say, of a four-element . . ."

"Last night," said Meg, "Mrs. Benning asked me again if I would like to stay with her."

"Oh, Meg."

"She said, 'Why won't your mother allow it? Just till the school year is over,' she said. She said, 'You know we'd love to have you. Does she think you'd be imposing? Would it help if I talked to her one more time?'"

"You'll be leaving us soon enough as it is," said Justine, stacking empty paper cups.

"At least we should consider my schooling," Meg said. "This is my senior year. I won't learn a thing, moving around the way we do."

"Teaching you to adapt is the best education we could give you," Justine told her.

"Adapt! What about logarithms?"

"Now I can't keep on and on about this, I want you to find the cat. I think she knows it's moving day. She's hiding."

"So would I," said Meg, "if I could think of a place." And she slid off the counter and left, calling the cat in her soft, sensible voice that was never raised even when she argued. Justine stood motionless beside the sink. When she heard footsteps she spun around but it was only her grandfather.

"Justine? There are neighbors here to see you off," he told her. He sniffed through his long, pinched nose. People who were not related to him ought to keep to themselves, he always said. He watched narrowly while Justine rushed through the house, hunting her keys and struggling into her coat and jamming her hat on her head. "Check your room, Grandfather," she called. "Turn off the lights. Will you help Meg find the cat? Tell her we're just about to leave."

"Knees?"

"And don't forget your hearing aid."

"They don't get better *that* fast, the cold has sunk into the sockets," her grandfather said. "Ask me again tomorrow. Thank you very much."

Justine kissed his cheekbone, a polished white blade. She flew through the living room and out the front door, into the chalky dawn. Cold air yanked at her breath. Frozen grass crunched under her feet. Over by the U-Haul truck, Mr. Ambrose was helping Duncan load the last of the mattresses. Mrs. Ambrose stood to one side, along with the Printzes and Mrs. Benning and Della Carpenter and her retarded daughter. And a few feet away was a newsboy Justine had never seen before, a canvas sack slung from one shoulder. Except for the newsboy they all wore bathrobes, or coats thrown over pajamas. She had known them for nearly a year and there were still these new things to be learned: Alice Printz favored fluffy slippers the size of small sheep and Mrs. Benning, so practical in the daytime, wore a nightgown made of layers and layers of see-through pink or blue or gray—it was hard to tell which in this light. They stood hugging themselves against the cold, and the Carpenter girl's teeth were chattering. "Justine, I never!" Alice Printz was saying. "You thought you could slip out from under us. But we won't let you go that easy, here we are at crack of dawn waiting to see you off."

"Oh, I *hate* goodbyes!" said Justine. She went down the row hugging each one, even the newsboy, whom she might after all know without realizing it. Then a light came on over the Franks' front door, three houses down, and Justine went to tell June Frank goodbye. All but the newsboy came along with her. June appeared on her cinderblock steps carrying a begonia in a plastic pot. "I had this growing for you ever since I knew you would be moving," she said, "and if you had run off in the night the way you're doing and not give me a chance to say goodbye it would have broke my heart in two." June rolled her hair up on orange juice cans. Justine had never known that before either. And she said not to thank her for the plant or its growth would be stunted. "Is that right?" said Justine, her attention sidetracked. She held up the pot and thought a minute. "Now why, I wonder?"

"*I* don't know why, I only know what my mother used to say to me," June said. "Justine, honey, I won't come any further, but you tell the others goodbye for me too. Tell that pretty little Meg and your sweet old grandfather, tell that handsome husband, hear? And I'm going to write you a letter. If my sister decides to get married again I have to write you first and ask you what the cards say. I wouldn't think of letting her go ahead without it. Can you manage such a thing long distance?"

"I'll surely try," said Justine. "Well, I won't say thank you for the plant then but I promise to take good care of it. Goodbye then, June."

"Goodbye, old honey," June said, and she grew sad all at once and came down the steps to lay her cheek softly against Justine's while the others looked on, suddenly still, tilting their heads and smiling.

Meanwhile Meg had settled in the rear of the battered Ford with an enormous gray tweed cat in her lap. The cat crouched and glared and Meg cried, causing a mist of tears to glaze the squat little house with its yellowed foundations, its tattered shrubs, the porch pillars rotting from the bottom up. In the front seat, her great-grandfather placed his hearing aid in his ear, adjusted a button, and winced. Duncan slammed the tailgate on the last of the mattresses and climbed into the truck cab. He turned on the headlights, coloring the gray and white scene in front of him—Justine being passed from hand to hand down a row of neighbors in their nightclothes. "Ho, Justine," he called softly. Of course she couldn't hear. He had to beep the horn. Then everybody jumped and screeched and a window lit up half a block down, but Justine only gave him a wave and headed for the car, unsurprised, because wasn't he always having to honk for her? She was late for everything, though she started out the earliest and the fastest and the most impatient. She was always leaving places the same way, calling scraps of goodbyes and then running, flying, bearing some shaking plant or parcel or covered dish, out of breath and laughing at herself, clutching her hat to her head as she sped along.

At nine o'clock in the morning, Red Emma Borden was wiping the counter in the Caro Mill Diner when these four unfamiliar people walked in—a man and wife, a teenaged daughter and a very ancient gentleman. Red Emma was about to have a cigarette (she'd been on her feet since four) and she wasn't eager to wait on anyone else. Still, it was nice to see some new faces. She had been born and raised and married and widowed in this town and she was sick of everybody in it. So she puffed up her orange curls, tugged her uniform down, and reached for the order pad. Meanwhile the strangers were trying to find acceptable seats, which was not all that easy to do. Two of the counter stools were broken, just topless aluminum pedestals, and another would tip you off as soon as you tried to perch upon it. They had to cluster at one end down near the exhaust fan. Even then, the old gentleman had a long tail of cotton batting dangling out from under him. But none of them made any complaint; they just folded their arms and waited for her behind four pairs of blue, blue eyes. "Well, now," said Red Emma, slapping down cracked plastic menu cards. "What you going to have?"

She addressed the woman first—a skin-and-bones lady wearing a hat. But it was the husband who answered. "Speedy here will have everything in the kitchen," he said.

"Speedy! I barely *inched* along," the woman said.

"I thought you had entered the Indy five hundred. And your seat belt flopping out the door, after I took all that time installing it for you—"

"I will take coffee and three fried eggs," the woman told Red Emma. "Sunny side up. And hotcakes, link sausages, and orange juice. And something salty, a sack of potato chips. Grandfather? Meg?"

Red Emma feared she would be cooking all morning, but it turned out the others just wanted coffee. They had the dazed, rumpled look of people who had been traveling. Only the woman seemed to care to talk. "My name is Justine," she said, "and this is my husband, Duncan. Our Grandfather Peck and our daughter Meg. Do you have the keys?"

"How's that?"

"We were told to stop here and pick up the keys for Mr. Parkinson's house."

"Oh yes," said Red Emma. She would never have supposed that these were the people for Ned Parkinson's house—a tacky little place next to the electric shop. Particularly not the old gentleman. "Well, he did say somebody might be by," she said. "Have you took a good look at it yet?"

"Duncan has. He chose it," said Justine. "You haven't told us *your* name."

"Why, I'm Red Emma Borden."

"Do you work here all the time?"

"Mornings I do."

"Because I like to eat in diners. I expect we'll run into you often."

"Maybe so," said Red Emma, breaking eggs onto the grill. "But if you come after noon it'll be my late husband's cousin, *Black* Emma Borden. They call her that because she's the one with black hair, only she's been dyeing it for years now." She poured coffee into thick white cups. "You say your husband chose the house?" she asked Justine. "He always does."

Red Emma flung him a glance. A fine-looking, straw-colored man. His conscience did not appear to be bothering him. "Look, honey," she told Justine. She set the coffeepot down and leaned over the counter. "How come you would let your husband choose where you live? Does *he* understand kitchens? Does he check for closet space and woodwork that doesn't crumble to bits the first time you try to scrub it down?"

Justine laughed. "I doubt it," she said.

Red Emma had once sent her husband to a used car lot to buy a family automobile and he had come home with a little teeny red creature meant for racing, set low to the ground, slit eyes for windows. It ate up every cent they had saved. She had never forgiven him. So now she felt personally involved, and she glared at this Duncan. He sat there as calm as you please building a pyramid out of sugar cubes. The grandfather was reading someone's discarded newspaper, holding it three feet away from him as old people tend to do and scowling and working his mouth around. Only the daughter seemed to understand. A *nice* girl, so trim and quiet. She wore a coat that was shabby but good quality, and she kept her eyes fixed on a catsup bottle as if something had shamed her. *She* knew what Red Emma was getting at.

"There's other places," Red Emma said. "The Butters are letting, oh, a *big* place go, over by the schoolhouse."

"Now on the average," Duncan said, and Red Emma turned, thinking he was speaking to her, "on the average a single one of the blocks in Cheops's pyramid weighed two and a half tons." No, it was the grandfather he meant that for, but the grandfather only looked up, irritated, maybe not even hearing, and turned a page of his paper. Duncan spun toward Meg, on his left. "It is accepted that wheels as such were not used in the construction," he told her. "Nor any but the most primitive surveying tools, so far as we know. Nevertheless, the greatest error to be found is only a little over five degrees on the east wall, and the others are almost perfect. And have you thought about the angle of the slant?"

Meg looked back at him, expressionless.

"It's my belief they built it from the top down," he said. He laughed.

Red Emma thought he must be crazy.

She flipped the hotcakes, loaded Justine's plate, and set it in front of her. "The Butters' house is a *two*-story affair," she said. "They also have a sleeping porch."

"Oh, I believe Mr. Parkinson's place is going to be just fine," said Justine. "Besides, it's near where Duncan's going to work. This way he can come home for lunch."

"Now where's he going to work?" Red Emma asked.

"At the Blue Bottle Antique Shop."

Oh, Lord. She should have known. That gilt-lettered place, run by a fat man nobody knew. Who needed antiques in Caro Mill? Only tourists, passing through on their way to the Eastern Shore, and most of them were in too much of a hurry to stop. But Red Emma still clung to a shred of hope (she liked to see people *manage*, somehow) and she said, "Well now, I suppose he could improve on what that Mr.—I don't recall his name. I suppose if he knows about antiques, and so on—"

"Oh, Duncan knows about everything," said Justine.

It didn't sound good, not at all.

"He hasn't worked with antiques before but he did build some furniture once, a few jobs back—"

Yes.

"The man who owns the Blue Bottle is Duncan's mother's sister's brother-in-law. He wants to ease off a little, get somebody else to manage the store for him now that he's getting older."

"We've used up all my mother's *blood* relations," Duncan said cheerfully. He was correcting the pitch of one pyramid wall. The truth that was coming out did not appear to embarrass him. "The last job was with my uncle, he owns a health food store. But no one in the family has a fix-it shop, and fixing is what I really do. I can fix anything. Do you need some repair work here?"

"No indeed," Red Emma told him firmly.

And she turned back to Justine, ready to offer her sympathy, but Justine was munching potato chips with a merry look in her eye. Her hat was a little crooked. Could she possibly be a drinker? Red Emma sighed and went to clean the grill. "Of course," she said, "I don't mean to say anything against Ned Parkinson's house. Why, in lots of ways it's just fine. I'm sure you'll all be happy there."

"I'm sure we will be," Justine said.

"And certainly your husband can handle any plumbing and electrical problems that might arise," Red Emma said, wickedly sweet, because she did not for a moment think he could.

But Duncan said, "Certainly," and started plunking his sugar cubes one by one back into the bowl.

Red Emma wiped the grill with a sour dish rag. She felt tired and wished they would go. But then Justine said, "You want to hear something? This coming year will be the best our family's ever had. It's going to be exceptional."

"Now, how do you know that?"

"It's nineteen seventy-three, isn't it? And three is our number! Look: both Duncan and I were born in nineteen thirty-three. We were married in nineteen fifty-three and Meg was born on the third day of the third month in nineteen fifty-five. Isn't that something?"

"Oh, Mama," Meg said, and ducked her head over her coffee.

"Meg's afraid that people will think I'm eccentric," said Justine. "But after all, it's not as if I believed in *numerology* or anything. Just lucky numbers. What's your lucky number, Red Emma?"

"Eight," said Red Emma.

"Ah. See there? Eight is forceful and good at organizing. You would succeed at any business or career, just anything."

"I would?"

Red Emma looked down at her billowing white nylon front, the flowered handkerchief prinked to her bosom with a cameo brooch.

"Now, Meg doesn't have a lucky number. I'm worried that nothing will ever happen to her."

"*Mama.*"

"Meg was due to be born in May and I wondered how that could happen. Unless she arrived on the third, of course. But see? She was premature, she came in March after all."

"I always ask for eight at the Barket of Cheer lottery," said Red Emma. "And I've won it twice, too. Forty dollars' worth of fine-quality liquor."

"Of course. Now, who's the fortune teller in this town?"

"Fortune teller?"

The grandfather rattled and crackled his paper.

"Don't tell me you don't have one," said Justine.

"Not to my knowledge we don't."

"Well, you know where I'll be living. Come when I'm settled and I'll tell your fortune free."

"You tell fortunes."

"I do church fairs, bazaars, club meetings, teas—anybody's, any time. People can knock on my door in the dead of night if they have some urgent problem and I will get up in my bathrobe to give them a reading. I don't mind at all. I like it, in fact. I have insomnia."

"But—you mean you tell fortunes *seriously?*" Red Emma asked.

"How else would I tell them?"

Red Emma looked at Duncan. He looked back, unsmiling.

"Well, if we could have the keys, then," said Justine.

Red Emma fetched them, sleepwalking—two flat, tinny keys on a shower curtain ring. "I really do need to have my fortune told," she said. "I wouldn't want this spread around but I'm considering a change in employment."

"Oh, *I* could help out with that."

"Don't laugh, will you? I'd like to be a mailman. I even passed the tests. Could you really tell me whether that would be a lucky move or not?"

"Of course," said Justine.

Red Emma rang up their bill, which Duncan paid with a Bank-

Americard so worn it would not emboss properly. Then they filed out, and she stood by the door to watch them go. When Justine passed, Red Emma touched her shoulder. "I'm just so anxious, you see," she said. "I don't sleep good at all. My mind swings back and forth between decisions. Oh, I know it's nothing big. I mean, a mailman, what is that to the world? What's it going to matter a hundred years from now? I don't fool myself it's anything important. Only day after day in this place, the grease causing my hair to flop halfway through the morning and the men all making smart remarks and me just feeding them and feeding them . . . though the pay is good and I really don't know what Uncle Harry would say if I was to quit after all these years."

"Change," said Justine.

"Beg pardon?"

"Change. I don't need cards for that. Take the change. Always change."

"Well—is that my fortune?"

"Yes, it is," said Justine. "Goodbye, Red Emma! See you soon!"

And she was gone, leaving Red Emma to pleat her lower lip with her fingers and ponder beside the plate glass door.

Justine drove the Ford down Main Street with the cat racing back and forth across the rear window ledge, yowling like an old, angry baby while people on the sidewalks stopped and stared. Meg sat with her hands folded; by now she was used to the racket. The grandfather simply shut his hearing aid off and gazed from his bubble of silence at the little wooden Woolworth's, the Texaco, the Amoco, the Arco, a moldering A&P, a neat brick post office with a flag in front. This time Duncan's truck was ahead, and Justine followed him in a right-hand turn down a side street lined with one-story buildings. They passed a drugstore and an electric shop, and then they came to a row of small houses. Duncan parked in front of the first one. Justine pulled in behind him. "Here we are!" she said.

The house was white, worn down to gray. On the porch, square shingled columns rose waist-high and then stopped, giving the overhang a precarious, unreliable look. Although there was no second floor the dormer window of some attic or storage room bulged out of the roof like an eyelid. A snarl of wiry bushes guarded the crawlspace beneath the porch. "Oh, roses!" Justine cried. "Are those roses?" Her grandfather shifted in his seat.

"This house is even worse than the last," said Meg.

"Never mind, here you'll have a room of your own. You won't have to sleep in the living room. Isn't that going to be nice?"

"Yes, Mama," Meg said.

Duncan was already pacing the yard when the others reached him. "I'm going to put a row or two of corn here," he told them. "Out back is too shady but see how much sun we get in front? I'm going to plow up the grass and plant corn and cucumbers. I have this plan for fertilizer, I'm going to buy a blender and grind up all our garbage with a little water. Pay attention, Justine. I want you to save everything, eggshells and orange peels and even bones. The bones we'll pressure-cook first. Have we got a pressure-cooker? We'll make a sort of jelly and spread that around here too."

Meanwhile the cat had streaked under the crawlspace, where she would stay till the moving was over, and the grandfather was climbing the front steps all hunkered and disapproving, muttering to himself, making an inventory of every splinter and knothole and paint blister, every nail worked loose, windowscreen split, floorboard warped. Meg sat down on the very top step. "I'm cold," she said.

Justine said, "Your father's going to take up farming. Maybe we'll have tomatoes."

"Will we be here to harvest them?" Meg asked nobody.

Justine found the keys in one of her pockets and opened the door. They stepped into a hall smelling of mildew, littered with newspapers and broken cardboard boxes. The kitchen leading off it contained a refrigerator with a motor on top, a dirty gas stove, and a sink on stilts. There was a living room with a boarded-up fireplace. In the back were the bathroom and three bedrooms, all tiny and dark, but Justine swept through flinging up windowshades and stirring the thick, musty air. "Look! Someone left a pair of pliers," she said. "And here's a chair we can use for the porch." She was a pack rat; all of them were. It was a family trait. You could tell that in a flash when they started carrying things in from the truck—the bales of ancient, curly-edged magazines, zipper bags bursting with unfashionable clothes, cardboard boxes marked *Clippings, Used Wrapping Paper, Photos, Empty Bottles.* Duncan and Justine staggered into the grandfather's room carrying a steel filing cabinet from his old office, stuffed with carbon copies of all his personal correspondence for the twenty-three years since his retirement. In one corner of their own room Duncan stacked crates of machine parts and nameless metal objects picked up on walks, which he might someday want to use for some invention. He had cartons of books, most of them second-hand, dealing with things like the development of the quantum theory and the philosophy of Lao-tzu and the tribal life of Ila-speaking Northern Rhodesians. But when all of this clutter had been brought in (and it took the four of them two hours) there was next to nothing left in the truck. Their furniture was barely enough to make the house seem inhabited: three rust-stained mattresses, four kitchen chairs from Goodwill, Great-Grandma's hand-carved rose-wood dining table, a sagging sofa and easy chair donated by a neighbor two moves back, and three bureaus of Justine's mother's, their ornate feet and bow fronts self-conscious next to the bedsteads Duncan had constructed out of raw pine boards that gave off a yellow smell. For dishes they had a collection of dimestore plates, some light green, some flowered, some dark brown with white glaze dripped around the edges, and thermal mugs given away free when Esso changed to Exxon. The cutlery with its yellow plastic handles had been salvaged from Aunt Sarah's English picnic basket. There were two saucepans and a skillet. (Justine did not like cooking.) They owned a broom and a sponge mop, but no dustpan, no vacuum cleaner, no squeegee, scrub bucket, or chamois cloth. (Justine did not like cleaning either.) No washing machine or dryer. When all the clothes in the house were dirty the family would lug them to the laundromat. Of course that was not much fun—the four of them struggling with their bulging pillow slips, the grandfather's head ducked way, way low in case of passers-by, all of them a little bedraggled in their very last clean clothes unearthed from the bottom of the drawer or the back of the closet—but wasn't it better than moving those shiny, heavy appliances from place to place? Why, by late afternoon they were completely settled in. There was nothing more to do. It was true that most of the boxes remained to be opened but that was nothing, some were still packed from the *last* move. There was no hurry. Justine was free to stretch out on her mattress, which had the piney-wood smell of home, and work her feet from her shoes and smile at the ceiling while the cat lay on her stomach like a twenty-pound, purring hot water bottle. Duncan could sit on the edge of the bed fooling with a stroboscope he had forgotten he owned. Meg could shut her door and unwrap, from its own special box, from seven layers of tissue paper, her framed photograph of a young man in a clerical robe at least a size too large, which she rewrapped almost immediately and slid to the back of her closet shelf. And in his room across the hall the grandfather could take a photo of his own from his pocket: Caleb Peck in tones of brown, framed in gold, wearing a hat and tie, his face stark and dignified, playing a violincello while seated in an open stable door twenty feet off the ground.

3
=

Duncan took a tour of the Blue Bottle Antique Shop with Silas Amsel, the owner. Since he had already seen it when he applied for the job, he was not very interested. He ambled along behind fat, bearded Silas, yawning and drumming his fingers on passing tabletops. Spider-legged spinet desks, clocks with cherubs and shepherdesses and Father Time, dusty goblets, mirrors framed in knobby gold plaster, occasional tables too weak to bear the weight of a lamp—what was the sense in all this? To tell the truth, he had never thought about antiques before. He had been reared in a world where they were taken for granted. No one ever *bought* them, no one bought anything; the rooms were crowded with mellowed, well-kept furniture that appeared to have grown there, and whenever children departed they took several pieces with them but left the rooms as crowded as ever, somehow, as if more had sprouted in the night. No, what interested Duncan was the bin of contrivances he had found behind Silas's counter: rusty cherry pitters, potato quillers, apple corers, fish scalers, an ingenious spiral cone for separating the white of an egg from the yolk. Beside the bin was a wicker valise that opened to make a chair for sitting by the seashore. Where had all that inventiveness got to, now? How had it faded away? The bin was marked with a felt-tip pen: *Your choice, $1.* The valise, which was broken, could be bought for $2.50, if anyone could find it among the boots and paper bags. When Duncan took over, he would put the valise in the front window. (He leered suddenly at Silas's broad, ponderous back.) He would polish the utensils and lay them out in rows. He would sell everything humdrum and buy ancient tools at barn auctions and flea markets, until the shop resembled a nineteenth-century inventor's workroom and he could sit inhaling a combination of machine oil and wood and oxidizing iron, his favorite smells.

"Oh, I'm getting old, getting old," said Silas, creaking up the steps at the back of the store to show him where the telephone was. "Be sorry to let loose of the reins but glad of the rest, believe me."

In fact Silas was a good thirty years younger than Grandfather Peck, who could have run the shop with one hand tied behind him, but Duncan was used to this premature aging among people outside the family. Besides, if Silas weren't retiring Duncan would still be looking for a job. He had thought, this time, that he might finally have used up all his mother's relatives. He had wondered if he would ever escape from the health food store, which he had turned into a paying proposition and then, out of boredom, allowed to run down again. Weevils took over the stone-ground wheat and mold got the soy grits and the unsulphured raisins turned to pebbles. He lost his natural gaiety and his recklessness, he fell back on bourbon, solitaire, and a flat-faced silence that not even Justine could penetrate. Was there anything worse than feeling you were *sealed* in a place, to grow old and stale and finally die? His careless bookkeeping and erratic hours, already a matter of principle, became so obvious no employer could overlook them. That was the pattern of Duncan's life—ventures begun light-heartedly, with enthusiasm but only half his attention, the other half devoted to plans for a perpetual motion machine made entirely of screen door springs or a method of breeding stingless honeybees or the entering of a contest, sponsored by an Englishman, for a one-man flying machine no bigger than an armchair. In the last twenty years he had been, among other things, a goat farmer, a photographer, and a cabinetmaker; he had worked in a pet store, a tobacconist's, a record bar, and a gourmet shop; he had taken census, shorn sheep, and fertilized the lawns of a suburban development on a toy tractor. Almost all these jobs had been enjoyable, but only briefly. He began to grow restless. He noticed that he was treading an endless round of days just as his pinched, unimaginative family had done before him. He would start going to work at ten and then eleven, four days a week and then three; and next came the bourbon, the solitaire, the silence in which to reflect upon the bars of his cage. Next another venture. He was his own perpetual motion machine.

Sometimes he worried about Justine. He didn't *want* to be the way he was, uprooting her yearly or even more often, switching Meg to still another school. He knew how the neighbors shook their heads over him. Yet it seemed he suffered from some sort of chronic dissatisfaction which came and went like malaria, and the only way to hold it back was to learn more and more new facts, as if continually surprising his mind. Now peculiar scraps of knowledge were stuck to him like lint from all his jobs. He knew a Toggenburg goat from a Saanen, he could measure a dachshund, by sight alone, for a plaid mackintosh with matching Sherlock Holmes-style hat. He was an authority on the making of yogurt and the application of poisons to broad-leafed weeds during dandelion season. He had also discovered that every shop, even the most unlikely, has a circle of daily customers who become its experts—the elderly gentlemen capping each other's list of imported cheeses, the ladies debating on the use of slippery elm bark, the teenagers intoning the life history of every member of every rock band. At the tobacconist's, college boys could spend hours recalling the time a legendary freshman had found a fully aged and yellowed, hand-carved meerschaum pipe sitting on the top of someone's garbage can. Perched on his stool behind the counter, gloating over the drawings for his pedal-driven flying machine, Duncan absorbed this stray knowledge like sunlight. Never mind that it was useless. And now he was about to find something else to learn, here among these ancient navigating devices and cracked foggy lanterns and ropes of amber beads like half-sucked butter rum balls.

"This is potassium lactate," said Silas, tapping a brown bottle on the telephone table. "We use it to replace the acids in the covers of old leather books."

And he looked surprised at the sudden light that flashed across Duncan's face.

"Now this pad I always keep handy, and the pencil chained. People will call with items to sell, you want to get their addresses. Here, by the way, is a message for you."

He ripped it off the pad. *Habit-Forming Entertainments called, come to lunch first Sun. in Feb.*

"What?" said Duncan.

"He said you would know him. He phoned four times in the last two days. He said if you couldn't make it call back, he's still listed as Exotico."

"Ah," said Duncan, and pocketed the slip. Silas waited but Duncan didn't explain.

"Well, then," Silas said finally, "if you can't think of any questions— but I'll be by, I'll drop by often, of course."

"Of course," said Duncan, and he sighed, but Silas was groaning back down the steps by now and didn't hear him.

Habit-Forming Entertainments, which had been Exotico, Inc., last year and Alonzo's Amazing Amusements the year before that, was located in a cow pasture on the outskirts of Parvis, Maryland. It was a carnival company, of sorts—the kind that is called a forty-miler, although in this case the circuit was considerably wider. It traveled from one tiny town to another, supplying the entertainment for firehouse fairs, church and school bazaars, homecoming celebrations, and the gala openings of new shopping malls. In between trips the entire company lived in trailers in the cow pasture, with a pumpkin-colored tent flying pennants in the middle. They worked year round. Even in the dead of winter, Habit-Forming Entertainments would come trundling across the frost-bitten Maryland countryside to whoever asked for them. They brought mechanical rides, two ponies, a concession stand, a few simple games of chance whenever local law allowed, and five girls to run the games in satin bathing suits with dirty seams. There was also a merry-go-round. It was hard to transport and something was always going wrong with it, the mechanism sticking or the animals toppling over, but Justine preferred it to any other merry-go-round she had ever known. It played only one piece: "The St. James Infirmary Blues." Whenever Justine heard that tune sawing through the air she had to climb on, she didn't care if she *was* too old. She sat astride a laughing white horse, hugging the mane and laughing herself or occasionally crying, because the music was so tinny and sweet and sad and made her nostalgic for times before she was born. And whenever she saw Alonzo Divich, who owned that merry-go-round and all the other equipment, he was whistling "The St. James Infirmary Blues" like a theme song. He said it was the only tune *he* knew, too. He and the merry-go-round: two clumsy, hopeful, cheerful creatures, lumbering along where you would least expect to find them.

He was whistling when Justine and Duncan arrived; they tracked him down by his song. They left the car at the edge of the field and made their way across the frozen stubble toward the trailers, which sat around the tent in a cold, huddled circle like covered wagons braced for Indian attack. In the spring, when the countryside was blooming, this sort of life could seem pleasant, but not today. Today everything was lit with a sickly white winter sun, the inhabitants were shut inside their trailers, the ponies hung their heads. "Oh, the poor things!" Justine cried, and she felt the same when she passed an orange ride all folded on its truckbed like a crumpled baby dinosaur. But the whistling continued, happy as ever, sailing out from behind a plowshed, and when they had rounded the shed there was Alonzo Divich looking untouched by cold or loneliness or time. He was sitting on a boulder braiding rawhide—a large, dark man with a drooping black mustache and drooping eyes. He wore too many colors of clothing, all a little soiled, greasy, strained across the stomach and crotch and under the arms: a rose shirt, a woven Mexican vest, suede dungarees and crumpled boots. When he stood to hug them, he gave off a smell of leather and honey. "Aha!" he said to Justine. "But you haven't changed at all! Even the hat is still the same! Is it rooted there?"

He had no accent—only a curious certainty to his speech. But where did he get his hybrid name, and his coloring, and his flashing gold molars and his habit of hugging other men so unself-consciously? Justine had asked him outright, once, what nationality he was. "You're the fortune teller, you tell me," he said.

"I read the future, not the past," she told him.

"Well, the past should be easier!"

"It's not. It's far more complicated."

But he had never told her, even so.

He led them to the tent, where folding chairs were grouped around long, wheeled conference tables. This was the company's communal hall, although in cold weather it was nearly empty. In one corner a blonde wearing slacks, gilt sandals, and several sweaters was combing out a miniature poodle. Two men in overalls were seated at a table drinking coffee from green mugs, but they left when Alonzo entered. "Aah, don't go," he said, flopping an arm toward their backs. He pulled out chairs at the center table, and seated himself at the head. Almost immediately a dark old lady appeared and spread a tablecloth. Then she brought a bottle and three small glasses, which she set before Alonzo. He filled the glasses exactly to the brim. The old lady reappeared with paper plates, plastic forks, and then trays of rice, hunks of meat in tomato sauce, eggplant, chicken dusted with some peculiar red powder, wrinkled black olives, bowls of beet soup and chopped cucumber in yogurt, great flat disks of bread and pitchers of green Kool-Aid. Steam rose from the platters, and from Alonzo's mouth as he talked in the cold, rubbery-smelling air. "Take some, don't be shy. First

Duncan, he's thinner than ever. He's stretching out tall and thin like a dandelion. How tall are you, Duncan?"

"Six two."

"Double rice for Duncan, Nana!"

The old lady shoveled a mountain onto Duncan's plate.

"Rice prevents heart attacks, stroke, and impotence," said Alonzo.

"It's the thiamine," said Duncan.

"More slivovitz?"

"Oh, I might as well."

Justine ate everything she was given and accepted seconds and thirds, egged on by the approving eye of the old lady who stood behind Alonzo's chair with her hands folded under her apron. Alonzo and Duncan mainly drank, though Alonzo outdistanced Duncan very early and even managed to work in a few slabs of bread stuffed with meat and rice, meanwhile talking steadily. "When I heard you were moving back to Maryland I thought, well then, I can wait. I was contemplating a certain action. But we'll go into that later. I had been thinking, now how will I reach Justine? Then I got your card. It came as a great relief to me."

He leaned back and laced his hands across his stomach, his face a buttery color in the light of the tent. Alonzo was a happy man but forever complaining, as if hoping to fool any jealous gods. Although he loved his carnival business he said that only a fool would stick with it. "Imagine," he always said, "some people suppose this life to be romantic, dancing around the wagons at night. If they were only in my boots! You need to be a mechanic, a lawyer, an accountant. It's all the assembling and disassembling of machinery, and repairs and insurance payments. I'm being robbed by my insurance agency. Disability and liability and major medical and fire and theft and acts of God. Then there is the social security, a headache in itself when you consider all these employees coming and going and the pregnancies and the girls deciding to finish school. And you have to negotiate in every town, some don't allow so much as a ring-the-bottle game, and there's the safety inspectors and the police and the church that wants to put a tray of cupcakes in your hot dog stand . . ."

It was Duncan he talked to; men were best for discussing business. But it was Justine he took away with him at the end of the meal, one large warm thumb and forefinger gripping her upper arm. "May I?" he asked Duncan. "Only long enough to say when I'll become a millionaire."

Duncan said, "Do you still have your mechanic?"

"Lem? Would I be here if I didn't? He's in the purple trailer. He knew you were coming; go right in."

Alonzo walked with his head down, still holding Justine's arm. "You must excuse the state of my place," he said. "I have too many people in it now. My wife has left me but one of her children stayed behind to keep me company. And also Bobby. You've met Bobby, my stepson. Actually my fourth wife's stepson, her ex-husband's boy by a woman from, Tampa, Florida. Would you care for Turkish coffee?"

"No, thank you," said Justine, and she stepped inside the little green trailer. Although it was crowded it was neater than her own house, with pots and pans arranged in rows in the tiny kitchen and account books stacked at one end of the corduroy daybed. There was a coffee table that had a stripped look, as if he had just recently cleared it. He smoothed it now with both hands. "For the cards," he said.

"Thank you," said Justine.

She sat down on the daybed. She removed her crumb-littered coat, although even here it was cold. From her carry-all she took the cards in their square of silk.

"Where did you get the silk?" Alonzo asked. (He always did.)

"They came with the cards," she said, unwrapping them. She shuffled them several times, looking off at the blue air outside the trailer window.

"And where did you get the cards?"

"Cut the deck, please."

He cut it. He sat down across from her and looked at her soberly from under curled black brows, as if his future might be read in her face.

Justine first met Alonzo Divich at a church bazaar in 1956, when she was telling fortunes in the Sunday school basement. She was with the white elephants and the potted plants; his carnival was outside. He came in to have his cards read. He was one of those people, she saw, who are addicted to outguessing their futures. Whenever he had an hour to kill, a layover in some town or a lull in his work, he would search out the local seeress. If there were five local seeresses, fine. He would go to all five. He would listen without even breathing. He had heard his fortune, he told Justine, from well over a thousand women, and it had not once been done right. He had not only had his cards read but also his palms, his skull, his moles, his fingernails, his dreams, his handwriting, his tea leaves and coffee grounds. He had been to astrologers and physiognomists, not to mention specialists in bibliomancy, clidomancy, crystal-gazing, and ouija boards. A lady in Montgomery County had set a gamecock to pick corn from a circle of letters; a Georgia woman studied smoke rising from a fire and another dropped melted wax into cold water, forming small nubbly objects that she claimed to be able to interpret. In York County, Pennsylvania, he had had to bake his own barley cakes, which were then broken open and examined under a magnifying glass. And in a marsh near St. Elmo, Alabama, a very old woman had offered to kill a rice rat and study its entrails, but he had felt that such an act might bring bad luck.

He had told Justine all this at once, leaning toward her across the table in her curtained booth while a line of church ladies waited their turns outside. Justine, although she did not know it, wore the tolerant, disillusioned expression of a doctor hearing that his new patient has been to forty other doctors before him, none of them satisfactory. It gave her a look of wisdom. Alonzo decided she was going to turn out to be special. "Lady," he had said, setting his palms on her table, "tell me the answer to my problem. I feel you can."

"What is your problem?"

"Don't you know?"

"How should I?"

"*You're* the fortune teller."

So Justine had to give the speech she had made more often than she could count, and would make many times again, sometimes even to him. "Now I am not a mind reader," she said, "and I have no way at all of guessing what you want to ask, or where you come from or anything else about your past. I read the future. I have a talent for predicting change. If you help me we can search for an answer together; but I'm not going to *outwit* you."

"My problem is this," Alonzo said instantly.

And he sat on a Sunday school chair and took his hat off—a sudden, changeable man, all black and bright and multicolored like a fire that could leap in any direction at any second. "My name is Alonzo Divich," he told her. "I own a carnival business." He jabbed a thumb at the merry-go-round music above them, "The St. James Infirmary Blues" spinning itself out among the cries of children and hot dog vendors, and teenagers clinging to the Tilt-A-Whirl. "I'm divorced, I have this kid. Now I've met a rich widow woman who wants to marry me. She likes the kid, too. She would even live in the trailer. I don't have to change one thing in my life for her. And I'm a marrying fool. I love being married, I tried it twice before. So what's the trouble? The same day we start the talk about a wedding, exact same day, a man I used to know calls and asks me to come and prospect for gold with him beside a lake in Michigan. He says he's onto something. He's going to be a wealthy man, and so am I. But of course there's the kid, and the mortgaged machines, and the woman who doesn't like Michigan. So which do I do?"

Justine was listening with her mouth open. When he finished she said, immediately. "Go look for gold."

"Huh? What about the cards?"

"Oh, the cards," she said.

So she let him cut them and she laid them down, her beautiful cards as limp and greasy as her baby's oilcloth picture books. She chose the simplest formation she knew. She pointed out the meaning while he hung over the table, not breathing: a happy journey, reunion with a friend, a pleasant surprise, and no possibility of money.

"Aha," he said, and she raised her face. "So it's lucky I ran into you. No money!"

"Mr.—"

"Divich. Just call me Alonzo."

"Alonzo, is the money all you're going for?"

"Well, but—"

"Go anyway! Go on! *Don't* just sit around hemming and hawing!"

Then she slapped his money back on his palm, for lack of any better way to show how she felt. And she gathered up her cards without looking at him even though he sat there a minute longer, waiting.

It was four years before she saw Alonzo again. On Independence Day, 1960, she set up a booth at a picnic in Wamburton, Maryland. Nobody there seemed much interested in the future. Finally she repacked her cards and took a walk toward the courthouse, where rides were spinning and balloons were sailing and the merry-go-round was playing "The St. James Infirmary Blues," sending out little shimmering catgut strings that drew her in. She started toward the wooden horses. And there beside the tallest horse was—why, Alonzo Divich!—wiping his face on a red bandanna and quarreling with a mechanic. Only when she came up he turned and stopped in mid-sentence and stared. "You!" he said. He ringed her wrist with his hand and pulled her away, toward a bench where the music was not so loud. She came, holding onto her hat. "Do you know how long I worked to find you?" he shouted.

"Who, me?"

"How often do you move? Are you some sort of forty-miler all your own? First I asked at the church, who was the fortune teller? 'Oh, *Justine*,' they said. Everyone knew you, but they didn't know where you lived. And by the time I found *that* out you had moved but left no forwarding address. Why? Did you owe money? Never mind. I haunted all your ladyfriends, I hoped you were a letter writer. But you are not. Then at the tobacconist's where your husband used to work they said—"

"But what did you want me for?" Justine asked.

"To tell my fortune, of course."

"I *told* your fortune."

"Yes, back in nineteen fifty-six. Do you think my life is so steady? *Now* that reading has no bearing at all."

"Oh. Well, no," said Justine, who saw that with him, that would certainly be true. She reached into her bag—at that time a leather pouch gouged by her neighbor's puppy—and pulled out the cards. "And you didn't go look for gold," she said.

"You *do* read the past!"

"Don't be silly. Here you are in Maryland; it's obvious to anyone."

"I didn't, no. I thought about it. Instinct said to follow your advice, but I held back. You know the rest."

"No."

"Yes, you do. I married the widow," he said, "who turned out to be a disappointment. She had no money after all, the kid got on her nerves, what she had wanted all along was to start us a troupe of belly dancers with her as the star. Belly dancers, when half the towns make our game girls wear sweatshirts! I said absolutely not. She left me. I haven't heard from my friend in Michigan but I expect he has a whole sack of gold nuggets by now and meanwhile here I sit, where I was to begin with, only I happen to be married again—oh, you were right! If I had listened to you, think where I might be today!"

"Cut the cards," Justine told him.

"My new wife is pregnant and I have too many kids already," said Alonzo. "She is morning-sick, afternoon-sick, and evening-sick. When I walk into the trailer she throws fruits and vegetables at me. I don't think we are getting along at all. However, that's not my problem, no . . ."

But what his problem *had* been Justine couldn't even remember now. There were so many years in between, so many different formations laid out for him on park benches, tent floors, and trailer furniture. Once he found her he never again lost track of her. He supplied her with change-of-address cards already stamped and filled out, with blanks left for the old address and the new. He adopted her entire family, unfolding for Duncan the mysteries of his diesel engines and his cotton candy machines and the odds on his games of chance, bringing Meg gaudy circus prizes for as long as she was a child, treating the baffled grandfather with elaborate old-world respect and sending Justine a great moldy Smithfield ham every Christmas. He would drive halfway across the state just to ask her a single question, and then overpay her ridiculously when she answered. He mourned her moves to Virginia and Pennsylvania and rejoiced when she was safely back in Maryland. He beat on her front door at unexpected times and when she was not home he threatened to fall apart. "I have to know!" he would cry to Duncan or Meg. "I can't make a move, I am utterly dependent on her!"

Yet the peculiar thing (which Justine had seen too often before to wonder at) was that he very seldom took her advice. Look at all his marriages: seven, at last count. Maybe more. And how many of those had Justine approved? None. He had gone ahead anyway. Later he would come back: "Oh, you were right. I never should have done it. When will I learn?" His wives tended to leave him, taking the children along. Then sooner or later the children drifted back, and there were always a few living in his trailer—sons and stepsons and others whose relationship was not quite clear, even to him. "My wives are gone and

I sleep alone but still I have three kids at me night and day, all ages. Next time I will listen to every word you say, I'll follow it to the letter," he said.

He said it now, nearly seventeen years from the day he had first ignored her advice, while Justine laid out the cards on the coffee table in the trailer. "I'm going to do everything you tell me to this time," he said.

"Ha," she said.

She bent closer and peered at the cards. "Money and a jealous woman. You're not getting *married* again."

"No, no." He sighed and stroked his mustache. "Who would marry me? I'm growing old, Justine."

For a second she thought she had heard wrong.

"I'm fifty-two," he said. "Do your cards tell you that?"

It was the only fact he had ever handed her. For some reason it diminished him. Alonzo, possessing an *age?* When she first met him, then, he would have been thirty-five—a young, unsteady number of years for a man, but Alonzo had never been young or unsteady. She raised her eyes and found a sprinkling of white in his hair, and deep grooves extending the droop of his mustache. When he smiled at her, creases rayed out from the corners of his eyes. "Why, Alonzo," she said.

"Yes?"

"Why—"

But she couldn't think what she was trying to say. And Alonzo shot his cuffs impatiently and sat forward on his stool. "Well, never mind *that*," he said. "Get on with my problem."

"Tell me what it is."

"Shall I sell the business to Mrs. Harry Mosely?"

"Who's Mrs. Harry Mosely?"

"What does it matter? A rich lady in Parvis, divorced, wants some kind of business different from all her friends."

"The jealous woman."

"Not of me."

"*Envious* jealous."

"She wears jodhpurs," Alonzo said, and shook his head.

Justine waited.

"Well?" he said.

"Well, what?"

"Do I sell or do I not? I'm asking."

"But you haven't said what the choice is," Justine told him. "What are you selling it *for?* Are you joining another gold rush?"

"No, I thought just something quiet. I have a friend who's in merchandising, he would find me something or other."

"*Merchandising?*"

"What's wrong with that?"

"I'm going to have to study these cards a bit," Justine said, and she bent over them again and rested her forehead on her hand.

"This life is hard, Justine," Alonzo told her. "That tent out there cost five thousand dollars and has a life span of only six years. I pay very high taxes on this pasture but Maryland has gypsy laws so we *have* to live here, it's too expensive to camp around. And occasionally people fail to pay me or the weather keeps the customers away, and a ride rusts to bits at exactly the time I clear the mortgage on it. I have so many people to be responsible for. Also these kids all the time. Can't you understand?"

"Yes, yes."

"Then why are you studying the cards for so long?"

"Because I don't know what to say," she said, and she laid an index finger on the six of hearts and thought a moment. "I see the woman and the money, but everything else is indecisive. No sudden fortune and no disasters. A few petty reverses, a friendship breaking off, but otherwise just—weak."

"Weak?" said Alonzo.

She looked directly at him. "Alonzo," she said. "Don't sell your business."

She left it up to him to decide whether it was she or the cards who spoke.

In the late afternoon, when the sun grew warmer, they sat outside on a collapsed sofa and watched two of Alonzo's teenaged boys pitching a baseball back and forth in the long grass behind the trailers. A girl was hanging out diapers, and a man was rotating the tires on his Studebaker. In the field beyond the baseball players, Duncan and Lem were fiddling with a hunk of machinery. Really it was time they started back, but Duncan said this machine was something special. He wanted to invent a ride for it to run. And the sun was warming the top of Justine's head right through her hat, and the dexterous twist of the baseball glove as it rose to meet the ball and the slap of leather on leather lulled her into a trance.

"If I were president, I would not have a personal physician in the White House with me but you, Justine," said Alonzo. "You could read the cards for me every morning before the Cabinet meeting."

She smiled and let her head tip against the back of the sofa.

"Till then, you can join my carnival. *Why* do you always say no? Coralette, who works the concession stand, she just takes her husband and kids along. They stay in the trailer and read comic books."

"Duncan doesn't like comic books," Justine said.

Out in the field, Duncan raised a sprocket wheel in one gaunt, blackened hand and waved it at her.

"And Meg, she's all grown up? She doesn't come on visits with you now?"

"She doesn't come *anywhere* with us," Justine said sadly. "She studies a lot. She works very hard. She's very conscientious. Other girls wear blue jeans but Meg sews herself these shirtwaist dresses and polishes her shoes every Sunday night and washes her hair every Monday and Thursday. I don't think she approves of us. To tell the truth, Alonzo, I don't believe she thinks much of carnivals either or fortune telling or moving around the way we do. Not that she says so. She's very good about it, really, she's so quiet and she does whatever we tell her to. It kills me to see her bend her head the way she sometimes does."

"Girls are difficult," Alonzo said. "Fortunately I never had many of them."

"I think she's in love with a minister."

"With a what?"

"Well, an *assistant* minister, actually."

"But even so," said Alonzo.

"She went to his church in Semple. She's religious, too. Did I mention that? She went to his young people's group on Sunday evenings. Then they started going out together to lectures and debates and educational slide shows—oh, very proper, but she's only seventeen! And she brought him to our house so we could meet him. It was terrible. We all sat in the living room. Duncan says she has a right to choose whoever she wants but he doesn't think she *chose* this man, she just accepted him. Like a compromise. What else could it be, with a man so meek and puny? He's one of those people with white shiny skin and five o'clock shadow. Duncan says—"

"But after all," said Alonzo, "better that than a motordrome rider. My first wife's girl married a motordrome rider."

"I would prefer a motordrome rider any day," Justine said. Then she sighed. "Oh well, I suppose nobody likes who their children go out with."

"It's true."

"When *I* was courting, my father locked me in my room one time."

"Oh?" said Alonzo. He squinted, following the arc of the baseball floating across the sun.

"I fell in love with my first cousin."

"Oh-ho."

"On top of that, my *shiftless* first cousin. He drank and ran around. For years he had a girlfriend named Glorietta, who always wore red. My aunts and my mother would whisper whenever they mentioned her, even her name. Glorietta de Merino."

"Ah, Glorietta," said Alonzo, and settled back with his face tilted to the sky and his boots stretched out in front of him. "Go on."

"He made terrible grades all through school and dropped out the first year of college. Nobody could ever find him when they wanted him. While *I!* I was an only child. I tried to be as good as possible. Would you believe, until I was twenty years old I had never tasted liverwurst?"

"Liverwurst," said Alonzo, turning it over lazily.

"Because my family didn't happen to eat it. Not that there was anything wrong with it, of course, they just weren't in the habit of ordering it from the market. I didn't know there *was* such a thing as liverwurst! The first time I tasted it I ate a whole pound. But that was later. First I fell in love with my cousin, and went on trips with him and rode in his unsafe car and had to be locked in my room. *Then* I discovered liverwurst."

"But what became of him?" Alonzo asked.

"Who?"

"The first cousin."

"Oh," said Justine. "Why, I married him. Who did you think I was talking about?"

"Duncan?"

"Of *course* Duncan," said Justine, and she sat up again and shaded her eyes. "Cousin Duncan the Bad," she said, and laughed, and even Alonzo, drowsy and heavy in the sun, had to see how happy she looked when she located Duncan's spiky gold head glinting above the weeds.

$$4$$

Duncan and Justine Peck shared a great-grandfather named Justin Montague Peck, a sharp-eyed, humorless man who became very rich importing coffee, sugar, and guano during the last quarter of the nineteenth century. On any summer day in the 1870's, say, you could find him seated in the old Merchants' Exchange on Gay Street, smoking one of his long black cigars to ward off yellow fever, waiting for news of his ships to be relayed from the lookout tower on Federal Hill. Where he originally came from was uncertain, but the richer he grew the less it mattered. Although he was never welcomed into Baltimore society, which was narrow and ossified even then, he was treated with respect and men often asked his advice on financial issues. Once there was even a short street named after him, but it was changed later on to commemorate a politician.

When Justin Peck was fifty years old, he bought a sycamore-shaded lot in what was then the northern part of town. He built a gaunt house bristling with chimneys and lined with dark, oily wood. He filled it with golden oak furniture and Oriental screens, chandeliers dripping crystal, wine velvet loveseats with buttons and more buttons up and down their backs, heavy paintings leaning out from the walls, curlicued urns, doilies, statuary, bric-a-brac, great globular lamps centered on tasseled scarves, and Persian rugs laid catty-corner and overlapping. Then he married Sarah Cantleigh, the sixteen-year-old daughter of another importer. Nothing is known of their courtship, if there was one, but her wedding portrait still looms in a Baltimore dining room: a child-faced girl with a look of reluctance, of hanging back, which is accentuated by the dress style of the day with its backward-swept lines and the flounce at the rear of the skirt.

In 1880, only nine months after the wedding, Sarah Cantleigh died giving birth to Daniel. In 1881 Justin Peck remarried, this time into stronger stock—a German cutler's daughter named Laura Baum, who rescued Daniel from the old freedwoman who had been tending him. Laura Baum's portrait was never painted, but she lived long enough to be known personally even by Meg, her great-great-step-grandchild. She was a sallow, straight-backed woman who wore her hair in a knot. Although she was twenty when she married, observers said she looked more like forty. But then she looked forty when she died, too, at the age of ninety-seven. And it was clear that she made an excellent mother for little Daniel. She taught him to read and cipher when he was only three years old, and she made certain that his manners were impeccable. When Justin suggested that she stop taking Daniel with her on visits to her father she agreed instantly, even ceasing her own visits although Justin had not asked that of her in so many words. (Her father was very obviously a foreigner, an undignified little man given to practical jokes. His dusty jumbled shop by the harbor was a hangout for seamen and other rough types.) "Always remember, Daniel," she said, straightening his collar, "that you must live up to your family's name." She never explained what she meant by that. Her darkies broke into hissing laughter on the kitchen stairs and asked each other in whispers, "What family? What name? *Peck?*" but she never heard them.

In 1885, Laura had a son of her own. They called him Caleb. He was blond like his half brother, but his tilted brown eyes must have snuck in from the Baum side of the family, and he had his Grandpa Baum's delight in noise and crowds. Even as a baby, being wheeled along in his caramel-colored wicker carriage, he would go into fits of glee at the sight of passing strangers. He liked anything musical—church bells, hurdy-gurdies, the chants of the street vendors selling hot crabcakes. When he was a little older he took to the streets himself, riding an iron velocipede with a carpeted seat. He and Daniel were confined to the sidewalk in front of their house, but while Daniel obeyed instructions, leafing through *The Youth's Companion* on the front steps with his chick-yellow head bent low, Caleb would sooner or later be tugged southward by the fire bell or the gathering of a crowd or, of course, the sound of a street musician. He followed the blind harpist and the banjoist, the walking piano that cranked out Italian tunes and the lady who sang "The Pardon Came Too Late." Then someone would think to ask, "Where's Caleb?" His mother came out on the front steps, a fan of creases rising up between her eyebrows. "Daniel, have *you* seen Caleb?" And search parties would have to be sent down all the streets running toward the harbor. Only everybody soon learned: if you wanted to find Caleb, hold still a minute and listen. Whenever you heard distant music somewhere in the town, maybe so faint you thought you imagined it, so thin you blamed the whistling of the streetcar wires, then you could track the sound down and find Caleb straddling his little velocipede, speechless with joy, his appleseed eyes dancing. The maid would touch his sleeve, or Daniel would take his hand, or Laura would grab him by the earlobe, muttering, "*This* is where I find you! Out with a bunch of . . . well, I don't know what your father is going to say. I don't know what he's going to think of you for this."

Only she never told his father. Perhaps she thought that she would be held to blame. Sometimes, from the way she acted, you would think she was afraid of Justin.

On Sundays the Pecks went to church, of course, and on Wednesday evenings Laura had her Ladies' Circle. On holidays there were the formal visitors: Justin's business associates and their wives, along with their starched, ruffled children. But you couldn't say that the Pecks had *friends*, exactly. They kept to themselves. They were suspicious of outsiders. After guests left, the family often remarked on the gentlemen's inferior brand of cigars, the children's poor manners, the wives' regrettable overuse of Pompeiian Bloom rouge. Daniel listened, memorizing their words. Caleb hung out the window to hear an Irish tenor sing "Just a Lock of Hair for Mother."

Daniel was a tall, cool, reflective boy, and from the beginning he planned to study law. Therefore Caleb would take over the importing business. In preparation for this Caleb attended the Salter Academy, walking there daily with his friend Paul and a few of the neighborhood boys. He worked very conscientiously, although sometimes his mother suspected that his heart wasn't in it. Coming home from school he could be waylaid by any passing stranger, he fell willingly into conversation with all sorts of riffraff. He had no discrimination. And he still followed organ grinders. With his pocket money he bought tawdry musical instruments, everything from pennywhistles to a cheap violin sold him by a sailor; he could make music out of anything. He played these instruments not only in his room but outdoors as well, if he wasn't caught and stopped. More than once he was mistakenly showered with coins from someone's window. When Laura heard about it she would grow dark in the face and order him to remember his name. She shut him in the parlor, where he continued to spill out his reckless, made-up tunes on the massive piano draped in fringed silk. Unfortunately the Creole gardner, Lafleur Boudrault, had taught him ragtime. A disreputable, *colored* kind of music. Justin, home in his study doing the accounts, would raise his head to listen for a minute and frown, but then he shrugged it off.

In 1903, Caleb graduated from the Salter Academy. The day after his graduation Justin took him down to his office to show him around. By now, of course, the importing business was very different from what it had been in the '70's. The old full-rigged steamers, which looked like brigantines with smokestacks, had given way to modern ships, and their spectacular journeys to Brazil and Peru and the West Indies had been discontinued in favor of the more profitable coastwise hauls, carrying manufactured goods south and raw materials north. The Merchants' Exchange had been torn down; Caleb would be spending his days in an office above a warehouse, behind a roll-top desk, dealing with ledgers and receipts and bills of lading. Still, it was a fine opportunity for a young man with ambition, Caleb. Caleb?

Caleb turned from the single, sooty window, through which he had been gazing even though it was impossible to see the harbor from there. He said that he would prefer to be a musician.

At first Justin couldn't take it in. He was politely interested. Musician? Whatever for?

Then the situation hit him in the face and he gasped and caved in. He felt for the chair behind him and sat down, preparing bitter, harmful words that would convey all his horror and disgust and contempt. But music was so—no young man would ever seriously— music was for women! For parlors! He felt nauseated by the sight of this boy's intense brown eyes. He could hardly wait to chew him up and spit him out and stamp on what was left.

Instead, all that came from his mouth were strange vowel sounds over which he had no control.

He had to be carried away in his office chair by two men from the warehouse. They laid him in his buggy and folded both arms across his chest, as if he were already dead, and then Caleb drove him home. When Laura came to the door she found Caleb on the topmost step with his father curled in his arms like a baby. But Justin's eyes were two hard, glittering pebbles, and she could feel his rage. "What *happened?*" she asked, and Caleb told her, straight out, while struggling upstairs with his burden to Justin's high carved bed. Laura's face grew as dark as coffee but she said not a word. She had the kitchen maid fetch the doctor from down the street, and she listened stonily to the doctor's diagnosis: apoplexy, brought on by a shock of some sort. He did not hold out much hope for recovery. If Justin lived, he said, one side would likely be paralyzed, although it was too soon to say for certain.

Then Laura went downstairs to the parlor where Caleb stood waiting. "You have killed your half of your father," she said.

On Monday, Caleb started work behind the roll-top desk.

Daniel, meanwhile, had finished his courses at the University in record time and was now preparing himself further by working at the offices of Norris & Wiggen, a fine old respectable law firm. He lived at home and often relieved Laura at his father's sickbed, reading aloud to him from the newspaper or from Laura's enormous Bible. Justin would lie very still with one fist clenched, his flinty blue eyes glaring at the wall. He had not recovered the use of his left side. It was apparent suddenly that he was a very old man, with liver spots across his dry forehead and claws for hands. Half of his face seemed to be melting and running downward. He spoke only with difficulty, and when people misunderstood he would fly into a rage. Because he could not bear to have his weakness observed by the outside world (which would take advantage immediately, he was certain of it), he had determined to stay in his bedroom until he was fully recovered. For he assumed that he was suffering only a brief, treatable illness, his convalescence hampered by a worse-than-useless doctor and a half-wit wife. Therefore he undertook his own cure. He had all the panes in his windows replaced with amethyst glass, which was believed to promote healing. He drank his water from a quassia cup and ordered Laura to send away for various nostrums advertised in the newspaper—celery tonic, pectoral syrup, a revitalizing electric battery worn on a chain around the neck. His only meat was squirrel, easiest on the digestive tract. Yet still he remained flat on his back, whitening and shriveling like a beached fish.

On Friday nights Caleb came and summarized the week's business in a gentle, even voice, directing his statements to the foot of the bed. Justin looked at the wall, pretending not to hear. As a matter of fact it seemed that Caleb was handling everything quite adequately, but it was too late now. The time for that was past, there was no undoing what had been done. Justin went on looking at the wall until Caleb left.

Laura brought out an old busybody she had—a mirror arrangement placed to reflect passers-by on the street below. She thought he might like to keep in touch with things. But when Justin turned his face to the busybody he saw Caleb just descending the front steps, turned faded and remote and long-ago by the blue glass of the windowpanes. He told Laura to take her nonsense elsewhere.

In February, 1904, the Great Fire burned out the heart of Baltimore, sweeping away every tall building in the city and most major businesses, including Justin Peck's. When it was over Justin insisted upon being taken to see the damage for himself. His sons carried him to the buggy and drove him downtown, through the peculiar yellowish light that hung over everything. It was the first trip Justin had made since his illness. From the satisfied look he gave to the rubble and the littered streets and the jagged remains of walls, it seemed that he credited the destruction not to fire but to his own absence. Without him Baltimore had gone up in smoke. Under Caleb's care the warehouse had caved in, the office had disappeared, the roll-top desk had dissolved into ashes. He turned to Daniel with a crooked, bitter smile and waved his good hand to be taken home again.

Now he developed a new obsession: he wanted to leave this combustible city entirely and build further north, way out on Falls Road. He dreamed his room was alight with flames and not a member of his family would come to rescue him. He called in the night for Laura, whose bed he had left some fifteen years ago following her third miscarriage, and he made her sleep by his side with her hand on a brass bell from India. He jarred her awake periodically and sent her out to the hall to sniff for fire. And Caleb, who was working around the clock to rebuild the warehouse, had to come to his father's room every evening and listen to interminable garbled, stammered instructions for the buying of land in Roland Park. Nowadays Caleb always smelled of smoke from the city and he moved in a deep, tired daze. He would rest his cheek against the doorframe and slump until his sooty white shirt appeared to have nothing inside it, while his father wove his tangled mat of words: builders, masons, two fire, two fireproof houses.

Two?

Well, Justin figured Daniel would be marrying Margaret Rose Bell.

Now Margaret Rose Bell was a Washington girl who had come to spend the winter with her cousins, the Edmund Bells. And although it was true that she and Daniel were often seen together, the fact was that she was not yet eighteen years old, and Daniel was still working at Norris & Wiggen. Customarily a man would wait till he was able to buy and furnish a house by himself before he would take a wife.

Yes, but Justin planned to have a great many descendants and he was anxious to get them started.

Land was purchased in Roland Park. Master builders were hired to supervise the construction of two large houses set side by side, with almost no space between them, although great stretches of land lay all about. And meanwhile Margaret Rose was fitted for a complicated ivory satin wedding dress with one hundred and eight pearl buttons running down the back. They were married in the summer. Because the houses were not yet finished Margaret moved into Daniel's boyhood room, where his wooden-wheeled roller skates sat next to his shelf of lawbooks. She was a small, vivid girl who generally wore dresses of soft material like flower petals, and at any moment of the day she could be seen running up and down the stairs, or flinging open windows to watch some excitement in the streets, or darting into Justin's room to see if he needed anything. At the sight of her Justin would begin blinking and nodding in his doddering old man's way, and he would go on nodding and nodding and nodding long after she had kissed the top of his head and left again. Oh, he hadn't been mistaken, Margaret Rose was what this house had needed. And she would be certain to provide descendants. Why, by the fall of 1905, when Justin Peck's golden oak and wine-colored household set off on a caravan of wagons to Roland Park, Margaret Rose was already holding a baby in her lap and expecting another. Things were working out just fine. Everything was going according to plan.

By 1908 they had bought a snorting black Model T Ford with a left-hand steering wheel and splashless flower vases. Each morning the two brothers rode off to work in it—handsome young men in hats and high white collars. Daniel had his own law office now, a walnut-paneled suite of rooms with an oil portrait of his father over the mantel. He was taking on no partners because, he said, he wanted to have his sons for partners, not just anyone. And Caleb had rebuilt his father's warehouse, bigger and better than before. He had a brand new rolltop desk with twice as many cubbyholes.

Whenever Caleb chose to marry, another house would be built beside the first two, but meanwhile he lived at home with his parents. He was a quiet man who became quieter every year. It was a known fact that he drank sometimes, but he never troubled anyone and he never became rowdy or noisy. In fact Margaret Rose said she wished he *would* get noisy, once in a while. She was fond of Caleb. Between them they had a few old jokes, which would cause Margaret to laugh in her low, chuckly way until Caleb, in spite of himself, would let his own mouth turn up shyly at the corners. He would come talk to her in her shady back yard, waiting patiently through all her children's interruptions and requests and minor accidents. And several times she gave evening parties expressly to introduce Caleb to one or another of her pretty cousins. Girls always liked Caleb. But though he might dance with them or take them for a drive, he didn't seem interested in marriage. More often now he stayed home in his room, or he toured the taverns, or he went someplace else, no one knew where. Really, not even Margaret Rose could say for sure what Caleb did with himself.

For Christmas one year, Margaret persuaded Daniel to buy Caleb a Graphophone. She thought it would be the perfect gift for someone so musical. Along with it came disc recordings of Caruso, Arturo Toscanini, and Jan Kubelik on the violin. But these discs affected Caleb the way formal concerts did; he became restless and absent-minded and unhappy. He started pacing across the carpet and up and down the hall and eventually straight through the front door and out of sight, and was not seen again for the remainder of the day. So the Graphophone was never taken up to his bedroom, as Margaret had intended, but drifted into Justin's room instead, where it amused the old man for hours on end. He seemed particularly fond of Caruso. He would order Margaret to stand beside his bed cranking the machine and changing the heavy black discs. Margaret was surprised. If this was the way he felt, why had he forbidden Caleb's music in the house?

For Caleb continued to spend all his money on musical instruments—wooden flutes and harmonicas and cellos and even stringed gourds that only colored people would think of playing. He kept them in his room, but he was not allowed to sound a note on them where Justin could hear. In fact, even the piano was forbidden now, and had been exiled to Daniel's house, where Margaret Rose could tinkle out Czerny without disturbing her father-in-law. If Caleb wanted to make music he had to go far away, usually to the old Samson stable on the other side of a field. He would sit in the loft door blowing whistles or sawing out stringy little street tunes, and only wisps of his music drifted up to the house, never as far as Justin's densely curtained sickroom. Yet Justin always seemed to know when Caleb had been playing, and he would turn his face away irritably when Caleb stopped by later to offer his meticulous, patient account of the previous week's business.

Meanwhile Daniel's house was filling up with children, and his practice was swelling, and he already had it in the back of his mind to become a judge someday while his sons carried on with the law firm. When he came home evenings, and Margaret ran up in her rustling, flowery dress to fling her arms around him, he would be remote and sometimes annoyed. His head was still crowded with torts and claims and statutes. He would set her gently aside and continue toward his study at the rear of the house. So for someone to talk to, Margaret tried giving afternoon tea parties. She invited her cousins and her girlfriends, who came tumbling in crying, "Maggie! Maggie Rose!" and kissing both her cheeks in the new way they had learned from Aunt Alice Bell, who had recently been to Paris. But Daniel said that he was not partial to these affairs. Oh, in the evening maybe, clients or business friends occasionally . . . he didn't want to be unreasonable, he said, but actually he expected his home to be a refuge from the outside world. And nowadays when he came in from a hard day's work he would be sure to find some unknown lady sitting on his leather chair, or a spectacular feather hat on the dining room buffet beneath Sarah Cantleigh's portrait, and once even the brass paperweight moved to the other side of his blotter, when everyone knew that his desk was forbidden territory. Besides, didn't she think she would be better off devoting those hours to her children?

They had six children. In 1905 Justin II was born, in 1906 Sarah, in 1907 Daniel Jr., in 1908 Marcus, in 1909 Laura May, in 1910 Caroline.

In 1911, Margaret Rose left home.

She had wanted to take the children to Washington on the train for her mother's birthday. Daniel didn't think she ought to. After all, she was a Peck now. What did she want with the Bells? Who at any rate were an undisciplined, frivolous, giggling lot. She said she would go anyway. Daniel pointed out that she was her own mistress, certainly, as everyone in his family had noticed more than once, but the children were *his*. And sure enough, there sat Daniel's children in a little bundle staring up at her, all Peck, blue Peck eyes and hair that matched their skin, solemn measuring Peck expressions, not a trace of Margaret Rose. She could go, Daniel said, but she couldn't take the children. And he expected her back on Saturday evening, as there was church to attend Sunday morning.

She went.

Saturday evening Caleb met the train but Margaret was not on it. When Daniel found out he merely pressed his lips together and walked away. Later he was heard telling his mother's servant Sulie to put the children to bed. Apparently no inquiries were going to be made.

On Wednesday Daniel received a letter from Margaret's father. He wrote in brown ink. Everyone knew that ink, because when Margaret's father wrote she would race through the house reading passages to different people and laughing at the funny parts. But Daniel read this letter in silence, and then went up to his room. When he came down again nothing at all was said about it.

In a month the children stopped asking for their mother. The baby stopped crying and the older ones went back to their games and nursery rhymes. Only Caleb seemed to remember Margaret Rose. He went up to Daniel one day and asked him point blank why he didn't go after her. Or Caleb himself would, though Daniel would be better. Daniel looked straight through him. Then Caleb went to Justin, who certainly loved Margaret Rose too and used to wait every day for the fluttering of her petal skirts against the banister. Now Justin merely closed his eyes and pretended not to hear. "But why?" Caleb asked him. "Don't you care? Life is not the same here when Maggie Rose is gone."

In all the accounts of the family history, told by all the aunts and uncles and upstairs maids, that was the only direct quotation of Caleb's that was ever handed down. Two generations later it was to ring in Justine's ears like poetry, taking on more depth and meaning than

Caleb had probably intended. But Justin was not moved at all, and he kept his eyes shut very tightly and waited for his son to leave.

Now Laura ran both households, upright and energetic as ever in her ugly brown dresses with her hair screwed back so tightly it stretched her eyes. To the Peck children she was the center of the universe, sometimes the only family member they saw for days. Justin was too old and sick to be bothered, and Daniel hardly ever came home before their bedtime. As for Caleb, he kept to himself. They might catch sight of him striking out across the field toward the Samson stable, the sunlight pale on his Panama hat; or leaving for work in the morning, already tired and beaten-looking; or returning late in the evening with his manner of walking curiously careful. He never played with them. Sometimes on those extra-careful evenings he even got their names confused. He did nothing to earn their attention. So they failed to notice how he appeared to be dimming and wearing through, almost transparent; and how his only friends now were the questionable types in taverns, and how the music from the stable had thinned and shredded until you almost couldn't hear it. Laura noticed. But what could it mean? She pondered over his long, unbreakable silences, the likes of which she had not seen before and would not again until the days of Caleb's great-nephew Duncan, as yet unborn and unthought of. She tried to shame him into more normal behavior. "Where is your common *courtesy?* At least think of the family." But he would only wander off, not hearing, and sometimes he would not reappear for days.

On a Saturday afternoon in the spring of 1912, Daniel was standing at the bay window watching Justin Two ride his bicycle. It was a heavy black iron one, hard for Two to manage, but he had just got the hang of it and he teetered proudly down the driveway. From out of nowhere, Daniel saw a small, clear picture of Caleb on his velocipede merrily pedaling after a flutist on a sidewalk in old Baltimore. The memory was so distinct that he left his house and crossed the yard to his mother's and climbed the stairway to Caleb's room. But Caleb was not there. Nor was he in the kitchen, where he most often ate his meals; nor anywhere else in the house, nor outdoors nor in the stable. And the Ford was parked in the side yard; he wouldn't be downtown. Daniel felt uneasy. He asked the others—the children and Laura. They didn't know. In fact, the last time anyone could remember for sure he had been walking off down the driveway three days earlier, carrying his fiddle. The children saw him go. "Goodbye now," he called to them.

"Goodbye, Uncle Caleb."

But of course that didn't mean a thing, he would surely have . . . Daniel went to Justin's room. "I can't find Caleb," he said. Justin turned his face away. "Father? I can't—"

A long, glittering tear slid down Justin's stony cheek.

Really, the old man was beginning to let his mind go.

Years later, whenever he was fixing some family event in its proper time slot, Daniel Peck would pause and consider the importance of 1912. Could there be such a thing as an unlucky number? (Justine would look up briefly, but say nothing.) For in 1912 it seemed that the Peck family suddenly cracked and flew apart like an old china teacup. First there was Caleb's disappearance, without a trace except for a bedroom full of hollow, ringing musical instruments and a roll-top desk with an empty whisky bottle in the bottom drawer. So then they had to sell the business, Justin's last link with the outside world. And after that Justin started dying, leaving his family in the same gradual, fading way that Caleb had until it was almost no shock at all to find him lifeless in his bed one morning with his bluish nose pointing heavenward.

In the winter of 1912 there was another envelope from Washington addressed in brown ink. After Daniel read it, he told his children that Margaret Rose had been killed in a fire. They were to pray for her to be forgiven. Now her children wore brown to school and could properly be called poor motherless orphans, although they continued to look surprised whenever some well-meaning lady told them so. They were calm, docile children, a little lacking in imagination but they did well in their lessons. They did not seem to have suffered from all that had happened. Nor did Laura, who continued as spry and capable as ever. Nor Daniel, of course—a man of even temper. Although sometimes, late at night, he would take the Ford and drive aimlessly over the moonlit roads, often ending up in the old section of the city where he had no business any more, and knew no one, and heard nothing but the faint, musical whistling of the streetcar wires in the dark sky overhead.

5
—

Justine's childhood was dark and velvety and it smelled of dust. There were bearded men under all the furniture, particularly her bed. When her door was shut at night blue worms squiggled through the blackness, but when it was open the knob stuck out exactly like a shotgun barrel sidling through to aim at her head, and she would have to lie motionless for hours pretending to be a wrinkle in the blankets.

In the mornings her father was away, either at the office or out of town, and her mother was in bed with a sick headache, and Justine sat in the living room with the curtains shut so that even to herself she was only a pale glimmer. She was waiting for the maid. First there was the scrabbling of the key in the apartment door and then light, air, motion, the rustle of Claudia's shopping bag and her thin cross mosquito voice. "Now what you doing sitting there? What you up to? What you doing sitting in that chair?" She would yank the curtains open and there was the city of Philadelphia, a wide expanse of blackened brick apartment houses and dying trees in cages and distant factory smokestacks. Then she would dress Justine in a little smocked dress and braid the two skinny braids that she called plaits. "Don't you *go* getting that dress dirty. Don't you *go* messing yourself up, I'll tell Miss Caroline on you." By that time maybe her mother's headache would be lifting, at least enough so that her parched voice could trail out from the bedroom. "Justine? Aren't you even going to say good morning?" Although not an hour ago she had buried her face in the pillow and waved Justine away with one shaky, pearl-studded hand.

Justine's mother wore fluffy nightgowns with eyelet ruffles at the neck. Her hair was the color of Justine's but tightly curled. She was the youngest of Daniel Peck's six children, the baby. Even total strangers could guess that, somehow, from her small, pursed mouth and her habit of ducking her chin when talking to people. Unfortunately she tended to put on weight when unhappy, and she had become a plump, powdery, pouchy woman with her rings permanently embedded in her fingers. Her unhappiness was due to being exiled in Philadelphia. She had never guessed, when agreeing to marry Sam Mayhew, that the Depression would close down the Baltimore branch of his company just six months after the wedding. If she had had any inkling, she said—but she didn't finish the sentence. She just reached for another chocolate, or a petit-four, or one of the pink-frosted cupcakes she grew more and more to resemble.

But Justine loved her mother's soft skin and her puffy bosom and the dimples on the backs of her hands. She like to huddle beneath the drooping velvet canopy of the bed, which was her mother's real home, surrounded by a circle of chocolate boxes, empty teacups, ladies' magazines, and cream-colored letters from Baltimore. Of course there were days when her mother was up and about, but Justine pictured her only in the dim rosy glow of the bedside lamp. She dwelt on the suspense of entering that room: was she welcome this time, or wasn't she? Some days her mother said, "Oh Justine, can't you let me be?" or wept into her pillow and wouldn't speak at all; but other days she called, "Is that my Justine? Is that my fairy angel? Don't you have one tiny kiss for your poor mama?" And she would sit up and scoop Justine into a spongy, perfumed embrace, depriving her of breathing room for a moment, not that it mattered. Then she flung back the ruffled pink sleeves of her bedjacket and taught Justine the games she had played when *she* was a child—cat's cradle and Miss Fancy's Come to Town and the doodle story, where you drew a map that turned out to be a goose. Or she would have Justine fetch scissors and she would cut, from the Baltimore newspapers, folded stars and paper dolls with pigtails and standing angels made from a circle cleverly slashed here and there as only she knew how. She would tell true stories, better than anything in books: How Uncle Two Scared the Hobo Away, How Grandfather Peck Fooled the Burglar, How the Mayhews' Ugly Dog Buttons Ate My Wedding Dress. She told how Justine was born in Baltimore thanks to split-second timing and not in Philadelphia as everyone had feared. "Well, luckily I had my way," she said. "You know how your daddy is. He didn't understand at all. When you started coming two months early I said, 'Sam, put me on that train,' but he wouldn't do it. I said, 'Sam, what will Father say, he's made all the arrangements at Johns Hopkins!' 'I just hope he didn't lay down a deposit,' your daddy said. So I picked up my suitcase that I had all ready and waiting and I said, 'Listen here, Sam Mayhew . . .' "

At six in the evening Claudia would leave, slamming the door behind her, and Justine's mother would look at the clock and her fingers would fly to her mouth. "How in the world did the time pass?" she would ask, and she would slide to the edge of the bed and feel for her pink satin slippers. "We can't let your daddy catch us lazing about like this." She would put on a navy blue dress with shoulder pads, and cover her rosebud mouth with dark lipstick, turning instantly from pink-and-gold to a heavy, crisply defined stranger like the ones hurrying down the sidewalk five stories below. "Of course my headache hasn't improved one bit," she would say. "I'd go back to bed but your daddy would never understand. He doesn't believe in headaches. He *certainly* doesn't believe in going to bed for them. It just is not his custom, I suppose."

To hear her talk, you would think Sam Mayhew was as different and exotic as an Asian prince, but he was only a small pudgy man with a Baltimore accent.

Then there were days in a row when Justine was not allowed in her mother's room at all, when she would puzzle and puzzle over what magic password had given her entry before. No one could go in but Claudia, carrying the latest string-tied box from the Parisian Pastry Co. Justine was marooned on a scratchy brocade chair in the living room and the bearded men beneath it were only waiting for her to lower one foot so that they could snatch her by the ankle and drag her down. Even Sam Mayhew's homecoming could not rouse his wife from bed. "Oh, go away, Sam, let me be, can't you see a crack is running down in front of my ears?" Sam and Justine ate supper alone, on the gold-rimmed plates that Claudia had laid out in the dining room. "Well, now, Justine, what have you been doing with yourself?" Sam would ask. "Did Claudia take you to the playground? Did you have a nice time on the swings?"

But he would quickly flounder and drown in her blank, astonished stare.

Day after day Justine on her brocade island looked at her mother's old *Books of Knowledge*—tattered maroon volumes with brittle pages, the only things she could reach without setting a foot to the floor. She lost herself in a picture of a train heading through outer space. It had been explained to her that this picture demonstrated the impossibility of man's ever reaching the moon. See how long it would take to cover the distance, even by rail? But to Justine it appeared all too easy, and she felt herself lightening and dwindling and growing dizzy whenever she saw that tiny lone train curving through the endless blackness.

Finally a time would come when she could raise her eyes from a page and find the air parting expectantly to make way for some change; she could always tell when change was coming. And not long afterward the telephone would ring, and Claudia would carry it from the foyer to the bedroom and rouse Justine's mother to shout long distance to Baltimore. "Hello? Oh, Father! Why are you—did Sam tell you to call me? What? Oh, not too well, I'm afraid. I said, not too *well*. Everything just seems to be going wrong, I can't quite . . ."

Justine would listen carefully, trying to discover exactly what had caused her world to collapse. She heard that her mother's nerves were acting up, her headaches were ferocious and no doctor could do a thing, the chandelier had fallen smack out of the ceiling, the landlord was impossible, Claudia showed no respect, there had been a very depressing story in the paper Sunday, Justine was turning sulky, Sam was out of town too much, and really it was entirely the fault of the City of Philadelphia. If he had any feeling, if he cared even a little, she knew it was asking a lot but she wished he would come and straighten things out.

He always came. She was his youngest daughter after all and very far from home, the only one of his children to leave the safety of Roland Park. Which was not to say that he approved of her. Oh, no. As soon as he stepped in the door, late that very night, he was curling his mouth downwards at the welter of pastry boxes and her crumb-littered, used-looking bed, and he was telling her outright that she had grown too fat.

"Yes, Father," Caroline said meekly, and she sat a little straighter and sucked in her stomach.

The next morning, when Justine got up unusually late after an unusually calm, dreamless sleep, she would find the apartment bright with sun and all the curtains open. Claudia was wearing a crisp white scarf and briskly attacking the dust in the cushions. Her mother sat in the dining room fully dressed, eating fresh grapefruit. And in the foyer her grandfather stood at the telephone announcing that he, Judge Peck, would personally drag the landlord through the entire United States judiciary system if that chandelier were not replaced by twelve noon sharp. Then he hung up and cupped Justine's head with his right hand, which was his way of greeting her. He was a bony man in a three-piece pinstriped suit, with fading hair like aged gardenia petals and a gold wafer of a watch that he let her wind. He had brought her a sack of horehound drops. He always did. Justine was certain that no matter what, even if he had rushed here through fires and floods and train wrecks, he would not forget to stop at Lexington Market first for a sack of horehound drops and he would not fail to cup her head in that considering way of his when he had arrived.

Generally during those visits Sam Mayhew would vanish, or if he did come home he wore a gentle, foolish smile and tried to keep out of the way. At any rate, the grandfather was never there for very long. He was a busy man. He came up over the weekend usually, just long enough to get his daughter to her feet again, and he left Sunday evening. Only once did he come on a working day. That was for Justine. She was supposed to be starting kindergarten, the first time she would ever be away from home alone. She refused to go. She wouldn't even get dressed. She became very white and sharp-faced and her mother gave in, sensing that there was no use arguing with her. The next morning when Justine awoke her grandfather Peck was standing by her bed carrying her plaid dress, her ruffled underpants with "Tuesday" embroidered on them and her lace-edged socks. He dressed her very slowly and carefully. Justine would have refused even her grandfather but his hands were so thick and clumsy, untying the bow of her nightgown, and when he stooped to pick up her shoes she could see the pink scalp through his thin pale hair. He even did her braids, though not very well. He even sat across from her and waited with perfect patience while she dawdled over breakfast. Then he helped her with her coat and they left, passing her mother, who wrung her hands in the doorway. They went down streets that were bitterly familiar, where she had shopped with her mother in the dear, safe days before school was ever thought of. At a square brick building her grandfather stopped. He pointed out where Claudia would meet her in the afternoon. He cupped her head briefly and then, after some fumbling and rustling, pushed a sack of horehound drops at her and gave her a little nudge in the direction of the brick building. When she had climbed the steps she looked back and found him still waiting there, squinting against the sunlight. Forever after that, the dark, homely, virtuous taste of horehound drops reminded her of the love and sorrow that ached in the back of her throat on that first day in the outside world.

In summer the leather suitcases would come up in the elevator to be packed, and Justine and her parents would board the evening train to Baltimore. Their arrival was never clear to Justine. She was half asleep, carried off the train and laid in the arms of some white-suited uncle. But when she awoke the next day there she was in Roland Park, all rustling with trees and twittering with birds, in her great-grandmother's white brick house, and if she went to the window she knew that all the houses within her view belonged to Pecks and so did the fleet of shiny black V-8 Fords lining one side of the street, and all the little blond heads dotting the lawn were Peck cousins waiting for her to come out and play.

Her mother would be talking in the dining room, but such a different mother—twinkling and dimpling and telling terrible giggling stories about Philadelphia. Aunts would be grouped around her, drinking their fifth and sixth cups of coffee. Aunt Sarah and Aunt Laura May were spinsters and still lived next door in the grandfather's house along with the bachelor Uncle Dan. Uncle Two's wife Lucy and Uncle Mark's wife Bea were Pecks by marriage only, and lived in the other two houses. They were not as important as the true Peck aunts, but then they *were* the mothers of the cousins. And of course, presiding over everyone was the great-grandma, a tidy, brownish woman. The white rims showing beneath her irises gave her a look of reproach, but as soon as she saw Justine she smiled and the rims disappeared. She offered Justine an enormous Baltimore breakfast—two kinds of meat, three kinds of pastry, and a platter of scrambled eggs—but Justine wasn't hungry. "Naturally," her mother said, laughing her summer laugh, "she's anxious to see her cousins," and she tied Justine's sash and gave her a pat and sent her off.

Justine had six cousins. All of them looked like her and talked like her, all of them knew the story of how Grandfather Peck had fooled the burglar. It was very different from Philadelphia, where her mother, coming to the school play, referred to "that *dark* little boy" and asked, "Who was the child who spoke with such a nasal twang?" With her cousins, there was no need to worry. Baltimore was the only place on earth where Justine would not be going over to the enemy if she agreed to play Prisoner's Base.

Yet even here, wasn't she an outsider of sorts? Her last name was Mayhew. She lived in Philadelphia. She did not always understand her cousins' jokes. And though they drew her into every game, she had the feeling that they were trying to slow down for her in some way. She envied them their quick, bubbling laughter and their golden tans. Occasionally, for one split second, she allowed herself to imagine her parents painlessly dead and some uncle or other adopting her, changing her name to Peck and taking her to live forever in Roland Park with its deep curly shadows and its pools of sunlight.

At such times Aunt Bea, coming out to the front porch to shade her eyes and check the children, would smile and sigh over poor little plain Justine, whose pointed face was wisped with anxiety so that it looked like crazed china or something cobwebbed or netted. And who ran so artifically, so hopefully, at the edge of the other children's games, kicking her heels up too high behind her.

In the evening they all went home. The four houses gave the illusion of belonging to four separate families. But after supper they came out again and sat on Great-Grandma's lawn, the men in their shirtsleeves and the women in fresh print dresses. The children grew overexcited rolling down the slope together. They quarreled and were threatened with an early bedtime, and finally they had to come sit with the grownups until they had calmed down. Sweaty and panting, choking back giggles, itchy from the grass blades that stuck to their skin, they dropped to the ground beside their parents and looked up at the stars while low measured voices murmured all around them. The oldest cousin, Uncle Mark's daughter Esther, held her little brother Richard on her lap and tickled him secretly with a dandelion clock. Nearby, Esther's twin sisters, Alice and Sally, were curled together like puppies with Justine in the middle because she was new and special. And Uncle Two's boys, Claude and Duncan, wrestled without a sound and without a perceptible movement so they wouldn't be caught and sent to bed. Not that the grownups really cared. They were piecing together some memory now, each contributing his own little patch and then sitting back to see how it would turn out. Long after the children had grown calm and loose and dropped off to sleep, one by one, the grownups were still weaving family history in the darkness.

In the winter of 1942, when Justine was nine, her father left for the war. The apartment was dismantled, a moving van came, and Justine and her mother took the train to Baltimore. Her mother cried all the way down. When they arrived she spilled out of the train and into her sisters' arms, still weeping, with her curls plastered to her face and her nose as pink as a rabbit's. Her sisters looked flustered and kept searching their purses for fresh hankies. The situation was new to them; no Peck had ever gone to war. It was believed that old Justin had mysteriously avoided the Civil War altogether, while every member of the family after him had possessed a heart murmur of such obviousness that they had been excused from even the mildest sports, the women cautioned against childbirth and the men saved from combat and long marches and the violence of travel by the unique, hollow stutter in their chests. Which did not prevent them from standing in a semicircle, bright-eyed and healthy and embarrassed, around their baby sister in the railroad station. It was their father who finally took charge. "Come, come," he said, and he herded them out of the station and into the line of Fords at the curb. Justine and her mother rode in his car, at the head of the procession. Justine's mother kept sniffing. Nothing irritated Grandfather Peck more than the sound of someone sniffing. "Look here, Caroline. We people don't *cry*. Get a hold of yourself," he said.

"I can't help it, Father. I just can't help it. I keep thinking of ways I could have been nicer to him. I mean I was never exactly—and I'm just certain he's going to be killed."

"He won't be killed," said Justine.

But nobody was listening.

They settled in Great-Grandma's house, since it had the most room. Justine was entered in the girls' school that Esther and the twins attended. Bit by bit she forgot almost completely the dark, bearded world of Philadelphia, and her mother grew carefree and girlish. Her mother seldom mentioned Sam Mayhew any more but she wrote him dutifully once a week, saying everyone was fine and sent him best regards. Only Justine, looking up sometimes from *The Five Little Peppers* or a game of backgammon, had a sudden picture of Sam Mayhew's sad, kind face and wondered if she had not missed out on something, choosing to be her mother's child alone.

Yet there were her cousins, always embarked on some new project. Esther wrote plays and her twin sisters shared a single role, speaking in unison. Justine played the princess in Aunt Laura May's blood-red lipstick. Little Richard would take any part you gave him, he was so happy to be included. And Uncle Two's son Claude was fat and studious; he was fine for rainy days, when he told horror stories in a hair-raising whisper in the gloom of the pantry stairwell.

But Duncan Peck was an evil, evil boy, and all his cousins worshipped him.

Duncan was prankish and reckless and wild. He had a habit of disappearing. (Long after she was grown, Justine could still close her eyes and hear his mother calling him—a soft-voiced lady from southern Virginia but my, couldn't she sing out when she had to! "Dun-KUNN? Dun-KUNN?" floated across the twilit lawn, with no more response than a mysterious rustle far away or a gleam of yellow behind the trees, rapidly departing.) While the rest of the cousins seemed content to have only one another for friends, Duncan was always dragging in strangers and the wrong kind of strangers at that, ten-year-old boys with tobacco breath and BB guns and very poor grammar. His cousins took piano lessons and hammered out "Country Gardens" faithfully for one half hour a day, but all Duncan would play was a dented Hohner harmonica—"Chattanooga Choo Choo" complete with whistles and a chucka-chucka and a country-sounding twang that delighted the children and made the grownups flinch. His great-grandma complained that he was impudent and dishonest. It was perfectly obvious that he was lying to any adult who asked him a question, and his lies were extreme, an insult to the intelligence. Also he was accident-prone. To his cousins that was the best part of all. How did he find so many accidents to get into? And such gory ones! He never just broke a bone, no, he had to have the bone sticking *out*, and all his cousins crowding around making sick noises and asking if they could touch it. He was always having a finger dangle by one thread, a concussion that allowed him to talk strangely and draw absolutely perfect freehand circles for one entire day, a purple eye or an artery opened or a tooth knocked horizontal and turning black. And on top of all that, he was never at a loss for something to do. You would never see *him* lolling about the house asking his mother for ideas; he had his own ideas, none of which she approved of. His mind was a flash of light. He knew how to make the electric fan drive Richard's little tin car, he could build traps for animals of all kinds including humans, he had invented a dive-proof kite and a written code that looked like nothing but slants and uprights. Tangled designs for every kind of machine littered his bedroom floor, and he had all those cousins just doting on him and anxious to do the manual labor required. If he had been a cruel boy, or a bully, they never would have felt that way, but he wasn't. At least not to them. It was the grownups he was cruel to.

Justine once saw him hanging from a tree limb, upside down, when the family was out on a picnic. He was safe but Aunt Lucy fretted anyway. "Dun-KUNN? I want you down from there!" she called. All Duncan did was unwrap one leg from the limb. Now he hung precariously, at an impossible angle, with his arms folded. Aunt Lucy rose and began running in ridiculous circles just beneath him, holding out her hands. Duncan grabbed the limb again—was he going to give in? What a disappointment!—but no, he was only readjusting himself so that now he could hang by his feet. All that supported him were his insteps, and it was not the kind of limb you could do that from. He folded his arms again and looked at his mother with a cool, taunting, upside-down stare that gave Justine a sudden chill. Yet wasn't Aunt Lucy laughable—flitting here and there crying, "Oh! Oh!" in a rusty scream. All the cousins had to giggle. Their grandfather set down his deviled egg and rose. "Duncan Peck!" he shouted. "Come down here this *instant!*"

Duncan came down on the top of his head and had to go to the emergency room.

Aunt Lucy, knitting soldiers' socks with her sisters-in-law, wondered and wondered what had made her son turn out this way. She considered all his flaws of character, his disgraceful report cards and the teachers' complaints. (He couldn't spell worth beans, they said, and had never learned that neatness counted. As for his papers, while there was no denying that they were ah, imaginative, at least what parts were readable, his hasty scrawl and his lack of organization and his wild swooping digressions left serious doubts as to his mental stability.) Now, where did all that come from? She reflected on her pregnancy: during her afternoon naps, she and the unborn Duncan had had, why, *battles!* for a comfortable position. Whenever she lay on her back, so the baby rested on the knobs of her spine, he would kick and protest until she gave in and shifted to her side. Of course she had only Claude to compare him with, but she had wondered even at the time: wouldn't the average baby merely have moved to a more comfortable position and let her rest?

The sisters sighed and shook their heads. The cousins, who had been eavesdropping in a row beneath the window, were very interested in pregnancy, but Duncan had a plan to weld all their bicycles together in a gigantic tandem and they couldn't stay to hear more.

When Sam Mayhew returned, his manufacturing company had reopened its Baltimore offices. There was no need to move back to Philadelphia. There was no need even to buy a place of their own, as his wife pointed out. Why bother, when Great-Grandma had three full stories in which she rattled around with no one but old Sulie the maid for company? So they stayed on in the white brick house in Roland Park, and Sam Mayhew rode downtown every day in a V-8 Ford behind his brothers-in-law. The Ford was a homecoming gift from the grandfather, who always had owned Fords and always would. To tell the truth, Sam Mayhew would have preferred a DeSoto. And he would have liked to buy a house in Guilford, which was where his parents lived. Somehow he never got to see his parents any more. But he was not a stubborn man and in the end he agreed to everything, only fading more and more into the background and working longer and longer hours. Once he took a three-day business trip and when he came home, only Sulie noticed he had been away. And *that* was because she had to count out the place settings for dinner every night.

His daughter, Justine, who had been undersized and pathetic when he left, was now a tall narrow beige girl. She had changed into one of those damned Pecks, clannish and secretive with a veiled look in her eyes, some sort of private amusement showing when she watched an outsider. And Sam was an outsider. Not that she was *rude* to him. All the Peck girls had excellent manners. But he knew that he had lost her, all right.

"What do those damned kids do all day? Don't they have any outside friends?" he asked his wife.

"Oh, they're all right. *We* were that way," she said serenely.

And she smiled out across the lawn at her brittle spinster sisters and her stuffy brothers who were all dressed alike, all lawyers as their father had wished them to be, and at the two wives who might have been chosen merely for their ability to be assimilated. Who *were* chosen for that. He looked down suddenly at his own colorless suit, so baggy that it seemed to be uninhabited. Then he sighed and walked away. Nobody noticed him leaving.

None of the girl cousins dated much in high school. At the mixers that were held with the boys' school up the road they were thought to be standoffish. Especially Justine, whose tense, pinched face stopped most of the boys from asking her to dance. Sometimes Sally, the prettier of the twins, might circle the floor with someone, but she tipped her pelvis away stiffly and seemed relieved when the music was over. As for the boy cousins, only Duncan had a steady girlfriend.

Duncan's girlfriend was a dimestore clerk named Glorietta de Merino. In an age when nice girls wore short skirts, Glorietta's swirled just above her ankles. She had a tumbling waterfall of black hair and a beautiful vivid face. There appeared to be sugar crystals on her eyelashes. Her waist was tiny and her breasts precisely cone-shaped, like the radio speakers Duncan was constructing in his basement. Anyone who talked to her appeared to be talking into the speakers—Grandfather Peck included, as Justine noticed when Glorietta came for Sunday dinner. Duncan was the only one who enjoyed that dinner. Even Glorietta must have suspected that things were not going exactly right. For afterwards, she never was seen in any Peck house again. Instead she took up residence in Duncan's car, a forty-dollar 1933 Graham Paige that smelled suspiciously of beer. Whenever the Graham Paige was parked outside, a green blemish in the row of Fords, you could glimpse a flash of Glorietta's red dress through the window. When Duncan taught Justine to drive, Glorietta rode in the back like a lap robe or a Thermos bottle, part of the car. She hummed and popped her chewing gum, ignoring the shrieking gears and the quarrels and near accidents. Later, when Justine had learned the rudiments of driving, Duncan sat in the back as well. Justine could look in the rear view mirror and see his arm cocked carelessly around Glorietta's neck, his face peaceful as he watched the passing scenery. She did not think *she* could ever be so relaxed with someone outside the family.

Once for a school bazaar Justine was asked to run the fortune-telling booth, which she knew nothing about. A very peculiar old biology teacher sent her to a seeress named Olita. "She is *my* fortune teller," she said, as if everyone should have one, "and she'll teach you enough to get by." Duncan and Glorietta drove Justine to a cleaner's in east Baltimore and parked to wait for her. Olita had a room upstairs, behind a plate glass window reading MADAME OLITA, YOUR DESTINY

DISCOVERED. Justine began to think this wasn't such a good idea. She turned back toward the car, planning to tell Duncan she had changed her mind, but she found that Duncan was looking squarely at her, half smiling, with a spark in his eyes. It reminded her of the time he had hung from the tree limb. She went on up the stairs.

Madame Olita was a large, sloping woman with a stubby gray haircut, wearing a grandmotherly dress and a cardigan. Her room, which was bare except for two stools and a table, smelled of steam from the cleaner's. Since the biology teacher had called ahead, she already knew what Justine wanted. She had written out a list of things to tell people. "Palms will be simplest," she said. "Palms take much less time than cards, and for a bazaar that's all that counts. Just sound sure of yourself. Take their hands, like so." She reached for Justine's hand and turned it upward, smartly. "Start with the—you could be telling fortunes yourself, if you wanted," she said.

"But I will be," said Justine.

"I mean *seriously* telling fortunes. You have the knack."

"Oh," said Justine. "Well, I don't think I—"

"Do you ever have flashes when you know something is going to happen?"

"No! Really," said Justine. She pulled her hand away.

"All right, all right. Here's the list, then, of the major lines of the palm. Life, mind, heart, fate . . ."

But later, when she had heaved herself up to see Justine to the door, she said, "This is really not a parlor game, you realize."

"No, I'm sure it isn't," Justine said politely.

"*You* know it isn't."

Justine couldn't think what was expected of her. She went on buttoning her coat. Madame Olita leaned forward and jabbed the back of Justine's left hand with one stubby finger. "You have a curved ring of Solomon, a solid line of intuition, and a mystic cross," she said.

"I do?"

"Even one of those denotes a superior fortune teller."

Justine straightened her hat.

"I have a mystic cross too," said Madame Olita, "but I've never found one on anybody else. They are very rare. May I see your right palm, please?"

Justine held it out, unwillingly. Madame Olita's hands felt like warm sandpaper.

"Well?" Justine said finally.

"You are very young," Madame Olita told her.

Justine opened the door to go.

"But you're going to enter into a marriage that will disrupt everything and break your parents' hearts," said Madame Olita, and when

Justine spun around Madame Olita gave her a small, yellow smile and lifted a hand in farewell.

Out in the car, Duncan and Glorietta were kissing in broad daylight. "Stop that," Justine said irritably, and Duncan broke away and looked up at her, surprised.

Justine wondered if some aura of Duncan's had rubbed off on her, so that Madame Olita had told the wrong person's fortune.

In the church hall after the sermon one Sunday a boy named Neely Carpenter asked Justine what time it was. "It's approximately twelve thirteen and a half," she told him.

"*Approximately* twelve thirteen and a *half?*"

"My watch says that, you see, but my watch is a little off," said Justine. "It's logical, really." She started laughing. Neely Carpenter, who had always thought of her as a spinster-faced girl, looked surprised for a moment and then asked if she would like a ride home from church.

After that he gave her a ride every Sunday, and he took her to the movies every Saturday night. Justine's mother said she thought that was very sweet. It was the fall of Justine's senior year, after all; she was seventeen. It was about time she had a steady boyfriend. And Neely was a doctor's son recently moved to Roland Park, a serious-looking boy with very straight black hair and excellent manners. "Why don't you invite this Neely boy for Sunday dinner?" Justine's mother asked her.

Sunday dinner was always held at Great-Grandma's house, with four leaves extending the table so that everyone could sit around it. Neely looked a little stunned when he saw how many Pecks there were, but he found a seat between Aunt Sarah and Uncle Dan and did his best to keep his place in the conversation. "Yes, ma'am. No, ma'am," he kept saying. Justine thought he was doing fine. She was proud of her family, too—her aunts in their new rust-colored fall outfits, her handsome cousins, her stately grandfather with his hair turned silvery white and his face puzzled-looking from the effort he had started having to make in order to hear. So she was surprised when later, after Neely had gone home, Duncan said, "You'll never see *him* again."

They were out on Great-Grandma's lawn, where Justine had gone to see Neely off and where Duncan, up to some project or other, was unrolling a gigantic reel of baling wire across the grass. When he raised his head to speak to her Justine was struck by his expression, which was almost the same as his grandfather's. "Why do you say that?" she asked him.

"Nobody takes Sunday dinner with the Pecks and comes back for more."

"Well! Just because *Glorietta!* And besides, you're wrong. He's already asked me to Sue Pope's birthday dance."

"Then he's a fool," said Duncan. "No, I don't mean because of you, Justine. I mean, who would willingly mix with that crowd in the dining room?"

"I would," said Justine. "I thought they were very nice to him."

"Ah, yes! 'Ask if your little friend there would like another potato, Justine.' Little friend! And, 'Tell me, is it true that you go to public school? How *are* the public schools?' And, 'I understand your father is a doctor, um, Reilly. How nice! It's a very rewarding profession, I hear, though a little—mechanical, don't you think? *We* are all lawyers, I suppose you know—' "

"What's wrong with that? They were only showing an interest," Justine said.

"Ho! And then when he asked Great-Grandma if he could help to clear the dishes. *Then* he got it *twice!* 'Oh, my, no, we have a servant, dear.' And, 'Besides,' Aunt Caroline says, 'it's the very best china.' "

"Well?" said Justine. "We do have a servant. And it was the best china."

Duncan stopped unreeling the baling wire. He straightened up and wiped his face on his sleeve. "You really don't see it, do you," he said.

But Justine wouldn't answer. She folded her arms against an autumn wind and looked instead at the four brick houses behind them, where everybody was getting comfortable now with newspapers and needle-work and cups of spiced tea. "You know what those houses remind me of?" Duncan said, following her gaze. "Hamsters. Or baby mice, or gerbils. Any of those little animals that cluster in one corner piled on top of each other even when they have a great big cage they are free to spread out in."

"Oh, Duncan," Justine said.

She knew he only talked that way because he was going through a difficult time. Next year he would enter college and he wanted to go to Hopkins instead of the University and study science instead of law. But Grandfather Peck and the uncles kept arguing with him, nagging, pushing him. Of course he could study science, it was a free country, they said, but all the same there was something so *materialistic* about science, whereas law . . . "Peck, Peck, Peck & Peck," said Duncan, referring to the family firm, which was actually called Peck & Sons. "What a perfect name for them." And he would shut himself away in his room, or go riding aimlessly with Glorietta so close beside him that if the Graham Paige were a matchbox (which it almost appeared to be) they would have tipped over long ago.

So Justine didn't worry when he spoke so bitterly. And sure enough, Neely kept on asking her out. He never came to Sunday dinner again but that was because he really had to eat with his *own* family, he said.

He did take her to movies and dances and birthday parties. He drove her home the long way around and parked some distance from the Pecks' in order to kiss her good night. He asked if she would like to move to the back seat where they would be more comfortable. "Oh well, oh no—" said Justine, uncertain of the proper answer. She really didn't know what she was supposed to do in this situation. None of her girl cousins could help her, either. All they knew about sex was what Duncan had told them when he was eight; that and the vague, horticultural-sounding information their mothers had given out. So Justine would flutter and debate with herself, but she always ended up saying, "Well actually I'm very comfortable where I am but thank you just the—" Neely, who might have been uncertain too, would look almost relieved. Going home he hummed along with "Good Night, Irene" on the radio. He was starting to talk about their getting married someday, after he was through with medical school. Justine thought he was the best-looking boy in Roland Park and she liked his eyes, which were gray and translucent like quartz, and his quiet, level way of speaking. It was possible that she might even love him, but she didn't know what her mother would say.

By the fall of 1951, Justine had started attending a girls' junior college nearby. She thought she would do English or preschool education or something. It didn't much matter. Although she had always been a fair student she didn't have any real curiosity and she couldn't think of any career she wanted to aim for. So she and Esther drifted off to college every day in the Ford their grandfather had bought them for commuting, their bright kerchiefs flickering and their hair whipping in the wind. Almost every evening Neely would come over (he was at Hopkins now) to study in the dining room with her. And there were still the Sunday dinners, the cousins alternating with grownups around the table to discourage mischief, and Claude's round face shining with the relief of being home from the University even if just for a day.

But Duncan!

Something came over Duncan that year. No one could quite put a finger on it. He had what he wanted, didn't he? He was studying science at Hopkins, wasn't he? Yet it seemed sometimes that he was more dissatisfied than ever, almost as if he regretted winning. He complained about living at home, which he had to do because Hopkins was so expensive. He said the expense was an excuse; this was just the family's way of punishing him. Punishing! To live at home with your own close family? He was morose and difficult to talk to. He did not appear to have any friends at all, at least none that he would introduce, and Glorietta was no longer to be seen. Well, of course he had always been somewhat of a problem. Surely this was just another of his stages, the aunts told his mother.

But then he started reading Dostoevsky.

Naturally they had all read Dostoevsky—or at least the uncles had, in college. Or *Crime and Punishment*, at any rate. At least in the abridged edition. But this was different. Duncan didn't just *read* Dostoevsky; he sank in, he buried himself in Dostoevsky, he stopped attending classes entirely and stayed in his room devouring obscure novels and diaries none of the rest of the family had heard of. On a soft spring evening, in the midst of a peaceful discussion on the merits of buying a home freezer, Uncle Two's branch of the family might be startled by the crash of enormous footsteps down the stairs and Duncan's wild, wiry figure exploding into the living room to wave a book at them. "Listen! Listen!" and he would read out some passage too loudly and too quickly for them to follow. A jumble of extravagant Russian prose, where emotions were stated outright in a surprising way and a great many extreme adjectives were used and feverish fancies kept darting and flashing. Paragraphs were layered and dense and complicated like chunks of mica. "Did you *hear?*" he shouted. His parents nodded and smiled, their embarrassed expressions giving them the look of sleepers dazzled by bright light. "*Well* then!" he would say, and off he spun, up the stairs. His parents stared at each other. His father went to talk to the grandfather, who understood it no better. "But I thought he was scientific!" he said. "What is he reading for?" And then, "Ah well, never mind. At least it's the classics, they surely can't hurt him."

But that was before Easter Sunday. On Easter Sunday, at the dinner table, the aunts were discussing Mrs. Norman Worth's extensive collection of eggshell miniatures. The uncles were arguing the details of a hypothetical legal problem: If a farmer, while turning on the water to irrigate the fields, accidentally startled another farmer's mule, which, in turn, kicked down the fence enclosing a prize-winning Angus bull, who thereupon . . .

"Neither of these subjects is fit table conversation," Duncan said.

Everybody thought about that for a minute.

"But what's wrong with them, dear?" his mother said finally.

"They're not real."

Great-Grandma, who had lived longest and was hardest to shock, poured more ice water into her tumbler. "To you they may *not* be," she said, "but I myself find eggshell miniatures fascinating and if I didn't have this tremor I would take them up myself."

"You owe us an apology, Duncan boy," said Uncle Two.

"You owe *me* an apology," said Duncan. "I've spent eighteen years here growing deader and deader, listening to you skate across the surface. Watching you dodge around what matters like painting blue sea around boats, with white spaces left for safety's sake—"

"*What?*"

"Can't you say something that *means* something?" Duncan asked.

"About what?" said his mother.

"I don't care. Anything. Anything but featherstitch and the statute of limitations. Don't you want to get to the bottom of things? Talk about whether there's a God or not."

"But we already know," said his mother.

What was so terrible about that? None of them could see it. But Duncan stood up, as wild-eyed as any Russian, and said, "I'm leaving. I'm going for good."

He slammed out of the dining room. Justine jumped up to follow him, but then she stopped in the doorway, undecided. *"He'll* be back," Uncle Two said comfortably. "It's only growing pains. Ten years from now he'll talk the same as all the rest of us."

"Go after him," the grandfather said.

"What, Father?"

"Well, don't just—*somebody* go. You go, Justine. Go after him, hurry."

Justine went. She flew out the front of Great-Grandma's house and paused, thinking she had already lost him, but then she saw him just coming from Uncle Two's with a cardboard box. He crossed the lawn and heaved the box into the back seat of the Graham Paige. Then he climbed in himself. "Duncan! Wait!" Justine called.

Surprisingly, he waited. She ran up out of breath, clutching her dinner napkin. "Where are you going?" she asked him.

"I'm moving."

"You are?"

She looked at the back seat. It was like him to leave his clothes behind and take his box of tools and scrap metal.

"But Duncan," she said, "what are we going to do without you?"

"You'll manage."

"What if we need you for something? Where will we find you?"

By now other members of the family were straggling onto Great-Grandma's porch. She could tell by the look he flashed over her shoulder. "Bye, Justine," he said. "I've already got a place, beside that bookstore on St. Paul, but don't tell the others."

"But *Duncan*—"

"Bye, Justine."

"Bye, Duncan."

At first the family assumed he would be home in no time. It was only his age. Everybody eighteen expected deep things of people, but it never *lasted*. Yet the days stretched on and there was no word of him. They began to question Justine more closely. "He's all right, he's got a place to stay," was what she had said earlier, but now that wasn't enough. Had he told her where? Because this was not some childhood game any more, surely she was mature enough to realize that. Wasn't she?

But she had promised Duncan.

Aunt Lucy said Justine was cruel and selfish. Justine's mother said there was no call for *that* sort of talk, and then Aunt Lucy broke down and cried. "Now look here. Get a hold of yourself," the grandfather said, which made her turn on him. Why couldn't a person let loose a little, after all? Where was the sin? How come a forty-four-year-old woman didn't have a right to cry in her own house, and state her feelings as she pleased, without a bunch of Pecks crowding around telling her she was not sufficiently dignified, and elegant, and tasteful, and respectable?

"Why, Lucy Hodges!" said Aunt Sarah.

Aunt Lucy gave her a look of pure hatred, there was no other way you could put it.

Justine was miserable. She would much rather tell and be done with it. But even if the grownup rules *were* different, Duncan was still playing by the old ones and he would be furious if she told. She hoped he would come home by himself—"turn himself in" was how she thought of it. Or that Uncle Two, strolling the Hopkins campus with false nonchalance during class break, would run across Duncan on his own. But Duncan didn't come and he wasn't seen on campus, and Uncle Two didn't want to ask at the Dean's office outright and involve other people in family matters. "You owe it to us to tell, Justine," he said. His face was tired and gaunt and there were shadows under his eyes. Aunt Lucy wasn't speaking. Even the cousins looked at Justine with a new edginess. How had she got herself into this? All she wanted was for the family to be happy together. That was the only reason she had run after Duncan in the first place.

She felt like someone who takes a single short step on solid ice and then hears a crack. She was halfway onto a drifting floe, one foot pulling out to sea and the other still on shore.

Then her grandfather said, "Have *you* been to see him?"

"Oh, I don't think he'd like me to, Grandfather."

"Why not? You're his cousin."

"I know."

"Yes, well," her grandfather said, and he pulled at his nose. "Well, never mind that. Go anyway. It's the only way we'll get any peace around here."

"Go visit him?"

"You didn't promise not to do *that*, did you? Go ahead. Don't worry, nobody will follow you."

But Justine half hoped someone *would* follow. Then life could get back to normal.

She knew the address because she had often gone with Duncan to the bookshop he mentioned—a cluttered place with creaky floorboards and great tilting stacks of used technical books. To the left of the shop was a paper sign, orange on black, saying ROOMS. When she opened the door she found narrow wooden steps, and at the top of the steps a dark hall with a toilet at the end. The doors reminded her of school, all thickly painted with scuff-proof brown and marked off with curly metal numbers. But she should have brought a flashlight to read the nameplates by. She moved down the hall very slowly, hunching her shoulders against a feeling of unknown things at the back of her neck, peering at the names scrawled on scraps of ruled paper or adhesive tape: Jones, Brown, Linthicum, T. Jones. No Peck. Only a door to her right with nothing at all, no name in the slot. And that, of course, would be Duncan.

She knocked. When he opened the door she held onto her hat, like someone who has just pressed a fun-house button with no notion of what to expect. But all Duncan said was, "Justine."

"Hello," she said.

"Was there something you wanted?"

"I'm supposed to see if you're all right."

"Well, now you've seen."

"Okay," she said, and turned to go.

"But you might as well come in, I guess. Since you're here."

His room was small and dingy, with stained wallpaper, a flapping torn shade, a speckled mirror, and a metal bed with a sagging mattress. Over in one corner was his cardboard box. He wore the clothes he had left home in, brown suit pants and a white shirt without a tie. He seemed thinner. "It doesn't look as if you're eating right," Justine said.

"Is that what you came to tell me?"

"No."

She sat down very delicately on the edge of the bed. She lifted both hands to her hat, making sure it was perfectly level. For some reason, Duncan smiled.

"Well!" she said finally.

Duncan sat down next to her.

"Your mother is really taking on, Duncan. She's crying where everyone can see her. Your father is—"

"I don't want to hear about that."

"Oh. Well—"

"I know what they're doing. I always know, I can tell, I can see as if I'm sitting there. They're talking about someone in the outside world. They're digging the moat a little deeper. They're pointing out all the neighbors' flaws and their slipping dentures and mispronunciations, they're drawing in tighter to keep the enemy out. Why do you think my mother's crying? Because she misses me? Did she say that? Think a minute. Did she? Did any of them? No. They're worried I might be with the wrong kind of people. They're upset to think a Peck is out there in the world someplace. I've lowered the drawbridge."

"Oh *no*, Duncan—" Justine said.

"Everything they do is calculated to keep others at a safe distance. Everything. Look at your hat!"

Justine's hands went up again, uncertainly.

"No, no, it's fine. It's a fine hat," he told her. "But what are you wearing it for?"

"Why, I *always*—"

"Yes, but why? Did you ever take a good look around you? Only old ladies wear hats any more, outside of church. But every woman in our family, even little girls, they all wear hats even if they're just off to the side yard for a breath of air. 'A lady doesn't *go* without a hat, my dear. Only common people.' Common! What's so uncommon about us? We're not famous, we're not society, we haven't been rich since 1930 and we aren't known for brains or beauty. But our ladies wear hats, by God! And we all have perfect manners! We may not ever talk to outsiders about anything more interesting than the weather but at least we do it politely! And we've all been taught that we disapprove of sports cars, golf, women in slacks, chewing gum, the color chartreuse, emotional displays, ranch houses, bridge, mascara, household pets, religious discussions, plastic, politics, nail polish, transparent gems of any color, jewelry shaped like animals, checkered prints . . . we're all told from birth on that no Peck has had a cavity in all recorded history or lost a single tooth; that we're unfailingly punctual even when we're supposed to come late; that we write our bread-and-butter notes no more than an hour after every visit; that we always say 'Baltimore' instead of 'Balmer'; that even when we're wearing our ragged old gardening clothes you can peek down our collars and see 'Brooks Brothers' on the label, and our boots are English and meant for riding though none of us has ever sat on a horse . . ."

He wound down like Great-Grandma's old Graphophone, and slumped forward suddenly with his long hands drooping between his knees.

"But Uncle Two is so *sad*," said Justine. "He wanders around the Homewood campus all day hoping to—"

"Justine. Will you please get *out*?"

She rose immediately, clutching her little suede purse. But in the doorway Duncan said, "Anyhow, thanks for coming."

"Oh, you're welcome."

"I meant it, Justine. I'm sorry I . . . really, if you wanted to come back sometime I wouldn't mind."

"Well, all right," Justine said.

Then of course when she got home everyone was furious with her, because she hadn't found out one concrete fact. What was he living on? Where was he eating? Was he going to school? Who were his companions?

"I just know he's taken up with some—trash, he does have such peculiar taste in friends," Aunt Lucy said.

And all of them wondered at Justine's sudden look of sorrow.

What Duncan was living on was a pittance paid him by a Hopkins professor. He was double-checking dry facts in a library, and then writing them into the blanks the professor had left in a very long, tedious book on paleobotany. He was eating saltines and peanut butter, washed down with a quart bottle of milk in his room. He had no companions at all, not even Glorietta, with whom he had had a terrible fight several months ago over her habit of saying "between you and I." Eventually he was going to go very far away, perhaps to British Columbia, but at the moment it seemed he just couldn't get up the energy. And no, he was not attending school any more. He was not even reading Dostoevsky, whose writing suddenly appeared to have the squirmy, eye-straining texture of plant cells. As a matter of fact, he thought he might be going crazy. He even *liked* the idea of going crazy. He waited for insanity as if it were some colorful character his parents had always warned him against, but every morning when he woke up his mind was the same efficient piece of machinery it had always been and he felt disappointed.

Several times a week, his cousin Justine would come bringing irritating, endearing gifts—a ridiculous pair of slippers, his striped bedspread from home, once his old blue toothbrush with Ipana caked in the bristles. Whenever he opened the door to her he felt deeply happy to see her thin, sweet face and her streamered hat, but before she had been there five minutes he wanted to throw her out. She had such a gift for saying the wrong thing. "Can I tell the cousins where you are? They want to come too."

"No. God."

"Do you need any money?"

"I can take care of myself, Justine."

"Grandfather gave me some to bring to you."

"Tell him I can take care of myself."

"But I can't give it back to him, Duncan. He was so—he just pushed it into my hand all clumsy and secret. He pretended he wasn't doing anything."

"Change the subject."

"Like in the old days when he gave out horehound drops."

"Justine, I wish you would go now."

She always went. But she always came back, too, and when she stood in his doorway again a few days later he was all the more touched by her stupid, comical persistence. From earliest childhood she had been his favorite cousin—maybe because she was a little more removed, a Mayhew, a Philadelphian, not quite so easy to know. But he was surprised that she would brave his dark stairs and his rudeness. Here she had always seemed so docile! He made a special effort for her, smoothing the spread and offering saltines from his roach-proof tin and suggesting she take her hat off, which of course she would not do. "Justine, I'm glad you came back," he said.

"Why, thank you."

"You may get on my nerves sometimes but at least you show things, you say things outright, you don't feel it's a sin. You were the only one to ask me not to go, the Sunday I left."

"But Grandfather told me to do that," Justine said.

Right away she had managed to get on his nerves again.

She always had an answer. She drove him up a wall. He reached the point where he would turn on her the moment she entered, letting loose a flood of arguments that he had been storing up. "You know what they're like?" (There was no need to say whom he meant.) "You know who they remind me of? People choosing a number on a radio dial. The way they ignore anything that isn't Peck, like flicking past stations that don't concern them, just a split second of jazz or ballgames or revivalist ministers and they wince and move on, and settle finally on the one acceptable station that plays Mantovani. Nothing uncomfortable, nothing extreme, nothing they can't tolerate . . ."

"They tolerated you at that Sunday dinner," Justine said. "Really you were as rude as can be and they tried to see your side of it and act reasonable. Who are you to say they can't talk about eggshells?"

Duncan said, "Nothing outside the family matters. Nobody counts if they're not Pecks. Not even neighbors, not even Sulie. Why, Sulie's been with us since our parents were children, but does anybody know her last name?"

"Boudrault."

"Hmm?"

"She married old Lafleur Boudrault, the gardener."

"Oh, details," said Duncan.

"He died in nineteen forty."

"Little church-lady Emily Post details and nothing underneath. And you're just like them, Justine, you always will be. Who asked you to come here and clutter up my life?"

But when she was gone, her smell of warm grass hung in the air and the memory of her imperturbable Peck face. At night her chilly little voice ran on and on, arguing, reasoning, imposing logic, even in his dreams. He would wake and punch his flattened pillow and toss beneath the spread that carried her smell too, even from its brief stay in her arms. He wished she were there to argue with; then he wished she were there to apologize to; then he wished she were there to lay her long cool body next to his on the sagging mattress and hold him close all through the deep, steamy Baltimore night.

Justine was not herself; everybody noticed it. Even summer vacation didn't seem to relax her any. She was strange and distant with her family. She began watching her aunts and uncles in a measuring way that made them uncomfortable. "What's the *matter* with her?" her father said once, but his in-laws only smiled blankly; they did not believe in asking too many questions.

It seemed that they accepted Duncan's absence now. Sometimes when Justine came back from visiting him they would forget to ask how he was. Or they would say, "See Duncan, did you?" and go on about their business. Even Aunt Lucy appeared resigned. But one day in August, a particularly hot Saturday morning, Aunt Lucy appeared on Great-Grandma's front steps with a small electric fan. Justine was drying her hair outdoors and reading *Mademoiselle*. "Justine, dear," said Aunt Lucy.

Justine looked up, with her mind still on her magazine. Her aunt wore the expression of a lady heading calm and smiling toward disaster.

"Justine, this is for Duncan," Aunt Lucy said.

"What? Oh, a fan. He could use it."

"Oh, I knew it! I'm so glad I—well, whenever you go to see him, then. Are you going today?"

"Today I'm going on a picnic with Neely. Tomorrow I might, though."

"Don't you think you might stop by this morning? Wouldn't you be able to work it in?"

Aunt Lucy's smile hesitated.

"Of course I could," Justine said, and she took the fan from her aunt's shaky hands.

It was not until she had parked in front of the bookshop that she noticed the little envelope dangling from the fan's grid.

Duncan's room was blasting with heat and he was so hot he seemed to have been oiled. He wore a grayish undershirt. His trousers were creased and limp. "Oh, it's you," was all he said, and then he sat back down on his bed and wiped his face with his balled-up shirt.

"Duncan, I brought you a fan from your mother."

"You've been telling her about my room."

"No, I haven't. She just *guessed* you would need this."

"What's that in the envelope?"

"I don't know."

He broke the string that tied it and pulled out a folded note. First he read it silently and then he groaned and read it aloud.

Dear Duncan,

I am taking the liberty of sending you the fan from my bedroom, now that it is so warm.

Everyone is well although I myself have had a recurrence of those headaches. Just a little tension, the doctor says, so I keep my chin up!

Your father has been working very . . .

"What about the fan from *my* room?" Duncan said. "There is one, you know."

"She gave you her own to show she cares, she didn't know how else to put it," said Justine.

"None of them do. Oh, you can tell who she married into. She's just like all the rest of them now. Too little said and too much communicated, so that if you fight back they can say, 'But why? What did *I* do?' and you won't have any answer. It all takes place in their secret language, they would never say a thing straight out."

"But that's tact. They don't want to embarrass you."

"They don't want to embarrass themselves," Duncan told her.

She said nothing.

"Isn't that right?"

"Probably it is," she said. "But so is the other. There *isn't* any right and wrong. I keep looking at them, trying to decide. Well, everything you say is true but then so is everything I say. And what does it matter, after all? They're your family."

"You know who you sound like? Aunt Sarah, Justine. You're going to grow up an old maid. Or you'll marry a stick like Neely and have him change his name to Peck. I can see it coming. I can see it in that flat straight face of yours, just watch."

But he had gone too far. Even he must have known that. When Justine turned away from him, fumbling for something in her purse, he said, "Anyway!" He jumped up and started pacing the floor. "Well, anyway, tell me all the news," he said.

"Oh . . ."

"Come on!"

"There's nothing much."

"Nothing? Nothing in all those four enormous houses?"

"Well, Aunt Bea has had to get glasses," Justine said.

"Ah."

"She's very shy about them, she wears them on a string tucked inside her blouse. She takes them off between sentences in a newspaper even."

"So Aunt Bea has glasses."

"And Mama's bought a TV."

"A TV. I might have known it would come to that."

"Oh, it's not so bad, Duncan. It's very convenient, don't you think, having a moving talking picture in your home that way? I wonder how they do it."

"Actually it's quite simple," said Duncan. "The *principle's* been around for decades. Have you got a pencil? I'll show you."

"Oh, I wouldn't understand," Justine said.

"Of course you would."

"But I'm not scientific. I don't see how you know those things."

"Those things are nothing," he said, "it's the others I don't get. The ones you take for granted. Like mirrors, for instance," and he stopped his pacing to wave at the mirror on the opposite wall. "I lay awake the other night going crazy over that. I spent hours trying to figure out the laws of reflected images. I couldn't measure the angles of refraction. Do you understand it? Look."

She stood up and looked. She saw herself in the speckled glass, nothing surprising.

"How come it shows my image and not yours?" he asked her. "How come yours and not mine? How come eyes can meet in a mirror when you're not looking at each other in real life? Do you understand the principle?"

In the glass their eyes met, equally blue and distant, as if the mirror were reflecting images already mirrored.

Duncan turned around and set his hands on her shoulders and kissed her on the mouth. He smelled of salt and sunlight. His grip on her was weightless, as if he were holding something back. When she drew away, he let his hands drop to his sides. When she ran out of the room he didn't try to stop her.

Justine wouldn't visit Duncan any more. Her grandfather kept coming around, pressing twenty-dollar bills into her hand, but she didn't know what to tell him and so she took the money in silence. She stuffed it haphazardly into her jewelry box, feeling like a thief even though she never spent it. She quarreled with her mother over a print dress, saying it was old-ladyish, although before she had worn whatever her mother picked out. When school started she studied indifferently and had trouble getting to class on time. Esther had graduated and was teaching nursery school, but now the twins were commuting with Justine and they objected to her late starts. "Is that what you call the point of life?" Justine asked them. "Getting to a class on the dot of nine o'clock?"

The twins looked at each other. Certainly they had never meant to imply that it was the *point* of life, exactly.

On a Saturday night in October, Justine was watching television with Neely in her great-grandma's study. Neely was stroking her neck up and down in a particularly rasping way, but she had been so short-tempered with him lately that she didn't want to protest. Instead she concentrated on the television: a mahogany box with a snowy blue postage stamp in its center, showing a girl who had become engaged due to cleansing her face with cold cream twice a night. She flashed a diamond ring at her girlfriends. *"Your* diamond's going to be *twice* as big,"* said Neely. "My father's already promised me the money."

"I don't like diamonds," said Justine.

"Why not?"

"I don't like stones that are transparent."

"You don't like *anything* any more, Justine."

On the television, a man held up a watch that would keep running steadily through everything, even a cycle in a washing machine.

"How about me?" Neely asked.

"What?"

"Do you like *me?"*

His finger kept annoying her neck. Justine winced and drew away.

A man in downtown Baltimore was interviewing people coming out of a movie theater. He wanted to see if they had heard of his product, an antibacterial toothpaste. "Goodness, no," said a lady.

"Well, think a minute. Say you have a cold and get over it. You wouldn't want to catch it right back again from your toothbrush, would you?"

"Goodness, no."

He stopped a man in a raincoat.

"Sir? Have you ever thought how risky it is, using the toothbrush you used when you were sick?"

"Why, no, now I never considered that. But you got a point there."

He stopped Duncan.

"Say!" said Neely. "Isn't that your cousin?"

Duncan was wearing some dark shade of jacket that Justine had never seen before. His face was clamped against the cold. There was no one in the world with such a pure, unwavering face. He stooped a little to hear the question, concentrating courteously with his eyes focused on something in the distance. When the man was finished Duncan straightened and thought a moment.

"Actually," he said, "once your body's built up enough resistance to overcome those bacteria in the first place it's very doubtful if—"

The man discontinued the conversation and ran after a fat lady.

Justine went to the front hall for her coat. "Justine?" Neely called. She ignored him. Probably he thought she was out of hearing, maybe gone to the kitchen for soft drinks. At any rate, he didn't call again.

All she told herself was that she owed Duncan a visit. He was her cousin, wasn't he? And she really should give him their grandfather's money. (Which was still crammed in her jewelry box at home.) She had herself convinced. But Duncan must have known exactly how her mind worked, because when he opened the door he stood looking at her for a minute, and then he drew her in and kissed her, and then he said, "Look, I can see the layers sliding across your eyes like shutters until you can properly explain this away." Then he laid her on his bed, with its hollow center that rolled her toward him so that she could feel his warm bones through the thin white fabric of his shirt. He took off her clothes and his. Still she didn't make a single objection, she said none of the things that she had said to Neely. She felt happy and certain, as if everything they did was already familiar. She seemed to be glinting with some secret laughter at this newer, more joyous mischief that they were just inventing, or at Duncan's Puckish face turned suddenly gentle, or at her own self in his mirror eyes, a naked girl wearing a Breton hat.

6
=

Duncan came home in March of 1953. He walked into his great-grandma's dining room one Sunday at dinnertime. "Duncan!" his mother said, half rising. Then, "What on earth is that you're wearing?"

He was wearing a peajacket he had bought from Navy surplus. His hair needed cutting. He had been gone nearly a year and in that time his face had changed in some indefinable way that made him an outsider. The grownups stared and his cousins gave him self-conscious, sidelong glances. All but Justine, who raised her face like a beacon and smiled across the room at him. He smiled back.

"Well, my boy," his grandfather said. "So you're home."

"No," said Duncan, looking at Justine.

But they didn't believe him. "Pull up a chair," his mother said. "Take mine. Get yourself a plate. Have you had one decent meal since you left us?"

"I'm going to get married," Duncan said.

"Married?"

The ghost of Glorietta flashed scarlet through their minds. All the grownups shifted uneasily.

"I'm marrying Justine."

First they thought it was a joke. A tasteless one, but just like him. Then they saw how grave and still the two of them were. "My God," said Justine's mother. She clutched suddenly at a handful of ruffles on her chest. "My God, who would have thought of such a thing?"

Though it seemed to all of them, now, that they should have thought of it long ago. Those visits Justine had paid him! Those trips!

Everyone knew she hated traveling as much as any other Peck. Yet day after day this winter she had packed a lunch in Sulie's kitchen and said she wouldn't be home till night. "I'm going on a trip with Duncan. Out to the country somewhere." "Yes, yes, go," they told her. "Keep an eye on him for us." She had cut classes, missed important family gatherings, stopped seeing Neely, grown distant from her cousins—"But it's good she's with Duncan," they told each other. "She's sure to be a good influence on him." How she had deceived them!

Only Sam Mayhew, slow of mind, seemed unable to make the mental leap the Pecks had just accomplished. He looked all around the table, from one person to the other, with his face set to laugh as soon as he saw the joke. "What? What's that?" he said.

The others waved him aside, too busy adjusting to the shock. But Duncan came over and stood squarely in front of him and spoke very quietly, as if to a child.

"Uncle Sam, I'm marrying Justine."

"But—you can't!"

"I'm telling you I am. I'm telling you, not asking you. Nothing is going to make me change my mind."

"You can't."

"Why, it must not even be legal!" said Caroline.

"Yes, it is," Duncan told her.

"*Oh* yes," his grandfather said.

"But—" said Caroline.

"Who's the lawyer here, you or me? Boy's right. It's true. And yes, I know, there's a lot to be said against it. But look at it this way. What nicer girl could he have picked? She's sure to settle him down some. And this way there's no adjustment for them to make, no in-law problems—"

"You ought to be locked up," Sam Mayhew said.

"Sir!" said Grandfather Peck.

"Haven't you heard of inbreeding?"

"Not at the table, Sam."

"Haven't you heard of *genes?*"

"Now, we come of good solid stock," the grandfather said. "No worries there." He picked up the carving knife. "Care for a slice of ham, Duncan boy?"

"He's a blood relative," said Sam Mayhew. "And he's only twenty years old, and he hasn't got a responsible bone in his body. Well, I'm not going to allow it. Justine won't marry Duncan or any other Peck."

"Then we'll elope," Duncan said.

"Elope!" cried Justine's mother. "Oh, anything but that!"

"You are a fool, Caroline," Sam Mayhew said. Then he stood and took Justine by the wrist and pulled her up and toward the door. But she was still calm and so was Duncan. Nothing seemed to disturb them. As Justine passed Duncan he gave her a slow, deep stare that caused the rest of the family to avert their eyes. "*Come*, Justine," her father said. He led her through the living room and up to her bedroom. She went without a protest. He set her in her room and shut her door and locked it, and put the key up on the ledge again before he went back to the others.

In her ruffled rocker, Justine sat and waited. The pointlessness of being locked in her room seemed more comical than annoying, and she was not worried about her family. Hadn't Duncan predicted everything? "Your father's the one who'll be upset. The others will get over it. Anyway, it's always been a bother adapting outside wives. Then your father will give in because he has to. There won't be any problems."

"I know there won't."

"There would be even less if you would just run away with me."

"I want to do this right, I said."

"Does it matter that much? Justine, why does it matter? They're just a bunch of *people*, just some yellow-haired, ordinary people. Why do you have to ask for their approval?"

"Because I love them," Justine said.

He didn't have any answer for that. Love was not a word he used, even to her.

She rocked and gazed at the wintry gray sky, while downstairs the battle went on and on. Great-Grandma soothed everyone, a dry brown thread weaving in and out. She thought this marriage was a wonderful idea; she had never heard of genes. When Sam Mayhew stormed, Grandfather snapped and cut him short. Uncles rumbled and aunts chirped and burbled. And over it all rode Duncan's level voice, sensible and confident. Justine could tell when he began to win. He continued alone, the others fell behind. The worst of the battle was over. All that was left was for the losers to regain face.

Justine felt suddenly stifled and bored. She went into her bathroom for her toothbrush, and took a pack of matches from her bureau drawer. She had not grown up with Duncan for nothing: heating the toothbrush handle very slowly, she pushed it little by little into the lock of her door and then turned it and walked out free. When she re-entered the dining room, they didn't seem surprised to see her. Only Duncan, noticing the toothbrush in her hand, tipped back in his chair and looked amused, but he sobered up when Justine's father rose and came around the table to face her.

"Justine," he said.

"Yes, Daddy."

"It has been pointed out to me that there's nothing I can really do to stop you. All I can hope is that you'll listen to reason. Justine, look. Don't you see why you're doing this? It's merely proximity, the two of you had no one else, *no* one in this family has anyone else. You were thrown too much together, at an age when naturally . . . and you were afraid to turn to some outsider. Admit it. Isn't that correct?"

Justine thought it over. "Well," she said finally, "it does sound correct, yes."

"Well, then."

"But then, *both* sides sound correct. I always agree with who I'm listening to."

He waited, expecting more. All she did was smile. "Aah!" he said suddenly, and turned away, throwing up his hands. "You even *sound* like him. You're a puppet. I've learned something today: set a bad and a good person down together and the bad wins every time. I always wondered."

"Say that again?" said Aunt Lucy. "Is it Duncan you're calling bad?"

"Who else?"

"*Duncan's* not a bad boy."

Even Duncan looked surprised.

"*Justine's* the one who kept the rest of us away from him. *Justine* wouldn't tell his own mother where he was staying! Blame your daughter!"

"Why, Lucy!" Justine's mother said.

Duncan let his chair tip forward. This might turn out to be interesting. But no, they were distracted by a new development: Sam Mayhew buttoning his suit coat. He worked with his elbows out and his clock-shaped face set impassively toward some point above their heads. They knew at once that something important was going on.

"I won't be attending this wedding," he said finally.

"Oh, Sam!" his wife cried.

"And I won't be living here."

"What?"

"I'm moving out to my parents'. I'm going to look for a house in Guilford."

He finished the buttons. He began pulling his shirt cuffs down, neat bands of white above his chubby red hands. "You may come too, of course, Caroline. And Justine if she decides against this marriage. But I warn you: if you come, we will only be visiting your family once a month."

"Once a *month?*"

"The first Sunday of every month, for dinner. We'll go home at three."

"But *Sam—*" his wife said.

"Make your choice, Caroline."

He continued to gaze above her head. Caroline turned to her family. She was still baby-faced, although the years had worked like gravity pulling on her cheeks. Her weight had settled in upon itself. She looked like a cake that had collapsed. To each brother and sister, to her father and her grandmother, she turned a round lost stare while twisting the pearls on her fingers.

"What's your decision, Caroline?"

"I can't just *leave* them like that."

"All right."

"Sam?" she said.

He walked over to Justine. Duncan rose instantly to his feet. "Justine," Sam Mayhew said, "you have been a disappointing daughter in every way, all your life."

Then Justine rocked back as if she had been hit, but Duncan already stood behind her braced to steady her.

The wedding was to be held in a church. All the family insisted on that. Duncan had not been to church in several years and detested Reverend Didicott, a fat man who came from Aunt Lucy's hometown and had a Southern accent that would surely double the length of the ceremony; but he said he would do whatever Justine wanted. And Justine, half willing anyway, went along with the others, submitting to a long satin dress, Sarah Cantleigh's ivory veil, and a little old lady consultant with an emergency cigar box full of pins, white thread, spirits of ammonia, and a stick of chalk for stains. "Oh, Duncan!" Justine said, as she sped by him on the way to the photographer. "I'm sorry! I know how you must hate this!" But he was surprisingly tolerant. He had agreed to give up his room and move home for the month preceding the wedding; he went without a word to buy a black suit that turned him stern and unfamiliar. During lulls in the excitement, he seemed to be observing Justine very closely. Did he think she would change her mind? Reading *Bride's* magazine, she felt his eyes upon her, weighing her, watching for something. "What is it?" she asked him, but he never would say.

Her mother was everywhere. She bustled and darted, giving commands, trilling out fitting schedules in a voice so gay it seemed about to break off and fly. "Really, no one would guess her husband's left her," Justine told Duncan.

"Don't speak too soon."

"Why?"

"Now she's got the wedding to keep her busy. What about later?"

Later Justine would be far away. One thing Duncan would not agree to was living in Roland Park. Nor even in Baltimore, not even long enough for Justine to finish school. And he would not go back to school himself. So they were renting a little house and a plot of land an hour's drive out in the country, where they used to go on their trips. Duncan planned to start a goat farm. It was what he had always wanted, he said. It was? Justine had never heard him mention it before. But he couldn't go on forever looking up facts for professors; and anyway, he kept losing those jobs, he gave in to a temptation to rewrite their material, making it more colorful, adding his own startling scraps of knowledge and a few untruths. And he and Justine each had a share of old Justin's trust fund. Because of the proliferation of heirs it amounted to almost nothing, but they could manage till the dairy started paying off. "You're strapping yourself in, boy," his grandfather said. "You want an education. And *renting's* no good, it's a shoddy way to do things."

"Sure, Grandfather."

But Duncan went on reading the *Dairy Goat Journal*, rummaging through his shocks of hair as he always did when he was absorbed in something. And a week before the wedding he helped supervise the loading of a Mayflower van containing ancient, massive furniture from the relatives and rolled-up rugs, crates of crystal stemware, gifts of silver and china, linens monogrammed by Aunt Laura May and heavy damask curtains, all meant for their three-room cabin. Justine wasn't entirely sure that everything was suitable, but how else would you furnish a place? She didn't know. Duncan made no comment, only watched without surprise as she directed the movers toward a claw-footed bureau, a tasseled floor lamp, a bedstead with pineapple knobs.

"Prepare your mother, now," he told her. "I mean it. Get her ready for doing without you, because it's going to be a shock for her once it happens."

"I will."

"Prepare *yourself*, Justine."

"Prepare for what?"

"Do you really understand that you'll be leaving here?"

"Of course I do," she said.

Well, naturally she would rather *not* be leaving. It made her sad just to think about it. But nothing mattered as much as the lurch in her stomach when she saw him. When they sat apart in Great-Grandma's study, some inner selves seemed to rise up and meet while their bodies remained seated. In halls and pantries and stairwells, they kissed until they were sick and dizzy. She missed Duncan's room downtown: his jingling bed, the warm pulse in the hollow of his throat, the leathery arch of his right foot curving exactly to the shape of her calf when they fell asleep.

"Still," Duncan said, "I wish I could be sure you know what you're getting into."

At the rehearsal, Esther took the part of the bride for good luck. It was terrible to see her up there so close to Duncan. Her emerald-green sheath showed off her figure, which was better than Justine's. "Tell me," Justine said to Duncan later. "Did you ever think of marrying Esther?"

"No."

"But why me?" she asked.

"Why *me*, for that matter?"

"I don't know," she said.

"Why are you marrying me, Justine?"

"Oh, well, Claude is too fat and Richard's too young."

She didn't understand the strange look he gave her.

On Justine's wedding morning, a pale cool day in April, her mother woke her by pulling open the curtains in her bedroom. "Justine," she said, "listen. Are you awake?"

"Yes."

"I want you to listen a minute."

She was wearing a slithery pink silk dressing gown and already her doll-like face was made up perfectly, her curls precisely flattened. She carried a torn scrap of paper. She sat on Justine's bed and held the paper out to her, smiling a coaxing smile like someone offering medicine. "Your daddy's telephone number," she said.

"My what?"

"Hear what I say, now. I want you to go out in the hall to the phone. I want you to dial this number. It's your grandmother Mayhew's. Ask to speak to your daddy. Say, 'Daddy, today is my wedding day.'"

"Oh, Mama."

"Listen! Say, 'Daddy, this is supposed to be the happiest day of my life. Won't you make it perfect and come give me away?'"

"But I can't talk like that," Justine said.

"Of course you can. And he has that fine suit that's still in the cleaner's bag, I know he took it with him. Why, it wouldn't be any trouble at all! Justine? I beg you, Justine."

"Mama—"

"Please, I've been counting on it. I know it will work. See, I've written the number so neatly? Take it. Take it."

She pressed it into her hands. Justine climbed out of bed, still unwilling.

"Go on, Justine."

In the hall, the telephone sat on a piecrust table. The window above it was partly open, so that Justine in her flimsy cotton nightgown shivered while she dialed.

"Hello," Sam Mayhew said.

She had been expecting her grandmother, a static-voiced old lady she hardly knew. She wasn't prepared for her father yet.

"*Hello*," he said.

"Daddy?"

There was a pause. Then he said, "Hello, Justine."

"Daddy, I—today is my wedding day."

"Yes, I saw it in the paper."

She was silent. She was taking in his soft, questioning voice, which reminded her of his baffled attempts at conversation long ago in Philadelphia. For the first time she realized that he had actually left. Everything had broken and altered and would not ever be the same.

"Honey," he said. "You can always change your mind."

"No, Daddy, I don't want to change my mind."

"I'm about to buy a house in Guilford. Wouldn't you like that? There's a room for you with blue wallpaper. I know you like blue. You could go away to college, someplace good. Why, you used to be a high-B student! Those Pecks think girls go to college to mark time but—it's not too late. You know that. You can still call it off."

"Daddy, will you come give me away at the wedding?"

"No. I can't lend myself to such a thing."

"I'd really like you to."

"I'm sorry."

Her mother tugged at Justine's nightgown. "Tell about the happiest day of your life!" she hissed.

"Wait—"

"Who's that?" her father asked.

"It's Mama."

"What's she doing there?"

"She says to tell you—"

"Did your mother put you up to this?"

"No, I—she just—"

"Oh," her father said. "I thought it was you that was asking. I wish it had been."

"I *am* asking."

"Justine, I'm not going to come to your wedding. Don't bring it up again. But listen, because these are the last sensible words you'll hear all day, or maybe all the rest of your life: you've got to get out of there."

"*Out*, Daddy . . ."

"You think you *are* getting out, don't you. You're going to farm chickens or something."

"Goats."

"But you're not really leaving at all, and anyway you'll be back within a year."

"But we're going to—"

"I know why you're marrying Duncan. You think I don't. But have you ever asked yourself why Duncan is marrying *you*? Why is he marrying his first cousin?"

"Because we—"

"It's one of two reasons. Either he wants a Peck along to torment, or to lean on. Either he's going to give you hell or else he's knotted tighter to his family than he thinks he is. But whichever, Justine. Whichever. It's not a business you'd care to get involved in."

"I can't talk any more," Justine said.

"What? Hold on there, now—"

But she hung up. Her teeth were chattering. "What happened?" her mother asked. "What *happened,* isn't he coming?"

"No."

"Oh! I see. Well."

"I feel sick."

"That's wedding jitters, it's perfectly natural," her mother said. "Oh, I never should have asked you to call in the first place. It was only for *his* sake."

Then she led Justine back to her room, and covered her with the quilt handstitched by Great-Grandma, and sat with her a while. The quilt gave off a deep, solid warmth. There was a smell of coffee and cinnamon toast floating up from the kitchen, and a soft hymn of Sulie's with a wandering tune. Justine's jaw muscles loosened and she felt herself easing and thawing.

"We're going to do without him just fine," her mother said. "I only wanted to make him think he was a part of things."

Later the minister, Reverend Didicott, told the assistant minister that the Peck-Mayhew wedding was the darnedest business he had ever seen. First of all the way they sat the guests, who were not numerous to begin with: friends clumped in back, and the bride's and groom's joint family up front. There was something dreamlike in the fact that almost everyone in the front section had the same fair, rather expressionless face—over and over again, exactly the same face, distinguished only a little by age or sex. Then the groom, who seemed unsuitably light of heart, followed him around before the ceremony insisting that Christianity was a dying religion. ("It's the only case I know of where *mental* sins count too; it'll never sell," he said. "Take it from me, get out while the getting's good." Right then Reverend Didicott should have refused to marry them, but he couldn't do that to Lucy Hodges Peck, whose family he had known down South.) The bride was given away by her grandfather, an unsmiling man with a mighty snappy way of speaking to people, although so far as was known the bride's father was in excellent health. The groom refused to kiss the bride in public. But the bride's mother was the strangest. Perfectly sedate all through the ceremony, if a little trembly of mouth, gay and flirtatious at the reception afterwards, she chose to fall apart at the going away. Just as the groom was enclosing the bride in his car (which was another whole story, a disgraceful greenish object with a stunted rear end), the mother let out with a scream. "No!" she screamed. "No! How can you just leave me all alone? It's *your* fault your father's gone! How can you drive off like this without a heart?" The bride started to get out but the groom laid a hand on her arm and stopped her, and then they took off in their automobile, which appeared to be led by its nose. The mother threw herself in the grandfather's arms and wept out loud. "We people don't *cry*, Caroline," he said. The most ancient Mrs. Peck of all put on a genteel smile and started humming, and Reverend Didicott looked inside the envelope the groom had given him and found fifty dollars in Confederate money.

Duncan told everyone they would be away on a honeymoon, but they weren't; he just liked to lie. Instead they went straight to the farm. For two weeks they were left to themselves. Duncan worked uninterrupted, settling in eight Toggenburg does and a purebred buck who smelled like a circus, transporting bales of hay and sacks of Purina goat chow, a block of pink salt and a vat of blackstrap molasses he claimed would increase milk production when added to the goats' drinking water. The weather had turned suddenly warm and he went about in his undershirt, whistling "The Wabash Cannonball," while inside their little house Justine threw open all the windows and tied the damask curtains back so they wouldn't hinder the breeze. She had made the place a replica of Great-Grandma's house, if you ignored the green paper walls and the yellowed ceilings. Rugs covered the flowered linoleum, and the four-poster bed hid the fungus growing beneath one window. She fought the foreign smells of kerosene and fatback by hanging Great-Grandma's china pomander ball in the hall. She worked for hours every day constructing meals from Fannie Farmer's cookbook, the one her aunts all used. In the evenings, the two of them sat side by side on the front porch in cane-seated rockers that used to be their grandfather's. They looked out across their scrubby, scraggly land, past the slant-roofed shed where the does stood swaybacked. Like an old country couple they rocked and watched the gravel road, where they might see an occasional pick-up truck bound for the Jordans' farm on the hill or a string of children carrying switches and weedy flowers, dawdling home. Justine thought she would like to stay this way forever: isolated, motionless, barely breathing, cut loose from everyone else. They were like people under glass. They rocked in unison side by side, almost touching but not quite, as if thin wires were stretched between them.

Then the letters started coming. "I keep busy, I go for a lot of walks," her mother said. "Not far, of course. Just up and down your great-grandma's side yard, up and down again." Aunt Lucy said, "We think of you often. Especially Caroline does, you can tell although you know she wouldn't mention it for anything." "Last Sunday," Great-

Grandma said, "we laid two places for you supposing you might be back from your honeymoon and would think to come for dinner, as it would do Caroline a world of good, but it seems you couldn't make it."

Justine felt stabbed in the chest. "Dear Mama," she wrote, "I miss you very much. I want to come home for a visit. Duncan says we will just as soon as we can, although of course goats are not something you can just walk off and leave. They have to be milked twice a day and watered, and Duncan has to stay pretty close by anyway because he has put an ad in the paper and soon customers will be coming . . ."

"Dear Ma," Duncan said on a postcard. "High! We're doing fine. Say hello to everybody. Sincerely, Duncan."

The family's ink was black, their envelopes cream. Nearly every morning a cream-colored accordion lay waiting in the mailbox at the end of the driveway. Once Duncan got there before Justine and he scooped the letters out of the box and flung them over his head. "Hoo!" he said, and tipped back his face like a child in a snowstorm while the envelopes tumbled all around him. Justine came running, and bent at the edge of the gravel to gather them up. "Oh, Duncan, I wish you wouldn't do things like this," she told him. "How will I know I've got them all?"

"What does it matter? Each one is just like the next."

It was true. Still she read them closely, often stirring or starting to speak, while Duncan watched her face. Each envelope let out a little gust of Ivory soap, the smell of home. She could imagine the leafy shadows endlessly rearranging themselves outside her bedroom window, and her grandfather's slow, fond smile when he met her at the start of a day. She missed her grandfather very much.

"If you like," Duncan said, "I'll take you this Sunday for dinner. Is that what you want?"

"Yes, it is," she told him.

But somehow they didn't go. Duncan became involved in cleaning the barn, or wiring the new electric fence. Or they simply overslept, waking too slowly with their legs tangled together and their blue eyes opening simultaneously to stare at each other across the pillow, and then the unmilked goats were bleating and there were always so many chores to do. "Maybe next Sunday," Justine would write. When the new sheaf of envelopes arrived she felt chastened and sorry even before she had opened them. But when she took the letters to Duncan out in the barn he only laughed. Like a teacher with a pointer, he would poke a stalk of timothy at stray sentences here and there—reproaches, transparent braveries, phrases with double and triple and quadruple meanings. " 'Of course we're sorry you didn't make it but we understand perfectly, as I had already told your aunts that perhaps we shouldn't expect you.' Ha!" he said.

Justine's face, then, would slowly ease, but she reclaimed the letters and stacked them carefully before she went back to the house.

Then one day a truck rattled up their driveway and a man climbed out, carrying a telephone on the palm of his hand. "Phone," he said, as if Justine should lift the receiver to answer it. But he swung on by her and up the porch steps, with a beltful of tools clanking around his hips. Duncan met him in the doorway. "*We* didn't order that," he said.

"Somebody did."

"Not us."

The man pulled a folded sheet of paper from his pocket and shook it open. "Peck and Sons," he said.

"That's someone else."

"Your name Duncan Peck?"

"Yes."

"This phone is for you, then. Don't complain. Bill goes to Peck and Sons. Wished *I* got presents like that."

"If we had wanted a telephone we would have ordered it on our own," Duncan said.

But Justine said, "Oh, Duncan, it's a *gift!* We can't hurt their feelings."

Duncan studied her a minute. Then he said, "All right."

Now the phone rang once, twice, three times a day even, and Justine would come running in from the fields or the barn to answer it. "Justine," her mother said, "I'm upstairs. I'm standing in the hall here looking into your room and your shelf of dolls along the wall, the Spanish lady with her real lace mantilla that your grandfather gave you in Philadelphia when you were only four, remember? She has the sweetest, saddest face."

"Mama, I'm helping Duncan dehorn a goat."

"Do you remember when Grandfather gave you the Spanish lady? You insisted on taking her to bed with you, though she wasn't a cuddly kind of doll. Your daddy and I came into your room every night after you were asleep and put her up on the bureau again. Oh, you looked so innocent and peaceful! We would stand there a while just watching you. Your daddy didn't have to travel so often then and it seemed we had so much more time together."

"Oh, Mama," Justine would say, "I wish I could be there with you. Don't take on so, please don't cry."

Aunt Sarah called, with Aunt Laura May on the upstairs extension. "She's started staying in bed, Justine, she never gets out of her bathrobe. She has these awful headaches. I called your daddy but I believe that man is possessed. He said he wouldn't come, she should come stay in *his* house and of course that is just not possible, he only has a weekly cleaning lady. Of course she would need more than that, it's all we can do to see to her wants even with Sulie helping out. We're running our feet off."

"We bring all her meals on a tray," Aunt Laura May said.

"We've moved the television up to her bedroom."

"The radio for daytime. *Stella Dallas*."

Justine said, "We'll come on Sunday."

"Do my ears deceive me?"

"We'll be there around noon," said Justine. "But we can't stay the night, you know, the goats are—"

"The goats, yes."

"Goodbye till then."

She went back out to the field. "Duncan," she said, "I think we'd better go for dinner this Sunday."

"You do, do you."

"It's been six weeks, you know. And they say that Mama is—"

"You don't have to keep harping on it, we'll go."

But in bed that night, when he had just stretched out alongside her and taken her head in his hands, the phone rang again and he said, "Bull's-eye."

"I'll get it," she said.

"Oh, your mother and her X-ray vision. She's worked on this, she's got it timed. She couldn't call when you were just reading *Woman's Day*, no—"

"Let me up, I'll answer," said Justine.

"No, don't. We'll ignore it." But then he said, "How can we ignore a thing like that? Nine rings. Ten."

"I'll only be a minute."

"Eleven," Duncan said. He had laid one arm across her to hold her down but he kept his head raised and his eyes on the black shine of the telephone. "We'll go out and sleep in the field," he told her.

"The *field*, Duncan!"

"Where else? If we answer, she wins. If we lie here and listen she wins. Hear that? Four-letter rings. Come on, Justine."

"Well, just let me get a blanket."

"Here's a blanket."

"I'll need a bathrobe."

"What for?"

"Do you want your pillow?"

"*No* I don't want my pillow."

"And insect repellent."

"Oh, for—"

Then he was off the bed and out of the room. "Duncan?" she said. "Duncan, have you changed your mind?" But before she could follow him he was back, waving the huge iron clippers he used for trimming the goats' hooves. Justine heard a single click. The phone gave a whimper and died.

"Oh, Duncan," Justine said, but she was laughing when she lay back down.

All the next morning the telephone sat silent on the bureau with its comical stub of a tail sticking out. In the afternoon, when they were leaving to do some shopping in town, Duncan locked the front door so that no repairman could come while they were gone. "You *know* the family is going to let them hear about this," he said. "They'll be sending undercover men with their little bags of tools." And sure enough, when they got back there was a card hanging from the doorknob. "What a pity, our telephone representative has been and gone," he said. Still, Justine only laughed.

But in the evening, when they were sitting on the porch, something stopped her rocking. She straightened suddenly and frowned. "Duncan," she said.

"Hmm?"

"I have this funny feeling."

Duncan had been reading a book on how to start a chicken farm, sliding a flashlight down the page because it was already dark. He raised the flashlight now and shone it into her face.

"Something terrible is going on at home," she told him.

"Something terrible's always going on at home."

"I mean it. This is serious. I really mean it."

"What, have you turned psychic?"

"No, but I can tell if there's going to be a *change* of some kind."

He rocked and waited.

"We have to go there," she said.

The flashlight clicked off.

"I'm sorry, Duncan. I'll go alone if you'd rather. But I just feel I—"

"All right, all right."

While she packed an overnight case, he drove up the hill to ask Junior Jordan to tend the goats. They could have done that weeks ago! But then, Justine knew that as well as Duncan. She waited on the porch, clutching her case, shivering a little although the night was warm. When she saw his close-set headlights bobbing toward her, she ran down the steps and opened the car door. "It's all set," Duncan told her. "Climb in."

The car seemed to be drawn down the road by two long yellow cones. Justine was reminded of other trips, before they were married, rushing home to beat a curfew. All through that silent drive she had the feeling that she was some younger, smaller self, anxiously chewing the ribbons of her hat while she wondered if she would be scolded for staying out so late.

In Guilford, at eight o'clock that morning, Sam Mayhew's cleaning lady had found him dead in his kitchen. He was wearing a bathrobe and there was a roll of Tums on the floor beside him. Apparently he had suffered a heart attack. By ten o'clock old Mr. Mayhew had called the Pecks, but at five o'clock that evening Caroline still knew nothing about it. Nobody wanted to tell her. Instead they huddled in small groups downstairs in Great-Grandma's house, whispering bulletins back and forth. "She's in her bed eating the chocolates Marcus brought her." "She's watching a program on flower arranging." "She's trying to get Justine on the telephone again." "Oh, if only we could just never tell her and this would all blow over!"

Then the grandfather arrived from work. He was forcibly retired now but he liked to prowl around his sons' offices, checking up. "What's this?" he said, seeing clusters of women everywhere. When they told him he shook his head sharply, as if getting rid of a fly. "What? But how old was he? Not even out of his forties! And had a *heart* attack? What kind of stock did the man come from, for God's sake?"

Then he went to break the news to Caroline. The others stood around downstairs, pretending to talk but trailing off in the middle of sentences. One by one the uncles came to find out where everybody was, and they had to be told too. Richard arrived with a girlfriend who was asked politely to leave, as there had been an unfortunate occurrence. Aunt Lucy, who had double-dated with Sam and Caroline when they were young, became a little upset and kept hanging onto her husband's arm until Laura May suggested that she fetch her afghan squares to get her mind off things. Then down came the grandfather, sober and dignified, checking his flip-top watch. "Well?" they asked. "How'd she take it?"

"Took it fine."

"What'd she say?"

"Didn't say anything."

"Shall we go up now?"

"Do what you like," he said, and then he went off to his own house, taking Esther with him to fix his supper.

The others tiptoed up the stairs. Caroline was sitting in her bed against stacks of pillows. When they came in she leaned over to lower the volume slightly on the television set. "Caroline, we're so sorry," they said, and Caroline said, "Why, thank you. It's so nice of you to take an interest."

"If there's anything we could be doing now—"

"I can't think of a thing! But I do appreciate your asking."

"Would you like to go over to the funeral home? Of course it's not as if you had still been *together* or anything, I'm not quite sure what is customary in this case but if you feel you—"

"Why, later, perhaps. Not just now."

"It's probably not customary anyway."

"No."

"Well, if you want us, then—"

"Oh, certainly! I'll let you know first thing."

They tiptoed down again. Although they should be going to their homes for supper, they seemed inclined to churn about in Great-Grandma's living room instead. They weren't quite sure just how they should behave. The last death in the family had been in 1912, too long ago for most of them to remember. "Yet after all," Aunt Sarah said finally, "it's not as if Sam Mayhew were really—"

"No. No."

"And after all, he did actually—"

"Oh, he acted like a man possessed."

"Always trying to turn her against us."

"Making *no* effort to understand her."

"And Caroline's so sensitive. It's the way she is."

"Refusing to give his own daughter away."

"But still," said Aunt Lucy, who sometimes grew overemotional, "Caroline loved him! I know she did, she must have, you could tell she was just torn. And now he's dead. Oh, what will she do now?"

"*Lucy,*" her husband said. "About time to feed me my supper, don't you think?"

"Well, all right."

"We'll try to call Justine from our house, Grandma. If the phone's not fixed, I'll drive out there in the morning."

"Oh, think of Justine. How will she ever forgive herself?"

Upstairs, cowboys sang lonesome songs around a campfire and the wind rolled tumbleweed across the desert with a howling sound.

At nine o'clock that evening, Caroline rose up in her pink silk gown and put on her feathered slippers. Before leaving the room she turned off the television set. She descended the stairs, stately and flowing; she crossed the front hall and went out the door. She drifted across the lawn and then onto the road, where she proceeded down the center with her arms out and her steps mincing and careful like a tightrope walker. To the first car that came, she appeared as monstrous and unexpected as a wad of pink bubble gum. The driver gasped and swerved at the last moment. The second driver was harder to surprise. "Do your drinking at *home*, lady!" he shouted out the window, and then he slid smoothly past.

She had to wait for six cars, all told, before she found one that would run her down.

Duncan brought Justine a cup of beef broth and a silver spoon and a linen napkin. He found her sitting in the living room of Great-Grandma's house, all alone, staring into space. "Oh. Thank you," she said. She set the cup on the coffee table.

"I made it myself."

"Thank you."

"Ma said coffee, but coffee has no food value."

She smoothed her dress.

"Broth has protein," Duncan told her. "You can go without protein for months and feel just fine, never notice, but underneath it's doing you harm that can never be repaired. Protein is made up of amino acids, the building blocks of the—"

"Duncan, I can't *believe* you're saying all this."

"I can't either," he told her.

He waited for her to try the broth. She didn't. He squatted beside her. "Justine—" he said.

But no, too late, the aunts had tracked them down again. "Justine? You mustn't sit like this, dear heart—"

They reminded him of ships. They traveled in fleets. Their wide summer skirts billowed and collapsed as they settled all around him, edging him out. But he didn't give in so easily. "We were just talking," he told them.

"She should be in bed."

"What for?"

"She doesn't look at *all* well."

She didn't. Even her hair seemed changed, hanging lank and lifeless around her face. In just four days she had developed a new deep hollow between her collarbones. She was already losing her country tan. If he could just carry her home, to the sunlit fields and their little house with its ridiculous damask curtains! But the aunts rustled and resettled, inching closer. "She ought to be left with us a while, Duncan. She just feels so *sorry*, you see. She's acting just like her poor dear mother did. You can't take her back to sit all alone in the middle of nowhere."

"Alone?"

"She needs looking after."

"*I* look after her," Duncan told them.

"Yes, but—and she could have her old room again, or maybe yours if hers would bring memories. You could go back to your cows or whatever and we would take good—Justine, do you like Duncan's room?"

"Duncan's? Yes."

"There, see?"

"Or she could come to us," Aunt Bea said. "At our house, you see, we have so much excitement, Esther and Richard rushing around and the twins so talkative, she'd just come out of herself in no time."

"Maybe she doesn't want to come out of herself," Duncan said.

"Oh, it helps to have a little company! All those young people making merry. Justine?"

Justine sat like a stone. The old secret, tucked-in smile she used to flash Duncan seemed gone forever. When he rose she didn't even look his way, and it seemed unlikely that she noticed when he left the room.

Now as she cruised through the darkening house she was aware of how everything here was attached to everything else. There was no such thing as a simple, meaningless teacup, even. It was always given by someone dear, commemorating some happy occasion, chipped during some moment of shock, the roses worn transparent by Sulie's scrubbing, a blond stain inside from tea that Sam Mayhew had once drunk, a crack where Caroline, trembling with a headache, had set it down too hard upon the saucer.

She went out the front door that was dented by Justin Peck's invalid's bed in the fall of 1905. She passed her grandfather's front porch, where Maggie Rose stood in the twilight waiting for a Model T. She climbed Uncle Two's front steps, surrounded by ghostly whispers and murmurs of love and scoldings and reproaches and laughter. Upstairs she found Duncan in his room among Erector Set machines he had built when he was twelve, a full-color poster of Princess Pet in the Land of the Ice Cream Star, the Monopoly board in which all seven cousins had played a thirty-eight-hour world series in the spring of 1944. But Duncan—oh, forever in the present!—was whistling "The Wabash Cannonball" and fiddling with a rectangle of lead-colored metal.

She didn't know how he could whistle.

When she came in the room he stopped. "Do you want to lie down?" he asked her. He began clearing his bed of everything on it, a jungle of wires and soldering irons, tubes of flux, glue, and paint. She sat on the edge of the mattress, but she didn't want to stretch out. It was barely eight o'clock. If she slept now she would lie awake for hours later on, as she had last night and the night before.

"Anything you wanted to say?" Duncan asked.

"No."

"I thought you might have come to tell me something."

"No."

"Well." He went back to whatever he was doing, but he didn't whistle any more. "This is a wire-bending jig," he told her.

She didn't comment.

"These pegs can be moved, see? Then you bend the wire around them any way you want. There are all kinds of curves and angles. I could make you a bracelet. Want a bracelet? Or a necklace, if you like."

She laid her fingers across her eyes, cooling them.

"I've got it," he said. "A nose ring. Want a nose ring?"

When she opened her eyes she found a curve of wire nearly touching her nose, giving off a gray smell, sharp at one end. She batted it away. "What are you trying to *do* to me?" she said.

He looked surprised.

"Are you trying to get me angry on purpose?" she asked him.

"Well, not on *purpose*, no—"

"Why are you acting this way?"

"Justine, *I'm* not acting any way."

"How can you play around with little pieces of wire when both my parents are dead, and you're the one that took me far off and cut the telephone cord and laughed at Mama's letters and wouldn't bring me to visit?"

"Justine."

"Daddy *warned* me," she said. "He told me straight out you were marrying me to torment me."

"Oh, did he?"

"Either that, he said, or to lean on me, but I don't picture *that* ever happening."

"Well, he certainly thought of everything, didn't he," Duncan said.

He went back to bending his wire. He adjusted a peg on the jig and turned a right angle.

"I'm sorry," Justine said finally.

"That's all right."

"I just feel so—"

"It's all *right*."

"Duncan, couldn't we just stay here a while?"

He looked up at her.

"We could live in Great-Grandma's house," she said. "Wouldn't that be nice?"

"No, it wouldn't."

"Please?"

"I should have known," he told her. "I didn't really believe you would come away with me in the first place."

"But I feel I'm getting *pulled*. I hate to just go away and leave them. And I can't stay here without you, but you wouldn't say a word against it when they brought it up."

"*I* don't want to pull you, Justine."

"But then they're the only ones doing it, and they'll win."

"Is that the only way you go anywhere? Being pulled?"

She was silent.

"All right," said Duncan. "I'd like you to come with me. It's important. It's more important than they are."

But she went on watching his face.

"Well, how am I supposed to do this?" he asked her. "I was too well trained, I don't feel *comfortable* saying things straight out. They got to me a little too, you know."

"Oh, Duncan," Justine said. "You've said everything straight out since you were four years old and told Aunt Bea she had hair like broccoli."

"No," said Duncan. "I a Peck. I not talk so good but I give swell presents."

Then he handed her his wire, a stick figure wearing Justine's flat hat and triangular dress, looking so straight-backed and light-hearted that even a tribesman in darkest Africa could tell that someone cared for her.

The family lined up to see them off, their faces papery in the morning sun. "I can't believe that you would be going like this," Aunt Lucy said. Justine kissed her. She kissed Aunt Sarah, who said, "Do you think your parents would have understood? Rushing off as if all that mattered was a pack of billy goats?" Justine kissed her way down the entire row, not skipping even Richard, who ducked and blushed, and when she came to her grandfather she hung onto him hard for a moment as if this, not the wedding, were her real leavetaking. "Oh, um, now, Justine," her grandfather said.

"Goodbye, Grandfather."

Duncan opened the car door and she climbed in. The seat covers had a fish-oil smell from the sunlight, and when she leaned out the window to wave the metal was pleasantly hot on her arm. In the trees above them, mockingbirds were singing. Even when the car roared up they didn't hush. "Scientists," said Duncan, "have been investigating the stimuli that cause birds to vocalize in the morning. So far they have determined only one. They sing because they're happy."

7

Duncan bought a dozen copper-colored hens and installed them in a shed he had built himself, complete with a box of oyster shells to assist in egg production and a zinc watering trough in which they all immediately drowned. But the goats flourished, and since only two customers had answered the newspaper ad there were quarts of surplus milk every day. Justine made butter and hand-cranked ice cream. Duncan boiled up kettles of Norwegian cheese. But no sooner had they finished one batch of milk than the goats gave more, and Justine dreamed at night of a white tide rising all around them. "Maybe we should cut down on the blackstrap molasses," she told Duncan.

"Well, I don't know if that would do much good. We seem to have started something we can't stop, here."

In the mornings Justine walked the gravel road with a basket of cheeses, peddling them to the neighbors, who bought them because they had grown to like her. Seeing her trudge up the driveway, in her country-looking hat and her plain cotton dress that was becoming a little faded, Mrs. Jordan would lumber out on her front steps and beam. "Why, it's Justine Peck! How are you, honey?" Justine smiled trustingly, holding out her basket. It was hard for her to ask people to buy things, but she did enjoy the visits. At each house she stopped for a few minutes to sit in the kitchen and talk, and gradually the smells of kerosene and fatback stopped seeming strange to her and she began to feel comfortable with the stooped, prematurely aged women who offered her buttermilk and ginger cake to put some meat on her bones.

Sometimes, though, alone at home, she felt a gust of sorrow blow through her like a wind and she would stop whatever she was doing, hands stilled, face stunned, and gaze into space for several minutes. Once when she was trimming the weeds that drained the fence's current the smell of cut grass swung her back over years and years and she found herself sitting on a twilit lawn, nestled between her parents, listening to the murmur of her family all around her. She dropped the clippers and reached for the nearest object; she gripped the fence until her knuckles turned shiny. The throb of electricity caused a distant, dull ache. Duncan had to pry her fingers loose and say her name several times before she would look up.

They had not been back to Baltimore after that first visit, but she did write home weekly and one or another of the aunts would answer. Occasionally her grandfather composed a solemn, formal, nineteenth-century note saying that everyone was well and sent best regards. If only she could reach out and touch his knobby hand, as if by accident! But all she said in her own letters back was that Duncan was fine, the weather was fine, the goats were doing nicely.

If the sorrow went on too long she drove to Buskville, where she walked the streets for hours. She had been raised to believe that the best cure for grief was shopping, especially for things to wear. But there wasn't that much money and anyway, she discovered she was incapable of purchasing clothes for herself. Putting on a dress that her mother had not picked out was a betrayal. She was reduced to buying little domestic articles in the dimestore: teaballs, lemon reamers, parsley choppers. It seemed very important to have everything that would make her house perfect.

One day in August, having exhausted all the dimestore's possibilities, she walked down a side street and discovered a hand-lettered cardboard sign reading MAGIC MARCIA, LOVE PROBLEMS. ADVICE. She swooped back through time and found herself on Madame Olita's doorstep, Duncan watching her teasingly with one arm hooked around Glorietta de Merino. After a moment she switched her Woolworth's bag to the other hand and rang Magic Marcia's bell.

The woman who answered was thin and dark, with a crimson slash of lipstick. She was not much older than Justine, but there were two little boys with runny noses hanging onto her skirt. Gray straps slid out from her scoop-necked blouse. Justine was sorry she had come, but it was too late to back out.

Then when she was settled at the kitchen table, over the remains of breakfast, it seemed she was expected to ask some specific question. She hadn't known that. "What is it?" the woman asked, flattening Justine's hand like a letter. "Husband? Boyfriend?"

"No, I—just general things, I wanted to know."

The woman sighed. She scratched her head and frowned at Justine's palm. Apparently she saw nothing unusual. "Well," she said finally, "you're going to live a long time, that's for sure."

"Yes," Justine said, bored. Really she had no particular interest in her future, which seemed certain to be happy and uneventful from here on out.

"Good marriage. Probably travel a little. Health is good. Probably have a lot of kids."

"I will?" Justine asked. Duncan didn't seem to want any children. But the woman said, "*Oh* yes."

A question began to tug at the edges of Justine's mind. She stared into space, not listening to the rest of her fortune. "Um, Magic Marcia," she said finally. "Could you tell me something? If your palm predicts a certain future, is there any way you can change it?"

"Huh?"

"If your future is having children, could you deliberately *not* have children? If your future is to cause someone pain, for instance, isn't there some way you could be very careful and *not* cause pain? Can't you escape your fortune?"

"What is written is written," said Magic Marcia, yawning.

"Oh," Justine said.

On Friday she went to Blainestown, having checked the yellow pages beforehand. She climbed the stairs to SERENA, MISTRESS OF THE OCCULT. This time, she knew exactly what she wanted to ask.

"Could I have avoided my future if my future was to do somebody harm?"

"Man does not avoid the future," Serena said.

On Monday she went back to Blainestown, this time to MADAME AZUKI, ALL QUESTIONS ANSWERED.

"It's in the stars. There is no escape," said Madame Azuki.

"I see."

On Wednesday she went to Baltimore. Duncan was inventing an automatic bean stringer and he only nodded when she told him she would be out for a while. She drove directly to a cluttered section on the east side of town. She found the dry cleaner's, which was exactly the same even to its fly-specked, faded posters showing women in 1940's suits. But Madame Olita's sign on the window above had become a few flecks of paint, and there was a padlock on her door. Justine went into the cleaner's. A large gray man was lining up laundry tags on the counter. "Can you tell me anything about Madame Olita?" she asked him.

"Ah, Madame Olita. She's gone."

"What, is she dead?"

"No, retired. She's not feeling so well, you know? But was she a fortune teller! I don't mind telling you, I used to go to her myself. Okay, so it's mumbo-jumbo. You know why I went? Say you got a problem, some decision to make. You ask your minister. You ask your psychiatrist, psychologist, marriage counselor, lawyer—they all say, 'Well of course I can't decide *for* you and we want to look at all the angles here and I wouldn't want to be responsible for—' They hedge their bets, you see. But not Madame Olita. Not *any* good fortune teller. 'Do X,' they say. 'Forget Y.' 'Stop seeing Z.' It's wonderful, they take full responsibility. What more could we ask?"

"Well, do you know where she is now? Could I just visit her?"

"Sure, she's right down the block. But I don't know how much she's up to. Well, tell her I sent you, Joe sent you. Maybe she could use the company. Five eight three, apartment A."

"Thank you very much," Justine told him.

"Hope you get the answer you want."

She let the door tinkle shut and walked on down the street, passing more cleaners and cut-rate pharmacies and pawnshops. At the end of the block was a large Victorian frame house surrounded by a veranda, and on the veranda sat Madame Olita in a Polynesian wicker chair. Although it was hot, she wore a crocheted shawl. She still had her stubby haircut, but she had lost an enormous amount of weight. Her clothes flopped and her neck was so scrawny that her face appeared to be lunging forward, vulture-like. She looked hollowed out. While Justine climbed the steps she watched without interest, perhaps assuming this was somebody else's visitor. "Hello, Madame Olita," Justine said.

"Hmmm?"

Madame Olita pulled herself together, wrapping the shawl more tightly around her shoulders.

"Joe sent me," Justine said.

"Oh? Joe."

"There's a question I wanted to ask. Would you mind?"

"Well, I'm feeling poorly these days, you see. I don't look into the future much."

"No, it wasn't about the future."

Madame Olita sighed. "Sit down," she said, pointing to the wicker chair beside her. She reached for Justine's hand, as if she hadn't understood.

"But I didn't want—"

Madame Olita bent Justine's palm back and frowned. "Oh, it's you," she said.

Justine felt pleased and shy, as if her unusual lines were her own accomplishment.

"Yes, I see," said Madame Olita, nodding and tapping her teeth with one finger.

"You said my marriage was going to disrupt everything," Justine reminded her.

"Did I."

"You said I would break my parents' hearts. How did you know that?"

"Oh, my dear," said Madame Olita, leaning back suddenly and dropping her hand. "Really, I don't remember. You were young and arrogant, and uncomfortable in my rooms, perhaps I just—"

"But it all came true!"

"Sometimes it does."

"Was that just luck?"

"It may have been. Sometimes it is, sometimes it isn't. Are you asking if I can truly see the future? I can. But more and more it seems to me that people are resisting change, digging in their heels against it. Which does make their futures easy to predict, but why bother? Fortune telling is only good when you forecast a *happening*. It falls flat when you say, 'Never fear, your life will continue in its present course forever . . .'"

She closed her eyes and then opened them and looked puzzled. "But I tend to go on and on," she said. "You had some question you wanted to ask."

Justine sat up straight and placed her hands together. "Madame Olita," she said, "if my fortune was to break my parents' hearts, is it true then that I had no way of avoiding it?"

"Oh, no."

"*No?*"

Goodness, no. You can change your future. I have seen lines alter in a hand overnight. I have seen cards fall suddenly into places where they refused to appear at any earlier reading."

"I see," said Justine, and then she sank back. It was the first answer that sounded right to her, but now she couldn't think why she had wanted to hear it. She felt limp and drained.

"Otherwise," said Madame Olita, "why take any action at all? No, you can always choose to *some* extent. You can change your future a great deal. Also your past."

"My past?"

"Not what's happened, no," Madame Olita said gently, "but what hold it has on you."

"Oh."

"If you are so interested, I will teach you the art yourself if you like."

"The—oh, well, I—"

"*Cards* would be your skill, I think."

"Thank you anyway," Justine said.

"Never mind. You'll be back. I sit here every day of the week, taking the air. You can always find me. Shut the front gate going out, if you will."

On Monday, Justine told Duncan that she was thinking of becoming a fortune teller. "Oh, really?" he said.

"Aren't you going to laugh?"

"Not yet," he said. "First I have to see how good you are."

So she drove off to Baltimore again, to the white frame house where Madame Olita nodded dimly in her Polynesian chair.

"These are ordinary playing cards," said Madame Olita, but to Justine they looked anything but. They were very old and the back of each was different: antique circus scenes of clowns, trapeze artists, dancing dogs, and bareback riders. "They once belonged to my mother. Who, though you wouldn't believe it to look at me, was a genuine gypsy lady with seven ruffled petticoats and tiny brass cymbals that attached to her fingers for keeping time while she danced. She was raised in an abandoned candy store on Gay Street. Not exactly a painted *wagon*, but still . . . unfortunately she married my father, a high school civics teacher. She left her old life entirely, she cut off her long black hair, she had two daughters whom she sent to Radcliffe. However, I would rather have been raised a gypsy."

She cut the cards. Justine sat across from her with her mouth open.

"It was my plan, after I graduated from Radcliffe, to join a caravan and marry a man with one gold earring. But it didn't work out that way. I looked then more or less as I do today. I never married anyone, let alone a gypsy. So I had to get a job in my father's high school, teaching algebra, but meanwhile I had learned fortune telling from my mother. Dancing I never mastered. I tried, though. My sister was quite good at it. But I bettered her at fortune telling. How I coveted these cards! My mother refused to give them to me. Cards like these are passed on only when the owner is dying, you see, and has no further use for them. Naturally I didn't want my mother to die. But shall I tell you? When she failed to wake from surgery at the age of fifty-seven, the first thing I thought was, 'Now I can have the cards.' I went home and got them out of her wooden chest, then I walked over to the school and resigned my position. I set up shop in east Baltimore, above the cleaner's. I have never laid eyes upon a caravan."

She laid the cards out in concentric circles on a wicker table.

"My sister," she said, "got the cymbals."

Then she frowned and stabbed a card with her forefinger. "But pay attention! These cards are not read like books, you know. They have meanings assigned that you can memorize in half an hour, but ambiguous meanings. The death card, for instance. So *called*. But whose death? The client's, or someone's close to him? And when? Is it real or metaphorical? No, you must think of these cards as tags."

"Tags," Justine said blankly.

"Tags with strings attached, like those surprise boxes at parties. The strings lead into your mind. These cards will pull out what you already know, but have failed to admit or recognize. Which is why palmistry works as well, or tea leaves or the Tarot or crystal balls, although I myself have yet to see a thing in a crystal ball. They all have validity, yes, but only when coupled with your own intuitions. You could take up astrology, even, but I already know: you haven't the scholarly mind for it."

"I prefer cards," said Justine.

"Yes, yes, I know. But pay attention to *everything*. Watch your clients carefully. There will only be two kinds. Most are bored and merely hope to be told that something will happen. A very few lead eventful lives but cannot make decisions, which may be *why* they lead eventful lives; they will ask you to decide."

"Which am I?" said Justine.

"Hmm? I don't know. Maybe neither. You have never asked me to read your fortune, after all."

"Oh. I guess not," Justine said.

"You're still looking backward, anyway," Madame Olita told her.

"No, I'm not!"

"Suit yourself."

After her lessons Justine drove straight home, but threads, strings, *ropes* pulled her in the direction of Roland Park and although she never gave in she had the feeling she was bleeding somewhere inside. "Well, you could go over for lunch," Duncan said, but she thought from the way he spoke that he dreaded her agreeing to it. And she knew that her family would be distressed if they heard about Madame Olita. Then her new accomplishment, which was still as thin and fragile as a freshly hatched egg, would never seem right to her again; that was the way her mind worked. She didn't go.

Did she believe in fortune telling herself? At Madame Olita's she did. She was drawn in, impressed and fascinated by those no–nonsense hands dealing out the future. But then at home she felt compelled to test her faith with Duncan. She laid out her Bicycle playing cards self-consciously in front of him. "Today," she told him, "I learned the formation used by Mademoiselle Le Normand, back in Napoleon's time."

"Le Normand," he said, interested, cataloguing the name in his mind.

"We practiced on Madame Olita's landlady, who is eighty-four years old. I predicted she was going to get married."

He grinned.

"But!" said Justine. "She is! She told me afterward."

"Good for you. Good for *her*."

"Madame Olita says just a little longer and I can set up in business."

"We'll retire and live on your earnings," he said.

She was relieved that he didn't laugh. This was the only special skill she had ever possessed, the only thing she knew that he did not. Once he started memorizing her list of significations, but he got side-tracked while shuffling the cards and worked out a proof for Bernoulli's Law of Averages instead.

There were days when Madame Olita was sharp-tempered and nothing would satisfy her. "Really, Justine, I despair of you!" she said. "Your mind! You have every qualification to be a good fortune teller but you will never be great, you're mentally lazy. You coast along in intuition."

"You said intuition was everything."

"Never! I never said it was *everything*. You have to know a few facts as well, after all. These cards are like a doctor's instruments. A good doctor has intuition too but he would never throw his instruments away on the strength of it."

"But you said they were just tags, you said—"

"Enough!" And Madame Olita would fling up her hands and then slump in her chair. "You'll spend your life doing readings for housewives and lovesick schoolgirls," she said. "I don't know why I bother."

But other days she was as mild as milk. Then she would tell stories about her clients. "Will I ever forget that first year? All the Negroes came for clues on how to play the numbers. 'Madame Olita I dreamed of handcuffs last night, which is number five nine eight in my Eye of Egypt Dream Book, but also razors, there was a cutting, eight seven three. So which do I play?' 'My dear,' I told them, 'you leave those numbers alone,' and after a while they gave up on me and never came back. But how I tried! I wanted to have some influence, you see, on their lives. I would give them demonstrations of my psychic ability. I would have them choose a card and sight unseen I would tell them what it was."

"I can't do that," Justine said sadly. Duncan had tested her once after reading an article on J. B. Rhine.

"No, I doubt very much that you would be psychic."

"Then how come I can tell the future?"

"People who have led very still lives can often sense change before others can," Madame Olita said.

"My life isn't still," said Justine.

Madame Olita only sighed.

At the last lesson, she gave Justine a test. "It's time for you to read *my* fortune," she said. Justine had been wanting to do that. She settled down happily at the wicker table, while Olita gazed off toward the street. It was one of her irritable days. "Cut the cards," Justine told her, and she said, "Yes, yes, I know," and cut them without looking. Justine chose a very complicated formation. She wanted to do this thoroughly, not missing a thing. She laid each card out with precision, and then sat back and drummed her fingers on her chair arm. After a moment she moved one card a half inch to the left and resettled herself. She frowned. She stopped drumming her fingers.

Madame Olita looked over at her with cool interest. Still Justine didn't speak.

"Never mind," said Madame Olita. "You passed."

Then she became full of bustle, issuing last-minute instructions. "Did I tell you that strangers should pay ahead of time? If they don't like their fortunes they tend to walk out, they'll walk right out on you."

Justine only gathered the cards in silence, one by one.

"Watch where you work, too. Some places have license fees, sometimes hundreds of dollars. It isn't worth it. Are you listening?"

"What?"

"Don't go to Calvert County. Don't go to Cecil County, don't go to Charles."

"But we live on a farm, I'm not going anywhere."

"Ha."

Justine wrapped the cards and set them on the table. She came to stand in front of Madame Olita.

"Be a little mysterious, I didn't tell you *that*," said Madame Olita. "They'll have more faith. Don't let on where you come from or how you learned what you know. Make a point of ignoring personal questions when you're giving a reading. Will you remember all this? What else should you know?"

Then she gave up. "Well, goodbye, Justine," she said.

"Goodbye," said Justine. "Could I come back for a visit?"

"Oh . . . no. No, I'll be going into the hospital for a while, I think. But I wish you luck."

"Thank you," said Justine. She turned to go.

"Oh, and by the way."

Justine turned back. Madame Olita, sagging in her chair, waved one hand toward the cards. "You might as well take those along with you," she said.

When fall came Justine worked up the courage to offer her services at the high school homecoming fair. She donated her fees to the school. After that people began traveling all the way out to the farm, several a week, mostly women, asking if they should get married, or divorced, or sell their land or have a baby or move to California. Justine was astonished. "Duncan," she said, "I don't want to be *responsible* for people. For telling them who to marry and all."

"But I sort of thought you believed in this," Duncan said.

She wound a strand of hair around her finger.

"Well, never mind," he told her. "Just don't say anything that would cause somebody harm. But I don't think people take *bad* advice. They've got intuition too, you know. In fact I'd be surprised if they take any advice at all."

So she continued receiving people in her small, warm kitchen, laying Madame Olita's cards across the surface of Great-Grandma's rosewood table. She became a gatherer of secrets, a keeper of wishes and dreams and plans. Sometimes when people very young or very old came in, full of vague hopes, unable or unwilling to say what they would like to ask, she merely reassured them. But sometimes she was so explicit that her own daring amazed her. "Don't sell any family possessions, particularly jewelry, particularly your mother's," she would say.

"How did *you* know?"

She hadn't known she did know.

Then sometimes people came whose flat, frictionless lives offered Justine no foothold at all, and she slid into whatever general advice came to mind.

"Don't rely too heavily on a man who bites his fingernails."

In the next room, Duncan snorted.

Justine charged three dollars for each reading. They needed it; their milk customers barely paid for the newspaper ad. Juggling the budget to meet the rent, scraping up money from half a dozen sources, Justine had the feeling that she had been through all this years and years ago. Then she remembered: Monopoly. When Duncan had wiped her out and she was selling back hotels and mortgaging her railroads and turning in her get-out-of-jail-free card, all to pay the rent on Boardwalk. Their present problems did not seem much more serious than that. She knew that Duncan would manage.

For Christmas they went home to Baltimore. The family was very cautious and tactful, circling widely around all delicate subjects. It broke Justine's heart to see what an effort they made. She worried about Duncan—would he say something new to hurt them? She went to bed each night exhausted. But Duncan was meticulously polite. He passed around the gifts that Justine had made by hand and he even invited the family to come and visit some Sunday. ("Oh, well, but it's so much more comfortable for you to come here, don't you think?" everybody said.) On the fourth day, when he became very quiet, Justine was quick to agree that they should head back early. She felt sad saying goodbye, particularly to her grandfather, but each time now it seemed a little easier than before.

In February, when money was especially tight, Duncan got a part-time job in town reporting for the Buskville *Bugle*. "But you can't spell!" said Justine.

"Never mind, you can."

For three weeks he ricocheted around the countryside, attending cornerstone layings, turtle derbies, zoning meetings, a Future Farmers contest in parliamentary procedure, a lecture on crop rotation. He enjoyed everything he went to, indiscriminately, and came home full of new scraps of information. "Did you know you can call up earthworms by vibrating a stick in the ground? If you harvest crimson clover too late it will turn into balls in your horses' stomachs. I've learned a quilting pattern from the eighteenth century." But then writing the articles made him irritable. He never did like going at something systematically. He would hand Justine great sheaves of yellow paper all scrawled over and crossed out, with doodles in the margins. When she ran through them with a red pencil, correcting his spelling and slashing through his long digressions, he lost his temper. "Occurrence, o-c-u-r-e-n-c-e," he said. "Why wreck it up adding extra c's and r's?"

"Because that's how it's spelled."

"A waste of letters. This language has no logic to it."

"I can't help that."

"Why'd you cross out my butterfly paragraph?"

"In an article on potato blight?"

"There happened to be a particularly fine great spangled fritillary sitting on the farm agent's shoulder, totally out of season, ignored by everybody, all the way through the lecture. You can't expect me to overlook a thing like that."

And he would type the article complete and hand it in to the office, where any reference to butterflies was immediately deleted.

"They have minds like a snake's intestinal tract," Duncan said.

The fourth week, he attended an amateur musicians' contest. His article that night began very well, describing the contest's history, its sponsors, and the instruments represented. The next paragraph switched suddenly to first person and related his own impromptu entry with a borrowed harmonica, playing "Chattanooga Choo Choo" for which he won fourth prize. In the third paragraph he reflected on the oddity of the word "impromptu," which could easily be mistaken, he said, for the name of some obscure Rumanian composer.

The newspaper editor said that, actually, they didn't need a new reporter as much as they had thought they would.

By March, Duncan was becoming restless. Justine was not sure why. Everything was going well, six does had been dried off in preparation for their kidding in the spring. But Duncan rattled around the house like a bean in a box, staring out one window after another, starting inventions he didn't finish, sending off to the Department of Agriculture for pamphlets on all sorts of impulsive projects: angora rabbits, fruit trees, popcorn. He painted half the kitchen yellow and then quit. He brought home a carload of rhododendron bushes with their roots balled up in burlap and he planted them all around the yard. "But Duncan," Justine said, "do you think this is the proper time?" They were still wearing overcoats to bed; the ground was still cold and gray. "Why do I have to do everything *properly?*" he asked. "Don't worry, I've got a green thumb. A green hand. I'm a whole green *man.*" And sure enough, the rhododendron took heart and started growing. But Duncan went off and forgot all about it; his strange mood hadn't eased in the least. "To tell the truth, Justine," he said, "this winter business is wearing thin. I imagined we'd be sitting by the stove oiling harness leather or something, but we don't *have* any harness leather. Don't you feel tired of it all?"

"No," Justine said.

She watched, frowning, while he measured the kitchen for some shelves. She didn't think he would ever finish them.

In April eight kids were born, all does. "Did you ever see such luck? We've got a whole damn *herd,*" Duncan said. Justine was glad because the bucks would have had to be killed. She spent hours playing with the kids, running across the field so that they would frolic behind her. They kicked up their heels and turned awkward half cartwheels. She set her face next to their muscular little muzzles; their yellow, slashed-looking eyes looked softly back at her. After the first few days they were switched to bottle feedings, and then to milk from a pan, while Justine crouched beside them and stroked their tufted spines. She fed them handfuls of grass to accustom them to solid food, and for most of the day she kept them in her yard. Meanwhile Duncan carried in endless buckets of warm milk, which he filtered and ran through the great silvery separator. There was suddenly a stream of customers with indigestion, allergies, or colicky babies, all desperate for goat milk, and the grocery store in Buskville had shown an interest in carrying Duncan's cheeses. "There," said Justine. "I knew it would work out!"

"Well, yes," Duncan said.

In May, all the kids died in one night from eating rhododendron leaves.

Justine wandered around forlornly for days, mourning as if the kids had been human. But all Duncan would say was, "Isn't it peculiar? You would think if rhododendron was poisonous they'd know it."

"All those lovely little brown soft furry babies," Justine said.

"But then, goats are fairly intelligent. Are intelligence and instinct inversely related?"

"At least we have the nannies still," Justine said. "We don't have to start *completely* over."

"No."

"And there'll always be a new batch next year, and I won't let them in the yard at all."

Duncan picked up her hand. "Justine," he said, "what would you think of getting out of the goat business?"

"What? Oh, Duncan, you can't quit now. Not after one little setback!"

"No, that's not the reason. I've been considering this for some time. I mean, there's no challenge to it any more. Besides, it keeps you tied down, you always have to be around at milking time. It makes me feel *stuck*, I feel so—and I was thinking. You know what I enjoyed most this year? Building that hen house. Putting things together, fixing them up. Now Ma's brother Ed has a sort of cabinetworks down in Virginia, making unfinished furniture and so on. If he could take me in—"

"Virginia? But that's so far. And *I* never knew you wanted to make cabinets."

"Well, I do."

"We're so nice and settled!"

"But I don't like being settled."

"And we would never get back to Baltimore. Duncan, I've already gone far enough, I don't want to go farther. I couldn't stand going farther."

He waited a moment, looking down at her. Then he said, "All right."

They didn't talk about it again.

People came filing through Justine's kitchen for advice on their spring problems: love affairs, unexplainable bouts of wistfulness, sudden waves of grief over people and places they had not even thought they liked. Justine laid her cards on the rosewood table.

"It will work out."

"Just wait through this."

"You will feel better a week from now."

Duncan plodded through carrying buckets full of milk.

He had grown very silent, although if she spoke to him he always answered. He began drinking bourbon at night after supper. He drank from his great-grandfather's crystal stemware. After the second glass his face became radiant and serene and childlike, and he would switch on a lamp in slow motion and start reading paperbacks. The technical books that he usually liked grew a film of dust while he worked his way through a stack of moldy, tattered Westerns the previous tenants had left in the barn. Whenever Justine looked over his shoulder stubbled men were crawling threats and cowboys were reaching for their guns.

"Duncan," Justine said, "wouldn't you like to sit out on the porch with me?"

"Oh, no thank you. Later, maybe."

But later he went to bed, moving dreamily through the house, not asking if she were coming too. She sat alone at the kitchen table and shuffled her cards. Then she laid them in rows, idly, as if she were her own client. She yawned and looked to see what had shaped up.

She saw journeys, upheavals, surprises, new people, luck, crowds, hasty decisions, and unexpected arrivals.

Which meant, of course, that Madame Olita was right: it was not possible to tell your own fortune.

All the same, if she had had a client with these cards! She imagined how she would glance at him, interested for the first time, amazed at his quicksilver life after all the stale ones she had seen up till now. She imagined possessing such a future herself, having to consult the cards every day, so much was going on.

Then it seemed to her that she was not reading her fortune after all, but accepting little square papers that told her what was expected of her next. She had no choice but to stand up, and gather her cards, and wrap them in their piece of silk before she went to the bedroom to wake Duncan.

This time they moved in a rented truck, which was cheaper than Mayflower. They left behind Justine's beloved goats, Duncan's chewed-looking rhododendron bushes and his empty, echoing, beautifully built hen house. They took most of the Peck furniture as well as ten years' supply of Bag Balm, which turned out to be excellent for chapped hands. And all the way to Virginia, his truck following behind the apple-green Graham Paige, Duncan studied the back of Justine's head and wondered what was going on in her mind. He knew she hated this move. She had joined up with him, he thought, as easily as taking the hand of someone next to her on a sofa. How could she guess that immediately afterward she would be pulled not only off the sofa but also out of the house, out of the city, off to another *state*, even, clinging fast in bewilderment and asking herself what had happened? And now look: she was so bright and reckless, rattling down the highway, he was reminded of her mother's terrible gaiety at the wedding reception. He knew that sooner or later she was going to break down.

Yet in Virginia, in their shallow hot apartment above Uncle Ed Hodges's garage, Justine remained cheerful. She hummed as she settled their belongings in—only, perhaps, taking a little less care this time, leaving the damask curtains unhung and giving Aunt Marybelle, without a thought, the huge walnut breakfront when it wouldn't fit through the apartment door. She located a church bazaar, where she told fortunes, and after that there was a steady trickle of clients. To Duncan they were indistinguishable from her Buskville clients—mostly women, faded housewives and very young girls—and their lives were indistinguishable too, and their futures, which even he could have predicted, but Justine was patient and kind with them and it was plain they all loved her. In the afternoons, if she had no readings, she came to the cabinetworks and watched Duncan build things. At first she was shy among the blunt, sawdusty carpenters, but she warmed up after a while. She made friends with them and told fortunes for their wives and kept their children. Sometimes she even helped out with the work, sitting on a board for someone or sanding down a tabletop. And always she was so joyous. How long could this last?

She said she wanted a baby. Duncan didn't. The idea of a family—a closed circle locking him in, some unlucky child whom *he* would lock in—made him feel desperate. Besides, he was not so sure that it was medically sound. Who knew what might be passed on? He pointed out their heredity; heart murmurs, premature births, their grandfather's deafness.

"But!" Justine said. "Look at our teeth! They're perfect, not a cavity in the lot. Nobody's ever lost one."

"Justine, if I hear one more word about those goddam teeth—"

But in the end he gave in. He agreed to a baby the way Justine, he imagined, had agreed to move to Virginia; he assumed it was necessary for her in some way that he would never understand. And all through her pregnancy he tried to take an interest. He listened to the details of every doctor's appointment, he practiced her breathing exercises with her until he grew light-headed. Twice he drove her to Baltimore for over-long visits with the aunts, who fussed and clucked around her while Duncan skulked nearby with his collar turned up and his hands jammed deep in his pockets. It seemed to him that his part in all this was so *incidental*. But when he steeled himself to suggest that she might want to go to Baltimore for the birth as well, Justine turned a sudden level gaze on him and said, "No, thank you. I'll have it here with you." How did her mind work?

By her seventh month she had started poring over old photographs in the evenings, particularly photographs of her mother. She sat squinting through a magnifying glass, her hard little knot of a stomach straining the faded dress she had worn since she was seventeen. For she hadn't bought any maternity clothes. Was she worried about the expense? In his experience, women *shopped*. He had expected a frilly layette to mount up in some bureau drawer, but the only things she had were what the aunts gave her. All the preparation she had made was to start building a cradle at the cabinetworks. And when he offered to get her a maternity dress himself her eyes spilled over with tears, something that almost never happened. "But I don't *want* anything. Nothing is right. I couldn't stand to buy anything in those stores," she said. Duncan was mystified. He did the only thing he could think of: he went out and bought three yards of flowered material and a Simplicity dress pattern. He assumed there was not much difference between reading a pattern and a blueprint; he could figure it out in no time and run it up on Aunt Marybelle's Singer. But when he got home Justine was in labor, and he had to take her straight to the hospital. It occurred to him during the trip that Justine was going to die. He thought he had known that all his life without admitting it: she would die at an early age because the world was so ironic. The sight of her calm face beside him—she was so *ignorant!*—made him furious. "You are *not* going to leave me with that baby to raise," he told her, and she turned and looked at him gently, from a distance. "No, of course not," she said.

She was right, of course. The birth was easy. Justine didn't die, she didn't come close to dying. He had been angry for nothing, and on top of that he had an eighty-five-cent pattern now which would never be used, because he'd be damned if they would ever go through this again.

Justine wanted to name the baby Margaret Rose, which was fine with him. But he was a little surprised. He had expected to have to argue against Caroline, or Lucy or Laura or Sarah, none of which he could stand. How long had Justine's fancy been taken by her runaway grandmother? Who was never mentioned, not ever, except by Sulie, who had loved Margaret Rose since first arriving to work for the Pecks at age thirteen. Certainly their grandfather never spoke of her. Duncan was curious as to what the old man would say now. Would he object? But no, when he came for a visit and they told him (Justine shouting it fearlessly into his good ear, which was turning bad like the other), he only nodded as if it meant nothing. Duncan should have guessed. *Justine* knew. In that family wrongdoers vanished without a trace, not even a hole to show where they had been.

They called the baby Meg for short. She was a blond, stocky, serious baby whose silvery eyebrows were quirked in a permanent frown. When she learned to walk, she *trudged;* if she laughed, it was only after a moment of study. Everything she did was laborious, even stringing wooden beads or feeding a doll or lugging around the large cardboard boxes that for several years she insisted on taking wherever she went. It touched Duncan to see her heaving her toys back into the toy chest every evening, unasked. As she grew older, as life became more hurried and scattered, she developed into a housewifely, competent little soul who always knew where things were, and what had been forgotten, and when they were supposed to be somewhere. By the age of six she had her own alarm clock, the only one in the house. For her seventh birthday she asked for a pop-up toaster. (She wanted to make toast like other people, she said, not in the oven.) She fixed her own breakfast, rinsed her own dishes, and hunted her own socks. Every afternoon when school was over she did her entire homework assignment without being told, her soft yellow head bent low, a pencil clutched tight in her fist. She asked to go both to Sunday school and church, neither of which her parents ever attended; she went alone, dressed in clothes from her grandmother, a bonnet and white gloves, clutching a quarter for the collection plate. Saturday afternoons she read her Bible assignment. "Meggie!" Justine would say, swooping down on her. "Come outside! Come play!" But Meg would have to finish and put everything away before she came. Then Justine took her out visiting other children, or hopscotching, or roller skating. If Justine stretched Meg's skates to the largest size she could wear them herself, and she demonstrated all she remembered from the old days. In a strong wind she stood still and was blown backwards, with her skirts pressed wide and flat. She leaned on the air like a figurehead, laughing, but Meg watched dubiously with her thumb in her mouth.

"This is a cricket," Duncan told Meg.

"Ooh."

"Do you want to know how he chirps?"

"No."

"Many people suppose that he does it with his legs but actually—"

Meg looked not at the cricket but at Duncan. Her eyes were transparent, and flat at the bottom.

He had not expected to feel like a father, but he did. Just the curve of her cheek could give him a wrench, or the blue veins inside her wrist or the stolid way she stood watching other children playing. But he was clearer-sighted than Justine, who thought Meg was perfect. He knew, for instance, that although Meg was of normal intelligence she had a mind that plodded and toiled, with narrow borders; that she was fiercely anxious for regularity, permanence, order. It seemed to him that he was the object of an enormous joke: he had feared all the genetic defects but the obvious one, total Peckness. She was more Peck than anybody, more even than stodgy Claude or the soft, placid twins. When she went to Baltimore for a visit she was the darling. There was not one facet of her that was foreign in any way. It was Duncan who was foreign. As she grew older she seemed to realize that, and more and more often the two of them found fault with each other, bickering pointlessly, defending their two worlds. Then Meg, silenced finally by his quicker tongue, would take on a closed, sad look, and he would be reminded of Justine as a child. He remembered how hopefully Justine would follow her cousins, her eyes anxious, her smile hesitant, her dress as carefully kept as when her mother had buttoned it in the morning. He softened, and gently tweaked a sprig of Meg's hair until she gave in and smiled.

But where was the child Justine had been? There was nothing hesitant about her now. She had become fast-moving, kaleidoscopic. There was a sort of dash to everything she did that surprised and fascinated him. When she flew down a street people turned to look after her: an angular, frayed, pretty woman who looked as if she had no idea where she was going. She still wore the washed-out dresses from her girlhood, their hems adjusted belatedly half a dozen times, either raised to stand out like a spare tire around her knees or lowered and showing all previous levels like lines on ruled paper; and on her feet, Mary Janes with neat little straps; on her head that everlasting Breton, which Duncan had had to replace, twice, when the crown broke through from all the times she had clutched it to her head on her wild, careening journey through life. Her days consisted of a string of unexpected events. Passing a crazy man talking to himself, for instance (whom Duncan pretended not to hear), Justine stopped to answer whatever question he had asked the clouds and ended up involved for years in the man's Houdini-like escapes from asylums. She was the only person Duncan knew who had actually had a baby left on her doorstep. (Later the mother changed her mind, but Justine had been prepared to keep him.) At any moment of the day he might catch sight of her driving seventeen third-graders in a fire engine down Main Street, or picketing a whites-only movie theater with the day's groceries still in her arms, or zipping past his shop window towed by two gigantic St. Bernards when an hour ago she had owned no dogs at all. And she moved so easily from town to town! Oh, at first, of course, she was always a little reluctant. "But I like it here. We were just getting settled." (She could get settled anywhere, he thought, in a cave or a coal mine even; she was like a cat.) "I don't want to leave all our friends," she would say. (Her friends, generally; Justine made friends by leaps and bounds while Duncan was more gradual. It seemed he had barely started getting close to people when it was time to leave a place.) "What do we have to go for, Duncan?" But it was plain what they had to go for—there he was, ever grimmer and bleaker, slogging through the days. "Oh, well," she always said in the end. "We'll move. We'll just move, what's wrong with that?" Then the two of them grew light-headed, as if spared from some disaster they had been dreading for weeks. Justine went off too far ahead of time to pack—her favorite occupation, which became easier every year as they left more and more things behind. She had very nearly stopped cooking, stopped cleaning; she had given away her wedding saucepans as if just *being* were enough to take all her time and attention. For dinner she served whatever came to mind, forgetting to eat herself and opening a window instead to beg a street Arab to let Meg have a ride on his horse. "Oh, *Mama*," said Meg, who would not think of riding such an animal and wished that her mother would not embarrass her by hanging out windows. But Duncan drifted on this turbulence happily; during lulls he felt something was missing. When he came home and Justine was out the air seemed empty and dead. He plowed through the rooms calling her name. He went to neighbors. "Is Justine with you? She's not at home, I don't see her anywhere." Until, having tracked her down, he could heave a long sigh and sink onto the nearest flat surface. "I couldn't find you. I didn't know where you were. I didn't know what had happened to you." Then life zoomed into full speed again, the unexpected fluttered all around them like confetti, and Duncan felt peaceful.

Sometimes he remembered that she had not always been this way, though he couldn't put his finger on just when she had changed. Then he wondered if she only *pretended* to be happy, for his sake. Or if she were deliberately cutting across her own grain, like an acrophobe who takes up sky diving. He became suddenly thoughtful, offering her perhaps a visit to Baltimore, although still, after all these years, the mere thought of his family filled him with a contrariness he seemed unable to control. Justine was still very fond of the family. When he pointed out for her the meaning beneath their words, the sharp edge beneath their sweet, trite phrases, Justine pointed out the meaning beneath *that* meaning, and he would have to admit some truth in what she said. She had the pathetic alertness of a child who has had to depend too much on adults; she picked up every inflection, every gesture and untied ribbon and wandering eye, and turned it over and over to study its significance. (Was that how she could read the future? She had foretold Great-Grandma's death, she said, when she noticed her buying all her lotions in very tiny bottles.) So with Justine's words fresh in his mind he would drive to Baltimore feeling charitable and enlightened, though that never lasted past the moment of entering staid chilly Roland Park with its damp trees and gloomy houses and its reluctant maids floating almost motionlessly up the hill from the bus stop, following their slow flat feet while their heads held back. And once they had arrived he kept watching her, trying to see if deep down she hated him for taking her away. But Justine was no different here from any other place. She gave everybody sudden kisses, knocked Aunt Bea's spectacles askew, swooped through the house causing all the fairy lamps and figurines to tremble on the tables, and once at supper she accidentally ate the little glass spoon from her salt dish. All the aunts jumped up and wrung their hands, but Duncan smiled and his forehead smoothed and he rested back upon the white, tumbling waters of life with Justine.

Now the aunts and uncles were old, the grandfather wore a hearing aid, and the cousins (Sally divorced, the rest unmarried, all childless) were developing lines and sags in their curiously innocent faces like aging midgets. The lawns had grown meager and the fleet of Fords was outdated. The only servant was old Sulie, who shuffled around angry about something, as she had been for years, stirring the dust back and forth with a wilted gray rag. Great-Grandma's house was inhabited by Esther and the twins, but Justine was the legal owner. Someday, everyone said, Justine and Duncan would want to come home bringing their sweet Meg, and when they did this house would be ready. Justine only smiled. Of course they would never live there. Yet always in the backs of their minds it waited as a last resort, if all else failed, if they ever were forced to admit defeat. It figured in back-up plans; it moved in on them, inch by inch, whenever money was tight and jobs were scarce, and over the years it had come to contain an imaginary life parallel to their own, advancing when theirs did. They knew what nursery school they would have sent Meg to if they had lived here, and then what grammar school; what pharmacy they would have patronized and where they would have gone for their groceries. Yet only one glance at that house, where it loomed beneath the oaks, was enough to make Duncan grow dark and hollow and he would suddenly lay a hand on Justine's thigh as if she were a square of sunlight on a windowseat, and he just in from the cold.

$$8$$
$$=$$

An inferior class of people tended to travel by bus. Daniel Peck glared at them: three sailors, a colored boy in a crocheted cap, and a sallow, weasely woman with four children whom she kept slapping and pinching. One of the children stuck out his tongue. "Look at there. Did you see that?" Daniel asked his granddaughter.

She glanced up from her magazine.

"Child made a face at me."

She smiled.

"Well, there's nothing funny about it, Justine."

Whatever she said, he didn't quite catch. It bothered him to go motoring with his hearing aid on.

They were returning from Parthenon, Delaware, where finally, after a great deal of tedious correspondence, he had located the youngest son of the past headmaster of Salter Academy. A Mr. Dillard. Mr. Dillard had already informed him by letter that he had never kept in touch with any of his father's students (who were older than he and not likely to be among the living anyway, he said tactlessly), but Daniel Peck knew that memory was not such a well-ordered affair. Sometimes little things could jog it, he knew, sometimes so small a thing as the smell of clover or the sight of a boy wobbling on a bicycle. So he had come in person, bringing his photograph of Caleb and prepared to offer any detail he could think of, a whole wealth of detail flattened and dried in his mind. "He was a tardy boy, always tardy. Perhaps your father mentioned having a student with a tardiness problem. And let's see, he was extremely sociable. Surely if there had ever been a class reunion of any sort he would have attended. Or just come visiting, don't you know. Perhaps come visiting your father years later, he would do that sort of thing. Can you remember such a visitor? Tall boy, blond, this picture doesn't quite show. He had a habit of tilting his head when listening to people. If you were a child he passed on his way to your father's study, for instance, he would most surely have spoken to you. Though he was not a *smiling* person. Did you see him? Do you know?"

But Mr. Dillard did not know. A stooped, red-faced man who wouldn't speak up. There were cartoon fishes all over his bathroom wallpaper. His wife was nice, though. Lovely lady. She offered them homemade butter mints, the first he had tasted in years, and gave Justine the recipe on an index card.

He set his face toward Justine, waiting till she would feel it and raise her head again. "Yes, Grandfather," she said.

"What'd you do with that recipe?"

She looked blank.

"Recipe card Mrs. Dillard gave you."

"Oh!"

"Don't tell me you lost it."

"Oh no. No, I—"

He didn't know the rest of what she said but he could *see* her plainly enough, rummaging through her crushed straw bag and then her dress pockets, one of which was torn halfway off. Gone, then. He would never have those fine butter mints again.

He removed a large leather wallet from the inner breast pocket of his suit coat. He took out a cream-colored envelope and a sheet of stationery. The envelope was already stamped and addressed. He was very well organized. His stepmother had taught him years ago: compose your card of thanks on the carriage ride home. Never allow an hour to elapse before writing a bread-and-butter note. "Then why," Duncan had asked as a child, "don't we write the whole *letter* ahead of time?" But no, that wouldn't do at all. You had to mention something personal that had occurred during the visit, don't you see. As Daniel did now, after frowning a moment at his pen.

Dear Mrs. Dillard,   *March 5, 1973*
    I write to express my appreciation for your hospitality. Your butter mints were extremely tasty, and it was very kind of you to take the time to see us. We shall remember our visit to you with a great deal of pleasure.

                                     Respectfully,
                                     Daniel J. Peck, Sr.

When he got back to Caro Mill or wherever he would type a copy of this note for his files. He liked to keep a record of all correspondence, particularly that regarding Caleb. His old Underwood typewriter, with its metal keys and high black forehead, was forever set up on the bureau by his bed; his file cabinet was packed solid with letters of inquiry, thank you letters, follow-up letters, for how many years back? How many years?

Well, his stepmother died in 1958. *That* was a hard time. She was the last person on this earth who called him Daniel. He had not realized that until she died. She had journeyed through all his life with him, minus the first few months: seventy-seven years. The only person who remembered his kid soldier doll, and his father's way of widening his eyes when displeased, and the rough warm Belgian blocks that used to pave the streets downtown. She left her house to Justine, and he knew why. (She was uneasy in her mind about that girl, the sweetest of his granddaughters and the most defenseless, dragged from pillar to post by harum-scarum Duncan, whom marriage had not toned down in the least.) But for months after her death Daniel would not enter her house or look at it, and although he allowed Esther and the twins to move in he told them to stay out of her bedroom. He would sort her things later, he said; he was just a little busy right now. He walked around feeling wounded, struck as if for the first time by the fact that the world kept progressing and people aged and died and nothing in life was reversible. Where had it all gone to? Whatever happened to that little brown German step-grandfather he used to have? Or Sarah Cantleigh's family, who cried whenever they saw him, were they all dead by now? Where was that silent, musical brother of his with the tilted head?

But he was a sensible man, and in time he recovered. Then he sent for Sulie with her ring of keys. They went to sort Laura's belongings. "Oh, my soul," Sulie kept saying. "My soul." She had been mad at Laura for decades, but she looked stricken as she gazed around the dark, stale room. Her eyes were triangular and the cords stood out in her neck. She had a wrinkled face like a yellow paper kite. "So this is what it all come to," she said.

"Now if you don't stop that," Daniel told her, "you can just go on back to the kitchen, hear?"

He left the clothes for the women to deal with; that was none of his business. What concerned him were her desk drawers, jewelry boxes, and knick-knack shelves, which held little momentos that should be parceled out among the family. He opened drawers guiltily, shamed by the puffs of lavender scent that rose from everything as if she were still in the room somewhere. "Well, I just don't know," he said to each new object they found, and then when he had laid it aside Sulie would pick it up and say, "Miss *Sarah* always admire this," or "Miss Bea always saying how she wish she had one like it."

"Take it to her then. Fine. Fine," said Daniel.

He kept nothing for himself. Those neat drawers, with everything arranged so precisely and all for nothing, took away his interest in life. And maybe Sulie's, too. At any rate, when he offered her the oval brooch that contained a plait of Laura's mother's hair and had only one little thing wrong with the clasp, Sulie's mouth turned downward. "I don't want it," she said.

"Suit yourself," he told her. Not everyone would put up with Sulie's rudeness the way he did.

In a desk drawer behind a stack of stationery he found an ancient brittle advertisement for Baum's Fine Cutlery. Beneath it, an envelope that looked as if it had been handled a great deal. Inside was a photograph of Caleb playing the cello in a stable loft.

Now, where did that come from?

He had never seen it before, but from the poor focus and the haphazard composition he guessed that it was the work of Margaret Rose that summer she got her Brownie. For a few months she had wandered everywhere, photographing the most unlikely things: Sulie stringing beans, Sarah on her rocking horse, Lafleur Boudrault playing cigar-box guitar and Mark with a mouthful of honeysuckle blossoms. (Daniel had known she was gone for good when he found all her photos of the children missing. But enough of that.) He peered at Caleb's blurred, sharp-featured face. So far as he knew this was the only picture of Caleb in existence. Not counting the one in the album: age two, wearing a ruffled dress and holding an open book he could not possibly have read. And of course all traces of Margaret Rose had been systematically destroyed long ago. Yet in a sense this was a picture of her too, a permanent record of her hasty way of doing things; and her presence could be inferred from the head-on, quizzical look Caleb directed to the camera holder—an expression he reserved for Margaret Rose. Daniel passed a hand over his eyes. "I believe that will be all for today, Sulie," he said.

"What, you quitting?"

"For now."

"Leaving this mess any which old way?"

"*Later* I'll tend to it."

When he left she was poking the piles of belongings with angry, crabbed hands, muttering beneath her breath. He didn't care to hear what she was saying.

Then for several evenings in a row he sat alone in his bedroom studying the photograph, testing the new feeling of sorrow that drove straight through his ribcage. And when that was absorbed (not lessened, just adjusted to) he became, he admitted, a little crazy. He began wondering if this photo didn't have some secret message to it. It was impossible for such an object just to *be*, wasn't it? He studied the angle of Caleb's hat, the set of his cello, the shreds left on the stable wall by some old poster. What was the significance? Meanwhile his bachelor son and his two spinster daughters whispered downstairs, wondering what he could be doing. When Laura May knocked on his door, he jumped and shoved the photo into his pocket. All she found was her father in his easy chair with his arms folded unnaturally across his front.

Then he went to Lucy, who played a little piano still. He pulled her aside one day when she was counting Mason jars in the pantry. "Lucy," he said, "*you* know music."

"Oh, Father Peck, I—"

"Look here. What note is this man playing?"

He showed her the photo. Surprise set little sharp pleats across her forehead. "Why, who—" she said.

"What note is he playing?"

"Oh, well, I don't—actually, it doesn't look to me as if he's playing *any* note."

"What? Speak up."

"Not any note."

"Why, how is that possible? No note at all? I never heard of such a thing."

"It looks to me as if he's just resting his bow on the strings, Father Peck."

"But that would be ridiculous."

"Oh, no, it's really quite—"

"I never heard of such a thing," he said, and then he slammed out of the pantry.

Already he knew he had made a mistake. For Lucy, of course, had to go and tell Two, and Two out of all the family was the most certain to recognize a description of Caleb. Then everybody knew, and everybody asked him what he thought he was up to. Caleb was best forgotten. He was surely dead by now. What did it matter what note he had played on a summer's day in 1910?

When Justine visited home that August, she came to where he sat in his slat chair beneath an oak tree. She kissed his cheek and drew back and looked at him. He could tell she had heard something. They had all been discussing him behind his back. He snorted. "You know, of course, that I am *non compos mentis,*" he told her.

She went on studying him, as if she took what he had said seriously. A literal-minded girl, Justine. Always had been.

"Could I see Caleb?" she asked finally.

"Pardon?"

He thought he had heard wrong.

"Your picture of Caleb."

"The others are asking *not* to see it."

"But I don't even know what he looks like," she said.

He frowned at her. Well, no, of course she wouldn't. Probably didn't know much of *anything* about him. Laura never let his name cross her lips; he seldom had himself; and to the others Caleb was nearly forgotten, a distant grownup uncle whom they had never found very interesting.

"Well," Daniel said.

He drew out the photograph, protected now by glass.

"My brother," he said.

"I see," said Justine.

"Generally he did not go about in his shirtsleeves, however."

Justine bent over the photograph. Her lowered eyelids reminded him of wings. "He looks like you," she said.

"But his eyes were brown."

"His face is the same."

"Yes, I know," said Daniel, and he sighed. He took back the picture. "The others, you see, they don't count him any more. To them he's a deserter."

Justine said something he couldn't catch.

"Eh? To me," he said, "he is still a member here. He goes back to nearly as long ago as I can recollect. I just like to think of him, is all. What's wrong with that?"

"Not a thing," Justine said.

"I would give all the remaining years of my life if I could set eyes on him again."

She said something else. He took a swipe at the air, protesting the curtain of muffled sound that separated them.

"If I could just walk to church with him once more," he told her, "only this time, paying closer *attention*, don't you see. If I could pass by the Salter Academy and look in the window and see him wave, or hear him play that foolish messy music of his on the piano in the parlor—if they could just give me back one little scrap of time, that's all I ask!"

"Oh, well," said Justine. "Come around to the front, Grandfather, see how Meg's grown." And then she took him by the hand, so that he had to rise and follow. In a way, he was a little disappointed in Justine. He had thought she might understand his viewpoint, but if she did she didn't let on.

In November of that year, on a cold, waterlogged day, he received an envelope postmarked Honora, Maryland, where Justine was living at the time. There was no letter, only a clipping from the Honora *Herald*, a whole page devoted to education. He was puzzled. Education did not much interest him. But wait: at the bottom was a very old-fashioned photograph of rows and rows of young boys. The caption said:

THE GOOD OLD DAYS

Above, the author's own school, Salter Academy in Baltimore, around the turn of the century. Note gaslights along the walls. Author is in seated row, second from left.

Daniel took off for Honora within the hour, driving his V-8 Ford. He arrived at Justine's house waving the clipping. Justine was in the kitchen reading some lady's future—an occupation he and all the family preferred to ignore. "Never mind that," he told her. "I want to see Ashley Higham."

"Who's Ashley Higham?"

"The man who wrote this piece, of course."

"Oh, then you *do* know him!" Justine said.

"No I don't know him, don't know him from Adam, but it says right here he went to Salter Academy, doesn't it? Says this is him seated, second from left, and not an arm's length away from him is my own brother Caleb, isn't it?"

"Is that right?" said Justine. She set down her cards and got up to have a look. So did the lady, not that it was any of her business.

"Now all I've got to do is find Ashley Higham," Daniel said.

"Oh, well, Grandfather, I don't really know where—"

"*I* know," said the lady.

So it was the lady who led the way to Ashley Higham. And Mr. Higham did, in fact, remember Caleb well, but had not seen him since graduation day in 1903. However, he had a remarkable mind and could reel off the name of every boy, his shaky white index finger slowly traversing the rows of faces. Daniel recorded each name on a sheet of paper. Later he would copy them into a pocket-sized ring notebook that he carried with him everywhere, gradually stuffing it fatter and fatter. For one thing led to another, one man remembered another who had been a friend of Caleb's and *that* man remembered Caleb's elocution teacher, who turned out to be deceased but his grandson in Pennsylvania had saved all his correspondence and from that Daniel found the name of the geography teacher, and so on. His files began filling up. His Ford clocked more miles in a year than it had in all its past life. And bit by bit, as the rest of the family grew more disapproving (first arguing reasonably, then trying to distract him with television and scrapbooks and homemade pie, finally stealing his car keys whenever his back was turned) he began staying for longer periods of time with Justine. Only visiting, of course. It would never do for Caleb to come home unexpectedly and find him vanished without a trace. His house still waited for him in Baltimore, his daughters still kept his room made up. But Justine was the only one who would hop into the car with him at a moment's notice, and go anywhere, and talk to anyone and interpret all the mumbled answers. And when he was discouraged, Justine was the one who bolstered his confidence again.

For he did get discouraged, at first. At first he was in such a hurry. He thought he was right around the corner from success, that was why. Then when he traveled clear across the state to find Caleb's oldest, dearest friend and learned that he had last seen Caleb in 1909, he grew morose and bitter. "I always assumed," he told Justine, "that people keep in touch, that if they lose touch they go back and pick it up again, don't you know. Of course I am more a *family* man myself, family's been my social life. But I would suppose that if you just watched a man's best friend long enough, you would be certain to see the man himself eventually. Well, not Caleb. In fifty years he has not once gone back to pay a call, and his friend has never done a thing about it. What do you make of that?"

Justine said, "Never mind, Grandfather. It will work out." (Was she speaking *professionally?*) And the next morning she was perfectly willing to set off again, cheerful as ever, never losing patience. So there was no need to hurry after all. He began to relax. He began to enjoy the search itself, the endless rattling rides, the motionless blue sky outside the window of his train. (For they had quickly switched to railroad, as his deafness had caused several near accidents and Justine's driving terrified him.) In the old days, merely a business trip to New York had made him feel like a ball of yarn rolling down the road, unwinding his tail of homesickness behind him in a straight line back to Roland Park. But now he learned to concentrate solely on the act of traveling. He liked to imagine that Caleb himself had ridden this very train. He bobbled along on the Southern Railroad Line or the

B & O, on dusty plush seats, occasionally stretching his legs on some small-town platform where, perhaps, Caleb had stood before him. And he returned home as confident as when he left, for there was always time to search further, next week or next month or whenever he felt up to it.

If Duncan minded this permanent visit, he never said so. In the beginning Daniel had asked him outright. (Well, as outright as he could get.) "Nowadays, people seem to prefer a minimum of adults in one household, have you noticed?" he had said. But Duncan only smiled. "Some do, some don't," he said. Another of those unexplained remarks of his. He did it on *purpose*. Daniel mulled for several days, and then he went to Justine. "Duncan of course has never kept close family ties," he told her, and waited, trustingly, for her to understand. She did.

"That's true," she said, "but he hasn't said anything so far."

And Daniel was careful to see that he never gave Duncan reason to. He held back from advice (which Lord knows the boy could have used) and praise and criticism. He accepted every change of address without question, although none of them were the least bit necessary. Didn't it occur to Duncan that other people had low periods too, and just sat them out instead of packing up bag and baggage? You endure, you manage to survive, he had never heard of someone so consistently refusing to. But never mind, he didn't say a word. He went uncomplainingly to each new town, he accepted Justine's half-hearted cooking and cleaning, which were, he assumed, the natural result of failing to give a woman any permanence in her life. Why should she bother, in those shabby, limp houses that looked flung down, that seemed to be cowering in expectation of the next disaster? And meanwhile Laura's fine place was sitting empty. (He didn't count Esther and the twins living there, for really they belonged at home with their parents.) But leave it be, leave it be. The only change he made in their lives was to deed his Ford to them once he quit driving. It made him nervous to ride about in the Graham Paige, for which Duncan had to haunt antique shows every time a part wore out. "But I don't like Fords," Duncan said. "I have a deep-seated *hatred* of Fords," and for half a year they had been a two-car family, Justine darting about in the Ford and Duncan in the Graham Paige, whistling cheerfully and looking down from time to time to watch the highway skating along beneath the holes in the floorboards. The engine, he said, was in fine shape, and no doubt it was, for Duncan was an excellent mechanic. But you have to have something to put an engine *in*, not this collection of green metal lace and sprung springs; and on moving day that year, without a word, Duncan had left it sitting in front of the house and driven off in the U-Haul. His grandfather pretended not to notice. He was a tactful man.

He lived in his own tiny, circular world within their larger one. While they moved up and down the eastern seaboard, made their unaccountable decisions, took up their strange acquaintances and then lost them and forgot them, Daniel Peck buttoned his collarless shirt and fastened his pearl-gray suspenders and surveyed his white, impassive face in the bedroom mirror. He wound his gold watch. He tidied his bed. He transformed even his journeys, the most uncertain part of his life, into models of order and routine and predictability. For Justine was always with him, he always had the window seat, she read her *National Geographic*, they carried on their spasmodic, elliptical conversations over the noise of the road. Now they had to ride the buses more and more often, since that was all most towns had these days. They would take long circuitous routes in order to join up someplace, somehow, with a railroad, and even *then* it was usually Amtrak, a garish untrainlike train where nothing went right, where certainly Caleb had never set foot in his life. But still Daniel traveled calm and expressionless, his hands on his knees, a ten-dollar bill pinned inside his undershirt, and his granddaughter's hat brim comfortingly steadfast in the right-hand corner of his vision.

They were drawing close to what's-its-name, Caro Mill. He noticed people rising to put their coats on, and lifting suitcases down from the rack. He noticed within himself a sudden feeling of emptiness. So they were back again, were they? He sighed. Justine looked up again from her magazine.

"We didn't get much done," he told her.

"Why, no."

To her it didn't matter. She thought he felt the same, he had ridden content beside her for so many years now. But lately he had had a sense of impatience, as in the old days when he first began his search. Did that mean he was drawing close to Caleb? Once he almost asked her outright for a reading from her cards—ridiculous business. Of course he had stopped himself in time. Now he stared bleakly out the window at a jumble of service stations and doughnut shops. "So *this* is where we're headed," he said.

"What?"

"It's not much of a place to come back to."

"Oh—" said Justine, and then something else he couldn't catch, but he knew it would be cheerful. Justine did not seem to be easily disappointed. Which was fortunate. Whereas he himself was leaden with disappointment, sinking fast. He felt there was something hopeless about the deep orange sunset glowing beyond an auto junkyard. "Grandfather?" Justine asked, in her most carrying tone. "Are you all right?"

"Yes, certainly."

The bus wheezed past a dismal hotel with tattered windowshades. It stopped in front of the Caro Mill Diner. Place couldn't have a regular terminal, no. Out they had to climb, in the middle of the street. The driver did not so much as give Justine a hand down the steps, or either of the other ladies; Daniel had to do it. He touched his temple for each one in turn as he let go of her arm. "Why, thank you," one lady told him. The other didn't say a word, or else he missed it.

In front of the diner sat the Ford, three feet from a hydrant, battered and dusty and bearing a long new dent in the rear bumper. He studied the damage. In the old days people left notes about such things, giving their names and telephone numbers. Not any more. When he finally climbed into the car he said, "Conscience has vanished."

"Excuse me?"

Justine looked at him, one hand outstretched toward her own door which was flapping open and snarling traffic. "What's vanished?"

"Conscience, I said. They dent your bumper and don't even leave a note."

"Perhaps I," said Justine, and something else.

"No, if you had done it I would have noticed. Besides, you've had this week's accident." His little joke. He laughed, covering his mouth with his fist to turn it into a cough.

Then, wham! He was jarred and knocked into the windshield. Aches and pains started up all over, instantly. It seemed that someone had reached down a gigantic hand and flung him like a doll. "Grandfather?" Justine asked. There was a long red welt on the inside of her arm, and a few dots of blood. Just past her, a car had stopped and a man was climbing out. And where the door had been swinging open there was nothing now at all, just clear blank air and then the man's angry face. The man was shouting but all his words were a blur. It didn't matter; Daniel was just relieved to see the cause of his shake-up. Of course, a door torn off! Yet he continued to feel disoriented. When the man had driven away, and Justine stepped out to drag the door to the trunk and heave it in, he was still so dazed that he didn't offer to help. He watched numbly as she slid behind the wheel again. "At least we're well ventilated," she told him. A strange thing to say, or perhaps he had misunderstood. He wished he were home. He raced through the hallways of his mind calling out for Laura, his father, Caleb, Margaret Rose. But really he should never have married Margaret Rose. A shared background was the important thing. If he had not been such a fool for her chuckling laugh and the tender, subtle curve at the small of her back he would have made a more sensible choice, a person he had known all his life. Who was that little girl who used to come visiting with her parents? Melissa, Melinda? But he had wanted someone new and surprising. A terrible mistake. How he hated Margaret Rose! The thought of her made him grind his teeth. He would like to know where she was now so that he could do something dreadful to her, humiliate her in front of all her fancy, tinkling friends. But no, she was dead. He was so disappointed to remember. As usual she had done something first, run ahead of him laughing and looking back at him over her shoulder, and for once he could not refuse to follow.

"Once you're alive, there's no way out but dying," he told Justine. She looked over at him.

"You've set a thing in motion, you see."

"It's like being pregnant," said Justine. Of course she couldn't *really* have said that. His ears were bad. His mind was bad. He was going to have to get a hold of himself. He straightened his back and looked out the window, a respectable elderly gentleman admiring the view as they rattled homeward.

Meg Peck and the Reverend Arthur Milsom were sitting in the living room waiting for Meg's parents. Or Arthur was sitting; Meg kept moving around. First she chose the armchair because she wanted to look proper and adult. Then she thought it was more natural to sit next to Arthur on the couch. They were about to ask permission to get married; what would they be doing across the room from each other?

Arthur had on his clerical collar, which wasn't absolutely required but it looked very nice. He was a young, pale, tense man, small but wiry. When he was nervous he cracked his knuckles and his brown eyes grew so dark and sober that he seemed to be glaring. *"Don't* be nervous," Meg told him, sitting back down on the couch. She reached over and took his damp hand.

The visit had been planned for weeks. The first Monday after she turned eighteen, he said, he would come talk to her parents. (Monday was a slow day at the church.) They had worked it out by letter. It was Arthur's feeling that Duncan was the important one, but as Meg pointed out they needed Justine there to smooth things over. For certainly Duncan would be at his sharpest. He didn't like Arthur. (How could anyone not like Arthur?) What they hadn't counted on was Justine's vanishing, taking Grandfather on one of his trips. Now there was no telling when she would be back, and meanwhile Duncan was coming home from work at any minute. They would have to handle him alone after all.

Meg always thought of her parents as Duncan and Justine, although she didn't call them that. It might have been due to the way they acted. They were not very parent-like. She loved them both, but she had developed a permanent inner cringe from wondering how they would embarrass her next. They were so—*extreme.* So irresponsible! They led such angular, slapdash lives, always going off on some tangent, calling over their shoulders for her to come too. And for as long as Meg could remember she had been stumbling after, picking up the trail of cast-off belongings and abandoned projects. All she really wanted was to live like other people. She tried to keep the house neat, like her friends' houses, and to put flowers in the vases and to hide, somehow, whatever tangle of tubes and electrical wires Duncan was working on at the moment. But then it seemed so hopeless when she knew how soon they would be moving on. "We're nomads," Justine told her, "think of it that way"—as if making it sound romantic would help. But there was nothing romantic about this tedious round of utility deposits, rental contracts, high school transcripts and interrupted magazine subscriptions. "He's ruining our *lives!*" she told Justine. Justine looked astonished. "But Meggie darling, *we* can't be the ones to say—" Then Meg's anger would extend to her mother, too, who was so gullible and so quick to give in, and she closed herself up in her room (if they were in a house where she *had* a room) and said no more.

She kept herself occupied with sewing, or pasting pictures in her scrapbook full of model homes—French windows and carpeted kitchens and white velvet couches. She straightened up her closet with all her shoes set side by side and pointing in the same direction. She ironed her own dresses, as she had since she was nine. (Justine thought there was no point to ironing, as long as things were clean.) At the age of ten she had baked her first cake, which everyone admired but no one ate because they were too busy rushing off somewhere; they seemed to live on potato chips from vending machines. Nothing ever worked on a schedule. She was encouraged to bring her friends home at any hour of the day or night. "This family is not a closed unit," Duncan told her—apparently his only rule, if you could call it that. But how could she bring friends when her parents were so certain to make fools of themselves? "Oh, I just love your folks," girls were always saying, little dreaming what agony it would be to have them for their own. For Justine might be found barefoot and waving her dirty playing cards, or sitting at the kitchen table with three or four unsuitable friends, or racing about looking for her broken straw carry-all in order to go to the diner whose food she preferred to her own. She had a high-handed, boisterous way of acting sometimes and she was likely to refer to Duncan publicly as "Meg's second cousin," her idea of a joke. And Duncan! Spouting irrelevant, useless facts, thinking out loud in startling ways, leaving her friends stunned and stupid-looking. *His* idea of a joke was to hang idiotic newspaper and ladies' magazine pages all over the house, bearing what he thought were appropriate messages. On Justine's birthday he pasted up a bank ad saying WE'RE INCREASING OUR INTEREST, and after Meg spent too much money on a dress (only because she wanted to look like the other girls for a change, not all homemade and tacked together) she found a page Scotch-taped to her closet door:

HAVE YOU EVER HAD
A BAD TIME IN LEVI'S?

Then she had snatched up the page and stalked in to where Duncan sat inventing a new keyboard arrangement for the typewriter. "Act your *age!*" she told him. But when he looked up his face was so surprised and unguarded, and she saw that he really *was* aging, there were dry lines around his eyes and two tiny crescents left by his wide, dippy smile. So she laid the paper down gently, after all, and went away defeated.

Now she sighed, remembering, and Arthur squeezed her fingers. "In an hour this will all be over," he told her.

"It will never be over."

"I don't understand."

"We're going to be demolished," she said. "I feel it."

But now she had insulted him. He straightened up, which made him look smaller. He said, "Don't you think I can have a reasonable discussion with my own girl's parents?"

"Yes but—"

"You forget, I'm a minister. I've convinced families who swore they'd cut off their daughters without a penny. I've convinced fathers who claimed that—"

"But it wasn't you their daughters were marrying."

"Now don't *worry*. If worst comes to worst we'll just go away quietly and have the ceremony in my own church."

But neither of them wanted that. They wanted everything perfect. Arthur wanted her to be happy, and Meg would only be happy with a white dress that dipped to a point at the waist, Sarah Cantleigh's veil, and a bouquet of baby's breath. She wanted to walk down the aisle of the family's church in Baltimore where her mother had been married; she would like to be guarded by rows and rows of aunts and uncles and second cousins, grave Peck eyes approving her choice. Bridal showers, long-grained rice, Great-Grandma's sixpence in her shoe. Arthur waiting beside the minister, turning his pale, shiny face to watch her procession. Whenever he looked at her, she felt queenly. All right, so he was not a handsome man, but would a handsome man treat her as adoringly as Arthur Milsom did? When they went to lectures she looked at the lecturer and Arthur looked at her. She felt the thin moon of his face turned upon her. He assisted her in and out of cars, through doorways, up the shallowest steps, his hands just barely brushing her. (The aunts would love his manners.) He devoted his entire attention to her, so much so that sometimes he said, he worried about his jealous God. Nobody had ever, in all her life, felt that way about her before.

A car drove up in front of the house, chugging and grinding familiarly. "There's Mama now!" Meg said. "Look, she beat him home after all." She rose and went out to the porch. Justine was still seated behind the wheel, straight-backed and prim, unguarded by even the vestige of a door. The car looked like a cross-section of something. But, "Certainly makes it easier to get in and out!" she called to Meg, and she waved gaily and stepped onto the sidewalk. "Coming, Grand-father?"

"Mama, I want to talk to you," Meg said.

But then up spoke Dorcas Britt, the lady next door, calling over the hedge in a large, rich voice that seemed to mock Meg's. "Justine, honey! I got to talk to you."

"A man came along doing eighty and flung Grandfather into the windshield," Justine said.

"Mama."

The house was swept suddenly with a variety of colors and shapes—the white, tottering grandfather, Justine flicking back her yellow hair, Dorcas all chartreuse and magenta on red patent-leather spike-heeled sandals. Arthur stood up with his fingers laced in front of him, as he did when greeting church members after the sermon. He wore a de-termined smile. Meg felt a twist; was she doomed to be embarrassed by *everyone*, all her life, even Arthur? "Mama, Grandfather, you re-member Arthur," she said. "Mrs. Britt, this is Arthur, my—Arthur Milsom."

"My baby has been kidnapped," Dorcas told him.

Her baby was nine years old and she was kidnapped regularly, always by her father, who did not have visiting rights, but Arthur didn't know that and he grew white around the lips. "Oh, my heavens!" he cried.

"Arthur. It's all *right*," Meg told him.

"All right?" said Dorcas. "To you, maybe."

"Grandfather was zonked in the forehead," Justine said.

Which caused Arthur to spin next in the grandfather's direction, full of a new supply of horror and sympathy. He hadn't learned yet. Such an expenditure of emotion would drain you in no time, living here. "*Arthur*," Meg said.

"The man was going eighty, at least," said Justine. "How else could he have ripped a door clean off like that?"

"It was already hanging by one hinge, Mama."

" 'You were going eighty,' I told him, but guess what he said? It's against the law to open a car door on the street side. Did you know that? How are we supposed to get into our cars?"

"Perhaps from the sidewalk side," Arthur said carefully.

Justine paused, in the middle of removing her hat, and looked over at him. "Oh. Arthur," she said. "Why, how are you?"

"I'm just *fine*, thank you, Mrs. Peck. How are *you*?"

"And Meg! Meggie, did you find my note? I forgot to tell you I was going off today. Did you have anything to eat when you came home from school?"

She didn't wait for an answer. She kissed Meg on the cheek—a breath of Luden's cough drops. Whenever she kissed people she gave them quick little pats on the shoulder. Meg drew away, trying to regather her dignity. "Mama, when you get a moment," she said.

"But I *have* a moment. All the time in the world. What can I do for you?"

"Don't you have to start supper?"

She meant, Can't you come out in the kitchen and talk without Dorcas? But Justine said, "Oh, I thought we would just have pick-ups tonight." The only one who understood Meg was Dorcas, who drew herself in while remaining, somehow, as billowy and bosomy as a featherbed. A fat blonde with tiny hands and feet. "*You* are not a mother," she said. "You have never had your baby kidnapped. This is not something I can just go home and forget until a more convenient time."

"Perhaps if you called the police," said Arthur.

"Police! Ha!"

"Mama, I want to talk to you a second."

"All right."

"I mean, privately."

"Honey, can't you talk here? Dorcas is a friend, we don't have to be private from *her*."

"I should say not," said Dorcas.

"Well, I'll wait till Daddy comes home," Meg said.

"Oh, Duncan! Where is he? Shouldn't he be here by now?"

And off she flew to the window, with Dorcas tripping behind her on her ridiculous shoes. "Look here, Justine, you got to help. Won't you lay the cards? I got to know where Ann-Campbell is."

"Oh, well, I'm sure she's all right."

Ann-Campbell would be all right anywhere. Meg pitied her kidnapper. But Justine gave in, soft-hearted as usual. "But maybe just a *quick* reading," she said. And off they went to the kitchen for the cards. Grandfather Peck stood teetering from heel to toe, peering after them. "Are they going to make supper?" he asked Meg.

"They're doing a reading, Grandfather."

"A what?"

"*Reading.*"

"What would they be reading *now*? It's suppertime."

He sat down suddenly in the armchair. There was a long knot growing on his forehead. "Grandfather, you're turning purple," Meg said.

"Ah?"

"Perhaps he needs medical attention," Arthur whispered.

But the grandfather, who could sometimes hear astonishing things, slapped his knee and said, "Nonsense!"

Then there was a blue-and-yellow flash in the door—Duncan, wearing the jeans Mr. Amsel had asked him not to. He sprinted across the hall and into the coat closet. "Daddy?" Meg said.

"Meg, where is that magazine I was reading last night?"

"I don't know."

"Do you have to put everything away all the time?"

"*I* didn't put it anywhere."

"Never mind, I found it."

Off he went again. The door slammed. Arthur began stroking his chin thoughtfully.

"Was that Duncan?" the grandfather asked.

"Yes, Grandfather."

"*You're* a pastor," he told Arthur.

"Assistant pastor, yes sir."

"Here's an idea for a sermon."

"Grandfather."

"All our misery comes from the length of our childhood. Ever thought of that?"

"No, sir, I don't believe I have."

"Look at it this way. Everything arises from boredom, right? Irritation, loneliness, violence, stupidity—all from boredom. Now. Why are we bored? Because the human childhood is so durned lengthy, that's why. Because it takes us so durned long to get grown. Years. Years and years just hanging around waiting. Why, after that just *anything* would be an anticlimax."

"Sugar," Duncan called, crossing the front hall again.

"How's that?"

"Eat more sugar."

"*What'd* he say?"

Duncan stuck his head in the living room door. "Sugar hastens puberty," he said. "All the Eskimos are growing up faster now they've switched to carbohydrates."

Grandfather Peck scratched his head.

"Daddy," said Meg, "we want to talk to you."

"Ah so, Meggie." But then he saw Arthur. "Why, looky there, a man of the cloth."

"Daddy, when Mama gets through—"

"Where *is* your mother?"

"She's reading the cards for Dorcas."

Arthur stood up. Next to Duncan he looked very small and stalwart. "Actually, Mr. Peck," he said, "I feel it would be quite enough just to talk to you."

"Oh, more than enough," said Duncan.

"When I became a man," the grandfather said, "I caught myself thinking, many times, so this is what it's like to be grown up! Plodding back and forth, between work and home. Even being a judge was not what I had hoped. Really you don't make judgments at all; you simply relate what happens today to what has happened yesterday, all the precedents and statutes and amendments. And when you've waded through that, what next? You get old. And you're old for years and years and years. Your hearing goes and your knees go. Some people's teeth go. I myself have kept all my teeth but I wouldn't say it has done much good. After all, whatever I eat I ate a thousand times before. In addition I have become more and more conscious of where the food comes from. Pork tastes like pigs, beef like cows, lamb like sheep's wool, and so forth. Milk chocolate, which I used to consider a treat, nauseates me now. I taste the smell of cow barns."

"I wonder," said Duncan. "If we ran some experiments with *goat's* milk chocolate—"

"The Chinese venerate age. If I were in China people would come to me and say, '*You're* old and wise. What's the meaning of it all?' "

"What *is* the meaning of it all?" Duncan asked.

"I don't know," his grandfather told him.

"Mr. Peck," said Arthur, "I would like to marry your daughter."

The grandfather said, "My daughter?"

But Duncan understood. He gave Arthur a long, clear, untroubled look, as if nothing such a man could say would bother him. Then he said, "She's seventeen."

"Eighteen," said Meg.

"Eighteen? Oh yes."

"And Arthur's twenty-six."

"Well, that's ridiculous," said Duncan. "When you're seventy he'll be seventy-eight."

"So?"

"And you're still in school."

"We're planning a June wedding," said Arthur. "She'll be graduated by then."

"And Daddy, you know I'm not the college type."

"Who is? Who cares about college? Did I ever say I wanted you to go to college? But I didn't say I wanted you to get married right off the bat, either, and go live in Simper, Virginia, sitting in the front pew every Sunday nodding all the flowers off your hat. It's a trap. Do you want to be trapped? I thought you would go off and do something, Meggie, travel somewhere. Leave old Caramel behind if you like, we're not trying to keep you for ourselves. Hitch-hike to California. Take a freight train. Take a *bus*. Learn to surf. Marry somebody unpredictable. Join the Foreign Legion."

"But I can't be that way."

"Try! Anything but this. Just settling for it doesn't matter who, any pale fish in a suit—"

"Mr. Peck," said Arthur, "I understand, of course, that in the heat of the moment—"

"How will you have babies, Reverend Mildew, osmosis?"

"Mama!" Meg called.

"Don't trouble your mother, Meg, I'll see him out myself."

"Unfortunately I am not that easy to discourage," Arthur said.

"That *is* unfortunate." But Duncan was guiding him toward the door anyway, and Arthur was allowing it. "Now," said Duncan, "if by any strange chance Meg still feels the same when she is of a decent age, Reverend, I admit there is nothing I can do about it. Meanwhile, goodbye."

"But I am of age!" Meg said.

The front screen slammed.

Meg looked at her great-grandfather, who smiled a weary smile showing every one of his perfect teeth. She crossed to the kitchen door and opened it.

"Meg," said Dorcas, "your mother's a marvel. My cards say Ann-Campbell is with Joe Pete and I'm to enjoy the rest while she's gone."

"Mama, listen."

Justine looked up. She was seated at the kitchen table, holding both hands rigid. Between each finger were long sprays of raw spaghetti. "Look, Meg!" she said. "I'm learning the I Ching!"

"Is that all you have to do?"

"Well, we should use yarrow stalks but we don't know what they are."

"I just want to tell you this," Meg said. "I blame you as much as him."

"What, Meggie dear?"

"The two of you are as closed as a unit can get, I don't care *what* he says."

"Closed? What?" said Justine, looking bewildered. She rose, holding out two spaghetti whiskbrooms. "Wait, Maggie darling, I don't—"

But Meg was gone. She ran across the hall and out of the house. There was no sign of Arthur or Duncan in the yard. Only the Ford, melting into the twilight, with a magazine page flapping in the space where the door should have been. WOULDN'T YOU REALLY RATHER HAVE A BUICK?

9

For the Polk Valley church's April bazaar Justine wore her very best dress—an A-line shift that Duncan had bought her five years ago at a nearly-new sale. She pulled her hair into a sprout on top of her head, covered it over with her hat, and dabbed at her mouth with a pink Tangee lipstick from high school. On her feet she wore her black Mary Janes, on her arm a gypsy bracelet borrowed from the Blue Bottle. Generally speaking, she thought she looked very presentable.

Because the car was in the body shop, Justine had to ask for a lift in Dorcas's baby-blue Cadillac. And Ann-Campbell had to come along, jouncing in the back seat, periodically nosing her sharp little freckled face between the two women to eavesdrop. Justine liked Ann-Campbell. She was certain she was going to lead a very interesting life.

On the way to Polk Valley Dorcas talked about her ex-husband, Joe Pete, whom she had married and divorced three times now. Every time she married him she had a large church wedding all over again, with Ann-Campbell as flower girl in a floor-length organdy dress to cover the scabs, scars, scrapes, bruises, and Band-Aids on her bony knees. Lately relatives had stopped attending, and the gifts had thinned out. "But," said Dorcas, "he's still my first husband, isn't he? I've never been married to anybody else, and neither has he. Why can't I have a wedding like I choose?"

Justine didn't want to think about weddings. They reminded her of Meg. She was worried sick about Meg, who had become very quiet the last few weeks, and whenever she talked it over with Duncan he acted so cross and stubborn that he was no help at all. He said Meg could marry anyone she chose, a Congo chieftain if she cared to, but not a man whose only quality was harmlessness. "Maybe she loves him," Justine said, but doubtfully. She *tried* to believe it. Whenever she saw Arthur she worked at being interested in him. She observed that he was kind-hearted, steady, polite . . . and then her mind would trail off to some other subject and she forgot he was there. She watched Meg, who appeared as placid as ever. But then Meg didn't show emotions, that was all. Of course she loved him or she wouldn't say she wanted to marry him.

Oh, the things she had prepared herself for, when Meg was born! Merely the fact of having a new person in the world implied a stream of unforseen events endlessly branching and dividing. As Meg grew into her teens Justine was braced for long-haired suitors, LSD, shop-lifting, pregnancy, revolutionists, firearms in the closet—anything, for her daughter's sake she could deal with anything! She just hadn't expected Arthur Milsom, exactly.

"Thursday night Joe Pete calls up. 'Will you be at home a while?' Where would I go to? On no alimony at all and six months behind in child support. And Joe Pete's a rich man, Britt Texaco. 'Joe Pete,' I told him, I said, 'all in the world that's left for me to do tonight is read my November seventy-two *Modern Movies*,' and he says, 'Fine, for I'm bringing back your daughter and you owe me forty-eight ninety-five for my new emerald rug which she dribble-bleached with a gallon of Clorox. I won't charge for the Clorox,' he says. 'Well and good,' I tell him, 'you can take that up with the FBI when they haul you in for kidnap.' *I'm* no fool."

"When he brought me back he stayed all night," said Ann-Campbell.

"It's his English Leather aftershave," said Dorcas.

Justine laughed.

The church parking lot was packed with cars, flashing the afternoon sunlight off their chrome, and ladies were swarming in the front yard and spilling down the hill as far as the cemetery. "I want to get a hot dog," Ann-Campbell said, "and you owe me a balloon from that time at the shopping center, and I need a caramel apple. If they have cotton candy, can I have some? If they're selling lemon sticks—"

"Ann-Campbell, you promised me you would act nice now if I let you stay out of school today."

"In school we do this math," Ann-Campbell told Justine.

"*Oh* yes," said Justine, who had disliked math.

"If five mothers are fighting over ten blond wigs, how many does each of them get? They want me to say two, but how can I be sure? Maybe one wig's ugly and nobody takes it. Maybe one mother's stronger than the rest and she gets five. Or one's got a head that's too big for the—"

"Ann-Campbell Britt, you are sending a shooting sharp pain right down between my shoulder blades," her mother told her.

If Justine had had to choose what child would most likely be Duncan's in all the world, she would have said Ann-Campbell. Never Meg.

The bazaar was in the church basement, down a flight of linoleum steps. It took Justine's eyes a minute to get used to the dimness. Then she saw rows of booths covered with crêpe paper, and more ladies bustling around in pantsuits and varnished hairdos. Justine hated pantsuits. Whenever she saw one she had an urge to tell the owner some scandalous fortune, loudly enough to be heard everywhere: "The father of your next-to-last baby has run off with a cigar-smoking redhead." But she kept her bright smile and waited, clutching her bag, until the woman in charge noticed she was there. Mrs. Edge's pantsuit was pale aqua, Justine's least favorite color. Oh, but she would have to get over this mood she was in. She widened her smile another inch. "I'm Justine Peck," she said. "I promised to come tell fortunes."

"Mrs. Peck? Why, I thought you would be darker. We've heard such amazing things about you, dear. Now *somewhere*, let me see now . . ."

Mrs. Edge led the way toward a card table. It was covered with a white cloth to which stars and crescent moons had been pinned. Justine followed and behind her came Dorcas, wobbling on her spike heels and humming. There was no telling where Ann-Campbell had got to.

"Now dear, this is your cashbox. I've laid a few dollar bills in for change. Is there anything else you'll be wanting? I do hope you won't be chilly. Perhaps you should have brought a wrap."

"Oh no, I'll be fine," said Justine, who was always burning up.

"Why! Here's Mrs. Linthicum, our pastor's wife. Mrs. Peck here is just a *wizard* telling fortunes, Mrs. L."

"Oh, then you can start on me," Mrs. Linthicum said. *She* was wearing a dress, and a little brown mushroom of a hat. She was a tall wispy woman with freckles seeping through her pink face powder. When she sat down in the folding chair she arranged herself so graciously, smoothing her skirt beneath her and then patting her bosom as if to make certain it was there, that Justine felt an unexplainable rush of sorrow. She reached over without planning to and touched Mrs. Linthicum's freckled hand. "Oh, is it the *left* palm you read?" asked Mrs. Linthicum.

"No, no, I don't read palms," said Justine, withdrawing her hand.

But she could easily have read that one, with its lengthwise groove and the worn wedding ring no wider than a thread.

She took out her cards and unwrapped them. "Why, how fascinating," said Mrs. Linthicum.

"Is there anything in particular you want to know?" Justine asked.

"Oh, nothing I can think of."

Dorcas leaned closer, giving off waves of Tabu, while Justine laid the cards down very, very gently. Madame Olita used to snap them down, but that was before they had started falling apart. When these went, where would she get more? She gazed into space, considering.

"I'm not afraid to hear, if it's bad," said Mrs. Linthicum.

Justine pulled her eyes back to the cards. "Oh, it's not bad, not at all," she said. "You're going to do just fine."

"I am?"

"You'll continue to have money worries, but not serious ones. You shouldn't be so concerned about your children. They will turn out all right. No trips in sight. No illness. You have true friends and a loving husband."

"Well, of course," said Mrs. Linthicum.

"All in all it's a very good life," Justine said. She cleared her throat and steadied her voice. "Anybody would be happy to have a formation like this one."

"Why, thank you very much," said Mrs. Linthicum. Then when the silence had stretched on a while she gave a little laugh and rose to pay her fee, pressing Justine's palm briefly with her cool, wilted fingers. When she left, Justine gazed after her for so long that Dorcas waggled a hand in front of her face and said, "You in there?"

Then others came, woman after woman, giggling a little in front of their friends. "No tall dark strangers? No ocean trips?" Several young girls filed through, a little boy in a baseball suit, a man in platform heels, an old lady. Justine tried to pin her mind to what she was doing. This was how she attracted future clients, after all. "You will have a minor car accident," she told one girl, relieved to see something concrete.

"Even if I drive slower?"

"No, maybe not."

"Then what's the point of all this?"

"I don't know."

"To warn you to *start* driving slower, Miss!" Dorcas cried. "Honestly, Justine! Where are you today?"

Oh, beautiful Dorcas, with her watery silk dress showing dimpled knees and her jangling bracelets and creamy throat! *Her* fortune altered from week to week. Which gave Justine a greater likelihood of error, but at least she enjoyed doing it.

During a lull they captured Ann-Campbell, who was winning too many prizes anyway tossing nickels into ashtrays, and Justine read her cards. Ann-Campbell leaned over her with a cone of cotton candy, smelling of burnt sugar and money. "You'll have to travel your whole life long to use up all the travel cards I'm seeing," Justine told her.

"*I* know that."

Then Dorcas, who had learned palmistry in high school, examined Ann-Campbell's little square hand—a mass of warts and deep, soiled lines. "I find travel too," she said, "but I don't know, Ann-Campbell gets carsick. Let me see yours, Justine."

Justine turned her palm up. Secretly she had become as addicted to the future as Alonzo Divich, now that life moved so quickly.

"Oh, talk about *travel!*" said Dorcas.

"What do you see?"

"Lots of trips. Oh, well, there's much too much to read here. You have an indecisive nature, there are lots of . . . but I'm not too sure what *this* means. And then a frequent change in surroundings and tendency to—"

"But is it a *good* palm?"

"I'm telling you, Justine! Of course it is, it's just full of things."

"No, I mean—"

Dorcas raised her head.

"Oh well, it doesn't matter," Justine told her finally.

She never did say what she had meant. She sat silent, frowning at the cracked square of silk in her lap, while beside her Ann-Campbell started firmly, grimly patting her arm with the hand that wasn't holding the cotton candy.

Duncan looked up from polishing a Cinderella pastry cutter and found Justine staring at him through the plate glass window, directly beneath his hand-lettered sign, ANTIC TOOLS WANTED. She was wearing her fanciest church bazaar outfit and there was a chain of safety pins dangling from the tip of her left breast. When he waved she waved back, but she kept on standing there. He rose and came close to the glass, popping his mouth like a goldfish. She smiled. "Come *in!*" he shouted.

So she came, leaving the door swinging open behind her. "I was just passing," she told him.

"You want to hear about my movie?"

"Yes."

"I'm going to buy a camera and walk around filming to one side of things, wherever the action isn't. Say there's a touchdown at a football game, I'll narrow in on one straggling player at the other end of the field. If I see a purse-snatcher I'll find someone reading a newspaper just to the right of the victim."

"What's the point?" Justine asked.

"Point? It'll be the first realistic movie ever made. In true life you're *never* focused on where the action is. Or not so often. Not so finely." He stopped and looked at her. "Point?" he said. "You don't usually ask me that."

"Duncan, I wish I knew what we should be doing about Meg."

"Oh. School called. She cut all her afternoon classes, they said. Is she sick?"

"Why, I don't know. I haven't been home."

"Every day this week she's had a headache."

"See there? No wonder I worry," Justine said. "I ought to go look in on her." But instead she sat down on a knobby piano stool he had been trying to get rid of for months. "I am forty and one-third years old," she said.

Duncan blew on the pastry cutter and started polishing it again.

"Doesn't it seem to you that things are going by very fast?"

"I have always thought everything moved too slowly," he said. "But I know I'm in the minority."

"How did we *get* here?"

But when Duncan looked up, she had her eyes fixed on the opposite wall as if she didn't want an answer.

He set down his work and rose to walk around the shop, passing his rows of polished tools and utensils. They did his heart good. He

ignored what Silas had brought in from his tours of the auction sales—
the china and scrolled furniture, which he allowed to pile up in dim
corners. He paused beside a nineteenth-century pressure scale and laid
his hand upon it gradually, delighting in its intricate, precise design.
Behind him he heard the familiar *plop, plop* of Justine's cards. What
would she be asking, all alone? But when he turned he saw that she
was laying the cards absent-mindedly, the way another person might
doodle or chew a pencil. Her eyes were on something far away; she
smoothed each card blindly as she set it on the sewing chest beside
her.

While he watched, she frowned and collected her thoughts. She
looked down at what she had laid out. "Why, Duncan," she said.

"What is it?"

"Why—"

"What is it, Justine?"

"Never mind, don't worry. Don't worry."

"Who says I'm worried?"

But she was already out the door, running down the street with
her hat streamers fluttering. It was the first time Duncan had ever
known her to leave her cards behind.

Daniel Peck was on the front porch, rearranging a sheaf of correspondence, when Justine came dashing up the walk between the rows of
sprouting vegetables. She looked wild-eyed and flustered, but then she
often did. "Grandfather," she called, "have you seen Meg?"

He tried to think.

"Meg."

"Well, now I wonder where she could be," he said.

"What time is it?"

He fumbled in his pocket and hauled out lengths of gold chain
hand over hand, raising his eyebrows when his fingers met up with a
watch. "Ah! Five twelve," he said.

She spun past him, into the house, clattering the screen door behind
her. He felt the noise rather than heard it. He felt his bones jar. Then
there was peace, and he returned to a letter dated April 10, 1973. He
squinted in the twilight at a ragged blue script.

Dear Mr. Peck:

In response to your query of March 17, I am sorry to say that I
do not recall my grandmother's ever mentioning a Caleb
Peck or, for that matter, any other young man she used to dance
with. I was not aware that she danced. However my cousin
Amabel Perce (Mrs. John M.) of Duluth, Minnesota may know
more. I myself was never at all close to my grandmother and am
certainly not the one to . . .

He sighed. Long white fingers entered his vision, fluttering another letter on top of the first.

> *Dear Mama,*
>   *I have gone to be married in Arthur's church. We will be living with Arthur's mother. Don't worry about me, I'll finish school in Semple. I will keep in touch.*
>
> *Love,*
> *Meg*

"Eh? What's this?" he asked Justine.

She merely lifted an arm and dropped it, as if she couldn't speak.

"Why," he said, "I didn't know it was proper for ministers to elope."

Justine went down the porch steps, back through the vegetables toward the street, drifting along slower than he had seen her in years.

"Justine? Wasn't that fellow a minister?"

She didn't answer. In the end he simply filed the letter away among his other correspondence and went on with what he had been doing before.

10

By May the whole front yard was a tangle of cucumber vines and little green stalks of corn. Neighbors began knocking on the door. "Justine, of course it's your lawn to plant as you please although frankly it seems . . . but never mind, what is that smell? What we want to know is, that *smell!*"

"Oh, just things from the blender."

"The—? When you turn down this street it's the first thing you notice. It smells like a zoo. A city dump. A *slaughter*house."

"I'll mention it to Duncan," Justine said. But her face was lit up and her eyes all curly, she was so happy to see somebody. She would reach out to touch visitors on the wrist or shoulder, drawing them in. "Since you're here, why don't you stay?"

"Oh, well . . ."

"We can sit out back. You won't smell a thing."

"Oh, well, maybe for a minute."

"I'll make you lemonade, or coffee. Anything. What would you like?"

The fact was, Justine hated to be alone. She had felt so restless and unhappy lately, wandering from room to room, trying to start up conversations with her grandfather when he was too busy with his own thoughts to answer. "Grandfather, isn't there any place you'd like to go?"

"How's that?"

"Do you want to *go* somewhere, I said."

"No, no."

She sank back and twisted a piece of her hair. It was impossible to drive off on her own; a car was so private. Like a sealed black box. She would end up speeding just to get her isolation over with, or she would run a stop sign because even horns and curses were better than silence. So instead of driving she walked to Duncan's shop, missing no opportunity to speak to passers-by. "Hello, Mr. Hill, did you get the money I said you would? Where's *Mrs.* Hill? Wait, Red Emma, I'll walk along with you," and she would run to catch up and travel three blocks out of her way, pausing at each house while Red Emma delivered the mail. She parted from people with difficulty, dragging it out, loitering on the sidewalk fiddling with a button and finding new things to say to them. She dreaded walking even half a block with only her own thoughts for company. And when finally she arrived at the Blue Bottle she would be full of pent-up words that exploded from her before she was fully in the door. "Duncan, Red Emma told me . . . Bertha Millar asked . . . oh, Duncan, I just had a thought, can we borrow a wayward girl from the police station?"

"A *what's* that?"

"Surely they must have some, wouldn't you think? We could leave our name and the next time the police arrest somebody they could bring her to us. I mean the house seems so—"

"Well now, wait a minute."

But she would be off to something new, picking up merchandise and putting it down. "Oh look, a locket like Aunt Bea's almost. And Aunt Sarah's dinner ring but the stone's a different color. Isn't it funny they call these antiques? They're only what our aunts wear every day of their lives. What's this thing, Duncan?"

"A Victorian slide pendant," Duncan said glumly. "If you ask me, it's junk. All this stuff is junk. Yesterday Silas brought in a whole carton full, he'd been to some flea market. 'Here, take this,' he said, 'and get rid of that mess on the table, it doesn't look nice.' Do you know what he called *mess*? A genuine chromatrope I bought from old Mrs. Milhauser, and a Boston bathing pan with a pump that still works . . . where is it now? I wanted to show you. He dumped it in some corner or other. He doesn't like tools and things with moving parts, he says they clutter the shop. We spend all our time shifting each other's merchandise into hiding places and out again, in and out. Look at that chair! He likes it. He wants me to ask a hundred and fifty dollars for it."

Justine looked at a chair with a curved spine that was all pointed leaves and flowers and little sharp berries. On one of its finials Duncan had impaled a liniment ad. "I've a good mind to quit this job," he said, but she didn't bother answering that. He would never quit in the middle of a fight.

She wanted him to come with her somewhere. "Maybe we could take a trip," she told him.

"All right."

"Just spur of the moment."

"All right."

"We might even stop and see Meg."

But then his face grew cold and stubborn. "Not a chance. Not until we're asked, Justine."

"But she *said*. She said in her letters."

" 'We'll have you over sometime soon,' is what she said. Pay attention."

He knew Meg's letters by heart, the same as Justine. It was all an act, his unconcern. ("Duncan," she had told him, "Meg has gone to marry Alfred, I mean Arthur," and he had grown motionless for one split second before continuing to close up shop.) "As long as we don't come for a meal," she said now, "why do we have to wait to be invited?"

"We're not going till we are, I tell you."

"Oh, that's ridiculous. She's our *daughter*."

"So what?"

"Remember when she was colicky, all those evenings you walked up and down with Meggie on your shoulder? You sang 'Blues in the Night.' Her head was straight up and wobbling, her forehead would get all wrinkled from trying not to miss a word."

"Merely singing 'Blues in the Night' to someone does not obligate me to pay them an uninvited visit seventeen years later."

"Eighteen," said Justine.

"Eighteen."

"You used to take her to the circus when she was too little to hold down a spring-up seat. For three straight hours you leaned on it for her so she wouldn't pop right up again."

"There was an intermission."

"Even so."

"Merely leaning on a spring-up seat for someone—"

"And she's not just *someone*. She's not just any old person that you would treat so formally the minute she hurt your feelings."

"Who's hurt?" Duncan said.

"Look at Grandfather. Do you know what I found him doing the other day? He was at the kitchen table all hunched over with his head in his hands. I thought something was wrong. Then he sat up and I saw he'd been studying this world map in the Hammond atlas. Not Maryland, not the United States, the *world*, Duncan. That's how far he let Caleb run before he would go after him. Are we going to do that too?"

"We're never going to forget that man, are we," Duncan said. "The one that got away." He set down a crimping iron. "However, we're wandering off the subject here. Meg has not vanished. We know exactly where she is. She writes us a letter once a week. All I'm saying is don't repeat history, give her a little breathing space. Let her ask us first."

"Oh, there's always some excuse."

"I'm just telling you what I think."

"Do you wish I hadn't come after *you*, when you left home?"

"No."

"Well, I wish it sometimes, Duncan Peck."

"No doubt you do," said Duncan.

"And if you ever walk off again, you realize I won't follow. I'll have them declare you legally dead, I'll remarry right away."

"Of course," he said serenely.

There was no way to win a fight with that man.

She stormed out of the shop and then stood on the sidewalk, wondering what to do with herself. Everything seemed irritating. The sunlight was too sharp for her eyes. The traffic was too noisy, a swarm of gigantic glaring station wagons. She hated the way the women drivers were poised at the Main Street traffic light, all lifting their arms simultaneously to orchestrate their hairdos. She turned in the other direction, toward home, which was not where she wanted to be but she couldn't think of any place else.

In the kitchen, her grandfather was washing the dishes. Periodically he had these spells of trying to make the house look cared for. He wore around his waist a striped linen dishtowel with an enormous charred hole in its center. He bent over the sink, unaware of Justine's presence, doggedly scrubbing a saucepan with a piece of dried gourd that Duncan had grown two years ago after reading about its scouring properties. The gourd looked like a chunk of hardened beige seaweed. From time to time he stopped scrubbing and examined it, frowning, as if he found it difficult to believe. Then he rinsed the saucepan and plodded over to the table with it, head bowed, shoulders hunched. "Hello, Grandfather," Justine said. "Grandfather?"

He started and looked up. "Eh?"

"You don't have to wash the dishes."

"I'd like to know what we'd eat off tonight if I didn't."

"We could always go to the diner," Justine said.

"Ha."

He dried the saucepan on a corner of his apron. Then he set it on a stack of meticulously cleaned, polished plates and trudged back to the sink. He was so stooped that, from behind, his head seemed to disappear. All Justine saw was his rounded shoulders, the elastic X of his suspenders in the hollow of his spine, and his trousers draped and formless as if he had no seat. Nowadays, everywhere Justine looked she found something to make her sad.

She would have liked to write Meg another letter, but she had sent one just this morning. So she went instead to Meg's bedroom, to open her closet and stare at the row of shirtdresses that seemed to be leading a gentle muted life of their own. Someday soon, Meg said in her letters, she would stop by for the rest of her things or her parents could bring them when they came to visit. But Justine felt comforted by what was left behind and she would be sorry to see the room stripped. She took a deep breath of Meg's clean smell: Ivory soap and fresh-ironed fabric. She stroked the collar of the nearest dress, with its precise top-stitching, and then she lifted the cover of the sewing machine to admire Meg's mastery of such a complex, wheeled invention. She would have opened bureau drawers, but Meg was particular about her privacy.

When Meg was a baby, Justine had realized for the first time that it was possible to die. She had felt suddenly fragile under the responsibility of staying alive to raise her daughter. (In those days, she expected to do it perfectly; she thought no one else could manage.) She developed a fear of fire that was so unfounded she couldn't even tell Duncan because of course he would laugh at her. Over and over again she imagined the salty smell of smoke in the air, or a flickering red glow reflected on the wall. If Duncan were home he could get them out of anything, but what if it happened in the daytime while he was at work? By herself she was so young and skinny and incompetent. Then gradually, she developed an escape plan. They were living in Uncle Ed Hodges's garage apartment at the time. If fire broke out she could snatch up the baby, climb out on the kitchen window ledge, and make a long, desperate leap to the roof of Uncle Ed's back porch. Once she had pictured all this she relaxed, and eventually she forgot her fear completely. It was not till years later, returning to Uncle Ed's for a visit, that she saw that such a leap would have been insane. It was not only too far, it was also upward. She would have had to soar through the air like some surrealistic figure in a painting by Chagall, feet set neatly together and arms primly clasping the baby. But in those days, she might have managed anything. She was so necessary. Even when Meg had left infancy, given up first Justine's breast and then her lap and finally gone to play in other rooms altogether, Justine had to *be* there. She had to be the feeder, the fixer, the sounding board for an endless stream of announcements. "Mama my dress is dirty, Sammy hit me, the violets are out. Mama there's a spider in my chocolate milk, a moth in my bath, a ladybug on the windowscreen. My stomach aches. My mosquito bites itch. Janie has a hamster, Edwin's in the asparagus; I broke the handle off my teapot, Melissa has a music box you can watch right through the glass." Justine nodded, barely listening; the only answer required was, "Yes, dear." Then Meg was satisfied, as if things came into existence only when she was certain her mother knew about them. And now what? Justine had raised her daughter without dying after all; she was freed from her fears. But at night she woke up shaky and sad, and she pressed her face against Duncan's chest and said, "I'm not necessary any more."

"To me you are," he said.

He didn't see what she meant. He hadn't had that feeling of being essential to Meg in the first place; he couldn't know how it felt to lose it.

She wandered to other rooms, to hers and Duncan's with its unmade bed and scattered clothing, to the hall where she tripped over a stack of lumber. Everything looked dusty and stale. She hung out the living room window to be revived by Ann-Campbell, who was taunting a playmate among the cucumber vines:

> Little boy your teeth are green
> And your tongue it is rotting away.
> Better gargle with some gasoline,
> Brush with Comet and vomit today.

She returned to the kitchen, feeling more cheerful. "Grandfather, let's take a trip," she said.

"A what?"

"A trip."

"But we don't have any leads right now, Justine."

"Why wait for leads? Oh, why won't anyone *do* anything? Are we just going to sit here? Am I going to get rooted to the living room couch?"

Her grandfather watched her, with his eyes wide and blank and his hands endlessly drying an Exxon coffee mug on the corner of his apron.

Justine took her grandfather to an afternoon concert in Palmfield, although she did not like classical music and her grandfather couldn't hear it. The two of them sat rigid in their seats, directing unblinking blue stares toward the outline of a set of car keys in the violin soloist's trouser pocket. Then they went home by bus with Justine as dissatisfied as ever, bored and melancholy. Each time strangers rose to leave she mourned them. Who knew in what way they might have affected her life?

She took Duncan, her grandfather, and Ann-Campbell Britt to the funeral of a chihuahua belonging to an old lady client. *"What* is this? *Where* are we going?" her grandfather kept asking. "Don't worry, just come," said Justine. "Why do you care? Just grab up your hearing aid and come, Grandfather. If you want things to happen you have to run a few blind errands, you know." So he came, grumbling, and they sat on folding chairs in a cow pasture that had recently been turned into a pets' memorial garden. "The casket cost one hundred and forty-five dollars," Justine whispered to Duncan. "It's all metal. But they could have settled for wood: thirty-two ninety-eight. Mrs. Bazley told me. She selected the hymns herself. The minister is fully ordained."

"Oh, excellent," said Duncan, "I wonder if he needs an assistant," and after the service he went up and offered Arthur Milsom's address to the minister. But Grandfather Peck wandered among the wreaths and urns looking baffled. Why had he been brought here? Justine could no longer tell him. She rode home beside Duncan without a word, swinging one foot and rapidly chewing coffee beans that she had taken to keeping in a tin container at the bottom of her bag.

On Sundays she drove her grandfather to Plankhurst for Quaker meeting, which used to be something she tried to get out of because she didn't like sitting still so long. Now she would go anywhere. Grandfather Peck was not, of course, a Quaker and had no intention of becoming one, but he resented regular church services because he claimed the minister wouldn't speak up. It made him feel left out, he said. Even the Quakers would sometimes take it into their heads to rise and mumble, perversely keeping their faces turned away so that he couldn't read their lips. Then he whispered, "What? What?"—a harsh sound sawing through the air. He made Justine write everything down for him on a 3 × 5 memo pad he kept in his breast pocket. Justine would click the retractable point of his ballpoint pen in and out, in and out, waiting for a five-minute speech to be over, and then she wrote, "He says that God must have made even Nixon," or "Peace is not possible as long as neighbors can still argue over a lawn mower."

"*That* took him five minutes?"

"Ssh."

"But what was he up there working his mouth all that time for?"

"Ssh, Grandfather. Later."

"You must have left something out," he told her.

She would hand back his pen and pad, and sigh, and check the Seth Thomas clock on the mantel and run her eyes once more down the rows of straight-backed radiant adults and fidgety children lining the wooden benches. After twenty minutes the children were excused, rising like chirping, squeaking mice to follow the pied piper First-Day

School teacher out of the room, breaking into a storm of whistles and shouts and stamping feet before the door was properly shut again. She should have gone with them, she always thought. The silence that followed was deep enough to drown in. She would plow desperately through her straw bag, rustling and jingling, coming up finally with her tin container of coffee beans. When she bit into them, she filled the meetinghouse with the smell of breakfast.

Once her grandfather wrote on the pad himself, several lines of hurried spiky handwriting that he passed to her. "Read this out when no one else is talking," he whispered. She struggled to her feet, hanging onto her hat. Anything to break the silence. "My grandfather wants me to read this," she said. " 'I used to think that heaven was—palatable? Palatial. I was told it had pearly gates and was paved with gold. But now I hope they are wrong about that. I would prefer to find that heaven was a small town with a bandstand in the park and a great many trees, and I would know everybody in it and none of them would ever die or move away or age or alter.' "

She sat down and gave him back the memo pad. She took the top off her coffee beans but then she put it on again, and kept the container cupped in her hands while she gazed steadily out the window into the sunlit trees.

One afternoon toward the end of May the doorbell rang and Justine, flying to answer it, found Alonzo Divich standing on the porch. Although it was hot he wore a very woolly sheepskin vest. He carried a cowboy hat, swinging by a soiled string. "Alonzo!" Justine said.

"I was afraid you might have moved," he told her.

"Oh no. Come in."

He followed her into the hall, shaking the floor with each step. Grandfather Peck was on the living room couch writing a letter to his daughters. "Don't get up," Alonzo called to him, although the grandfather was still firmly seated, giving him that stare of shocked disbelief he always wore for Alonzo. "How's the heart, eh?" Alonzo asked. "How's the heart?"

"Hearth?"

"Nothing's wrong with his heart," said Justine. "Come into the kitchen, Alonzo, if you want your cards read. You know I can't do it right with Grandfather watching."

While she cleared the remains of breakfast from the table, Alonzo wandered around the kitchen examining things and whistling. "Your calendar is two months ahead," he told Justine.

"Is it?"

"Most people's would be behind."

"Yes, well."

She went to the living room for her carry-all. When she returned

Alonzo was standing at the open refrigerator, looking into a bowl of moldy strawberries. "How is my friend Duncan?" he asked her.

"He's fine."

"Maybe I'll drop by and see him. Is Meg out of school yet?"

"She's married."

"Married."

"She eloped with that minister."

"I'm sorry, Justine."

He shut the refrigerator and sat down at the table to watch her shuffle the cards. He looked tired and hot, and the grooves alongside his mustache were silvered with sweat. A disk with Arabic lettering gleamed in the opening of his shirt. Last time it had been a turquoise cross. She didn't ask why; he wouldn't have answered. "Alonzo," was all she said, "you have no idea how it gladdens my heart to see you. Cut, please." He cut the cards. She laid them out, one by one. Then she looked up. "Well?" she asked.

Alonzo said, "You realize, last time I took your advice."

"You did?"

"When you told me not to sell the business."

"Oh yes. Well, I should hope so," said Justine.

"It was the first time you ever said to keep on with something I was already doing."

She stopped swinging her foot.

"But I was tempted to disobey you anyway," he told her. "I admit. I went to see my friend, the one in merchandising. He has these clients, you understand, department stores and such, they come to him for ideas on . . . but anyway. I said I might join up with him. 'Oh, fine,' he tells me. But then he starts suggesting I wear a different style of clothes. Well, that I can follow. I am practical, I know how the world works. But he doesn't see, he's still trying to convince me. 'Face it, Alonzo,' he says, 'we all have to give in in little ways. Look at *me*. I'm a tall man,' he says. And he is, a fine tall man. 'Well,' he says, 'when important clients come, know what I do? I try to stay seated as much as possible, and if I stand I kind of squinch down. I don't *stoop*,' he says, 'that's too obvious. Just bend at the knees a little. Understand, it's not something I think of so consciously. But you can see a client, important fellow like that, he wouldn't feel right if I was to tower over him. You got to keep a watch for such things, Alonzo.' "

He shook his head, and pulled his great silver belt buckle around to where it wouldn't cut into his stomach so.

"Justine," he said, "do you know that I have never before done what you told me to do?"

"I'm not surprised," she said.

"I mean it. You're always right, but only because I go against instructions and things turn out badly just the way you said they would.

Now I discover things turn out badly anyhow. Is that your secret? I've found it, ha? You give people advice they'll be sure not to follow. Right?"

She laughed. "No, Alonzo," she said. "And I'm glad you didn't sell the carnival. *Whatever's* gone wrong."

"My mechanic's been arrested."

"Lem?"

"He robbed a bank in nineteen sixty-nine. They *say*."

"Oh, I see."

"Now, here's what I want to know. Is he coming back, or not? I mean if he's coming soon I'll hold the machines together somehow and wait it out, but if he's guilty, on the other hand—"

"Well, I don't think I'm supposed to say if someone's *guilty* or not."

"Look here! What do I care about guilt? All they lost was two hundred dollars, let him keep it. Besides a little matter of a shooting. I want to know about my *business*. I want to know if I should just give up, because to tell the truth this fellow Lem was a man I relied on. He saw to everything. Now, merchandising is out but there is always something else, and the jodhpur lady still wants my carnival. Shall I sell, after all? Is the man gone forever?"

Justine frowned at a card.

"You see what I've fallen to," Alonzo said. "I used to ask about beautiful women. Now it's financial matters."

"Well, Lem is not coming back," said Justine.

"I knew it."

"But you shouldn't sell the carnival."

"How can you keep saying such a stupid thing?"

"Don't argue with me, argue with the cards. Have you ever seen anything like it? I've turned up every jack in the deck, you'll have all the mechanics you want."

"Oh, of course," Alonzo said. "One after the other. The first one drinks, the second leaves with my ponies—"

"And look at the women! Look, Alonzo, you're not paying attention. See? Here you are, the king of hearts. And here's the queen of hearts, the queen of clubs, the queen of diamonds . . ."

Alonzo sat forward, peering at the cards, resting his hand upon his knees.

"Here is the good luck card, the card of friendship, the celebration card . . ."

"All right, all *right!*" Alonzo said.

She sat back and smiled at him.

"Oh, Justine," he told her sadly, "sometimes I think I would like to go live in a cabin in the woods, all alone. I'd take a lifetime supply of slivovitz, my accordion, plenty of food, perhaps some books. Do

you know I've never read an entire book? Just the good parts. I think
about hibernating like a bear, just eating and drinking and sleeping.
No tax, insurance, electric bills, alimony, repairs or repainting or Rus-
toleum, no women to mess up my life, no one shooting bank guards,
no children. Then here you come galloping along in your terrible hat
and your two sharp hipbones like pebbles in your pockets and you
tell me all these things I may expect, a life full of surprises. How can
I refuse? I feel curious all over again, I like to know what will happen
next."

And he shook his head, stroking downward on his mustache, but
he did not look so tired as when he had arrived. All his tiredness
seemed to have passed to Justine, who sat slumped in her chair with
her hands limp on the cards.

Duncan and Justine were on the front steps, watching the fireflies spark
all around them. "Today I sold an antique garden engine," Duncan
said.

"What's a garden engine?"

"It's this big wheeled thing to spray water on your flowers. What
a relief! I bought it with my own money in a moment of weakness. I
kept it sitting in the back room; I had to open the double doors to get
it in and then I was afraid it would go right through the floorboards.
A man named Newton Norton bought it. He's just started reconstructing
this old-time farmhouse out in the country."

"Well, that's nice," said Justine.

"He also bought some fuller's shears, and all my carpenter tools."

"That's nice."

He looked over at her.

"When I went into Meg's room," she said, "and found her note
telling me she'd gone, I never read anything that hurt so. But then I
looked up, and there I was reflected in the window that was just starting
to go dark outside. There were these deep black shadows in my eyes
and cheekbones. I thought, 'My, don't I look interesting? Like someone
who has had something *dramatic* happen.' I thought that!"

She laid her face against Duncan's sleeve. Duncan put his arm
around her and pulled her closer, but he didn't say anything.

Lucy Peck had to ride in the suicide seat, beside her husband Two, who was driving. Laura May and Sarah got to sit in back. Lucy had to put up with the hot air rushing in Two's open window and Mantovani playing much too loudly on the radio. She had to say what roads to take when she couldn't even *fold* a map right, much less read it. "Now the next thing is you're going to turn left, about a quarter-inch after Seven Stone Road. Or, I don't know. What would a little bitty broken blue line seem to mean?" Her husband set his front teeth together very, very delicately, not a good sign at all. A bumble bee flew in past his nose, causing Lucy to cry out and fling her road map into the air. And meanwhile there sat Laura May and Sarah, protected by layered hats with brown veils, contemplating two separate views peacefully like children being taken for a drive.

It was the sixth of June and they were on their way to Caro Mill, Maryland, to celebrate their father's ninety-third birthday. Unfortunately his birthday fell on a Wednesday this year, which meant that no one who worked could come along. And Bea was confined to her bed with lower back pain. It was up to them: Lucy and the maiden aunts, and Two, who was now retired. Between them they had loaded the car with presents and fruit, a Thermos of Sanka, Laura May's needlework, Sarah's knitting, insect repellent, sunscreen, Bufferin, Gelusil, a Triple-A tour guide, a can of Fix-a-Flat, a fire extinguisher, six emergency flares, and a white banner reading SEND HELP. They had had the Texaco man check the gas, oil, water, brake fluid, transmission fluid, tire pressure, and windshield cleaner. Then Two nosed the car out into traffic and they were on their way, with enough horns honking behind them to remind Lucy of an orchestra tuning up. Young people nowadays were so impatient. Luckily Two was not a man who could be fussed, and he went on driving at his same stately tempo. In his old age he had shrunk somewhat, and was made to seem even smaller by his habit of tipping his head back as he peered through the windshield. His eyes were narrow blue hyphens. His mouth was pulled downward by two ropes in his neck. When he decided to turn left from the right-hand lane he signaled imperiously out the window, still facing front, maintaining his cool Apache profile for Lucy to marvel at while behind them more horns honked. "Kindly check the odometer, Lucy," was all he said. "I would be interested in knowing our mileage on this trip."

"Yes, dear."

Once they hit the open road they were dazzled by too much

sunshine and too wide an expanse of fields. It was some time since they had been in the country. (One year ago today, to be exact.) Lucy longed for her wing chair in which she could sit encircled, almost, with the wings working like a mule's blinders to confine her gaze to the latest historical romance. The upholstery was embroidered in satin-stitch, which she loved to stroke absently as she read. Then in the back yard her Sea Foam roses were just opening; there were going to be more this year than ever before and she was missing one entire day's worth. And it was so much cooler and greener at home, so shadowy, so thickly treed that when you spoke outdoors your voice came echoing back, clear and close, as if reflected from a vaulted green ceiling not far above your head. Here the sun turned everything pale. Pinkish barns sped past and bleached gray roadbanks, and beige creeks spanned by wooden bridges like dried-up, whitening bones. Lucy turned and sought out her sisters-in-law—a double pair of webbed eyes reluctantly drawn to hers. "Really, traveling makes me sad," Lucy told them. But they didn't answer (Lucy always said such *personal* things), so she faced front again.

At Plankhurst there was a very confusing crossroads and she sent Two thirteen miles out of the way before the mistake was realized. "Oh, I'm just so—I just can't tell you how badly I feel about this," she said. Two grunted. In the back seat her sisters-in-law gave her disappointed looks that made her want to cry. "I just seem to do everything wrong," she said. Nobody denied it.

Two hours out of Baltimore they began to encounter signs for Caro Mill, although still it seemed they were in the depths of the country. The only buildings were farmhouses, widely scattered, and occasionally a little grocery store patched with soft drink ads. Then they swooped over a hill and there was the town all spread out before them, a clutter of untidy buildings. They had traveled this Main Street annually for years, although each time in a different location. They had passed this very Woolworth's, diner, pizza parlor, fabric store displaying dingy bolts of cloth turning gray along the creases. Still, Lucy sat up straighter and began perking the lace at the neck of her dress. Two pressed his thin white hair flat against his head, and in back there were rustles and whispers. "Oh, I do hope Father likes the—" "Remind me to ask Father if he wouldn't care to—" But Duncan was the one Lucy thought of, not her father-in-law at all. It was for Duncan she had bought this hat (only wouldn't he think the wooden cherries were—old-ladyish, maybe?) and put on these coins of rouge and her eighteen-hour girdle and the Sunday pearls. (Only come to think of it, hadn't he always laughed at the family's fondness for pearls?) She twisted her rings. "Perhaps he won't be home," she said.

"Who?" Two asked, although of course he knew.

"It *is* a working day. Though Justine said he comes home for lunch. But perhaps he won't. I mean, one time—"

One time when they visited he had gone fishing with a friend. A *plumber* or something. Another time he had wandered around the house all afternoon wearing earphones on a very long cord, following a baseball game. You could only grasp the depth of the insult when you remembered that Duncan did not like sports and would prefer to do almost anything but listen to a game. "*One* time—" she said, but Two's voice cracked across hers like a whip.

"Leave it," he said. "What'd you do with Justine's letter?"

"Letter?"

"Her *letter*, Lucy. Telling us how to get to their house."

"Oh. Oh, why I—"

She remembered suddenly that she had left the letter at home on the dining room buffet, but she didn't want to say so. "Why, *someplace* here," she said, riffling through her pocketbook. Two let out a long puff of air. He slowed and beckoned from the window, startling a fat lady standing on the median line. "Pardon me," he said. "We are looking for Watchmaker Street. For twenty-one Watchmaker Street."

"Oh, *Justine*," the lady said.

Everyone flinched. Justine's name was always bandied about so. Like common property.

"Why, you just turn left at the next light," she said, "go two blocks and turn left again. That's Watchmaker Street."

"Thank you."

He rolled the window all the way up.

Now they were silent, concentrating on the view, wondering what sort of house they were headed for. Hoping, just this once, for something really fine. But no. Of course: there it was, a flimsy, no-account little place. Tacked to the screen was what appeared to be a magazine ad for traveler's checks. YOU ARE FAR, FAR FROM HOME, it said, IN UNFAMILIAR TERRITORY . . . But then out flew Justine, barefoot, glowing, in a dress with a lopsided hem. "Uncle Two!" she cried. "Aunt Lucy! You got here!" She hugged them—some of them twice over. She called for her grandfather, who naturally couldn't hear. She showed Laura May and Sarah up the rickety steps and into the house to find him, and then she ran out again to help Two and Lucy unload the trunk. "Duncan will be here in a minute," she said. "He's coming for lunch. Oh look! This is Aunt Bea's gift, I know the wrapping. Will you look at that bow?" But then she dropped it. Fortunately it was not breakable. Lucy had often wondered: was accident-proneness *catching*? Justine had been such a careful little girl. "I wrote and asked Meg to come too but they're having final exams," Justine said. "It seems to me these birthday parties get smaller every year. She sent her love to all of you."

"Oh, bless her heart," Lucy said. "Well, some of these things are her wedding presents. Did we tell you we're giving her your great-grandma's silver?"

Not a one of them was tactless enough to comment on Meg's manner of marrying.

"Now," said Two. "Tell me straight. How's Duncan's business going?"

"Oh, fine, Uncle Two. Just fine."

"What is it again? Jewelry?"

But then Grandfather Peck came down the steps, bending in an odd flimsy way at the knees, and he had to be greeted and fussed over. Lucy kissed his bristly white cheek, Two shook his hand. "Happy birthday!" Lucy shouted.

"How's the what?"

"Happy birthday!"

He looked at her for a moment, considering. "Oh, very well, thank you," he said finally.

"You don't have to shout, Aunt Lucy," Justine told her. "Only narrow *in*. You know what I mean?"

"Oh yes," said Lucy, although she didn't. They went through this on every visit.

Once they were inside the house, there was the usual difficulty in knowing what to say about it. Certainly *some* comment seemed called for. But the rooms were small and dark. The windows were curtained only by great tangles of plants all merging and mingling and sending long runners clear across the floor. There were not nearly enough places to sit. In one of the little back bedrooms, Lucy was horrified to glimpse an absolutely bare, rust-stained mattress, striped blue and white. It reminded her of the time her church group had toured a flophouse for their social service project. "Justine, dear heart," she said, "have we interrupted your bedmaking?"

"My what? Oh no, I'm going to run the sheets down to the laundromat this evening."

"Perhaps I could help you put the fresh ones on."

"But I don't have any others," Justine said.

Lucy sat down very suddenly on a chrome-legged chair that had been dragged out of the kitchen.

Grandfather Peck never would open his presents until after lunch. He had them taken to the table, and meanwhile he and Two settled themselves in the living room and discussed business affairs. Since both of them were retired, it was a vague, wistful, second-hand sort of discussion. "Dan I believe is very much involved with that Kingham matter," Two said. "*You* remember Kingham."

"Oh yes. What was that again?"

"Well, let's see, I'm not quite . . . but he says it's moving just fine."

"Fine, is it."

Perhaps Two should not have retired just yet. But he would feel better when his brothers joined him—Dan in two years, Marcus the year after that. (Sixty-eight was the age they had agreed upon.) Then Claude and Richard could run things on their own. There was no point in working yourself straight into the grave. Still, Two seemed bored and listless as he sat sunk in a corner of the threadbare couch. His father nodded opposite him. His father was so aged that he had reached a saturation point; no new wrinkles had been added in years. He looked not much different from the way he had at seventy. Not much different from Two, as a matter of fact. They might have been brothers. This was how they all ended up, then: arriving at some sort of barrier and sitting down to wait for death, joined eventually by others who had started out later. In the end, the quarter-century that divided their generations amounted to nothing and was swept away. Lucy passed a hand over her own wispy, corrugated forehead. She looked at Two, a handsome man whom she had determined to call Justin back when they were courting, but finally she had given in and called him what his family did. They won, as they always had. Everything was leveled, there were no extremes of joy or sorrow any more but only habit, routine, ancient family names and rites and customs, slow careful old people moving cautiously around furniture that had sat in the same positions for fifty years.

But just as she felt herself sinking into a marsh of despair, she heard Duncan's light quick step across the porch. She saw him fling the screen door open—such a tall boy, or man rather, with his eyes lit from within and that awning of fair hair flopping over his high, pure, untouched forehead. She rose and smoothed her skirt down and held her purse more tightly to her stomach. "Duncan, darling," she said. His kiss was as hurried as ever, brief and light as a raindrop, but she felt her heart floating softly upward and she was certain that this time everything was going to go wonderfully.

For lunch Justine served baked ham, potatoes, and snap beans. Everyone was pleasantly surprised. "Why, Justine," said Two, "this is excellent. This ham is very tasty."

"Oh, Grandfather did that."

"Hmm?"

They stared at her. She seemed perfectly serious. Her grandfather was absorbed in salting his beans and could not be contacted.

For dessert they had a layer cake with nine large candles on it and three small ones. Lucy watched closely while it was sliced. "Is it a mix, dear?" she asked.

"Oh, no."

"You made it from scratch?"

"Grandfather made it."

This time, he looked up. He gave them a shy, crooked smile and then lowered his white eyelashes. "Why, Father Peck!" Lucy said.

"I did the ham too," he said. "She tell you that?"

"Yes, she did."

"Also the potatoes. I baked them first, you see, then scooped them out . . . found it in Fannie Farmer. Some people call them potato boats."

Two looked at his watch.

"The cake is what is known as a war cake," said the grandfather. "It makes do with considerably less butter and eggs than we would normally use, you see. After all, we're living in reduced circumstances."

He seemed to savor the last two words: reduced circumstances. Lucy thought they sounded smugly technical, like devaluated currency or municipal bonds. For a very brief moment she wondered if he didn't almost *enjoy* this life—these dismal houses, weird friends, separations from the family, this moving about and fortune telling. If he weren't almost proud of the queer situations he found himself in. But then Sarah said, "Remember Grandma's orange peel cake?" and his face became suddenly thin and lost.

"Oh. Oh yes," he said.

"She used to mix it secretly in the pantry. Remember? She said she would give the recipe to Sulie but Sulie says she never did. Although of course we can't be too sure of that."

"I wonder what was in it," Justine said dreamily, and she paused so long with her knife in mid-air that Two grew impatient.

"*Come* on," he said. He looked at his watch again. "It's one thirty-two. Do you always have dinner so late?"

"Mostly we don't have dinner at all," Justine said.

"I ask because last year we ate around noon. Dessert was served shortly before one."

"Was it?"

"The year *before* that, we ate even earlier."

"Did we?"

"Is this a new hobby of yours?" Duncan asked Two. "Are you planning to graph us?"

"To—no. No, it's just a little matter of timing, you understand. I thought the presents would be opened by one o'clock. Maybe we could do them before dessert."

"But I had counted on enjoying my cake," the grandfather said.

He and Two stared at each other, a pair of old, cross men. "This is a matter of timing, Father," Two told him.

"Of what?"

"*Timing!*"

"Speak up."

Two groaned.

"The worst of it is," Lucy whispered to Justine, "now Two is growing a teensy bit deaf himself."

"I most certainly am *not*," Two said.

"Sorry, dear."

Two picked up a small flat package. "From Sarah," he said. "Happy birthday."

Two's father took the package and turned it over. How many times had Lucy watched him painfully untie a bow, peel off the Scotch tape, remove the paper and fold it carefully for future use before he would look to see what he had been given? Year after year he received this cascade of shirts and socks and monogrammed handkerchiefs, all in glossy white boxes and handsome paper, tied with loopy satin bows. To each gift he said, "Why, thank you. Thank you very much," after which he replaced it in its box. Probably none of these things would ever be used. Except, of course, Justine's: a crumpled white sack of horehound drops that honestly seemed to delight him, although that had been her gift for as long as anyone could remember. "Can you figure it out?" he said. "Stuff's practically impossible to find any more but every year she manages. Expensive, too. *Justine* makes do with Luden's cough drops but I fail to see the resemblance myself." He popped a lozenge in his mouth and passed the sack around. Only Justine took one. Nobody else could stand them. "Last chance till next year," he told Lucy, flooding her with his pharmaceutical breath. Lucy shook her head.

Duncan of course gave nothing at all, and would never allow Justine to pencil his name beside hers on the sack of horehound drops. He didn't believe in celebrating birthdays. He would give presents any time, to anyone, sudden surprising *touching* presents, but not when the rules said he was supposed to. And this year there was no gift from Meg either. Lucy was watching. Not so much as a tie clasp or a bureau top organizer. She felt a brief surge of wicked joy: now Duncan himself knew the pain of having an ungrateful child. Perhaps he had thought, when Meg eloped, So this is what it feels like! This is what my parents have had to put up with all my life! But then she was ashamed of herself, and she felt truly sorry that her granddaughter had somehow forgotten such an important occasion.

Next to last came Laura May's gift: needlework, as usual. This year a family tree, embroidered on natural linen with a wooden frame. "Why, thank you," said her father. "Thank you very much." But instead of setting it back down, he held it in both hands and looked at it for a long, silent moment. A diamond shape, that was what it was. Lucy had never noticed before. Justin alone began it and Meg alone ended it. In between there was a sudden glorious spread of children, but what had they come to? Nothing. Claude, Esther, the twins, and Richard stood alone, unmarried, without descendants. (Laura May had tactfully left off all record of Sally's divorce and Richard's annulment.) Only Duncan on the far left, son of the oldest child, and Justine on the far right, daughter of the youngest child, were connected by a V-shaped line that spilled out their single offspring at the bottom of the diamond. There was no room for anyone below Meg's name. Lucy shook her head. "But," said Justine, "maybe Meg will have six children and things will start all over again!"

Maybe so. Lucy pictured the diamond shape endlessly repeated, like the design on the border of a blanket. But the thought failed to cheer her up.

Then came the last gift, the largest, a gigantic cube two feet square. The card was the largest too. It had to be. *Birthday greetings and many happy returns from your sons Justin II, Daniel Jr., and Marcus.*

"Well now," said Grandfather Peck.

Two began chuckling. The wrapping was a joke.

First the striped paper, then a large white box. A slightly smaller box inside, then fleur-de-lis paper covering another box, then another, another . . .

Grandfather Peck grew bewildered. Mountains of ribbon and tissue rose around him. "What's all this?" he kept asking. "What's . . . I don't understand."

"Keep going," Two said.

He and his brothers had spent an entire evening working on the wrapping. Ordinarily they were not humorous men, but while fitting cartons inside cartons on Lucy's dining room table they had chortled like schoolboys, and Lucy had had to smile. She smiled now, seeing Two's face all squeezed together to keep the laughter in. "Go on, go on," he kept saying.

A hatbox, containing a shoebox, containing a stationery box, containing a playing card box, containing a matchbox. And finally the gift itself, wrapped in white paper. Two was laughing so hard that the corners of his eyes were damp. "It's a joke," he explained to Duncan. "See?"

"Typical," said Duncan.

"No, see? They did it at this office party, when Dan's secretary got married. They wrapped a little tiny present in a great big box, funniest thing you ever saw."

"It would be funnier if they had wrapped a great big present in a little *tiny* box," said Duncan.

"No, see—"

Grandfather Peck removed the Scotch tape from the minute rectangle of paper. He opened the paper carefully, but for once did not fold it and set it aside. Perhaps because it was too small. Perhaps because he was too shocked: his present was a single calling card.

" 'Worth and Everjohn, Inc.,' " he read out. " 'Your Local Domestic Investigating Agency. 19 Main Street, Caro Mill, Maryland. Why Stay in Doubt? Call Us and Find Out. All Reports in Strictest . . .' " He looked up at Two. "I don't quite understand," he said.

But instead of answering Two rose and left the room. They heard him open the front screen door. "All right now!" he shouted.

The man he brought back with him looked like Abe Lincoln, even to the narrow border of beard along his jawline. He wore a black suit, a very starched white shirt, and a string tie. Probably he was in his thirties, but his weary, hungry expression made him seem older. Runlets of sweat streaked his temples. There was a pulse in the hollow of one cheek. "Sorry to have kept you out there so long," Two was saying. "I know you must be hot."

"Oh, I didn't have nothing else to do."

"Father, this is Mr. Eli Everjohn," Two said.

Mr. Everjohn held out his hand, which seemed to have an unusual number of bones in it. Grandfather Peck peered into his face. "I don't understand," he said.

"Your birthday present, Father."

"Oh, naturally," Duncan said to no one. "I'm surprised they didn't gift-wrap the man himself."

"Well, they thought of it," Lucy told him.

"Father, Mr. Everjohn's a detective," said Two.

"Yes?"

"He tracks people down."

"Yes, of course," said Grandfather Peck. He waited patiently, ready to smile as soon as he saw the point.

"He's going to track Uncle Caleb for you."

"How's that?"

"See, Dan and Mark and I pooled together and hired him. We thought, why not get this thing settled? I mean determine, once and for all, that Uncle Caleb is . . . I mean *you're* not getting anywhere, Father. Now we'll spare no expense. We've picked a man who's located here so that you can keep tabs, help out in any way that's needed, and no matter how long it takes we're prepared to foot the bill. Understand? That's our little gift to you. Happy birthday."

His father stared at him.

"Didn't you hear?" Two asked.

"But I don't . . ."

Mr. Everjohn's hand remained outstretched, motionless. You would think that he went through this every day.

"I don't believe I require any assistance, thank you just the same," Grandfather Peck told him.

"But Father! It's your birthday present."

"Then it's his to refuse," Duncan said.

"Stay out of this, Duncan."

Duncan rose and came around the table. He shook Mr. Everjohn's hand. "I believe," he said, "that my grandfather likes to track his own people."

"Certainly, for fifteen *years!*" Two shouted.

But he was not a shouting man. Even his sisters, fluttering their hands toward their ears, couldn't hold it against him. This was all Duncan's doing, some germ he spread. "Two, dear," Lucy told him, and right away he lowered his voice.

"Oh," he said, "don't think I don't know why you've let him live here, Duncan. You *like* to see this happening, your grandfather chasing rainbows on the Greyhound bus line. But consider him, for once. At the present rate, how long will it be before he's successful?"

"Forever, probably," Duncan said. "But at least he's happier than most other Pecks I know."

Everyone looked at the grandfather. He stared blandly back, not giving away a thing.

"And I doubt if success is what we want here," said Duncan. "What would you do with Caleb now? Where would you fit him in? In the end you'd just have to let him run on, like a fox after a foxhunt."

"Oh, was he a sportsman?" Mr. Everjohn asked.

"What? I don't know. No."

"Of course not," said Two.

Mr. Everjohn took a spiral notebook from his shirt pocket. He uncapped a Bic pen and wrote something down. In the sudden silence Justine said, "Maybe you'd like a seat."

"What for?" Duncan asked. "He's not staying."

And his grandfather said, "Yes, actually *Justine* and I—"

"That's just what we're trying to spare you," Two told him. "These endless, fruitless searches, wandering about the country like a pair of— let a professional do it." He turned to Duncan. "As for what to do with Caleb," he said, speaking very low and fast, "I seriously doubt that that problem will arise. If you follow me."

"What, do you imagine he's dead?"

Two gave his father a sidelong glance.

"You can't stand to think he's alive and well and staying away on *purpose,*" Duncan said. "Can you? But he's a Peck and he's not even ninety, barely in his prime. I'll bet you a bottle of bourbon he's sitting in an old folks' home this very minute watching *The Dating Game.*"

Grandfather Peck slammed a hand down on the table. Everybody stared.

"I've stood a lot from you, Duncan," he said, "but not this. *I do not have a brother in an old folks' home.*"

If he had spoken to Lucy that way she would have crumbled and died, but Duncan only raised his eyebrows. (And though she blushed for him, she felt a little thrill that nothing these Pecks could do would ever really touch him.)

"Mr. Everjohn," said the grandfather, "I'll tell you all I know, and then you get to work. I am not a drinking man but I want to collect a bottle of bourbon from my grandson here."

Then he stood up and led Mr. Everjohn to the living room. Two went with them but the others stayed in the kitchen, gazing down at their slices of cake, which no one had the appetite for. Lucy tore her napkin to shreds and wondered where the Gelusil was. Sarah fanned herself with a sheaf of folded wrapping paper. Justine was chewing on a birthday candle and Laura May had picked up the family tree to admire her own embroidery. Only Duncan, circling the table aimlessly, seemed to have any energy left. He whistled something unfamiliar. He touched a strand of Justine's hair as he passed. He looked over Laura May's shoulder at the family tree. "Has it occurred to you," he asked her, "that someone somewhere may still be searching for Justin?"

By four o'clock Two still hadn't made a move to go. And he was the one who hated night driving! He said he had to get everything straight with the detective first. Lucy could tell he was beginning to regret his choice, not that there *was* much choice in a town like Caro Mill. This Mr. Everjohn was turning out to be a little peculiar. The more peculiar he got the grimmer Two's face grew, and the gayer Duncan's. Justine became downright hospitable and offered Mr. Everjohn root beer and birthday cake. By now they were all in the living room, the aunts in a row on the couch and the others in kitchen chairs, having been lured there one after another by the goings-on. Grandfather Peck was giving Mr. Everjohn the names of every classmate Uncle Caleb had ever had. Every teacher, friend, and business associate. Where did he get them all? Then Uncle Caleb's church, school, barber, tailor, doctor, tavern . . . she had never known a Peck to frequent a tavern. But Mr. Everjohn did not look surprised. He continued filling his spiral notebook, scribbling away at unexpected moments for unexplainable lengths of time. He requested and pocketed the grandfather's treasured photo, saying he would have a copy made, but why, when it was half a century out of date? He listened to a recital of the entire attendance sheet of a vacation Bible school that had opened, and closed forever, in the summer of 1893. Whole strings of names were allowed to slip by, but then he would pounce on one and fill two pages. What was he writing? Lucy sat up very straight, but she couldn't see into his lap.

Now another peculiar thing was, how a man of business could spare so many hours. Naturally a detective was not like a *lawyer* or anything, but still you would think he had appointments and commitments. Mr. Everjohn seemed ready to give the Pecks the rest of his life. He sat without fidgeting, keeping his sharp knees clamped together and his elbows close to his body. One trouser leg was rucked up to show a shin like a stick of timber. He wrote with his pen held so awkwardly that it made Lucy's hand ache. When he asked questions, they were always the least likely. For instance, he wanted to know Uncle Caleb's smoking habits, the name of his childhood nursemaid, his mother's birthday, and his preference in shoes. He asked about Laura's reading matter and Justin's will, about religious beliefs and shipping schedules. The stranger the questions, the more excited Grandfather Peck became. It was like going to the doctor for a headache and having him examine your toenails. What undreamed-of things he must know! Even when Mr. Everjohn asked about Margaret Rose, Grandfather Peck barely flinched. "Of course, that's something I never think about," he said. "I've forgotten her entirely."

"Ah," said Mr. Everjohn. When he opened his mouth like that, his face became impossibly long and his cheeks sank in.

"Anyway, she left before Caleb did," said the grandfather.

"Now where was it she went to?"

You could have heard a pin drop.

"Washington," said the grandfather.

"Oh yes."

"She got a job. But she died."

"What kind of job?"

"There's not much point in going into this," the grandfather said.

"I got to know anyway, Mr. Peck."

"Uh, she laundered money."

"Money."

"She worked for the U.S. Treasury. She washed old bills."

Mr. Everjohn's deep, bruised-looking eyes searched mournfully around the room.

"It's perfectly possible," Duncan told him. "They used to wash them and coat them with rosin. For crispness. In the past they weren't so quick to throw things away. They had a machine that—"

"I see," said Mr. Everjohn. "Cause of death?"

"Boardinghouse fire," said Grandfather Peck.

"She live in a boardinghouse?"

"Her parents wouldn't *let* her stay with them, you see. In those days women were expected to be better behaved. They tried to make her come back to Baltimore. Her father wrote and told me."

"Now. You sure she really died."

"They buried her, didn't they?"

"I was thinking maybe that was where your brother went to: Washington. Maybe the *two* of them. You ever consider that?"

Lucy had. But Grandfather Peck was merely impatient. "If he were such a scoundrel, why would I be looking for him?" he asked.

"*Oh* yes," said Mr. Everjohn, and he seemed perfectly satisfied. He slipped the notebook and pencil back into his pocket. "Well, I think I got something here to start on."

"We certainly appreciate your making a housecall, Mr. Everjohn," Two said.

"Why, that's all right."

"I never expected to take so much of your time, but of course I am fully prepared to—"

"Think nothing of it," Mr. Everjohn said. "To be honest, this town don't keep a man very busy." He felt beneath his chair for his hat and then rose, unfolding foot by foot. With a hat on he looked more like Lincoln than ever. The crown was even slightly squared, the brim oddly curved. "There's so little call for us, me and my partner have to shadow each other's wives for practice," he said.

"Really," said Two.

"Women's lives are right dull, I've found. My partner's wife goes to one store for toothpaste and another for mouthwash, just to get herself two outings."

"Well, I know you have to be getting back," said Two.

"Now *my* wife takes *lessons*. She will sign up for anything. You wouldn't believe the places Joe has got to follow her to."

"May I expect your bill on a monthly basis?"

"Pet grooming. Exotic dance. Kung-fu. Stretch-'n-Sew."

"Oh, Eli!" cried Justine, making one of her shocking leaps to a first-name friendship. "Won't you take your wife a piece of birthday cake?"

"She's on this diet," Mr. Everjohn said gloomily. "She goes to Weight Watchers and Slenderella, and every Thursday from two to four she's got her this class in low-carbohydrate food preparation." He shook Justine's hand too hard. "I'll keep in touch," he told her.

"Well, drop in any time. Grandfather will want to hear."

"And thank you again for your patience," Two said.

But the minute Mr. Everjohn was out the door, Two collapsed in his chair. "I knew we should have used a Baltimore man," he told Lucy.

"Well, there, dear."

"I must have the names of twenty good detectives back home. But no, Marcus said it had to be a Caro Mill fellow. That way Father could handle things, he said. Otherwise *we'd* be the ones to—"

"Well, I thought he was very nice," Justine said, returning from the front door.

"If you children would live in a civilized area, Justine—"

"Caro Mill is civilized."

Two turned to Duncan, who was playing with what looked to be an auto part over by the window. "You need to come back to Baltimore, boy," he said. "What's stopping you? Jobs? You know there's lots to do in a law office that wouldn't take a degree. Your cousins could fix you up. Quick mind like yours, there's *lots* to—"

"Thanks anyway," Duncan said.

"Do Justine good. See there? She's looking a little tired."

Lucy glanced over at her. Why, she was. It was true. Now that she was not running or laughing or talking too much, her face seemed strained and pale. Blame Meg, that's who. Children! She shifted her gaze to Duncan, an aging little boy. Secretly her favorite son, and she had always imagined what a fine man he would be once he was grown and mellowed. But that had never happened. He was preserved forever as he had been at ten, reckless and inconsiderate, not kind at all, not ever willing to make allowance for other people's weaknesses. He had needed a good strong wife to settle him down and round his sharp edges, but he hadn't got one. Only Justine. Was Justine the way she was *deliberately*? Had she just flat out decided one day that she would refuse to take responsibility, that Duncan could go caroming straight to hell taking wife and daughter along before she would say a word? Something made Lucy speak up suddenly, when she hadn't even known she was going to. "Oh," she said, "if only poor dear Caroline could have been with us today!"

The look Duncan gave her was as cold and hard as glass, but Lucy felt her little triumph warming all her bones when she saw how still Justine grew.

By the time they were back in the car it was very nearly twilight. Even so, Lucy took the preaddressed envelope out of her purse and unfolded a sheet of stationery and wrote, as Two had taught her to:

> Dear Justine, June 6, 1973
> Thank you so much for the lovely time! As always you made a perfectly charming hostess, and the War Cake was delicious. We shall remember our visit with a great deal of pleasure.
> Love,
> Aunt Lucy

She placed the note in the envelope and sealed it. "Whenever you notice a mailbox, Two . . ." she said, but then she trailed off, bleakly tapping the letter against her purse. Two moved his lips as he drove. In back, Laura May and Sarah sat side by side beneath veiled brown hats and looked out the windows at their separate views.

12

Now Justine and her grandfather had no place to go. At first they hardly noticed; they traveled less during the summer months anyway. But as June dragged on, hot and humid, and then July took over, Justine grew unhappier. She didn't have enough to do with herself. There was some troubled feeling gnawing at the back of her mind. Uneasiness drove her into quarreling with Duncan, snapping at her grandfather, telling skimpy, half-hearted fortunes for her clients. She spoke with an unplaceable foreign accent for days at a time. She insulted Dorcas. The cat moved out of the house and into the crawlspace behind the rose bushes. Her grandfather sat on the porch, unusually still, with his face slack and vacant.

"Look, Grandfather," Justine said, "isn't there someone you would like to look up? How about that man in Delaware? Maybe he's remembered something new."

"It wouldn't be any use," her grandfather said.

"Well, I don't see why not."

"That detective fellow didn't even take his name down. Took hardly *any* of those names. Seemed to think they would serve no purpose whatsoever."

"Oh, what does *he* know," Justine said.

She had begun to resent Eli's odd, probing questions and the mysterious silence that followed all answers. After each of his visits she felt tampered with. He had a way of arriving when no one was home and settling himself to wait on the front porch. When she and her grandfather returned he would loom up, tall and black as a raven, with his squared-off hat centered over his chest. "Eli!" she always cried, but her heart grew thick, as if preparing against invasion. And her grandfather, who made a point of remembering every passing name, said, "Mr.—ah," and stood scowling down at his shoes like a foregetful schoolboy. But Eli was humble and awkward, and he began by discussing something harmless—his shadowing practice, his wife's calligraphy lessons. After all, he was in no hurry. Then Justine warmed to him all over again, to his absurd fringe of a beard as precise as the brush on a typewriter eraser and his preposterously long, multiple-jointed fingers fumbling at his hat; and her grandfather relaxed enough to grow politely bored. "Come inside, Eli," Justine would say. "I'll make you some iced tea." But at that very moment his face would narrow, his fingers would grow still. "What all were the records your family owned?" he might ask.

"What?"

"*Recordings.* For that old-timey phonograph."

She had to turn to her grandfather, who scuffed the porch floor-boards petulantly. "Caruso, I remember," he said finally. "Other things. Red Label discs."

"Oh yes. Red Seal."

"In the beginning they were called Red Label."

"Ah," said Eli.

"Don't you know *anything?*"

"But what besides Caruso? Any more?"

"I don't recall."

"It's something I got to find out," said Eli, but he wouldn't say why. "Well, I reckon I'll just have to go to Baltimore again. You've kept them, now."

"We've kept everything," said Grandfather Peck. And when he went inside he would slam the screen door. Yet it was plain that Eli's questions intrigued him. For the remainder of the day he would be thinking hard, frowning until his eyebrows met. "Can you tell me why he would ask such a thing? What has he got up his sleeve? That fellow must know something we just have no idea of, Justine."

But for the grandfather, after all, finding Caleb was the only goal. For Justine the point of the search had been the trips themselves, and now she felt bereft and useless. She wandered from room to room, absently carrying her straw bag around with her as if she were a visitor, long after her grandfather had settled himself in the armchair to plan what he would say first when he and Caleb met.

Meanwhile Duncan was selling antique tools by the dozen, by the gross, faster than he could stock them. Why did things always work out this way? Newton Norton, the man who had bought the garden engine, was reconstructing his ancient farm down to the last pitchfork in the barn. He haunted the Blue Bottle, seizing on old rusty pliers and milking lanterns, blacksmith's implements, kitchen utensils. "If you could see Silas's face!" Duncan told Justine. "Sometimes Newton Norton has to call for a truck just to take his purchases home."

"He must be crazy," said Justine. "What if he has to move someday?"

They were on the front porch, Duncan sitting on a stool while Justine gave him a haircut with the kitchen shears. His hair was thick and straight, audible when it fell. She cut it in layers down the back like a shingled roof, and then when she combed it the layers sifted magically together and evened out. She combed again, floating off into a trance among the shimmering yellow ribbons. She cut another inch off. "Maybe I should have been a barber," she said.

"Let's not get carried away here," Duncan told her.

By now it was August and their corn was so tall it blocked their view of the street. Cars swished by unseen, almost unheard. (Duncan was interested in the effect of greenery upon the decibel count.) People walking past were no more than disembodied voices.

"Hello!" they called, apparently taking it on faith that someone was there to answer. "Well, hi!" said Justine. She waved her flashing shears in the air. Duncan didn't look up. He had his mind on other things.

"I told Silas, 'See there?' He wouldn't let me buy that old sewing machine of Mrs. Farnsworth's, now he's sorry. Newton Norton tracked it down himself and gave her twice what it was worth. But you know Silas. 'Yes,' he said, 'but once he's got this farm of his set up, what then? Hmm?' Well, yesterday Newton Norton opened his place to the public, a fully working nineteenth-century farm. Admission two dollars. Fifty cents for children. *Plus.* Cooking lessons. A six-week course in old-time American cooking. You learn in this kitchen that has a wood stove and a fireplace big enough to roast an ox. You make cabbage custard and codfish cakes—well, to tell the truth, none of it sounded edible. But *somebody* must like it. All this morning women were coming in asking for sausage guns. Bird's-eye maple sauerkraut mashers. They snatched up these hand-cranked machines that I hadn't even quite figured out yet, things to pare cucumbers and strip corncobs and peel potatoes. By noon I'd sold every utensil in the place."

"Think of that! You're a success," said Justine, trimming around his ears.

"That's what they call it."

But he spoke through a yawn, and then sneezed when a snippet of hair landed on his nose. His face glinted all over with stray blond sparks. He didn't *look* like a success.

On the fourth Sunday in August, the three of them drove to Semple to visit Meg. They were supposed to go earlier but always at the last minute Duncan claimed that something had come up. He had to attend an auction, or a special flea market, now that Silas was urging him to buy more tools. Yet he returned without any tools whatsoever—only, once, a carton of rusty Prince Albert tobacco tins. "These are antiques?" Justine asked. "Imagine, they used to be garbage. I used to see them in the weeds along Roland Avenue. But where are the tools? What about the kitchen utensils?"

"None of them appealed to me," said Duncan. "Only Prince Albert."

"In the end, the silliest things get valuable. We shouldn't throw *anything* out."

"It doesn't seem to me that we do," said Duncan.

Now he wanted to cancel the trip yet another time (he said there was a Tailgate Treasures near Washington) but Justine had caught on to him. "It's not possible," she said. "You know how long we waited for Meg to invite us. Now we've put her off twice. What will she think?"

"Maybe just you and Grandfather could go. I could go to Washington alone."

"What on, bicycle?"

"I could borrow Silas's station wagon," he said.

"Besides, I don't want to go just with Grandfather. I'd really like you with me this time."

"Maybe in the fall, when things are quieter."

"I don't understand you, Duncan," Justine told him. "What is it you have against this visit?"

But then he grew touchy. He always did object to the way she dragged his secret feelings into the open.

Still, on the fourth Sunday in August there he was, maybe a little grimmer than usual but resigned to the trip, heading the Ford along a gritty two-lane highway toward Semple with Justine sitting beside him and Grandfather Peck next to the window. On the rear seat was a stack of Meg's summer dresses and a paper bag containing a dozen ears of corn. ("But the corn will be wasted," Duncan said. "Reverend Mildew will try to eat it with a knife and fork.") Meg's other belongings—her set of Nancy Drew mysteries and her pennants and bottles of cologne—remained in her room. Duncan had thought they should bring everything in one fell swoop but Justine preferred not to. "All she asked for were her summer dresses," she said. "Maybe she doesn't have space yet for the rest."

Duncan, who never dragged anyone's secret feelings into the open if he could possibly help it, merely nodded and let her have her way.

They reached the outskirts of Semple at two in the afternoon. *Welcome to Semple, Va., "Prettiest Little Town in the South,"* the sign said, looming above a stack of pine boards weathering in a lumberyard. They bounced over railroad tracks, past rusty, gaping boxcars. "Now *there* was a town," said Grandfather Peck. "Had its own train."

"Only freight trains, Grandfather," Justine said.

"Pardon? Freight? Didn't we go to Nashville once from here?"

"That was from Fredericksburg. Three years back."

"Oh yes."

"Here we had to take a bus to Richmond and *then* catch a train."

"Nashville was where that boy played the banjo," said her grandfather. "His great-uncle taught Caleb how to work a stringed instrument when they were both fourteen."

"That's the place," Justine said.

He slumped, as if the conversation had taken everything out of him.

On Main Street Justine saw someone she knew—old Miss Wheeler, who used to ask the cards whether she should put her father in a nursing home—and she wanted to stop and speak to her, but Duncan wouldn't hear of it. "I'd like to get this over with, Justine," he said. Going back to places always did make him cross. When they passed the Wayfarer's Diner and then the Whole Self Health Food Store, whose tattered awning and baggy screens leapt out like familiar faces, Justine could feel the edginess in the skin of his arm. "Never mind, we're only visiting," she told him. But she had trespassed again and he drew himself in, moving slightly away from her so that their arms no longer touched and there was a sudden coolness along her left thigh.

Arthur Milsom's church was a large brick building on the other side of town. Justine had never attended it, but of course Meg had pointed it out to her—she remembered how the steeple had seemed sharper than necessary, barbed with some glittery metal at the tip. The rectory was brick also, but the house of the assistant pastor, next door to the rectory, was a small white cottage without trees or shrubs, set on a square of artificial-looking grass. There was a bald picture window with a double-globed, rosebud-painted lamp centered in it, and beside the front walk a hitching post in the shape of a small boy with a newly whitened face and black hands. Duncan stopped to study it, but Justine took her grandfather by the elbow and hurried him up the steps. "*Where* is this?" he asked her.

"This is Meg's, Grandfather. We're visiting Meg."

"Yes, yes, but—" And he revolved slowly, staring all about him. Justine pressed the doorbell, which was centered in a brass cross with scalloped edges. From somewhere far away she heard a whole melody ringing out in slow, measured, golden tones. Then the door opened and there was Meg, thinner and more poised, with longer hair. "Hello, Mama," she said. She kissed Justine's cheek, and then her great-grandfather's. When Duncan had turned from the hitching post and climbed the steps she kissed his cheek as well. "Hello, Daddy," she said.

"Well, Meggums."

"I thought you might change your mind and not come."

"Would I do a thing like that?"

She didn't smile.

She led them across sculptured blue carpeting into the living room, where Christ gazed out of gilt frames on every wall. Most of the furniture seemed to come in twos—two identical tables flanking the sofa, two beaded lamps, two ice-blue satin easy chairs with skirted ottomans. On the spinet piano in the corner there were two framed photographs, one of Arthur in a clerical robe and the other of Meg with some sort of shiny drapery across her bare shoulders—but so retouched, so flawlessly complexioned, her hair so lacquered, that it took Justine a moment to recognize her. Besides, what right did some unknown woman have to set Meg's photo in her living room? Justine picked it up and studied it. Meg said, "Oh, that's my—that's just the picture we put in the paper when we—" She snatched the photo away and set it down. "I'll get Mother Milsom," she said.

Justine sought out Duncan, who was slouched on the sofa leafing through a *Lady's Circle*. His feet, in enormous grease-spattered desert boots, were resting on the coffee table. "Duncan!" she said, slapping his knee. He looked up and then moved his feet carefully, picking his way between china rabbits and birds, candles shaped like angels, a nativity scene in a seashell and a green glass shoe full of sourballs. Justine let out a long breath and settled down beside him. Across the room, her grandfather paced the carpet with his hands clasped behind his back. He did not like to sit when he would have to struggle up again so soon for the entrance of a lady. He paused before first one Christ and then another, peering closely at a series of melancholy brown eyes and lily-white necks. "Religious art in the *living* room?" he said.

"Ssh," Justine told him.

"But I was always taught that that was in poor taste," he said. "Unless it was an original."

"Grandfather."

She looked at the door where Meg had disappeared. There was no telling how much could be heard. "Grandfather," she said, "wouldn't you like to—"

"They've got him in the dining room too," said Duncan, peering through the other doorway. "Praying in the garden."

"Oh, Duncan, what do you care? When did you ever give a thought to interior decorating?"

He frowned at her. "So you're going to take their side," he said.

"I didn't know there were sides."

"How's that?" asked her grandfather.

"Duncan thinks I'm defecting."

"Hmm?"

"*Defecting*."

"Nonsense," said her grandfather. "You're as smart as anybody."

Duncan laughed. Justine turned on him. "Duncan," she said, "I certainly hope you're not going to go into one of your silly fits here. Duncan, I mean this. For Meg's sake, now, can't we just try to—"

But then whispery footsteps crossed the carpet, and a lady in white entered the room with Meg just behind her. "Mother Milsom, I'd like you to meet my mother," Meg said. "And my father, and my great-grandfather Peck." Meg's face was stern and her forehead was tweaked together in the center; she was warning her family not to disgrace her. So Duncan rose to his full height, keeping one thumb in his magazine, while the grandfather touched his temple and Justine stood up and held out her hand. Mrs. Milsom's fingers felt like damp spaghetti. She was a long, wilted lady with light-brown hair parted in the center and crimped tight to her head, a pale tragic face, eyes as black and precisely lidded as a playing-card queen's. Her dress, which was made of something crêpey, hung limp over her flat chest, billowed hollowly at the waist and wrists, and dripped in layers to her skinny sharp legs. She wore pointed silver pumps from the Sixties. When she smiled her eyes remained wide and lusterless, as if she were keeping in mind some secret sorrow. "So finally we meet," she said.

"We would have come before but Duncan was buying Prince Albert tins," Justine told her. Nervousness always did make her talk too much.

"*I* understand. Won't you be seated? Margaret, darling, would you care to serve the iced tea?"

Meg looked at her mother. Then she left the room. Mrs. Milsom floated slowly downward into one of the satin chairs, parts of her appearing to settle whole minutes after other parts. She laid her hands delicately together. "Arthur I hope will be joining us shortly," she said. "At the moment he's napping."

"Arthur naps?" said Duncan.

"It's a fourth Sunday. His day to preach. Preaching takes so much out of him. Naturally we had been hoping that you would be here in time to hear his sermon, but apparently things did not fall out that way." She gave Justine a deep, mournful look.

"Oh well—" said Justine. They would have come for the sermon, even Duncan—anything for Meg—but Meg had specifically told them not to arrive till after lunch.

"Generally on fourth Sundays he awakes with a headache," said Mrs. Milsom, "and sustains it during the entire service and even afterward, until he admits that I am right and takes to his bed. He suffers real pain. This is not some ordinary headache."

"Maybe he should switch to *fifth* Sundays," Duncan said. "Sixth, even."

Justine shot him a look.

"Where's the minister?" asked Grandfather Peck, settling creakily into an armchair.

"*Grandfather*, turn on your—"

"Arthur is napping, Mr. Peck," said Mrs. Milsom. Her voice was thinned to just the right pitch. "I know all about the deaf," she told Justine. "My father was afflicted. In his later years he would go so far as to sing the 'Doxology' while his congregation was on 'Bringing in the Sheaves.'"

"Oh, your father was a minister too," Justine said.

"Oh yes. *Oh* yes. All my family."

"And your husband?"

"No, ah—he was in construction."

"I see."

"But *my* family, now they have been clergy for a great many years. I myself am a healer."

"Is that right?" said Duncan. He stopped rolling up his magazine. "You heal by faith?"

"I certainly do."

She smiled at him, her eyes like black pools. Then Meg came tinkling and clinking through the doorway with a tray, and Justine tensed because she herself, of course, would have spilled ice cubes into Mrs. Milsom's snowy lap or tripped over the veins in the carpet. She forgot that Meg was as graceful and confident as her maiden aunts. The tray paused at each person, dipping neatly, holding steady. Mrs. Milsom watched its progress with her lower lip caught between her teeth. She was tense too, as if Meg were *her* daughter. It wasn't fair. She had no right. Justine snatched a tumbler off the tray and a disk of tea flew onto the sofa cushion, but Duncan instantly covered it with his *Lady's Circle*. "Mama. It's sweetened," Meg whispered.

"What?" Justine said aloud.

"It's *sweetened*."

"The tea is sweetened," said Mrs. Milsom. "Thank you, Margaret. Won't you take some yourself?"

"I was thinking I might go see if Arthur's awake."

"Oh no, dear, I wouldn't do that just yet."

"He did say to wake him when they came."

"If we do he'll have his head till tomorrow, believe me," said Mrs. Milsom. "I know him." She smiled and patted the arm of her chair. "Come sit with us a while."

So Meg came to perch at Mrs. Milsom's side, and Justine averted her eyes and concentrated on her tea. It was a fact that the only thing she couldn't stand was sweetened tea. It made her gag. She would feel sick and heavy for the rest of the day. Still she drank it, searching with her tongue for the nearest ice cube to dilute the sugary taste. Duncan, who didn't care one way or the other, finished his own drink in one breath and set the glass down upon the polished table. "Well," he said. "So you've got your diploma, Meggie."

She nodded. Her hair touched her collar, a little less neat than it used to be. Maybe she was trying to look older.

"So what next?" Duncan asked her.

"Oh, I don't know."

"Going to get some kind of a job?"

"Mr. Peck," said Mrs. Milsom, "being a minister's wife *is* a job."

Duncan looked over at her. Justine grew worried, but in the end all he said was, "I meant, *besides* that."

"Oh, there's nothing besides that. Believe me, I know. I'm a minister's daughter. And I've been standing behind Arthur all this time filling in until he found himself a wife: attending teas and sewing circles, helping at bazaars, fixing casseroles—"

"Meggie, your mother must know people," Duncan said. "All sorts of people with jobs to offer, I'm sure of it. How about Pooch Sims? The veterinarian." He turned to Justine. "*She* could use someone."

"Oh, Mr. Peck," said Mrs. Milsom. She laughed and her ice cubes rattled. "Margaret wouldn't want to do that."

Everyone looked at Meg. She stared down into her glass.

"Would you, Meg?" Duncan asked.

"No," said Meg, "I guess I wouldn't."

"Well, then, what?"

"Oh, I don't know, Daddy. Mother Milsom's right, I do have a lot to do already. I've taken over the nursery at church and I have so many calls to pay and everything."

Justine's teeth seemed to be growing fur, and still she hadn't made a dent in her drink. She longed for something sour or salty. She had a craving for pickles, lemon rind, a potato chip even. But Mrs. Milsom gazed at her so reproachfully that she raised the glass and took another swallow.

"Mainly of course the minister's wife is a *buffer*," said Mrs. Milsom. "She filters his calls, tries to handle the little things that so clutter his day—oh, Margaret can tell you. We've been teaching her all about it. Arthur is not terribly strong, you see. He's allergic to so much. And he has these headaches."

"But I thought you were a healer," Duncan said.

"A healer, yes! I have a little group that meets on Sunday evenings. Anyone can come. I inherited the gift from my father, who once gave sight to a blind man."

"But your father was deaf."

"He still had the *gift*, Mr. Peck."

"I meant—"

"Of course the gift must be kept alive by prayer and faith, it has to be nurtured along. That's what I tell Arthur. I feel that Arthur very definitely has the gift. I am working with him on it now. So far there has seemed to be some—I don't know, some sort of *resistance*, I'm just not—but we're working, I'm sure we'll get there."

"How about Grandfather here?" Duncan asked. "*He* could use some help."

She hesitated.

"Think you could just clap a couple of hands on his ears to oblige us?"

"Well, I'm not—is it nerve deafness, or what?"

"Oh, if faith only heals certain *kinds*," said Duncan.

Both Meg and Justine stirred, uneasily. Duncan gave them a wide, innocent smile that did not reassure them. "But never mind," he said, "my real interest was headaches."

"Headaches, Mr. Peck? Do you suffer from headaches?"

"No, your son does."

"My son."

"Arthur."

"Oh, *Arthur*," she said blankly.

"Didn't you say that Arthur got headaches?"

"Why, yes."

Duncan looked at her for a moment, honestly puzzled. "But then," he said, "why can't you heal him?"

Mrs. Milsom clasped her hands tightly. Her mouth became blurred and her eyes filled with what must surely be black tears; but no, when they spilled over they were clear and they made white tracks down her hollow white cheeks.

"Oh, Duncan," Justine said. But what had he done, after all? Nobody understood, except perhaps Meg, who quickly buried her nose in her tea glass. Then Mrs. Milsom straightened and darted an index finger beneath each eye, quick as a frog's tongue. "Well!" she said. "Haven't we had nice weather for August?"

"It's been very nice," Duncan told her gently. And he must have been planning to stay that way to the end, sober and courteous; he would never willingly hurt anybody. Except that Justine chose that moment to reach toward the green glass shoe on the coffee table—sourballs! right under her nose!—and choose a lemony yellow globe and pop it into her mouth, where she instantly discovered that she had eaten a marble. While everyone watched in silence she plucked it out delicately between thumb and forefinger and replaced it, only a little shinier than before, in the green glass shoe. "*I* thought we could have used more rain," she told the ring of faces.

Duncan made a peculiar sound. So he *was* going to have a silly fit after all. Justine had to sit as straight as a statue, dignified enough for the two of them, while at intervals Duncan steamed and chortled like an electric percolator on the couch beside her.

When Arthur was up (pale and rumpled, inadequate-looking in a short-sleeved Hawaiian shirt) they moved out to the back yard to admire Mrs. Milsom's flowerbeds, then over to the church to see the new red carpet just recently installed in the aisles. They tiptoed through the vaulted, echoing nave with their faces very serious. They were all particularly careful of one another, if you didn't count Duncan's pinching Justine when he didn't know Mrs. Milsom was looking. They were so appreciative, so soft-voiced and attentive, that by the time they had assembled beside the Ford to say their goodbyes everyone was exhausted. But Mrs. Milsom held out both hands bravely for the sack of sun-baked corn, and Arthur insisted on taking the entire burden of wedding silver from the trunk. He staggered off, stringy-armed, sway-backed beneath his load. Meg remained beside the car with her pile of shirtwaist dresses. "Well," said Justine, "I suppose we'll be seeing you soon." She felt bruised by disappointment. She had imagined that this visit might, in some way, wrap things up—that whatever had gone wrong in their family might finally be straightened out, or at least understood; and that having seen Meg settled and happy she could let her go at last. She had supposed that care and responsibility could be shucked like old skin, leaving her cool and smooth and lightweight. But Meg's face was screwed so tight it made her ache, and she would never be free of Meg's old, anxious eyes. "Meggie, is there anything you need?" she asked. "I mean, if you think of something, anything at all—"

"I'm sorry about the tea," Meg said.

"Tea?"

"I told her you didn't drink it sweetened."

"Oh, that's all right, honey."

"She was making it after lunch and I said, 'Don't put sugar in it, Mama likes hers with just lemon.' But she said, 'Oh, everybody likes their tea with sugar, it's so refreshing.' I said, 'But—' "

"Meg, I don't care," said Justine.

"I said I would mix a separate glass then," Meg told Duncan, "but she doesn't really like me in her kitchen."

Duncan studied her. Grandfather Peck stroked his chin.

"She does everything, even makes our bed up. She says I don't know hospital corners. You never taught me about hospital corners, Mama."

"I'm sorry, honey."

"I wanted to have you for lunch today, I said I would cook it myself. You know I can cook. Simple things, at least. Fannie Farmer. But she said it wasn't possible because her group was coming over for supper, these people in her healing group. She had to have the kitchen to herself. The people in her healing group are all old and strange, they have chronic illnesses and they think she helps, and then sometimes they bring her someone new and they all pray together holding hands."

"Does it work?" Justine asked.

"What? No. I don't know. I thought when I got married we would be so—regular. I thought finally we—I didn't know all this would be going on. When I met her she was like anybody else. Except for wearing white. She did wear white all the time. But I didn't know then about this healing. She wants Arthur to learn healing too and she even wanted to look at *my* hands, she wondered if I have the gift."

"Do you?" Justine asked.

"Mama! I wouldn't go along with a thing like that."

"Well, I don't know, at least it would be a new experience."

"I don't want new experiences, I want a normal happy life. But Arthur just won't stand up to her, really he—and now she wants him to develop his gift because hers is going. She thinks it's because of her age. At the meetings they pray and cry, you can hear them everywhere in the house. She reminds God of what she used to accomplish: once she stopped a man in the middle of a heart attack."

"She did?"

"She says she has so much left to do, she should be allowed to keep her gift. She says it's unjust. There are people sick just everywhere, she says, and blind and crippled and suffering pain, and here she is powerless and she can't even stop her own son's headaches any more. She goes on and on about it, calling out so everyone can hear: just because a little time has passed, she says, *that's* no reason to let her dwindle down this way."

"Well, I should say not," said Justine.

Meg paused and gave her a look. "Are you listening?" she asked.

"Certainly I'm listening."

"I live among *crazy* people!"

"You should leave," Duncan told her.

"Oh, Duncan," said Justine. She turned to Meg. "Meggie darling, maybe you could just—or look at it this way. Imagine you were handed a stack of instructions. Things that you should undertake. Blind errands, peculiar invitations . . . things you're supposed to go through, and come out different on the other side. Living with a faith healer. *I* never got to live with a faith healer."

"That's what you're going to tell your daughter?" Duncan said. "Just accept whatever comes along? Endure? Adapt?"

"Well—"

"And how would people end up if they all did that?"

Justine hesitated.

"Never mind, Mama," Meg told her. "I didn't mean to mention it, anyway."

So Justine got into the car, but untidily and with backward glances because so much seemed still unsettled. The troubled feeling was nagging at her mind again. She couldn't quite put her finger on it. She felt as if she had mislaid an object somewhere, something important that would thread through all her thoughts until she found it. But she sat forward briskly and called out the window, "Meggie darling!"

"What is it?"

"If you do have to do bazaar work, you know, if you need any help, I'll be happy to drive down any time and tell fortunes."

"Thank you, Mama."

"You know I have a lot of steady clients here."

"Well, that's very nice of you, Mama," Meg said. But Justine could tell that she had made a mistake. She should have offered something plainer and sturdier—anything but more gifts from heaven.

By the time they reached Caro Mill it was night, and the streets had a dismal abandoned look. The only place open was the diner, eerily lit and vacant except for Black Emma swabbing the counter. "Maybe we could stop for coffee," said Justine. But the car slid by, and neither Duncan nor her grandfather answered. (They had not spoken all the way home, either one of them. Only Justine had chattered on and on until she wondered herself when she would shut up.) "Duncan?" she said. "Couldn't we stop for coffee?"

"We have coffee at home."

"I don't want to go home," she said. "I have this peculiar feeling. I wouldn't mind staying the *night* somewhere, even. Duncan?"

But he said, *"Endure,"* and turned sharply down Watchmaker Street. She blinked and looked at him.

In front of their house, when the engine had died and the headlights had faded, the three of them sat motionless for a moment gazing through the windshield, as if being borne along on some darker, more silent journey. Then Justine touched her grandfather's arm. "Here we are," she said.

"Eh?"

He stumbled out, latching the door inconclusively behind him, and Justine slid after Duncan out the driver's side. They went single file up the walk between looming rustling cornstalks. At the porch, they stopped short. A shadow unfolded itself from the steps. "Eli!" Justine said.

"Eh?" said her grandfather.

And Duncan said, "Well, Eli. What have you found for us?"

"Caleb Peck," said Eli.

13

Eli Everjohn drank his coffee white, preferred Jane Parker angel food cake to taco chips, and was perfectly comfortable sitting on a chrome-legged chair in the kitchen. He had to make all that clear before they would let him get on with his report. "Listen here," he kept saying. "Listen. It struck me right off—" But Justine would interrupt to ask, couldn't she take his hat? wouldn't he be cooler in his shirtsleeves? And old Mr. Peck trudged around and around him, thinking hard, occasionally offering interruptions of his own. "I believe I ought to fetch my notebook, Justine."

"Yes, Grandfather, I would do that."

"I believe that windowscreen is torn. Where else would these mosquitoes be coming from?"

"I'll find the swatter."

"Oh, leave it, leave it. Mr. Everjohn here has something he wants to say to us."

But when Eli took a breath Justine halted him. "Wait, I've been wanting something sour all *day*. Don't start without me."

"*Justine—*" Duncan said.

Eli Everjohn was a patient man. (In his business, he had to be.) Still, he had been dreaming of this moment for a good long time now. He had come over on a Sunday evening expressly to bring this news, which he thought might cause him to burst if he left it till Monday: in just under three months, he had accomplished what a whole family could not do in sixty-one years. He had performed a spectacular piece of deduction, and now he wanted to tell about it in his own slantwise, gradual way so that everyone could admire how one clue had built upon another, one path led to the next, with sudden inspired leaps of the imagination to bridge them. True detective work was an art. *Finding* was an art. He was grateful to the Peck family for handing him this assignment. (How could he ever again settle for guarding anniversary gifts or pretending to read *Newsweek* in front of beauty parlors?) So he cleared his throat, and pushed his coffee cup a certain distance away, and plaited his long fingers on the table before him and began as he had planned. "It struck me right off," he said, "that there was one thing the same in all accounts of Caleb Peck."

"You'll have to speak up," said the old man.

"Oh. Sorry. It *struck* me—"

"Justine, I think my battery's going."

"Will you let the man *speak?*" Duncan said.

So that Eli, with the last of his patience worn away, ended up blurting it out after all and ruining the moment he had planned for so long. "Mr. Caleb Peck," he said, "is in Box Hill, Louisiana, alive and well."

It had struck Eli right off that there was one thing the same in all accounts of Caleb Peck: he was a musical man. To his family that was only a detail, like the color of his eyes or his tendency to wear a Panama hat just a little past the season. But to Caleb, wasn't it more? Eli pondered, sifting what he had heard and endlessly rearranging it. He traveled a few blind alleys. He scanned the alumni lists of several well-known music schools, including Baltimore's Peabody Institute. He checked the family's old phonograph records for performers whom

Caleb might have been moved to seek out. He inquired as to Caleb's piano teacher—someone young and pretty, maybe? Someone inspirational, to teach him those Czerny exercises he found crumbling away on top of the piano in old Mr. Peck's Baltimore parlor? But no, the Czerny was Margaret Rose's, said Mr. Peck. Caleb had not liked Czerny. He was not, to tell the truth, very fond of the classical mode. And he had never had a music teacher of any kind. Only little Billy Pope passing on his fiddle lessons, and a leatherbound book telling how to play the woodwinds (which in those days were really made of wood—see the ebony flute in Caleb's old bedroom?) and for the piano, Lafleur Boudrault, who taught him ragtime.

Was this Lafleur Boudrault young and pretty, by any chance?

But Lafleur Boudrault was the Creole gardener, not pretty at all—a scar down one cheek and a permanent wink. Long dead now. Survived by his wife Sulie. He wouldn't have helped out anyway: a cross-grained sort.

Eli traveled once again to Baltimore and sought out Sulie, who was moving a dustcloth around and around the attic. Nowadays all she did was dust. She would not give up her cloth, which had to be pried from her fingers in her sleep as you would pry a pet blanket from a child in order to wash it. And what she dusted was not helpful at all—never the furniture, which Lord knows could *use* a dusting, all those bulbs and scallops and crevices; but only the hidden places that didn't count, the undersides of drawers and the backs of picture frames and now these trunks and cartons in the attic, which she had been on for weeks and weeks. They couldn't get her to stop. They wanted to pension her off; didn't she have family somewhere? They were almost certain there had been a daughter. But Sulie only laughed her cracked, rapid laugh and said, "*Now* you wants to do it. Now you wants." Oh, she was mad, no question about it. But Eli needed Caleb's contemporaries and there were not all that many to pick and choose from. He climbed the narrow, hollow, pine-smelling steps to Laura's attic, submerging first his head and then his shoulders and then his wool-wrapped body in a heat so intense that it seemed to be liquid, and at the last he was merely floating upward in a throbbing dull haze. He swam between crazed china hurricane lamps and slanted portraits, across rugs rolled and stacked like logs, toward the spindly figure briskly polishing an empty Pears soap box down where the dusty light fingered its way through the louvers. "Mrs. Sulie Boudrault?" he asked, and without looking up she nodded and hummed and went on polishing.

"Widow of Lafleur Boudrault?"

She nodded.

"You wouldn't happen to know where Mr. Caleb Peck has got to."

Then she stopped polishing.

"Well, I thought they wouldn't never ask," she said.

She settled him on a china barrel, and she herself sat on a stack of *St. Nicholas* magazines with her dustcloth clutched daintily in her lap. She was a very small woman with stretched-looking skin and yellow eyes. Her manner of speaking was clear and reasonable, and her story proceeded in a well-ordered way. No wonder: she had had over half a century in which to arrange it.

"When first Mr. Caleb had left us," she said, "I told Lafleur, 'Lafleur, what do I say?' For I know where he had went to yet I would hate to give him away. 'Lafleur, do I lie?' 'That ain't never going to come up,' he say. 'Them folks don't think you know *nothing*.' Well, I was certain he was wrong. I waited for old Mrs. Laura to fix me with her little eyes. She the one to watch for. Mr. Justin the First couldn't do nothing, maybe wouldn't have anyhow, but he had that Mrs. Laura so scared she would do it for him and more besides. She was one scared lady, and it had turned her mean and spiteful. Watch out for Mrs. Laura, I told myself, and so I watch and waited and plan how to answer what she ask. But she never do. Never once. Never even, 'Sulie, do you recollect if you served Mr. Caleb breakfast that day?' Never a word."

Sulie set her skirt out all about her—a long draggled white eyelet affair that hit halfway down her skinny calves, with ankle-high copper-toed work shoes swinging below them. After thinking a moment, she dug down into her pocket and came up with a handful of Oreos, mashed and limp. "Have you a cookie," she said.

"Thank you," said Eli.

"She never ask. Nor none of the others. Took me some time to see they never would. 'Why, looky there!' I say to Lafleur at last, and he say, 'Told you so. They don't reckon just old us would know *nothing*,' he say. So my eyes was opened. That was how. I made up my mind I wouldn't tell till they say straight out, 'Sulie, do you know?' And Mrs. Laura I wouldn't give the time of *day* even. I never did. She live forty-six years after Mr. Caleb had went and I never spoken to her once, but I don't fool myself she realize that. 'Sulie is getting so *sullen*,' was what she say. Even that tooken her five or so years to notice good."

Eli finished the Oreo and dusted off his hands. From his pocket he took a spiral notebook and a Bic pen. He opened to a blank page.

"Now," said Sulie.

She stood up, as if to recite.

"Mr. Caleb was a musical man," she said.

"I had heard he was."

"He like *most* music, but colored best. He like ragtime and he copied everything Lafleur do on the piano. He like stories about them musicians in New Orleans, which is where Lafleur come from. Lafleur had got his self in a speck of trouble down there and couldn't go back, but he would tell about the piano players in Storyville and what all went on. Understand this was back *long* time ago. Didn't many people know about such things.

"Then times got hard and Miss Maggie Rose left us. I had to move on over to Mr. Daniel's house and tend the babies. I was not but in my teens then. I had just did get married to old Lafleur. I didn't know much but I saw how Mr. Caleb was mighty quiet and maybe took a tad more to drink than was needed. But I never thought he'd leave. One night he come down cellar to our bedroom, me and Lafleur's. Knocks on our door. 'Lafleur,' he say, 'this fellow down at the tavern is talking about a trip to New Orleans.'

" 'Is that so,' say Lafleur.

" 'Wants me to go along.'

" 'That so.'

" 'Well, I'm thinking of doing it.'

" 'Why, sure,' Lafleur tell him.

" 'Permanent,' Mr. Caleb say. 'Unannounced.'

"But still, you see, we didn't have no notion he was serious.

"He ask Lafleur was there someplace to go, to stay a whiles. Lafleur mention this white folks' boardinghouse over near where his sister live at. Mr. Caleb wroten it down on a piece of paper and fold it careful and left. We didn't think a thing more about it. Come morning he arrive for breakfast, sometime he would do that. Eat in Mr. Daniel's kitchen. 'Fix me a lot now, Sulie,' he say. 'Can't travel far on an empty stomach.' Well, I thought he meant travel to *town.* I fix him hotcakes. I set out his breakfast and when he had done finished he thank me politely and left. I never did see him again."

She considered her fingernails, ridged and yellowed like old piano keys.

"Could I have that boardinghouse address?" Eli asked her.

"Yes, why surely," she said, and she gave it to him, slowly and clearly, having saved it up on purpose all these years, and he wrote it in his notebook. Then she faded off, so that Eli thought she had forgotten him. He rose with care and tiptoed to the attic steps. He had already dipped one ankle into the coolness below when she called him. "Mr. Whoever-you-are!"

"Ma'am?"

"When you tell how you found him," she said, "make certain you put in that Sulie known the answer all along."

So now he had an address, but it was sixty-one years old. He knew he couldn't expect too much. He caught a plane to New Orleans that night. He took a cab to where a boardinghouse had stood in the spring of 1912. All he saw was a supermarket, lit inside with ghostly blue night lights, hulking on an asphalt parking lot.

"I reckon there's no sense hanging around," he told the cab driver.

Eli registered at a small hotel from which immediately, despite the hour, he called every Peck in the telephone book. No one had an ancestor named Caleb. He went to bed and slept a sound, dreamless sleep. On the following day, he set out walking. He picked his way past suspicious-looking hidden courtyards and lacy balconies, secret fountains splashing, leprous scaly stucco, monstrous greenery and live oaks dripping beards of moss, through surprising pockets of light where the air seemed to lie like colored veils. In various echoing buildings, archives both official and unofficial, he wandered gloomily with his hands in his pockets peering at yellowed sheet music, clippings, menus, and sporting-house directories under glass, as well as cases full of dented trumpets and valve trombones that appeared to have come from the dimestore. In the evenings he attended nightclubs, where, wincing against the clatter of brass and drums, he sidled between the tables to stare at the curling photographs on the walls and the programs once handed out during Fourth of July celebrations. There was no Caleb Peck. There was never that stiff, old-fashioned white man's face or Panama hat.

Eli's wife called, sounding lank and dragged out with the heat. "But it's hotter here," he told her. "And you ought to see the bugs." She didn't care; she wanted him home. What was he doing there, anyhow?

"I'll be back in another week," he told her. "In a week I'm going to have this thing wrapped up."

It was August eighteenth. Although he did not have a single new clue, he was beginning to feel excited.

Now he started shadowing the gaudy, sunglassed tourists, who seemed to know something he did not. They were always in possession of secret addresses: the lodgings of palsied old sax-hornists, clarinetists, past employees of the Streckfus Excursion Lines and granddaughters of Buddy Bolden's girlfriends. (Who was Buddy Bolden?) Eli slipped in behind them through narrow doors, into dingy parlors or taverns or bedrooms. Sometimes he was ushered out again. Sometimes he would pass unnoticed. Then he introduced questions of his own, all of them out of place:

"You wouldn't know a jazz *cellist*, by some chance."

"Any good musicians out of Baltimore?"

"Whereabouts were you in the spring of nineteen twelve?"

Ancient, dusty eyes peered back at him, but never ancient enough. "Nineteen twelve? What kind of memory do you think I got, boy?"

By imperceptible degrees the Pecks had altered Eli. He had begun to ignore the passage of time, as if it were somehow *common*. He felt irritated that ordinary people could not do the same.

Days were tiresome, yes, and hard on the feet, but nights were worse. The string of clubs, bars, cafés, dance halls, and strip joints went on forever, and all the music sounded the same to him: badly organized. Eli slipped into a place and out again, into the next. He ducked away at any mention of cover charge, waved off waiters and hostesses. When pressed, he ordered Dr. Pepper; mostly he left before things had gone that far. The scent of success discouraged him. He wanted failure, spooky little hole-in-the-wall cafés. For surely, he was thinking now, Caleb himself was a failure. Whatever he had ended up doing, it had not left any mark upon this town.

He entered bars that smelled of mildewed wood, that had names like The High Note or Sportin' Life, where a few musicians played raggedly and without much interest. A black man sang above a guitar:

> My train done left, Lord, done left me by the track,
> My train done left, Lord, done left me by the track.
> Tell the folks in Whisky Alley
> I ain't never coming back . . .

Eli shook his head. He slid past a drunkard and returned to the sidewalk, where he milled among the tourists in a greasy, neon-lit, garlic-smelling night.

The following morning, he was up unusually early. He ate breakfast in a coffee shop near where he had been the night before, and he strolled past the same bars, but they were closed now. Farther down, an aproned man was sweeping the entrance of a strip joint that looked cheerful and homely by daylight. "Tell me," Eli said to him. "You know that little old bar back there? Easy Livin'?"

The man squinted. "What about it?"

"You know what time it opens?"

"Most likely not till evening," said the man. "You got a wait, fellow."

"Well, thank you," Eli said.

This morning he did not delve any further into the archives of jazz. He bought a paper and read it in a park. He had a second cup of coffee and a glazed doughnut. Then when the movies opened, he toured the city catching Jimmy Stewart films. Eli very much admired Jimmy Stewart.

At six o'clock he had a plate of scrambled eggs in a diner, followed by another cup of coffee and apple pie à la mode. then he set off toward Easy Livin'—on foot, since it wasn't far. He took his time. He nodded soberly as he walked and he looked about him with a well-meaning expression such as Jimmy Steward might have worn. When he reached his destination, he straightened his string tie before stepping through the battered door.

Easy Livin' was dark even now, when it was barely twilight. There was a bar with a brass rail, a few scarred tables, and at the end of the room a raw wooden platform for the entertainers. At the moment, there were no other customers. Only a boy behind the bar, and on the platform the black man who had sung the night before. He was squatting to hitch up some sort of electrical wire. He didn't even look around when Eli came up behind him.

"Say," said Eli. "Could I ask about a song?"

The singer grunted and then rose, brushing off his dungarees. He said, "This here is not one of them jazz joints, baby. Go on up the street."

"Last *night* you were singing," Eli said.

"Only the blues."

"Ah," said Eli, who did not see the difference. He pondered a moment. The singer looked down at him with his hands on his hips. "Well," Eli said, "you were singing this here song I was wondering about."

"Which."

"Song about a train."

"*All* songs got trains," the singer said patiently.

"Song about Whisky Alley."

"Mm-*hmm*."

"You recall it?" Eli asked.

"I sung it, didn't I?"

"You know who wrote it?"

"Now how would I know that?" the singer said, but then, all of a sudden: "Stringtail Man."

"Who?"

"The Stringtail Man."

"Well, who was that?"

"*I* don't know. White fellow."

"But he's got to have a name," Eli said.

"Naw. Not that I ever knew of. White fellow with a fiddle."

"A fiddle," said Eli. "Well—I mean, ain't that a little peculiar for jazz?"

"Blues," said the singer.

"Blues, then."

"Now I don't know a thing more than what I told you," said the singer. But he hunkered down, anyway, getting closer to Eli's level. "This fellow was *away* back, long before my time. He was lead man for White-Eye, old colored guitar man that used to play the streets. Now White-Eye was blind and the fiddler would lead him around. But whenever he fiddled, looked like the music just got *into* him somewhat and he would commence to dancing. Old White-Eye would hear the notes hopping to one side and then to the other and sometimes roaming off entirely if the music was fast and the fiddler dancing fast to match. So White-Eye hitched his self to the fiddler's belt by means of a string, which is how we come by the Stringtail Man. *Anybody* roundabouts can tell you *that* much."

"I see," said Eli.

"How come you to ask?"

"Well, there used to be this tavern in Baltimore, Maryland, called Whisky Alley," Eli said. "Close by the waterfront."

"So?"

"You don't recollect where this Stringtail fellow was *from,* by any chance."

"Naw."

"Well, how about White-Eye?"

"Him neither."

"No, his name. Didn't he have a name?"

"White-Eye. White-Eye. White-Eye—Ramford!" said the singer, snapping his fingers. "Didn't know I could do it."

"I'm very much obliged," Eli said. He dug down in his trousers pocket. "Can I buy you a Dr. Pepper?"

The singer looked at him for a moment. "Naw, baby," he said finally.

"Well, thanks, then."

"Nothing to it."

By noon the following day, Eli had contacted every Ramford in the telephone book. He had located White-Eye Ramford's great-grand-daughter, a waitress; from there he had gone to see a Mrs. Clarine Ramford Tucker, who was residing in the Lydia Lockford Nursing Home for the Colored and Indigent; and from there to a Baptist cemetery in a swampy-smelling section outside the city. The sight of Abel Ramford's crumbling headstone, a small Gothic arch over a sunken grave obviously neglected for years, smothered by Queen Anne's lace and chicory, brought Eli up short, and for a long time he stood silent with his hat in his hands, wondering if this were the end of his road. Then he took heart and went to see the caretaker. He learned that Mr. Ramford's site had no visitors at all, so far as was known; but that every year on All Saints' Day a bouquet of white carnations was brought by Altona Florists, a very high-class flower shop with lavender delivery trucks.

And Altona Florists said yes, they did have a standing order for that date: a dozen white carnations delivered to this little colored cemetery way the hell and gone; and the bill was sent to Box Hill, Louisiana, to a Mr. Caleb Peck.

That was Saturday, August twenty-fifth. It had taken Eli exactly eighty-one days to complete his search.

Because he had been warned not to approach Caleb in person ("I want to do that much myself," Mr. Peck had said), Eli came home without that final satisfaction. But it was almost enough just to tell his story in Justine's kitchen and watch the old man's astonishment. "What? What?" he said, even when he had clearly heard. He started circling the table again, kneading his hands as if they were cold. "I don't understand."

"He's in Louisiana, Grandfather."

"But—we never did go anywhere near there. Did we, Justine?"

"We didn't know."

"We never thought of it," said Mr. Peck. "Louisiana is one you forget when you're trying to name all the states in the Union. What would he be doing there?"

"Eli says—"

"I always suspected that Sulie was no durn good."

"Now Grandfather, you didn't either, you know how you used to rely on her."

"She took advantage," he said. "Why, if we somehow missed asking her—and I don't believe for a minute that we did—it was an oversight. Just chance! How long are we going to be held accountable for every little slip and error?" He frowned at Eli. "And you say Caleb is a—"

"Fiddler."

"I don't understand."

"*Fiddler.*"

"Yes, but I don't—" He turned to Justine. "That doesn't make sense," he told her.

"You always did say he was a musical man," she said.

"It's the wrong Caleb."

"No sir!" said Eli, lifting his head sharply. "No indeed, Mr. Peck."

"Bound to be."

"Would I come to you if I wasn't sure yet?" Eli fumbled in his breast pocket, brought out his notebook, and turned the curly, gray-rimmed pages. "Here. I checked this man out, listen here. Caleb Justin Peck, born February fourteenth, eighteen eighty-five, Baltimore, Maryland. Who else could it be?"

"How'd you learn all that? I told you not to go near him."

"I called and spoke to a nurse at the Home."

"Home?"

Eli flipped back one page in his notebook. "Evergreen County Home for the Elderly, two fourteen Hamilton Street, Box Hill, Louisiana."

Mr. Peck felt behind him for a chair and sat down very slowly.

"If you say a word," Justine whispered to Duncan, "I'll kill you. I'll kill you."

"I wasn't going to say anything."

Eli looked from one face to the other, confused.

"But of course he's not *in* the Home," said Mr. Peck.

"Why, yes."

"He just lives nearby. Or visits some acquaintance there."

"He's a resident."

"He is?"

"Room nineteen."

Mr. Peck rubbed his chin.

"I'm sorry," said Eli, although previously he hadn't felt one way or the other about it.

"My brother is in a Home."

"Well now, I'm sure it's—"

"My own brother in a Home." His eyes flashed suddenly over to Duncan, spiky blue eyes like burs. "You will want your bottle of bourbon or whatever."

"Forget it," said Duncan. He looked somehow tired, not himself at all.

"Why!" said Mr. Peck. "Why, Caleb must be *old!*"

Nobody spoke.

Mr. Peck thought a moment. "He is eighty-eight years old," he said at last.

Telling the news was not as much fun as Eli had expected it would be.

14

> 21 Watchmaker Street
> Caro Mill, Maryland
> August 27, 1973

Dear Caleb,
    I take pen in hand to

> 21 Watchmaker Street
> Caro Mill, Maryland
> August 27, 1973

Dear Caleb,
    When I heard you were alive, Caleb, my heart

> 21 Watchmaker Street
> Caro Mill, Maryland
> August 27, 1973

Dear Caleb,
    This is your brother writing. My name, in the very likely event that you have forgotten, is

21 Watchmaker Street
Caro Mill, Maryland
August 27, 1973

Dear Caleb,

I take pen in hand to express my hope that you are in good
health and spirits.

Originally I had planned to visit unannounced, extending personally an invitation to stay with us here in Caro Mill. However my
grandson reminded me that perhaps you had no wish to see your
family again. I told him that of course this would not be the case.
Is it?

A great deal of water has flowed under the bridge. Altogether
now I have seven grandchildren and one great-grandchild. I regret
to inform you that both of our parents passed on some time ago, as
well as the baby, Caroline. My sons and two grandsons are running the firm etc.—but it is difficult to impart all this via the post.
I am hoping that soon we shall be speaking face to face instead.

My grandchildren Duncan and Justine, who live at the above
address and with whom I often visit, second my invitation and
look forward to making your acquaintance. Should you find yourself
short of cash at the moment I would be willing to provide the
airplane ticket. I understand that one may fly from New Orleans,
journeying from Box Hill by Greyhound bus which if I am correct
is the only recourse in those parts.

I have flown by airplane myself on several occasions. Airplanes
are now quite a common occurrence and what the Ford has developed into will be difficult for you to believe.

Of course it is no disgrace to find oneself residing in a Home, if
alternatives are lacking and one's family has all passed on. In your
case I do not know about the alternatives, but I do know that your
family has not all passed on. They are mostly alive and would
never consider allowing one of their number to enter a Home for
any reason whatsoever. You must surely have guessed this and yet,
by some manner of logic which utterly confounds me, chose not to
call upon your own flesh and blood in an hour of need.

But we will let bygones be bygones.

But in what way did the family ever injure you? If our father
was, perhaps, overmuch involved in business, our mother a trifle
strict, was that so important that you must ruin your life for it
and then, having completed the ruin, fail to turn to us for aid?

But there is no point in dwelling upon such things.

I neglected to mention that I was made a Judge, though now of
course retired. It is my understanding that you entered the musical
world in some capacity, which is not quite clear to me though I
hope to hear more about it when we meet.

My grandson says that you have a right to be left alone, and that surely you would have contacted us long ago if you had any desire to see us. Of course it is not my intention to intrude where I am not wanted.

You could have sent us a telegram collect from anywhere in the country and we would have come immediately, yet you chose not to. This to me, Caleb, speaks of some spitefulness, for surely you knew that it would pain us to think of a Peck in any such Institution. You were always contrary, even as a child, and caused our mother much worry, due to your stubborn nature which, as I gather, you never managed to overcome.

But enough of that. It is all over now.

My grandson says that your whereabouts is your own secret, to keep or not as you see fit, and consequently I must not let the rest of the family know without your permission. He has instructed the friend who found you not to notify my sons until you allow it. He says we had no right to run you to the ground this way. I told my grandson that I did not believe you would view it in such a light. Surely you understand that my only desire was to see you once more and perhaps have a little talk, not about anything in particular, which there never seemed to be enough time for back in 1912.

To tell the truth, Caleb, it appears that my ties to the present have weakened. I cannot feel that what happens today is of any real importance to me. I am not overly connected to my own descendants, not even to my granddaughter. She means well of course but is so different from me and so unlike my earlier recollections of her, perhaps I would not know her if I came upon her unexpectedly in the street. Consequently it is my hope that you will answer this letter, and that you and I may soon meet to talk over those years which once seemed so long ago but now appear clearer than they were even while we lived them.

I remain

> *Your brother,*
> *Daniel J. Peck, Sr.*

15

Justine stood on her front walk, ignoring a shower that was more mist than rain, talking to Red Emma. "Say you mailed a letter August twenty-seventh," she said. "Or I don't know, it was afternoon; maybe it went out the twenty-eighth. No, because he sent it direct from the post office. He has stopped trusting the corner boxes ever since they changed to red and blue. Say you mailed a letter August twenty-seventh, and it was going to a little town in Louisiana. How long would it take?"

"Airmail?" asked Red Emma.

"He doesn't trust airmail."

"He doesn't trust *anything!*"

"There've been so many plane crashes lately."

"Well, I would give it three days," said Red Emma. "And considering he didn't mail early in the day and it's going to a little town, make it four."

"So it got there August thirtieth," Justine said.

Red Emma nodded. Tiny droplets clung to her curls like the dew on a cobweb, and her face was shiny and her mail pouch was growing speckled.

"Then how long back again?" Justine asked. "Four more?"

"I would say so."

"Plus a day in between for the answer to be written."

"Well, if it would *take* a whole day."

"September fourth," said Justine. "A week ago. I don't think Grandfather can stand to wait much longer."

"Really he ought to develop some other interest," Red Emma told her. "Join the Golden Age Club."

"Oh, I don't think he'd like it."

"But he would be so popular! With his fine head of hair and all his teeth."

"Maybe so," said Justine, "but I don't picture it."

She waved goodbye and went back to the house with her mail—a sample packet of salad dressing mix and a postcard from Meg. "Here," she said to Duncan. He was playing solitaire on the living room floor. When she tossed him the postcard he picked it up and squinted at the picture, which showed thousands of people stretched out nearly naked on a strip of sand. He turned the card over. " 'Dear Mama and Daddy and Grandfather,' " he read. " 'Here we are with the Young Marrieds Fellowship having just a wonderful time and wish you were . . .' "

He passed the card to his grandfather, who was sitting on the couch doing nothing at all.

"What's this?" said his grandfather.

"Card from Meg."

"Oh, I see."

He set the card very carefully on the couch beside him and went back to staring into space.

"Grandfather, would you like to play cribbage?" Justine asked him.

"Cribbage? No."

"It's just as well, you always forget the rules," Duncan told her.

"Would you like a game of chess, Grandfather?"

He looked at her blankly.

"Or a trip in the car. You don't want to just *sit*."

"Why not?" he asked her.

Duncan laughed.

"It isn't funny," Justine told him. "Oh, when is this rain going to stop?" She swept tangles of plant vines aside in order to peer through the window. "I wish we had somewhere to go. I wish we could just get in the car and drive, or catch a train somewhere."

"You know," her grandfather said, "my feelings won't be hurt at all if he doesn't ever answer."

Justine turned to look at him.

"Anyhow, what was I thinking of? It would be so tiring, having to bring him up to date on all that's happened. Too much has gone on. I might not know him. He might not know *me*. I might look old to him. Now I recall we were often short-tempered. Why, we couldn't sit and talk five minutes without one or the other of us losing patience! And he never showed much interest in the children. And I wouldn't know *what* to say about his music and all. Then look at that place he's living in. Who knows what goes on there? Probably they have this schedule of activities, and special shelves to put your pajamas on and rules and medication and refreshment hours and seating arrangements that I would just have no inkling of. We have nothing in common. Know what I dreamed last night? No, maybe *two* nights ago. I dreamed that I saw Caleb driving down the street. Looking fine, just as fine as always. But his car! Peculiar little foreign station wagon, with a pinchy face and windows too big for it like one of those durned chihuahua dogs you see around. 'Caleb!' I called to him, 'what are you *doing* driving that thing?' and all he did was turn and wave. You would think that he belonged in it."

"Grandfather, it will work out," Justine told him. "All week I've had this feeling of change coming. He's going to write any day now. We'll send him a plane ticket and settle him in Meg's old room."

"Then what?"

"What?"

"*Then* what, I said. Then what will we do? 'Oh, it will work out, it will work out.' You're always so blasted cheerful, Justine. But where is your common sense?"

"Why, Grandfather—"

"Sometimes it gets too much for me," he told Duncan. "*You* expect me to have the patience of a saint."

"Not at all," Duncan said.

"You think I shouldn't say how I feel. Underneath, you think that."

"Do what you like, I don't care."

"In my childhood I was trained to hold things in, you see. But I thought I was holding them until a certain *time*. I assumed that someday, somewhere, I would again be given the opportunity to spend all that saved-up feeling. When will that be?"

Nobody answered. Justine stayed braced against the windowframe, Duncan lowered a three of spades and stared at him. Finally their grandfather rose and went off to his room, leaning on each piece of furniture as he passed it.

At noon Justine had to eat lunch alone. Duncan had left for the shop and her grandfather, when she knocked on his door, said that he was busy. From the sudden squawk of metal on metal she guessed that he was rearranging his filing cabinet. "But maybe you could just come out and have some coffee," she called.

"Eh?"

"You could keep me company."

"How's that?"

She gave up and went back to the kitchen. She opened a bottle of pickled onions and set it on the table, went to the drawer for a fork, and then suddenly straightened and frowned. This premonition of hers was pressing now against her temples and the small of her back. She returned to her grandfather's room and knocked again. "I was wondering," she called. "Would you like a cup of tea, instead?"

"Justine."

"I asked if—"

"Justine, I don't feel so well."

She opened the door instantly. Her grandfather sat on his bed holding a sheaf of papers. His face was white and slick and the papers were trembling. "What is it?" she asked.

He passed a hand across his eyes. "I was standing over there, you see," he said, "just rearranging my files a bit. I was just *standing* there when I felt so—"

He trailed off and looked at the shaking papers.

"Lie down," Justine told him. When he didn't seem to hear she touched his shoulder, pushing him gently backward until he gave in. She bent to scoop his feet up and set them on the bed. Now he lay half on his side, half on his back, breathing a little too quickly. "Are you sick to your stomach?" she asked him.

He nodded.

"*Oh*, then. Probably just . . . are you dizzy?"

He nodded.

"Well . . . but your chest doesn't hurt."

He nodded again.

"Does it? Say something."

"Yes."

"I see," Justine said.

She thought a moment. Then she went to the open window and leaned out. Next door, Ann-Campbell stood in a wading pool wearing bikini underpants, tilting her face into the rain and singing,

> We are fine mermaids of high pedigree,
> We eat baby sharks and we pee in the sea . . .

"Ann-Campbell!" Justine called. "Go get your mother. Hurry. I want her to call the ambulance in Plankhurst."

Ann-Campbell broke off her song.

"Hurry, Ann-Campbell! Tell her to call Duncan too. My grandfather's having a heart attack."

Ann-Campbell darted off, all flashing angles and freckles and patches of peeled skin. Justine turned back to her grandfather. "A what?" he said, bewildered. "Having a what?"

"Well, maybe not."

He pressed a hand to his chest.

"Is there anything I can get you?" she asked him. "Do you want a drink of water? Or—I don't know, maybe you aren't supposed to. Just lie still, Grandfather."

He did not look capable of doing anything else. He seemed to be flattened, sinking into his mattress. Nevertheless, his neck was tightly strung as if he were determined to keep his head just slightly off the pillow; it was not dignified to be seen in a horizontal position. Perhaps he even wished she would leave him in privacy, but she couldn't. She paced around and around the tiny room, willing into him all her strength and her burning, aimless energy. She kept being drawn to the window, which opened onto the side yard and would not have shown her the ambulance even if it could come so soon. "Oh, I wish Caro Mill had a hospital of its own!" she cried.

"I would never agree to a hospital," her grandfather said. He closed his eyes.

Then the screen door slammed and Justine could breathe again. "Duncan?" she called. "Is that you?"

But it was only Dorcas, clattering across the floor on her spike-heeled sandals. She stuck her bubbly head in the door and rounded her eyes at Grandfather Peck, who pretended to be asleep. "Justine honey, I called right away," she said. "They're sending an ambulance. Now I'm going to stand on the corner and wave it down."

"And Duncan? Did you call Duncan?" Justine asked.

Dorcas was already leaving, but her voice floated back. "He's coming too, he'll be here in a minute."

Justine went back to the bed and sat down on the edge of it. She laid a hand on her grandfather's cold, damp forehead. His eyes flew open and he gave her a look she had not seen him wear before: he seemed to be asking something from her. "What is it?" she said.

"Justine, I—there seems to be a considerable amount of pain starting up."

"Oh, where is Duncan?"

"I believe that I'm having a heart attack."

She picked up both his hands, which passed on their shakiness to her. His eyes withdrew and he thought something over in the gray of the ceiling. "Well," he said finally, "I had certainly hoped for more than *this* out of life."

"Don't talk!" she told him. She jumped up and ran to the window again. "Oh, where is—"

Then something made her turn, some sound much smaller than a click, and she saw that her grandfather had let his head rest at last and his hands were still and his face was calm and dead.

While she waited for Duncan she went into the living room, but it made her sad to abandon her grandfather and she returned to the bedroom. Even now, after all, there was that pinstriped collarless shirt and the silvery slant of hair, those perfect teeth glinting between the thin Peck lips, the waxy gray cord of his hearing aid and the deep-socketed eyes, closed but still leaking their blueness into the white of the lids. There was more to him than soul; there was this body, which would have looked different worn by any other man. She memorized the single stark line running alongside each corner of his mouth, drawn by pride and firmness of purpose. She willed his gnarled hands to press into hers, one more time, a bitter oval of horehound, but she did not reach out to touch him. He was too much present still, and would not have approved. Instead she slightly altered the position of his pillow, causing his head to lie straighter; and when the movement set up a resulting of papers she pulled from beneath his shoulder the sheaf of letters he had held, his carbon copies on onionskin. Their new creases and the blurred gray softness of the type made them seem to have come from someone already long dead and forgotten. "Dear Caleb," she read, from the top page. "I take pen in hand to express my hope that . . . ." Her eyes slid down, line by line. When she reached the end of the letter she lowered it and stared at her grandfather's closed, set face.

"Justine!" Duncan called.

She spun around.

"Justine? Dorcas says—"

He stopped in the doorway, and then walked in and picked up his grandfather's wrist. "Well," he said after a moment, and when he set the wrist back down he was so gentle that there was no sound at all. Then he came to stand in front of Justine. "I'm sorry," he told her.

She held the letter out to him, and he took it from her to read it. First he sighed, then he smiled; then he stopped reading and looked over at her.

"Oh, Duncan," Justine said, "how could he write such a thing?"

But when he reached for her, she dodged his hands and went to the opposite side of the room.

16

Down the curved, gleaming staircase (which in her girlhood she used to descend holding onto her chest, to prevent exercising off what little she had), across the porch where her great-grandmother had often sat listing the three permissible excuses for typing a note of condolence (paralytic stroke, severed tendons, and amputation) Justine moved dimly beside her husband, wearing the suit she had worn to her mother's funeral and clutching one frayed white glove. (She had not been able to find the other.) She entered her Uncle Mark's car; she rode through Roland Park, alighted in front of the church, and climbed the steps leaning backward slightly as if she feared what she would find inside. But inside there was only a density of carpet and shadowy pastel light from the windows, and up front an anonymous coffin. Then a cemetery as flat and well mown as a golf course, rows upon rows of glazed granite headstones including PECK Justin Montague, PECK Laura Baum, MAYHEW Caroline Peck and finally an admirably well cut rectangular ditch beside which the coffin lay like something forgotten, abandoned at the brink, while more words were said. Afterwards the family went home to receive their callers, who had been streaming in for the past two days and continued even now that it was over—elderly gentlemen, ladies in hats and gloves and veils and crocheted shawls in spite of the heat. "My," they said to Justine, "are *you* that little girl of Caroline's? But you used to be so—well, you certainly have—now, this is your husband, isn't it? *Him* I recognize."

Him they recognized. From her new distance Justine turned and looked at him, at his boyish pointy chin and his gawky way of standing, twining one leg about the other and rocking slightly with his hands in his back pockets so that his elbows jutted out to spear passers-by. The upturned corners of his mouth made him appear to be smiling mysteriously, teasingly, and perhaps he was. "Why, Duncan!" said Justine, dropping her glove. "You haven't changed a bit!"

An old lady mumbled, embarrassed at her mistake. Plainly these two were not married and perhaps not even related, in spite of the resemblance. Then Duncan stooped for the glove and handed it formally to Justine, and Justine turned and went off alone.

Not only had Duncan remained the same but so had her aunts and uncles, solidified in their flowery dresses and summer suits, and her cluster of cousins passing trays of tea cakes as they had when they were children. Only Justine stood swaybacked, chewing the empty finger of her glove, in a distant corner of the room.

"You were that little girl who used to be so sweet," a spindled-shanked lady told her. "And still are, I'm sure. You used to bring me little handfuls of flowers. You would never stay and talk because you were too shy."

Justine removed the glove from her mouth and gave her a sweet, shy smile, but the lady was not deceived and moved on immediately.

When the guests were gone Duncan escaped to bed, but the rest of the family had a light supper in the kitchen, working around Sulie, who was dusting the pipes under the sink. They laid out memories of Grandfather Peck, one by one. Aunt Lucy cried a little. Aunt Sarah became irritable and informed Justine that there was no call to wear a hat in her own family's house. "Oh, I'm sorry," said Justine, removing it. Then she didn't know what to do with it. She balanced it on her lap, leaving her sandwich untouched. She was feeling very tired. Really she would have liked to go off to sleep. But she stayed on, and by the time the aunts and uncles had risen to go she had her second wind and remained in the kitchen with the cousins, who discussed memories of their own. *They* remembered their grandfather's expression at that picnic for which Duncan had made him a Noxzema and olive sandwich, and first they sputtered into their iced tea and then laughed outright. Justine looked around at each blond, lit-up face, remembering times when she had been a member here. When she and the girls were eleven and twelve and thirteen, what on earth had they all found so funny that it made them laugh until they squeaked?

Esther was now the supervisor of a nursery school. Alice was a librarian, while Sally, the prettier twin, had returned from her month-long marriage a little less outgoing than she used to be and now taught piano in the privacy of Great-Grandma's house, on a modern blond upright that looked peculiar in the wine-colored parlor. Richard had a high-rise apartment downtown, and Claude lived over the garage behind Uncle Two's and spent all his money on steel engravings that nobody liked. New little lines were pricked in all their faces and their hair was dryer and duller, their hands growing freckles; but still they were the same. Only Justine was different, and when she tried to talk to them she had the sense of swimming hard against a strong current. Frustration made her clumsy, and she spilled a glass of ice cubes into Claude's lap but everyone said it didn't matter a bit.

Upstairs, in her old pink-and-white bedroom, she undressed in the dark so as not to wake Duncan and lay down beside him. It was going to be one of those nights when she couldn't sleep. She felt a familiar alertness in her legs, as if she were tightrope-walking on a rubber band. Voices swam in and out of her hearing: Duncan at twelve, explaining shotgun poker; Richard asking if he could come too; Aunt Bea naming all the wedding gifts she had received in the summer of 1930; and her grandfather calling, "Wait for me, Justine! There's no need to rush so." But she had rushed anyway. She had been so quick and brash, so loud, so impatient, which must explain that constant look of puzzlement he had worn in his later years; for where was the old slow, tender Justine?

"Wait for me," she heard Meg say, and she clearly saw Meg's five-year-old face, apple-round, rosy with heat, in the shadows of a spiral staircase in a lighthouse on the New Jersey coastline. They had stopped there on the way back from an unsuccessful job interview. (Justine had always wanted to live in a lighthouse.) Justine had climbed up and up, tumbling over her feet in her haste to see what was at the top, while Meg trudged panting behind. There were two hundred and seventy-eight steps, a sign outside had said. But when Justine reached the top, she found the catwalk enclosed in clear plastic, which clouded the view. The only room was a small dark alcove in which a uniformed park guard sat tipping his chair, reading a paperback Mickey Spillane. So she didn't want to live there after all. She descended more slowly, still breathless from her upward run, and on the next to the last flight she found Meg sobbing on a windowsill while Duncan tried to comfort her. "Oh, *honey!*" Justine cried. "I forgot all about you!" But had that taught her anything? She had only speeded up with every year, gathering momentum. Racing toward some undefined future and letting the past roll up behind her, swooping Meg along under one arm but neglecting to listen to her or to ask if she wanted this trip at all. So Meg grew up alone, self-reared, and left home alone for a sad stunted life she had not really wanted; and Grandfather Peck became ever more lost and bewildered stumbling through a series of paper shanties. And Justine awoke one day to wonder how it had happened: what she had mislaid was Justine herself.

But Duncan, who had changed her whole life and taken all her past away from her, slept on as cool as ever, and on the crown of his head was the same little sprig of a cowlick he had had when he was four.

In the morning everyone suggested they stay a while, but Duncan said he was anxious to get going. He barely tolerated the lengthy discussion on traffic conditions, alternate routes, and whether or not to take a Thermos. He acted jittery and exasperated during the loading of the car trunk, while the uncles were padding more of Meg's wedding presents with the flowered sheets that Aunt Lucy had insisted they accept. ("I can't forget that bare mattress in your little home," she had said, shuddering. "*Nobody* just washes their linens and puts them right back on. You give them a rest in a cupboard first, which increases their life span by sixty-six percent.") Then there were the ritual cold drinks out on the porch, with Duncan finishing first and nervously rattling his ice cubes while waiting for Justine. Justine took extra long, to make up for him. She kept gazing around her at her family. "If only you could have got in touch with Meg!" Aunt Sarah told her.

"We'll call and break the news as soon as she gets back from the beach."

"She'll feel terrible, missing the funeral."

There was a quavering in the air, thin sad thoughts hovering among them. Uncle Two cleared his throat sharply. "Well!" he said. "I never asked how the health food business was going."

"Antiques," Duncan said.

"Antiques, then."

"It's okay." He looked off across the lawn and tapped his glass. "Justine, we have to get started if we want to beat the heat."

"Oh. All right," she said. But she would rather have stayed. It gave her a tearing feeling to have to rise and kiss each soft, kind face in turn.

The family descended the steps with elaborate care, proving their reluctance to say goodbye—except for Duncan, of course, who danced down the walk ahead of them tossing and catching a spangle of car keys. "Duncan, boy," said Uncle Mark, "if your grandfather left any unpaid bills, now, medical expenses and so on—"

"I'll let you know."

"And I suppose I'd better write those detective fellows, tell them to close their case." He opened the car door for Justine. "Durned people have been spending money like water anyway," he told her. "I'm glad to be shed of them."

Justine threw Duncan a glance, but he wouldn't meet it. He had made her promise to keep Caleb's secret forever, unless he changed his mind and wrote. So all she could say to her uncle was, "I'll tell Eli myself, if you like."

"His latest expenditures are downright *bizarre*," her uncle said. "Why would he want to bribe a florist?"

"I'll take care of it."

She climbed into the car, and Duncan started the motor. "Finally," he muttered. Then they were off, zooming down the road scattering a cloud of maple-seed propellers while Justine leaned out the window to wave. Aunt Lucy shouted something. "What?" Justine called. Aunt Lucy shouted again.

"Duncan, stop," said Justine. "Your mother's trying to tell us something."

Duncan slammed on the brakes. The car whined into reverse. "What?" Justine called.

"I said, *Don't forget to rest your linens!*"

Duncan clapped a hand to his head, but Justine only nodded and called, "Thank you, Aunt Lucy," and blew her a kiss, and then more kisses for all the others, until Duncan jerked the car into forward again and bore her away.

17

Duncan had been playing solitaire for months now, but nobody guessed it had been that long because at first he had kept it a secret. At first he always did. Like an alcoholic hiding his bottle while everyone else drinks in public, he had stashed decks of cards in out-of-the-way places and he played in uncomfortable and poorly lit corners. At the smallest sound he was ready to scoop his game together and look up with an innocent face and a smile. (He did not like to be caught depending on things.) But gradually, drugged with patience and canfield and accordion, he forgot his surroundings and forgot to hide the cards, then failed to notice when someone came upon him, then finally wandered into the living room absent-mindedly and laid out his game in the center of the floor where everyone had to stumble over the great spread V of his legs. He played throughout meals, visits, family quarrels, and his grandfather's wake. He returned from Baltimore carrying a suitcase in which a single deck of cards had scattered itself through everything—interleaving with the pleats of Justine's funeral skirt and standing upright among the bristles of her hairbrush. But he didn't bother collecting them. He took instead a double deck that had been waiting all this time behind a begonia pot, and he settled himself on the floor and laid out a hand of spider, which was his favorite, most absorbing game, requiring hours and days of deliberation and strategy and intricate plotting. He kept losing and laying out new set-ups. Justine wandered through the rooms still wearing her hat.

At the Blue Bottle, when he went, he played on a scarred wooden desk behind the counter. He swept away stacks of bills, circulars, and correspondence, clearing the large space that spider required. When the bell tinkled over the door he didn't hear. If he had to answer a question or ring up a purchase he was annoyed, and showed it. Couldn't they see he was busy? By now he despised antiques. He despised the people who collected them—artificial-looking ladies who had, no doubt, thirty years ago thrown away the identical beechwood rolling pins that they were now rebuying at such exorbitant prices. And to make it worse, Silas Amsel had become a nuisance. Once the shop had proved a success, he *expected* things of Duncan. He was always waiting to hear good news. Duncan couldn't stand to have things expected of him. Gradually he sold less and less, bought fewer tools, behaved more rudely toward the customers. Silas began to complain. He mentioned trivial lapses: the few times Duncan had forgotten to lock up, and the mornings he was slightly late. There was a misplaced bronze he claimed had been stolen. (As if anyone would bother stealing an object so ugly, or so heavy.) There were little spats and insults every time Silas came to the shop. And he came more and more often, and stayed longer, and meddled more. He would start grumbling even before he was fully inside. He would stand in the doorway, shaking his head. Duncan pretended not to see him. (Sometimes he *really* didn't see him.) He remained seated, pondering over a vast network of playing cards, one finger hooked in a bottle of Old Crow. He felt the air turning gluey with the weight of other people's disapproval, suspicions, hopes, preconceived notions. Only Justine allowed him to go unclassified.

Justine trailed through the shop and out again with the crumpled streamers of her hat fluttering indecisively.

"I'll be finished in a minute," he called, and she said, "Hmm?" and returned, vaguely. She did not shut doors behind her; so for her the antique sleighbell was forever still, a fact he appreciated. She lacked finality. She was the other shoe which never dropped. He looked up from his cards and sent her a smile so deep and sudden that it would surely have wiped all the forlornness off her face if she had seen it, but she didn't. She was studying a chipped paperweight. She looked lost. Nowadays all she would talk about was her grandfather, his wishes she had not granted and gifts she had not thanked him for. She did not mention Caleb. Duncan waited for her to, but she didn't. Now it was October and if she were disappointed, leafing through the mail every morning with her listless, uncertain fingers, she didn't show it. She merely returned to the same old subject: she unwrapped the past endlessly, untying the ribbons, removing the tissue, untying more ribbons. "Do you remember when he took us on the train? I don't know where to. He took all us children, it was some kind of outing. Some patriotic occasion of some sort. I believe he was sorry before we'd even left the depot but it was too late to back out and he didn't want—"

Duncan couldn't remember. He suspected that he had been left at home. But he didn't say so to Justine. He watched her turning the crystal paperweight, and peering into it, and then raising her eyes to examine without interest her own reflection in an ormolu mirror. "Look at me," she said, "I'm one of those eccentric old ladies you see on the street, with a beat-up hat and a shopping bag."

But to him she was an awkward girl-cousin wearing very long shoes, and the comical up-dip at the ends of her hair was enough to make him leave his cards and come set a kiss on her cool cheek.

"You might find me going through a trash basket," she said, still to the mirror. She ignored his kiss.

"Maybe we should take a trip," Duncan told her. "Somewhere we've never been."

"Children would make bets on what I carry in my string bag."

But her bag was straw, not string, and he *knew* what she carried. Coffee beans, and salty things to nibble on, and the future wrapped in a square of rotting silk. Hadn't she always? She turned from the mirror, as if guessing his thoughts, and opened the bag to show him. He saw neither food nor cards but only sheaves of yellowed photographs belonging to her grandfather. Aunts and uncles standing around in the ocean, by waterfalls, beside new cars; cousins holding up fish and diplomas and Bible-study trophies; Grandfather Peck carefully posed, 8 × 10, behind an enormous empty desk, beneath a parade of *Maryland Digests* and *ALR* volumes; somebody's bride; somebody's baby; Duncan laughing; Great-Grandma guarding her soul against theft by camera; more uncles; more aunts at someone's garden party, clustered together with their faces frozen in surprise. (They would run to a mirror just beforehand and then run back, level, bearing their chosen expressions as carefully as jellies on a platter.) Justine snapped her bag shut again. She gave him a long measuring stare that turned him cold. "That's what I carry," she said, "but don't tell the children."

Then she walked out. The bell quivered but kept silent. Duncan thought of going after her—asking at least where she was headed, or whether she would be there to fill the house for him when he got home. Or most important: what he had done to make her look at him that way. The way other people had looked at him all his life. All his life they had marked him as thoughtless and mischievous, wicked even; yet he had continued to feel that somehow, underneath, he was a good man. With Justine, he *was* a good man. Had she changed her mind about him? He didn't want to know. He didn't want to ask, and have to hear her answer. In the end all he did was return to his game of solitaire.

In an airport waiting room, at eleven thirty in the morning, Justine sat in a vinyl chair with her straw bag balanced on her knees. She was watching a group of students on standby. The regular passengers had already filed through, and now an official took a stack of blue tickets from his podium and began calling out each standby's name. They cheered and came forward, one by one. They accepted their tickets like Oscars, smiling at the official and then waving triumphantly to their friends, who clapped. Justine clapped too. "Mr. Flagg!" the official called. "Mr. Brant!" Mr. Flagg beamed. Mr. Brant kissed his ticket. "Mrs. Peck!" And though Justine had no one with her, she was so carried away by all the gaiety that she beamed too, and turned back to bow to the empty row of chairs before she headed through the gate marked *New Orleans*.

18

At night, in his narrow white cot, with old men wheezing and snoring all around him, he lay flat on his back and smiled at the ceiling and hummed "Broken Yo-Yo" till the matron came and shut him up. "Just *what* do you think you're doing?" He didn't answer, but the humming stopped. A fellow at the end of the row called out for a bedpan. The matron left, on dull rubbery heels. The fellow went on calling for a while but without much interest, and eventually he fell silent and merely squeaked from time to time. Caleb continued smiling at the ceiling. What no one guessed was that "Broken Yo-Yo" was still tumbling note on note inside his head.

From four a.m. till five he slept, dreaming first of a cobbled street down which he ran, more agile than he had been in years; then of fields of black-eyed Susans; then of grim machinery grinding and crumpling his hands. He awoke massaging his fingers. The ache was always worse in the early morning hours. He lay watching the darkness lift, the ceiling whiten, the sky outside the one gigantic window grow opaque. The tossing forms around him stilled, signifying wakefulness, although none of them spoke. This was the hour when old men gave in to insomnia, which had been tracking them down all night. They would rather not admit their defeat. They lay gritting their gums together, tensed as if on guard, betraying themselves only by a dry cough or the occasional sandpapery sound of one foot rubbing against the other. Caleb was stillest of all, but now "Stone Pony Blues" was spinning between his ears.

At six o'clock the matron came to snap on a switch. Long after she had gone, fluorescent tubes were fluttering and pausing and collecting themselves to fill the room with glare. The sky appeared to darken again. Morning came later now; it was fall. In December he would have been here seven years and he knew every shadow and slant of light, all the sounds of night and morning and mealtimes, which he tabulated with a sense of contentment.

Those who could manage for themselves began to struggle out of bed and into their bathrobes. Caleb's bathrobe was a rubberized raincoat, whose belt he tied clumsily without moving his fingers. He had asked Roy's wife Luray for a real bathrobe this coming Christmas and he was fairly certain she would bring him one. He slipped his feet into paper scuffs and went off across the hall to the toilets. Already a line had formed. While he waited he hummed. The old men went on discussing their constipation, indigestion, leg cramps, and backaches. They were used to his humming.

For breakfast there were grits, shredded wheat bisquits, and coffee. The men sat on long wooden benches, eating from tin plates with compartments. The women sat on the other side of the dining hall. They could have mingled with the men if they wished but they didn't, perhaps preferring not to be seen in their flowered dusters, with their veiny white legs poking out and their scalps showing through the thin strands of hair. Caleb, however, bowed and smiled in their direction before taking his place on a bench.

After breakfast they went to the social room. Some watched television, most just stared into space. Those who were crippled were wheeled in and parked like grocery carts. A gin rummy game started up in one corner but lapsed, with the players merely holding their cards and sitting vacantly as if frozen. A man with a cane told another man how his son had done him out of a house and five acres. Caleb himself did not have anyone to talk to at the moment. His only friend had died in August. Jesse Dole, a horn player who had been recorded several times in the days when you blew into a large black morning glory and it came out of another morning glory in someone's parlor. They used to sit in this very spot between the radiator and the Formica coffee table, arguing the fine points of their different styles of music. Then one night Jesse died and they collected him in his bedsheet and swung him onto a stretcher, leaving Caleb to spend his days all alone with the vinyl chair beside him empty. The others thought he was a little odd. They didn't have much to do with him. But Caleb was accustomed to making friends with anyone, and he knew that sooner or later he would find somebody or somebody would find him, maybe some new man coming in with new stories to tell. Till then, Caleb sat tranquilly in the social room with his knotty hands resting on his knees and his eyes fixed upon the green linoleum floor. For lack of anything else he had begun thinking back on his memories, which wasn't like him. He had never been a man to dwell on the past. Leaving places, he forgot them, always looking ahead to the next; but he had supposed that someday he would have the time to sit down and take a look at where he had been and this must be it.

New Orleans in the early part of the century: jitney dances at the Okeh Pavilion and the faint strains of quadrilles, schottisches, and polkas, and musical beggars one to a block playing anything that made a fine noise. White-Eye Ramford bowling along the sidewalk with his buckle-kneed gait, plucking notes like little golden fruits and singing and stumbling so you thought he was drunk, till you saw his flickering black paper eyelids and the blind, seeking roll of his head. He had lost his sight at twelve or maybe twenty, his stories differed; and by the time he reached middle age he should have learned how to navigate but he hadn't. He was hopeless. A plump, clumsy, hopeless man with a mild face, wincing when he stumbled and then moving on, resigned, plucking more notes from his cracked guitar. He wore a ragged white carnation in his buttonhole, and a derby on his head. It was the fall of 1914. Caleb was on his way home from the sugar refinery and he stopped and stared. Then he followed behind. Till the blind man called, "Who that?" and Caleb melted into a doorway. The next day, the same street, Caleb brought along his fiddle. When he heard the guitar he started playing. High haunting notes wailed and rose, commenting on the tune, climbing behind it. He had known immediately what this sort of music required. The guitar readjusted, making way for the fiddle, and the two of them continued down the street. Someone dropped a coin into a lard bucket hanging from the guitarist's belt. "Thank you," said Caleb, always well mannered. The guitarist spun around. "*White* man?" he cried. Caleb was so pleased at his surprise that he hardly noticed he was left standing foolishly alone. He was certain (because he wanted it so much) that the two of them would meet again, and that he would go on playing his fiddle behind the cracked guitar until he was accepted. Or tolerated, at least. Or recognized to be unavoidable.

In 1912 or 1913 you could run into Caleb Peck in just about any sporting house or dance hall in the city, always propped against the piano or the edge of the bandstand, puzzled and wistful, worn down from his menial daytime job, hoping to be allowed to fill in for some musician, though no one was that eager to have him. After all he did not play any brass, and most had no use for a fiddle. As for piano, he was a musical Rip Van Winkle. He had learned from a man who left New Orleans in the nineteenth century, when jazz was still spelled with two s's. So in 1912 and 1913 Caleb merely hung around the edges of places, with a thin strained face from so much listening, from absorbing so much, from trying to understand. But in 1914 he discovered the blues, which he understood instantly without the slightest effort, and for the next twenty years you could find him in the same small area of the Vieux Carré, linked to a blind man by a length of twine and playing a fiddle above a slippery song.

While he stared now at the streaks of detergent on the green linoleum, he could hear White-Eye's loopy thin voice and the twang he made sliding a bottleneck down the strings of his guitar. He sang "Careless Love" and "Mr. Crump." He sang what Caleb made up— "Shut House" and "Whisky Alley" and "Cane Sugar Blues." Then "The Stringtail Blues," which some people credited to Caleb too but it was plainly White-Eye's, telling how a blind man felt leaning on other people. Caleb's fiddle shimmered and lilted, the guitar notes thrummed beneath it. Caleb had turned shabby, and not quite clean. It took money to be clean. He was surprised sometimes when he caught sight of himself in a window: that lanky man in a grimy frayed suit. Often he bore welts from the bedbugs in his rooming house, where he continued to live alone, unmarried, year after year. He had a great many friends but they were mostly transients, disappearing unexpectedly and resurfacing sometimes months later and sometimes never. Only White-Eye was permanent. Yet you could not say that they were friends, at least not in any visible way. They hardly talked at all. They never discussed their personal affairs. But some people noticed how their two stringed instruments spoke together continuously like old relations recollecting and nodding and agreeing, and how when Caleb and White-Eye parted for the night they stood silent a moment, as if wishing for something more to say, before turning and shambling off in their separate directions. At night White-Eye went to a wife he never named and an unknown number of descendants. Caleb went to work as watchman in a coffee warehouse; otherwise he would have starved. (He took no more than a deceptive jingle of coins from the lard bucket.) For twenty years he existed on four hours of sleep a night. He did it for the sake of a single body of music: those peculiarly prideful songs celebrating depression, a state he had once known very well. He could no longer imagine any other kind of life. If you asked where he came from, or who his family was, he would answer readily but without real thought. He never pictured the city he named or the people. His mind veered away from them, somehow. He preferred the present. He was happy where he was.

The other street musicians dwindled to a handful, and Storyville was closed and the jazz players went off to Chicago or the excursion boats or the artificial bands hired by debutantes' mothers. But White-Eye and the Stringtail Man continued, supporting themselves more or less even through the Crash in 1929. They had become a fixture.

Though not famous, they were familiar; and the poorest people were willing to give up a coin in order to keep the world from changing any more than it already had.

In 1934, on a Monday morning very early in the year, Caleb set out searching as he always did for the first faint sound of White-Eye's guitar. (Their meetings were never prearranged. You would never suppose, at the close of a day, that they were planning to see each other tomorrow.) But he had not gone two blocks when a brown woman wearing a shawl came up and touched the scroll of his fiddle, and told him White-Eye was dead. She was his widow. On the very morning of the wake she had taken the trouble to locate Caleb and break the news and invite him to the funeral—a fact that he appreciated, though all he did was nod. Then he went home and sat for a long time on his bed. He wouldn't answer when his landlady called him. But he did attend the funeral the following afternoon and even accompanied the family to the cemetery, a remote little field outside the city. He stood at the edge of the swampy grave between two tea-colored girls who stared at him and giggled. Throughout the ceremony he kept brushing his hair off his forehead with the back of his hand. He was, by then, nearly fifty years old. It was the first time he had stopped to realize that.

Now Caleb traveled the streets alone. Since he had never been a singer he merely fiddled. (No one guessed that White-Eye's voice still rang inside his head.) The solitary strains of his music had a curious trick of blending with street sounds—with the voices of black women passing by or the hum of trolley lines or a huckster's call. First you heard nothing; then you wondered; then the music separated itself and soared away and you stood stock still with your mouth open. But when people offered him a coin, moved by what they thought they might have heard, they found no tin cup to drop it in. They tucked it into his pockets instead. At night Caleb would find all his pockets lumpy and heavy and sometimes even a crumpled paper bill stuck into his belt. He could not always remember where it had come from. He merely piled it on top of his bureau. But as the months passed the dazed feeling left him, and one noon when he was sitting in a café eating red beans and rice he looked up at the waitress pouring coffee and realized that life was still going on.

He stayed in New Orleans two more years, and might have stayed forever if he had not fallen in with a pair of cornetists who talked him into taking a trip to Peacham. Peacham was a small, pretty town just to the north, still suffering like anyplace else from hard times and unemployment. But the mayor had hit upon a solution: he planned to make it a resort. (Nobody thought to ask him who would have the money to go there.) He published a three-color brochure claiming that Peacham had all the advantages of New Orleans with none of the crowds or city soot: fine food, lively bars, two full-sized nightclubs rocking with jazz, and musicians on every street corner. Then he set to work importing busloads of chefs, waitresses, and bartenders, as well as players of every known musical instrument. (In all the native pop-ulation there were only three pianists—classical—and the minister's daughter, who played the harp.) References were unnecessary. So were auditions. In a creaky wooden hotel on the wrong side of town musicians were stacked on top of one another like crated chickens, venturing out each morning to look picturesque on designated corners. But there was no one to drop money in their cups. The only visitors to Peacham were the same as always—aging citizens' grown sons and daughters, come to spend a duty week in their parents' homes. One by one the new employees lost hope and left, claiming they had never thought it would work anyhow. Only Caleb stayed. He had landed there more or less by accident, reluctant to leave New Orleans, but as it turned out he happened to like Peacham just fine. He figured he could enjoy himself there as well as anyplace else.

Now he worked days as janitor for an elementary school, and in the evenings he played his fiddle on the corner he had been assigned. He ate his meals at Sam's Café, where a large red kind-faced waitress gave him double helpings of everything because she thought he was too skinny. This woman's name was Bess. She lived just behind the café with her two-year-old boy. It was her opinion that Caleb's hotel charged too much for his room, and bit by bit she persuaded him to move in with her instead. It wasn't hard. (He was so agreeable.) Before he knew it he found himself settled in her kerosene-lit shack, in her brown metal bed, beneath her thin puckered quilt, which smelled faintly of bacon grease. If she was, perhaps, not the one he would have chosen out of all the women in the world, at least she was cheerful and easy-going. Sometimes he even considered marrying her, in order to give her son Roy a last name, but they were already so comfortable together that he never got around to it.

By 1942 Bess had saved enough money to buy a café of her own in Box Hill, a town some twenty miles away. Caleb wasn't sure he wanted to go; he liked it where he was. But Bess had her mind made up and so he followed, amiably enough, lugging his fiddle and his pennywhistle and a flute and a change of clothes. This time he took a job as short-order cook in Bess's café. He found a park to do his fiddling in, a new crowd of children and courting couples to hear him in the evenings. Only nowadays more and more of the men wore uniforms, and the girls' clothes too were uniform-like—square-shoul-dered, economical of fabric—and he wondered sometimes, playing his same old music, whether people could really understand it any more. In his head, White-Eye Ramford still sang of despair and jealousy and cruel women and other rich, wasteful things. The couples who listened seemed too efficient for all that.

There was some trouble with Caleb's fingers—a little stiffness in the mornings. His bow hand could not get going at all if the weather was damp. And by now his hair was nearly white and his whiskers grew out silver whenever he went unshaven. On several occasions he was startled to find his father's face gazing at him from mirrors. Only his father, of course, would not have worn a dirty Panama hat, especially in the house, or a bibbed white apron stained with catsup or trousers fastened with a safety pin.

Bess's café was close to the freight tracks, between a seed store and a liquor store. There were some tough-looking men in those parts, but nothing that Bess couldn't handle. Or so she said. Till one evening in March of 1948 when two customers started arguing over a mule and one drew a gun and shot Bess through the heart by accident. Caleb was fiddling at the time. When he returned, he thought he had walked into a movie. These milling policemen, detectives, and ambulance attendants, this woman on the floor with a purple stain down her front, surely had nothing to do with the real world. In fact he had trouble believing she was dead, and never properly mourned her except in pieces—her good-natured smile, her warm hands, her stolid fat legs in white stockings, all of which occurred to him in unexpected flashes for many years afterward.

Of course now Caleb was free to go anywhere, but he had the responsibility of Bess's boy Roy, who was only thirteen or fourteen at the time. And besides, he liked Box Hill. He enjoyed his work as short-order cook, frying up masses of hash browns and lace-edged eggs in record time, and since the café now belonged to Roy what else could they do but stay on?

Year by year the café became more weathered, the sign saying "Bess's Place" flaked and buckled. Roy grew into a stooped, skinny young man with an anxious look to him. They took turns minding the business. Evenings Caleb could still go out and fiddle "Stack O'Lee" and "Jogo Blues." But his hands were knotted tighter and tighter now, and there were days when he had to leave the fiddle in its case. Then even the pennywhistle was beyond him; there was no way to tamp the airholes properly when his fingers stayed stiff and clenched. So he set about relearning the harmonica, which he had last played as a very young man. The warm metal in his hands and the smell of spit-dampened wood reminded him of home. He paused and looked out across the counter. Where were they all now? Dead? He wiped the harmonica on his trousers and went back to his song.

Roy said they needed a waitress. This was in 1963 or so. They had the same small group of customers they always had, railroad workers mostly and old men from the rooming houses nearby. Caleb couldn't see that they had any sudden need for a waitress. But Roy went and got one anyhow, and once he had then Caleb understood. This was a pretty little blond girl, name of Luray Spivey. Before six weeks had passed she was Mrs. Roy Pickett and there was a jukebox in the corner playing rock-and-roll, not to mention all the changes in the apartment upstairs, where he and Roy had lived alone for so many years. She covered the walls of Roy's bedroom with pictures of movie stars torn out of magazines, mainly Troy Donahue and Bobby Darin. She brightened the living room with curtains, cushions, plastic carnations and seashells. She followed Caleb around picking up his soiled clothes with little housewifely noises that amused him. "Hoo-*ee!*" she would say, holding an undershirt by the tips of her fingers. But she wasn't the kind to run a man down. She knew when to stop housekeeping, too, and sit with Roy and Caleb and a six-pack of beer in front of the second-hand television she had talked Roy into buying for her. In the café she cheered everybody up, with her little pert jokes and the way she would toss her head and the flippy short white skirt that spun around her when she moved off to the grill with an order. All the customers enjoyed having her around.

Then the twins were born, in the fall of 1964. Well, of course life is hard with twins; you can't expect a woman to be as easy-going as ever. Plus there was the financial angle. Certainly people require more money once they start having children. Luray was just *frazzled* with money worries, you could see it. She wanted so many things for her babies. She was always after Roy to take a second job, maybe driving a cab. "How we going to even eat?" she would ask him, standing there scared and fierce in her seersucker duster. (Once she had ordered her clothes off the back pages of movie magazines, all these sequined low-necked dresses and push-up bras.) So Roy took a job with the Prompt Taxi Company from six to twelve every night and Caleb ran the café alone. Not that he minded. There wasn't much business anyway and he had just about given up his evening fiddling now that the park was gone and his hands were so stubborn and contrary. (Besides, sometimes lately when he played he had the feeling that people thought of him as a—character, really. Someone colorful. He had never meant to be that, he only wanted to make a little music.) So he would putter around the café fixing special dishes and talking to the customers, most of whom were friends, and after the plates were rinsed he might pull out his harmonica and settle himself on a stool at the counter and give them a tune or two. "Pig Meat Papa" he played, and "Broke and Hungry Blues" and "Nobody Knows You When You're Down and Out." The old men listened and nodded heavily and, "Now that is so," they said when he was done—a much finer audience than any courting couple. Till Luray came down from upstairs with her hair in curlers and her duster clutched around her. "What all is going on here? Caleb, you have woken both babies when I had just slaved my butt off putting them down. What is everybody sitting here for? Shoo now! Shoo!" As if they were taking up seats that someone else wanted, when it was clear no more customers were coming; and anyway, they were having fun. There was no point to hurrying off when you were having fun.

Then Luray got back in her transparent white uniform and said she saw that she would have to start waiting tables again; men customers would leave her tips that they wouldn't leave Caleb. "Well, naturally," Caleb said. "They're personal friends, they wouldn't want to embarrass me." "It don't embarrass *me*," said Luray, tossing her head. She would open the stair door, listening for the babies. Caleb worried about her leaving them alone but she said they would be fine. She was saving up to buy them an electric bottle sterilizer. Caleb didn't think a sterilizer was all that necessary but he could see that, to Luray, there was always the chance that some single magic object might be the one to guarantee that her babies would live happily forever; and maybe the sterilizer was that object. So he was not surprised when after the sterilizer was bought she started saving up for a double stroller, and after that a pair of collapsible canvas carbeds although they didn't own a car. And he didn't hold it against her when she started criticizing his work, although certainly there were times when she got him down. "What do I see you doing here? How come you to be using pure cream? What you got in mind for all them eggs?"

The fact was that Caleb was pretty much a custom chef by now. He had known his few patrons a very long time, and since he was not a man who easily showed his liking for people he chose to cook them their favorite foods instead—the comfort foods that every man turns to when he is feeling low. For Jim Bolt it was hot milk and whisky; for old Emmett Gray, fried garden-fresh tomatoes with just a sprinkle of sugar; and Mr. Ebsen the freight agent liked home-baked bread. The narrow aluminum shelves behind the counter, meant to hold only dry cereals, potato chips, and Hostess cream-filled cupcakes, were a jumble of condiments in Mason jars and Twinings tea from England, Scotch oatmeal tins, Old Bay crab spice, and Major Grey chutney. The café appeared, in fact, to be a kitchen in the home of a very large family. It had looked that way for years, but this was the first time Luray noticed. "What kind of a business *is* this?" she asked. "Do you want to send us all to the poorhouse? Here am I with these two growing babies and lying awake at night just wondering will we manage and there you are cooking up French omelettes and rice pudding, things not even on the menu and I don't even want to know how much you're charging for them . . ."

Luray took over his job, whipping an apron around her little tiny waist. She acted as if she thought Caleb had grown weak in the head. She sent him up to tend the babies. Caleb had never been good with children. The sight of them made him wretched; he was so sorry for humans in the state of childhood that he couldn't stand to be near them. When one of the babies cried his insides knotted up and he felt bleak and hopeless. So he tended them as if from a distance, holding himself aloof, and as soon as it was nap time he hurried downstairs to socialize with the customers. He sat turning on a stool, talking and laughing, a little silly with relief, plunking down money from his own pocket to pay for a cup of coffee so Luray wouldn't send him off. He would fish out his harmonica with stiff, thickened fingers and give the men "Shut House" or "Whisky Alley." Till Luray stopped in front of him with her hands on her hips and her head cocked. "Hear that? Hear what I hear? Hear them babies crying?" Then Caleb put away his harmonica and went back upstairs on slow, heavy feet.

In the fall of 1966, Luray found out she was pregnant again. She was not very happy about it. Money seemed scarcer than ever, the twins were getting to be a handful, and already the apartment was cramped. Caleb slept on the couch now, and the babies were in his old room. When he got up in the night he stumbled over blocks and wheeled toys and cold soggy diapers all the way to the bathroom, where likely as not Luray had shut herself in ahead of him. "Go away!" she would shout. "Go back to bed, you old skunk!"

One morning she went out all dressed up, leaving Roy to tend the café and Caleb to mind the babies. When she came back she told Caleb she had found him a place to move into. "Oh! Well," Caleb said.

He had thought a couple of times himself about moving, but not so concretely. And then there was the money. "This café just can't *support* two apartments, Luray," he said.

"It's not an apartment."

"Oh, a room? Well, fine, that'll be—"

"This is a place the county helps out with."

Then she flashed Roy a sudden look, and Roy hung his head in that bashful way he had and his face got red. But still Caleb didn't understand.

He understood only when they deposited him in the gray brick building with the concrete yard, with attendants squeaking in their rubber-soled shoes down the corridors. "But—Luray?" he said. Roy wandered off and looked at a bulletin board. The back of his neck was splotchy. Only Luray was willing to face Caleb. "Now you know they'll take good care of you," she told him. "Well, after all. It's not like you were any real relation or anything." She was balancing a baby on each arm, standing sway-backed against their weight—a thin, enormously pregnant woman with washed-out hair and cloudy skin. What could he say to her? There was no way he could even be angry, she was so dismal and pathetic. "Well," he said. "Never mind."

Though later, when the nurse told him he couldn't keep his harmonica here, he did feel one flash of rage that shook him from head to foot, and he wondered if he would be able to stand it after all.

Now he had to hum to make his music. Unfortunately he had a rather flat, toneless voice, and a tendency to hit the notes smack dab instead of slithering around on them as White-Eye Ramford used to. Still, it was better than nothing. And as time went by he made a few acquaintances, discovered a dogwood tree in the concrete yard, and began to enjoy the steady rhythm of bed, meals, social hour, nap. He had always liked to think that he could get along anywhere. Also he did have visitors. Some of these old men had no one. He had Roy and Luray coming by once a month or more with their four little towheaded boys—Roy as young as ever, somehow, Luray dried and hollowed out. But she was very kind now. When the clock struck four and the matron shooed them from the visitors' parlor Luray would reach forward to touch Caleb's hand, or sometimes peck his cheek. "Now we'll be coming back, you hear?" she said. She always said, "Don't see us out, you sit right where you're at and stay comfortable." But he came anyway, out the steel door and across the concrete yard, to where the gate would clang shut in his face. He would wave through the grille, and Luray would tell her boys to wave back. And maybe halfway up the street, heading toward the bus stop, she would turn to smile and her chin would lift just as it used to, as if she were letting him know that underneath, she was still that sweet perky Luray Spivey and she felt just as bewildered as he did by the way things had worked out.

In his patched vinyl chair in the social room he hummed old snatches of song, joyous mournful chants for St. Louis and East St. Louis, Memphis and Beale Street, Pratt City and Parchman Farm. But it was a fact that he never hummed the "Stringtail Blues" at all, though White-Eye Ramford sang it continually in the echoing streets of his mind:

Once I walk proud, once I prance up and down,
Now I holds to a string and they leads me around . . .

The morning the letter came he had been sitting like this in the social room. He remembered that when the attendant tossed the envelope into his lap he had expected a good half hour, perhaps, of studying pictures of floral arrangements. (Altona Florists were his only correspondents.) Bouquets named "Remembrance," "Friendly Thoughts," and "Elegance," which you could send clear across the continent without ever setting foot in a shop. But when he ripped open the envelope what he found instead was a typewritten letter of some sort. He checked the outside address. Mr. Caleb Peck, yes. All the postmark said was "U.S. Postal Service Md." Whatever had happened to postmarks?

Maryland.

He shook the letter open. "Dear Caleb," he read. He skipped to the signature. "Your brother, Daniel J. Peck, Sr." A stone seemed to drop on his chest. But he was glad, of course, that his brother was still alive. He remembered Daniel with affection, and there were certain flashing images that could touch him even now, if he allowed them to—Daniel's yellow head bent over a schoolbook; the brave, scared look he sometimes gave his father; the embarrassed pride on his face when Maggie Rose came down the aisle in her wedding dress. Yet Caleb shrank in his vinyl chair, and glanced about the room as if checking for intruders. Then he read the rest of the letter.

It seemed that Daniel was inviting him to pay a visit. He was asking him to come to a place called Caro Mill. Caleb had never heard of Caro Mill. He found it difficult to imagine his brother anywhere but Baltimore. And when he pictured accepting the invitation he pictured Baltimore still, even with this letter before him—a streetcar rattling toward the sandy, shaded roads of Roland Park, a house with cloth dolls and hobbyhorses scattered across the lawn. Daniel descending the steps to welcome him, smiling with those clear, level eyes that tended to squint a little as if dazzled by their own blueness. Caleb smiled back, nodding gently. Then he started and returned to the letter.

He learned that his parents were dead, which of course he had assumed for many years. (Yet still he was stunned.) And the baby, Caroline, whom he had forgotten all about. But where was Maggie Rose, had she ever returned? Daniel neglected to say. Caleb raised his eyes and saw her small, dear, laughing face beneath a ribboned hat. But she would be an old lady now. She had grandchildren. Her sons were lawyers, her husband a judge. It was 1973.

Yet the language in this letter came from an earlier age, and the stiff, self-conscious voice of the young Daniel Peck rang clearly in Caleb's ears. All the old burdens were dropped upon him: reproaches, forgiveness, reproaches again. An endless advancing and retreating and readvancing against which no counterattack was possible. "You must surely have guessed . . ." "But we will let bygones be bygones." But, "You were always contrary, even as a child, and caused our mother much . . ." Then Caleb reached the final paragraph, skimming rather than reading (so that none of it should really soak in). "To tell the truth, Caleb," his brother said, and held out his hand and stood waiting. As in the old days, when after weeks of distance he would climb all the steps to Caleb's room simply to invite him for a walk; or some other member of the family would, for they were all alike, all advancing and retreating too, and Caleb had spent far too many years belatedly summoning up his defenses only to have them washed away by some loving touch on his shoulder, some words in that secret language which, perhaps, all families had, but this was the only one Caleb had ever been able to understand. He was angry and then regretful; he rebelled against them all, their niggling, narrow ways, but then some homeliness in the turned-down corners of their mouths would pull at him; then he reached out, and was drowned in their airless warmth and burdened with reminders of all the ways he had disappointed them.

So he asked an attendant for writing paper, chafing and excited for the three hours it took her to bring it, but once it came the stony feeling weighed him down again and he found it impossible to form the proper words. Besides, his hands ached. His fingers would not grasp the pencil firmly. He folded the blank page and stuffed it in his pocket, where Daniel's letter was. Days passed. Weeks passed. For a while his family infiltrated every thought he had, but eventually they faded, returning only occasionally when he put on the coat that served as bathrobe and a rustle in the pocket cast a brief shadow over his morning.

For lunch there was chicken à la king on toast. After lunch came nap time. Wheelchair patients were laid out like strips of bacon on their beds, but most of the others—rebelling in little ways—wandered in the aisles or stood at the window or sat upright in bed in nests of thin, patched blankets. Caleb himself lay down but did not sleep. He was mentally playing the fiddle. Anyone watching closely could have seen the fingers of his left hand twitch from time to time or his lips just faintly move, uttering no sound. He was playing the "Georgia Crawl" and every note was coming just the way he wanted.

After naps they were supposed to stay in the social room till supper. Caleb, however, wandered out into the yard, and since he always went to the same place nobody tried to stop him. He sat on a bench beneath the little dogwood tree growing from a circle in the concrete. Its upper branches were dry and bare. Lower down, a few red leaves shook in a cold wind. Caleb turned up the collar of his raincoat and huddled into himself. Before long it would be winter and they wouldn't let him come here any more. By next spring the tree might have died. He was not much of a nature lover, but the thought of sitting in utter blankness, unsheltered by even this cluster of dry twigs, made him feel exposed. He glanced around, suddenly wary. All he saw was a woman in a flat hat picking her way across the concrete.

Now visiting hours were well under way and outsiders would be everywhere, their unexpected colors turning the Home drabber than its residents had realized. Perhaps this one was lost. She moved toward him as if fording a river full of slippery stones. Her straw-colored hair, hanging gracelessly to her shoulders, made him think of the very young girls of his youth, but when she came closer he saw that she was middle-aged. She looked directly at him with a peculiarly searching expression. She held out her hand. "Caleb Peck?" she asked.

"Why, yes."

He took the hand, although she was a stranger. He would go along with anything; he always had.

"I am Justine Peck."

"Oh?"

He looked at her more closely, past the helter-skelter hat and the aging clothes to her sandy face, sharp nose, blue eyes. He would know her anywhere, he thought. (But he hadn't.) A sad kind of shock went through him. He continued holding onto her bony hand.

"I am Daniel Peck's granddaughter."

"Oh yes. His granddaughter."

"Whom he didn't feel connected to," she said.

"Yes, I seem to remember . . ."

He let go of her hand to reach toward his pocket, the one that rustled.

"I have bad news," he heard.

His—niece? Great-niece. Sat beside him on the bench, light as a bird. He knew what she was going to say. "Daniel is dead," he told her. How could he have awakened this morning so contented, not guessing what had happened?

"He had a heart attack," she said.

He felt cheated and bitter. A deep pain began flowering inside him. His hand continued automatically to his pocket, found the letter and pulled it out. "But I hadn't yet answered," he said. "*Eventually* I was going to."

"Well, of course."

Which was not what he had been afraid she would say.

He opened out the letter, blinking through a mist, and smoothed it on the bench between them. Daniel's typing was conscientious and stalwart and pathetic. This wasn't fair; it was like having him die twice. "It isn't fair," he told Justine.

"It's not. It's not at all."

She sat watching a pigeon while Caleb reread the letter. The margins wobbled and shimmered. Now everything came clear to him. He saw kinder, gentler meanings in Daniel's words; the other meanings were no longer there. He understood the effort involved, the hesitations, searches for the proper phrase, false beginnings tossed in wastebaskets.

"I should have written," he told Justine.

She went on watching the pigeon.

"It always seemed to work out with them that I didn't do what I should have. Did do what I shouldn't have."

Her gaze shifted to him, transparent blue eyes whose familiarity continued to confuse him.

"How did he find me?" he asked her. Before, he had barely wondered.

"A detective did it," said Justine, "but we'd been hunting for years."

"I thought they would just forget about me."

She started to say something, and stopped. Then she said, "I used to read the cards for you."

"The—?"

"Fortune-telling cards."

"Oh yes," he said.

"I asked, would Grandfather ever locate you? The cards said yes. However there was always room for error, because Grandfather didn't cut the cards himself. He wouldn't have approved. I never thought of asking would he actually *see* you."

Caleb folded the letter and put it back in his pocket. He was not sure what they were talking about.

"Uncle Caleb," said Justine, "will you come home with me?"

"Oh well I—that's very kind of you."

"You know we'd love to have you. Duncan and I. Duncan is another grandchild, I married him. You'd like him."

"Married him, did you," said Caleb, unsurprised. He sniffed, and then blotted both eyes on the sleeve of his raincoat. "*Well* now," he said. "Whose little girl are you?"

"Caroline's."

"Caroline's? I thought she was the baby, I thought she died."

"Only after she grew up," said Justine. "Duncan is Uncle Two's."

"Two's? Oh, Justin Two."

He contemplated the pigeon, whose feathers reminded him of a changeable taffeta dress that Maggie Rose had once worn. Justin Two was the most demanding of all her children, he seemed to remember; the loudest and the shrillest, the most likely to interrupt a conversation. "Tell me," he said, "is he still the same?"

"Yes," said Justine, as if she knew what he meant.

He laughed.

Justine said, "Listen. You can't stay here! I went to that office in there to ask for you and they said, 'He's out by the tree, but you've only got twenty minutes. Then visiting hours will be over,' they said. I said, 'But I've been traveling since yesterday! I am his great-niece Justine Peck and I've come all the way from Caro Mill, Maryland. I *have* to spend more than twenty *minutes!*' 'Sorry, Miss,' they said, 'rules are rules.' You can't stay in a place like this!"

"It's true," said Caleb, "they do like rules."

"Will you come? We could leave this evening."

"Oh, well you see they'd never let me do it," Caleb said. "No. You weren't the person who signed me in here, they'd never just let me . . . or if they did, there'd be so much paperwork. It would take some arranging. Perhaps several weeks before they would allow me to—"

"*Allow* you?" Justine said. "What, are you in prison?"

Caleb blinked and looked around him.

"Never mind, just come," said Justine. "You already have your coat on. There's nothing you want from inside, is there? We can go over the wall in back, where it's lowest. They won't even see us leave."

"You mean—*escape?*" said Caleb.

"Won't you just come away with me?"

People had been saying that to him all his life. He had still not learned to turn them down.

19

Every now and then Justine would catch a glimpse of Caleb—as he passed a doorway, or skimmed in and out of view in front windows while walking the porch—and she would mistake him for Grandfather Peck and her heart would leap. She had never managed to believe that some people truly will not be seen again. Look, there was that jutting head, the glint of silver hair, the long nose pinched white at the tip! But then she would notice his eyes. The shock of brown eyes in her grandfather's face. Or she would call and he would answer instantly, wincing if she spoke to him too loudly, which she was always doing, out of habit. Or his clothes gave him away—her grandfather's, yes, but on Caleb they looked scruffy and poorly cut. She sank back, wherever she was, and Duncan looked at her curiously but said nothing.

Duncan was playing Battue now, moving yellow plastic disks among a triangle of pegs. For him it appeared to be another game of solitaire, not a puzzle; he had solved the puzzle years ago. The disks clicked steadily like the beads of an abacus or a rosary, their rhythm dictated by the churning of private thoughts. What were Duncan's private thoughts? He wouldn't say. He kept the bourbon bottle beside him, always nearly empty, it seemed, its cheap wavery glass perfectly clear down to the inch or so of yellow in the bottom. Occasionally he smoked a doll-sized metal pipe containing foul-smelling leaves and seeds and stems. Then he would grow dreamy and whimsical, although the leaves were so old now (having been stored nearly forever in an oregano bottle in the kitchen) that Justine suspected they had lost all their potency. He suggested unusual projects—for instance, planting the little round seeds on some village green. "Once a year we could have a new ritual, the Burning of the Green. All the villagers could sit around breathing the smoke and getting happy on a specified day." Justine looked sideways at Caleb to see if he were shocked. He didn't seem to be. He was not above accepting a slug or two of bourbon himself (those rigid, grandfatherly lips poised at the rim of a bottle!) and perhaps would have tried the pipe as well, if smoke did not make him cough. Nevertheless, Justine continually felt the need to tell him, "You mustn't think Duncan's always like this."

"He's not?" said Caleb.

"No, really he's just—it will pass."

Then she wondered why she bothered explaining, for Caleb only looked disappointed. He had some sort of expectation of them that Justine couldn't understand. On the trip, for instance, his moods had kept shifting until she hadn't known what to think of him. First he was elated, almost all the way to New Orleans. It was her favorite view of Caleb so far: his face alight, looking much like Duncan's, just as she had always known it would. He was tense with excitement and his hands moved rapidly as he spoke. (Yet Justine had been taught that a Peck does not gesticulate.) He told her his whole life, everything that had happened to him since leaving Baltimore—*buckets* of life, torrents of names and places, snatches of song broken off and sentences left unfinished. She had the feeling that he had been saving it up for sixty years, until he could locate a family member. But then when he had finished and she questioned him on the fine points—"Whatever happened to the friend you went to New Orleans with?" "What sort of man was White-Eye Ramford?" "Did you ever think of coming home?"—he became morose and short of words. "I don't know. I don't know," he muttered. Thinking to cheer him up, she said, "When we get to New Orleans we'll buy you some shoes. You can't get on a plane in paper slippers." But if anything, that only deepened his gloom. He looked out the window, his thumb and middle finger steadily stroking the corners of his mouth in a way that made her uncomfortable. But of course: he was mourning his brother. She should have thought. No doubt he had only been making an effort for her sake, earlier, and it had worn him out. So she let him sit in silence, and when they reached New Orleans she didn't mention his shoes again. He did, though. He became suddenly brisk. "Say now!" he said. "Weren't we going to change out of these paper scuffs?" We can't go back to the family looking unkempt."

"Well, if you want to," Justine said carefully.

"Unfortunately I am out of funds at the moment but—"

"Oh, I'll take care of that."

In that respect, at least, he showed his background. He did not make any sort of unseemly fuss over financial matters.

They had to stay overnight in a very poor hotel, for which Justine was apologetic, but Caleb didn't seem to mind. He retired early after eating a large quantity of salad; fresh fruits and vegetables were some sort of obsession with him. When he waved good night in the corridor he looked just fine, but the next morning on the plane he was up and down, up and down. Talkative, then moody. Mostly moody. He asked her unlikely questions. "How many ships do you have?"

"Ships? What?"

"Do you own or lease them now?"

"*Ships!* Oh," said Justine. "We're not importers any more."

"You're not?"

"The family sold it all."

"Why! When did they do that?"

"Right after you left," said Justine.

Then he sank into himself again, and hardly spoke until they had landed and caught the two connecting buses to Caro Mill. When she led him up Watchmaker Street she felt she was *laboring* with him, he looked so dismal. But at her front walk he stopped short. "Here?" he said. "Is this where you live?"

For the first time she noticed how unsteady the house appeared, how the screens bagged and the steps buckled. She wondered what that rusty motor was doing on the porch. "Yes, it is," she said.

She felt him staring at her. She focused on the tips of her shoes.

"This is your *house?*"

"Yes."

"And what is this yellow stuff in the yard?"

"Why, cornstalks."

"I mean—*eating* corn?"

"Well, Duncan wanted to grow some, you see, and he said the back didn't get enough sun. He said we could grind up the garbage for fertilizer and spread it on the—"

She felt herself growing desperate, trying to convince him that really their life was perfectly logical. But she shouldn't have bothered. For when finally she raised her eyes (just a glance at his face to see how she was doing) she found the corners of his mouth perked upwards like Duncan's, his expression bright and merry again. He was back to being cheerful. And he remained cheerful ever after, growing more light-hearted day by day. He fit right in. She couldn't understand him.

Sometimes Duncan let the Battue disks fall silent a moment while he read the newspapers. Help Wanted, of course. "Look, Justine, someone in Virginia wants a zoo keeper."

"You've never been a zoo keeper, Duncan."

"Right."

"I mean you don't know the first thing about it."

"Right."

"You have a job. Duncan, you *have* a job, and you should have been there three hours ago."

Then he would rise, steady on his feet but a little slow, his face luminous and calm and angelic as only bourbon could make it, and he would very, very carefully button himself into his jacket. "If you really want to know," he said (but speaking in Caleb's general direction), "I don't believe in people sacrificing themselves for the sake of other people."

"But neither do I, Duncan," she said.

He didn't have any answer for that.

So he would give a little salute to Caleb, and turn up his collar as if facing winter winds before he set off for the antique shop. Where there would be no customers anyway, now that opening hours were so uncertain. Where antiques lay in a jumble, dusty and neglected, and half the lightbulbs were out and the window was patched with adhesive tape. Look at this very newspaper column, spindled now on a Battue peg. WANTED *antique shop mgr. must be reliable apply Silas Amsel Box 46 Caro Mill.* But Justine was firm and cool and deliberate. Like her grandfather, she stiffened her pointy chin and set her head at a commanding angle. "It's time we learned to stay in one place," she told Duncan every night when he came home.

"Whatever you say, Justine."

There was something underneath, some considerateness in his voice that made her turn on him. "Don't you think so?" she asked him.

"Whatever you say."

"Not what *I* say. Don't you think so yourself? We've been moving around forever."

"That's very true," he said.

"Why do you keep agreeing with me? Do you feel you have to humor me in some way?"

"No, no."

But he did. She knew he did. It was because of her fetching Caleb. Wasn't it? Duncan seemed to think she had gone crazy, or senile—or who knows?—running off like that to get Caleb. (She had assumed he would understand. She had called the antique shop from Box Hill: "I'll be away overnight, I think, Duncan, I don't think I can find a plane out of New Orleans till tomorrow." "New Orleans? Is that where you are? I thought you had left me," he said. "I went home for lunch and you weren't there." She said, "*I* wouldn't leave you"—forgetting altogether that up till that afternoon she had been seriously considering it. She was so excited about meeting Caleb. And it was so good to hear Duncan's voice on the telephone. It had completely slipped her mind how angry she was with him.) When she came back from New Orleans, Duncan gave Caleb a long look and then shook his hand. But the look he gave Justine was longer—a gentle, sad, *pitying* look, which she was going to remember till the end of her days. What could he be pitying her for? He didn't even know that she had done all this illegally, so to speak. Yet during supper that night he had been so soft-voiced and solicitous, as if she were sick. When really there was nothing more natural than having your great-uncle come to stay with you.

Not that Duncan minded having Caleb. He got along with him very well. Better than Justine herself did, in fact. They had long discussions on jazz and blues and Creole food. Duncan would ask about Lafleur Boudrault, and Whisky Alley, and musical funerals and old-time cathouses, about which (Justine was surprised to hear) Caleb seemed to know everything. Caleb played Duncan's harmonica, drawing forth from it such beautiful, disreputable sounds that Justine stood motionless and open-mouthed. *This* was her great-*uncle?*

But he didn't like to be called Great-Uncle, or even Uncle. Perhaps he had been without relatives too long for such titles to sit easy on him. "Just 'Caleb' will do," he said. And there had been so many difficulties in the way of his paying the rest of the family a visit. He was too tired from the trip; he was just getting used to Caro Mill; his arthritis was acting up. Thanksgiving would be better, he said. They could arrive unannounced and take the family by surprise. "Thanksgiving!" said Justine. It was barely November. Was it fair to keep everyone in the dark for so long? She was all for going this Sunday, perhaps, for Sunday dinner at Uncle Two's. But Caleb refused, offering a dozen shiftless excuses. ("I'm scared I wouldn't know anybody's name," he said.) Justine sighed. She had to admit there were times when Caleb disappointed her.

No, more than that. Tell the truth. There were times when she almost disliked him.

He had gone so far afield, it seemed. He had journeyed such a distance from his family. Now it appeared that the return trip was not that easy, maybe even impossible. He had a hundred habits and qualities that the Pecks would not have tolerated, skills they neither possessed nor wanted, bits of knowledge they would not know existed. Often he said things that horrified her. "Maybe," he said, "we could just *never* let the family know, have you thought of that?"

"Why, Caleb!"

"I mean—Justine, I'm happy here with you and Duncan. Why go anywhere else? It would be like meeting strangers."

"That's ridiculous! It's ridiculous."

"I don't have anything in common with them, Justine."

"How can you say such a thing?"

"Do you think a one of them would recognize me?"

No. Not a one of them. Deep down, she knew it, and he and she would stare at each other in absolute agreement even while she continued to protest.

Sometimes she shut herself in her room and pulled out Caleb's old photo, which she had taken from her grandfather's pocket after he died. She studied it as if it could be read, not merely looked at. The gleam of Caleb's Panama, the set of his shoulders, the perfect crispness of his tie. Nowadays he did not even wear a tie. His old jauntiness had become, somehow, *boldness*; his speech had a sharp, unpleasant tang. There was something spineless and lackadaisical in the way he walked. And she could not help noticing that still, wearing Daniel's clothes and Duncan's aftershave, he had the musty cabbage smell of a public institution.

Well, after all, he had been away so long.

Yes, but he had gone by degrees, traveling only where led, merely proving himself adaptable, endlessly adaptable.

As Justine herself had.

Then a trembling would rise from the soles of her feet, turn her stomach queasy, pass through the hollow of her chest to beat in her throat like a second heart. She stuffed the snapshot beneath a stack of magazines and hurried out to join the others.

In the afternoons, with Duncan asleep on the floor beside his disks, Justine brought Caleb up to date on the family. Even though he seemed not to care, she sat at the table earnestly filling him with history. She was amazed at how little time it took to tell—all those events unfolding over months and years, summed up now in minutes. "Richard did get married but it was annulled, the girl's father had it annulled because she was under age, and since then he's lived downtown in a—"

"Now, which was Richard?"

"Why, Uncle Mark's son," she said.

When she told how her mother died she spoke without inflection, as if hoping he wouldn't catch it, but of course he did. He made no comment. When she talked about fortune telling he only looked interested. What did he really think? She imagined that he was about to define her; that at last, after clearing his throat, he would sum her up, announce where she had been heading all her life. She tensed expectantly whenever she caught him looking around the house, or glancing at her clothes, or staring at some toothless woman in socks and Wedgies who came to have her cards read. Surely he was judging their life, whose skimpiness she had just begun to realize. Any moment now he would give his verdict. But he never did. She kept trying to explain herself, even so. "You see we have always just—Duncan has kept wanting us to move around," she told him.

"Is that right," said Caleb.

"He likes to travel."

"But he hasn't traveled *far*."

"What?" She searched her memory for other family news, meanwhile absently cracking a coffee bean with her teeth. "Now Aunt Lucy, she always says—"

"Lucy? I didn't remember Daniel had a Lucy."

"Lucy is Two's wife, Caleb. I told you that."

"Ah yes." He nodded. "It must be hard trying to keep all this straight."

"I don't have to *try*. They're family. Now, what was I telling you about Aunt Lucy?"

"You said—who did you say she was?"

So that she grew exasperated. "Don't you have any *memory?*" she asked him. "Don't you feel any connection at all?"

"Memory, yes. Connection, no."

She believed him. At night, tossing in her bed, she told Duncan, "We might as well have picked a stranger off the streets."

"What makes you think so?"

"He's not connected, he says. He *admits* it. That scroungy old man—if he had written a letter when he should have I bet Grandfather would be alive today. He doesn't have a trace of the family left in him and he tells me so as if he's proud of it. He doesn't have a trace."

"He does, though."

"What are you talking about?"

"Oh, use your head, Justine. Who do you know who acts more like a Peck? Consider that he has remained alone his whole life long, never let in anybody who wasn't a blood relative. Never got close to White-Eye, never married that waitress, never was a father to Roy. Can't you read between the lines? Look at what Luray said: it's not as if he were a real relation. You say the Pecks haven't left a trace?"

"You don't know the first thing about it," Justine said. "Of course he didn't get close to White-Eye. He was careful and respectful. He had *tact*." And she would flounce over on her side away from him, preparing for another night of insomnia.

Then the next afternoon, facing Caleb, who wore his brother's pinstriped shirt, she was full of new hope and energy. "I think you're going to like my cousin Claude," she told him.

"Oh yes?"

"He collects engravings. He's the only one besides you who's interested in the arts."

But, "I believe I'll make coffee out of some of those beans, Justine," he said. Then she would notice how metallic his eyes were, and how there was something raw and uncared-for about his skin, which was stretched too tightly across the bridge of his nose.

He had taken over the kitchen by now, as if he guessed how she felt about cooking. (The first supper she served him was hot dogs scorched in a skillet.) He prepared every meal so seriously and so tenderly that it tasted like a gift. "Eat it all," he told them at suppertime. "If you don't finish it, how can I make more? I want to get started on something new." He would hum as he worked, clattering pots, cursing the scarcity of equipment. "But that's all right, I can make do with anything. Put me in the pokiest diner and I will cook you up a seven-course meal. Why did I ever retire? I let Luray talk me into it. Here I've been thinking I had no means of support, but I do! I'm going to get a job and contribute to the household, I have it all worked out."

But even Duncan looked doubtful when he heard that. "Well, look," he said. "I wouldn't want to discourage you, but *age* might stand in your way, don't you think?"

"Never mind my age," said Caleb. "Oh, for the quality places, yes. But there is always some little café by the tracks or the water where they don't give a hang, and that's where I'll ask."

"Well, at least why don't you wait a little. If we move or anything, you don't want to go through a whole new job application."

"But we're not moving," said Justine.

"Oh, no hurry," Caleb said. "I play it by ear. I wait to see what falls out and who is going in what direction. I always have." He smiled. "It's funny," he said, "I'd forgotten the taste of garlic. Can you beat that? It's peculiar how you associate some foods with people. Or times you used to have, or places . . . Bess always liked garlic-buttered popcorn. The two of us must have eaten bushels of it. Now you could bring me some and I don't know, it would taste so *unfamiliar* somehow. I suppose everybody's like that. Best friend I ever had liked Blue Peter sardines on saltine crackers, but maybe if I were to track him down today I'd find he doesn't even remember them any more."

Duncan listened so hard he forgot to eat. Justine slid a salt shaker back and forth. Why did Caleb have to talk about food all the time? No one else in the family did. All they asked was that their meals be nourishing, and not too unusual in taste. They tended to like white things, foods baked in cream sauce. They would have been horrified by the peppery shrimp casserole that Caleb had served tonight. "Listen!" Justine said suddenly. "How can we be sure you're Caleb Peck?"

Both men stared.

"How do we know you're not some impostor?"

"Justine," said Duncan.

She ignored him. She was watching Caleb. "But who else would bother?" Caleb asked her.

"You're not like them in any way."

Caleb shrugged. (A foreign gesture.) "For that matter," he said, "how do I know *you're* a Peck?"

"We're not even sure that Eli's honest," Justine said. "Maybe he just picked up some stranger and coached him. Maybe the two of you framed this whole story together. After all, there must be money involved. Caleb's share of the will must have been drawing interest for sixty years."

"Caleb didn't *have* any share of the will," Duncan told her. "Justine, I wish you would—"

But Caleb only nodded, sober and proud somehow, as if he were receiving compliments.

In the night there was a pounding on the door, and shouting and the beam of headlights across the bedroom ceiling. Justine, wide awake as usual, crawled over Duncan and threw a bathrobe around her shoulders. "Just a minute," she called. Duncan stirred and then sat up. From Caleb's room came the rustle of bedclothes. Justine ran through the hallway, breathless and shivering. Someone had died. Something was wrong with Meg. She had never realized how many possibilities there were for disaster, or how calm and joyous her life had been until this moment.

But it was only Tucker Dawcett, whose wife had her fortune told weekly to see if he were faithful and never believed it when the answer was yes. Tucker was just a sweet skinny man with buck teeth. He jogged in a sweatsuit every morning and worked as a, let's see—

Policeman.

Her teeth started chattering again.

Tucker coughed, and then showed her his identification in a plastic envelope. (Why on earth?) For all she knew it was his YMCA card. "Oh. Tucker," she said.

"Could I speak with you a moment, Justine?"

From the hall doorway, Duncan said, "Do you know what time it is?"

"Police business," said Tucker.

Duncan came up behind Justine without a sound.

"Now I have to ask you folks this question," Tucker said. "Are you all related to a Mr. Caleb Peck?"

"You get us up at one a.m. to ask us that?" Duncan said.

"Now I know, I know how trying this must be," Tucker told him. Through the screen his face looked grainy; out of tiredness or embarrassment he kept his eyes down. "Fact is I was sacked out at home myself. Doug Tilghman called from the station asking me to run this little errand. I wanted to wait till morning but he said we would look pretty silly if Louisiana called back in a couple hours and we hadn't done a thing."

"Louisiana?" said Duncan.

"See they got this lady down there claiming a Mr. Caleb Peck has been kidnapped."

Duncan looked at Justine.

"Seems like he was in a home of some sort. This lady, Mrs. Luray Pickett, went to visit him last Sunday and found he'd disappeared. Home hadn't noticed. Seems somebody at the office remembered a

Justine Peck come from Caro Mill to visit him, and he was never seen again."

"So?" said Duncan.

"Well, I believe that would be kidnapping, or stealing at least. See, the man was institutionalized. He didn't have no right to be leaving on his own free will. Or would it be aiding and abetting? Well, look. *I* don't care about it. Let an old fellow go where he wants, I always say. But Doug Tilghman said I had to just ask, because some lady somewhere is fit to be tied. Mrs. Luray Pickett. I said, 'Look, Doug, can't this wait till morning? I mean what will the Pecks think of us for this?' I said, and he said, 'Tell them I'm just as sorry as I can be but these policemen in Louisiana have this lady name of Mrs. Luray Pickett who is kicking up a storm, calling them and visiting, asking why they're not doing more. She says she put the man in a Home herself and saw to his every need, never let a month go by without . . . and here he has been removed and not so much as a by-your-leave. She says if anybody thought she wasn't taking proper care they could just come to her in person, there was no need to steal the man, and she will thank the police to get him replaced or she'll know the reason why. And also—' Well, and it's true there's not many Justine Pecks. I mean the *name* is odd. And especially from Caro Mill. Of course you do have that old man staying with you now . . ."

"Tucker," said Duncan, "don't you know that all our family is from Baltimore?"

"That's true, they are."

"And have you ever heard either one of us mention a relative in Louisiana?"

"Well, not directly," said Tucker.

"So," said Duncan.

"Well, I knew there was nothing to it," Tucker told him. "Sorry to have woken you folks up." And for the first time he raised his eyes to meet theirs. "I'll tell the wife I saw you," he said. "Night, now."

"Night," said Duncan.

He turned on the porch light and shut the door. Justine waited, but he didn't say a word. Maybe he was angry. She should have told him from the beginning. Only at the beginning he had been so odd, and after that it was never the proper moment. Now what? Would he make her send Caleb back again? Then it occurred to her that all this time Caleb must have been listening, bolt upright in bed, terrified they would give him away. "That poor old man!" she said, and slid past Duncan to open Caleb's door.

He was gone.

His bed was unmade, and his pajamas lay at the foot. His rubberized raincoat no longer hung from the closet door. Duncan's harmonica was missing from the bureau. And the window was wide open, empty and black, the paper shade lisping in the wind. "Duncan!" Justine called. "Hurry, we have to find him!"

She already had one leg over the windowsill before he stopped her. He took hold of her arm and said, "Let him get a little head start again first, Justine."

20

Duncan sat on the floor with a twelve-hundred-piece jigsaw puzzle, "Sunset in the Rockies." He had found all the straight edges and constructed the frame; but now he was simply moving pieces around, picking one up and tapping it against his teeth while he stared into space, setting it down, picking up another, turning several over to expose their gray cardboard backs. He considered turning the whole puzzle over and doing it all in gray.

He considered moving Justine back to Baltimore.

"Is that what you want?" he asked her when she came through wearing her hat.

She looked startled. "What?"

"I asked if you wanted to move to Baltimore."

"Baltimore?"

"Baltimore, *Maryland*, Justine."

She stared at him.

"We'll live in Great-Grandma's house. *Your* house," he told her. "I'll find some kind of busywork with Peck and Sons. You know Dad's always said I could."

"You mean, stay forever?"

"No reason not to."

"Never again move?"

"Not unless you liked."

She thought a while, biting her lip.

"But you might not be happy there," she told him finally.

Which was her way of saying yes. He felt the answer settling on him by degrees, like a large heavy blanket drifting down. He was done for. Yet at the same time he had a sense of relief, almost. What else would you call this sudden giddiness? The other shoe had fallen. He nearly laughed.

Underneath, he must have known all through their marriage that this was where they were headed.

* * *

Justine fit books into cardboard boxes. Then machine parts. Duncan let his jigsaw puzzle dissolve and scatter while he took up a new kind of solitaire. Lately he had become talkative and fanciful, almost silly; he was emerging from his silence. But the bourbon and the solitaire remained, because he had lost his job by now and if he didn't look occupied in some way Justine would ask him to help her. That was one thing he could not do. He would feel like a child repacking his pathetic provisions—blanket, alarm clock, teddy bear—after half a night of running away. Or like some sea animal, declawed and deformed by battle, scuttling back to his shell with whatever scraps of himself he could salvage. He remained on the floor, pretending to be deep in his game. Meanwhile his mind had sprung awake again and was playing games of its own. He composed a list of all his favorite words, aloud. "Luncheon. Reality. Silver salver. Ippolitov-Ivanov." Justine sat back and wiped her hair off her forehead.

"Sometimes I wonder why we travel with so much *stuff*," she told him.

One of the puzzling things about Justine was that she always seemed to be shaking lately, and it hadn't stopped when he decided to move her to Baltimore. The streamers of her hat trembled gently, and whenever she drank coffee (which was the only thing she would touch) she spilled it. She reminded him of a fragile tree full of birds. But what could he do that he hadn't already done? He tried diverting her thoughts. "Justine," he said. "You know? In twenty years I firmly believe we will be traveling instantaneously by transposition of matter. You get in this glass box, see, if you want to go to, say, Omaha, and someone in Omaha gets in *another* glass box—"

"I travel fast enough as it is," said Justine, "and way too far."

"You haven't traveled so far," Duncan said. "Then bulletin boards would spring up everywhere: 'Gentleman from Detroit wishes to go to Pittsburgh; does anyone in Pittsburgh wish to go to Detroit?' There would be new hope for the unemployed. Bums could make money being transposed to Cincinnati when someone in Cincinnati wanted to get out. You go to a park bench. 'Look, fellow,' you say—"

"But it would always be me who ended up accepting," said Justine. She rose, and for no apparent reason examined her face in the speckled metal switchplate on the wall. "I can turn into anyone. That's my curse."

Her curse was her ability to see all sides of every question, but that wasn't something Duncan wanted changed and so he didn't mention it. Finally Justine turned away and bent to pack another box.

She was fitting some things of Meg's in now. Each object she handled very gently and lovingly, taking much longer than necessary. She rolled a stray belt meant for a dress Meg might not even be wearing any more, and she tucked it in beside a mildewed high school almanac.

She took the lid off a tin of pebbles that Meg had collected on a Virginia beach in the summer of 1965, and she held each pebble up to the light and smoothed it with her fingers before replacing it.

At mealtimes, if he remembered, Duncan made sandwiches and poured two glasses of milk. But Justine seemed to have given up on eating. She didn't even go to the diner; she didn't go anywhere. When he urged her she would take one bite of her sandwich and then set it down. "Come on. Eat," he told her. Though he could see that it wasn't possible. He could tell from the way she chewed; her mouth was too dry, or too small, or something. Never mind, she would eat when she got to Baltimore. Aunts would take her in hand. He thought of the aunts for the first time with gratitude, imagining how they would relieve him of Justine's dull white face and her limpness. Then he caught himself and looked away from her eyes, which were fixed on him too steadily.

He could always leave her, of course. He could settle her in Baltimore and then go off again on his own. But he knew that he wouldn't. If he didn't have Justine he wouldn't even know how to see things, what to look at; nothing would exist for him if he couldn't tell Justine about it. The first flat-brimmed hat in a department store window would break him. He would be unable to last the night without her rustling, burning wakefulness guarding his sleep. So he put away all thoughts of leaving, and he wrote the letter to Peck & Sons asking for work. But when the answer came, he didn't want to open it. He stuffed it in his pocket, angry already at the phrases he knew it would contain. Finally Justine found it, and opened it for him. "Well? What does it say?" he asked.

"Oh . . . they'll get you something."

"But what does it *say?*" Are they glad I'm finally listening to reason? Do they say they always knew we would end up coming home?"

"No, they don't mention it," Justine said.

He snatched the letter away from her—his Uncle Mark's signature beneath a secretary's crisp black typing. Probably, his uncle said, there would be some employment for him although it was hard to say what, on such short notice. And no, the firm had no need of a fix-it man, what kind of a question was that? And of course it was true that Great-Grandma's house was legally Justine's, although really the family had been the ones to see to its maintenance all these years and Esther and the twins were so accustomed to living there . . .

All in all, Duncan thought the letter sounded disconcerted. As if secretly the family had *enjoyed* having the two of them ricocheting around somewhere. He had not expected that. Nor had he expected to feel so offended, once he found it out.

But the wheels were set in motion, anyway, and now they gave notice to the landlord and made arrangements with the movers. ("I'm not hiring a U-Haul," Duncan said. "I don't have Grandfather." But really he was just indulging in his new policy of floating to places. He pictured the Mayflower men hauling out the living room rug by its corners while he remained seated on it, steadily playing forty thieves.) They notified the electric company and the water department, breaking off ties, unplugging all their cords to Caro Mill and reeling them in. They wrote a letter to Meg giving their new address. ("Although," Justine said, "there is no way we can ever let Caleb know . . .") Nowadays when Duncan passed the Blue Bottle he saw an unfamiliar young man established behind the counter, picking his fingernails and gazing idly out the reglazed window with its display of gilded china teacups.

At Thanksgiving they stayed home, since they would be going to Baltimore anyway in another few days. They ate dinner on the living room floor: a combination pizza that Duncan had bought from a takeout place. "Really you shouldn't have," Justine said. She meant because of the cost; their money was nearly gone. They were living on Bank-Americard. "But it wasn't expensive," said Duncan, "and I thought you *liked* combination pizzas. I told them to put extra anchovies on. Why aren't you eating?"

She took a bite. She didn't seem to be tasting it.

"Isn't it good?"

"If Caleb were here we'd be taking him to the family today," she said.

"If he were here, yes."

"And they wouldn't have liked him."

He leaned forward and tapped her plate. "Eat," he told her.

The morning after Thanksgiving Dorcas came to have her cards read. She was considering marrying a movie house owner named Willis Ralph McGee. "How do you like the name Dorcas McGee?" she asked Duncan.

Behind her, Ann-Campbell said, "It stinks."

"Who asked you?"

Now that it was cold Dorcas wore a car coat heaped with blond fake fur, but her feet were still in spike-heeled sandals. Blood-red toenails glinted beneath nylon, overrun the next moment by the last of Duncan's forty cards. She moved her toes a fraction of an inch away. "You said I would meet somebody soon, Justine, and so I did," she said. "Now I want to know what kind of husband he would make."

"Lousy," said Ann-Campbell.

"Will you hush that?"

"My daddy, Joe Pete Britt, is not ever going to stand for this," said Ann-Campbell. "Here, Justine, I brung in your mail. There's a bill from Howard pharmacy, a Korvette ad—"

"Just *give* it to her, Ann-Campbell."

Justine set down a roll of binder's twine and took the letters. "Well, here is something from Mayflower," she said. "I just hope they're not putting off the moving date."

"I hope they *do!*" said Dorcas. "Just years and years."

"Here's something from—who do we know in Wyoming?"

Justine tore the envelope open. Duncan laid down a nine of clubs, which Dorcas immediately stepped on. "Now I don't want to hurry you or anything," Dorcas said, "but me and Ann-Campbell are going out to Woolworth's for a hot fudge sundae and we were just stopping by *briefly* to get my fortune told."

"You prick a balloon," Ann-Campbell told Duncan, "and see what number is wrote on it. That's the price of your hot fudge sundae. Could be a nickel. Could be a penny."

"Is that so," said Duncan. "Would you move your foot a little, Dorcas?"

"Could be forty-nine cents," said Dorcas. "It always has been."

"Well!" said Justine.

They all looked up at her, but it seemed she was reading a letter. She would read for a moment and then look up, then start reading it all over again. "What is it?" Duncan asked her.

"Well, it's a—"

He waited, but she went back to the letter.

"Reason I'm in a hurry is that tonight we have this special date," Dorcas said. "I have a feeling he's going to propose. Now I don't want to answer without knowing what the cards say, do I?"

"Certainly not," said Duncan.

"Justine? If you don't want to do it all you have to do is tell me."

"Look at this, Duncan," Justine said.

He took the letter, a cream-colored sheet crumpled and gray around the edges.

November 20, 1973

Dear Justine,

I want to apologize for taking so long to write, but circumstances prevented me up until now.

It was very kind of you to invite me to stay with you. The frankfurters you cooked were delicious, and I shall remember my visit with a great deal of pleasure for a long time to come.

Love,
Caleb Peck

Duncan laughed—a single, sharp sound. He handed the letter back. "It's a thank you note," said Justine.

"That's right."

"A bread-and-butter note."

"That's what they call them."

"I just want to ask you one thing," Dorcas said. "And I want an honest answer. Hear? Now Justine, you have been putting me off all morning and it's not the first time. Other people have noticed too. Nowadays you just *drift* the cards down like your heart's not in it. Anything anybody asks you definite, should they do it or should they not, you don't want to reply. You just shuck it off, like. Well, what I want to know is, do you not really care to read the future any more? Are you trying to phase it out? Because all you got to do is say the word, Justine. Not to keep on going with your mind on something else the way you have been lately."

"What?" said Justine.

Dorcas looked over at Duncan.

"Oh, your *fortune*," Justine said.

"That's right."

"Well, let me find my . . ."

She fetched the straw carry-all, unwrapped the cards from their square of silk.

"My great-uncle Caleb wrote a thank you note," she told Dorcas.

"Now isn't that nice."

"Thanking us for his visit."

"You can always tell good upbringing, is what *I* say," said Dorcas, but her eyes were on the cards, which Justine was gently shuffling over and over again. "Aren't you going to want a table to lay those out on? Or you're just going to go on shuffling evermore."

"*Oh* yes," said Justine. And they went off to the kitchen, leaving Ann-Campbell behind. Ann-Campbell squatted next to Duncan. "Will Justine let Mama say yes to Mr. McGee?" she asked him.

"I don't know."

"Will she tell her to marry daddy again, Joe Pete Britt?"

"Tune in next week and find out," said Duncan.

"Huh?"

"Nothing." He tipped back his head for a swallow of bourbon.

"Who is this great-uncle Caleb man?"

"That old guy we had around for a while," Duncan said. "Who is either very dumb or very very smart, it's hard to tell which."

"If she marries Mr. McGee I might just come along to Baltimore with you all," said Ann-Campbell, edging closer. "I think that might be what's going to happen. Justine will tell her to go ahead."

"Justine won't tell her *anything*, don't worry," Duncan said. "She hardly opens her mouth any more."

But just then he heard her laugh, a clear light sound that startled him, and he looked up from his cards and met Ann-Campbell's speckled green eyes fixed thoughtfully upon him.

* * *

After lunch Justine worked in the yard a while, pulling up yellowed cornstalks. She returned with her face pink. Starchy-smelling air trailed behind her. "Feel," she said, and laid her stinging hands on Duncan's cheek. He drew back. "Doesn't it make you want to get outdoors?" she asked him.

"Not exactly."

"Aren't you tired of sitting here?"

She spun away from him and went off toward the kitchen. A minute later he heard her running water in the sink, clattering dishes, but she must have grown tired of that, because very soon she was back in the living room. She stood at the window a moment, and then took a second pack of cards from the sill and settled down on the floor with them, not far from where Duncan sat playing forty thieves. He could hear her murmuring to herself as she laid them out. ". . . the queen of change, beside the king. The wish card, the journey card . . . why so many journeys? Look how far the loved ones are! This is the card for journeys beyond other journeys, I've never had that one before. The card for, what was it?"

She fell silent. Duncan looked up to find her chewing a thumbnail and staring into space.

Shortly afterward she left, sliding into an old lumberjacket that used to be Duncan's. She didn't say where she was going. Duncan heard the Ford start up, a burry sound in the frozen air. First he was pleased, but then he wondered if she would keep her mind sufficiently on her driving. He noticed how empty the house felt. There was a strong wind blowing up from the north, whistling through all the cracks. The sky was white, and the room seemed lit by a bleak cold glare that hurt Duncan's eyes. Everywhere he looked there was something dismal to see: packing cases, dry dead plants on the windowsill, a sprawl of tomato-stained pizza wrappings from the day before. He rose and went to the bedroom. He was only planning to rest; he lay on the unmade bed with one arm across his eyes and thought about the turn his life was taking. But then he fell asleep and dreamed about antiques— jewelry that came in clusters and jungles of carved chair legs. Even in his sleep it was impossible to find any space that was pure and simple and clean of line.

When he woke it was dark. Justine was still not back. He got up and felt his way to the kitchen, where he turned on the light and made himself a peanut butter sandwich. The cat watched him from the stovetop. "So this is what it's like to be grown up!" Duncan told her. She blinked and looked away, offended. He took his sandwich into the living room and settled down again beside his unfinished game. It was clear he was not going to win. Still, he shifted cards doggedly and pondered a choice of moves, munching meanwhile on his sandwich. There was nothing else to do.

Then the Ford drove up, and a minute later Justine's quick footsteps crossed the porch. When she opened the door he kept his eyes on the cards; she would never guess how glad he was to see her. "We're out of peanut butter," was all he said.

"Oh, are we?"

He moved a deuce.

"I think I'm losing," he said.

"Never mind." She came to kneel in front of him, a flash of red plaid, and scooped his cards up. Some were left on the rug and some flew out of her hands. "Well, wait a minute," Duncan said.

"Shall I tell your fortune?"

She had never told his fortune in all his life. He stared at her. But Justine only smiled—bright-eyed, out of breath, her hat a little crooked—and began laying cards in a disorderly row that she didn't even glance at. "You are about to alter your entire way of life," she said, smacking down some jack or king. She was watching Duncan's face.

"Yes, well," said Duncan, reaching for his bottle.

"You are going to become a fix-it man for a carnival."

He set the bottle down.

"Your wife will be their fortune teller. You'll have a purple trailer in Parvis, Maryland, and live happily ever after. How do you like me so far?"

"You're crazy," he said, but he was smiling, and he didn't even protest when Justine spilled all the rest of his bourbon while leaning over the cards to give him a kiss.

21

On moving day they got a late start, which was fine because there wasn't that much to move. They were taking only their books and clothes, plus Duncan's spare parts and inventions, packed in a little orange U-Haul van. They were leaving everything else behind. Furniture would be supplied in the trailer. Built in. Justine liked the idea of having everything built in. She enjoyed telling people they were traveling light, and would have thrown away even some things they needed if Duncan hadn't stopped her.

It was a clear, frosty morning in December, with a sky as blue as opals and a pale sun. Some of the neighbors had come to see them off. Dorcas Britt and her husband Joe Pete, and Ann-Campbell with Justine's cat struggling in her arms. Red Emma, Black Emma, old Mrs.

Hewitt and her poodle. Maureen Worth from across the street, still in her bathrobe, and Mrs. Tucker Dawcett, who stood a little apart and looked sad and wistful, as if she expected even now to be handed news of her husband's unfaithfulness like a parting gift. Justine went from one to another, setting her face against theirs and giving them little pats and making promises. "Of course we'll be back. You know we will." Duncan was rearranging boxes in the U-Haul, and from time to time he cursed and stopped to rub his hands together. Red Emma threw him a dark, sullen look that he failed to see. "You tell him to bring you on weekends, hear?" she said. "Don't you let him just keep carting you off every which way." She kissed Justine's cheek. Mrs. Hewitt hugged her. "Oh, it just seems like people are always *going,* leaving, moving on . . ."

"But it's not far," said Justine. "And you can all come visit."

"In a trailer? In a cow pasture?" Dorcas said.

"You're going to love it," Justine told her. "*We're* going to love it. Oh, I can feel good luck in my bones, I know when we're doing something right. Besides, next month it will be nineteen seventy-four. Add all the digits and you get twenty-one, add those and you come up with three. Our lucky number. Did you ever see a clearer sign?"

Someone pushed a pot of ivy into her arms. Then a rubber plant. She was carrying so much they had to open the car door for her and help her settle things in. "Just put them anywhere," she said. "The front seat is fine." The front seat was already full of food for the trip—Fritos, Cheez Doodles, salt herring and coffee beans and a box of Luden's. This year she was the only person in the car. Though next year, who could tell? She took the cat from Ann-Campbell, and then once the cat was in she had to get in herself and slam the door, fast, and roll down the window no more than a slit. "Ask Duncan if he's ready to start," she said. The clanging of the tailgate was her answer. "Well, I guess I'll be saying goodbye then." For the first time her voice was sad, and appeared to drift out too slowly on the mist of her breath. "We don't want to hit the rush hour." She stuck a cold silver key in the ignition and kneaded her fingers. Hanging from the gearshift knob was a National Safety Council ad torn out of a magazine: cupids with black straps slanted across their chests, I LOVE YOU, WEAR YOUR SEAT BELT. She turned and looked at the cat, who glared at her from behind a begonia plant. "Well, then," she said, and roared the engine up and left, waving her hand out the slit in the window.

Behind her the U-Haul's engine started too, and the crowd of neighbors moved over to Duncan. "Have a good trip!" "Drive safely, hear?" The truck rolled off. "Oh, aren't you ashamed," Red Emma called suddenly, "taking her away from us like this?" But Duncan only waved. He must not have heard. Or else he was too intent on catching up with Justine, who by now was only a puff of smoke in the distance.

ABOUT THE AUTHOR

ANNE TYLER was born in Minneapolis, Minnesota, in 1941, but grew up in Raleigh, North Carolina, and considers herself a Southerner. She graduated Phi Beta Kappa from Duke University at age nineteen, and twice won the Anne Flexner Award for creative writing. She has done graduate work in Russian studies at Columbia University and worked for a year as the Russian bibliographer at the Duke University Library.

Miss Tyler has published eleven novels, and her stories have appeared in such magazines as *The New Yorker*, *The Saturday Evening Post*, *Redbook*, *McCall's*, *Harper's*, and *The Southern Review*. Her most recent novel, *Breathing Lessons*, won the 1989 Pulitzer Prize. She is married to a psychiatrist, Taghi Mohammed Modarressi; she and her husband live in Baltimore, Maryland, with their two children.